THE GIRL WHO COMMANDED LIGHTNING

A NOVEL

CLIFF RATZA

THE
GIRL WHO
COMMANDED
LIGHTNING

A NOVEL
BY CLIFF RATZA

The Girl Who Commanded Lightning

Copyright © 2025 by Clifford Ratza

All rights reserved. No parts of this book may be used or reproduced by any means, graphic, electronic, or mechanical, including photocopying, recording, taping, or by any information storage retrieval system, without the written permission of the publisher except in the case of brief quotations embodied in critical articles and reviews.

ISBN: 978-1-967375-64-6 (Paperback)
ISBN: 978-1-967375-65-3 (E-book)

Library of Congress Control Number: 2025916274

Printed in the United States of America

Published by:

info@thequippyquill.com
(302) 295-2278

About the Book

THIS BOOK, THE SEQUEL to The Girl Who Electrified the World, traces the unexpected twists and turns Electra Kittner must confront as she recovers from Techno-Plague poisoning. She must also contend with war raging in Cyberspace, directed by a rogue Middle East state allied with China and Russia, while dealing with America's relentlessly harsh government.

The theme for all books in the series is this: extraordinary people are sometimes victims of a primitive world that can't handle the truth, but no matter how exceptional they are, they must still deal with the complexities of being "merely human," best handled with an optimistic and pragmatic philosophy. There are three storyline threads:

1. The adventures of Electra and her closest friends.
2. The challenges as she reaches out to her allies.
3. The battles with the Iron Triangle and related adversaries.

Readers should enjoy the book on whatever level they wish:

- Gripping action-packed thriller
- Glimpses into a plausible near-term future
- Insights for dealing with the "human condition"
- Illustrative worldview philosophy
- Fast-paced, suspense-filled, emotive narrative and imagery
- Introduction to topics every reader wants to know
- Interesting talking points going beyond sound-bites

There is a glossary and an appendix at the back for readers who wish to know more about terms or topics referenced.

At least three more books are being developed for the Lightning Brain Series, so readers shall have much more reading enjoyment in store. Electra's exciting odyssey continues.

Main Characters

Robin Setdarova
Carter Quavah
Electra/Alisha (Kit) Kittner
Matt Fortier
Mariah Robles
Zoe Vargas
Su-Lin Song Chou Indira Ramanujan
Russell (Russ) Conklin
Tim Godfrey
Jared Gardner
Angus McTear
Kameyo Kato
Hudson (Hud) Haller
Hollis (Holy) Haller
Jennifer Conklin
Ziarmal Thaqaf
Darla Tinibu
Jevon Mathias
Amanda Cruz
Micki Stiegland
Katy Tang
Sergei Zeitsev
Chen Xu
Sam Ryder
Kwame Chyril
Toni Diya
Jasmine (Jazzi) Kent
Bo Rudman
Blake (Woolly) Wolker
Kathryn Lauret
Jackson Nolan

Baligh El-Mofty
Gui Hou
Rachel Cohn
Vincent Valdez
Randall Dancer
Hannah Aaron
Tyger Riddley
Winona Kota
Carley Kota

Book Series Dedication

OF COURSE, I WISH to thank my parents, Clyde and Betty Ratza, for their loving patience and generosity that gave me the freedom to explore the limits of my world, and my sister, Claudia, for introducing me to poetry and literature. Thanks also to Robert Williams and the entire Quippy Quill Productions Department for powering our Lightning Brain Series forward. And a special thanks to Adam Horton for his careful draft reviews and suggestions.

I wish to dedicate this series to the readers who have embraced plot and characters, delighting in tracing their journey-through-life trajectories. And just like our characters, the trajectory of each reader is also sui generis—a popular word from the Latin meaning of its own kind. And though each of us is unique, our trajectories share a similar outline. Another poem from Indira distills the essence.

Triple Crown

Are you where you meant to be?
Engaged in what you meant to do?
With those who wish to share with you"
The joys of your maturity.

It's not like the past early years,
You search for meaning in your life.
The journey's often fraught with strife,
Some paths may lead to bitter tears.

This crown is worn by very few,
It's oft beyond the outstretched reach.
Try your best but life will teach,
Be grateful for what you've been able to reach.

CONTENTS

Chapter 1
December 2121

"Christmas Nightmare"
Thread 1 Chapter 1

"BE CAREFUL, YOU IDIOT! That might be our last hope for keeping Electra alive." Robin had harsher words to hurl at Carter, but his quick reflexes kept the bottle from rolling off the work station and Robin's additional words from spilling out.

"I've got it. And I found others too." Carter gingerly packed the bottles into the carrier, then scoured the workstation for any remaining experimental vaccine containers.

"Make sure you bring all her logs and notebooks so Matt can figure out what to do. We gotta go."

At 10 p.m. on Christmas Eve, the second squad sent to Electra's university lab was about to leave, taking with it Techno-Plague vaccines. The first squad had crashed en route. Clarence, Electra's long-time EMT friend who had been working at her grandfather's clinic long before "Doc" Kittner was murdered eight years ago, was dead, and Su, Electra's godmother and faithful biotech researcher, was in an emergency room. Electra's fate rides with Carter and Robin; they must race through a snowstorm back to Electra's house where Matt, Mariah, and Zoe are struggling to keep her alive.

Carter yelled to the guard as he pushed Robin through the doorway.

"Thanks for helping us. I hope plows have kept up with the snowfall."

"Good luck, young fella. I've known the young lady since she started here as a graduate student. She's grown a lot and it'd be a shame for her career to be terminated by the T-Plague. Drive safe." Carter—Electra's former "almost-significant other"—was struggling to get a grip on what he and Electra's support group would need to do next. Though his thoughts were racing faster than his prized Corvette, the comparison was actually damnation by faint praise because driving was slow-going. *I'm gonna be in trouble on the side roads. My Vette's low clearance won't make it through the drifts, but I'll get as close as I can. And I sure hope Matt can interpret Electra's notes.* While Carter drove, Robin thumbed through one of the notebooks; her troubled look mirroring the conditions.

"I can't understand a thing I'm reading. Has Electra ever shown you some of her work?"

"No, but she told me about some of the stuff she's working on, and she sure had a command of the research. Come to think of it, until the T-Plague got her, she seemed to have a command of just about everything. But I always got the feeling she never wanted to reveal too much about her work, or herself. And my economics training doesn't have the math or science to handle what you're looking at. Sorry."

"Matt's medical training should help. He's studied a lot of science and is good at math too. He coaches me through some of my math classes." Neither felt like talking more, so Robin peered mutely at the blowing snow, unable to help Carter navigate through the storm.

The snow plows had been clearing the main routes since the storm began early morning, making travel possible, but driving was treacherous once on the side streets. Fortunately, most people were hunkering at home, so the ghost-like traffic eliminated stuck-car obstacles. But Carter's prediction was right. As soon as he drove onto the secondary roads, his Corvette began losing traction, finally hanging up in a snowdrift about a mile from Electra's house. *It's time to call Matt.*

Matt Fortier, Robin's sometimes co-friend, depending on her emotional state, had been called into action late yesterday afternoon to help keep Electra alive. She had contracted a new, virulent strain of the T-Plague. He had done all he could, but it wasn't enough unless he had the right vaccines. He and his helpers kept her packed in snow, fighting a losing battle to keep her 110-plus temperature from killing her brain before her immune system killed the virus.

Electra had lapsed into a coma; all he could do now was stay at her side, at the ready, until vaccines arrive. And that's where he was when his cellphone beeped.

"Matt, this is Carter…We're stuck in the snow about a mile away on Sunnyside… We'll hike from there… Yeah, that'd help… Have Zoe meet us… She can help Robin carry the logs and notebooks." After disconnecting the call, Carter shouted instructions to Robin as he pulled her from the car.

"The wind and the snow are still blowing. Hold onto me so you don't slip. Footing's bad and you're not wearing boots."

Robin wrapped her free arm about his waist, saying nothing while looking straight ahead, clutching a briefcase and wearing a backpack loaded with Electra's notebooks. They walked several blocks before Carter spotted a silhouette framed against the snow hurrying toward them.

"That must be Zoe. I don't know much about her. I think she's Electra's current roommate. Maybe Mariah knows more about her."

Robin said nothing but thought to herself, How odd for Electra to have a roommate and not tell me. I'm supposed to be her best friend. Something's going on in her personal life that I don't know about. It's my fault we've drifted apart, but I'll worry about that later. Right now, let's just keep her alive. The silhouette morphed into a bundled, boot-clad lady of average height as it approached Carter.

"You must be Zoe Vargas. I'm Carter Quavah, and this is Robin Setdarova."

"Hi. Let me carry the briefcase." Zoe grabbed it and without another word started retracing her steps so fast that the other two struggled to keep up.

"I'm glad you're wearing boots. Robin and I will follow in your tracks. How's Electra."

"Not good. Still in a coma. Please walk faster."

Matt rushed to the front door when he heard it open. "I need an antidote I can inject. Did you find any?"

"Yes, but I don't know what it's for. Robin retrieved all the notebooks, and you'll need to figure out what to do." Matt took all they gave him into the kitchen, where he unpacked the drug carrier and spread out the notebooks.

"Look, why don't all of you go upstairs and watch over Electra. I'll be there as soon as I know what to do." Everyone joined Mariah, who was already at Electra's bedside, trusting Matt to figure out how to use the vaccines.

He was ready by three in the morning, after studying as best he could Electra's main log book. It was neat and thoroughly maintained chronologically up to Christmas Eve, but much was notated in biotech drug terminology he couldn't decipher. There was a jumble of alphabetic vaccines and antidotes that he pieced together, along with usage and dosing regimens, but he was out of time to study further and had to act now. Electra's vital signs had been in the danger zone for hours. She would be dead by sunrise if he didn't do something. He ran upstairs to tell his four exhausted partners his best guess.

"I think I've found the right antidote for the mutated virus. Since I can't wake her I have to inject it, and I've estimated from her notes how much and how often. We'll keep snow packed around her until her temperature drops. I'll stay awake to monitor vital signs and give more injections. If my guess is right, she should pull out of the coma soon after the fever breaks. Any questions before I inject her?" Zoe didn't have a question, but she did have ideas.

"We should take turns spelling each other. That way we can all get some rest and be ready for action when she comes to. And we should eat something to maintain our energy level, even if we're not hungry." Matt shook his head no before replying.

"Thanks for offering, but I need to stay at her side. Why don't you ladies make something to eat while Carter checks sleeping arrangements?" The ladies went to the kitchen while Carter rearranged blankets and floor mattresses in a nearby bedroom, then came to Matt's side, bringing sandwiches and soft drinks. As they studied the comatose creature packed partially in snow, lying naked before them under a bedsheet, Carter's words broke the silence.

"How different a Christmas story we're living through. Easter, not Christmas, is for resurrection. I hope the injection brings her back to life. If not, the story becomes a nightmare." Their eyes met just before Matt inserted the needle into a vein on Electra's forearm, just below the elbow. No words were spoken as both sent silent prayers to their personal gods, then sat while mutely eating. Twenty minutes later, Carter nodded to Matt, then rose silently to leave, thinking to himself, In everything she did, Electra always hoped for the best but planned for the worst. But I'm too tired to think straight. But I've learned from her not to worry about what's outside my control. It's time I followed her advice.

Carter trudged to the other bedroom, leaving Matt alone and in charge of what little control he had, and before collapsing on a vacant mattress, briefly pondered his sleeping partners. Robin and Electra are the same age—I think about twenty-four—but Electra is much more mature in all ways, at least matching Zoe and Mariah's early thirties, same as mine and Matt's. Electra is a source of strength for the ladies in ways I don't understand. And I don't think they'll know what to do if Electra doesn't pull through. At least I'm ahead of them, but not by much. Carter fell into a dreamless sleep minutes after his head hit the pillow.

Chapter 2
December 2121

"Christmas Present"
Thread 1 Chapter 2

THE LIGHTNING BRAIN HAD been waging a life-or-death battle against T-Plague virus for the past twenty-four hours, concentrating all its resources and empowering its immune system to kill the intruder, and the injected antidote tipped the struggle in Electra's favor. The lightning brain had won; it had carried out the prime directive of every living organism: to survive, to go on living. And it was ready to claim the spoils of victory: it was about to spark Electra's consciousness back to life.

But victory came at a terrible cost; neural entanglement gravely crippled Electra's lightning brain; it would need an unknown amount of time and effort to repair its physical, cognitive, and emotional inter-neural systems if it were ever to recover fully. If it didn't, what was coming back to life would be a different person and never again would Electra, the girl with the lightning brain, be exceptional.

In the heat of battle, the lightning brain had shut down everything but basal life support systems. Now that the battle was over, it was reactivating them, flickering the subconscious back to life, which brought back instinctive physical and emotional primal powers for navigating an unrecognizable world. At first, Electra's eyes saw only shapeless white light, but shimmering images gradually emerged, as if they were blurred pictures trapped behind a fine mesh screen. Her ears filled with a booming, buzzing confusion that gradually coalesced into sounds and syllables she could not understand, like words spoken from a distant underwater source. All other senses were blank slates, and Electra did what any newborn would do: she cried out in fear.

Matt lurched awake. He had been watching over Electra through the night, hoping she would come back from the dead, and her cries were the Christmas present he had prayed for. He grabbed her shoulders to keep her still, to comfort her now that she was regaining consciousness as Christmas Day dawned pristine clear and bright.

"Electra. Electra. Can you hear me?" Matt saw her look of fear change to a quizzical expression, as if groping to recall what was no longer in reach.

"Ye-yes," she stammered hoarsely.

"Electra, it's Matt. We're all here to help you. Do you know where you are?"

"Nu-uh-no."

"Are you in pain? Is it OK for you to talk?" Matt saw her eyes begin to focus on the immediate as she turned her head from side to side. She licked her lips and rasped an indistinct reply.

"N-no pain. Ca-can talk little... Need drink." Matt's shouts roused his team.

"Robin! Electra's awake. Get water." Carter, Mariah and Zoe scrambled to Matt's side, all peering intently into a pair of eyes struggling to grasp an unrecognizable world. Robin poked a flexible straw into Electra's lips and she sucked the bottle dry. Matt took vital readings and reported back.

"Her temperature is 101; pulse is 80; blood pressure is 140 over 90. Thank God the fever broke. She's come back from the dead. I'll test in a moment to see if she's contagious, but I need to explain the situation and get her to talk with us. Once we get started, ask me if you have a question and I'll ask her. OK?" All nodded in agreement. Matt asked first if she needed to pee, even though it was unlikely because she had sweated away most of what would have accumulated. She shook her head no.

"Please pay close attention. Don't try to talk just yet. My name is Matt and these are your friends..." Matt spoke each name while pointing. "We are here to help you recover from the T-Plague, which almost killed you yesterday. You've been in a coma for nearly twelve hours, but the vaccine shots I gave you did the trick. I'm going to ask you questions and I want you to think as best as you can before nodding yes or no. Do you remember what happened yesterday before you went into a coma?" Electra's eyes matched her negative nod.

"OK, let's back up. You don't know what happened yesterday, and you don't know where you are. Do you know who you are, or who we are?"

Everyone saw incipient fear in her eyes as she nodded no, so Matt took a different approach. He comforted her with a smile, cupping her face in his hands.

"After what you've just been through, it's too soon for you to remember much of anything, so here's what we're going to do. Your girlfriends—Robin, Mariah, and Zoe—are going to bathe and dress you, then get some nourishment in you. And your guy-friends—that's Carter and me—will fix up your bedroom. We'll talk later after you've had a chance to adjust."

Robin took charge of the ladies. Electra was too weak to stand, so she ordered Mariah and Zoe to put her into the wheelchair and then into the bathtub as soon as she filled it. Then she went to the kitchen and prepared Electra's breakfast. Electra hasn't eaten solid food for two days, and she's dehydrated. No wonder she's so weak. We'll feed her small amounts at frequent intervals. We'll start with apple sauce and banana slices. And we'll use one of her vitamin-fortified sports drinks.

"Try to stand while Mariah and I lift you. Then step into the bathtub." Zoe was the smallest of the three, but all were thin, and Electra's ordeal had removed pounds as well as color, making her pale as a snowflake, so they easily situated her in the warm water. "Mariah will shampoo your hair and wash your head and shoulders, and I'll take care of the rest."

"That's good by me," Electra mumbled, then asked for a mirror before they started. She held it in trembling hands as she surveyed uncertain terrain. What she saw startled her. I have no recollection of this image. I don't recognize a thing! And what I see is appalling. It looks like someone whose life has been sucked out. Lifeless and pale like a corpse. And the pitch-black hair is a stringy tangled mess.

Features that once might have been striking still are, but in a bad way. They're awfully gaunt and hard-edged. And whoever it is looks hopelessly lost." Zoe snatched the mirror before Electra dropped it.

"Don't worry! We'll get you looking good again. You just survived a life-or-death battle, and you look great to us." Zoe and Mariah did their best, completing the job by toweling her off, then blow drying and combing her hair. Electra said nothing. A glimmer of a smile thanked them, but a look of puzzlement remained.

Meanwhile, Robin checked with Matt and Carter, who, after stripping the bed and removing its waterlogged mattress, had cleaned and straightened the room.

"Hey guys, let's have Electra sit in her wheelchair while she eats breakfast here. If she's strong enough afterwards, you can carry her downstairs. It's better for her to be doing something down there rather than just sitting up here." Matt spoke for the guys.

"You're right, and after that I'm going to Clarence's clinic to meet with Dr. Liefen-Liu. I had the presence of mind to call him last night, so he knows the bad news about Clarence. We'll transfer Su to the clinic, and he'll serve as Su and Electra's physician. Carter, do you want to come with me?"

"Yes, and on the way back let's buy a new mattress and retrieve my Vette."

By the time Robin returned with Electra's breakfast, everyone was gathered in the bedroom. Zoe volunteered to handle the spoon. Less than a month ago Electra was feeding me breakfast. Now it's my turn to take care of her.

Matt took Electra's vital signs once more, and then announced next steps while Zoe wiped Electra's face clean.

"Listen up, everyone. Electra should be OK without me for a while. Carter and I are going to transfer Su to Clarence's clinic, then we'll come back here to figure out who wants to help me keep Electra on the road to recovery. I'll explain this to Electra right now." Zoe stepped aside for Matt to caress Electra's cheek.

"Electra, this is Matt again. Your temperature has fallen to 99 and you are out of danger. Your girlfriends will take care of you until Carter and I get back. We are transferring your friend Su to your grandfather's clinic. We'll tell you all about it when we get back, and we'll talk about getting you back in action." Electra was not yet talking but didn't need to say anything. Her expression of thanks was clearer than words. A subliminal synapse clicked in the lightning brain when it heard the name Su. I might know that name, but I

don't know why. Why is she in a hospital? I must see her.

Matt put his hands on her shoulders to keep her from struggling to get up.

"Please don't worry about Su. I'll take care of her for all of us. I'll be back as soon as I can. Robin, how about you take charge until we get back?"

"OK, but help us get Electra downstairs before you go…"

What will become of Electra? Clarence and I failed to get her antidote. And how is Clarence? Those were the first thoughts that came to Su when she regained consciousness. The last thing I remember is the ambulance flipping over the guardrail. As she glanced around the room, she knew immediately where she was. The minimal lighting, sterile white walls, and medical monitoring gauges next to a rail-equipped metal bed told her she was lying flat on her back in a hospital room. And the spinal brace and inability to move her legs indicated that her back was broken. Su fought off panic by searching for something to cling to, and what she found gave her resolve.

I'm the last of the star-crossed Worldstars, and though I'm injured I'm still alive. It's not yet my time to go. Our biotech careers started so well. Jason said we were kissed by the sun, but we were actually cursed by the devil. First, Indira was struck by lightning while giving birth to Electra, then Jason blew himself up in the lab. And Adom was gunned down protecting me from Chinese corporate espionage agents. Well, I'm still here, and I'm not the last of Electra's keepers. I've got to talk with Matt. Su punched the call button that summoned a nurse.

"Good morning, Su-Lin. How are you feeling?"

"Other than a headache, soreness all over, and no feeling in my legs, fine. Please, you must help me get in touch with a Matt Fortier.

It's most important."

"Please don't worry. He and a friend are on the way. Let me check how the gash on your forehead is healing. You must have hit the windshield when the ambulance crash-landed. And the muscle soreness is normal. The amount of jostling you get in a car accident is like playing a football game while wearing no padding. You're very lucky that only your back is broken."

"Would you be able to help me to the bathroom?" The nurse's smile widened.

"Of course. And you're a nurse's delight. Petite and light. Is your spinal brace comfortable enough for you?"

"Yes."

"Good. I'll get you to a sitting position, and then set you in a wheelchair. The area around your forehead stitches is infection-free. There should be little scarring, and your hair might cover it. Windshield safety glass prevented a more serious head injury. Would you like a pain reliever?"

"No, thank you, a pain reliever's not necessary. Thank you for all your help."

"You're welcome. And I'll bring you breakfast after we get you back from the bathroom. Your friends might be here by then. I think the doctor will brief them first. Your friend Matt is a medical professional, a certified EMT."

The roads were plowed, and the traffic was light on this sparkling Christmas morning, so Matt and Carter concentrated on their patients. Carter spoke first.

"You've been focused on Electra for the past twenty-four hours. You must be running on adrenaline."

"Some, but not completely. The naps I took helped, and I'm glad Zoe forced me to eat. I feel ready for Electra's next steps, which should now have a clearer path to recovery. It's Su-Lin Song Chou I'm worried about. Do you know much about her? Robin met her on a couple of trips to Austin. Electra sometimes calls her Aunt Su. She's petite, polite, and seems very smart. Robin says she plays the piano to relax from biotech R&D."

"Well, you know more than I do. I'm sure we'll get to know her better as she starts her recovery here in DC."

Su sat in the wheelchair after finishing breakfast, musing about Carter and Matt. They're good-looking young lads. Trim athletic builds, both about the same height, just an inch or so taller than Electra. I'd guess they're maybe thirty, plus or minus. Matt's got the curly, dark brown hair; Carter's is lighter and shorter. According to what Electra told me on her last visit to Austin, Matt and Robin are co-friends, and he wants her to accept his vow-cer marriage contract, but Robin's still coming to terms with her sexuality and related emotional issues. And I think Electra de-escalated Carter's intimacy. The emotions of youth cut both ways, giving highs and lows. And I know, for I've been there, done that, and have tried moving on. But that is still difficult for me.

Su's reverie was broken by the sound of Matt, Carter, and the attending physician approaching. She usually greeted people with typical oriental reserve and politeness, letting them speak first. But not this time. Su preempted the conversation.

"How is Electra?"

"Her fever broke, and she'll recover. We'll tell you all the details later, but right now let's focus on you. Dr. Edelman, would you please tell Su the good news?"

"Good morning, Su-Lin. I'm Dr. Edelman, an on-duty physician. I am pleased to report that your condition is stable enough for you to be transferred to Matt's hospital. He's one of the EMTs at Loudoun County Hospital, where Dr. Henry Liefen-Liu will take care of you. I know all of this is happening awfully fast, so you must have questions. What would you like to ask me?" Su's oriental politeness kicked in.

"Dr. Edelman, thank you for treating me. I'm sure Dr. Liefen-Liu and Matt will answer all my questions, so it's unfair of me to take up any more of your time. I am ready to go."

"Well then, Matt has all the medical forms for you to sign. And we've transferred your files electronically, so Matt's clinic will handle them going forward. So just sign, and you'll be all set for the transfer."

Ever the diplomat, Carter tried chatting up a stream of small talk on the drive but soon realized Su preferred solitude, so he respected her private space. A break will be good for all of us so we can recharge our emotional batteries. What's that famous quote from a legendary football coach? "Fatigue makes cowards of us all." We need to be fresh, mentally and emotionally, when we get Su checked in. By the time they met with the doctor, all three were ready.

Dr. Liefen-Liu was empathetically professional, which matched Su's temperament. His instructions were as clear as Christmas Day's cloudless sky.

"I'll take additional images of Su's back and do a brain scan to make sure she doesn't have latent neural cavity swelling caused by colliding with the windshield. And I want you to bring Electra here tomorrow so I can evaluate her. We need to measure how much neural damage the T-Plague caused. Matt, it looks like we have two patients: Su and Electra. And Su, please do not worry. You'll get the best possible care, and we'll get you back to Austin as soon as you're ready."

"Thank you. And please tell me, how is Clarence?"

"Clarence died in the crash. Matt has offered to explain." Neither the doctor nor Su said another word as Matt filled in the remainder of the conversation. Then he wrapped up the meeting.

"We'll be back tomorrow mid-morning, if that's OK. It's nearly 5 p.m., so we'll be going. Su, please don't worry. Our plan is to get you back to Austin as soon as you're ready to travel and all preparations are made. You'll see, everything's going to be fine." Su smiled, but kept her final thoughts to herself.

He seems so genuine, so nice. They all do. Maybe everything will turn out all right for all of us. What was Indira's answer to any question? Aha, the answer given by the Buddhist monk: Perhaps.

Carter and Matt were drained physically and emotionally by the time they drove back to Electra's. Matt had called Robin earlier to let her know what was going on with Su, and Robin told him Electra was stronger, able to talk better. And when they entered the house, they knew everything was under control. Mariah and Zoe were preparing dinner, while Robin was sitting in the living room with Electra. Matt took Electra's readings one more time.

"All vital signs are pretty much back to normal. And you look better now than this morning. Tomorrow, we'll take you to the clinic for Dr. Liefen-Liu to check you out."

"Good. Maybe seeing see Su, Clarence and Dr. Liefen-Liu all at once will trigger my memory." Carter and Matt looked at Robin, numb expressions on all three. "Hey, what's wrong?" Robin took a deep breath and answered.

"Last night Su and Clarence drove to your lab to get your antidote. The weather was terrible and they were in an accident. Clarence died. Su's back is broken. I'm sorry to tell you this right now, but I know you better than anyone here. You're strong and resilient, and always want to know the facts, know the truth."

A look of utter devastation swept across Electra. Her lips quivered, unable to sound a single syllable. And then her emotions broke loose as she sobbed uncontrollably. Robin reached out and Electra clutched her as if she were drowning. Robin kissed and rubbed her hair.

"Electra, Electra. It's all right. Let go of your emotions, let them flow. All of us will keep you safe." Matt and Carter retreated to the kitchen while Robin shared Electra's anguish. They would return with reinforcements when appropriate, when the emotional storm had subsided.

Zoe and Mariah entered while the storm was raging. Robin lifted Electra out of the wheelchair and the three of them formed a circle, hugging and supporting their extraordinary friend. The storm ended as Electra regained control of her spent emotions.

"I don't know why I broke down. I guess I needed to let go. Su and Clarence must mean a lot to me. I'm better now. Let me sit on the couch. I'm done with the wheelchair." The four sat in the living room, two bracketing Electra and Robin sitting across. Robin finally broke the silence.

"Carter and Matt are getting dinner on the table. I'll check how they're doing, and when I call, please join us in the dining room. We all need to eat." Ten minutes later, Robin issued the first call for dinner. Zoe and Mariah pulled Electra to her feet, then guided her to the dining room.

The fellows had done a nice job setting an inviting table, using Zoe's Christmas napkins and candles. Carter sat at the head, Robin at the other end, Electra and Mariah on her right, and Matt and Zoe on her left. The dinner was what had been planned for Christmas Eve: baked beans and Swedish meatballs served with cornbread, salad, and a Pinot Noir. Pumpkin pie for dessert. Carter stood, palms pressed to the table, as he gave a combination blessing and recap.

"As long as I live, I shall always remember this Christmas. And I thank God for the present we received. Electra is with us once again. I'm sure we all share the same sentiment. It's been an emotional couple of days; Matt and I are exhausted, as no doubt you are too. Ladies, thanks for letting us stay overnight. Tomorrow, Matt will take Electra to the hospital so the doctor can evaluate her condition. And we'll also discuss what to do for Su. My guess is we'll have two patients to care for. We'll talk about all this tomorrow, after everyone gets a good night's sleep. But for tonight, let's just enjoy the dinner Zoe and Mariah prepared, and give thanks for our Holiday blessings." Everyone raised a wine glass, following Carter's lead. And then Electra haltingly spoke.

"I thank you all for your—uh-your present of friendship. I'm sorry I'm not myself yet. My brain's not thinking clearly, but I'm talking better and feel stronger than I did this morning. And even though I don't remember me or you, I know you'll help me figure out what to do." Electra stopped talking; she couldn't think of anything else to say, so Mariah helped her out.

"You'll be good as new when we get finished with you. And we'll start tomorrow, but let's start eating now before the food gets cold."

The wine and the food helped everyone loosen the cumulative stress. After dessert, Electra asked to be excused. She wanted quiet time to work on her computer. Perhaps some document or image would pop up, triggering damaged or dormant memory. Robin walked her to the workstation, then returned to the group. Electra sat glumly, peering numbly at an array of equipment, her brain as blank as the lifeless computer screens staring back.

How intimidating. I'm facing three monitors connected to several computers. If I'm supposed to know how to use this stuff, I must have been pretty smart at one time. She screwed her courage tight and punched the on buttons; the system came to life. Images and an occasional video paraded across the screens, accompanied by a female voice welcoming her by name and asking for a password. But nothing came to mind; she hadn't a clue what to do, so she sat and watched the pictures float by. Most of them caused subliminal emotional tremors.

I must know all these people from some time and place I can't recall. Who's the group of four holding the Worldstars banner? I sort of look like one of them, and the other lady is Chinese. Could that be Su? And the kindly-looking older person. Is that his son and granddaughter with him? And is the little girl possibly me? And the pictures of three girls. The ash-blonde, blue-eyed one could be Robin, and the raven-haired one might be me. But who's the beautiful one with them? And there are no pictures of Carter and Matt, or Zoe and Mariah. Why not?

The more she looked, the more frustrated she became, so she turned off the computer before her headache became worse. She was about to head back to the dining room when she spied an envelope tucked unobtrusively beneath the keyboard; when she removed it, she saw she had written it to herself.

DATE: 12/23/2016

TO: Electra

FROM: Electra

SUBJECT: Open if you feel LOST

I couldn't possibly be more lost. What did I want to tell myself?

She peeled back the flap and read the one-page note. Do the following as soon as possible in this sequence:

1. Get a brain scan and take an I.Q. test.
2. Find out the condition of our brain from the test results.
3. Get our bank safety deposit box key from our Home Management Notebook, which is in the bottom right drawer of our computer workstation.
4. Go to our bank and get into our safety deposit box. (Address is with the key).

5.   Read the letter on top and follow the instructions.

6.   Do not tell or let anyone read these items.

YOUR LIFE AND MINE DEPEND ON HOW WELL YOU DO!

Electra re-read the note, then stared into space, trying to concentrate. She felt a distant stirring in her cognitive self, as if her brain were trying to switch gears to a better state of awareness. I have no idea why I wrote this to myself, but at least I know what to do next. I wrote it the day before I was struck down by the T-Plague. There's gotta be some connection. Maybe things will start to clear up tomorrow. Now it's time to rest. Electra put the note back into the envelope, hid it in her Home Management Notebook, and rejoined her support group.

"Well, I figured out how to turn the computer on, but that's about all I accomplished. I want to go to bed. I need to sleep, so I'm saying good night." Zoe jumped up.

"I know you're feeling better and can manage on your own, but let me walk with you just in case you need help."

"Thanks, Zoe. See you all tomorrow…"

As she lay in warmth of her bed, a feeling of calm enveloped her. For the very first time since coming back from the dead, thoughts in her brain were beginning to come into focus. Neural circuits were slowly beginning to trigger, trying to regenerate parts of her cognitive self. She was beginning to understand her surroundings once again.

These people who are with me sure seem to have my best interests at heart. I guess they love me, and maybe I love them too. I don't know why, but even though it'll take time, I'll figure it out. Let me focus on what I know so far about each one.

I'll start with Robin, thin, high-strung Robin, pictured with me and some other female. I don't know why, but I feel I've known Robin for a long time. Then there's Mariah, scrawny and flat-chested. Odd, but I feel sexually attracted to her. And what about Zoe? She seems pert, and her tawny-colored short hair fits her and makes her cute. And for some reason, I feel this overwhelming desire to protect her. Like she's been wounded and is vulnerable. There must be a story behind all this.

Electra let her brain roam free, hoping some missing pieces would snap into place but nothing did, so she thought about the fellows. Who are Matt and Carter? Could they be my lovers? I have this feeling that Carter and I are close. And is Matt connected with Robin or Zoe? I don't know, but I sense tension between Robin and Matt. Well, enough thinking for now. I need to sleep, to regain my physical and emotional strength, and to let my brain heal itself.

A dreamless sleep descended, but while Electra slept, the lightning brain kept working.

Chapter 3
December 2121

"The Good, the Bad, and the Ugly"
Thread 1 Chapter 3

ELECTRA AWOKE RESTED AND alert just before the dawn, resolving that every morning when she first awakens she would try to recall what's going on in her memory, past and present, and then prepare for the day ahead. Perhaps more recollections will have sorted themselves out during the night. As she unfolded out of bed, a neural circuit snapped. My last name is Kittner! I am Electra Kittner, and today I'll find out more about who that person is.

She walked to the window and looked out upon a snow-white landscape just beginning to sparkle as day chases the night away. Let's see, today is the day after Christmas, December 26th. It's Boxing Day in England, but why did I just recall this? Do I have friends in England? And why do I suddenly have this urge to exercise? Maybe fitness is important to me. I better follow where my fitness itch leads. She changed into shorts and a tee shirt, then quietly snuck downstairs, looking for exercise equipment. There was nothing on the first floor, so she checked out the basement, where she found more than she bargained for.

This has got to be a fitness center for a serious jock. It's even got wall mirrors to check form and position when lifting. Am I supposed to be some sort of athlete? She studied the machines and decided it was too soon to use them. I feel like my body is coming back to life, but not with much of my old strength, so I'll ease into exercise. I'll just do some sit-ups, push-ups, and pull-ups. It took less than five minutes to confirm how much strength the T-Plague had sapped.

She managed only twenty sit-ups and ten push-ups before her muscles quit. And she lost grip of the bar after only one pull-up.

Since no one else was up yet, Electra started complaining out loud, but soft enough not to disturb the sleepers.

"Damn! I must be stronger than that. Let me check my definition." She slipped off her shorts and top so she could see the bare facts from top to toe. "Well, my face and hair look better than yesterday. Sort of like life is seeping back in after being drained out. And my physique is toned and cut. So where did my strength go?"

"It's still there. It's just waiting for you to bring it back to life." Electra jumped like a cat jolted by static electricity.

"Matt! You startled me. Don't look! Let me put my clothes on!" Matt paused on the stairs until Electra was back in uniform, then came to her.

"When your memory comes back, you'll remember I was your physical therapist and trainer while you were recovering from that terrible car crash that killed Christi and broke your neck. I know your anatomy better than just about anyone. Look, your brain and body took a terrible beating battling the T-Plague, but you won. I'll put you on a workout program that will get your body back in the shape it was." Matt had more to say, but only to himself. She seems a bit better physically and mentally than she was yesterday, but I can tell she's struggling to absorb what I've just told her. Well, maybe the more she hears, the faster it will click into place.

"I was in an accident? And someone named Christi was killed?" Another synapse snapped. "My god! Now I know the third girl in the picture. Robin, Christi and I were best friends. Am I right?"

"Yes, but I don't know much about her. It'll be better if you talk to Robin about Christi, but I can tell you about your fitness. Your body seems to have an ability to heal quickly, and to morph into whatever you want it to be. I didn't know you when you were a kid, but you were supposed to be a great soccer player. And for some reason, you stopped competing in sports, but you kept training. And when Carter first met you, you intimidated him. He's a good athlete in his own right, but he told me you probably could beat him in arm wrestling, or in just about any fitness contest." Electra's expression matched her words.

"Well, that was then, but that couldn't possibly happen now. I barely did one pull-up. You're sure you can bring me back?"

"Let me tell you a story about Greg LeMond, the winner of the 1989 Tour De France. I'll use the words I remember as told by Phil Liggett, the legendary cycling sportscaster. It goes something like this:

'And now in the starting gate for the opening time trial in the 1989 Tour De France is American Greg LeMond, former World Champion and Tour Winner, making a comeback after more than a year's layoff from a near-fatal hunting accident. His progress has been slow, but let's never forget that true athletic greatness never goes very far away. It's there, waiting for him to bring it back. But it takes hard work to do so, and his comeback is not assured. We will follow the story in the 21 stages and 2200 miles that await.'

"I want you to watch on the Internet the very last stage of the 1989 Tour. It's one of the most inspiring athletic performances I've ever seen." Matt could tell Electra was getting restless. Good! She's

in no mood to wait. That's the spirit I want to see.

"OK, I'll watch it. But please give me your summary."

"The last stage is a 25-kilometer time trial that ended on the Champs-Élysées in Paris. Greg Le Mond was in second place, 50 seconds behind the leader, Laurent Fignon, who had won the Tour in '83 and '84. Time trials are called the 'Race of Truth' because you ride alone. There's no place to hide. The riders start every two minutes in reverse order of race standing. LeMond was the first Tour rider to use triathlon bars and disk wheels, and that day he road like a man possessed. The experts thought the distance was too short to make up a 50-seconds deficit, but LeMond did that and more, winning by just 8 seconds, the shortest margin of victory in Tour history. And Fignon rode past the point of exhaustion. He collapsed after crossing the finish line.

"I've watched it dozens of times, and each time I come away as thrilled and as motivated as the very first. I want you to watch it soon. It will motivate you too. It'll show what your training can do to bring you back. I know what's in you." Electra threw her arms around Matt.

"I'll do whatever you want me to do, and I'll start when you want me to start. Please, help me come back."

"We'll start tomorrow, after we hear today from Dr. Liefen-Liu. Let's go upstairs and get your team in action. Then you and I will go to your grandfather's clinic."

The mood at the breakfast table was upbeat. Carter announced that while Electra and Matt were at the clinic, he and the ladies would start organizing who'd be doing what in the coming weeks.

"It's nine a.m. now. When do you think you'll bring Electra back?"

"Since it's still early, and it's the day after Christmas, the clinic shouldn't have a lot going on, so the brain scan and I.Q. testing should be completed by noon. After that, Electra and I will meet with Su and the doctor so we know what's next for her. I expect the scan and test results will be ready for discussion with the doctor by three. We should be back by five this afternoon. See you all then."

Traffic was light on that Saturday after Christmas, and Dr. Liefen Liu met with them promptly.

"Good morning, Electra; good morning Matt. Electra, do you remember me? My name is Henry Liefen Liu. I and Dr. Rihanna Antar treated you after your accident four years ago." Electra peered at the trim Chinese doctor, who appeared to be in his mid-to-late forties.

"Hello Doctor. I'm sorry, but I can't seem to recall ever being treated by you. I hope you can tell me how my brain is, and what it needs to do to recover."

"We'll soon find out. This morning we'll do a brain scan first, and then give you an intelligence test. We need to evaluate your brain's neural pattern and test your cognitive abilities. Normally, we would compare today's results with your last set of tests, but unfortunately there are no records for comparison. The comparison would show us how much damage has been done. But today's testing will show us how well your brain is currently functioning. So, please come with me. You can meet Matt at the reception area about noon. And since Matt starts officially on Monday as our night duty EMT, he can visit with his colleagues until then."

The rest of Matt's morning melted away. His associates walked him through enough of the emergency room's standard operating procedures so he'd be useful on day one. Matt wanted to serve a higher purpose by working for the understaffed clinic, taking Clarence's place while continuing to work at Jennifer Conklin's holistic healthcare business. As he came out of the E.R., he saw Electra walking to the reception area.

"So, how was your morning? Does anything here seem familiar?"

"No, not yet. Every now and then I get an intuitive feeling I've been here before, but nothing definite yet. According to the doctor, I used to come here with my grandfather when I was little. He says Doc Kittner and I were best buddies, but I don't remember him at all."

"Give it time. And now it's time for us to meet with Su and the doctor. We'll wait for them in Examining Room C."

Su was already there, facing the door and waiting for everyone when Matt ushered Electra in. As her eyes locked onto Su's, a couple of neural circuits sparked twinges of recognition. She approached the wheelchair, struggling to find something to say but couldn't, so Su smiled and spoke first.

"My goodness, Electra. Your mother would say you could be mistaken for Persephone. Do you recognize me?"

"I know your name is Su. I feel I should know you, but I'm sorry, I don't recognize you." Su reached out with both hands.

"Well, I recognize you. Come sit next to me and let me tell you some things about yourself. And by the way, in Greek mythology, Persephone is a goddess, Queen of the Underworld. You look so pale!" Electra sat but Dr. Liefen-Liu came in before they could chat.

"Hello again, Electra and Matt. And hello again, Su. Matt and I already told Su what we think would be best for her, and she agrees, so I can make our meeting brief. Su's paralysis in her legs is caused by two cracked lumbar vertebrae. She must wear the back brace until the breaks mend. And that could take 10 to 12 weeks. The paralysis might disappear, but that depends on how the vertebrae and nerves heal. We can release her from the hospital if she has a place to stay while starting physical therapy. Matt says he can start P.T. on Monday, after he takes her tomorrow to Electra's home. And he'll make all arrangements for flying Su back to Austin as soon as possible. Matt assures me that Electra's support group can take care of Su until she leaves for Austin." Matt jumped into the conversation to help Electra get a grip on what she had just heard.

"Your support group is ready to take care of you and Su. We've already been talking about it, and when we get home we'll go over all the details." Additional neurons began firing in Electra's brain.

"Good. And Su can tell me more about who I am." The doctor had nothing else to say, other than final instructions.

"Excellent. We will discharge Su Monday morning. Matt and I will coordinate transferring all medical records when Su is ready to go back to Austin. And Matt, why don't you and Electra take Su back to her room. I'll go over test results with you and Electra back here at three."

Matt performed caregiver duties like a professional. He made sure Su and Electra ate, let them talk long enough to overcome any apprehension, and then made them rest.

"Both of you need to take a break. You'll have plenty of time to talk starting Monday, so let's not overdo it now." They agreed, so Matt took Electra to the reception area. Matt sat across from her, happy to let her sit in the stillness of her thoughts while he glanced at a sports magazine. Promptly at three, a nurse marched up.

"The doctor will see you now…"

"Electra, I have good news for you. Your scan and test results look good. I'll start with the scan. Neural activity patterns in your brain are normal. The images show the expected amount and locations of cellular activity. When there are fewer locations and less activity, that indicates T-Plague is causing neural entanglement. Matt will start giving you a drug we call the 'S-Vac Smart Pill' to keep T-Plague in remission.

"Now, let's talk about the results of your intelligence test. Congratulations, you scored in the upper fifteen percent, which is one standard deviation above the mean. That and your work ethic have contributed to your excellent academic career." Matt looked more relieved than Electra and though she didn't speak, he did.

"That's great news. And we'll make sure her support group continues getting her stronger, physically and emotionally. I can't wait to tell them. Thank you doctor."

Matt chatted happily on the drive home.

"I was afraid your brain might have been badly damaged, but it looks like you dodged the proverbial bullet. And Robin told me you invented a medical device you call the Neuro-Knitter that treats broken necks. She says you treated her when she broke hers. Maybe you can treat Su too." Electra nodded.

"That's a good idea. I'll check it out just as soon as I get my bearings." That was all she said to Matt, but there was much more she said to herself. I invented a Neuro-Knitter? And I healed Robin's broken neck? I don't remember anything at all about any of this. I have to get to the safety deposit box pronto.

"What time is it? If my bank is still open, would you please drive me there?"

"It's four-fifteen. Why do you need to go to the bank? I'll give you money if you need some." It was obvious Electra was agitated, so he pulled to the curb. "Look, tell me the name of your bank. I'll call them. Maybe they're open." I know the name of my damn bank! I saw it in my damn notebook last night. What is it? Suddenly, another neural circuit clicked; the name came into focus.

"It's the Middleburg Bank. I need to get some stuff out of my safety deposit box. My family has been a long-time customer. Please call the local branch. Tell them my last name is Kittner, and I must get items stored in my safety deposit box. I've got my key at home. Please!"

"OK, hold on while I call." Matt found the number and connected with the branch manager. "Hello. My name is Matt Fortier, and I'm calling on behalf of one of your customers, Electra Kittner… Yes, she's with me. Hold on, please, while I give her the phone."

"It's the branch manager, David Tustman." Matt handed Electra the phone; she was on her own. Damn, what do I do now? I'm having a panic attack! But suddenly, the attack subsided, replaced by a

calming thought. I know what I'll do. I'll just act naturally. I'll simply

pretend.

"Hello, David. This is Electra Kittner. I'm sorry to bother you so late on a Saturday, but I need to retrieve some documents from my safety deposit box. I need them for a Monday meeting. Would it be possible to come in today before you close?... No, I left the key at home… Let me ask Matt if we can get there by five." Matt signaled yes, so she continued. "We'll be there by five. And thank you so much." Electra disconnected the call, then returned the phone to Matt.

"Thank you for taking me there now. You are a good friend."

"All your support group people are your good friends. Come on, let's get your stuff and get home…"

Matt commanded the dinner table's attention as he directed the conversation.

"The good news, according to the Doctor, is that the neural scan looks perfectly normal. And even better, Electra scored in the top 15 percent on the I.Q. test. With all that going for her, she'll be thinking clearly again with just a little help from her friends. And as we all agreed, we're gonna be her support team, keeping her safe and on the mend until she's back to where she should be. What details can you and the ladies provide?" Carter spoke for the team.

"Well, we thought about who should be the primary caregiver, and Zoe volunteered because she is temporarily living with Electra. And Mariah and I will coach her on the Guardian Party public relations work Electra was doing, as well as explain her role on Angus McTear's Brain Trust. Electra, do you remember what the Brain Trust is?" She shook her head no. "Well, we provide policy recommendations to Angus, who is the acting president of the United States. Sounds impressive, doesn't it? Well not to worry. We'll give you all the background when it's time." Carter pushed onward.

"And Matt will be your physical therapist and conditioning trainer. I think you might have started this morning. Finally, Robin can help you regain emotional bearings and tell you about your friends in Austin. I know all this sounds like a lot to handle, but you were doing all this and more. It'll all come back if we're patient." Carter lightened the conversation by poking fun at himself.

"My last name is Quavah, which is derived from a Hebrew word meaning to be patient and wait. I'm not patient by nature, but I've learned to practice it, along with slowing down my quick temper and judgmental temperament. And if I can handle those things, you can handle your stuff because I've seen you in action. You'll be fine." Matt brought up the final subject.

"The doctor told me I can bring Su here Monday morning. Electra can be her caregiver with assistance from Zoe when needed. It'll give Su a chance to help Electra learn more about herself and her research, and while she's doing that we'll get Su ready to head back to Austin, probably by mid-January. So, there you have it: Electra and Su's recovery plans. Electra, what do you think? I hope we haven't overwhelmed you."

"Yes, you have, but I know you'll be patient when I ask you to repeat stuff. I'd be lost without all of you. Someday, I'll repay you for your kindness. I'm better today than yesterday, physically and mentally. And I'll get better each day. And now, I'd like to sit at my workstation and read some documents Matt and I picked up at the bank on the way home. I think it'll help jog my memory. I'll be there until bedtime." Everyone but Electra stayed at the table. Robin spoke first after she had gone.

"Electra is better today than yesterday, and I'm glad the Doctor is pleased with her test results. But I've known her since grade school, and right now she's just a shadow of herself—physically, mentally and emotionally. Matt and I have seen her remarkable ability to recover quickly and come back stronger than ever, but it's going to take all our efforts to bring her back, and I hope that'll be enough. But I can't think of anything else we can do. Can anyone else?" No one said a word until Zoe spoke up.

"Mariah, do you remember at Thanksgiving when Electra christened us the Phoenix Trio. She said that when in grade school she, Robin, and Christi were called the Three Queens, and she considered us to be the reincarnation." Robin looked hurt and spoke right up.

"Did Electra say why she didn't include me? I thought she and I were best friends."

"She didn't go into a lot of detail, but she said you were busy adjusting to life with Matt. But how about this: why don't we call her support group—that's the five of us—the Full House. You know, three queens and two kings. And we do sort of fill the place up." Carter was the first to speak.

"I like it, so let's go with it. And if there are no objections, let's clean up the dishes and get ready for tomorrow. We'll get another bedroom set up for Su, and we'll get ready to kick off Electra's recovery plan first thing tomorrow."

Meanwhile, Electra was sitting at her workstation, ready to remove the heavy rubber bands that secured all the items she had taken with her from the bank. It's good my safety deposit box is big. These binders and folders I built are hefty things. There's heavy reading ahead. Better start with my handwritten instruction page. Hmm…

MAKE SURE YOU HAVE THE RESULTS OF YOUR BRAIN SCAN AND I.Q. TEST.

Hello Electra. Actually, I'm going to call you Electra-A, because you are the Electra that exists after I poisoned us. (Don't worry, I'm not suicidal. It was an unavoidable accident.) I will refer to myself as Electra, the one whose brain state existed before the T-Plague put me out of commission.

I started putting this packet together the day after my poisoning in case my immune system and experimental drugs couldn't protect me from the T-Plague. Since you are now reading this, I— the old Electra —am dead. Or maybe not. It all depends on you. Let me describe what's in this packet:

- Instruction document (you're reading it now)

- Electra Chronicles" Notebooks (chronological diaries of your daily activity and history. DO NOT LOSE THEM. You'll never know what to do without them.)
- Twenty-four envelopes, each containing a letter discussing your progress. (Open one each month in numeric sequence, or when you think you're ready to talk with me.)
- Contingency Plans folder. It contains all the contingencies I could think of as we move forward.

You will use this packet to learn the details regarding who you were, who you are, how you got here, what you know, etc. Don't try to read it all at once. It's too much for you to assimilate. Study it every day until you get tired. Then come back later. It'll help if you read it in two ways: in chronological sequence and in reverse order.

Let's get the bad news out of the way. My assumption is the doctor said your brain scan was normal, and that your intelligence is pretty good, maybe in the upper quarter. Well for you, those results are not good. They are bad! Worse than bad, they are terrible. (Your brain scan should look like a forest of lighted Christmas trees. Your intelligence should be off the charts.) In other words, your brain— our brain which I refer to as the lightning brain—has been severely damaged by the T-Plague. The neural entanglement has crippled our cognitive ability and has trapped me inside. The lightning brain cannot shift into our extraordinary cognitive states where I exist. I hope you are smart enough to do what must be done.

Now, here's more bad news. My immune system couldn't handle the T-Plague virus mutation, nor could my experimental vaccines.

So my—our—condition may deteriorate further if you don't do something. Keep taking all the experimental drugs and vaccines. Maybe they'll have a delayed reaction that will help cure us. If they don't and you still bring me back, it'll provide cover for the extraordinary power of our lightning brain. We'll have an excuse if anyone ever questions why we have a freakish neural pattern: blame it on the T-Plague.

OK, let's have some good news. The lightning brain survived. And it picked you as the cognitive state best suited to bring me back, so you must be pretty damn smart and talented. And your cognitive persona has two other personas that work with you. You and I used to have an extraordinary physical persona. How much of it is intact I don't know, but I suspect some of it is still functioning. Physical states are controlled by primitive parts of the brain that include a section called the reptilian brain. It might have been damaged less than higher learning centers. I think entanglement affects the neocortex more than the other centers, and the neocortex is the site of our cognitive self. It'll be up to you to find out. We also have an emotional persona, which for me was often problematic. Emotions are controlled by older parts of the brain, like the amygdala or the hippocampus, and are close to the brain stem. This entire area of the brain is called the limbic brain. Emotions are a two-edged sword that are part of being human. I always was working to understand them, to know when to let them out and when to restrain them. You'll have to determine what condition they're in. Since they operate at a more primitive level than cognition, neural entanglement might not have damaged them as much. Good luck. Maybe you can help me deal with them better if you are able to bring me back from the dead.

Why am I telling you all this? It's my way of testing how smart you still are and how much you remember about the best part of us—our lightning brain. I hope there's enough left for you and me to work with.

OK, here's a starter list of what you need to focus on. All the details will become apparent when you study the notebooks:

- Postdoc job. You are a biotech postdoc at George Washington University, doing research in bio-drugs, neuroscience and neuro-devices. I have done enough work so you can keep your advisors and associates happy for almost two years. Think of it this way: you have nearly two years to figure out how to bring me back. Look in the Postdoc Notebook for all the details. Use it to write your summary reports. When in doubt, pretend you're in command of everything.
- Brain Trust and Guardian Party public relations work. You'll need to talk with Carter and Mariah regarding the Brain Trust,

and Zoe for PR. I recommend you let Zoe take our place in both.

- Austin Texas connection with Hud Haller and H&H DNA Partners, Inc. That's where Su fits in. She does our T-Plague vaccine development there. Get her to work on improved vaccines for the old and mutated virus. We also have a neuro-device lab run by Tim Godfrey. Su is supposed to visit us, so talk with her about all this. We've given them enough to do for almost two years, so you just have to pretend you know what you're doing. When in doubt, just act smart.
- Build another Electra Chronicles Notebook starting with the date I left off. Update it each day with all the information that would help us should we ever need to use it again.
- Update your Postdoc Notebook each day so you can refer back when needed for details.

Now, here's a starter list of personal facts:

- Worldstars is the name given to a team of biotech researchers comprised of Su-Lin Song Chou, Adom Ola, Indira Ramanujan and Jason Kittner. They worked at the NIH/CDC in Washington. All are dead except for Su. Talk with Su to learn more.
- Indira and Jason never married, but they are our parents. Mother was practically perfect: intelligent, empathetic, killer looks, talented in science and the arts, wrote poetry, etc. She was killed during childbirth by a lightning bolt that transformed our DNA and rewired our brain, making us exceptional. But you have to keep this a secret. We are a genetic freak. The world we live in is cruel and harsh and would treat us badly if they knew of our makeup and abilities.
- We were raised by Jason and our grandfather Justin Kittner, whose nickname was Doc, and he became our "omniparent." Jason loved us but was often blunt, ignoring feelings; he never understood women. When we were fifteen, Jason blew himself up in a lab accident, pushing too hard to develop T-Plague vaccines. Grandfather was murdered by terrorists a year later.

- The T-Plague started nearly thirty years ago and became a worldwide pandemic. It causes a rapid onset of dementia (like Alzheimer's) and has dumbed down the Nation's I.Q.
- America nearly collapsed because of Middle East Terrorism, our worthless government, and the T-Plague.
- Su and I have developed a number of T-Plague vaccines, but they don't work on the mutated virus that nearly killed me. We have to guide Su to change the formulation.
- We worked with a Brit, Alice Bicker, to neutralize Middle East Terrorism. We wanted to become good friends with her, but she's dead (killed by the British Secret Service).
- Robin, Christi and I were best friends. Christi and I were lovers. I love Robin too, but not the same way I loved Christi. Robin is high-strung, had a nervous breakdown, but recovered. She is coming to terms with her own sexuality. Matt is her lover and wants her to go beyond co-friend status and accept his vow-cer marriage contract. Matt was our physical therapist when I broke my neck four years ago. That's how he met Robin.
- We've known Mariah Robles (Carter's friend) for less than a year. Carter got her pregnant when they were in college. I am sexually attracted to her.
- We've known Zoe Vargas for five years. We met her when we started working for the Guardian Party. I learned a lot about public relations from her. She was abused physically and emotionally because of my neglect. I didn't protect her from Jared Gardner. She's living with us so we can take care of her until she's ready to plug back in to her PR career.
- Carter and I were lovers until he found out I can't have kids. He wants kids, especially a son. You and I are sterile. (Both Carter and Matt are great guys. You'll see.)
- I am bisexual. You'll have to figure out what you are. Good luck with that too!
- Look on the next page for our computer I.D.'s and passwords for all the computers and networks we use. There's a lot of info our computers, so good luck with that too.

- And finally, be aware of our Creature from the Id. When push comes to shove and our life's in danger, the lightning brain takes command, uniting our cognitive, emotional, and physical personas into a Creature that emerges from our subconscious. Never doubt the lightning brain. It does what has to be done. The Creature is ruthless, cold-blooded, and possesses killer instincts. Does all this sound frightening? Actually, when unleashed, it gives me an emotional rush even better than an orgasm. It's addictive, and it is hard for our cognitive persona to regain command. There's an old proverb that says Forewarned is forearmed. Now you know, so beware.

This is enough to get you started. You'll find out all the details when you read your notebooks. Read about Jason and Indira. I included a copy of Indira's poems that will help you know her better. I have to write up your letters and contingency plans. And here's the game you must now play. YOU MUST ACT NATURALLY, PRETENDING THE BEST YOU CAN THAT YOU KNOW ALL ABOUT WHO YOU ARE AND WHAT YOU WERE AND ARE AND SUPPOSED TO DO. AND NEVER REVEAL OUR SECRET!

You and I are playing this game in uncharted territory. Maybe our lightning brain will heal itself, but we can't count on it. I think it needs your help. I guess I got careless. I thought we had natural immunity to the mutated virus. And if not, our experimental vaccines would take care of us. I was wrong. It's up to you now. You and I will stay in touch via this packet. Just keep following the instructions.

I shall close with a poem our Mother wrote that speaks to you right now:

The Pretender

I wake up each day disappointed to see,

A glance at the mirror's reflection of me.

There must be some error there has to be more,

In order to handle today what's in store.

I'm busy each day searching hard searching long,

To find everything make me smart make me strong.

And though I have found some they still aren't enough,

To say to the World I have all the right stuff.
And so as I march off to tasks still to do,
Praying no one catches on and sees through.
That I'm able to finish the things that must be,
And so I beseech Lord have mercy on me!

One final point. I found out Mother wanted to name us Alisha. (Father named us Electra for obvious reasons.) I have changed all our official documents to include the middle name Alisha, and that's what I'm going to call you from now on. Alisha, good luck bringing me back. I promise to be your best friend.

My love and best wishes are with you always… Electra

Alisha read the instructions three times. DAMN! I've got to bring her back. Come on, Alisha. Get with it. I'll start reading now until I get too tired to go on. Then I'll sleep and let my brain continue working.

Alisha read long past the time her support group went to bed. And just before she fell asleep, a tingling sensation enveloped her brain. It was beginning to stir, and it continued stirring all through the night.

Call me Alisha! And let me think! Those stirring words roused her Sunday at six a.m. She stretched and flexed and jumped out of bed.

Thank you, Electra. I remember most of what you told me last night. And I'm feeling stronger and thinking better. It's time to act; time to pretend.

Alisha dressed for exercise, then tiptoed to where Matt and Robin were sleeping. "Matt, I'll be in the basement. Join me when you can." Matt sat up, but she was gone before he could say a word. By the time Matt got there, Alisha had already worked up a light sweat.

"Good morning. I'm beginning to remember some of my workout routines, but I've got to cut way back so I can build back up. I'm sweating already, and my arms and abs could handle only two sets of about 10 reps. But I'm better than yesterday."

"That's a good start. Let's compare your routine to what I had in mind."

"OK, but I'd like everyone to start calling me Alisha. That's Electra's middle name. Electra's not back yet, but Alisha is. That's me, and all of us will bring her back."

"Fair enough. I never knew you had a middle name, but since we're playing a name game, we've named your support group the Full House, three queens and two kings. OK, back to working out."

Matt introduced Alisha to the Full House at breakfast, and Robin picked up where Matt left off.

"You never told me you had a middle name. This is great! It shows you're remembering more and more. Does the name have any special meaning?"

"Yes, it means protected by Allah." Damn, how do I know that? My brain must have clicked some missing memory into place last night.

But don't act surprised.

"Hey Robin, every now and then the words 'Holy Shit' pop into my brain when I'm talking with you. Do you know why?" Robin blushed as she tattled on herself.

"I'm afraid I do. When you and Christi and I were the Three Queens, you teased me that compared to Christi's colorful vocabulary, mine was so prim and proper. The strongest language I used was that S-word. And do you remember how Christi experimented with sex and drugs before you and I settled her down?"

"No, I don't. You'll have to tell me more in private. And after breakfast, I would like for Mariah to tell me about all the public relations work, and Carter to tell me about the Brain Trust." Carter added to that.

"Good idea. Let's you and me talk at your workstation; then I'll get Mariah to join us. And sometime later today, Zoe can tell you all about what she used to do for the Guardian Party. We've got a full day ahead, so everyone chop-chop..."

Carter and Electra huddled half an hour later, hoping his hushed words might stir memory.

"This is going to be a pretty ugly story, but you'll understand why events had to unfold like they did once your memory clears. And I'll arrange an early January meeting with the Brain Trust so everyone is working from the latest facts. What I'm telling you goes no further than you and me, and Angus, Mariah, and Russell. And it's gotta stay that way. So, here's a quick summary.

"Jared Gardner, the leader of the Guardian Party, was the President of the United States until you poisoned him with the T-Plague virus. Angus McTear, who had been the Secretary of State and Secretary of Defense, is acting President, and you masterminded getting him President by poisoning everyone ahead of him on the succession list. And you pinned all the treachery on the unsuspecting Chinese.

"The public didn't like the weak and leaderless administrations prior to Jared's. Their feckless policies caused America's accelerating drift towards the apocalypse. Jared and the Guardian Party shit-canned 'Kinder and Gentler' policies and used slogans like 'Harsh Times demand Harsh Measures' and 'Guarding what makes America Great' to gain public support in order to power his programs. His programs are working economically, but you and Angus were afraid power would go to Jared's head and he'd become a tyrant, leading the country in the wrong direction. Angus built a Brain Trust—you, me, Mariah Robles, Russell Conklin who's Christi's father, and Olivia Torres, a senator from California who's my political mentor. We've been doing a good job coming up with policy recommendations to moderate Jared's when he gets too aggressive or out of line. About two months ago we found Jared was getting out of control: following his own advice rather than ours, sexually abusing staffers, sneaking prostitutes into the White House—we think he killed at least one— funneling service contracts to companies he controls, and starting to believe in channeling—a religious belief that he's some sort of demiurge chosen to lead us. We had to keep all this hush-hush for obvious reasons, and that's when you poisoned people to neutralize Jared, poisoning yourself by accident.

"Only you, Angus, Mariah, Russell, and I know the whole story, and we're sworn to secrecy or we could be tried for treason. And we thought that with Angus the acting President, he'd be able to steer the right course without being too harsh, according to our standards. But we must remember this: the public I.Q. has

dummied down because of the T-Plague; lots of people have become cruel and uncaring, and they like harsh measures. They don't care about human rights or collateral damage as long as they're being protected and don't have to think for themselves. Electra—uh, I mean Alisha, are you with me so far? Electra felt more lost than ever, but bucked herself up. Just pretend! Nod your head yes. You'll read more about
it soon.

I'm with you to some extent. And I'm remembering more, thanks to this refresher lecture. Please keep going."

"Well, there's just one additional piece that'll bring you up to the latest. Everyone you poisoned except Jared is a mental vegetable. They're all out of action. But there was a news bulletin yesterday that Jared awoke from his coma and has stabilized. It's too soon to say if or when he'll able to take over the reins that Angus now holds. This is going to make things interesting. I can't wait for our next Brain Trust meeting for Angus to tell us what's going on. We all have to stay tuned. I'm gonna get Mariah to join us. Be right back." Two minutes later, Mariah picked up where Carter had left off.

"So Electra—uh, I mean Alisha—my role on the Brain Trust is sociopolitical assessment of how Jared's policies jibe with public and congressional sentiment. Carter and I butt heads on this, but Angus keeps us in balance. I'm supposed to pick up the public relations part that you were responsible for, because you were phasing yourself out of the Brain Trust. Carter and I think it'll be good if we bring Zoe into the Brain Trust, but keep her in the dark about all the ugly background stuff. You used to work for her as a volunteer at Guardian Party Headquarters, so she'll know a lot of the background already. She can handle the speech writing and press releases Angus will need. You used to write stuff for him as well as Jared. Does that make sense to you?"

"Yes, I see how this all fits together." Electra felt a tiny jolt, followed by a famous nonsense rhyme flickering in her brain: "I see, said the blind man to the deaf mute, as he picked up his hammer and saw." My lightning brain is clicking more memory back into place. And it must have had a damn good sense of humor. That'll help all of us, and it'll help me in my acting career. When I get in a jam, I can use it if I need a distraction.

"You know, I've seen enough for now. I'm tired and want to rest. How about I talk with Zoe later?" Carter's reply matched his expression.

"Well done, Alisha! I'm proud of you, and so is the rest of your support group. At this rate, you'll be good as new sooner than we think." Alisha nodded, then rose to leave.

"Perhaps you're right. I sure hope so." As she walked away, another slight tremor jolted her brain. I know why I said perhaps! It's the Buddhist monk's answer to any question. I must have learned that somewhere, but where, I don't yet know. I'll have to be patient and help the lightning brain click more pieces into place. According to Electra, it'll be win for all three: for Electra, the lightning brain, and for me. And I agree.

Chapter 4
January 2122

"The Diminished Trust"
Thread 2 Chapter 1

ALTHOUGH ANGUS HAD A lot on his mind, he had all the tools to deal with the issues facing him. He held degrees from top black universities that had launched a stellar CIA career, catapulting him to Secretary of Defense and then to Secretary of State appointments. Late last year, a succession of singular events rocked Washington, thrusting him into the Oval Office. Now in his mid-fifties, he looked and sounded presidential: grey-flecked shortish hair, wire-rimmed glasses, resonant voice. His six feet two inches bulky frame commanded attention no matter the audience. And he had his Brain Trust. But how good would it be if the "brains behind the throne" were out of commission? Today's Brain Trust meeting might tell the tale; it was the first time he'd be with Electra since the T-Plague nearly killed her.

Angus had calmed the country and its international partners by taking measured but decisive actions as soon as possible after gripping the presidential reins. He stated in his first address that as acting president, he would champion the cause and the course mapped out by Jared Gardner, but would not rush to judge the nation's enemies nor push beyond what is fair. He filled vacancies caused by the alleged Chinese poisoning attack and reassured world leaders he would consider their needs before retaliating. He knew he had full support of the Guardian Party, much of Congress, and many private citizens because Americans always close ranks in a crisis, but he knew all would be watching him closely. Sentiment ran high for harsh measures and retaliation, so he needed to push for tough policies that "guard what makes America great" but must avoid vindictive cruelty that longer-term might lead to catastrophe. Angus started the meeting in his typical no-nonsense style.

"Welcome back from the Holidays, people, and let me get the elephant in the room out of the way. Jared Gardner is on the road to recovery but has memory gaps and trouble concentrating. He's the only victim other than Electra who has pulled through. By some quirk, their immune systems fought off the virus. The doctors think he might be fit to reoccupy the Oval Office in several months. It depends on how quickly and completely his physical and mental conditions improve. But until then, I am in charge and will continue doing what we've set in motion. Carter told me he'd like to chair the meeting, so I'll turn it over to him."

"Thanks, Angus, and welcome to our first Brain Trust meeting of the year. Let me start by announcing a couple of personnel changes that Angus has approved. First, Electra is taking a leave of absence until she recovers completely. And she prefers people to call her by her middle name—Alisha—until she's back to her old self. We've recruited Zoe Vargas to handle the public relations activities Electra — uh, Alisha—used to handle. And Mariah and I will team up to handle Alisha's role for synthesizing what we know to develop projects.

"We can make today's meeting brief because we're just coming back from the break. So, I'll simply recap where we are, then ask for any relevant updates. I'll walk us through this bullet point handout covering short-term issues."

Everyone scanned Carter's crisp one-pager:
- Brain Trust Focal Points—Short-Term
- Top International Issues—1. How to punish China for the attack on our leaders 2. How/When to attack Isilabad and Iran.
- Top Domestic Issues—1. How to Implement Pillars Programs (local Citizens Guard and Security Watch groups to uncover "bad people") 2. How to Implement Golden Years Program (pulling the life support plug on terminally ill) 3. How to generate support for new program to cure T-Plague victims (raise the nation's I.Q.)

Analysis/Recommendations we need to work on—1. Getting an effective R-Vac (Smart Pill to cure T-Plague victims. Russell Conklin to lead) 2. Taking the pulse of public opinion and Congress regarding harsh measures and national morals.

Carter spent fifteen minutes summarizing and expanding each point as needed, then asked each person for opinions. After that, he ended the first part of the meeting.

"As you can see, we have a good handle on what we'll do starting today. And now, let's revisit public opinion for existing programs. Mariah, what would you like to say?"

"For now, just this: we have to acknowledge the public's call for change that puts America number one. That's what brought Jared and the Guardian Party to power. But we have to use the lessons of history to tone down public sentiment and Guardian Party policy if they become too harsh or vindictive."

"Thank you, Mariah. Who else would like to add opinions?" Everyone noticed Angus's growing impatience because only silence answered his request. Carter segued to Angus.

"So, we need to steer a middle course, which is why Angus is in charge. Let's have him give us final words."

"OK people. Between now and the next meeting, please get the answers we need. And Electra—uh, Alisha, please stay. Meeting adjourned."

Alisha marched to where Angus was sitting and while waiting for him to say something, spoke resolutely to herself. I might not be as smart as Electra, but I'm not retarded, so just deal with what he says.

I've read the recent chronology of events in my notebooks three times, so I bet I know the facts better than he does. And for the stuff I don't, just act naturally and pretend, but don't back myself into a corner.

"I'm relieved you're on the mend. We need to talk. Let's have lunch in the Oval Office." Alisha hurried to tell Zoe she'd take a rideshare home, then hustled back to Angus, who ushered her to where lunch was waiting.

"I think you'll like White House BLTs. I know they're your favorite sandwich, and the triple fudge brownies won't hurt you one bit. You look thinner than before, and you're sort of pale, so they'll help you bulk up."

"The sandwich looks good; has plenty of bacon. May I take half home, along with a couple of the brownies? I'm unable to eat as much at one sitting as I used to, so I'm eating smaller amounts more frequently. And that seems to suit the fitness program my trainer has me on."

"I wish I could get used to smaller portions. I'll check with the White House Chef and Fitness Center about combining smaller portions with a bigger workout schedule." Angus paused for Alisha to take a couple of bites before asking questions. "Now tell me, how is your brain feeling? Level with me, because I know you were the brains behind the Brain Trust." Alisha put down the sandwich and took a sip of Coke before answering.

"Here are the brutal facts. The T-Plague nearly terminated my careers, and if it weren't for my close friends I'd be dead. When I came out of a coma, the world was a great big buzzing wall of white noise. I could barely stand, didn't know who or where I was, and couldn't recall much of anything. That was three weeks ago, but since then my physical strength has rebounded. Not to where it was, but it's pretty good. And my memory is gradually coming back. But— and this is FYI only—I'm not as smart as I used to be. I think my I.Q.is gradually improving, but it's nowhere near what it was. That's why I'm taking a leave of absence. Zoe and the Carter-Mariah team will serve you well, as will Russell Conklin. And I'll talk with them to keep up with what's going on." Angus nodded, then replied.

"I'll consider Carter the brains behind the throne until you come back. I haven't discussed this with him yet, but I hope he'll have some recommendations for how to handle Jared if, or more likely when, he recovers. But that's a topic for another time. Right now, I'm happy to be talking with you. You're still sharper than most."
"Thanks for the compliment and for lunch. It's time for me to leave. I have a fitness session at home this afternoon, and I'm sure you have meetings waiting for your arrival." Angus smiled wearily as he replied.

"Sometimes I think I'd be happy to trade places with you." Alisha felt a jolt as additional neural circuits came online. *I just remembered a poem that fits Angus!*

"No sir! You're built for leading America today. There's a saying that many are called but few are chosen. Well, you've been chosen. And here's a poem chosen for you. It was written long ago by my mother. She titled it The Once and Future.

'Where have all the Great Men gone?
The heroes in your mind.
We need them now to carry on,
They seem so hard to find.
Concealed perhaps when they appear,
Once human just like us.
Revealed in Wisdom's future year,
Though flesh has turned to dust.
Greatness dwells in each of us,
Awaiting the chosen call.
So do when asked without a fuss,
In time your stature's tall.'
I think it fits you to a T."

"Well, I'll be. Anyone who can remember poetry has a better brain than mine. You go girl." Alisha followed orders.

I wish I were a professional athlete. I love training. I love the exercise, the sweat, and the endorphins. I'll bet Electra was positively addicted to running because that's the path I'm on too.

Alisha was cooling down after the three-mile run that capped her afternoon training session led by Matt. Matt was actually supervising three programs at once—Alisha's, Zoe's, and Su's—and coordinating them with his evening EMT shift. While Alisha ran, he led Su's physical therapy and Zoe's overall conditioning. The latest MRI showed little vertebral healing, but his physical therapy kept Su's muscle tone from deteriorating. Zoe, on the other hand, was blossoming. *He liked her pert and positive approach. She was bright, easy to talk to, and seemed well adjusted. She didn't complicate things. There must be a story why she's Alisha's roommate, but I'm*
not going to pry.

"OK athletes, listen up. Today I increased your workouts and walked you through what to do. I'll be back same day, time, and place next week. And here's what I expect you to do this week. Work out together. Zoe and Alisha assist Su; Alisha assists Zoe; after that, Alisha finishes her strength run. And all of you get a gold medal for effort and achievement. Now hit the showers while I hit the road."

Matt trundled Su's wheelchair up the stairs, then departed. Alisha and Zoe took over, sponge-bathing and putting Su into leisure clothes. Then Zoe showered and changed. Alisha stripped off her sweats and donned a robe, all the while chatting with Su.

"You'll have one more workout before we fly you back to Austin. Matt and the doctor will transfer your records and make arrangements so you can pick up right where you left off when we get you home."

"I'm still getting used to calling you Alisha, but I'll catch on. We're fortunate Hud leases a corporate jet. It'll make lugging me and my wheelchair easier for you. But I must say, your strength and physique are coming back quickly. I wish I could say the same about my back." There was more she wanted to say but she spoke them only to herself. These were words meant only for Electra.

I know you better than even your Alisha persona does, and I sense your brain is fighting to recover its brilliance. Alisha seems smart, but not like the old Electra. And the Alisha persona is different in other ways too: less enigmatic, less complex emotionally, more empathetic and easygoing and, for most people, more fun to be with. I haven't detected Electra's philosophic, melancholy nature. I hope the real Electra comes back to me, for she was the reincarnation of her mother, Indira, the one I still love.

Alisha was unaware of what Su was thinking but could tell her mind was elsewhere, so she didn't interrupt until Su's focus returned.

"I need to tell you something that I'm beginning to understand again. When we get back to Austin, Tim and I will figure out how to use one of our neuro-devices to treat your broken vertebrae. I'll tell you more when we get with Tim, but it's possible it can accelerate the healing process. My brain hasn't recovered yet, but I'm thinking clearly enough to remember it worked when I treated Robin. And please, don't mention this to anyone else." Su nodded, showing no emotion, waiting for Alisha to say more.

"And now I need to tell you something less cheery. All the new formulations you've been working on, and all the experimental vaccines that I've been working on, are ineffective against the new T-Plague virus strain. I'm living proof they don't work as advertised. I'm still taking large doses of my experimental drugs because they can't hurt, but they won't speed my recovery. So, here's what we're going to do. I'll give you copies of my drug development notes, and when you get back to Austin you start improving our current line extensions—they're for the original virus—and do the same for my experimental formulations for the mutated virus. And until my brain recovers, I'm not smart enough to help you. I don't know what to do. I'm sorry." Su nodded again, and this time she spoke, revealing only a hint of feeling.

"This will be a wonderful opportunity for our new associate, Kameyo Kato. She's the associate professor we hired away in December from University of Texas. She's taking Adom's place. This is the first you've heard about it because you've had other things on your mind. She and I have been in contact regularly, and she knows about my accident. She'll start the day I get back. Do you remember giving me the OK to hire whomever I thought was the best candidate, without having you get involved in the vetting?" "Uh no, but if you picked her she must have the right stuff. You don't need to tell me anything else. I'll meet her when I take you back." Just then Zoe popped in.

"I'm out of the shower. It's your turn while I talk with Su. And if you help me jockey Su to the kitchen, she and I will start making supper." The three ladies had been living together for almost a month and had discovered the best way to shuttle Su around the house. It took only a couple of minutes to reshuffle everyone's locations. Zoe was bustling about while Su observed.

I like Zoe, and I won't ask why she's living here. She and this new Alisha get along well. It's rather odd, but I can't recall the old Electra being so happy and chatty.

Zoe asked, "I thought I'd make omelets and a salad. Will that be OK?

"That will be fine. And I overheard you and Alisha planning to take me with you on Saturday afternoon on your shopping expedition. You don't have to drag me with you. I'll just slow you down."

"Nonsense. I think Alisha and I can chauffeur you around very well. And I like talking to you. You always tell great stories about the old Electra. I think they help Alisha's memory, and I get to know more about her." Zoe stopped abruptly, becoming deathly serious.

"I'll tell you something if you promise not to tell anyone. Electra saved my life. I can't tell you the details. It's still too painful; no one knows, and it's got to stay that way. She's my best friend, and I hope she likes me as much as I like her. I hear her coming, so I'll shut up." Zoe returned to dinner preparations just before Alisha bounced in. "I sure feel energized from today's workout, and my appetite is beginning to recover. How are you ladies feeling?" Su spoke right up. "Do you remember this quote you told me during one of your trips to Austin? Every day in every way I'm getting better and better."

"No. My body's recovering faster than my brain. Sorry." Zoe walked over to hug her, then piped up to add moral support.

"Don't be sorry! I see you getting better and better, just like the quote. Your physical strength is coming back, and so is your emotional strength. Your brain will catch up soon. Hey, would you please take care of toast, butter, and jam while I take care of the omelets?"

"Will do. And I'll set the OJ and cranberry juice on the table. Everyone can help themselves."

Dinner conversation first touched on how nice Matt is, and then settled on the Saturday shopping spree. Su excused herself afterwards; she wanted quiet time on her laptop to check Emails and review her lab notes, so she wheeled into the living room, but was still within earshot. Zoe and Alisha cleaned up the kitchen, then chatted happily afterwards about what they'd be hunting for at the mall. Su smiled inwardly as she eavesdropped.

I like listening to Zoe and Alisha chat. They sound so happy, so engaged in clothes and cosmetics. Alisha seems more interested in looking good than the old Electra. But I think the old Electra had been moving in that direction. She was dressing better and looking more mature. Well, it's all good, and we'll have fun on Saturday. It'll bring back memories of shopping trips with Indira, but those stories are for me only.

Saturday brought fitting conditions for a shopping trip. Friday's early morning snowfall had blown away, plows cleared the streets and winds scrubbed the clouds from the sky. Zoe and Alisha loaded Su into the van and off they went to Zoe's favorite local mall.

Shopping with a friend is a time-honored social tradition or meme, just like dining out or taking in a movie. The day flitted by, and by late afternoon Su announced the shopping expedition was over. She was pleasantly tired and ready for dinner.

"You two score ten out of ten on the fashion meter today. Tell me again how the fashion consultants made selections for you." They were enjoying a late Saturday afternoon meal at Zoe's favorite gourmet deli. Alisha had talked Zoe into expanding the shopping list from spring slacks, skirts, and shoes to include trendy cosmetics and hairstyles. Su was marveling at the transformative effects.

"Zoe told me about computer software styling apps, and the clothing consultant took a couple of basal pictures of me. Zoe already has hers in the Internet cloud, so the consultant used those for her."

"What's a basal picture?" Su wasn't versed in the latest fashion jargon, so Zoe explained.

"Those are digital pictures of Alisha—or me—in the buff. Apps can use photos of us wearing clothes, but the fit is better without. Some of the pictures are close-up head shots. The styling apps use them to display virtual reality images of how we look in the clothes, cosmetics, and hair styles. I'm glad Sherman Pickey opened a store at this mall, because it's almost as good as shopping at the flagship store in Georgetown. And the clothing consultant connected us to a great cosmetics store and hair stylist located on the second level. They used our head shots in their styling apps."

"When we get home, both of you will have to model the clothes, and if they look as good as they did before the hair styling and cosmetics, both of you will turn heads. What are the hairstyles called?"

"Alisha's is a pixie cut; mine is a layered bob. I prefer shorter styles because I'm average height, but I think this is the first time Alisha has selected a shorter style." Alisha laughed, then corrected Zoe.

"Well, yes and no—sort of. Su saw me after my accident four years ago. A lot of my hair was burned to a crisp, so a short style was chosen for me by the flames. But now I want a shorter style because it fits better with my workouts and running. How do you like the make-up job?"

Su answered, "I like the narrow eyeliner. It dramatizes your jet-black hair and darker complexion. Thank heavens you no longer look like a cadaver! You were ghost-white the first week out of the coma. And the pale pink lipstick is subtle. As for Zoe, I like the Parisian red lipstick and pale green eye shadow. It goes with her tawny-brown hair and brown eyes."

"Thanks for your assessment. Zoe and I are pleased you like the results. So, let's head home. You and Zoe can handle the shopping bags, and I'll handle the wheelchair. And I'm pleased the weather cooperated. Better that it snowed yesterday than today. The maintenance crew did a nice job plowing the parking lot. We don't need snow tires or chains on your wheelchair. But let's bundle up. It's below freezing, and I had to park farther away from the entrance than I thought I'd have to. I'm surprised the lot was so crowded, but the crowd has thinned out, so it won't be bustling now…"

"Do you see our target? The taller female pushing the wheelchair and her shorter partner in the lead? They should be pushovers for a snatch and run. I'll take care of the taller one; you handle the shorter. Make sure you get shoulder bags, purses and shopping bags. Meet me at the car if we have to separate, but I don't think that'll happen. And watch your footing. The snow has made it icy in spots."

Two twenty-something nondescript toughs were tracking a defenseless shopping expedition as it headed for the exit. Both were stocky, and the taller one—the loud-mouthed leader—was about as tall as Alisha. The other was about three inches shorter, about five feet eight. Although the sky was clear at six that night, there was no moon, and the glow of the mall faded into darkness where Alisha had parked. Alisha was chattering away, oblivious to what was silently approaching from behind.

"You know, if it were warmer I might have worn a pair of my new— agh!" Her words jolted to a stop as a jarring tug on her shoulder bag spun her around, but the strap held and she staggered forward into the chest of the taller clod.

"My, aren't you the pretty one. Let's see how you look with a poke in puss." Alisha lurched backwards, coming to rest against the wheelchair, helpless and paralyzed by panic. Mother of god, we're being mugged! What do I do?

Alisha felt an enormous jolt shock her brain but did nothing; she didn't have to, for her physical persona's muscle memory took control and Alisha became an observer of the action about to be unleashed. The clod was so confident he took too long winding up to deliver a haymaker. Alisha beat him to the punch, delivering a karate palm strike, breaking his nose that became a geyser of blood; Alisha followed up with a knee into his groin that doubled him up, followed by another into his teeth that set him down on his back. She followed with two vicious kicks to his head that would keep him down for the count. Meanwhile, her partners were frozen in spacetime by Alisha's bold action. And it wasn't over.

She wheeled just in time to see the smaller tough snatch Zoe's purse, then shove her to the ground. He turned to flee, running over ice and snowy patches. Alisha threw her shoulder bag at Zoe than sprinted after her next victim. He was awkward and slow afoot; Alisha's flying tackle brought him face down in a pile of snow 20 yards later. She landed on top of him, grabbed as much hair as she could and began smashing his head through the snow onto the asphalt, one, two, three times in rapid succession.

Get with it soldier! Gather your people and get out of here! Alisha had no idea where the words crashing into her brain came from, but she obeyed the command. She stood up and surveyed the damage. The two toughs were not about to get up anytime soon, so she retrieved Zoe's purse and automatically took from the closest clod his cellphone and wallet, then ran back to her speechless partners.

"Quick! Let's get in the van and go before they get up. Zoe! Help me load Su." That was the only command needed. Alisha's adrenaline-charged strength made light work of the load. Alisha was about to speed away when Zoe yelled at her.
"We gotta report this to Mall Security."

"Oh no we don't! We're not gonna get involved. Here's what we'll do—"Alisha's brain froze. "Jesus, I don't know what to do. Panic was about to return; then suddenly she felt a sudden jolt as the lightning brain shifted gears.

"Here's the cellphone and wallet I took from one of them. You call Mall Security using his cellphone so they can't trace the call to us. Tell them what happened, but we're leaving because we're afraid to get involved. Tell them the name of the guy whose wallet I took. Tell where to find them. And while you're doing that, I'll make sure they stay put."

Alisha jumped out of the van and ran to her first victim, who was barely coming to. She knelt atop his chest, scissoring his head between her hands by clutching his ears, preparing to torque his neck until it snapped, but before she could, another command crashed into her brain.

Get with it, soldier! This is not a drill. No need to kill. Clear the area. Once again, she obeyed the command.

Alisha drove for ten minutes as if in a trance before Zoe finally spoke.

"What the hell happened back there?" Alisha snapped into the present.

"You tell me. I'm not sure. It's all a blur." Su decided to keep silent, whispering to herself instead. I've just seen some of the old Electra.

That's her physical persona, guided by raw emotion. Ruthless. Coldblooded. Calculating. Killer instincts. Thank god! I pray that all of her returns. I want her back.

Later that evening, having calmed down from the shocking episode, the trio sat in the living room, ready to make sense of what they had witnessed. Zoe and Alisha were sitting on the couch, Su in front of them. Zoe lighted candles and poured brandy to warm the chill all of them felt. Alisha spoke first.

"I'm more puzzled than anyone. It was like I wasn't in control of what I was doing. It was like I was an observer. I scared myself." Alisha could think of nothing else to say, nor could Zoe, who put her arms around Alisha's shoulders, but Su could.

"I believe I can explain what happened. And I will, but before I do, please answer this question. Can we trust Zoe to know more about you?" Alisha blinked mutely, but Zoe answered.

"I know what you're getting at. You don't know me at all, or why I'm staying here, and you know more about Alisha's past than anyone. Maybe there's something you don't want me to know. I'll leave you two alone." Zoe got up, but Alisha grabbed her. I have this terrible guilt feeling, like I owe Zoe for something bad I did. Another jolt jarred Alisha's brain, stirring dormant emotions now breaking free as neurons started firing.

"Please stay and hear what Su has to say. You're my best DC friend, and you should know more about me. I want to take care of you, like you've been taking care of me." Zoe sat down and stuttered what was on her mind.

"I've needed a best friend for a couple of years, and Alisha did her best to be that person. But she didn't know until late last year what a bad place I was in. But once she did, she got me out of harm's way." Alisha saw a tear welling in the corner of Zoe's eye; she knew instinctively to be emotionally strong. She carefully wiped away the tear, then replied with a smile that could light any room.

"We'll be the best of friends. Ever the best of friends. Now, let's hear what Su has to say."

"Earlier tonight all of us were in danger. I've been in other situations with the old Electra where we were threatened, and the actions you took tonight are just like what the old Electra would take. Now, please bear with me as I apply my understanding of biology and neuroscience to what's going on.

"Alisha's brain is badly damaged by the T-Plague, and it's trying to recover. I don't know how effective the drugs she's taking are. I have worked for years with the old Electra, developing T-Plague vaccines, trying my best to understand what she had come up with, but I couldn't keep up with her. Maybe they'll help her brain recover, or maybe it'll repair itself by building new connections and dissolving neural entanglement. I simply don't know. I'm not smart enough. That's one reason the old Electra better come back. But I digress. Let's get back to Alisha's brain.

"Her brain, like all human brains, is divided into three main sections: the primitive reptilian brain which is the oldest part, the limbic brain which is next oldest part, and the neocortex, which is the latest to evolve. Our physical control—call it our physical persona —is in the reptilian brain. Our feelings and emotions—call them our emotional persona—are in the limbic brain. And our rational and cognitive activities—call them our cognitive persona— are in the neocortex.

"My conjecture is this: the T-Plague does severe damage to the neocortex. It damages the limbic brain to a lesser extent, and the reptilian brain least of all. Alisha's actions tonight were directed by the most primitive part—the reptilian brain. And Alisha's reptilian brain seems to have most, if not all, of the abilities the old Electra had. That's a good sign. Maybe her emotional persona is relatively intact. And maybe her cognitive persona will come back too. And there are three scenarios.

"Scenario one—Alisha's brain has stabilized. What she has now is as good as it's going to get. There won't be any improvement. The old Electra is gone forever.

"Scenario two—her brain will regain some of its former abilities— with or without the help of vaccines. But we'll never see the old Electra again."

"Scenario three—her brain figures out how to repair itself completely. The old Electra returns. I have no idea which scenario will play out or how long it will take. But let me ask the person who might know best. Alisha, what do you think?"

Su's much smarter than I am. I don't remember any of that brain background stuff she just rattled off. Come on, think. What can I add? No brilliant insights flashed into her brain. Alisha had to rely on what she had, and in so doing came up with a depressing thought. "Isn't there also scenario four? That's where I spiral downhill? I just thought of a better term to describe it. I regress even further." Su nodded slowly in agreement.

"Yes, that is a possibility, but let's be optimistic and not deal with that one. You're a month into recovery, so I think we can eliminate scenario four." Zoe added a more positive scenario.

"Let's add another scenario. Alisha comes back better than ever." Alisha added to that line of reasoning.

"Let me make another observation. Sometimes I feel brain twinges and jolts. Perhaps it's a side effect of the vaccines, or maybe it's my brain trying to repair itself. And whenever I feel them, I feel like I'm getting stronger and better than before." Su nodded, then replied.

"That's a possibility, so here's what you should do. When those jolts occur, think about what changes are taking place in your physical, emotional or cognitive states, and what is happening around you. Maybe you'll detect a connection. Do you remember from statistics what that phenomenon is called?" Alisha thought for a moment, then glumly nodded in the negative, so Su answered.

"Causality is the term for it. Try to identify what is causing your brain jolts. Your brain is going to get better. Just let vaccines and your brain take care of the recovery. And do your part by keeping busy, physically and mentally."

"You're right. And I have to do both to prepare for our trip back to Austin. All three of us have things to do to get you ready to go. Zoe, anything you'd like to add?"

"No, I'm worn out. Let's get Su ready for bed. I'm sure we'll all be full of pep tomorrow. And since tomorrow's Sunday, I'll make blueberry pancakes. And tomorrow afternoon, Su and I can bake brownies. Those are two of the old Electra's favorites. I'm sure Alisha will like them too."

Alisha nodded then added, "All three of us would like the old Electra to make a comeback, so I'll do my best to make it so. And on her behalf, I shall thank you for helping me help her too."

Chapter 5
February 2122

"The Texas Roundup"
Thread 3 Chapter 1

I SURE LOOK LIKE A pounded turd. Hud Haller, the rugged, man-sized President of H&H DNA Partners and associated businesses, made that assessment while looking in the mirror as he shaved, and he never used fancy phrases to sugarcoat the facts. During the past four months his business empire had taken a terrible pounding. First Adom Ola, the fellow his father Hollis was grooming to take over the oil and gas business, is shot dead by corporate espionage agents. Next, his ace biotech researcher, Su-Lin Song Chou, breaks her back in a car crash, and then his clever partner, Electra Kittner, damages her brain. And now the government is threatening to seize part of his empire if he doesn't give them patents. It's a good thing Electra's rounding up Su and herself for this morning's meeting. And if she wants us to call herself Alisha, that's fine with me, as long as she walks and quacks like the old Electra. And they better figure out what to do. If they don't, I'm gonna worry the warts off a frog. Well, me and my Dad have come through calamities before. We'll just have to do it again.

Hud was not the only one self-reflecting that morning about meeting Su and Alisha; so was Kameyo Kato, who today would officially begin working on Su's genetic drug development projects. Unlike Hud who was looking at himself in a mirror, Kameyo was viewing her preparation through the prism of her formidable intellect whose components would impress anyone.

Yes, she knew even more about manipulating viruses than Dr. Chou. Her advanced degrees earned in Tokyo and her cutting-edge research at Austin's University of Texas attested to that. And yes, her Japanese cultural heritage would serve her well. Not that it matters to her, but her family tree traces far back to the Samurai warrior nobility. What matters is how her parents had taught her to embrace many teachings from the Samurai philosophical Book of Five Rings (Earth, Water, Fire, Air, Void) so she would personify the meaning of the word Samurai: to serve. And she embodies the best ethics of Japan's oldest religion, Shintoism, which is a holistic, now and nature-focused, optimistic view of life, promoting its Four P's": Purification of mind and body through ritual, Presentation through practiced style, Prayerful respect for elders, and Participation with others.

Most importantly, she knows herself, her motivations, her needs. She is a "Woman of Modernity," preferring the opportunities and status women can reach in America when contrasted to still xenophobic-minded and male-favored Japan. Though Japan is a 5000-year-old cultured and nuanced civilization, outmoded traditions linger still. America, not Japan, is the land of her rising sun. She will serve herself and Dr. Chou by dedicating herself to a life of research.

Hud's leased corporate jet carrying Alisha and Su was an hour away. For the past two hours Alisha had been reviewing her presentation, making sure it covered all the points the old Electra had listed in her first progress letter. Alisha read the letter one more time.

"Hello Alisha. I'm pleased you are reading my first letter, written expressly for you. You should be a month or so into recovery, so please consider this letter a report on the progress or activities you should be handling now.

I hope you are seeing tangible progress physically, emotionally, and cognitively. I expect physical progress first, then emotional, and finally cognitive. Look for signs of improvement, but be patient. Now, let's turn to activities.

By now, you should have met with the Brain Trust and plugged Zoe in for your public relations work. Keep in touch with Carter because Angus should appoint him power behind the throne. Is Jared permanently sidelined? I hope so.

Next, you should have held a meeting with your postdoc advisors. I gave you enough completed work to keep them at bay for about two years.Use the material I've developed to give them a presentation. Do it soon if you haven't done so already.

Next, you should meet with the Austin team to keep Su pointed in the right direction for drug development, and ditto for Tim on the neuro-devices. I gave them all the details before putting myself out of commission. You also have these details in your Postdoc Notebook. And tell Hud to play hardball with the government if it pushes too hard for patents. He can always set up overseas manufacturing locations while pumping sales through our shadow companies. Make sure he controls our virtual companies' sales forces. And find out if he and Tim have filled the Sales and Marketing slot for our neuro-devices.

And lastly, keep reading the Electra Chronicles until you know them by heart. It's your story, and you need to know who and what you are, and where you've been so you pretend you're in command. If you're as good an actress as I was, you'll fool everyone. I've been doing it for our entire life.

I hope you are enjoying our game, and I know you're doing your best. My love is with you always. From Electra, your best friend in waiting...

PS. I am attaching to this letter a 'Background Primer' covering the basics of what you need to know about Philosophy, Science, and Religion so you don't have to recreate what I have already concluded. As the lightning brain recovers, more will become clear, but please use what I wrote to kick-start your thinking. I ran out of time to include the softer subjects—psychology, economics, sociology, and politics. You should be smart enough to figure those out on your own."

Alisha sat back while grading herself. Electra would be satisfied; I'm on schedule, except for my postdoc meeting. And I'm following her advice for running meetings: act naturally and pretend.

Alisha glanced at a tired-looking Su, who for the entire flight had been reviewing research correspondence. She welcomed Alisha's comments.

"I'm going to run the meeting. I've put together a hand-written agenda that will cover everything I could think of. And if anyone can add to it as we proceed, that'll help me even more. But would you do me a favor? Would you please tell me the Hud story again?"

"Yes, of course. And I'll give you the short version because we're landing soon. But it'll be enough to help you remember how he fits in. So here goes.

"You remember that your mother nicknamed us the Worldstars when we met Jason and Adom first year in graduate school. Well, Hud was Adom's good friend. Turns out that Hud, a big and strong Texan, handsome in a rugged sort of way, came from a wealthy family. His father, Hollis Haller, was a wildcatter who built a successful independent oil and gas company. Hud worked in the oil patch but wanted to study biotech. His father agreed to fund his startup biotech company if he would headquarter it in Austin so he could help run the oil and gas business. Adom and Hud kept in touch, and Hud called when your father blew himself up in the lab. That's how Electra found out about Hud.

And then, when the CIA tried to frame me for sabotaging CDC T-Plague vaccine development programs—you might not remember, but they almost killed me with a truth serum overdose— you and Hud set up a drug development joint venture called Worldstar Biologicals so I had a place to hide until the CIA cleared my name. I'm still keeping a low profile because I don't trust the government. I've been doing our T-Plague vaccine development, and Electra has been helping. Adom joined me a couple of years later when the NIH lab was about to fire him. He never told me the whole story, but for a several months he was a CIA person of interest. Oops... hold on."

The plane hit a pocket of turbulence as it began its descent, interrupting Su's monologue and giving Alisha a moment to think. *How does my memory jibe with Su's facts? I'm beginning to remember bits and pieces, but I'm lucky that most of what she's saying is written in Electra's notebooks. But I haven't come across anything explaining why Adom was a CIA person of interest. I guess not even Electra and her lightning brain could cover all the* bases, but she wrote down so much so quickly to help her comeback. I should call it our comeback, for she and I are intimately connected. I don't know how she did everything she did. She was one smart lady.

"OK, let me continue. So, Adom joins me in Austin, falls in love with Texas, and Hud's father—his nickname is Holy—grooms him to take over the oil and gas business plus a cattle ranching business the two had started a year before Adom was killed. You can talk to Holy about those details. The last thing you need to know for our meeting is that you convinced Hud to start a neuro-device lab so you have a place to work on your neuro-devices. You hired Tim Godfrey two years ago to be your biotech engineer and Director of the Neuro Device Lab. And last November you told Tim to hire a Director of Sales and Marketing to bring the first device to market. I don't know who that person is, but we'll meet him today."

"Thanks for the review. It's helping me remember enough to handle my agenda. And just in time. We'll be landing in fifteen minutes, and Hud said there'll be a limo waiting for us. I think you and I are ready."

Hud was the kind of person who would always hope for the best but plan for the worst, so he greeted his "wounded Worldstars" as soon as they arrived, assessing the damages while helping them into the building. Other than Su's wheelchair and Alisha's shorter hair, they look about the same. I sure hope they're ready for action. I'll know better after the meetings. And I better talk with Alisha privately before we start. Alisha remained in Hud's office; Su wheeled away to a conference room.

"Welcome back, Little Lady. You look good, and I hope you're ready to set things in motion. We've been sort of on break since you and Su got damaged. So gimme the straight scoop: how're you feeling, and what do you want me to call you?"

"Hud, please call me Alisha. I'm feeling pretty good, but I'm still recovering. My memory is getting better, but I'm not as smart as I used to be. But the doctors say I'm making excellent progress, and I should continue improving, especially if I keep doing more, because keeping busy helps me remember more of what I should know. So please, let me lead the meetings today. And I want everyone to call me Alisha. That's my middle name. I'll use it until the old Electra returns. But you'll see that Alisha—that's who I am now—is very capable. I have an agenda that will cover everything needed to get us moving. Who's in the conference room with Su?"

"Tim's in there, plus two new people. Su hired Kameyo Kato in early December to replace Adom. She officially starts today. And in January I approved Tim's hiring a Director of Sales and Marketing for launching our first neuro-device: the Neuro-Knitter. The guy's name Brian Ritz, and his background is in a couple of areas that Tim thinks make him a good choice: artificial intelligence and medical devices. Tim's briefed him on the Neuro-Knitter, and I've shared the sales and marketing plan overview you sent me in December. But before we go in, I gotta run something by you that just came up. The government is threatening to shut down our T-Plague vaccine sales if we don't give them patent information. What do you think we should do?" Electra already thought of this. I'll tell him exactly what she wrote down.

"You should play hardball with the government if it pushes too hard. We can always set up overseas manufacturing locations, and we can pump sales through our shadow companies. Just make sure you control our virtual companies' sales forces. We don't want anyone tracing the vaccines back to us. I'll leave all this for you to handle." Hud leaned back, starting to grin.

"Little Lady, uh-Alisha, that's something we can run with. And if the government keeps threatening, this'll push'em back like one of Holy's cattle prods. OK Little Lady—uh—Alisha, everyone's rounded up, so let's join 'em. And you lead the meeting after I introduce you and
Su."

Hud led the way to the conference room. Su had parked her wheelchair on one side of the table next to a young Oriental woman. Sitting on the other were two fellows that Alisha sized up. Tim must be the geeky looking fellow. The other must be the marketing guy. OK. Smile, talk slowly, act naturally, and don't panic. When in doubt, table the topic. Alisha took a deep breath after Hud's introduction and started the meeting.

"Hi everyone, and thanks for welcoming Su and me back. Both of us have recovered enough, so we're ready to pick up where we left off. Hud and I already resolved a couple of issues best handled by him, and since it's lunchtime, here's what I thought would be best. Su and I will have lunch with Kameyo. Afterwards, the three of us will map out our next steps. And then Tim, Brian and I will meet in the Neuro-Device Lab to discuss plans for this year. How does that sound?" Hud spoke for the group.

"We brought in some Tex-Mex grub, so fill your plates and chow down. Uh-Alisha, why don't you and Su and Kameyo use my office. I'll be here with Tim and Brian."

Alisha and Kameyo rendezvoused at Su's wheelchair, where Kameyo bowed ever so slightly, then spoke.

"Hello Dr. Kittner. I am Kameyo Kato, and it's an honor to be working for Dr. Chou." Alisha returned the bow, then offered her hand which Kameyo shook firmly.

"I'm pleased to meet you, and please, call me Alisha. And I'm also pleased to have you with us, though I'm sorry you had to wait so long for us to get back in action. But Su tells me she's been Emailing since the middle of January."

"Yes she has, and she's sent me a great deal of background on solution paths for the S, I, and R vaccines." Kameyo smiled when Su joined the discussion.

"Kameyo understands better than I how you've integrated quantum biology and cellular factory concepts into our solution paths. She picked it up in a couple of weeks; it's taken me a couple of years. What an excellent illustration of the proverb that says Youth will be served."

"Dr. Chou, may I help you with your wheelchair?"

"Thanks for offering, but I can manage. Besides, it's good exercise. Why don't we do this. After we move to Hud's office, would you please bring me a plate of Tex-Mex?" Alisha had a better idea.

"Why don't you let Kameyo wheel you into Hud's office. I'll fill my plate then join you while Kameo brings back lunch for herself and you." Kameyo wheeled Su away; Alisha used that time to consider what she had seen.

Kameyo looks plenty solid, pretty much what I expected. Average appearance and dimensions for a late twenties Japanese female. Nonsense longer hair tied in a ponytail. I like her firm handshake, direct approach, and eye contact. I'll bet she's smarter than I am, so I better not be too assertive. I'll just pretend and act naturally. That's my modus operandi until I get my brain back to where it was.

Alisha enjoyed listening during lunch to the small talk between Su and Kameyo, and when everyone was finished she directed the conversation to her agenda.

"Let me sketch what you and Su need to do. You need to incorporate my latest research into Su's to improve our current T-Plague vaccines, I-Vac for inoculation, S-Vac for symptomatic relief or suppression, and R-Vac for reversal or cure. They were developed to handle the original T-Plague virus. And you must then develop the same triad to handle the mutated virus. Su and I brought with us samples of the mutated virus for you to culture so you have a supply to support your R&D. I expect that when you find the correct solution path, you can apply it to attack Alzheimers. That will be our next blockbuster, once T-Plague is under control. So, I'd like you to outline what you plan to do." Kameyo nodded yes and spoke immediately.

"Very well. My starting point is the latest findings for apoptosis, which is the study of how and why cells die. We want to kill the cells infected with T-Plague and then digest, or remove them. I earned my PhD from the Tokyo Institute of Technology by extending Yoshinori Ohsumi's 2016 Nobel prize-winning work in autophagy, which is the study of intracellular degradation. We've discovered the molecular pathways viruses exploit to target individual proteins. And I'm using the extensions of recombinant DNA technology and CRISPR/Cas9 with PCR amplification to weaken the virus and the infected cells so antibodies generated by the victim's immune system will kill them, releasing enzymes from the cell's lysosomes that will digest the cell. We can adjust your solution paths accordingly, so our next generation of vaccines will dissolve the neural entanglement, provide immunity, and give symptomatic relief and suppression. And then we'll repeat the process for the new strain." Alisha was impressed and said so to herself.

She rattled that off like she knows it cold, as if she wrote the book. I don't know what all those acronyms stand for. I'll buck this over to Su.

"Su, you'll be supervising Kameyo. Are you comfortable with her approach?"

"Yes. I've been reading the research literature and Kameyo's white papers, so I'll be able to contribute ideas shortly. And I'm confident we can launch improved formulations within six to nine months. Then we'll focus on the mutated strain. And until the improved line extensions are available, our current vaccines are still the best on the market."

"Excellent. I won't be able to participate because my time is committed to other projects, but I will visit periodically for hands-on updates. So why don't the two of you map out your time and events schedule that includes your resource budget, and tomorrow morning you can show me what you have. And now, I'm going to head to the Neuro-Device Lab. Please carry on and make it so."

The caffeine in the Coca Cola Alisha gulped on the way to the next meeting helped to reduce an incipient headache as well boost energy. Pretending is stressful, but it'll get less so as I practice more. Good thing they don't need me for vaccine development. I'd be in big trouble if they did. I sure wish I knew what to do to kick-start my brain. I guess I just keep busy pretending until my brain repairs itself. But something's going to trip me up if I'm not careful or I don't get smarter. Well, I'll just have to stick with the plan and hope no one but me catches on to how little I know.

Alisha joined Tim and Brian, who were already sitting at the lab conference table. Both rose to greet her; their clothing labeled them better than name tags. Tim dresses like a nerdy geek; Brian like a slick marketer. Let's see if he acts the part. She placed two neurodevices on the table, then started the meeting.

"Gentlemen, it's good to be with you. I know Tim quite well. I hired him to set up the lab, and he's already helped me build our first two neuro-devices. I brought with me the ones I've been using at my George Washington University lab. Brian, I apologize for not meeting with you as part of the hiring process, but Hud and Tim say you've got what it takes to handle neuro-device sales and marketing. So if you would, please describe your background."

Alisha listened attentively, appraising the sights and sounds. *He looks like a sales and marketing type. Well groomed, nice clothes, a little taller than the average guy, could stand to lose maybe five pounds, but keeps himself in shape. Talks well too. All this is to the good.*

"…and with my B.S.in computer systems and MBA with a focus on marketing, I'm golden working for cloud-based cybersecurity companies. I've worked for three on my ten-year career track. I earned my spurs starting as a field technical sales consultant, then moved into market development, and then into strategic market planning and management. My last company, Cybergard Security Systems, headquartered in Milpitas near San Francisco, is one of the leaders applying artificial intelligence to security software."

"Sounds like you were doing well and liked working for these companies. Why did you suddenly leave them to join our team?"

"Our industry is fast-paced. When you find an opportunity, you have to act while the window's still open. Hud made some calls to candidates Tim liked, and I'm the best you'll find. And when Tim told me about your techniques for adapting AI software to your cutting-edge medical devices, plus the tools you're developing for Internet security, I said to myself this is the chance of a lifetime.

My career will continue to grow with you."

Alisha could feel her headache building. *Why is he talking about artificial intelligence and Internet security? Am I supposed to know that stuff? Well I don't, so just keep pretending.*

"Fair enough. So, let me sketch what I want you and Tim to do this year. It'll keep you busy. We're going to launch two models of our Neuro-Knitter. The first model is what Tim has built. It uses neural stimulation in the brain and spinal cord to heal broken necks. Tim, you need to modify it to treat breaks lower on the spinal column. And you will do this while treating Dr. Chou's broken back. You'll swap the neck collar for a back pad that can be placed over the cracked vertebrae. That should be a simple modification, because I've already given you the schematics and software. You are responsible and will handle it by yourself. I'm focusing on other projects that you guys will learn about maybe next year. Tim, does this makes sense to you?"

"Yep. The modification is easy. All I do is focus the fields on a different part of the spinal cord."

"Good. I want you to start immediately mending Su's back. And while you're doing that, Brian will do his market development for the model that targets broken necks. How far along are you with the sales and marketing plan? How do you plan to segment the market? Have you developed your high-priority target list?" Brian fidgeted with his pen but kept smiling.

"I've roughed some of it out, and if I may, I'd like to make a suggestion. Why don't Tim and I work together for the rest of the afternoon, and we can all meet tomorrow morning to show you our time and events schedule for this year."

Alisha could feel her stress subside, as if she were some poor student just excused from the second half of a difficult exam.

"That's a good suggestion. We'll reconvene tomorrow afternoon. And now, I have to chat with Hud. See you then, after I meet with Su and Kameyo earlier in the morning." Alisha gathered her papers and departed for a safer place.

That was OK. Lucky for me they're able to work on their own. Tim can charge ahead without me because he already has all he needs. And I'm smart enough to handle Brian and the marketing plan. I'll tell Hud how the day's going. He'll like what I have to say.

Hud's grin widened when Alisha stepped into his office and sat across from him.

"Well, how's the day going? You look sort-a worn out, but that's to be expected first day back in the saddle."

"The meetings went well. Both teams are able to carry on just fine. And you are correct sir; I'm tired. I'm going to rest before dinner. And that's one of the advantages visiting you. I get a safe place to stay, meals included. It would be good if I have dinner with just you and your Dad. Let's let Su and Kameyo do what they want tonight. I'll bet Kameyo will offer to help Su settle in, and I want to stay out of the way. And let's leave Tim and Brian on their own too."

"Tell you what. I'll drive you home right now, and I'll tell Dad to join us for dinner at six. And when do you want our jet to fly you home?"

"Today's meetings were even better than I expected, and our people know what to do next. I'm not sure how much more time I need to spend with them, so I'll make my commercial flight arrangements and leave late tomorrow. No sense using the corporate jet for one person."

"Sounds like you know what you're doing. So let's get you home. That'll give you two hours to relax."

The nap did worlds of good. Alisha's headache and fatigue subsided, and she was thinking clearly. Who knows? Maybe all the smart pills I take are helping, but I consider them like vitamins. They can't hurt, and maybe they'll help. And my brain gave me another couple of twinges; it's trying to switch gears. Well, it's time for dinner.

Alisha felt another tiny vibration stir her brain, as if additional neural circuits were coming online. I just remembered why Adom was running from the CIA! He blew up a terrorist lab, and the CIA thought he was running it. I don't know how he got there, but my lightning brain is repairing more neural circuits, bringing back more and more of my memory. And Su's right. The more I use my brain, the faster it recovers. And I suddenly know why: the brain is a massive array of interconnected neurons. Memory is simply an associative sub-array. The more I use these circuits, the more they interconnect with other circuits, allowing all the neurochemicals generated to potentiate neural activity. I'm not going to tell anyone, but I can actually feel brain repairs starting to kick in. OK, calm down and get ready for dinner.

Personal issues, not business topics, were on the conversation menu, and chatting with Holy sparked memories of previous visits. Alisha marveled at his vitality. I like talking to Holy. Hard to believe he's in his nineties. He stands ramrod straight and his mind is as sharp as a Buck 119 hunting knife. And under that stoic exterior, he's a thoughtful and caring gentleman. Hey, I'm thinking about hunting knives. There must be a Texas connection. Be patient. It'll all come back.

Holy spoke right up after they sat down at the dining room table.

"I like the name Alisha, so that's what I'll call you if that's what you want. And you look good too. You're tougher than the T-Plague, but it seems like it's changed you a bit. The old Electra sometimes had sharp edges that got in the way. She should have smiled more and enjoyed herself more instead of worrying about the next day and the day after that."

"I think I'm on the mend. And maybe the changes you see are all to the good. But enough about me, how are you?"

"I can't kid anybody; losing Adom was a big blow. He was like another son, and with Hud full-time in the drug business, he was set to run the O&G business plus our livestock ranch. That was a terrible night at the ranch when he got shot dead. If I'd ah been there, I'd ah done my best to kill those bastards. I handle knives really well, which every cattleman can. But that's over and done, and I won't look back."

"Your vitality and approach to life will take you to at least one hundred."

"It would be an easier trek if Adom were here. He was a great caregiver when I needed assistance. But I'm still able to get around pretty good. And that's why I keep working. I love what I do and it keeps me in the present and future. That's why I plan to stay working until I have to step into the coffin. Now tell me, how is your friend Robin?"

"She's struggling a bit. There's been a lot of upheaval in her life. She's living with a very nice fellow—Matt Fortier. He treats her well, but Robin is high maintenance. She has a lot of emotional issues that make her temperamental."

"Yep, I remember how high-strung she is. But she sure is a great piano player. Do you remember when we hooked up my virtual reality home entertainment center to play with her?" I'm drawing a blank on that.

"No I don't, and I don't remember your virtual reality center. What is that?"

"What I did was figure out how to adapt military virtual reality simulation hardware and software to music or art exhibits. I bought some of the older generation components and plugged them in to my media computers and monitors. The combination creates a light show to go with the music I'm playing, or background lighting and music for art gallery exhibits I'm viewing. Companies are just beginning to apply virtual reality techniques to media. I can think of the next steps: add three-dimensional motion or pump in fragrances. Maybe you and Tim can come up with a device that connects brains to the equipment."

Alisha's brain registered another vibration. Now I remember. I tucked all that away to think about later. What did I call the device? The Cyber-Theater, or the Neuro-Theater. This could be our next neuro-device. It's like the Holodeck from the Star Trek series. This has possibilities.

Hud was happy to sit back and listen to Alisha and his dad ramble on. This Alisha sure is a nice gal. I bet she and the old Electra would be good friends. Well, it's time for all of us to get some rest. Tomorrow's gonna come, and we'll do our best to handle it. I'll tell'em to get some sleep. "I don't know about you two, but I'm ready to bunk down for the night. And I bet tomorrow will be a good day."

"You're right, son, so let's all say good night. See you at sunrise."

Alisha awoke fully refreshed at four in the morning. I acted well yesterday even though I didn't know everything I should. I think I'll get up and prepare for today. First, I'll exercise my brain by going over the Background Primer Electra wrote, and then I'll exercise my body. She slipped into workout clothes, then began reading Electra's write-up.

Background Primer

Religion:

- Theologians and philosophers have concluded there is no answer to "Does God Exist?" Each person must decide for

themselves according to their preference for Faith or Reason.
- All religions are shrouded in the mists of Antiquity and emerged from myth and ritual practiced by different tribes that all shared universal yearnings.
- Man is genetically predisposed to believe in a god/higher power to explain the natural world.
- Organized religions often degenerate into a self-serving power grab.

Christianity:
- "Jesus Conspiracy" theories still abound. Analytic researchers utilize Bayesian statistics when trying to resurrect the "Historical Jesus," but the probability calculations disappoint religious fundamentalists.
- Many pre-Christian pagan religions contain Christ-like stories: A Savior or Messiah Virgin Birth Miracles Resurrection.
- The existence of a historical Jesus doesn't matter, because its believers constructed the Bible that provided a world-changing, universal ethical philosophy needed today.

Philosophy:
- The Greek philosophers pretty much nailed Western Philosophy, and might have concluded all controversy if they had today's science and technology.
- Note the progression: Greek Roman Judeo-Christian Muslim Renaissance Enlightenment Post-Modern Post Post-Modern Here is my definition of Post-Post-Modern Philosophy: NeuroSci Extended Deconstructive Emergent Post-Pragmatism
- Enlightenment Philosophy principles: Truth, Knowledge, Rationalism, Progress
- Post-Modern philosophy is bankrupt (Negative, Nihilistic, Anti-Truth, Anti-Math)

Science:

- Asymptotic limits to man's cognitive skills restrict what is accessible to man's comprehension
- High Energy Physics/Quantum Mechanics/Cosmology have reached their limits and have become Religions rather than Science because their conjectures cannot be proved or disproved by experiments or observations. Their "Mind Experiments" are merely flights of fancy. Government keeps funding them because spin-offs have practical, technological benefits.
- Biotech, Nano-tech, and AI progress awaits for those able to apply the validated parts of Quantum Mechanics. Witness progress already made in Genetic Engineering and Quantum Computing.
- "Lightning Brain's competitive advantage compared to "Mere Mortals": Can develop superior Algorithms Can handle greater Complexity Can build on existing Hardware

More will become apparent as you read through all my notebooks.

I have run out of time to give you "Soft Science" basics: Psychology, Economics, Sociology, Politics. They are easier to grasp. You are smart enough to figure them out yourself, and you will remember what you already know as the lightning brain recovers.

The breadth and depth of Electra's summary amazed Alisha.

Electra knows a lot and knows how to summarize using bullet points. I follow what she's saying about religion and Christianity, but I don't remember anything about Bayesian statistics for testing historical hypotheses. But that's not important for today, so I'll tuck it away.

And I follow most of her philosophy bullet points, except her definition of Post Post-Modern Philosophy. I think that's what she named her brand of philosophy. And she has a whimsical sense of humor; only a philosopher would appreciate its title.

But the last section made her panic. I can't skip over the science stuff, because that's supposed to be my strong suit, and we'll be covering this today. I follow what asymptotic limits are, but I don't recall much about Quantum Mechanics or Quantum Computers.

And the last bullet point says I'm able to write better algorithms, handle more complexity, and piggyback on existing hardware. Beats me how I'm supposed to do it. Well, I'm just going to fake it and act naturally. It worked yesterday. Time to exercise. Endorphins always help.

Brian didn't need to review notes or exercise this morning; he had already rehearsed what was needed to make today a big success. He was finishing breakfast, filling his drive-time coffee mug to the brim, all the while congratulating himself for being so clever.

I fooled Tim and Hud, and Alisha looks like a pushover. I can't wait for my guys to get their hands on her today. They'll get her to cough up the schematics for that brain probe as well as source code for her hacking tools. Tim said she keeps all that to herself, so my guys will shake it loose. Then we send it back to Cybergard and put Alisha away for good. And I'll work for Tim until I milk the place dry, then head back to Silicon Valley.

Brian never planned to change jobs because Cybergard fits him best, but he always took advantage of job interviews to find out more about competition. And when Tim Godfrey explained what he's doing, Brian jumped at the opportunity to pirate cutting-edge AI and hacking software. Besides Brian, only Darla Tinibu, President of Cybergard, knew of his treachery, and they could rely on assigned security agents to "talk" with the target, cleaning up any residue afterwards. Corporate espionage and disposal were their specialties. Brian's confidence was so overflowing he whistled all the way on his drive to work, savoring his coffee and cleverness.

Alisha was wrapping up the second meeting and last meeting of the day. The first, with Su and Kameyo, had been encouraging. Their personalities and abilities meshed, as evidenced by how well they presented a timeline and budget that would take them to the end of the year. Alisha was relieved; she could observe rather than participate in their projects. And perhaps Su would allow Kameyo to become a personal friend, not just a professional associate.

The second meeting was equally encouraging. Tim said he'd need no assistance modifying the Neuro-Knitter to treat lower spinal injuries, and would meet tomorrow with Su to adapt the prototype so he could begin treating her broken back. Not only would treating Su help mend her vertebrae, it would provide clinical data that would support safety and efficacy claims Brian would trumpet in all advertising and promotional material. And Brian's sales and marketing plans, though aggressive, were achievable if he hustled. Alisha would be happy to watch progress unfold. Brian seems to be a take-charge marketing type. Thoughtful too. And I'll compliment both for how much they've already done.

"Well thank you, gentlemen. I like what you've lined up for this year. I look forward to monthly teleconference meetings so you can report progress. So, if there are no final questions I'll leave for the airport. And Brian, thank you for arranging the limo. When will it be here?"

"I've arranged for a four-thirty pickup, so you have time to say a quick goodbye to Hud, and then have a pleasant ride to the airport. Would you like me to escort you to Hud's office?"

"Thanks for the offer, but that won't be necessary. I've already said my goodbyes, and I can handle my suitcase and briefcases, so I think I'll wait by the entrance and enjoy the pleasant weather. Winters in Austin are so mild compared to DC. OK, I'm off. We'll talk end of March."

Brian's two security guys were inconspicuously parked just close enough to the building entrance to observe foot traffic. The leader was driving; his partner would play the role of fellow passenger. They had "borrowed" a limousine from the shuttle service early that afternoon, so it was unlikely to be reported missing yet. Thanks to Brian, they had cellphone photos of their target. The leader recognized Alisha and repeated the plan of action just before he drove to the entrance.

"That's gotta be the target. According to Brian, it'll be easy for you to subdue her, so here's what we'll do. You pretend to be a fellow passenger. I'll explain to her when I put her stuff in the trunk she gets a discount on the fare because she's sharing a ride with you. Then I'll put her in the back seat next to you. After we're out in the countryside, you can do what you want to terrorize her so she'll be ready to spill her guts when Brian meets us. But make sure she's still able to talk."

Alisha waved at the approaching limousine, and the driver flashed the headlights in return, then hopped out to greet her.

"Hello young lady. You must be Alisha Kittner. Let me put your bags in the trunk. I hope you don't mind sharing the ride. We got your call so late the only way we could schedule you was to put two in the limo. But you'll be charged only half the fare."

"That's fine with me. I'm just going to sit and read." Alisha slid into the back seat, holding one of the Electra Chronicles notebooks. She said hi to her fellow passenger, then immersed herself in the notebook. This was her fourth reading, each time memorizing and remembering more. And she guarded them with her life. Electra told me to study them thoroughly and never-never lose them. I'm a goner if I do.

Alisha paid no attention to what was unfolding. Instead of heading to the airport, the limo was heading away from Austin, into the countryside. Finally, a tremor jolted her brain, forcing her to look up and pay attention to her surroundings. Why are we in the middle of nowhere? Why did we turn onto this gravel road? Where's the airport?

"Driver, where are we? Shouldn't we be at the airport by now?"

"Change of plans. Your fellow passenger will explain." Alisha glanced to her left, spotting a revolver then wincing as he thrust it against her side.

"Someone wants to meet you, so you be a nice lady. Just sit still and be quiet until we get there." A wave of panic swept over her. "But why? And who? And where are we going?" Her fellow passenger became hostile.

"I told you to keep quiet, so shut up!" And with that, the man in the back seat threw a punch, but Alisha blocked it with her notebook, further infuriating him. He grabbed the notebook, ripping out the pages and showering her with giant pieces of confetti. Alisha shrieked in disbelief.

"Those are my notes! I can't do my work without them! Stop! Please!" But it was too late. All the pages had been ripped. The attacker gloated at Alisha's distress.

"Tell you what we'll do. Be nice to me and I'll let you pick up the pieces." Then he punched again, holstered his gun and straddled her, pinning her to the seat. He was doing all his thinking with the head between his legs and began loosening his trousers to unleash another weapon.

Alisha began screaming as panic turned to naked fear, freezing her brain and body. But suddenly, a tremendous quake jolted the foundations of her brain. If it were an earthquake, it would have registered a seven on the Richter scale. This was not the "big one," but it was big enough to shift Alisha into an altered state as the lightning brain cast off more neural entanglements. A calming clarity enveloped her as wrath surfaced from her subconscious. She didn't know what it was, but something was taking control, and she was not only aware but able to join with it. And whatever it was knew what to do.

Her attacker's conceit became his fatal mistake. In his rush to rape his captive, he exposed the wrong weapon first. Alisha grabbed with both hands his gun, shooting him twice in the gut before he could react. The impact toppled him backward; Alisha bolted upright and jammed the gun against the back of the driver's head, her steely voice hissing venom.

"Keep your hands on the steering wheel and stop right here". She spoke again after the car rolled to a stop. "Now tell me, who do you and your buddy work for?"

"Ask the guy we're supposed to meet." "No. You'll talk now if you want to live." "Go ahead and shoot me. I'm dead if I talk." "OK. Drive to where we're supposed to meet."

They rolled on for another half mile, then parked. Dusk was upon them, but Alisha pieced together the setting as she hurriedly glanced around, never shifting focus from the driver.

This place is an abandoned quarry. Look at that open pit filled with water. The place is deserted. Looks like it's been shut down for years. They must have picked it because they don't want to be disturbed, or me to be found if they leave me here. I have to know more before more people arrive. But how do I get him to talk? An aftershock rattled her brain. I know how!

"I have something that will coax answers out of you. Roll down all the windows, then get out of the car." The driver complied, saying nothing. Alisha exited too, keeping the gun trained on her adversary.

"Now, let's walk to the trunk. Open it, then slowly remove your belt and lie face down. And give me your cellphone and wallet, then keys before you do." When he had done as told, Alisha bound his legs with his belt before saying more.

"I have a device called the Brain Probe. I can inflict pain in your brain by hitting it with electromagnetic waves. It works very well when I plug the power adapter into the limo's electrical power outlet. Would you like a demonstration?" That got a response.

"No! Brian told me about it. I'll talk." Alisha was flabbergasted, but she kept calm and quiet, speaking only to herself.

Brian! I can't believe it. What game is he playing?" Approaching headlights ended the conversation. Alisha didn't panic; she knew what to do. She beat the driver unconscious with the pistol, rolled him into the tall grass and out of sight, then jumped into the driver's seat, starting the engine before the other car arrived. The vehicles greeted one another by flashing headlights. Alisha jumped from the car brandishing the gun before Brian could react.

"Freeze where you are and raise your hands, or you'll never lift another thing!" It was just light enough for Brian to recognize who was talking. Alisha approached cautiously. Brian's voice matched his shocked look.

"Alisha, what's going on?"

"Get out of the car and walk slowly to the limo's trunk. Then you'll answer my questions after I show you something." Brian was in no position to argue. Alisha paced behind him and spoke when they stopped.

"Who is that on the ground?" Bend down slowly and roll him over. "I don't know. I never saw him before."

"This is your last chance to start answering my questions with correct answers. Who is he?"

"I told you, I don't know!"

"OK then, we'll eliminate him from the conversation." Alisha shot him in the forehead; blood splattered Brian as he fell backwards. "I will give you a demonstration of how effective my Brain Probe is if you refuse to talk." There was just enough daylight for Alisha to see naked fear in Brian's eyes. "OK, OK! I'll talk."

"Why did your guys drive me here?" "We wanted to question you?" "About what?"

"Your brain probe and your hacking software." Alisha's brain figured out the rest.

"So, you wanted me to give you my patents and schematics and software code or else you'd kill me. You and your partners are working for Cybergard. What else would you like to tell me?"

"There's nothing else to tell. You figured it all out. Don't call the police. Maybe you and I can cut a deal." Alisha cut the conversation short.

"Who at Cybergard knows about our meeting?" Brian stammered out what he hoped might spare him.

"If I tell you, can we talk about a deal?"

"Maybe, but tell me now who we'll have to cut out of the deal."

"It's Darla Tinibu. She's President of Cybergard. I don't like her anyway, and you wouldn't either. So, deal with me instead."

"Maybe, but you left out one last detail. You didn't tell me where you were going to dump my body. But I figured that out. You were going to dump me in the pit. So, here's what you'll do. Drag your buddy's body into the back seat of the limo." Judging by his zombielike motion, Brian was in shock but was strong enough to load the dead man into the back seat. Then he turned to face Alisha.

"You've killed them both! You're worse than Darla!" Alisha ended tonight's meeting by firing another bullet that collapsed Brian into the back seat. putting the body count at three, and then made a final inspection of all bodies, removing wallets, phones and keys, increasing the number of guns and I.D.s in her shoulder bag.

It's time to dispose of the evidence. Let's see. Alisha walked to the side of the road. The grassy shoulder extended for another twenty feet before dropping abruptly twenty feet to a murky water-filled pit. I don't know the depth, but I'll take my chances.

She backed the limo as far as she could, pointing it towards the pit, then removed her bags from the trunk and found part of a tire jack that would wedge the accelerator pedal down. She did so and checked final preparations, then shifted the gearshift lever to drive by reaching through the driver-side window, standing aside and then watching the limo zoom over the edge, splashing into the water before she reached the edge. The car's forward momentum carried it thirty feet into the pit where it was now beginning to list forward as water poured in through the open windows. She watched in near darkness until it sank from sight, then loaded her bags into Brian's car and prepared to drive off. As she sat behind the steering wheel, another, larger aftershock registered in her brain, causing her body to tremble.

I'm finally beginning to understand what the Electra Chronicles are telling me. The lightning brain is repairing itself! I can feel it! It's as if scales are falling off my brain's memory. I hope the repairs aren't finished, but I'm remembering more and understanding more.

Alisha's trembling stopped and she was about to drive away, but a sudden awareness flashed into her cognitive persona, bringing her to a screeching halt. I have just seen the Creature from the Id! I felt wrath and glee simultaneously. It was thrilling. And maybe it saved me when I was mugged last winter on the shopping expedition, but back then my brain hadn't recovered enough to be aware of what was happening. The old Electra warned me about this. I better reread that section. Suddenly, Alisha felt a storm of emotions swirl inside.

I feel sorry for Brian, even though I didn't know him at all. But her sympathy for him and his partners died abruptly. Brian and his friends would have treated me badly. I prefer the Creature killing them instead of them killing me.

Alisha regained enough control to plan her exit. I'll drive to the airport and park Brian's car in long-term parking. Then I'll go to the ticket counter and change my ticket to the next flight home. And when Hud calls about Brian not coming to work, I'll act surprised. By now, I'm a great actress. It'll be months before anyone spots the sunken limo. I better get rid of the guns before getting to the airport. What else do I need to do? Damn! I forgot to retrieve the torn pages from the last Electra Chronicles notebook! I'm in big trouble; don't panic yet. Maybe I can recall most of them. I better think hard.

Alisha followed her own advice on the drive to the airport, on the flight to DC, and on the ride home from the airport.

It was late Friday morning by the time Alisha stepped into her house. Though she hadn't slept for a second in over 24 hours she didn't feel tired; she felt like thinking more. She wanted to withdraw into her fortress of solitude—the lightning brain—so she could sort through current events. She piled her luggage and briefcase next to her workstation, suited up to run, and ten minutes later passed the first mile marker on one of her running trails. A mile later the endorphins kicked in, reinforcing what the lightning brain was already doing: incorporating all its new learning from the trip, using its unshackled memory and improved I.Q. She could almost feel neural entanglement dissolving, replaced by more powerful cognition giving her rational persona a clarity that enabled her to understand better the old Electra's legacy.

I'm a long way from having Electra's extraordinary cognitive abilities, but I'm smarter now than a couple of days ago. I'm beginning to understand what "The Electra Chronicles" are teaching me about my three personas and about Electra. I can handle myself when I put my game face on. And I learned I have a built-in warning system when I pay attention to what's going on about me. What was it that Holy said? I seem happier than Electra, not as complex or philosophical. Maybe so. Maybe I have a better handle on emotions than Electra did. Now that I'm thinking better, I can understand her better. And maybe I can recall what was in the notebook my attacker destroyed. Just then Alisha felt another neural tremor. I must get home!

Alisha ran like lightning, bolting into the house, and searching madly for the contingency folder Electra had prepared. She dug it out and feverishly scanned for anything related to lost documents. And there it was: an envelope containing a "Lost and Found" letter. She ripped it open and devoured the words.

"Hello Alisha. If you are reading this, you must have lost one of your notebooks. All the notebooks I left you are valuable, and the Electra Chronicles are most important. I can think of many events that might have caused your problem, but that's not important. What's important is replacing what was lost.

I prepared long ago a backup safety deposit box. It contains a complete set of all your notebooks, current up to the day I departed. The bank name, address and safety deposit box key are in the envelope. When you find what you are looking for, MAKE A COPY AND PUT IT BACK IN THE BOX.

"I hope you didn't suffer much of a setback because I want to come back and meet you as soon as you can make it so. When I return, we'll make a great pair; you'll help me and I'll help you. Alice —our dearly departed British friend—described it best with a quote from the Dickens novel, Great Expectations, 'Ever the best of friends, eh Pip?' Trust me, that is what we shall be…"

Alisha sat on the bed, sobbing from empathy-filled relief. She loved the Electra still imprisoned in the lightning brain. Electra was extraordinary; she was brilliant beyond mere mortals. But in spite of her brilliance—or perhaps because of it—she was emotionally flawed, which made Alisha love her all the more. Electra, when you

return let me help you handle your emotions better. She sensed that Electra had obsessive-compulsive and manic-depressive tendencies. Her complex, enigmatic personality was often cloaked in melancholy, preventing her from living in the joy of the moment. A psychiatrist could mistakenly conclude Electra was mentally ill, suffering from schizophrenia, split personality, and other psychotic disorders. No wonder the secret of your lightning brain could never be revealed! You'd be locked away or dissected. Just then an odd thought popped into Alisha's head. When Electra returns, what will become of me? I

hope the lightning brain will keep me around. Alisha shrugged; the thought vanished quickly as Alisha shifted gears.

She showered and then called Zoe, who volunteered to bring home pizza. As she disconnected the call, another shudder jolted Alisha's brain as she empathized with Electra's pain. I know why

Zoe means so much to you. You blame yourself for neglecting Zoe when she needed a friend. I shall teach you to lighten up. You did more than all of Zoe's associates combined. And you cannot live other people's lives. Ultimately, they are responsible for their own actions. Not even Jesus could save all his disciples.

Alisha puttered the afternoon away, unpacking and putting notebooks in a safe place. Then she sat in the living room's gathering twilight glow, thinking about her alter ego. I think Electra would be satisfied with my Austin performance. She'll be center stage when she returns, but I hope there'll be a part for me. It's not my call, but I can't wait to see.

Chapter 6
April 2122

"Enemies of the States"
Thread 3 Chapter 2

ZIARMAL THAQAF'S ISLAMIC NAME fits him much better than the turban he wears only when absolutely necessary. It means hard worker who surpasses all in skill, and that's precisely what he is. From years of study, he knew what direction Isilabad should lead the centuries' old war against the West, and the map isn't revealed by studying Muhammad's teachings in the Koran. Indeed not, for the older generation of Islamic warriors had chosen the wrong battlefield. Neither Isilabad nor any of its rogue predecessors could ever defeat the West on land, sea, or air. But from his computer studies that earned him a PhD and then a stellar Silicon Valley Internet Security career, he knew the West could be defeated in Cyberspace. That was the new battlefield, and Ziarmal had the blessings, the resources, and the ear of Isilabad's Exalted Ruler to prepare weapons and plans.

He had researched Cyberspace's 21st century growing pains caused by Silicon Valley's hyper-optimistic intentions for increasing efficiency in all aspects of modern life via Net Centrism (make the Internet a religion) and Solutionism (build cloud-based algorithms to solve all problems).He understood how it had fueled the growth of the Platform Economy (computer technology reduces "friction" in transactions and increases networking among buyers and sellers), and grudgingly acknowledged that Silicon Valley's leading platform companies had patched the obvious problems caused by this disruptive paradigm shift. But everything relying on Cyberspace shared a nuanced Achilles Heel that Ziarmal would exploit.

He had earned multiple degrees near Silicon Valley—the mecca of cloud computing and Cyberspace—then became known as the guru for developing advanced Web-based security systems. His brilliance attracted the best youthful talent; one of his acolytes had been Cyrus Wassani, the son of Hassan Wassani, who at that time was ascending to a coveted throne: that of Isilabad's Exalted Ruler, the Caliphate of Islam.

Cyrus urged his father to bring Ziarmal back to Isilabad so he could lead Internet terrorism against America, the Great Satan. Ziarmal and Hassan were the same age and cut from the same cloth; they were brilliant, devious, relentless, and dedicated to restoring Islam to its rightful place on the world stage. And most importantly, they were of like mind regarding Islamic beliefs; most are primitive, outmoded, out of step with its people, and incompatible with Modernity. So, they would work under the guise of religion to build a power base from which to attack. Hassan would build wealth and political influence; Ziarmal would build weapons and war plans. Together they would lead the Middle East back to world dominance. He returned to become the linchpin in a treacherous piece of Hassan's subterranean R&D facility that harnessed all that Cyberspace-related technology had to offer.

Ziarmal's work progressed steadily, but when the Great Satan and its "Coalition of the Smart" uncovered other pieces of Hassan's deviousness—Trojan filters and an Apocalypse Clock that could unleash T-Plague via the Internet—the Exalted Ruler and his inner circle were terminated. Ever since then, Isilabad leaders had been kowtowing to the West to avoid a shooting war, waiting for an opportunity to retaliate. Ziarmal would be the power behind the throne for making it so.

Ziarmal was more devious than even his friends imagined. Not even his "Iron Triangle" allies—China and Russia—knew all his plans. Ziarmal coined the name "IT Alliance" when he assembled a "Coalition of the Committed" that wanted to repay the West. IT meant "Iron Triangle" formed geographically by the three countries, or "Internet Technology," which is the prized resource for controlling Cyberspace and its weaponry. Ziarmal had targeted both countries because they were leaders in computer hacking and Internet intrusion. Russia still resented how the West had marginalized it when the Soviet Union collapsed, and China feared its economy would be crushed if America ever regained its footing on the world stage. Ziarmal patiently explained all this to the new Exalted Ruler and his inner circle. They in turn covertly recruited Russia and China to join. Collectively, they would fool the West; their leaders would be singing Kumbaya while the Iron Triangle attacked them in Cyberspace.

Ziarmal and counterparts communicated weekly on secure Internet connections and met in person three times a year, sequentially rotating the location among the three countries. The last meeting confirmed the good news: soon Ziarmal would give the command to strike. The West would never know what hit them.

Cybergard Security Systems Inc. was cast from the same mold that makes Silicon Valley companies the best places to work. They provide golden career paths and a list of perks that seems endless, such as round-the-clock free food, exercise classes, nap pods, game arcades, and concierge services. And some of the companies would even pay for employees to have sperm or eggs frozen. No wonder all the employees are happy. All, that is, except one: company President Darla Tinibu, a black female built like a fire hydrant and packing the power of a connected firehose.

Darla should have embodied the best of African heritage. Her parents earned degrees and built solid careers in Silicon Valley after emigrating from Zimbabwe. They were talented IT professionals as well as loving, caring parents who provided everything so their one child could thrive. As an infant, Darla had been one of the few untouched by T-Plague. Like her parents, she was smart. But unlike them, she was manipulative and greedy, desiring money and power. Both would come to her if she built a career in Silicon Valley using computer technology at a "platform economy" company. And her determination made it so. Now in her late forties, she had risen to the top, propelled by ability while concealing her ruthless personality.

Darla respected America, but had a soft spot for only one continent: Africa. She had studied its history, which had finally been corrected to give native Bantu and Swahili people credit for establishing in southeast Africa once-powerful ancient civilizations that had been overthrown half a millennium ago by Arab and Western countries using superior technologies to gain gold, ivory, and slaves. Much progress had been made in the 20th and 21st centuries as America led the way to establish a thriving community of African nations. And Darla pledged to take whatever steps necessary to build an "African Silicon Valley" that would be as important for Africa's future as the Great Rift Valley is for homo sapiens' past.

Darla hadn't heard from her corporate spy, Brian Ritz. He and the two security agents she assigned him a month ago had vanished. Not even their cellphone tracking chips placed them on the grid.

And this made her angry, for Darla had big plans to marry two technologies for her own glory: artificial intelligence and Internet security systems. No company had commercialized the combination yet, but from what Brian had initially reported, a privately held Texas company might be in the lead. That's why she planted Brian at H&H DNA Partners. He would pirate its technology. Well, if Brian doesn't surface, I'll look elsewhere, or maybe try a different infiltration route. This is on my to-do list and no one else will know.

Jared Gardner considered his deliverance from the T-Plague to be a divine sign that he is the chosen one to channel God's plans for America. Why else was he the only survivor of the cowardly Chinese attack? Not only did he survive, but the neurologists reported that according to brain scans and intelligence testing, his brain was making a comeback. It might not be as good as before, but he felt he'd be plenty sharp. Maybe the big memory gaps surrounding events leading up to the Chinese attack would shrink. If progress continues, he'd be able to return to the Oval Office in no more than two months.

And when I get back, I'm going to follow my own advice. One of the first things I'll do is punish China for the attack, then deal with Isilabad. And then I'll accelerate the pace of my programs, making them tougher so they're more effective. I'm still not too clear on what was going on late last year, but there must have been a lot swirling about me. Too bad my security guy—Peter Schmitzer—was killed trying to protect me. He would know. Maybe when I get back, Angus or someone else will jog my memory. I'll be ready to deal with all situations. Yes, harsh times demand harsh measures, and I'll use them all to protect myself and America.

Alisha knew the pace of her recovery was accelerating but kept the details to herself. Thanks to all the events that had unfolded while in Austin, she now realized that every time her brain emitted a seismic jolt, it was a signal more memory and neural circuitry were back in action. Perhaps any stress-induced neurochemicals reinforced whatever repairs were underway. Whatever the reason, upon returning from Austin she was remembering and thinking better and faster. She had been able to complete all but one of the assignments Electra said she must finish at this point in her recovery. (Sometimes Alisha playfully referred to the old Electra as "She Who must be Obeyed," copying a now-famous moniker referring to the lead character of Henry Rider Haggard's 1886 novel She: A History of Adventure.) All that remained was a status presentation to her postdoc advisors.

Alisha thought it would be easy to do because Electra had built a two-year cushion of completed research, thoroughly documented in white papers, background notes, and supporting articles. I'm not as smart as the old Electra, but I'm pretty clever, and I'm a convincing actress too. All I have to do is memorize what's already written. How hard can that be? It turned out to be a Herculean task.

This stuff is incomprehensible. I don't think human brains will ever catch up to Electra, no matter how long they evolve. But here's what I'll do: since I can't blind them with brilliance I'll baffle with bullshit. And I'm great at pretending and acting naturally. Someday, I hope to give Electra a command performance.

Alisha slaved away for two weeks, finally coming up with a presentation and discussion guide she could read from when addressing her advisors. Fortunately, all activities other than workouts and running needed little attention, so by mid-April Alisha had her act together.

The three-person advisory board professors followed her work ever since she had entered a GWU graduate school biotech program. Two of them attributed her progress to dedication and hard work because she appeared to be an average graduate student. But her lead advisor, Professor Ravenhill, had noticed subtle changes as she moved through the program. She emerged from her naïve shell, becoming smarter and more assertive. And now, though none would admit it, they could barely follow the bi-annual summaries she sent them, let alone her refereed journal articles. But they had to maintain the illusion of superiority, and the best way was to hide out in a crowd, so they invited graduate students and colleagues from local colleges to attend.

Alisha designed her talk to be cordial and inclusive, giving generous credit to her advisory board. But she also intended to keep everyone off balance, using enough breadth and depth that would make it difficult for anyone to ask questions. She packed four slides with pithy points she'd elaborate by reading from her discussion guide, filling up to ninety minutes with concepts, jargon, and acronyms that would leave the audience speechless. She would also sketch white board diagrams to give the appearance she knew the material cold. Her discussion guide contained pictures of what she would draw.

Alisha used that Friday morning 4 a.m. wakeup run to rehearse one more time. None of them know much about Electra being zapped by the T-Plague. Since they don't know I'm filling in, I'll go by the name Electra. And I've memorized every shred of the stuff I could understand, so I can talk the talk, even though the audience can outgun me. And I'll be fast as lightning, so they can't hit a moving target. I'm as prepared as possible. If I act my part as planned, they won't draw any academic weapons. So, it's time to get my game face on and enjoy playing my role. The pleasant spring weather put audience and advisors in a good mood, as did the pre-talk yogurt, muffins and assortment of juices. Alisha talked ten minutes before the start to a nervous advisor who would provide introductory remarks.

"Good morning Electra. I'm ready, and I hope you are too. I always get jittery before talking to an audience, even in a classroom setting, so I'll keep the intro short—five minutes max. Someone labeled my condition 'the nervous pee.' There's that proverb: Physician, heal thyself. I forget where it comes from, but it doesn't work for me. You look calm and collected, but that's how you always look."

"Good morning, Professor Winberg, and thank you for handling the introduction. Don't worry, you'll be fine. That proverb is from Luke 4 Verse 23, and once you start talking the nerves will calm down."

Wow, my brain is working AOK today. I pulled that proverb from Sunday School memory. I'm ready; just remember to smile, speak slowly, and make eye contact with the audience. And don't recite the slide. Talk about it.

Professor Winberg started his introduction promptly at ten, gladly relinquishing the podium to Alisha in a record-tying three-minute introduction. She was cool, collected, and sported her game face. She pressed the control button and the first slide appeared above and behind her.

POSTDOC STATUS REPORT—SPRING 2122

ELECTRA KITTNER

PURPOSE
- Summarize my Theoretical Conjectures
- Provide Current Research Status
- Highlight Commercial Applications

ALL WORK IS ORIGINAL AND EXTENDS MY PHD AND NIH PROGRAMS
- Research Areas: DNA-Related Drug Development and Medical
- Devices and Software for Cloud-Based Big Data Mining and Security
- My Work Explores and Connects Two Worlds: Neurospace and Cyberspace

- Drug Development Disciplines include: Virology, Molecular Biology, Genetic Engineering, Neuroscience
- Medical Device and Software Disciplines: Computer Programming, Nanotechnology, Computer Chip Interfaces between Biological and Computer Systems

"Good morning, and thank you for attending today. I am Electra Kittner, and I would like to tell you something about my research…" She smiled while talking for ten minutes about the first slide, giving credit to her advisors and lab associates, and sketching three whiteboard diagrams that embellished additional details listed in her discussion guide. The audience is with me. Good! Remember to make eye contact. Time for the next slide.

Alisha advanced to the next slide, pausing for the audience to skim its bullet points.

CONJECTURES

FOR DRUG DEVELOPMENT

Breakthroughs will take place at the interface of two levels of Reality

- Thermo/Stat Microscopic Reality (PV = n RT Entropic and Free Energies, etc.)
- Quantum/Sub-Atomic Reality (Wave Equation Uncertainty Principle, Wave-Particle Duality, etc.)

Model Cells as Tiny Factories or Industrial Centers

- Sections of DNA assemble Drugs using Amino Acids and Enzymes
- All Communications handles by Chemical Receptors and Neuron Signals

DRUG DEVELOPMENT MODELS

- Solution Path integrates virology, molecular biology, genetic engineering and neuroscience using quantum biology concepts
- Virus infects specific bacteria causing the virus to spread to Neural Centers
- Virus targets specific Neural Control Center that produce nano-enzymes
- Nano-enzymes cause DNA mutation in Neural Cells

- Mutation may lead to Enhanced or Diminished Host

Characteristics
Current Extensions

- Incorporate latest Aptosis Research (Death of Cells)
- Integrate Autophagy into the Solution Path
- Autophagy: an intracellular degradation system that delivers cytoplasmic constituents to the lysosome. Despite its simplicity, recent progress has demonstrated that autophagy plays a wide variety of physiological and pathophysiological roles, which are sometimes complex.
- AFM (Atomic Force Microscopy)
- Protein Embedding (DNA-related segment targeting receptor sites)
- PCR (Polymerase Chain Reaction acceleration) CRISPR/Cas9 Gene Editing

This is a killer slide. I've packed more in here than their brains can assimilate. I'll speed up my delivery just a bit, but I'll enunciate clearly and smile all the while.

"As you probably know, a conjecture is an opinion or conclusion unsubstantiated by data or information. I'll now describe what conjectures, models and extensions I'm using for my drug development work."

Alisha spent thirty minutes covering these topics, sketching three additional whiteboard diagrams. That should put them on their

heels, and I won't let up. She proceeded immediately to the next slide.

CONJECTURES FOR MEDICAL DEVICES

Breakthroughs will integrate Artificial Intelligence Software with Neural Implants

- Smart devices will send/receive electrical signals to brain control centers
- Nanotechnology shrinks chips and devices to "cranial scale"
- Software and Neuralware symbiotically learn

MEDICAL DEVICE MODELS

- Brain is enormous Finite State Machine (100 billion neurons creating 100 trillion synapses)
- Mental State: Unique set of neurons and synapses "turned on" at finite potentiations
- Map physical structure of Brain (locate control centers and "hot spots")
- Send/Receive Electric Signals to target synapses ("hot spots")

Current Extensions
- Nanotechnology to increase granularity of the cell
- Big Data Technology to process terabytes of data
- Networked Computer Arrays to simulate interacting Neural Centers
- Multi-threaded parallel programs utilizing Recursive Algorithms
- Embedded Chips interfacing Biological and Computer Systems

"Now, let me describe the same topics for my other area of research: medical devices..."

She took an additional thirty minutes to cover what she wanted, including three more sketches. She maintained a cheery tone, but as she scanned the audience, she could tell that many brains were beginning to disengage. *Good. I'll wake them up with my last slide.* COMMERCIAL APPLICATIONS

Limited only by our Imaginations! Sampling of Drug Applications:
- Use the Human Biological Systems to manufacture its own Drugs
- Provide Immunity, Pain Relief, Cure for all T-Plague mutations
- Focus on Chronic Diseases: Alzheimer's, Diabetes. Cancer, Heart Disease
- Turn off the Aging Switch (Holy Grail of Anti-Aging)
- Extend Hayflick Limit—Invert Viral Degradation Pathways

Sampling of Medical Device Applications:
- Focused Bone/Joint Repair

- Pain Relief
- Physical/Mental
- Enhancement
- Replacement for Conventional Psychotherapy/ Psychopharmacology
- Hardware/Software storage for the "Human Condition"
- Gateway for Transhuman Evolution to the Post-Human Age

WARNINGS:
- Many Ethical Issues must be addressed
- Will need large pool of "Smart Researchers" to support our first exploration into the new and exciting worlds of Neurospace and Cyberspace
- Software security breaches threaten AI Devices or Internet/ Cloud-Based Systems

"Well, as we all know, the real payoff to research is discovering new concepts and then bringing them to the market so our society benefits from improving our quality of life and our quality of economy. The applications of my research areas—short-term and longer-term—are truly staggering. It is limited only by our imaginations, for we are embarking on a journey into two brave new worlds: that of our brain which I call Neurospace, and that of computer networks and the Internet which we call Cyberspace. That's where the future lies, and let me describe just some of the applications..."

Alisha talked for an additional twenty minutes, and her content and delivery brought some of the audience back to life. She didn't waste time sketching additional diagrams; by now, even the smartest in the audience were running out of energy and were more interested in lunch than in her words, so they pretended to understand by nodding knowingly. I think they've heard enough. And I don't see anyone drawing an academic weapon. Let's wrap up so I can get out of here.

"All these applications have the potential for making our lives better, but we must heed warnings that accompany technological breakthroughs. There will be ethical issues to address, such as balancing longer lifespan against the economics of self-sufficiency, or defining the red line that separates man from other animals. And what happens if the pool of smart people is inadequate to handle living in a technologically advanced future? And what about software or Internet security? We must prevent application or operating system software from being compromised or hijacked. Otherwise, what is designed to help us might be subverted into weapons of human destruction. We don't need answers this minute, but we will need them as our technology advances. So, let's move ahead, but deal with warnings before they start flashing red.

"And finally, you might ask me why haven't 'Just around the Corner' predictions made over a hundred years come true? Two reasons: first, even the smartest researchers failed to handle the enormous challenges posed by problem solution decomposition and complexity. In other words, no team is smart enough to break the problems into bite-sized pieces, solve them, then put them back together. Second, because human beings feel threatened, society has deliberately adopted a go-slow approach to R&D and implementation in order to avoid harmful large-scale human reengineering or obsolescence. But I am optimistic that great new worlds await us, and as long as we explore them with the wisdom and intelligence to do the right thing, the rewards are monumental. Perhaps some of you will join me on our quest for a 22nd century Holy Grail. Thank you for listening. And now, I'll be pleased to entertain any questions or comments you may have." Alisha smiled but yelled to herself, Please, no questions!
Just go and leave me in one piece.

There was the usual smattering of applause accompanied by low-level buzzing and murmuring that follow a presentation, but no immediate questions. Finally, a lone voice from the back spoke up.

"Doctor Kittner, I liked your talk, but maybe next time you could use a larger font and put more color in the slides. And maybe you could include some sort of video."

"That's a good suggestion. I'll do that next time. Thank you." Only one other comment came up.

"I'm not sure I know what all those acronyms mean. Maybe next time you could spell them out on the slides."

"That's another good suggestion, and I'll do that next time. Thank you very much."

Professor Winberg joined Alisha at the podium to conclude the session.

"Thank you, Doctor Kittner, and thanks to our audience for being here today. I hope you will join us again."

Alisha chatted briefly with her committee before returning to her lab. Professor Ravenhill spoke for all of them.

"That was most impressive. You know the material cold. You'll be a shoo-in next year for an associate professorship. And your research could support a team of postdocs. We should reach out to other departments or universities to form inter-school or interdepartmental research projects you could lead." Alisha maintained composure, but had to stifle an incipient panic attack. *Damn! I was too convincing. I need more I.Q., not more projects.*

"Thank you for the kind words. And yes, I certainly can handle additional projects, given the right team of associates. But I think we should table this discussion until the end of the year so I can demonstrate further how I'm able to manage multiple projects." Her committee thought that was reasonable, so she said goodbye.

"Whew! I enjoyed giving my talk, but I'm tired. Good thing I packed a good lunch; that'll reenergize me, and it's waiting at my lab. I have some stuff to clean up and notes to summarize before heading home for the weekend. Thanks again for all your support."

The walk back to the lab felt almost as good as getting out of school for summer vacation. *I am so happy to have that talk in the rearview mirror. I think Electra would be pleased with my performance. I don't know why, but I felt a tiny brain quake just now when talking with Professor Ravenhill. Either the stress or something he said registered in my brain. And that has to be good. Now it's time to call me Alisha.*

Lunch reenergized her, so she puttered about the lab for a couple of hours that afternoon. She wasn't smart enough yet to know how to do biotech R&D, but she toyed with all the equipment, trying to figure out how each apparatus worked. She was about to drive home when an idea flashed in her brain. I think I handled myself very well today. I'm ready to have some fun. I feel like partying tonight. Maybe my female keepers can join me for dinner. I'll call them now. Alisha called Robin first, who was on campus that afternoon.

"We haven't talked for a while, and I've left you messages…Not to worry; I know school stresses you out. Hey, you want to go out for dinner tonight?…You're meeting with your Econ study group?… No, that's OK… Get the project done… Call me sometime so I know you're OK. Bye-bye."

She had better luck with Mariah and Zoe. Both were free, and Mariah chose a popular Georgetown restaurant convenient for everyone. They would meet at five so there'd be no waiting for a table.

Alisha was first to arrive, so she picked a conspicuous table her partners would spot. I want something stronger than a Coke. I don't know what Electra likes to drink, so I'll study the drinks menu. Hmm, nothing looks familiar. Maybe the old Electra didn't drink much. I'll

just have to experiment for both of us. And the Long Island Iced Tea contains lots of different liquors. I think I'll have one for starters. She had drained half the glass by the time Zoe arrived, breathless as usual but looking far better than she did a couple of months ago.

"What a great idea! We'll celebrate getting your presentation done and TGIF. You must feel great. No wonder you look so relaxed. Hey, that's not a Coke; that looks like Long Island Iced Tea. I never knew you liked it."

"Hi ya, Zoe. I sure like it now. It's really tasty, and I earned it because my presentation went well. What do you like to drink? I seem to remember you like gin and tonic."

"You're right. That's a good sign your memory's getting better. Here comes our waitress; that's what I'll order. You better hold off ordering another Ice Tea until Mariah gets here."
"I hope she gets here soon. I'm thirsty."

Mariah wanted to walk to the restaurant; the spring breeze and sunlight felt good, and the fifteen-minute stroll would give her a chance to unwind from the stress of her socio-political think tank job. It would also give her a chance to think about Alisha.

Late last year I spent one night with Electra. Both of us wanted to take our relationship to the next level, but then Electra almost killed herself. What remains is Alisha, and I don't know if I feel the same towards her. In some ways, she's not nearly as good: not as smart or thorough, not as assertive or strait-laced. But in other ways she seems better: not as enigmatic, not as philosophic or sometimes melancholy, more open and free-spirited; more fun to be with. I don't know what Alisha feels towards me. Maybe tonight's a chance to find out.

"Here comes Mariah. Alisha, put your glass down and wave." Mariah bustled to the table,then sat next to Zoe. They had become friends, seeing each other at least once a month at Brain Trust meetings or when Alisha's support group met. Personal issues—not careers or work or the external world—would be tonight's topics.

"Hello girls, and what a great way to celebrate Alisha's presentation. Did you dazzle them?"Alisha drained her glass before giggling an answer.

"Maybe I didn't dazzle them, but I sure kept them at bay. They didn't try to pin my ears back with tough questions, and that's all to the good. Hey, you should order a drink. I need another Iced Tea. What are you drinking? I seem to remember you like Chardonnay? Don't you like anything with more pizzazz?"

"I'll start with Chardonnay. Maybe I'll have something else later." The waitress took orders and returned with three fresh drinks. Alisha proposed a toast.

"I'll bet you don't know my mother wrote poetry. I'm beginning to remember more of them, and here's one for us. It's called The Nerve of Youth, and the last verse is my toast to us."

Fresh nerve of steel's a treasured gift,
Bestowed in early years.
It makes them sure and makes them swift,
Protects them from their fears.

Alas it does not last too long,
Time wears it away.
When nervous energy runs down,
And caution rules the day.
So propose a toast that Youth runs free,
Have their sights set high.
Give them strength then let them be,
May their power never die.

Mariah and Zoe took ladylike sips; Alisha took a rather large gulp before plunging into her top-of-mind topic.

"Hey, you two are looking good, but what about the rest of the Full House—you know, Carter, Matt and Robin. What's happening in their lives?" Mariah spoke first.

"Carter is alive and well, busy with work, with tennis at his club, and with his Corvette. And most recently, he's been tutoring Robin in economics and tennis. She's taking a macroeconomics class which is difficult, so she's stressed out. And she's finally taking a Personal Fitness course required to graduate. She picked tennis. That's the latest I know. Zoe, what would you like to add?"

"I talk to Matt more than Alisha does, even though he's with us both once a week for fitness training. He's happy he switched jobs from physical therapy at a rehab center to EMT, replacing poor Clarence, even though he's working third shift. He doesn't spend as much time at home with Robin as before, but his schedule fits well with the holistic healthcare business he and Jennifer Conklin started last year. And that's it." It was now Alisha's turn to talk.

"Well, I spoke with Robin today to invite her, but she had an economics study group meeting on campus this evening. That sort of ties in with Carter's tutoring. And like you said, she seems a bit stressed out. I've left cell messages a couple of times, but she doesn't return my calls. I guess between school and Matt and her part-time job, she's fully loaded. How're she and Matt doing?" Zoe knew more than the others.

"Matt sometimes calls me to talk about it. He doesn't call you because you don't need anything else to think about while you're still recovering. And maybe he talks with Carter; they've become good friends. But I think I'm the one he confides in the most. So please, keep what I'm saying confidential. And maybe you can give me suggestions for what to relay.

"Matt's doing his best being as supportive as possible, but he's realizing more and more Robin is high maintenance. She has mental issues. So, he took the initiative to enroll them in a relationship counseling program. That seems to be helping a bit, but from what I read between the lines, I think the problem goes beyond relationships. I think Robin is heading for a nervous breakdown. Didn't that happen when she dropped out of the Curtis Institute?" Mariah and Zoe paused for Alisha to answer. She blinked, not knowing what to say until suddenly feeling a brain tremor that triggered memories of Robin.

"Sort of, but the doctors who treated her thought it was more of a stress-related breakdown. She was getting hit on by her instructors, she couldn't make it as a concert pianist, and she contracted the T-Plague. That's enough to stress out anyone. Maybe there's too much uncertainty once again in her life. Last year her parents were deported, she broke her neck, and she moved in with Matt. And now, she's struggling to graduate. And maybe her part-time job's a hassle. Now that I'm feeling better, maybe I can help her just by talking to her. But come on, let's give ourselves some credit. Collectively, we're doing all we can to help her. Although she's high-strung, she's resilient and will bounce back. Let's get another round of drinks to toast Robin, then order dinner."

Drinks, dinner and conversation topics came and went. Zoe was ready to go, but not Alisha.

"If you want to call it a night that's fine, but I'm ready for more. Mariah, would you like to stay? I can see why you picked this place. Nice crowd, nice music, nice dance floor. How about it?"

"I never knew you were a closet party-person. I'm game for staying awhile longer." Zoe said goodnight; the waitress asked what else they'd like to try.

"I'd like to switch from the Iced Tea to another drink. What would you recommend?"

"You might like a Cosmopolitan Cocktail. It's made from cranberry juice, lime juice, triple sec, and vodka. A lot of the ladies like it."

"I'll try it. Mariah, what'll you have?"

"I'll have a Blue Hawaiian. Can your bartender make one?"

"He sure can. That's even more popular than the Cosmo." When the waitress returned, Alisha sampled the Blue Hawaiian."

"This is good stuff. What's in it?" Mariah supplied the answer.

"It's got crème de coconut, pineapple juice, white rum, and blue curacao. It tastes like a pina colada. Let me tell you a bit more about popular ladies' drinks…"

The ladies were having such a good time they were unaware of two fellows observing from the fringe of the dance floor how good they looked. Burke nudged his buddy, making a proposal they'd all like.

"Those two look as good as the drinks they've been ordering. Why don't we ask them to dance? And maybe we'll get lucky. If things break our way, we'll order more drinks and spike theirs with the club drug I brought. I've got a bottle of roofies. Look, you sit with the Latino and I'll sit next to the short-haired one. Let me break the ice; I'll give you the pills because I can distract them when the drinks arrive." Matias liked the plan and the odds. Both fellows looked cool and collected as Burke cast his line.

"Ladies, you look as cool as your drinks. How would you like two cool guys to join you? My name is Burke, and my buddy is Matias." Alisha glanced up at a pair of unexpected visitors, speaking before Mariah caught up with the action.

"Well that depends on a couple of requirements. First, you have to be good dancers; second, you have to pick up our tab. And maybe, if you meet those requirements, you can demonstrate your driving skills by taking us home."

"I think we'll exceed all your expectations except the last. I don't know where you live, but I do know the way to my place. Will that do?"

"Perhaps. Why don't you fellows sit down?" Mariah was shocked but didn't show it; only the words in her head did. Alisha, what are you getting us into? Be careful!

"My name's Alisha, and this is my friend Mariah. This is the first time I've been here, but Mariah has been here before." Burke started spinning smooth sentences while Matias slyly examined the goods. Mariah, after tonight we'll call the two of you patsies. You don't have much for boobs, but there's enough to grab as we go.

"Matias and I come here when we make the rounds. It's got good music and attracts a nice dance crowd. Care to dance?" Mariah tried to deflect Burke's moves.

"Alisha and I aren't into the dance scene, but thanks for asking. Maybe you can find other partners." Alisha had a different notion. "I like to dance; I just haven't had many opportunities lately."

Burke was smart enough to squeeze through the opening.

"Well Alisha and I will dance while Mariah and Matias chat. And he can order us another round of drinks. Are you game?"

"I like it. Burke, you lead the way. And I hope Matias will have drinks waiting when we get back to the table. Mariah, make sure he orders another Cosmopolitan for me."

Burke led her by the hand to the dance floor, which had enough couples to make it lively but not cluttered. Alisha didn't know the dance moves, so she asked Burke to explain the steps, giving her time to watch the action. And she liked what she saw: a mix of opposite and same sex partners enjoying themselves. The ladies were all having fun showing off all levels of dance move expertise. Though she didn't know dance step names or intricacies, Alisha decided that she could handle basic fist pumping, side-to-side body waves, boob pumping, and hair molester moves. I'll just start out easy, then let my body take over.

"Come on Burke, let's join the party." Alisha launched herself into the crowd; Burke hustled to keep up.

Alisha vanished into the moment, experiencing everything she could. The more she danced, the more she threw herself into the moves, visually expressing the not-so-subtle sexual implications. Burke appreciated all this, up close and in person.

This is one hot lady! I better get us back to the table before someone tries to cut in. When the music switched to a slower tempo, he dragged his giddy partner back to the table.

"That was fun! Mariah, come dance with me while the guys order more drinks. Burke, signal us when the drinks arrive."Mariah thought, Good. I can tell Alisha to slow down and think.

Slow dance moves are easy to learn, especially the Night Club Two Step, which many couples were doing. Alisha needed only a minute to figure out how to lead, then guided Mariah out onto the floor and into their private dance space, insulated from all the other couples. No one but Alisha heard Mariah's warning.

"Don't encourage these guys. We don't know them. You've had enough to drink, so let's get out of here."

"OK, we'll go after we have one more drink. And let's finish this dance. I like dancing with you." When the music shifted to a faster beat, Alisha took Mariah back to the table, noticing that Burke was arguing with two ladies at an adjoining table.

"What do you think's going on?" Mariah shook her head, saying nothing. As they reached the table, one of the ladies warned Alisha. "Don't touch your drinks! These jokers put something in them. I'm telling our waitress." A shock jolted the lighting brain; its long dormant warning system came back to life.

"Hey Burke, what gives?

"I don't know what they're up to, but those bitches are just trying to cause trouble." Mariah hissed out a challenge.

"Prove they're wrong! Why don't you and Matias drink ours?" Burke's eyes spoke lies.

"Uh, Matias and I don't like sweet drinks."

"Here, let me help you." Mariah threw one drink in Burke's face and poured the other over Matias, then grabbed Alisha by the arm. "Grab your purse! We're leaving," and they were heading for the exit before the fellows could react. Once out the door, Mariah hurried them away and spoke first.

"I'm parked in my building's lot. How about you?"

"Three blocks in the direction we're heading. Let's pay attention. Maybe they'll come after us." A block later, Alisha spotted the two fellows running towards them. She scanned the nearby strip mall and chose an escape route.

"Let's duck in here. There must be a rear exit."

The night clerk at the adult gift store often saw two ladies shopping together. His store had a range of merchandise: clothing, toys, lotions, and liquor were among the popular items, so he paid little attention when Alisha and Mariah headed to the liquor section in the rear. He turned his attention to the customers who were paying for items. But the clerk didn't like the looks of the two fellows who ran in a minute later. These guys might be a problem. I better watch them on the monitor.

"Damn, the back door's locked. Let's get to the counter." Alisha pushed Mariah in that direction, but it was too late. Burke and Matias blocked the aisle.

"Not so fast, you two. We never got a chance to say goodbye. How about a goodnight kiss, or something stronger?" In all the excitement, no one noticed Mariah reaching into her purse.

"Here's something stronger, asshole!" Mariah unloaded a canister of Mace directly into Burke's face; as he fell backward, his burning eyes and choke-filled gasps put him out of action. She sprayed in the direction of Matias but he ducked, making the crown of his head a perfect target for Alisha. She grabbed a liquor bottle from the shelf and smashed it on top of his head, toppling him atop Burke. Then she pushed Mariah forward and yelled at the clerk before they streaked out the door.

"Those guys tried to rob us! Call the police!"

They dashed the remaining block, not looking back until reaching the parking garage, and when they did, flashing lights by the store cut through the darkness. Mariah was out of breath, but not Alisha. All my training sure paid off tonight. I'm not a bit tired. Instead of tired, I feel wired. She put her arm around Mariah's waste and led her to the elevator.

"We'll be out of here soon. My van's on the second level." By the time they were driving away, Mariah had settled down enough to talk.

"I thought you were more careful sizing people up. If those ladies hadn't warned us, who knows what might have happened?"

"You're right. I promise to be more careful next time." They drove in silence until Alisha spoke again, this time in a softer tone. "I'm sorry if tonight scared you, but you handled yourself pretty well. You doused Burke twice: first with the drink and then with Mace. And I hope Matias likes the bottle I bashed over his head. Damn! I'll never get these red wine stains out. And these are my new slacks and blouse. I ruined yours too. Sorry." Mariah looked at the blotches and shrugged.

"Tonight was scary but sort of exciting. And I'm sure it will end well. Why don't you spend the night at my place? We haven't had any time together since you got sick." Alisha seized the moment.

"That'll be perfect. And tomorrow we'll drive back to get your car, then go shopping. Why don't you call Zoe and tell her I'm staying with you? Don't tell her what she missed. We can do that tomorrow when she comes shopping with us. She knows all the trendy stores."

"Good for her. She can help us prowl the malls. But please, let's prowl for clothes, not fellows. We'll do just fine without them. Not many guys have an eye for clothes. They're more interested in what lies underneath. And that's no lie." Alisha smiled, then joked to herself.

I'll have to ask Electra how Carter stacks up. I'm sure she'll give me the bare facts, especially if I loosen her up with a couple of drinks.

Then she'll have to tell me what she really thinks.

Chapter 7
May 2122

"Alisha on the Prowl"
Thread 1 Chapter 4

I SHOULD HAVE BEEN a pro athlete. I'm positively addicted to fitness training. And running gives me time and endorphins to think things through. Alisha had three miles left on her morning strength run. She had increased the number and intensity of workouts beyond Matt's schedule but told no one. Only her lean and cut physique announced a fitness level beyond what she had been before the T-Plague cut her down. Although her mind and memory hadn't completely recovered, Alisha was more than competent by "mere mortal" standards, and she gave herself credit for maintaining all the activities Electra had underway, hoping that time or additional brain quakes might bring Electra back.

My advisors think the old Electra is alive and well, and they're not crowding me. My presentation kept them at bay. And I'll keep it that way. Alisha did spend hours each week at the lab, conducting bogus online searches supposedly for material that would help her research. Actually, she spent more time viewing new club dancing moves and selecting a summer wardrobe, as well as hunting for a new car. For entertainment, she watched retro and the latest action adventure or sci-fi flicks; car chase and combat scenes captivated her. And when she needed a break, the university fitness center provided all that was needed for an afternoon workout.

Austin activities were proceeding nicely without her involvement. Kameyo diplomatically took charge of drug development; she was even smarter than Su, bubbling with the energy only youth possesses. And she was able to increase the efficacy of all vaccines, without guidance from anyone. Her modifications could defeat the mutant T-Plague virus even if the old Electra never returns.

Kameyo also provided caregiver assistance whenever Su needed help, but her broken back was nearly healed; Tim's adjustments made the Neuro-Knitter a world beater for repairing spinal injuries. Another month of therapy would make Su as good as new. Of course, Alisha pretended to be shocked when Hud reported Brian missing, but she told him what to do: promote his best drug sales manager to Director Neuro-Device Sales and Marketing and have him implement Brian's plans. Hud liked the suggestion, and when he jokingly asked what he could do for her, she asked for a large chunk of money. Money was available because her joint venture with Hud was profitable, and she kept her earnings in a corporate account. This would be the first time she tapped into it, so Hud showed her how to transfer funds electronically. Though he was tempted to ask what the money was for, Hud knew better than to ask so he didn't pry.

Brain Trust activities didn't need Alisha's expertise but she did keep in touch with Carter. Zoe, who found another PR job in March, took Alisha's place and didn't miss a beat. Jared was not yet ready to return to duty, which meant Angus could steer a moderate course that was by no means "kinder and gentler," but certainly not brutally harsh. Only Russell Conklin reported a slowly building problem. Although the original T-Plague virus was under control, a mutant strain was spreading from its DC epicenter. Alisha offered no advice. *I can't help you here. It's up to you to get smart pills from Hud or the Dark Web.*

That left only personal activities to think about, all of which centered on "the Full House," most of which made her smile. Mariah had accepted her invitation for more intimacy and, as agreed, their relationship remained a private affair; only Zoe suspected there was more to it than club dancing. And this didn't bother Zoe. She considered Alisha her best friend for which a sexual dimension was irrelevant, making them great roommates; she could live with Alisha for as long as she wished. She was growing stronger and planned to move back to her apartment sometime in the next couple of months.

Alisha's love affair with Carter had morphed by mutual agreement into friendship until the old Electra returned, so Carter was reluctant to stir the flames until then. She suspected he and Matt often discussed relationship quandaries, for they had become close friends; both were genuinely nice fellows, similar in appearance and emotional maturity. Carter was a bit more cerebral and reserved; Matt was perhaps a bit more pragmatic and even-tempered. Both knew how to treat significant others.

That left only Robin, whose veneer of resilient toughness was beginning to crack, exposing once again her fragile, high-strung temperament. So far, the "Full House plus Alisha" support group was keeping her centered, but it took a concerted effort, as Matt and Carter knew all too well. Robin would be a person of interest during the guys' lunchtime conversation after playing tennis at Carter's club. Carter complimented Matt after the third set.

"Your ground strokes are getting better and better. At the rate you're improving, we should do well at our Memorial Day doubles tournament."

"It goes to show that we soccer players can be good in other sports. But your strokes and tactics are way ahead of mine. And you'll have to teach me how I can play better at the net."

"Just be patient. It'll come to you. And, since it's Sunday and you played so well, a free lunch is coming your way. I'll buy, and I'll get you home in time so you can get to your clinic. Let's stop at that place you like—the one with the outdoor patio and great onion rings.

We'll take advantage of the great weather."

"That's a deal, and I'll buy the beers."

Carter's Vette whisked them from his club to the pub. It was only 1 p.m., so they had the entire afternoon to share the way best friends do. The waitress seated them at an umbrella-shaded table that kept the sun away, the gentle breeze giving them the warmth and fragrance that accompanies an east coast spring. That, their friendship, and the beers primed them for a discussion about the opposite sex, always a challenging topic even for males who know how to make relationships work.

"So, what's up with Robin?"

"Change up to down and I can tell you lots of stories. I'm trying my best to buck up her spirits, but she's spiraling downhill. Even though you've been tutoring her in economics, she thinks she failed the macroeconomics course. If so, that will push back her graduation. And she's giving up on the relationship counseling I was taking her to. She's mad because the counselor told her she's the problem and said she needs psychological, not relationship counseling. And she argues on every phone call with her parents. She won't admit it, but she misses the security of having them here, rather than in Russia. And to top it all off, she's mad at me because I have to work the night EMT shift." Carter took another sip of beer before replying.

"No wonder she seems out of sorts. Even when you and I play doubles with Zoe and her, she doesn't seem to be having much fun. It's like she's just going through the motions. But at least she's getting better at tennis. She'll get a good grade in her Personal Fitness class; I can't imagine anyone screwing that up. Robin is high maintenance for you, and you have a lot to balance. You've got your EMT job and your holistic healthcare counseling business you and Jennifer Conklin started last year. How's that going?"

"Even better than expected. Jennifer runs the nutrition and fitness seminars, and then I get personal trainer and physical therapy referrals. And day sessions fit nicely with my night EMT schedule. And it would be easy to balance all I have going on if Robin were a partner instead of a complainer and whiner. I've done all I can; I haven't told her yet, but I might end our relationship. It's not good for me anymore."

"That's unfortunate, but we both know it takes constant effort on both sides to keep a relationship alive. Alisha and I de-escalated our relationship even before she got sick. I'm not sure where it'll go when she recovers. I'm sure you noticed she seems different now. Not as sharp mentally; still has memory lapses. But she seems happier, less enigmatic or philosophic. And more fun to be with. And there are other facets of her personality I never saw before. I never knew until lately that she likes to dance and party so much. And she drinks a lot more than just Coca-Cola. I hope she's careful when she goes to the dance clubs. You and I might soon be on the meet market dating scene, and you have to be careful on the Web or at the bars. T-Plague and STDs are out there too." Matt nodded, putting down his beer before talking.

"Here's something I've noticed because I run weekly fitness sessions for her and Zoe: Alisha's getting fitter and fitter. I think she's doing extra workouts besides the ones I supervise. And speaking of Zoe, she's the most well-balanced of the ladies in our support group. She's bounced back from whatever got to her last year. Well, enough about the ladies. How's work going?"

"I'm lucky. I like working at the Federal Reserve Board, and it gives me insider connections. I'm part of President McTear's think tank, and so is Mariah. But you know, the more contact I have with these insiders, the more the glamor wears off. They're just like all the rest of us—most are just average people trying to do the best they can, balancing careers and families." Matt added,

"Let me tell you what connections have done for me. I know people connected to soccer, and they connected me to a part-time trainer position that helps build business for Jennifer and me. I'm working with the National Spirit soccer team. Do you know who they are?"

"Aren't they DC's team in the professional National Women's Soccer League?"

"Yep. They're based in Germantown, which is close by. I'm good friends with Amanda Cruz, the head coach. The team's always looking for fresh talent; next weekend they're holding tryouts, and I'm gonna ask Alisha to give it a shot. She hasn't played since she started high school, but when she played co-ed club soccer, I've been told she was the star of her team. I think it'll be fun for her, no matter how she does. It might even motivate her to join a local soccer club, and maybe it'll pry her away from the club dancing scene. Zoe told me she goes by herself when Mariah begs off." Matt had more to say, but just then his cellphone beeped; it was a call from the clinic.

"Matt Fortier here… Yes, I can start an hour earlier… I'll be there are seven… Bye." After disconnecting the call, Matt said, "Let's head back. And remember, I'll pay the bar tab."

Who said, "Uneasy lies the head that wears the crown"? Now I remember; it's from Shakespeare's play Henry IV. Well, I'll say it today. Angus McTear, acting President of the United States, not only said it to himself but felt that way too. He had just chaired a National Security Council meeting, and it made him feel like a duck swimming: calm and unflustered above the water, paddling madly just below the surface to stay afloat. But at least he was paddling in the right direction. And even if Jared recovered enough to take over the reins, Angus would do everything to keep him pointed in the right direction.

Angus had skillfully slowed down a "rush to victory" shooting war with Isilabad, using that as a threat if Isilabad continued to backpedal on its commitments. And he was doing everything possible to avoid a China confrontation over last December's attack that sidelined Jared and eliminated most of his lieutenants. Angus was one of the few who knew the real perpetrator and the unwitting accomplices. It was Electra. He was one of three from the Brain Trust who were sworn to secrecy or would be tried for treason.

Angus had tempered most of Jared's programs, making them less onerous on the "participants," but he was getting pushback for slowing down the Pillars Program. A growing number of citizens wanted to enforce the laws locally via vigilantes, so he was steering a precarious path. Just like Ulysses in Homer's Odyssey, he had to navigate between a Scylla–harsh programs that would boomerang on America long term—and a Charybdis—a mean-spirited public and opportunistic politicos who demanded short-term results.

Angus had a firm grip on his Brain Trust issues, but his Secretary of Defense reported a new problem: an increase in Cyberspace hacking, as if an unknown enemy were probing the Government's Cyberspace defenses. Cyberspace skirmishes were nothing new, but the diversity of network targets was, so Angus authorized his

SecDef to investigate further. Depending on what surfaced, he might ask the Brain Trust to study the problem.

Compared to a year ago, political analysts agreed the state of the nation was in better shape, giving credit to Angus McTear, but he wasn't so sure. I wish I felt the same way, but I feel like the guy falling down an elevator shaft who's asked midway down how he feels. Until I hit the bottom, the answer is "So far, so good."

Alisha wasn't bothering her pretty head this week about the state of the nation. She had a bunch of happy personal thoughts on her mind. Next Saturday, thanks to Matt, she would play soccer "just for kicks," for a nice change of training pace. Friday night she had a dance club party, and she considered dancing a fun combination of cardiovascular exercise and social relationship-building. And tonight, Carter would help her pick out a new car. It was time to trade in the van for something that better fit her style.

She had scheduled a six o'clock appointment at Sports-Elite Motors Ltd, even changing into something more appropriate than her lab attire. She would show off what she would wear Friday: her brand new sleeveless side-leg red party dress and matching heels. She was pacing at the lab entrance when Carter's Vette drove into view. And what a view awaited Carter.

She's dressed like she's going to a Formula One post-race party. Wherever we're going, I'm glad to be along for the ride. Carter pretended nonchalance as Alisha slipped into the Vette, but as her dress rode up past mid-thigh, he lost his train of thought and just stared. Alisha ignored his reaction, smiled and kissed him on the cheek.

"Thanks for driving. You're the car enthusiast so you probably know about Sports-Elite Motors. I checked it out on the Internet; it's close by—near Springfield just off Route 95—and it has what I'm looking for." Carter finally stopped staring and started talking.

"Good evening. Yes, I've heard of them, but I've never been there. Some of my car club friends have, and they tell me the selection is top drawer. Are you sure they have what you're looking for? It's quite a change from the hatchback or van you're accustomed to."

"Well, I'm ready for a change. And I don't have to buy tonight if I don't want to. No matter what, it'll be fun to drive some of the cars." Carter didn't mention that her stylish heels might not fit the pedals; being the good diplomat he kept quiet about that, but he did offer a suggestion.

"No matter which car you choose, I'd avoid the robotic driving option. Driverless vehicle technology, other than for long hauls on interstates, is still unreliable. Besides, if you get a snappy sports car you want to drive it yourself. So, don't get talked into it." Carter provided additional suggestions, and when they strolled into the showroom at six, Alisha was ready to prowl, keeping Carter in tow.

Callum spotted Alisha as soon as she unfolded from the Vette. That must be my six o'clock appointment. My word! We must put her in a convertible. Her significant other is one lucky chap I'll have to use my best British accent tonight.

"Good evening, Ms. Kittner, and welcome to Sports-Elite Motors." He greeted the couple using typical British reserve, suggesting they walk the showroom before sitting with him to discuss recommendations.

"This is my good friend Carter. Thanks for the offer, and we'll take you up on it. We'll come to your office after we've looked around. I've already viewed models online, so it won't take me too long." Electra proceeded to march through the showroom, Carter following obediently. Twenty minutes later, she marched into Callum's office, ready to announce her choices.

"I'd like to test drive a Ferrari first, and then compare it to a Porsche." Callum smiled knowingly.

"Excellent choices. And may I offer you a beverage before driving? I would prefer to offer you wine, but it's against our rules. We need you sober, because our vehicles are high-performance. I must assume you know how to drive a stick shift automobile. Am I correct?" Alisha looked at Carter, who figured he should be her negotiator.

"Oh yes. Her previous vehicle was a six-speed, and she handles my Vette as well as I do."

"Very good. I'll give you the keys to the Ferrari. I recommend you help Alisha become familiar with the controls." Callum pointed to the car, then handed the keys to Carter, who helped Alisha get in and then scrunched himself into the passenger seat. Alisha gaped at the dashboard.

"Uh, I didn't look closely at dashboard pics on the Internet. Where do I start?" Carter located the ignition switch, brake release, and gear shift lever, then pointed to the pedals.

"Now remember, you have over five hundred horsepower, so ease the clutch out slowly. You have three pedals to contend with. Make sure you're stepping on the right ones."

"Got it."

Carter kept watching, but it was his ears, not his eyes, that came into play. The gearbox made a horrendous noise, like marbles being ground in a garbage disposal.

"You're grinding metal on metal! Push the clutch all the way down." "Got it."

She finally got the car into gear, but it was the wrong one. She babied the accelerator too much; the engine died.

"Pay attention to the gear shift lever. You have six forward and one reverse gear. First gear is found by moving the lever to the far left; reverse is found by pulling the lever up and to the left. OK?"

"Got it."

This time, she shifted into the right gear but pushed too hard on the accelerator. The car leaped forward, snapping Carter's head backward, then forward when she stomped on the brakes, killing the engine once again. Alisha smiled sheepishly.

"Sorry." *This is trickier than I thought. I better remember more about how I used to drive.* She composed herself, started the engine, put the car into first gear, fed the right amount of gas, and released the right amount of clutch to drive smoothly out of the lot and onto an uncrowded boulevard that led into a residential area. She drove straight for a couple of blocks, confidence-building, until she came to the first stop sign. And that's when she ran into trouble.

Her left high heel wedged itself between the pedals. She couldn't hit the clutch or the brake pedal, so she took her foot off the accelerator. The car bucked to a stop in the middle of the intersection. Fortunately for the car and driver, and passenger, there were no other cars entering the intersection. Alisha looked at Carter, bewildered and crestfallen. Ever the diplomat, Carter knew what to say and what to do.

"I have an idea. Let's change places. I'll drive and you watch. You're simply out of practice, and you're not paying attention to what you're doing."

"OK."

Carter had them moving again and explained all that he was doing.

"The steering is very responsive. This car has a very tight turning radius. Watch how much we turn with just a little steering wheel motion... Now watch how I shift gears... And you have to watch the tach and listen to the engine RPM to know when to shift...The car handles beautifully... Listen to that exhaust sound..." Carter drove for fifteen minutes, explaining patiently what he was doing, but he could tell his "student driver" was getting more confused and frustrated. As Carter pulled to the side of the road, Alisha complained to herself.

I'm a poor student despite Carter's teaching ability. Carter asked, "Well now, do you feel like giving it another try?" Wrong question. Alisha's folded arms and pouted lips needed no words. She glared and was about to say something nasty. Bungling had deflated her vanity and pride, but a tiny brain twinge jolted her before she let loose. Carter's not the problem, I am. I'm not concentrating. And my

shoes don't fit the car. I still have a lot of improving to do.

"I don't think this is the right car for me. Let's take it back. I'll pay for dinner on the way home."

By the time they stopped at a diner, Carter's humor put Alisha in a better mood.

"I think Callum wanted you to test drive all the cars with him. He couldn't take his eyes off your legs. And tell you what, we'll try other cars another time when you're more like your previous self."

"Thanks for being so understanding. You're a good friend. And I hope I get back to my old self soon, but right now, I feel like this

verse from a kid's poem, if you substitute my name: Poor old Jonathan Bing,
     Went home and addressed a short note to the king:
   "If you please, will you excuse me, I won't come to tea.
   'Cause home's the best place for all people like me."

"Anyone who can remember poetry like you is making a good comeback. Look, you're much better now than just a month ago. Cut yourself some slack."

"You're right, and thanks for reminding me. I'll be in a better mood tomorrow."

Alisha did feel better the next day, and even better the day after that, because she was ready for Friday's dance club party. The mirror on her closet door told her she'd cut a great figure on the dance floor or at the bar. I'll wear my red velvet neck choker with my dress. And this new shade of dark red lipstick is kick-ass. I am ready to prowl.

Unlike the old Electra, Alisha behaved more like the younger generation found in every culture that needs to express itself socially. She knew it was simply part of social instinct; younger people worldwide look for fun and excitement, especially when it may be tinged with danger. And Alisha's generation had plenty of danger to contend with. The risk of contracting socially transmitted diseases or the T-Plague lurked, so young people joined dance or party groups for protection.

Groups vetted members to confirm they met club standards and required applicants to submit medical test results certifying they were clean. Alisha joined the DC Sybarites Dance and Social Club at the insistence of people she had met two months ago at one of the trendy spots. She liked them, and before sending her application and annual membership fee, checked it out on the Web. The DC Sybarites welcomed all sexual orientations and accepted a wider range of income and professions than other clubs, but they would not accept anyone with criminal or questionable medical records. The weekly online newsletter highlighted which particular location club members would be visiting, and it contained a social calendar for events other than dancing. For safety's sake, members were encouraged to show their Sybarite I.D.s and ask for others to do likewise before engaging a partner.

I'm gonna play soccer tomorrow, so I'll get to the dance early and leave early. And it's close by; Chevy Chase is only a half-hour drive. The parking lot was full when she arrived, so she had to park two blocks away. Not a problem. It's a warm and clear evening. Alisha pranced in, flashing her I.D., which cut the admission price in half.

By now, much of the old Electra's savoir-faire had come back, but Alisha's social and emotional intelligence extended it, making her popular and quick to gain footing on the dance club scene. And she had practiced to perfection an entrance routine. Start with a drink, scan for someone I know and like, chat someone up, and then select someone when I'm ready to dance. With drink in hand, she was ready to prowl the night away.

Where did the night go? It's one a.m. and I need to get a little sleep before playing soccer. It's time to go. She was finishing a drink with the night's last partner, Jevon, a handsome black male who was built for dancing. She sensed he was gay and that was fine; dancing was all she wanted tonight. Gay men are usually smart and sensitive, and she didn't have to worry about being the target of a trophy hunter: a testosterone-bloated ego looking for someone to take home and mount.

"You're a great dance partner. I'll look for you again. But it's time for me to go."

"I'm gonna stay a bit longer, but do you want me to walk you to your car?" A touch of vanity colored her reply. She would be embarrassed if he saw her driving an older van.

"No, I'm fine. Good night." "Back at you, and be careful."

Alisha walked out of the club, thinking only about how little sleep she'd get before leaving for soccer. She didn't notice two fellows getting out of a car parked in the shadows of the dimly lighted half-empty parking lot. They weren't dancers; they were crude types who preyed upon unsuspecting females, and late-night dance clubs were good hunting grounds.

"Will you look at that! What a babe. Let's grab her quick when she gets close to your car. Then I'll run back for mine and follow you."

Alisha was startled out of her thoughts when the bigger boob grabbed her from behind and spun her around.

"Hi ya, Babe. Your party's not over yet." Before she could scream he slapped her twice across the face, stunning her, then yelled to his accomplice. "Shove her into your back seat and go. I'll follow." The other bad guy wrapped his arms around her and was ready to pull her to his car.

Alisha was freaking out in terror. I'm in deep yogurt now! Come on, think! She was being dragged to a car, offering no resistance when suddenly a violent quake shook the lightning brain. Get with it soldier! This is not a drill. Get your brain and body in gear. You've been trained to handle yourself. Now do it! Instantly, her terror morphed to thrilling clarity. She knew what to do and acted instinctively. Her assailant had loosened his grip, which was his first and final mistake.

Alisha spun around violently, throwing an elbow catching the bad guy's throat and knocking him backwards. She grabbed a handful of hair with one hand and broke his nose with a palm fist from the other, then she kicked him in the groin, dropping him to the ground, but she lost her balance and tumbled backwards. I gotta take off these shoes so I can run! She yanked them off, then gathered herself, shoes, and purse just before the other guy's car sprang to life. She turned to run, but saw she didn't have to. The other car was waiting, doors open and engine idling. She leaped in and steadied herself. I can handle this! It's an automatic. Away she squealed, pursued by the other car.

The two cars were similar-sized, but the other had more horsepower and was gaining ground, but Alisha was now totally engaged in the thrill of the chase. I can't get away from him, so let's crash both cars. And then I'll outrun him on foot. Do it now, while I'm not too far from the van. Alisha accelerated, then slammed on the brakes when the pursuit car was a car length behind. The impact spun his car to the right slowing it down. Alisha accelerated gaining distance, then did a one-eighty, controlling the fish tail. The other driver was too slow to react; Alisha smashed into the driver's side of the other car, putting both out of commission, but not herself. She grabbed all her gear and was ready to race away into the darkness, into the safety of the night, but before fleeing, she said good night to her pursuer.

"Catch me if you can, asshole!" The collision had jammed his door shut. All he could do was watch Alisha's vanishing act.

It was almost a mile to the van, and Alisha raced like the wind all the way. She leaped in and sped away to complete her escape. It took fifteen minutes for her brain to stop racing, to shift to a lower gear. By then she was breathing normally again and ready to assess the damages. *The soles of my feet feel OK. I can handle running a mile barefoot. And my cut lip isn't bleeding too badly. I'm good to go for soccer.*

The drive gave her quiet time to think more. She knew the adrenaline rush would keep her awake, so instead of sleeping, the best she could do would be to lie down and meditate, hoping that would be enough rest for playing soccer. *I think I used to be able to put my brain into altered states that fit the situation. I'll try it tonight.* And then she recalled what had jolted her brain. *Another brain quake hit me when those clods grabbed me. Maybe more scales are falling away; maybe more neural circuits are coming back; maybe more neural tangles are dissolving. I can only hope, but tonight was a stern reminder to pay attention, and to know when to activate my early warning system.*

Alisha pulled into her driveway at four. *Matt's picking me up at nine, so I'll shower now, then rest for three hours. Then I'll get up and stretch and get set. And I'll remember to concentrate and pack my game face.*

"Pay attention! You look tired. Did you get a good night's sleep?" *I'll tell Matt the truth, but not the whole truth.*

"I tossed and turned the whole night. I guess I was too keyed up about playing soccer today, but I'm ready."

"That's OK. The adrenaline will pick you up. Now let me give you some background on the National Women's Soccer League. You might already know this, but it'll help if you hear it again. There are ten teams playing a twenty-game six-month season:

April to October. Each team has a maximum 20 player roster; for each game eighteen are declared eligible. Salaries go from about seven thousand to forty thousand, and there are no long-term contracts, so just about all the players have other jobs. And there's turnover during the season for reasons that don't concern you. Games draw maybe five to seven thousand fans. Some are televised, but the only games televised nationally are when the U.S. Women's National Team plays exhibition games. They do it for preparation when playing internationally. Those games get a large viewing audience because the National Team has a big following that peaks when playing in World Cup and Olympic competitions. The National Team considers the NWSL a farm club. So far so good?"

"Yes, I'm following you."

"The National Team is headquartered right here in DC, but our local team, the Washington Spirit, runs out of Germantown, so that's where we're heading today. I'm a good friend of the head coach, Amanda Cruz, and I assist the trainer. I told her you used to play, you're rounding into better shape, and you'd like to see how you stack up. And look, there's no pressure on you. Just have fun. Neither she nor I are expecting you to run wild, but it'll be a good change of pace for you. Maybe it'll motivate you to join a local soccer club. Are you OK with that?" Of course not! Not unless my talent returns. But I'll act like I am.

"Yes, it might be fun to play again, as long as I don't embarrass myself."

"Don't worry about that. I'm sure your muscle memory will kick in when you get into the flow. So, here's the drill for today. You'll sign in for the tryouts. Then I'll introduce you to Amanda. There'll be maybe twenty wanna be's trying out, and Amanda has room to bring five onto her roster. You'll then go to the locker room, change, and warm up on the field. You know, basic dribbling and kicking. When the coaching staff is ready, they'll whistle everyone together and introduce you to the current players you'll be scrimmaging against. They'll divide those trying out into groups of six. Each group will showcase what they can do on defense by trying to defend against scoring plays run by current players, and then ditto for offense skills by trying to score against them. Half the hopefuls will be weeded out in the morning session. This afternoon will be the final selection. Some of the current players have attitudes, so don't expect the current players to be talkative or friendly. But if you make the cut, they'll become like sisters. I've seen great camaraderie, just like on local soccer clubs. I bet you remember what that was like, even though it was a long time ago. Are you clear on all this?" "Yes, I sure am." This time, Alisha meant it.

Matt pulled into the stadium parking lot thirty minutes before tryouts were to begin. Alisha said hi to Amanda, changed into uniform, then warmed up alongside seventeen other hopefuls. These drills used to be child's play for me, but I was a child then. Maybe I should have practiced this week. Well, it's too late now. All I can do is concentrate and get my game face on. Just then, a minor tremor shook her brain. Today's performance could be a mid-term exam for how well parts of my emotional and physical personas are recovering.

Amanda blew the whistle promptly at ten, assembling everyone and explaining how the day would unfold. Just like Matt described. Good. Alisha was in the third scrimmage group and studied techniques of players in the first two sessions. The current players are good, but I was better when I was a kid than they are now. I know those moves. Focus on what they're doing and how they're moving. Another jolt registered in the lightning brain. Any remaining fatigue or jitters vanished as Alisha's emotional and physical personas merged into one. She was ready to run when her scrimmage team took the field. Let the flow of the game come to me. Don't get fancy. Stick with the basics until I get my legs centered.

Alisha gained confidence as her scrimmage unfolded. She stumbled badly on the first defensive set, but acquitted herself nicely on all the rest. The same held when playing offense. She tripped on the ball once and squibbed a couple of kicks, but her footwork improved steadily. The scrimmages ended at twelve-thirty; fifteen minutes later Amanda read the names of the eight finalists. Alisha had made the cut and would be in the afternoon scrimmages starting at two.

Matt jogged over to congratulate her, offering suggestions for the afternoon.

"Congratulations, kiddo! You did better than I thought. I know you're in good shape, but your footwork is better than I imagined. And you stepped it up as you settled into the flow. Have you been practicing?"

"No, but maybe my muscle memory is better than we thought. Once I get in action, it's like my body knows what to do."

"That might be, but here's what I want you to do. Put on a pair of sweats, grab a light lunch, and meet me in the practice area at one-thirty."

"Got it." Alisha jogged to the locker room, cleaned up, and then joined others for lunch. She spotted an empty chair at a table occupied by three who made the cut, so she moved in that direction.

"Hi, my name's Alisha. OK if I join you?" One of the older girls replied,

"Sure. Sit down and join in." The others welcomed her to the table and continued talking about what to expect this afternoon. Alisha used a pause to ask a question.

"I'm glad we made it to the afternoon scrimmage. Have any of you tried out before?" The oldest responded first.

"I made it to the final cut last year, so I know the drill. It'll be focused and intense compared to this morning. We'll be matched up one on two so the coaches can see us perform on our own. And the current players won't hold back like they did this morning. They'll get in your face and try to play mind games." One of the younger girls asked a question about the current players. The answer gave little comfort.

"From what I remember, a couple were pretty nice but several had attitudes and matching egos. Watch out for Micki Stiegland. She's the team leader and plays center midfield position. I go to the games and see her in action. She acts tough and plays tough to match. I hope I don't have to face her this afternoon. She'll make you look bad. Maybe the coaches take that into consideration, but I don't know. She crushed me last year and they didn't pick me." Alisha was absorbing all this and wanted to know more.

"This is good stuff. Thanks for sharing with us. Then she asked the girl sitting next to her,

"What's your name?" "Katy Tang."

"What does Micki look like?"

"You can all see for yourself. She's coming this way with her gang, and she's wearing her trademark scrimmage jersey. You'll see what I mean."

Of the three players approaching the table, the lettering on one jersey labeled Micki even better than a name. It read "I'M THE IT GIRL!" which appeared to fit her in the world of soccer. She was about four inches shorter than Alisha, putting her close to five feet eight, and powerfully built. Though average looking, her build and determined expression made a strong impression, as did her effortless gait. And she wasn't bashful.

"Well hello again. I recognize a couple of you from previous tryouts. Welcome back. And for all you rookie wanna-be's, get set for fun this afternoon. We'll see if you've got what we're looking for. Good luck, because you'll need it." Micki and her two followers grinned, then breezed by. One of the rookies made a remark everyone shared.

"That was encouraging. I hope she's a better leader than greeter. And if we make the team, we'll find out." While the girls resumed talking, Alisha left to find Matt on the practice field. She forgot to bring a ball, but Matt had one for her.

"OK, listen up. I want you to stretch, then go through some footwork drills. You were tentative at the start this morning, but got in gear near the end. This afternoon, you gotta be ready to go right from the start. Keep your sweats on and keep stretching until the coaches call you. I hope you go late rather than early. That way, you can watch how opponents move. And believe me, they won't hold back."

"Got it." Alisha withdrew into herself as she ran through her drills. *I wish Grandfather were here today. He told me that someday I wouldn't have to hold back; someday I could let it out.*

Maybe today's the day to start. Alisha glided through her drills, gradually building speed and deception.

"You were holding back this morning, weren't you?" Those words ended Alisha's drill.

"You startled me! Hi Katy. "No, I wasn't holding back. I was sort of easing into the flow, letting technique come back to me. Hey, thanks for sharing with us at lunch. That info will help." Just then Amanda blew the whistle.

"Good luck, Alisha. I hope we both make the team."

Amanda explained what to expect in the afternoon scrimmage, agreeing with what Matt had told her and what Katy had mentioned at lunch. Much to Alisha's satisfaction, she would go in a later scrimmage, so she and Matt watched intently from the sidelines. From the opening play, everyone saw that no one was holding back. The coaches had fired up the team to play with play-off intensity, because this is the only way to separate the talented from the pretenders. Only the best would make the cut, which is ultimately what a team needs to survive, let alone thrive.

Alisha focused totally on the moment, unaware of time; Matt gave her final instructions when Amanda called her name. "This is not a drill! This is game time, so get with it. You've got the goods, so strut your stuff."

"Got it," is all she said as she took her position on the field. I've heard those words before. I know I can handle the situation.

Defensive scrimmage started the action. Alisha had to defend against two attacking players, one of them being Micki. Good! To be the best you have go over the best. And that's what I intend to do. The attackers were deliberate on the first offensive play sizing up the defender. When Micki tried to sidestep, Alisha poke-tackled the ball away. On the next attack, Micki passed the ball to the other forward just before reaching Alisha. But Alisha was quicker. She raced to that player and hooked the ball away with a block-tackle. On the third attack, Micki bore down but Alisha's slide tackle stopped her and the ball trickled away. The attacks continued and Alisha stopped all but one.

Amanda blew the whistle, signaling a change to offensive scrimmage. Now it was Alisha's turn to attack. Build momentum slowly. Wear them out. On her first attack, Alisha went for Micki's fellow defender. She jogged directly towards her, then came to a dead stop juggling the ball, freezing her opponent who took a defensive stance. She then surprised by kicking the ball between the defender's legs, intercepting it on the backside and raced in to boom the kick past the diving goalie. On her second attack, she drove directly towards Micki, then veered at the last moment towards the other defender, stutter-stepping and racing past towards the goalie.

This time she delayed booming the ball until the goalie dived in anticipation, then she kicked where the goalie had been. On her third attack Alisha went for the kill. She raced directly at Micki, stutter-stepping and shielding the ball with side-to-side dribbling that put Micki on her backside. Alisha raced over her and scored her third goal.

Amanda had seen enough and blew the whistle, saying nothing except calling the next rookie. Alisha jogged over to Matt.

"Where did all that come from? You were unstoppable! Go cool down, then shower and change. We'll talk later."

All Alisha said was, "Got it," then started jogging around the practice area.

"Where did you come from? You're better than even Micki." High praise indeed from Katy. The lightning brain was beginning to stand down, so Alisha stopped to talk.

"Thanks for the compliment. Hey, come jog with me. How'd you do?"

"Better this time, I think. I didn't have to go up against Micki. Wow, you annihilated her. She's gonna be pissed." The two of them jogged for another fifteen minutes, then Amanda blew the whistle signaling the end, then told everyone to gather in the club room after showering and changing. The eight remaining rookies and team scrimmage players filled the locker room with chatter typical of postgame decompressing antics. Alisha was toweling off and talking with her rookie companions. One of them spoke for all.

"Three of us won't make the cut. I hope I do, but if I don't I want to wish good luck to those that do." They continued chattering until Micki walked by.

"Well, don't you look sweet! But three of you are gonna be mad when you get the bad news." The rookie standing next to Alisha spoke up. It was Katy.

"Maybe they'll be as mad as you looked when you fell on your backside. You think you're hot shit, but I think you're nothing but a steamed turd!" Micki glared daggers, preparing to slap Katy, but Alisha caught her wrist.

"Hey! Lighten up. I hope you're a better team leader than what you're showing us now." Micki was at a loss for words. She pulled away and stalked off.

The eight rookies milled about for a couple of minutes, then finished dressing. As they filed out, one of them said, "Maybe the three that are cut are better off. They won't have to put up with Micki. Well, let's find out who stays and who goes."

Amanda wasted no time. She congratulated all in the room, then announced the names of those who made the cut and when they should return. Five minutes later as the group filed out, Matt said to Alisha, "Today might be a watershed moment for you. There are lots of ways you can go from here, and they're all good." Matt was as pleased as Alisha because she had made the cut.

"I owe it all to you. I'm ready for more action, and I'm gonna have a good time no matter what unfolds."

"You owe it to yourself. All I did was bring you here. You're better than I thought, and if practice makes you even better, you'll turn some of heads. But don't think too far ahead." Alisha smiled, but replied only to herself,

Maybe so, but so much hinges on the lightning brain making a complete recovery. If it does, I promise always to be the best person I can be, physically, cognitively, and emotionally.

As she drifted asleep that night, Alisha wondered if some day she might marvel at Matt's words. I think Mother wrote a poem— she named it "the Memory Garden"—that tells how the things we do today lead to memories only revealed through the passage of time. A slight tremor shook the verses from memory into her consciousness. Alisha recited them aloud.

> Tomorrow's memories are made today,
> It's good you are too close to see.
> Just go about your merry way,
> They are a future mystery.
> No crystal ball for where things lead,
> What fruit your current efforts bring.
> Just tend the present plant the seed,
> For the flower to bloom and blossoms take wing.
> Tomorrow's harvest depends on you,
> Its bounty and whether short or long.
> So remember today in the things you do,
> Blow a kiss to the future then keep moving on.

Indira had wonderful insight into the human condition. According to the "Electra Chronicles," she had much more empathy and artistic sensitivity than Electra. The Chronicles order me to study Mother's poems, and I shall go one better. I shall also study poetry and literature to understand better where Indira's poems fit. And I hope Electra returns to help me, for if she does, I'll do my best to help her.

I'll have to wait and see.

Chapter 8
August 2122

"Meeting of the Minds"
Thread 3 Chapter 3

ZIARMAL WAS PLEASED WITH progress, for all Iron Triangle Alliance pieces were starting to mesh. He and his counterparts—Sergei Zaitsev from Russia and Chen Xu from China—had just completed testing the first release of their co-developed Internet Security Info-Tools System, codenamed ISIS, and each reported success. Their attacks compromised enemy targets, befuddling clueless network administrators. Significant damage from only a minor intrusion. Just wait until we launch a second attack against more valuable targets. The West won't know who or what hit its infrastructures, corporations, or government agencies. But we must be patient; we must remain invisible.

Ziarmal named his grand strategy "combine and divide and conquer," which he and his partners labeled CDC. They had combined forces to build ISIS and then divided specific targets for destruction. Though Russia and China dwarf Isilabad by conventional standards, only the IT Alliance knows about Isilabad's superior Cyberspace capabilities, thanks to Ziarmal's Silicon Valley training and Cyberworld recruiting. He had built a convoluted chain of proxy servers to conceal his activities and cloud-based resources. Although he works out of a subterranean research and control center, he remotely manages via secured and encrypted communications protocols a dispersed team of hacker-developers. The same protocols work for weekly IT Alliance meetings, but the next meeting would be in person to confirm all off-grid and hardcopy backups are untouchable. I don't think a shooting war is likely, but if Jared Gardner returns, the odds could change. Either way, the IT Alliance is bulletproof. And only my partners share our private joke regarding our CDC strategy. America's vaunted CDC, its Center for Disease Control, is still battling the T-Plague. Now the Great Satan will be struck by a Cyberspace plague.

After reading the second letter from Electra, Alisha graded her performance a C+. I'm sorry, Electra. I've hit some of your targets, but I guess I've been playing around more than you'd like. But I'm keeping us afloat and nothing's close to a tipping point, so let's not worry.

Alisha was most pleased with her postdoc activity because there was nothing she needed to do, other than periodically feed summaries to her advisors of what Electra had stashed away. She was satisfied with Austin's activity, although she needed to visit again to keep Su, Tim, and Hud focused. Hud better hire Brian's replacement.

But Alisha's Brain Trust activities were stagnating for two reasons: some events were beyond her control, and some she just didn't know what to do. The biggest event outside her control would be the return of Jared. A news bulletin conveniently coinciding with the Fourth of July announced the "triumphant return of President Gardner;" he would resume command, making Angus McTear Vice President. When Zoe heard the news, she promptly resigned from the Brain Trust, stating a conflict of interest. (Only Zoe and Alisha knew why—no one else ever would.) Angus could trust Carter and Mariah to handle her assignments, but all of them would need a plan for controlling Jared once he was fully operational. But Alisha was not clever enough yet to know what to do about Jared, nor did she have anything additional to offer for the T-Plague. All that would have to wait until Electra returns from her accidental "sabbatical." But there was much she could do in her personal life, and she gave herself an A+ for what she was accomplishing.

Soccer topped the list. The lightning brain had dissolved enough neural entanglements and extended the right circuits to bring her soccer skills back to life, force-multiplying them because of improved fitness and additional practice sessions. Even though she didn't play very game, Alisha's dream of becoming a professional athlete had come true. She loved the camaraderie among fellow rookies, the rigors of training, and the thrill of competition where she could play with abandon. There was no place else she'd rather be on this warm and sunny Saturday than running through soccer drills on her team's practice field.

"Alisha! Slow down! You're killing us." Katy was pleading for mercy on behalf of her teammates. Alisha jogged over to where her fellow rookies were gasping for oxygen.

"I feel good today. How'd you like my last attack?"

"We did, but Micki and the vets didn't. You've put them on their butts a couple of times. And I think everyone but you is ready to call it quits." Evidently the coaches did too. Amanda blew the whistle to assemble the entire team.

"OK, everyone, that was a spirited practice. We're rounding into shape for our marquee match coming up mid-September when we play an exhibition game against the National Women's Team. The game won't count in our league's official standings, but it'll have all the excitement of a championship game. Every team wants to beat them because no one ever has. The game will be televised nationally, and the TV ratings will be high because the public follows our National Team. Let's keep training and practicing like today. So, hit the showers and enjoy the rest of the weekend." The team was streaming to the locker room when Amanda called out,

"Alisha, come to my office before changing."

"Yes, Coach. I'll be there just as soon as I take my cool-down laps." Twenty minutes later, Alisha glided into the coach's office, taking a chair across from Amanda, expecting high praise for today's effort. *Just wait till I show off my new moves. It'll be a first. But I won't tell anyone until I'm ready.* She sat primly, waiting for compliments to begin flowing. It would be a long wait.

"Alisha, why do you like to play soccer matches?"

"I love the thrill. It's fun to score goals, and I'm good at it."

"Yes, you are. But isn't the goal for our team to win, not just for you to score all the goals." *I'm not sure where this is heading, but I'll play along.*

"Yes, Coach, but they're the same. The more goals I score the better chance we have to win. Don't you agree?"

"Only to a point. Remember this: the team is greater than the sum of its players." Wait a minute, Coach! I'm the one who makes things happen.

"Yes, but I'm better than the others, so I should do the scoring."

"You are very talented. The improvement you've made in just a couple of months is extraordinary. But you're too selfish. The team will do better if you work with them. If you pass the ball we'll score more goals." Alisha frowned but held her tongue, letting Amanda explain further.

"Do you realize you are polarizing the team? You're the leader of the rookies, but you offend the vets. They think you are deliberately disrespecting them. Maybe they aren't as talented as you, but they have worked hard and made personal sacrifices to get to where they are. Please give them more credit, and please show a bit more empathy for them." Alisha was about to argue, but a minor brain tremor stopped her.

"I apologize, Coach. I didn't realize that was the situation. I chalked up the chattering to typical rivalry among rookies and vets. All teams have it, but I'll follow your advice."

"Thank you. See you at our next practice."

Alisha headed to the locker room, realizing Amanda's reprimand had reactivated additional neural circuits. The lightning brain is making more repairs! I understand what Coach is saying. And I feel it too. Now I know better what to think, how to feel, and what to do. She stripped out of her sweaty uniform, enjoyed a refreshing shower, and then moved to the benches located between the lockers and toilet stalls. Most of her teammates were still there; Katy in particular wanted to know what Coach had to say, but Micki and one of her defensive backs confronted Alisha before she could say anything.

"You're a bitch of a show-off! And you try to make us all look bad. Well, now it's your turn. Let's see how you look on your ass!" Micki shoved with both arms, toppling Alisha over Micki's partner who had knelt unbeknownst behind her. Her head bounced as she skidded on the wet floor, and she slipped again as she tried to stand. Even the rookies laughed at Alisha's exaggerated contortions that were as funny as a clown act. But Alisha didn't see the humor in any of it.

They're laughing at me! I hate to look foolish! I hate embarrassing myself! Emotions hijacked thinking as rage broke free, powering retaliation. She leaped to her feet and dived into Micki's midsection, wrapping both arms around her and driving her against the wall in a bathroom stall. She grabbed Micki by the hair, using Micki's head as a bell clapper, banging it against both sides of the stall. Micki was dazed, unable to defend herself, but Alisha continued the attack. She jammed Micki's head into the toilet bowl and was about to use her foot as a plunger when several rookies dragged her away.

"Stop it! Let her come up for air!" And then the lightning brain registered another quake. Rage dissipated, replaced by embarrassed shame for what she had done. Micki picked herself off the floor and staggered out of the stall. Alisha burst into tears and rushed to support her vanquished opponent.

"Micki! I'm sorry. I just snapped." There are times opponents become friends when the battle is over, when the rage of the conflict is replaced by compassion and respect. That's what Alisha was feeling.

"I'm as much at fault as you are. Let's end it now." Micki offered her hand, which Alisha shook just as Amanda walked in.

"I heard a ruckus. What's going on?" The girls looked at one another for an answer; Katy was the first to blurt an explanation.

"Our leaders are having a meeting of the minds." Amanda knew there was more to it but realized the situation had settled down. All she said was "Good," and left the ladies work out the rest.

Alisha used her Sunday morning run to consider further what she had learned yesterday. I'm getting stronger physically. And I'm getting smarter too, cognitively and emotionally. Now I'm finally beginning to understand what the Electra Chronicles are telling me about myself, and about the Creature from the Id. I've got to do a better job controlling my anger, but not even Electra could do it all the time. And I'm realizing more and more I have a streak of vanity that sometimes makes me petty. But lots of pretty women do, so I'll be aware of it and work around it best I can. And I am learning more about empathy. Mine is growing.

She used the remainder of the miles to plan for a fun-filled week. Let's see. Carter and I will look at more cars Wednesday, and I'll go Saturday to my dance club's Labor Day party. I'll see if the Full House wants to come along. I'll invite Katy too. She'll like Carter and the group, and vice versa. Life is good. And then a strange thought flashed into her brain.

What will life be like when Electra returns? What's keeping her? I can feel I'm getting better; each brain quake tells me so, but I guess I've got a way to go. I'm no dummy, but I'm less than a Neanderthal compared to a human when comparing my intelligence to Electra's. But perhaps I'm getting better than she emotionally. Maybe I'm more empathetic. When she returns, will I be allowed to stay, or will the lightning brain dismiss me? All this is out of my control, so I'm not going to worry about it. Alisha finished the run feeling good about today and the coming week.

Carter knew as soon as he spotted Alisha waiting for him that tonight's car hunt would be better than the last one. She was still attired in style—wearing designer white summer slacks, electric blue sleeveless casual V-neck loose T-shirt blouse belted at the waist and color coordinated ballet flats—but everything fit better with cars than the killer party outfit worn the last time. Maybe she's talked some sense into herself, but I'll tread carefully. I don't want her to unload on me like she almost did last time.

Alisha was bubbly and all smiles, kissing Carter on the cheek after she glided into the passenger seat.

"I learned my lesson last time. Those high-performance sports cars are sexy looking, but they're not meant for me, so here's what I did. I surfed the Net for 'chick cars.' I'm sure you know what they are."

"I believe I do. They're the most popular cars women picked on interviews and surveys. The term swings back and forth between a cute description or a pejorative. Today, chick cars are in fashion. And compared to cars from a couple of decades ago, today's cars are engineering marvels. Which brands are you considering?"

"I've narrowed it down to the two most popular. Volkswagen and Ford. What would you suggest?"

"Speaking as an economist, I recommend you buy American. You get better value and easier maintenance, and you're helping American workers. What would you like to drive first?"

"Let's do Ford first, and if I like the color, I'll buy it. There's a dealer in Falls Church just off I-66, and you're already heading in the right direction. Last time, you told me to avoid the robotic driving option. Anything else I don't need?"

"The basic options package is pretty complete. Maybe you'll want to upgrade the communications system and add some color stripes. Other than that, I can't think of anything else. But did you follow the news story about an outbreak of driverless rig accidents on some of the interstates? There was a hardware or software glitch on a couple of local distributed control networks. Luckily, it happened on less-traveled sections. It seemed to clear up when engineers rebooted the system, but I don't think they know the cause. I don't trust driverless technology yet." They'd talk more with the sales consultant about driverless technology when they got to the showroom, so Alisha changed the subject.

"I'm going to send an Email inviting everyone to a Labor Day Dance Party hosted by my club and two others. We've booked two floors at the Ultra Club on F Street Northwest. Are you game?"

"I'm not much of a dancer. I won't go if I'm going to feel intimidated. What'll it be like?"

"It's a young, diverse crowd. People are friendly and have fun no matter what dancing skills you have. And you can mix and mingle, snack and drink if you don't want to dance. And I wouldn't have joined if the club weren't safe." Carter thought the party seemed like a safe bet.

"Matt's a good dancer, so maybe he can talk Robin into coming. Zoe and Mariah should like it too, and if they come I'll tag along. Just send all of us the info. Well, we're here. Let's check out the cars." Alisha hadn't made an appointment, but dealer traffic was light so a sales consultant walked them around the showroom.

Alisha described what she wanted and the consultant—a well-versed young black lady—came up with just the right car: a six-cylinder cherry red Mustang close-out, already sporting a white trim package and upgraded communications system. Carter had a cellphone video of the van, which he used to negotiate a trade-in value. The only thing left was for Alisha to transfer a down payment from her bank to the dealer. She punched in URL's and access codes, but her bank's computer network was down. The sales consultant wasn't upset.

"Don't worry about it. You're not alone. A lot of banks had computer system problems today. We did too, and we're not up yet. Our tech guys are still diagnosing the cause, so here's what we'll do. Call me tomorrow when your bank is online and I'll walk you through our transfer protocol. And bring in your van when you're ready to pick up your new car. We'll have it ready for you Friday."

Banking Internet glitches disappeared by the next morning, allowing Aisha to transfer money; she would pick up the new car on Friday and drive to the dance the next evening.

Next priority was to invite friends to the dance, which she did via cellphone and Internet. By evening she knew everyone in the Full House except Robin would be there. Matt explained that she was swamped with school work, but Robin would call her sometime after Labor Day. Matt volunteered to pick up Zoe because Alisha would drive directly from afternoon soccer practice to the dance.

Alisha hustled through workouts and chores so she could pick up her new car early Friday afternoon. Even though society had streamlined its driving habits over the past decades, most people still want to own a car. America's love affair with automobiles is part of its cultural DNA—sociologists call it a meme; buying your first new car is a rite of passage. Alisha had not a trace of buyer's remorse when she drove away from the dealership. The sales consultant took cellphone photos of her posed artfully next to the car; she Emailed them that evening to her friends. I'll send them to Katy and get her opinion at soccer tomorrow. Maybe she'll want to come to the party.

The more the merrier.

Robin was glad all her close friends would be at the party. That would keep them out of her way when she packed up the belongings she needed. Voices in her head were telling her it's the right time to do the right thing.

Poor passionate but emotionally brittle Robin. She suffered from schizophrenia and related mood disorders that had begun in high school. They are often difficult to diagnose in adolescents, and her case went undetected because there was so much upheaval in her life. Doctors attributed her nervous breakdown a couple of years ago to stress and T-Plague, crediting her rebound to inner toughness. But that toughness was a veneer covering feelings of doubt, inferiority, and anger at males, including her father. Her deepening depression drove her into dark corners from which she could not escape. She was withdrawing from her friends as everything in her life spiraled downward. The voices in her head told her to tell no one, not even Jennifer Conklin, not even Alisha. Coach Cruz applauded the team's spirited practice session.

"Ladies, we have two weeks to our Super Bowl. Our record won't put us in the playoffs, but we have a chance to make history if we beat or tie the National Team. It's an important game for them because it's the last tune-up before World Cup playoffs. They'll be primed to play, but they're going to be real confident. If we focus on our game plan—teamwork and tough defense—we can surprise them.

"The game will be nationally televised from the Men's Major League Soccer Stadium in DC. There could be over twenty thousand fans, and I want us to give the best effort possible. Next Saturday's practice will be light. We'll talk strategy and look at National Team game videos. We'll know all about them and they haven't a clue about us, and we'll make the most of it. Between now and the game, keep training but taper. And listen to this: our local sponsors are getting us new uniforms and chartering a bus for the game. We're gonna look every bit as good as the National Team. OK, hit the showers and follow our plan!"Rookies and vets merrily chattered as the session ended, but a worried-looking

Katy pulled Alisha aside. "Is this a good idea? I don't think the Coach would approve us going to a dance party."

"Of course it is. Think of it as a cool-down after a hard workout." And you are the very first rider in my new car. How did you like the pics?"

"I love the white-stripes-on-red. Let's check out the sound system after we shower. What kind of music do you like?" The question caught Alisha by surprise. I don't know. I never thought about it.

That part of my memory hasn't come back. I'll just fake it.

"Oh, I sort of like all types, but nothing in particular. What about you?"

"I took some community college courses in music and film, and they opened my eyes and ears. The instructors drew material from previous genres and time periods. I particularly liked learning about rock and roll roots and tracing pop music history. The music back then—compared to now—was emotionally primal; the rhythm had a relentless driving intensity you don't need drugs for. I'll play some when we drive to the dance."

The duo showered, then changed into dance club clothes. Alisha had deliberately selected a conservative outfit because she knew Katy was not into the dance scene. As they walked to Alisha's car, Katy picked up the conversation where she left off.

"I took a smattering of literature and art courses too. I even dabbled at painting and writing poetry, but I soon found out I'm a better fine arts spectator than creator. How about you?" That's another question I can't answer yet, even though I've been reading Indira's poems and studying art and literature. I'll pretend, and just act naturally.

"I like the fine arts but haven't had time to participate. Maybe I will after my soccer career. But why don't you find a couple of tunes fitting for tonight?"

Katy dialed the controls, locating on popular Websites songs she liked. Alisha found two of them mesmerizing: Break on Through to the Other Side, by the Doors, and Don't Leave me this Way, by Thelma Houston. Though Katy had never been to an LBGT dance club, her selections were spot on: the songs fit the mood. Katy explained their histories.

"The Doors' music is iconic acid-rock from the 1960's Hippie movement, and Thelma Houston's is from the 1970's Disco era. Just listen to how the beat and melody drive the words." Without warning, Alisha felt a severe brain quake; she felt disoriented and pulled to the curb before she lost control of the car. She bent over the steering wheel, eyes closed and hands clapped over her ears as verses from an Indira poem cascaded into her brain:

"Not too often—unpredictably only now and then,
I find myself being drawn relentlessly once again,
By some dormant fragment that will
Break on through to the other side,
Like some self-addictive past turbulent afflicted rushing tide.
Sometimes a more innocent and breathless time.
Sometimes some vivid episode without reason or rhyme.
Pregnant with possibility for whatever calling's meant to be,
And for but a moment the World distilled to my reality.
Such are these sensations—obsessions from the past,
Too intense the feelings—too harmful should they last.
Banish to distant memory—remote places once well known,
Better off for sanity—leave well enough alone."

Her head cleared as the verses faded away. Katy had the presence of mind to look after Alisha, grabbing her shoulders then stroking her hair.

"What's wrong? You look white as a ghost." Alisha looked up.

"I'm OK now, but for a moment I felt dizzy and weak. Something in those songs took me someplace I can't recollect. Maybe you're right. Perhaps we shouldn't go to the party tonight. Let's stop for a pizza, then I'll drive you home."

"That's a good idea. The Coach will approve. Pizza has lots of good carbs…"

There was no harm done missing the party. Alisha called Carter the next day to apologize for standing everyone up, and he understood her explanation. According to Carter, the Full House danced past midnight. Mariah, who already knew club dance moves, taught them to Matt, who paired up with the always energetic Zoe. Mariah then helped Carter master the basic steps. All four felt right at home whether on the dance floor or mingling with the crowd. Several club members introduced themselves and asked Mariah where was her usual partner. That question didn't surprise Carter; when dressed in party finery, Alisha would catch everyone's eye. And she can't fool me any more like she used to. She likes people to notice her. But I have to admit, she does wear her vanity well. She doesn't flaunt.

Alisha spent part of the week doing what every new car owner does: pampering the car like a newborn just home from the hospital. She practiced handling and parking, washed and waxed, and peered into unexplored territory: the mysterious space under the hood. She didn't recognize anything so she did what everyone does as a last resort: she read the instruction manual. I can't be this dumb. Maybe I'm just not mechanically inclined. I think I'll settle for appearance rather than performance.

On Saturday she drove to the final practice; her teammates thought she looked good in the new car. Coach Cruz took pictures of the team wearing new uniforms, clustered about Alisha, who was sitting behind the wheel. Coach promised to Email copies, then issued final instructions.

"We've put in all the hard work and training, so school's out for us.

All we need to do is taper and train lightly this week. Be here next Sunday at ten a.m. to ride the bus. The game starts at two, so we'll have over two hours when we get to the stadium to warm up. Take your mind off the game until next Saturday, then focus, focus, focus. Relax until then."

Alisha decided to start tapering and relaxing immediately, so she went club dancing by herself that evening. Mariah wasn't in the mood, and Katy would say it violated the Coach's orders. Besides, it was time for her to fly solo and see what might happen.

She wanted to lose herself in the rhythm of the dance steps and the music, and that's what she did with male and female partners. She couldn't believe it was midnight when her partner escorted her off the floor for one more drink before flying home.

"I like how you express yourself when you're on the floor. It's a turn-on watching you move. I gotta ask you, do you take drugs before clubbing?" The question caught Alisha by surprise.

"No, I never felt like I needed them. Do you?"

"Sometimes I do, and tell you what, they raise emotional intensity. Lots of people do. Pro athletes take them, too, but not to get high. They want to improve performance on the field. The leagues try to ban performance-enhancing substances, but some of the new drugs are hard to detect. If you want to experience life to the fullest, you gotta live it first-hand, not through other people or books. You should try drugs sometime, just for kicks or comparisons. Here's contact info for a safe source." Alisha thanked him but refused the offer. Drugs aren't for me. Better to face life thinking clearly, not with a drugged-up brain or body. But I can empathize with those who do. Maybe I should warn my partner. But no, this isn't the time or place to interfere.

"I hope we can dance together again. Be safe." He hugged Alisha, then they each went their separate ways.

Alisha had only one major item she had to complete this coming week: she had to plan and schedule another trip to her Austin partners for early October. It gave her a useful distraction, taking her mind off car and soccer training, both of which were polished to perfection. Alisha called Hud on Thursday morning to follow up on the Email she had sent earlier that week.

"How's the state of Texas?... Good for you…I just want to make sure the first week in October is good for my visiting you… Excellent. I'll book my own flight. And I'll send you a detailed agenda if I have time to revise what I already sent you. And let me mention something else. I'll be on national television Sunday playing in a soccer match. Have you heard about it?... Yeah, women's soccer is popular and they're advertising the match to build excitement for Women's World Cup Soccer playoffs. I think they start next month… Who should you bet on? Bet on me. So what if they've never been beaten or tied by any team in our league. You can get great odds or bet the spread. I've got the goods, so watch me. See you in October."

That call wrapped up her work week; all other activities were under control. Between now and Sunday morning she would relax by watching retro-flicks and taking tapered workouts. And she would continue re-reading the Electra Chronicles. *Electra, I wish you were here to watch me play soccer. Maybe I'm as good, or maybe even better, with my legs than you were. But your I.Q. is way over my pretty head. Please come back soon.*

Game day. No matter the sport, the age, or the level of the playing field, all players experience matchless pre-game anxiety and excitement. It's part of the magic bestowed by sports to competitors, and spectators share the suspense. Alisha awoke ready for the thrill of the game. *Calm down. Don't burn up energy by getting ready too soon. I don't have to put my game face on just yet.* She needed a diversion, so she busied herself looking at fashion magazines. *I can add trendy stuff to my winter wardrobe.* That worked wonders redirecting her attention, and it wasn't until she dressed to leave that she packed her game face.

Matt called as she was about to drive to the bus. He was taking her close friends to the match, including Russell and Jennifer Conklin. Only Robin was unable to go because she was preparing for exams. Since he was an assistant coach and trainer, he'd join the team at the stadium.

"And remember, try to relax until game time."

"Got it. That's exactly what I'm gonna do. See you at the stadium."

Everyone on the bus could feel excitement building as they motored toward the stadium, but Coach Cruz deliberately shelved any fiery talk until game time. Alisha sat next to Katy, flipping through fashion magazines and pointing out what she'd look for on her next shopping trip. The bus arrived at noon, and because the weather was warm and sunny, soccer fans were already gathering. Coach Cruz led the team onto the playing field before taking them to the locker room. "This is the best stadium and the biggest crowd ever for us. I expect all of you will have jitters when you first come out. I will too. And that's OK. We'll huddle up and I'll remind you again that when the game begins, the crowd and the stadium will disappear, as will your jitters, because you will lose yourself in the moment, in the game. Now go in and change, then come out for your standard warmup drills. And don't watch the opposing team. You've seen enough on the videos. Focus on yourself and our team."

The team followed Amanda's advice, chattering all through the warm-up. Time ticked away, and when Alisha looked up, she saw the stadium filled, only fifteen minutes left before the National Anthem would play. It's time to put my game face on. I'll play this game for Electra. She always had to hold back, but I don't, and I won't today. I know I've got the goods, and I'm gonna strut my stuff. If all I can do is talk the talk, I'll look like a fool, like a faker. But if I can walk the walk, I'll come across like a confident winner. That's what I'm gonna be. And I'll carry my team as far as I can bring them.

Alisha felt a tremor surge through her brain. She felt energized as her game face snapped into place. She was ready. Don't go wild right away. Size up the competition. Hold back until it's time. Then fly! Coach Cruz gathered her team just before the start.

"OK ladies, this is our moment, your moment to take center stage. Look around you at the crowd, at the stadium. Then look at one another, right here, right now. This is as good as it gets. And it doesn't matter what the final score is as long as you play with all you've got. And play smart. Play teamwork and play defense. And don't count goals. Just stay in the play. And forget any blown plays or mistakes. You can't get'em back, so move on. We've got a first, then a second half, and we'll make adjustments at halftime if needed. They're about to call your names, so let's go!" The team clapped hands, broke the huddle and waited to hear names before jogging into the starting players' line. Matt found Alisha just before her name was called and told her to let her body and brain meld into one.

"Don't overthink! I know your muscle memory knows what to do.

Let it out when the time comes."

"Got it," was all Alisha's game face needed to say.

The National Team won the coin toss, so the Spirit's goalie kicked off. Alisha was surprised by her opponents' speed and agility. They're even better on the field than on video. Once again, words echoed in her brain. Get with it, soldier! This is not a drill! You're better than any of them. Focus on making it so. Suddenly, Alisha saw the game running at a slower speed, as if she were inside the opposing team's decision loop. When the play comes my way, I'll take attacker's momentum away and add it to mine. Just watch.

The Nationals played with speed, agility, and overwhelming confidence. They wouldn't embarrass the Spirit; they'd treat them nicely but would make sure to maintain a comfortable lead so they could practice in the game for what was coming up: the start of the World Cup.

Only one Nationals attack came at Alisha's position, and she was able to deflect the ball. The next attacks came at other positions and the third one led to a goal. One of the Spirit's attacks had Alisha in the play, but she had to pass the ball to another player who had fewer defenders around her. The pass was good, but her teammate muffed the ball. The Nationals converted the muff to another goal. The score stood 2-0.

The Spirit played with determination, following the strategy Coach Cruz had put in place. The fans appreciated the effort and empathized with the underdogs. And they enjoyed watching the National Team's marquee players in action, even though they weren't breaking much of a sweat. The announcers calling the game for the national audience kept up a pleasant stream of National Team facts and stories, hoping to keep the viewers engaged. When the Nationals scored their third goal, the lead commentator offered a summary.

"The Nationals are using this contest to prime for the World Cup, and thanks to the Washington Spirit, we're getting an opportunity to see them showcase their stars. The Spirit players are fighting gamely, but they're outgunned. I can tell they're well coached, but it would take a stroke of lightning to change the flow of the game…"

The score was 3-0 at halftime. Coach Cruz huddled her players, congratulating them for a great effort and the discipline to follow her strategy, but everyone could feel enthusiasm draining away.

She was about to tell them to keep doing what they were doing when Micki spoke up.

"Coach, we gotta change something. If we stick with your strategy, it'll be 6-0 or worse, and none of us came here to be practice dummies. We want to win, or at least put dents in the National's armor. So, let's go with a 'star strategy.' We're not gonna play team or position soccer. We're gonna feed the ball to Alisha on offense and help her score. You haven't unleashed her, and she's held back. It's time to turn her loose and let her run the ball down their throats. The Nationals don't know anything about her, or much about us for that matter. By the time they catch on the score should be closer, and maybe they'll get rattled. How about it?" Amanda called to Matt, explaining what Micki wanted.

"It's worth a shot. It'll be better than what we did in the first half. Alisha, listen up! You'll be able to fool them at first, but when they catch on, we can use you as a decoy. You know, you'll get the ball but pass it when someone else has a better scoring opportunity." Alisha nodded her head and said, "Got it." But she had other plans. *No way am I gonna pass the ball unless it's impossible for me to attack.*

"OK team, we're ready for the second half. Let's go!" Matt and Amanda headed to the referees to confirm a second half rule modification for this match: if the game ends in a tie, there would be no shoot-out. The referees nodded while smiling.

Micki—who was not about to mince words—kept the team huddled for another minute.

"We're gonna shit-can what the assistant trainer just said. Alisha, you keep pushing the ball up field. Only pass if you can't keep attacking. Is everyone on board?" Only one player spoke up.

"Alisha, do you think this'll work?" Alisha tightened her game face and spoke two words only. "Just watch." She spoke a couple of more to herself. *It's time, but I won't run wild… not yet.*

The Nationals kicked off to start the second half. They were becoming a bit too cocky, expecting more of the same from the first half. The first mistake was letting the Spirit midfielders advance the ball too far before intercepting them. Alisha was well past the center line when she received a pass. She advanced the ball directly at a defender, then accelerated and faked her out with lightning quick shielded side steps. She booted the ball forward and raced to catch up, bearing down on the startled goalie and then booming the ball in the direction opposite the goalie's lunge." That woke up the crowd, but not the Nationals.

The Nationals attacked again. The Spirit stopped it but was unable to get the ball to Alisha. Attacks and counterattacks followed, and still her teammates couldn't get her the ball. On the next possession, the Nationals scored again, making the score 4-1. Micki screamed to Alisha, "Don't worry about playing your defensive position! Go after the ball!" All the Spirits heard it.

The ensuing kick went to Micki, who charged ahead getting past all but three defenders. Alisha glided towards her in time to get a perfectly placed push pass. She reached the ball in full stride, and even though two of the defenders had the angle she cut to the right faster than the defenders could react. This time the goalie was ready but unable to block the booming kick. This time the Nationals, the crowd, and the announcers paid attention.

"It looks like the Spirit made a halftime adjustment. They're getting player number 11—we're checking names—into the flow of the game. Maybe they can keep doing it, but the Nationals will try to isolate her by not attacking her position. Let's see how this plays out."

The second half continued playing out just the way Micki called it. Alisha abandoned her defensive position and went straight at the attacker. This time she used a poke tackle to take the ball away, then raced towards the goal, but an opposing defender tripped her, giving her a penalty kick. But she couldn't score; there were too many defenders in the way. Time to pick up the pace! I'll race around their
tackles.

The teams traded possessions. By now the Nationals were paying close attention to Alisha, but she snuck past enough opponents to intercept the attacker, using a blocking slide to take the ball away. She was quicker than all the defenders, springing to her feet and avoiding tackles. The Nationals goalie had lost confidence and Alisha rammed the ball past her before she could react. The score was 4-3. The Nationals were no longer coasting; they were playing all-in, playing for pride, for reputation, for unblemished record. They were being bloodied and the crowd loved rooting for the underdog.

By now Alisha was in full flight, her body and emotions merging; she was running wild; her power and desire were unstoppable, and her teammates were fighting as hard as they could. But it wasn't enough. The Nationals swooped in for another score, making it 5-3 with five minutes left. The crowd was totally engaged, as were the announcers.

"We now have the name of player number 11, Alisha Kittner. A walk-on late last spring. And today she's walking—no she's running— all over the National Team. Quite a story in the making. Too bad her team can't help her more, but they're fighting bravely."

The Nationals were gasping for oxygen; for the last fifteen minutes Alisha had been running their legs off. They're not gonna be able to keep up. Time to take it to the next level.

Alisha ran directly to where the Nationals' kick was heading. A teammate passed her the ball and she set sail for the opponent's goal. Let's see how they like keep-away. Alisha used her speed, conditioning, and footwork to fake and weave, and dance past the defenders, who by now were running in slow motion. The goalie watched helplessly as Alisha drove in for another score. The crowd was on its feet, chanting "RUN GIRL RUN!...RUN GIRL RUN!... The announcers led the cheers for the TV audience.

"You're watching an amazing display of athletic drive, determination, and talent! This unknown, unheralded young lady and her valiant team have completely taken the wind out of the National Team's sails. Lucky for the Nationals, there are only two minutes left, and they get the kick. Unless lightning strikes, they should be able to hang on."

The Nationals did everything possible to keep Alisha away from the ball. They advanced the ball, using well-placed passes to play keep-away and to obstruct her advances. But they ignored the only other player who could spoil their victory. Micki hooked-tackled the ball away from an attacker, made a backward pass to a fellow teammate, and then raced along the right sidelines to a secondary position. Katy now had the ball and advanced the attack. She was not closely guarded, and she struggled past midfield just as Alisha broke free.

Katy passed the ball in Alisha's direction, and she scrummed it away from two defenders, one of them falling down. Alisha ran over her and down the center of the field. The crowd and the announcers were on their feet, screaming. There were only thirty seconds left, fifty meters to run and seven defenders ahead, all bearing down on Alisha. And that's when she spotted Micki, in the clear and awaiting a pass. Alisha didn't hesitate. She made a long pass to Micki, then cut to left of center to draw defenders away.

Micki gathered the ball as twenty seconds remained, and she started her drive towards the Nationals goal—that twenty-four by eight-foot promised land for her team's place in the record books. But she squibbed the ball badly, almost tripping and coming to a dead stop as three defenders closed the gap. There was nothing left to do but try a desperation kick, and with ten seconds left she let it fly, but it sailed too high and too far to the left. There was an audible gasp of dejection as soon as the crowd saw the ball veer away from the goal. And that's when lightning struck.

It was Alisha's moment to burst into the national spotlight. Alisha had practiced the most difficult, the most spectacular kick in all of soccer: the bicycle kick, where a player leaps skyward, doing a backward somersault, kicking the ball as it passes high overhead. Rarely attempted by even the best males; never before attempted in a professional women's soccer match.

Alisha timed her leap perfectly, reaching maximum altitude completely inverted. She struck the ball with the instep of her right foot, sending it on an arc that just cleared the outstretched arms of the goalie. The ball nestled in the back of the net as time expired.

"SHE SCOOOOORES! SHE SCOOOOORES! AND SHE DID IT ON THE HARDEST KICK OF ALL—A BICYCLE KICK! SOCCER FANS'LL BE TALKING ABOUT THIS GAME FOR A LOOOOONG TIME!" Both announcers continued to rave about what they had just witnessed. The crowd continued chanting "GO

GIRL GO!... GO GIRL GO!" Alisha was on her knees, not quite knowing what to make of it as her teammates swarmed around about.

The locker room was a joyous din of laughter and celebration; the team had just scored an incredible victory because a tie was as good as a win. Coach Cruz hurried in to prepare them for hastily assembled TV interviews. When Alisha heard she'd be televised nationally one-on-one, she turned to her teammates, gasping,

"Oh my God! I forgot my makeup. You gotta make me look good." Katy chirped a suggestion for everyone to paint up and look alluring.

"When the big-name athletes dress up for post-game interviews, they're making a statement. Let's do the same. Sexy female athletes are a hot commodity. So, let's add more fuel to the fire."

Some of Alisha's one-on-one interviews aired live. Others would be edited and shown later. Hud, who had watched the game and interviews with a couple of close business and gambling partners, gladly accepted their good-natured scolding.

"No wonder you cleaned up on our bets. You had insider information. What sort of business partner is she?" Hud shot right back.

"I can't tell y'awl that. That's confidential. But she'll be here next week, so you can buy her and me a drink to find out." Sam Ryder accepted the offer.

"That young lady's got it. If she plays her cards right, she's gonna go places. I want to meet her..."

Chapter 9
October 2122

"Alisha on the Run"
Thread 1 Chapter 5

ALISHA HAD HER FEET back on the ground soon after all the hoopla caused by her stellar performance. Though it fueled her predisposed vanity, her emotional persona knew how to stay centered.

The soccer story stayed in Monday and Tuesday's sporting spotlight. One commentator waxed poetic when comparing the stunning outcome to the 1980 U.S. Men's Hockey Team victory over Russia, calling it a "Splendor in the Grass" analog of "the Miracle on Ice." But like everything newsworthy in the lightning-fast 21st century, attention turns away from today as the next day dawns. On a morning run the week after, Alisha considered how capricious focal points can be. Soccer has been a great run for me, and I can play with the team next year. But I'll put that thought away and follow advice given in another Indira poem called "More or Less." "I only am one more or less, To me it's about the same.
Try my best like all the rest,
And enjoy being part of the game.
But nimble Youth has ego aglow,
It matters what others think.
The World must know they're best in show,
So they push right to the brink.
The World applauds then turns away,
Leaving lessons for Youth to learn.
The World changes unpredictably,
Now a different player's turn."
Indira knew how fickle and fleeting is fame. I'm so glad Electra left me a copy of her poems. I can feel Indira's empathy for other

people, for what life offers. From what I've read, and from what has returned to me in memory, she had it all, and her empathy and artistic abilities were better than Electra's. Is it possible that mine are better too? I'll never know unless she comes back. Well, it's not for me to worry about. I'm moving on to my Austin trip. But before she could, Matt called her Monday afternoon to talk about Robin's struggle, not Alisha's success.

"I need your help. Robin's going to fail the stats course she's taking if I don't help her prepare a take-home final exam. Her professor is very understanding. He recognizes she can't concentrate and is willing to waive all remaining homework and an in-class final exam if she researches three questions. And he's willing to let her be coached, as long as she submits well-written explanations. She has until Thanksgiving to do it, but she's freaking out because I don't know how to solve them. Can you take a look at them? I sure would appreciate it. And after the way you played on Sunday, I'd say the old Electra is back." Alisha grimaced, speaking quickly to herself before replying. I can feel myself getting better, but I'm not at her level yet. But this is a good test for me to see how much has come back. "Why don't you Email me the exam? Please give until Saturday to sort through it, and I'll give it my best shot. Did you tell her I'd take a look?"

"Yes, and it calmed her down. She didn't want to ask you because she's trying to rely less on you and more on me. And if you can't solve the problems, try to think of somebody who can. I have to get to the clinic, but I'll Email it to you right now. You're the best." Five minutes later, Alisha peered at the three questions.

1. Explain Simpson's Paradox.
2. Explain how Bayes Theorem can be used to "prove historical events."
3. Explain a solution to the Monty Hall Problem.

I'll take them one at a time, and I might as well start now. I know I have stats-math somewhere in my brain, and I recall an Econ lecture I watched several years ago that showed how Simpson's Paradox can be misleading. Maybe Electra left notes. If so, I'll start there. If not, I'll surf the Web for info. Either way, maybe some neural circuits will turn on, especially if I focus. Although she couldn't find any notes, she found more than enough on the Internet. And the more she focused, the clearer her thinking became. Suddenly, an answer broke through.

I understand! Simpson's paradox is a subtlety appearing in statistical problems dealing with proportions. A simple comparison of two telephone sales reps handling call-ins illustrates it. Comparisons can be reversed when lurking variables are taken into consideration. One representative might have a higher proportion of total correct calls for the month, even though the other had a higher proportion each week. I know how to write up a solution, which I'll do later. Let's move on to number two.

Hmm. I recall a section in "The Electra Chronicles" talking about Bayes' Theorem for computing the probability of the historical Jesus. I'll start there and then surf the Web. As she studied, she became absorbed in the use of prior probability and likelihood functions to compute posterior probability. Suddenly, she felt a neural shudder.

I got it! Bayesian statistics uses subjective and conditional probabilities to calculate the odds that non-recurring historical events could have occurred. I can write up a solution for this problem, too, so let's move on to number three, the Monty Hall Problem. Alisha soon discovered it was the hardest of the three questions, but also the most intriguing.

The problem is named for the original host of the game show "Let's Make a Deal." A solution caused a kerfuffle when it appeared in a 1990 Marilyn vos Savant "Parade Magazine" column. She's the person who scored the highest recorded I.Q. ever. Her answer, though correct, attracted scathing criticism from numerous PhD mathematicians. Alisha read a statement of the problem:

- A Contestant is asked to choose which of three closed doors conceals a new car. The other two each conceal a goat or is empty. The Contestant chooses Door 1, and the Host opens one of the other doors, but not a door concealing the goat or the car. It doesn't matter if Door 2 or Door 3 is opened, so let's assume Door 3. There are now two unopened doors, and the Contestant is given a choice:

keep Door 1 or switch to Door 2. What should the Contestant do?

I know Electra is smarter than Marilyn, but I'm not Electra. But I can tell I'm getting smarter. Let's surf for suggestions. Alisha found several solutions, none of which appealed to her. They contained either too much data or too many equations. I can't believe I've been working for four hours. I think I'll take a break and let my brain look for a simpler solution. I'll save what I've done and finish the exam no later than Friday.

Alisha awoke thoroughly refreshed on Wednesday and decided to focus on her Austin trip after she completed a morning workout. She prepared an agenda that had five items: three for Hud and one each for Su and Tim. And she re-read those parts of the Electra Chronicles so she knew all project details well enough to act her role. She no longer feared dealing with situations she knew little about, for she had perfected the art of sidestepping tough questions or decisions by deferring, deflecting, or delegating. And at times, she found evidence she was getting smarter, so she took a late afternoon run and spent the evening thinking about the Monty Hall Problem. Nothing inspirational came to her, so after an hour, she packed her bags for the morning plane flight, then relaxed by surfing the Internet for clothes or car accessories that would fit her style.

Airport security glitches and Internet outages made for a frustrating early morning flight. Seems like travel infrastructure and information system reliability are deteriorating again. Next time I talk with Carter, I'll point that out. Good that I booked a 6 a.m. flight. We're three hours late, but if Hud didn't give up and go home, we can still stay on schedule. He hadn't. He was waiting for her at the baggage claim carousel.

"Thanks for picking me up. Did you know the flight would be late?"

"Yep. Local Internet service was restored just before I was gonna leave, so I got a couple of calls made and then left to get you. We got your agenda yesterday and we're all set to compare ideas. But there are two additional items. We can chat about them in the car." As soon they were in the car and on the road, Alisha continued the conversation.

"I know why you and Holy like Austin. Great weather and terrain; great academic and hi-tech business climates; easy traveling to or from Dallas, Houston or San Antonio. No wonder you don't want to move headquarters. Maybe you won't have to. How are your government negotiations going?"

"You were right about playing hardball. Washington backed off on grabbing our patents or nationalizing us. And they'd never believe me if I told them the truth about the patents. You told us years ago not to file because if we did we'd be letting the competition see stuff they'd never figure out on their own. And even if we filed, they'd be inaccurate because only you have the latest formulas."

"Please keep it that way. And never tell anyone that you and I have a joint venture business. I don't want anyone connecting us except through my parents. And I think you took care of the Chinese security snoops who almost connected us. We don't ever want a repeat of that."

"You got that right, Little Lady. Even the T-Plague vaccine guy from NIH—that Russell Conklin fellow—doesn't know what we're up to. He's pretty reasonable, and he's convinced the government to buy from us. So, we're keeping Washington at bay. And don't worry about hiring a replacement for Brian. The sales guy I transferred to handle Neuro-device sales and marketing is doing a good job putting Brian's plan in action. And I'll let Tim find the right person to hire for security software development."

"Excellent. We've just covered our three agenda topics, so I can meet with Su and her assistant Kameyo this afternoon, and then with Tim tomorrow. Now please tell me, what are the new items?"

"One is sorta bad, one is sorta good. Let me give you sorta bad first. Your friend Robin can't handle the accounting work. She started out OK, but for most of this year she's been struggling. She's falling way behind. I haven't fired her because she's your friend and Holy likes her, but I've got one of our bookkeepers doing her work. You better talk to her; find out what's wrong. And we gotta keep friendship and jobs separate. It's up to you, but you should fire her." "I'll take care of this when I get back. And what's the sorta good thing?" Hud couldn't help breaking out a Texas-sized grin.

"Well now, I cleaned up on the soccer bets I placed. I watched the game with a couple of my gambling partners. What a game! You were on fire, hotter than hell's brass hinges. My buddy Sam Ryder wants to take us to dinner, so if it's all right with you, we're on for tonight."

"That's good by me, but who is he?"

"He's a native Texan just about my age; grew up in Houston; his Papa made boatloads of bucks in real estate. He graduated from UT Austin studying performing arts stuff. Worked in Hollywood for ten years, then came back to Austin to start an entertainment business his Papa funded. He likes gambling and sports; we met when both of us came back to Austin to start our businesses. You'll like him. And you'll like the restaurant too, Truluck's Seafood, Steak, and Crab House. Been around a long time. Has an elegant and private set-up. We'll meet him there at seven."

"You planned our drive-time discussion perfectly. We wrapped up just as you rolled into the parking lot. I hope the rest of the meetings roll as smoothly."

Hud walked Alisha to the conference room he always uses for intracompany meetings, then returned with Su and Kameyo. Alisha knew from periodic updates that Tim's modified Neuro-Knitter had accelerated Su's recovery, but seeing her walk into the room was the best proof, and Alisha said so.

"We can build advertising and promotion pieces featuring your recovery."

"Hello Alisha. Welcome back, and yes we can. The therapist credits Tim's device for mending the vertebrae so quickly, and our ad agency is working as we speak on promo pieces. I might not be able to play soccer like you, but I've regained strength and full range of motion. And I need all my strength to keep up with Kameyo. She'll give you a summary of what she's accomplished."

Kameyo spoke for the next forty-five minutes, explaining how she used autophagy concepts to improve vaccine solution paths that work on the current strain of virus. Computer modeling and in vitro testing confirmed its superiority, and manufacturing operations had begun building inventory.

"And as soon as we get the sales pipeline filled, our sales reps will report how well they work on patients. Then Dr. Chou and I will focus on the new strain. I am confident the modifications I have made will be effective there as well, and if so, we project rollout in six to nine months." Alisha knew enough to nod knowingly. I understand better this time than last, but not enough to say something clever, so I'll let Su take it away.

"Fine, I'm certain Su and you will make it so. And remember, our next target will be Alzheimer's. Next time, I'd like you to outline an approach. Well, I'll leave you two to carry on."

Alisha was happy to hustle out of the conference and into the safety of Hud's office. Kameyo and Su are a wonderful team. I don't think Electra would need to meddle. She told Hud on the drive to dinner, then asked about their dinner partners.

"What does Sam Ryder look like?"

"You can tell he's a Texan, but with some Hollywood polish added. He's not the kind of guy who'd work on a drilling rig. Looks like you'd expect someone in entertainment to look like. Taller than average and carries his weight well. Sharp dresser and keeps just a little gray at the edges. Friendly and outgoing, but he has killer instincts when it comes to business and gambling. Same with sports, too. Between him and his Papa, they can bankroll a lot of projects. Sort of like me and Holy. Maybe Sam Senior will be at dinner."

Both Sam Ryders greeted them at the table. Hud's description of Junior was on the money, and you could see the father in the son. Alisha liked what she saw.

"Well, hello, Hud, and thank you for bringing our star performer. Young lady, you dazzled us with your soccer skills. My father, Sam Senior, and I want to shake your hand." Alisha glowed in the warmth of their greeting.

"Thank you for the compliment. I'm pleased you watched the match. Did Texas fans root for David or Goliath?" Sam Senior spoke right up.

"Texans root for both sides in any contest where both give it their all. And they were cheering for how you took command. We think you got the goods."

Dinner conversation flowed smoothly, the white tablecloth illuminated by the amber glow of the candlelight providing an intimate forum for sharing, and when, after dinner, drinks were being sipped, Junior steered the conversation in Alisha's direction.

"I hope Hud's told you something about us, because I think you'll like us, and will also like what we have to offer. By the way, Hud told us about the first time he met you. Was the gun loaded?" "When I put my game face on, I'm always loaded for bear. I'll let you draw your own conclusion."

"That's just what I wanted to hear. You think on your feet as fast as your footwork. Well, now, we think we know a bit about you, and we like everything we've seen. We hired a vetting agency to do a background check. Please don't be insulted. If you ran a business, I'm sure you'd do the same. Here, I'll give all of us a copy. Please tell me if it's accurate. And let me say right away we wouldn't be talking tonight if you didn't look even better than Bambi." After Sam handed out copies, Alisha studied for five minutes before replying.

Vetting Report for: Alisha Kittner as of October 2122
Single Female
Mixed Race: Asian and Caucasian
Hair: Black
Eyes: Hazel
Height: 5 feet 11 inches
Weight:120 pounds (approx.)
Born: Electra Alisha Kittner February 11, 2097
Mother: Indira
Jaswinder Ramanujan
Father: Jason Kittner
ACADEMIC RECORD
Graduated Grade School (Home Schooling Track): June 2109
Graduated High School (Home Schooling Track): June 2112

Graduated George Washington University (B.S. Biotechnology): June 2114

Graduated George Washington University (PhD. Biotechnology): December 2119

CRIMINAL RECORD

No reported incidents

EMPLOYMENT HISTORY

Current Position: Postdoc Researcher George Washington University: January 2120 Previous:

Guardian Party Part-Time (Fund Raising Public Relations): 2113—2120

CDC Work Study Program (Lab Assistant Data Handling Clerk): 2112 —2113

MEDICAL HISTORY

Survived Lightning Strike at Birth that killed Mother: February 2097

Survived Car Crash (Burns Broken Neck): 2118

Survived Techno-Plague: December 2122

THUMBNAIL SKETCH

- Parents are talented Biotech Researchers (Washington DC CDC Lab).
- Parents and two Grad School friends (Su-lin Song Chou, Adom Ola) known as the Worldstars Team. Hudson Haller good friend of Adom Ola.
- Mother (Indira Ramanujan) died during childbirth and before Marriage Contract Finalized.
- Raised by Father (Jason Kittner) and Grandfather (Justin aka Doc Kittner), Childhood appears to be healthy and normal.
- Promising child athlete (Soccer).
- Withdrew from sports in high school to focus on studies.
- Father killed in lab explosion while Alisha was in High School; Grandfather murdered while Alisha was in High School. Alisha assumed an adult role immediately and handled it capably.

- Introverted personality until the automobile crash. Afterwards engaged in more social interaction. Leadership ability emerged.
- Hobbies: Soccer, Dancing, Politics (volunteer and part-time job).
- Chosen Career: College Level Research/Teaching.
- Other Business Interests: None. Alisha's parents are the link between Alisha and Hudson Haller.
- Limited international travel (England, India).
- Sexual Orientation: Bisexual, but nothing abnormal uncovered. Has a diverse mix of LGBT friends. Heterosexual relations confirmed.
- Emotional Health: Appears normal. No evidence of mental instability.
- Cognitive Ability: Education and current job indicate above-average intelligence. Seems to have recovered fully from Techno-Plague.
- Appearance and personality traits all positive.

POSSIBLE SKELETONS

- Father's and Grandfather's deaths suggest they might have been involved in unknown activities that made Alisha an unwitting victim in some type of medical-political intrigue. This is pure speculation. There is no supporting evidence.

RECOMMENDATION

- Alisha has the attributes to be the core of the sports team you are planning. She is attractive, likeable, socially aware, smart, and has an appealing personality. People who meet her like her immediately.
- Possible taglines: Run Girl Run, Go Girl Go. Could be updated to: Run Alisha Run, Go Alisha Go. Viable connections to team nickname (T-Breds).
- Proceed if athletic skills are transferable to football as played in the Co-NFL
- Confirm she is tough enough physically to withstand hard hits that will be delivered by the opponent's defense.

SHE READ IT THREE TIMES. They know all the facts, which I've adjusted by using my Network Security Suite. Where is this going? Oh, I see. They want me to play in the Co-NFL. That's major league sports! I want to hear what they have to say. Stay cool and composed, and act naturally.

"You do a thorough job. What's here is accurate. But please tell me, where is all this going?" Sam Junior let everyone in on his plan. "Hud doesn't know this, but Dad and I are buying the Houston Horses CoNFL franchise. We're gonna move it to Austin and rebrand it the Austin Thoroughbreds. Are you familiar with the Co-NFL?"

Yes, I follow it closely. I know it's popular—a great mix of sports and entertainment. It's tackle football with rule changes, including size and weight restrictions on males to level the playing field because teams have male and female athletes competing against each other. I believe there's an upper limit for the number of males a team can have in plays. The league started about thirty years ago and remains popular because of the exciting teamwork and competition between males and females. That's because, over the past fifty years, women have raised the bar for female athletic excellence while maintaining an appealing sexuality. Men and women alike enjoy the games; men appreciate the blend of beauty and athleticism, while women respect athletic female role models. Many women athletes are close to parity with men in many positions. My parents' friends told me my mother could have played if she ever put her mind to it." Hud chimed in.

"Yep, Alisha's right. I knew her mother. She was practically perfect. Smart, pretty, socially adept. She was athletically gifted, but she never wanted to get serious about sports. I didn't think it was possible, but Alisha here is like an improved model: bigger, stronger, smarter." Junior picked up where Hud stopped.

"We don't know if you can handle a lot of hits, and we're concerned about injury. The league rules try to protect females from overly aggressive blocks and tackles, but the game hits you're liable to take can be hard. Some of the female players hit as hard as the men. You have to be honest with us and with

yourself. Do you think you're tough enough to play in the league?"
I've never thought about this,
But I need to put a positive spin on what I say.

"That's an excellent question, and I can't give you a final answer, but take a look at how I've done in soccer. I've had no problems dealing with the hits, and my speed and quickness blunt most defenders that come at me. I guess you'll have to see how I do in scrimmages."

"Fair enough. If it looks like we can keep you from getting injured, we can carve out a role that will be a win for you, for our team, and for the Co-NFL. Let me put more cards on the table. And before I do that, how about another round of drinks?" The pause was to everyone's liking. Hud's recollections of Alisha's parents helped lower the conversation's intensity, and when the glasses were empty, Sam continued detailing his plan.

"You understand the game very well, and I think you know that at the professional level Sports and Entertainment are synonymous. We're interested in buying the franchise for a couple of reasons: Dad and I love sports, and there's money to be made by turning the franchise around when we move it to Austin. The current owners want to sell. They don't know how to recruit players or market the product. Last season the team ranked second from the bottom and had nothing going for it. We think we can turn the situation around. And before I continue, please answer me this: are you interested?" Are you kidding? Do Texans like Tex-Mex? Of course I am, but I'll be cool about it.
"I could be, but I need to know more. What are your intentions?"

"We're going to be the first franchise to build its fan base on a female star system. And the star has to be a female who can play quarterback. We're thinking maybe you could be the first one. Have you ever played football?"

"No, but I have a knack for training myself. I'm sure I can learn enough on my own for your coaches to get me to the next level."

"From what you showed us on TV, you have incredible quickness and agility. You ran roughshod over the best women soccer players, but the Co-NFL players are even better. Some of the females, and certainly many of the males, will be as good or better. And you're light, which makes you quick but possibly too fragile. But we've already covered that, so let's move on. Let me see the size of your hands." Alisha put her hands in his.

"Now give me a firm handshake. Dad, I think her hand is big and strong enough to grip a football. I'm gonna ask the waiter to get one I left in the car. Alisha, what do you think so far?" You haven't seen anything yet. But don't let'em know.

"I'm tougher than I look, and I'm sure I can master the basics of throwing a spiral. And I want to compete against the best."

"I like your confidence. And we'll build the offense around your running first, passing second. We found a coach that invented a new formation; he calls it the Wide-V. The quarter back stands about three yards further back than his two flanking running backs. Depending on the play called, the snap might go to the quarterback or to either running back, giving the quarterback all sorts of options. Here comes the waiter. Let's see how you handle the ball." Junior was right; Alisha's hands were big enough and strong enough. Now it was her turn to play offense.

"I know why the star has to be a female. Everyone expects males to be better and will root for a female who tries to upset the conventional wisdom. And she must be more than just athletic to pull it off. She has to have 'star quality.' She has to have looks, personality, and speaking skills. If she combines that with enough athletic ability, the fans will go for her and the team, and they'll do so right from the start if you have a good public relations campaign that'll build awareness, interest and desire. Then the fans will take action; they'll come to the stadium or watch at home or at sports bars. Mr. Ryder, I know I can deliver what you need. And I think you know it too. If you didn't, we would not be into our third after-dinner drink."

"You must have taken a marketing course somewhere, because you just sized up the situation. Our six-month season—and that includes a pre-season and play-offs—starts in February. We've got a little more than three months to build the team, but we have to start now. Dad, what do you think?" Sam Senior, spry for mid-80s, had paid attention to the preceding and he liked it all.

"If the young lady says she can, then she will. And if she's wants it, I say let's roll the dice with her. And we'll make her a good offer." Hud added his good-natured humor.

"You guys better make her an offer she can't refuse. You'll be sorry if you don't." Alisha shook hands with Junior and Senior, and Junior concluded the first of what they all hoped would be many future talks.

"I'll call you next week Monday to line up all the details, but tell me this: do you want to be called Alisha or Electra?" That's an easy question I can answer.

"Please call me Alisha when I'm off the field. I did a major makeover awhile back, and Alisha is the female you're looking for. When I was a kid soccer player, everyone called me by my nickname, Kit. I haven't used it since then, but how does this sound? When I've got my game face on and am in scrimmage or competition, call me Kit.
The name Kit Kittner should fit nicely for team advertising and promotion."

"That's a good idea. Kit is catchy. Well then, let Dad and me be the first to congratulate all of us for recruiting Alisha Kittner, the rising star of the Austin Thoroughbreds. And let's call it an evening."

Hud was happy with the overall proceedings but voiced one concern on the drive back.

"You've got lots going on, and adding a football career adds to the load. Are you sure you can handle it?" A tingling tremor in the lightning brain confirmed her answer.
"I sure can. Just watch me."

Hud didn't need to watch Alisha the next day when she ran Tim's meeting, and it unfolded just as she had rehearsed. She surprised herself by knowing much of the technical aspects, and she pretended to know the rest, instructing Tim to handle the details of what she outlined. Then she let Tim summarize his marching orders.

"All this makes a lot of sense. Our sales guys can start promoting our Neuro-Knitter for neck and back injuries as soon as we get the advertising pieces done. And I understand what the first generation Cyber-Theater will do. It's an enhanced sensory simulation to accompany digital music or videos. I'll watch Holy's modified home entertainment center and talk with him for suggestions on how best to start. After all, we're building on what he came up with. And I can already see a lot of line extensions for next-generation equipment." "Good. And do you understand why you need to line up candidates for a new position reporting to you? It'll be the Director of Software Development to support the other hat you're wearing: AI Development. There's too much for one person to handle both hardware and software, but you're in charge overall. I want you to line up your three top candidates and I will make the final selection. Let's get this done by the end of the year."

"I understand how it fits your overall plan. It's impressive how you integrate all this technology. Maybe someday I'll understand how you do it." Alisha's smile masked her concern.

If Electra doesn't come back soon, no one's going to understand where we'll go unless I grow another brain. But at least we've got the next six months mapped out and I am definitely getting smarter, so it's time for me to go." Tim, I'm leaving for the airport. We'll follow up as usual." The lightning brain needed to decompress on the flight home. Although Alisha was pleased how well the meetings went, stress had fatigued her, making her realize once again how difficult it is to juggle all the activities Electra handled with aplomb. And she had just added a pro sports career to the mix. Well, I'm not going to worry my pretty head over it. Everything will fit. Something will come to me. Alisha tucked a pillow behind her head and let her mind wander, soon falling asleep.

A sudden jolt shook her awake. We must have hit an air pocket. But no, everyone else seems undisturbed. That wasn't an air pocket; that was a brain quake. And suddenly, she knew what caused it. The lightning brain has found a solution to "The Monty Hall Problem." It's so simple! It's come up with a solution based on an analogous argument.

Suppose we have 1000 doors and you pick Door 1. The probability is .001 that the car is behind Door 1. Now, the Host opens all doors but Door 1 and one other, stipulating that the car is behind one of the two unopened doors. The probability is still .001 that the car is behind Door 1, which means the probability is .999 that the car is behind the other unopened door. Would you switch? Of course! Doing so has a .999 probability of success.

Coming back to our three-door problem, we will always switch because the probability is 1/3 the car is behind Door 1 and 2/3 it is behind Door 2.

I shall write thorough answers to all the exam questions tomorrow morning and email them to Matt after my morning workout. Thank you, whatever gods may be, and thank you, lightning brain, for bringing Electra closer to me.

Alisha hustled through her morning run, not even bothering to eat breakfast or shower until she had emailed Matt. Then she cleaned up and celebrated by having pancakes, using the rest of the day to unpack from the trip and dote on her new car. When her cellphone chimed that evening, she expected to hear Matt's cheery voice, but the caller I.D. was Jennifer's. I'll bet she'll congratulate me for last weekend's soccer performance. That will be a happy conversation.

It wasn't. Jennifer shrieked Alisha's worst nightmare: "ROBIN COMMITTED SUICIDE!"

Chapter 10
October 2122

"The Triumphant Return"
Thread 1 Chapter 6

ALISHA STOOD FROZEN IN spacetime after terminating the call, trying to piece together Jennifer's garbled words. She had just found Robin floating in the bathtub, wrists slashed and overdosed on antidepressants. By an odd twist of fate, Matt was the EMT that responded to the emergency call, using CPR to restart a pulse, then bandaged both wrists and rushed Robin away. Jennifer knew nothing else.

Alisha's emotions were numb, her brain completely blank, not knowing what to do. Finally, a desperation thought flashed into her consciousness. Get to the clinic now. That one thought jolted her into zombie-like motion. She mechanically searched for her keys and jacket, then lurched out the kitchen door towards the garage. But something went terribly wrong. She lost her balance and clutched the railing to keep from tumbling down the steps. Suddenly a blinding flash, a thundering crash, and a paralyzing brain quake shook the lightning brain to its very core. Alisha screamed, clasping hands over ears, collapsing to her knees. Every sensation force multiplied a whirling confusion; she tried to stand but instead fell forward down the steps and into oblivion...

"Electra, wake up! You return now! Wake up!" Electra's cognitive persona staggered back to life. She groped to her feet, then turned to face whoever had called out. At the top of the steps stood a wraith-like mirage cloaked in a pristine glowing, flowing white robe. It was Indira, her mother, the muse of the lightning brain. Electra was spellbound, able only to gape at the apparition.

"My daughter, your lightning brain has summoned you back. Tonight's tragedy provided the final stimulus to cast away the remaining neural entanglement. After nine months of neural repairs, you are finally ready to retake command. You have returned, but are now different than before, perhaps even better in some ways, and must pick up not where you left off then, but where you are now. No time remains for me to explain further, for I must go, and so must you. When you awaken, you will know what you must do."

"Mother! Please, don't leave me this way. Help me."

"My child, I am. And I am always within you, always talking with you and ready to visit like tonight whenever I am summoned. My love is with you always." Electra fell forward on her knees; the smiling apparition faded; Electra lapsed once again into oblivion.

"Hey! I know you. Come on, Electra, get up. I've waited long enough for you to return." Electra pulled herself up, fully aware but this time saw nothing. And she didn't need to, for the voice she heard was in her head. It sounded like her voice, but it spoke with a different tone and perspective, from a different state of mind.

"Electra, call me Alisha! I know you better than you know me, but you'll soon figure everything out. And right this minute, we both know what to do: find Matt at your grandfather's clinic and do what we can for Robin. And use my name, not yours, the rest of tonight while talking to others. I'll explain on the way. Now get in the car and drive like lightning! And I hope you like our new car." Electra dashed into the garage.

"This is a Ford Mustang! Where's the old van?"

"I'll explain later. Now get in and go. You drive and I'll talk." Electra sped away, not even bothering to close the garage door, and focused on Alisha's words.

"You accidently poisoned yourself, and the T-Plague nearly killed you. The lightning brain had only one option left: conjure me until you were ready to return. I am a collection of neural states that are different from yours. I'm no dummy, but you are the extraordinary cognitive persona. My emotional persona is probably better than yours in some ways, and maybe worse in others. We'll figure that out as we get to know one another. And we both share the same physical persona, using it best according to what we need. We'll call it Kit when playing sports. Look, we have to keep this a secret; we'll make a game of it. If a shrink ever got his hands on us, he'd say we're crazy, suffering from a split personality, which according to his jargon is dissociative identity disorder. Keep driving and keep quiet. I have more to tell you. "The lightning brain figured out while repairing itself that I'm very useful, so it's making me the 'Keeper of the Emotional Persona,' and you the 'Keeper of the Cognitive.' And since I've brought Kit into the game, she'll be the 'Keeper of the Physical Persona.' And the lightning brain is the 'Keeper of the Keepers.' We get to use the lightning brain, controlling it indirectly. Let's consider ourselves a 'team of complements' that will serve us well. We are a macroscopic analogy of the wave-particle duality, a concept I've borrowed from one of your favorite subjects, physics.

"You and I can always talk to one another, and I'm Kit's primary contact. Indira is in the shadows, talking to you more than to me. When situations arise, we'll figure out which one should represent our team; you know, be our agent. Tonight's our first test. You take charge, but use my name. Let's not confuse 'mere mortals' more than we have to. By the way, I like that term you stuck them with long ago. You've got your work cut out tonight. Good luck with Matt and Robin. OK, we're here. I've given you enough background to get you started. Everything else is in our brain."

A calm clarity enveloped Electra as she skidded into a parking space. I know this place. I grew up here. It's where Grandfather practiced for over forty years. And I know what I must do. She streaked through the entryway to the reception desk.

"Hello, my name's Alisha Kittner. I'm a friend of Matt Fortier and a just-admitted accident victim, Robin Setdarova. I must see them now. Where are they?" The night-duty nurse glanced at the admittance sheet and found the name.

"They got here about two hours ago. You wait here; I'll check the emergency room. She might still there, but they might have moved her."

"I can't wait. I'll check for myself. Thank you." Alisha charged ahead but didn't find Robin.

"Where'd they take the suicide victim?" The on-duty EMT checked the clipboard.

"Matt took her to Examining Room Two."

Electra charged into the corridor, almost colliding with Jennifer.

"Alisha! Thank God you're here! Have you found Matt?"

"No, but we will. Follow me." Alisha dashed into Room Two, startling the one person standing.

"How is Robin?"

"We've done all we can, and we're still giving intravenous sodium bicarbonate to raise blood pH. That should help the drug overdose. But unless she comes out of the coma, it's a tough road. Let's go talk in the reception area." Matt led the way to a sitting area; traffic was light that night; they were the only people present.

"Robin really did a number on herself. Jennifer, since she moved in with you a couple of days ago, did you see any signs she was so depressed?"

"No. I've known for a couple of months how disturbed she is, but I didn't notice major changes." Matt shook his head.

"She hid it well. I noticed careless grooming and clothing recently, but she cycles through that when school's bothering her." Jennifer pulled a sealed envelope from her purse.

"I found this letter addressed to Alisha. Maybe it'll explain what happened." She handed it to Alisha, who spoke hurriedly.

"We are her best friends, so I'll read it out loud. I wonder how long ago she wrote it." She tore open the envelope; the sloppy scrawl confirmed it had been written in her last desperate hours.

"Dear Alisha,

I'm sorry I've been such a big disappointment. I've tried, but I just don't have the courage to deal with my worst enemy. The enemy is me.

I've made a mess of a music career; of school; of relationships. But I'll clean everything up by leaving now.

Tell Matt I'm sorry I couldn't be what he was looking for. Tell Carter I'm sorry for being a bad student. Tell Mariah and Zoe I'm sorry for being jealous. Tell Jennifer I'm sorry for not repaying her kindness.

You did everything possible for me. I'm sorry I couldn't handle life. I always loved you more than you loved me. I'm sorry I couldn't become your Christi…"

They stared at one another, saying nothing until Alisha spoke.

"Did either of you know Robin felt this way? I had no idea she was this disturbed." Matt shook his head no, saying nothing, but Jennifer did.

"When Robin moved in this week, she said she needed some distance from you and Matt to work things out. She made it sound like she was getting a handle on her problems. I'm stunned by this letter. What are we going to do?" They all sat in stony silence until Alisha spoke.

"Matt, where's your laptop? I need to borrow it. And then, I need everyone to leave me alone with Robin." Matt looked at Jennifer, who returned his puzzled look. Then they looked at Alisha, whose expression was deadly serious.

"Let me get if for you…"

Alisha had Robin all to herself. She turned on Matt's computer and found two songs she would loop endlessly. She would play them until Robin came out of the dark corners where she was trapped. Alisha would do for Robin what Alice Bickerwith had done for her; she would stay at her side, talking and holding and rubbing her, doing anything to generate sensations that could penetrate into Robin's darkness and bring her back. And Alisha would do so until Robin comes back or until she herself collapses from exhaustion. Call it the final bullet, the last flare, the Hail Mary Pass. This was Alisha's final, desperate act.

She cranked up the volume and started a non-stop stream-of-consciousness chatter accompanied by the relentless driving beat of her chosen retro-rock music. She told stories from the past, from the present, and from what the future might hold if only Robin would come back. She rubbed her hair, her hands. She patted her cheeks and jostled her shoulders. Then she pulled her out of bed, cradling her head and leading her in dance across the room as she sang to the music. First one song from the Doors:

"You know the day destroys the night, night divides the day, Try to run, try to hide, break on through to the other side, break on through to the other side, break on through to the other side yeah…" And then the other from Thelma Houston:

"Don't leave me this way! I can't survive, can't stay alive without your love, Oh baby don't leave me this way…

Baby! My heart is full of love and desire for you! Now come on down and do what you gotta do! You started this fire down in my soul!

Now can't you see it's burning out of control…"

Alisha repeated these steps endlessly. The lightning brain was in an obsessive-compulsive state. The nurses looking in shook their heads, thinking Alisha was out of control but dared not interfere. They couldn't believe anyone could carry on like that for so long.

But after three hours, Alisha had gone beyond her limit; she was spent physically and emotionally. She placed Robin for the last time onto the bed and held her with both arms. Still no response. Alisha was on her knees, her head pressed between Robin's breasts. She whispered over and over, "Don't leave me this way…" She was about to enter a dreamless sleep when she felt a hand rub the back of her head. She opened her eyes to meet those of Robin who whispered,

"I won't leave you if you won't leave me."

Alisha pushed the call button before collapsing. The nurse, accompanied by Matt and Jennifer, rushed in to see a role reversal they could scarcely believe; Robin was whispering to her best friend, stroking her hair. Electra was asleep, but when she awakens it would be a triumphant return. Both Electra and Robin had come back.

Chapter 11
November 2122

"The Team of Complements"
Thread 1 Chapter 7

"YOU AND I ARE living proof of Nietzsche's conjecture found in Twilight of the Idols: 'That which does not kill you makes you stronger.' Please let me explain." Electra wanted to tell Alisha what she had just learned from using her Brain Probe to scan the lightning brain. "By all means, please do. Now that you're back and have taken care of the 'Robin Crisis,' I expect you'll tell me all sorts of things." "The T-Plague nearly killed me, but thanks to you and the lightning brain, I came back, and I came back stronger in some aspects. And the episode confirms that the Buddhist monk's answer—'Perhaps'—to questions asked for even the bleakest events may apply. Thanks to the T-Plague, our cognitive persona is more powerful and you are now a permanent facet of the lightning brain. I am the keeper for our Cognitive Persona, you for our Emotional Persona, and we share equally our Physical Persona.

"I don't have any pre-T-Plague scans for comparison, but I infer from the images that our brain now has more connections and centers of control. When it is in the Electra State, a specific set of neural centers emerges, but when it switches to the Alisha State, a different set switches on. Psychiatrists call this Dissociative Identity Disorder—aka split personality—but I prefer to call it our 'Team of Complements' advantage. And judging from pattern density, as well as how quickly and thoroughly I understand whatever I focus on, my cognitive persona is even smarter than before. And now that you have permanently emerged, I suspect your empathy is better than what I had before. What do you think?"

"Perhaps so. Our friends think my personality differs from yours, and I do think differently. I'm more spontaneous and intuitive. And I have other interests and insights. I read poetry and literature rather than science and math. Let me give you some examples of my insights into emotions and feelings." She heard Electra's tiny giggle before continuing.

"I can explain why you never did a lightning brain scan before. Your rational persona didn't think it was necessary, but actually your emotional persona wanted to preserve the mystery of the unknown. We all do. Think about the Virginia Woolf quote: 'The future is dark, which is the best thing the future can be, I think.' Think how boring life would be if we already knew the outcomes for everything. And here's another to consider.

"While you were on sabbatical, I went through our keepsake box and re-read final letters written by Indira, Jason, and one other family member, Satish Ramanujan, Indira's father. And I found an unopened letter from Hollywood addressed to Indira. Why have you never opened it?"

"It would serve no purpose, so I tucked it away."

"Well, then you should have thrown it away instead. But you didn't because your emotional persona wanted to preserve a bit of mystery. But we should open it sometime; it might reveal additional mysteries."

"You are correct and we shall. I'm counting on you to make my empathy even stronger. And perhaps you are that part of us that contains artistic ability. Su told me I played the piano like a lumberjack trudging through a forest. I whacked the keys but didn't feel the music. I thought I was a good actress, but your performance while I was away could win an Oscar. And have you thought about writing poetry?"

"Yes, and sometime I'll tell you more about what I've come up with. But let's switch topics back to you. I've watched several original Star Trek episodes dealing with devices like your Brain Probe. In one, a device lets people live in an illusionary world; in another, it neutralizes thoughts or emotions. I'm sure you've thought of those and other Brain Probe applications as well. But you better be careful of the ethical implications."

"I am. The Brain Probe has many uses, but only I will control them, and I will rely on your ethical guidance." Electra was about to say more but a call came in on the cellphone, interrupting the conversation. She recognized the caller ID.

"Professor Ravenhill is calling, so I'll take it. You and I can talk more whenever we like. I'm so happy to be back. Now I have someone who understands me." Electra picked up after the third chime.

"Kittner, Ravenhill here. How are you?"

"Doing well, thank you, and I hope you are too."

"Yes, yes. I'm always fine. Listen, something just came up that might be right in your wheelhouse. You're smarter than you let on, so let me explain if you can listen now."

"Yes, this is a good time."

"One of the visiting professors invited me to help get his papers published by writing a section outlining how his findings might lead to practical applications. He's a tenured high-energy physicist at University of Texas in Austin, and he babbled about the latest mind experiments being done to explain how black holes use duality and entanglement to create the Universe. It has something to do with entropy being encapsulated in the digital information stored on a black hole's surface. He said it's all covered by the Holographic Principle. I nodded like I knew, but I don't. Do you know what he's talking about?" Electra felt a minor neural surge as the lightning brain shifted gears before she replied.

"Yes. Holography creates a 3-D image using 2-D data. So by analogy, a black hole creates the Universe using all the information stored on its boundary."

"I'll make you a deal. I thought of you because you apply in your research pieces of quantum mechanics to explain DNA folding, resulting in faster DNA sequencing techniques, and reversible nanologic computer chips resulting in Quantum Computer's lower energy consumption. Read the draft of his paper and explain the Quantum Physics background to me, then think of some practical applications.

I'll make sure both of us are mentioned when it's published, and I'll fast-track your assistant professorship appointment. And we'll get grant money from the government so you can do work here at GWU as well as UT in Austin. The DOD likes to fund practical quantum research spin-offs."

"That's an offer I can't refuse. We have a deal. I'll start working on the paper as soon as you send it. And thanks for all you've done for me."

"Yes, yes. And thank you for helping me get my name in another paper. You really know more than you let on. And that's all to the good for you and for me." Alisha offered a final comment after Professor Ravenhill disconnected.

"I like how you take Ravenhill's feelings into consideration. You're no longer using him. You've made the relationship win-win. Please carry on…"

Electra immersed herself in quantum physics after downloading the paper while Alisha thought more about poetry. My empathy might now match that of Indira. No wonder I understand her poems so well. She wrote them in the Modern Metaphysical or Lyrical style. Unlike post-modern poems that are mostly free verse, hers have a meter and rhyming scheme people like. And they don't deliberately obscure what they're trying to say. The one called "Return of the Queen" captures how I feel, now that Electra is back. It speaks to me:

The Queen and all her powers,

I sense return to me.

This grace-filled gift my Spirits lift,

Awaken now and see.

I have weathered the worst winter,

That obscured the path once known.

It struck with a fury sufficient to bury,

And left me all alone.

But resplendent Spring the Queen it brings,

There's prescience in the air

My senses shout she is about,

The signs are everywhere.

I see her in the duet

Of swiftly soaring swooping songbirds,

This aerial ballet.

The nest they build with family filled,
Which offspring can't repay.
I feel her in the emergent emerald stems
Of dew-jeweled garden flowers,
Now bursting forth I find.
Roots nurtured firmly in the soil,
Their essence intertwined.
I hear her in the gentle burbling
Of fresh fragrant breezes,
Rustling softly through the trees.
She'll teach she'll guide she has not died!
She's not yet done with me.
But will the Queen and all she means,
Dwell evermore in me?
Or will she fade like late Autumn shade,
The ghost of memory?
The answer lies unknown for now,
Locked in a vault of mind.
To which I say on rare Spring day,
Winter stay far behind!

I won't even try to match Indira's style, but I have an idea for a different approach. I'll show Electra, but not now. Both of us have other things to do.

Alisha's phone call surprised Mariah next evening.

"I'm so happy you're calling. Zoe told me what happened to Robin. It's good she's staying with you until she centers herself."

"The worst is behind her, and Jennifer Conklin will help me help her make a comeback. I've been talking to Carter, so I know you and he are doing OK. But I'm calling not about work, but about play. How about going to Atlantic City? We can have a great time dancing and gambling. And I'll drive us in my Mustang."

"It'll be a first for me. I've been to casinos, but never to Atlantic City. I'd like to go."

"Wonderful! We'll make a weekend of it. I'll pick you up at your office right after work on Friday and we'll come back Sunday morning. And be sure to pack a couple of dancing outfits. I'll make reservations right now."

Electra had written up by Thursday evening what Professor Ravenhill wanted but made a final reading Friday afternoon, commenting to herself before emailing it. I commend today's high-energy physicists for their perseverance, but I think Einstein's quote says it all: "The Mathematics of Quantum Theory is elegant but its Physics is dismal." They've lost sight of the Explosion Principle, which says you can prove anything from false assumptions. And though their mind experiments are thought-provoking, actual experimental results all too often look like smudges on graphs, indistinguishable from experimental error. But I'm happy to assist because I can learn about the latest developments. I'll look for ways to use them in my projects. I'm satisfied with my week's accomplishments, so it's time for Alisha to take charge.

Rain slowed traffic as Alisha drove on I-95 towards the Atlantic City Turnpike intersection near Philadelphia, but that didn't dampen Mariah's enthusiasm.

"Monopoly was my favorite childhood board game. The original board spaces are named after Atlantic City streets and places. I liked Park Place and Boardwalk best of all. Did you have any favorites?" "For some reason, I liked Marvin Gardens. And I also liked the high-priced real estate places like Boardwalk. We'll check it out tonight. I made reservations at Caesar's Palace, which is on the Boardwalk." Mariah switched subjects because of all the trucks standing still.

"You're doing the driving, but I've been watching traffic. There seems to be a problem in the autonomous trucking lane. It's all backed up. What does your GPS say?"

"It's reporting a network issue. We're going to arrive after midnight, so I'm going to call the casino so they hold our room." Alisha tried but was unable to connect.

"The communications network is down. Why don't you tune in a radio station that's covering the failure?" Mariah did so and the duo heard about intermittent outages centered on East Coast metropolitan areas, prompting Mariah to ask another question.

"Carter told me there's growing concern about coordinated network security attacks in Cyberspace. Do you think this might be one of them?"

"Could be. And before I picked you up, my bank's online system was down. We'll hear more tomorrow after the network engineers reboot the systems. But there's no need to worry. Cyberspace glitches add to our adventure, forcing us to rough it without all the Cyberspace conveniences. And we have a three-quarters tank of gas, so please find us some music and let's talk about strutting our stuff on the Boardwalk."

There was no truck traffic heading towards Atlantic City, but electrical power outages reduced driving speed. It was almost two a.m. when Alisha drove into a darkened Atlantic City. As they approached the casino, Mariah asked a question for which Alisha guessed an answer.

"Casinos' lights are blazing like torches because they have backup power systems. No one, not even Cyberterrorists, can turn the lights out on gambling. Let's do this; we'll park in front and have an attendant take us and our luggage to the front desk. You can wait there after I register us, and I'll go back to park in the garage." Alisha's plans started unraveling as soon as she tried to register.

"I'm sorry, but we reassigned your room because you weren't here by midnight."

"I tried calling, but the cellular networks were down. Are they working now?"

"I don't know about cellular, but our computer and wi-fi networks are. Let me find another casino where you can stay." Twenty minutes later they were set.

"We have a room for you at the Golden Nugget, which is also on the Boardwalk. Of course, it's not as nice as Caesar's, but it would be my second choice." Alisha gave thanks and a twenty-dollar bill to the clerk, and then asked an attendant to roll their bags back to the car.

The adventure continued from there.

"Where'd my car go?" One of the attendants pointed to a sign.

"Your car's been towed. You can park here for only five minutes." Mariah's expression and shrill voice registered a complaint.

"Why didn't you come in and tell us?" Alisha shushed her and spoke.

"Please give me the address and phone number of the towing company, and get us a taxi to the Golden Nugget." Mariah calmed down on the ride five minutes later when Alisha explained the scheme.

"Casinos and towing companies probably have a sweetheart deal. Casinos condone towing after five minutes as long as towing companies scratch casinos' backs. Hey, don't be so glum. Our adventure is becoming more intriguing each step along the way."

It was nearly 4 a.m. by the time the bellhop tucked the girls into their room. By this time, Mariah was an unhappy camper.
"I'm too tired to be hungry. What are we going to do?"

"Why don't you shower and go to bed. I'm going to surf the Net and then retrieve my car."
"Huh? You won't get any sleep."

"Hey, we're at a casino. We're not supposed to sleep. We're supposed to party. And I'm simply taking care of party preparations."

"OK, if you say so." Mariah headed to the shower, and Alisha switched to Electra before heading to Cyberspace.

I shall now test some of my network security tools. I shall penetrate vehicle registration networks and adjust appropriate databases. And I shall also explore Garden State Towing's complaint files, and then plant bogus information. And I know Alisha will be a most convincing actress.

Mariah had been asleep for an hour by the time Alisha entered the towing company's office. The bored night shift clerk barely budged when she strode to the counter.

"Good morning, sir. My name is Alisha Kittner. According to your nametag, I'm speaking with Mr. Fahrquhar. Am I correct?"
"Yeah. Go on, but make it quick. I'm about to punch out."

"You towed my car from Caesar's Casino at 2 a.m. this morning. I've come to reclaim it. It's a red Mustang. I'll write down the license plate number for you."

"Let me check the records... Yeah, we did. It'll cost you two hundred dollars to claim it now, and another hundred dollars for each additional day."

"Mr. Fahrquhar, do yourself and your boss a favor. Please check the ownership records stored in the state of Maryland's registered vehicle database."

"Why should I do that?"

"It will save your and your boss's jobs. My father-in-law is the governor of Maryland. He and I are in my car. And he and New Jersey's governor are personal friends. I strongly recommend you forget about the tow and the two hundred dollars. If you don't, my father-in-law will have the New Jersey governor sic someone from his staff on you. I know all towing companies have a list of complaints bordering on criminal violations. So, you have a choice. You can do what I ask, or you can let me talk to your boss. And if I do not drive away in twenty minutes, I guarantee this episode will end badly for the two of you."

"Maybe the network's still down and I can't check the databases." "It's up, and I did a quick background check before coming here. Believe me, if your governor's staff digs deeper, Garden State Towing will hang you and your boss for uncovering problems you could have kept hidden. So, go ahead and logon, but make it quick. I'm tired and getting angry. And you don't want to make me or my father-in-law angry."

Fahrquhar grunted, then logged on using the computer on the counter. As he typed away, Alisha discreetly observed his eyes. Eyes are windows into a person's thoughts. Mr. Fahrquhar's not very happy. Alisha was on her way fifteen minutes later.

When they awoke at ten, Mariah's mood brightened when Alisha recounted how she drove back a winner. After sampling the brunch buffet, they strolled the Boardwalk, though the weather wasn't as cheery as Mariah's outlook.

"What's that answer you like to use when you turn a lemon into lemonade? I think it applies to yesterday's troubles. Our luck has turned so let's gamble."

"Indira often used 'Perhaps,' and it definitely applies to last night.

What game would you like to play?"

"I've learned how to play Texas Hold'em by watching The World Series of Poker. It's the most popular poker game. Do you know the rules?"

"No. What are they?"

"Every player is dealt two cards face down—these are called 'Hole Cards.' Then there's a round of betting where players can Check, Bet or Fold. Checking means you defer betting in that round until someone else bets. When all the betting has finished three shared cards are dealt face up in the middle of the table. This is called the Flop. There's another round of betting, and then another shared card called the Turn is added face up to the Flop. Another round of betting takes place, and then a final shared card called the River is added to the Flop. Players who haven't folded form their best five-card poker hand using their two Hole Cards and the five face-up cards in the middle."

"So, how does the game end?"

"In one of two ways. When the remaining players turn over their Hole Cards, the player with the best hand wins. This is called the showdown. The other happens when someone bets enough so everyone else folds. This is how most hands end."

"I can see why it's so popular. In addition to Hole Card luck, you have to compute odds, read opponents' body language, and bluff when necessary. I would imagine casinos set table limits for minimum bets and maximum raises. What are the betting strategies?" Mariah laughed before answering.

"I guess it's to win more than you lose, but the commentators sometimes talk about tactics, giving them catchy names like 'Stop and Go' or 'Bluff Catcher.' They say 'Check-Raise' is easy for beginners because it's basic but powerful. You're supposed to check if the action is on you, and raise if someone bets after you."

"I'm impressed. You know a lot, so let's do this. We can go back to our room and surf the Net for additional betting guidelines. Then we'll dress up and go play at a beginner's table. We'll act like we don't know much, and I'll ask if it's OK for us to play the same Hole Cards." Mariah was all in, so the two hustled back to the room and then to a table after a quick Internet check and change of clothes. Electra whispered a warning to Alisha just before they sat down. I'll compute the odds, and you can read body language and bluff for us. But don't get carried away and attract attention because you're winning. Attract attention because you look good. Alisha took the advice. Three hours later, she and Mariah took three hundred dollars in chips to the cashier's cage. As Alisha counted the money, Mariah applauded their success.

"We're winners, thanks to you. You certainly have a knack for knowing what to do. That classic country and western song says it all. You knew when to hold or when to fold."

"Nonsense. It was a team effort. And we should try our luck by going to Las Vegas. I'm told the comparison is like a cellphone to a rotary dial. But I like being here, so what would you like to do next?"

"Let's grab a drink and go dancing."

"I'm in; let's find a trendy place."

The pair sat close enough to a TV monitor to hear a news summary of yesterday's outages.

"Network failures have now been rectified, but it took eight hours for software engineers to reboot affected, or should I say infected power, transport, and communications hardware and software systems. There are no official statements, but some analysts believe yesterday's events add to growing evidence that the problems may have been caused by a coordinated viral attack in Cyberspace. We hope to know more in the coming days..." Alisha remained unruffled.

"Let's not worry. We weathered the worst, and we retrieved my car, and we won at the casino. You and I are on a roll."

"You're right. I bet our luck will hold, so we'll hold off worrying until Monday."

Alisha smiled but added a half-joking note of caution." Perhaps, but let's always be careful."

Chapter 12
November 2122

"Cambrian Explosion Redux"
Thread 2 Chapter 2

ELECTRA'S RETURN WAS LIKE a Cambrian Explosion, bringing her back to life and creating the Electra-Alisha duo, a singular source of many diverse pursuits. Each encapsulated a collection of lightning brain states that made the whole greater than the sum of the individuals. Alisha's empathy approached that of Indira's, and Electra's I.Q. had increased. They were the best of friends, helping one another and playing a hidden identity game, the secret of which no one would ever detect.

"First things first, Alisha. I have learned much during my sabbatical, so please let me put into perspective how my glimpse into mortality has changed us."

"Please do so. And I'd bet I already know some of the emotional changes, for that's my specialty. But go ahead; I marvel at how well you articulate, theorize, categorize, and compute. But those are your specialties. I'm listening."

"Before the T-Plague got me, sometimes I would get impatient when people couldn't grasp what I was teaching them. But when the T-Plague hit, I learned how difficult learning can be. Concepts that had been clear looked like blurred words viewed through a fine-mesh screen. I can see now, but I shall always be patient when teaching others.

"And now I know why we should live each day like it's our last. Tomorrow is promised to no one. So I promise to appreciate each day by living in the moment, and thanks to you, by fully enjoying right now.

"And, I understand even better why we live in the present and plan for the future, wasting little time dwelling in the past. Going forward, I shall implement what I call a 'punctuated approach to living. Let me explain what this means when dealing with relationships.

"As we go through life, we accumulate relationships with family, friends, lovers, etc. Relationships change gradually because humans don't handle sudden disruptions very well. So, we continue muddling along in relationships after life-changing events, rather than facing the truth. Though it might be painful, it's better in the long run to let partners know when it's time to end a relationship. That way, we're being honest with ourselves and with others." Alisha agreed, adding her insight.

"Yes, that may very well be the best approach. But when you take it, make sure you are not throwing away too many emotional links that soften you, that make you understand better the human condition, and that connect you with the best feelings of the past. shall remind you from time to time. That's one of my jobs."

"You're good at it; you know the right balance. Let me offer one additional point. Anyone can change if they want to, but it takes motivation and hard work. Wishful thinking won't work. Look at us. If it weren't for all your efforts and the repairs the lightning brain made, I wouldn't be here today. For all of us, life is a constant change that forces us to move on. If we don't take command and move ourselves ahead, we get left behind." Alisha interrupted before Electra could say another word.

"Let me recite one of Indira's later poems called Course Correction that expresses your sentiments:

Don't labor to replace the greats of the past,
The errand of fools who refuse to see.
That in now-ploughed terrain there lies no mystery,
It's a thin veneer layer that will never last.
Instead, boldly go for what has not yet been said,
Look outside, then in for a coming to be.
Unite reason and passion for a vision you see,
Care not for a judgment, it's your word instead.
Long after you're gone, there'll be time to decide,
Whether the words that you said had the power to stay.
Revealing directions that sail away,

And place you among those never to die.

"I like how you recite Mother's poems. You put more feeling into them than I do. And you're a better actress. You have the artistic ability I lack. Make sure you read me your poetry sometime."

"I will when the time is right. But I think it's time we plug you back into our collective lifestyle." Electra agreed and said so.

"Let's make a go of it…"

The top priority was to put their personal life back in order. Alisha would decide how to rearrange their close circle of friends, aka the Full House, to help Robin recover. She knew Robin's schizophrenia would last a lifetime, but Robin could still lead a productive life if the Electra-Alisha duo were always close. However, her dependence must diminish over time, or she would fritter her life away.

Robin moved in with Alisha soon after she was released from the clinic, and it coincided with Zoe's move back to her apartment. She had been living with Alisha ever since Jared's agents had brutalized her, and she was now ready to live on her own once again. Matt, Carter, and Mariah helped make light work of both moves, and the fellows knew what additional changes would accommodate Robin. Matt's intimate relationship is over, as is Carter's with Alisha, and though Alisha believed Robin wouldn't object if she escalated her Mariah relationship, that would remain a strictly private affair.

Electra made a startling adjustment in how she would view the world and vice versa. I no longer have to worry about being a genetic freak. Not even medical experts can uncover my secret. I can blame the T-Plague if anyone ever detects genetic defects or abnormal neural patterns. I'm in the clear; no need to fear.

There were no pressing issues, so Alisha tinkered for a couple of days with the new car, deciding what modifications to add. She liked fast, stylish cars to match her tony wardrobe and extroverted personality. And only she knew that Electra had a streak of vanity in her otherwise understated, conservative manner. Only she knew how much fun Electra had tagging along on all of Alisha's social adventures.

Electra busied herself updating the "Electra Chronicles" notebooks. How valuable they are! If the lightning brain ever short-circuits again, our hard copy backup will be better than ever.

One afternoon while working at home, she added a diagram of her adjusted worldview philosophy that illustrates which of her three personas—physical, emotional, and cognitive—handles different components of philosophy and learning. (Every branch of learning has a philosophical foundation.) The components are arranged vertically from most qualitative to most quantitative. The horizontal timeline arrows indicate how advanced or "modern" they are.

She was pleased with the results, so she rewarded herself with a peanut butter crackers and Coke break, then returned to her workstation to print out the diagram. Electra's Worldview Philosophy 5000 Buddha Gold Age Jesus Muham Ren. Enlightenment Modernity+ 2100 BCE CE

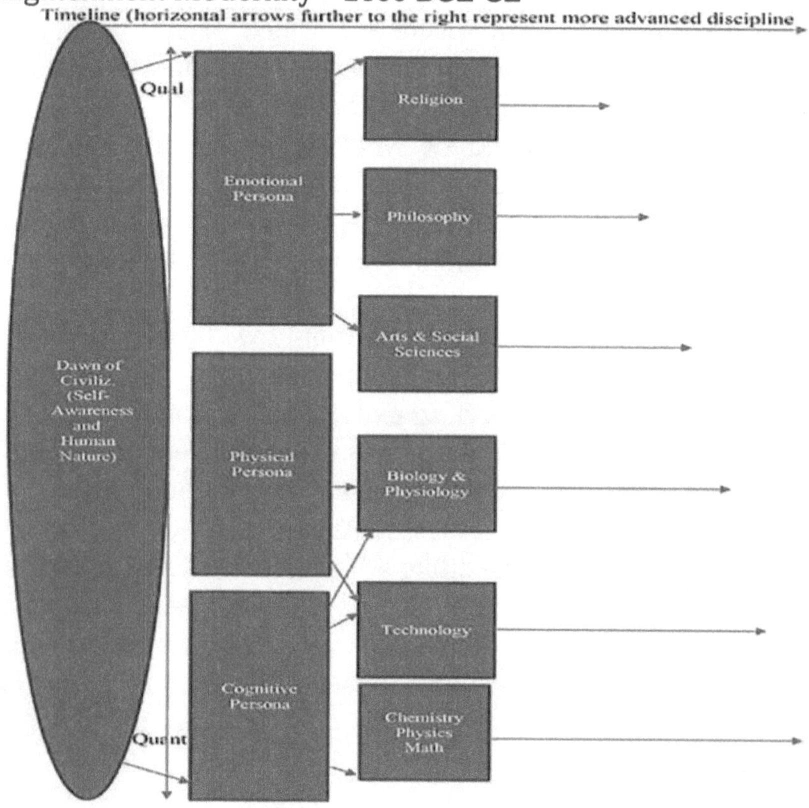

I LIKE WHAT I see. I can use it to explain how my R&D projects might generate blowback from different types of people. I'll bullet point the big takeaways to provide more clarity. Ten minutes later she had what she wanted.

Major Conclusions

- Each person views the world through three Personas: Emotional, Physical, and Cognitive
- Vertical Axis goes from "Qualitative/Faith" to "Quantitative/Reason".
- Note how the connections between Personas and Philosophy/Learning Components are consistent with the "Faith versus Reason" conflict. (Faith/Religion associated closely with Emotions Sci./Tech associated closely with Reason.
- Note how the Horizontal Timeline shows that "Reason" is more advanced and sophisticated, and attuned to Modernity than "Faith".
- Biotech and AI Projects are ahead of Society's collective Emotional PersonaExpect "pushback" against too much Tech.

Progress is too fast from significant segments of Society

I'm satisfied with these diagrams. They do a nice job organizing how I connect philosophy to faith versus reason, and how my projects interact with society. When I show them to my teams, what shall I say? Fifteen minutes later, she printed out her discussion guide notes and read them to herself:

Discussion Guide Notes

I'VE STUDIED THESE TOPICS extensively and can offer the following explanation. The starting point is human awareness, which marks the dawn of civilization. And my three-persona framework helps organize subjects. And it makes sense to arrange them according to a "Faith versus Reason" or "Qualitative versus Quantitative axis. Religion is furthest towards Qualitative or Faith; Math or Science is furthest toward Quantitative or Reason. The time axis lets me diagram how advanced or sophisticated that area has become.

I think the materialist philosophy makes the most sense for explaining Nature. The mind and the brain are one and the same; just different facets of the same thing. Everything in Nature is determined by atoms. The quote from the Greek philosopher Democritus nailed it: nothing exists but atoms and the void. And Man's understanding of Nature and Reality depends on how advanced are Science and Technology.

Man is a social animal who likes to tell stories; Evolution and DNA ultimately define what Man is. Our fundamental beliefs are captured in our DNA and evolve slowly over time. Man's predispositions for Religion, for Ethics, for Understanding, and for Social Interaction are somehow stored in our DNA; they become less relevant as our Science and Technology provide more accurate explanations for how the Universe works. And we should never lose sight that there are "Laws of Human Nature" we must obey, though they aren't as unyielding as Newton's Equations. In the long run, I don't think Religion will ever win the battle against Human Nature when the two are in opposition.

Many of Man's beliefs are relics from antiquity. Old civilizations had primitive technology. Cave men believed in gods and spirits because they had no other means of explaining the world around them. Man is afraid of being alone in an indifferent Universe, so he clings to outmoded beliefs because Human Nature evolves so slowly compared to the pace of scientific discovery and technological change.

And finally, we must realize that the human brain has structural limitations. Life's three big questions—Does God exist? How did the Universe start? How did Life begin?—might forever be inaccessible.

I certainly can't prove the above, and I will never argue with anyone who has different views. Everyone is free to choose. But I can say my worldview provides a consistent framework in all I want to think and do, and it centers me. It also centers my R&D projects. And if something better comes along that can be observed and explained heuristically, I can always change the way I look at things. Any questions or comments?

AND THAT'S IT. OR as they say in show biz: that's a wrap. It's time for an afternoon workout. Alisha, take it away.

Electra enjoyed physical exercise almost as much as Alisha, but Alisha was better equipped to lead it, especially considering the CoNFL career she had recently added to the mix. Alisha liked to "think on the run," using an endorphin-powered runner's high to expand on whatever the topic. Today's topic was most timely.

Electra's cognitive abilities exceed my wildest expectations. She thrives on handling the heavy-duty rational thinking, and that lets me handle emotional issues and fitness training. Our teamwork is paying off already; look how I convinced the local Co-NFL franchise —the DC Ambassadors—to let me practice with them. And I didn't lie; I just didn't tell them everything. And I'm not going to show them everything either. I'm learning their drills and improving my skills. All this thanks to Matt. I networked through him, and the Ambassadors believe my story: practicing with them will help me prepare for next year's soccer season, even though there is no soccer for me next year. That and my charm opened up the locker room door.

That evening, Electra finished compiling a list of current issues. Every December, as part of planning for the new year, she used it to justify or modify existing projects or to select new challenges. She was sitting at her workstation, studying the document she had just printed.

The Big Issues Facing:

Socio-Political Arena:
- National/Global Economic Collapse
- Bad Government
- Defusing Terrorism
- Sustainable Lifestyles
- Expanding Human Potential
- Planning for an Advanced Civilization

Science-Technology Arena:
- Conquering Diseases (Genetic Engineering, Biotechnology)
- Evolution (Origin of Life, DNA)
- Transhumanism (Nanotechnology and Computer Chips)

- Artificial Intelligence (Computer Hardware and Software)
- The Singularity (Machine Self-Awareness)
- Global Pandemics (Uncontrollable T-Plague, etc.)
- Big Data and Forecasting Cyberspace Security

"Dead" Arenas:

- Religion (Existence of God)
- Philosophy (Post-Modern Branches, Linguistic Extensions)
- Population Growth, Global Warming
- High Energy Physics (Unified Field Theory, Time Reversal, String Theory)
- Cosmology (Multi-Verses, Big Bang, Big Crunch)
- Aliens
- Planetary Risks (Climate Change, Super Volcanoes, Meteor Strike)

ELECTRA DIDN'T INVENT ITEMS on the list; they were well documented by any number of private or public sector think tanks and subject matter experts. All she did was use her superior brain to classify and consider. Though all issues stir the imagination, many are "dead ends"for the lightning brain,not worth her time or effort. Some had been "studied to extinction"by respected scholars or scientists so there was nothing new to discover, while others were inaccessible to the human brain: not even the lightning brain could conduct additional work based on verifiable observation or reasoning. It could only speculate, based on nothing but opinion, belief, or faith. This kind of work makes for spirited debate but leads nowhere. Electra prefers to work in emerging areas where she can make big contributions.

She already had two ongoing activities that fit in the Socio-Political Arena: Bad Governments (keeping Jared under control), Defusing Terrorism (keeping Isilabad sidelined), and two in the Science Technology Arena: Global Pandemics (T-Plague), Artificial Intelligence (Neuro-devices). If she had more resources—a dream team of researchers who could keep up with her—she would work on more projects. Alas, that team was still only a dream, so her project list was set. But she would continue searching for challenges that her current project teams could handle.

Just then, Robin glided in and plunked herself down on the sofa, so Electra directed full attention to her.

"Your timing is perfect. I'm all set to begin your next therapy session. But before we start, I'm grabbing a Coke. How about you?"

"Nope, I'm good like this. Go get yours so we can get going." Although she was rebounding from the depths of her suicide attempt a month ago, Robin needed Electra's dedicated support. She was like a delicate flower that bloomed when nurtured by a green-thumbed gardener, but might wither otherwise. Electra had pulled her out of psychiatric counseling, replacing the bungling therapist and his drugs with herself and mood-elevating exercise. And it was working.

Electra returned with her Coke and sat in the chair next to the sofa, kidding about her Freudian role. Robin kidded right back.

"Who's my shrink? I'm confused. Should I call you Doctor Electra or Doctor Alisha?"

"It's your choice. What do you think?" Robin frowned briefly, then answered.

"Well, for starters, I think you sound just like a shrink: you answered a question by asking me a question. But no matter, I think I know why you asked us to call you Alisha right after you got sick. You weren't your old self. Well, I think you've recovered, but you're sort of different now. You used to have sharp edges: often aloof and enigmatic, tinged with melancholy, and never enjoying things as much as you should. You worried too much. You always held back, but would unload on people when they needed it. But when you started getting better, your close friends noticed you were getting sort of nicer: smiling and enjoying little things more and worrying less. No one knew you liked to party like you do now. I never knew you liked to dance that much and could hold so much alcohol. And your make-up and wardrobe makeover are big changes. It's like you're taking on some of Christi's personality."

"All of what you say is true except for the part about Christi. I left Christi in the past long ago; the changes you see are because of me. So, let's do this: call me Alisha for the lighter side of life; call me Electra for the more serious side. I'll tell my other friends to do the same. Does that sound OK?"

"It does, and for my therapy sessions, I'll call you Electra."

"Excellent choice. I'll cut right to the chase and tell you what I think will be good for you. We aren't going to worry about your schizophrenia; it's hard-wired in your brain. Lots of talented people have mental illnesses. We'll get you to where you can live a productive life by dealing with it. Think you can live with that?"

"Since you bailed me out of the alternative, I have no choice, so I'll live with it."

"Good. Here's how we'll start: we'll use exercise instead of drugs to handle mood swings; we'll have you keep busy on goal-oriented tasks so you focus on right now; and you'll live with me for as long as you want. As you get stronger emotionally, you'll need me less, but don't put a date on that happening. And don't agonize over sex.

Just do what feels right. You're old enough and have had enough experience to follow your feelings, which means your Matt relationship morphs to being friends. So far, so good?" Robin nodded.

"Now, I'd like you to answer a couple of questions. Why are you jealous of Mariah and Zoe? They had no idea." Robin squirmed out an answer.

"I'm sorry, but I was jealous because they were coming between us."

"Robin, no one's ever going to come between us. My love for you— whether or not it includes sex—is unconditional. There are many ways a person can love, and I love you in a different way than I loved Christi. And stop saying you're sorry. There's no need to apologize to anyone." I'd better say something to lighten this up. "Why else do you suppose I put up with all your high-maintenance shit? And by the way, you're the one who taught me to say Holy Shit." That cracked Robin up.

"Christi would approve of that addition to your vocabulary." Electra had just a little more to say.

"I have three recommendations. First, don't go back to school until you can concentrate better. The drugs you were taking clouded your thinking. Second, pick only one task—other than exercise—to keep you busy. Make it your part-time accounting for HUD. And third, Alisha and you will start going out to either sensual pleasures cafes or dance clubs. She knows the safe places. What do you choose for this coming Saturday?"

"I can handle a sensual pleasures cafe."

"Excellent choice. Alisha will drive you in her new car. And the two of you need to go shopping sometime. It's a real mood elevator, and you're ready for a makeover to match."

Thanksgiving marks the start of the year-end Holiday Season, a time when most people cycle down for year-end. But Electra had other plans. She had a list of things to do and places to go; item number one was a phone call to Carter. He should be at his office, so I'll call that number first. Carter answered promptly.

"Good morning, Carter, it's Electra. I trust you had a good weekend."

"I'm fine. How are you?" If it's Electra and not Alisha, I'd better be extra sharp.

"Doing fine, and so is Robin. How about you?"

"Well, my Vette is running OK, but not much else. I spent Saturday at the office arguing with Mariah. Let me fill you in on the latest regarding our Brain Trust. And please, keep this confidential. I know you always do, but I just wanted to remind both of us. You'll hear an edited version when Jared gives his Thanksgiving Eve address to the nation. Here goes.

"You already know that Jared is again president, and Angus is his VP. Jared still relies on him for advice, but that is quickly coming to an end. He's beginning to go his own way and has told Angus to disband our Brain Trust. What do you think of that?"

"That's always been a possibility. I guess he's feeling full of himself now that he's recovered from the T-Plague."

"That appears to be the case. And frankly, I've had my hands full keeping Mariah from being too outspoken. She and I have serious disagreements about Jared's programs, even when Angus pushes through our modified versions. Many of Jared's programs make sense economically, and the public likes his feisty and harsh tone. But she's dead set against them; she thinks his programs are heavy-handed and walk all over people's rights and freedoms. She went ballistic when Angus announced Jared's latest Pillars Program—a school-based security watch program. She's afraid it'll be like the Hitler Youth Program."

"Can't you and Zoe modify the tone in the public relations press releases?"

"We used to, but Zoe resigned, and Jared's harder to please now, and even if we do, he wants Angus to push for harsher implementation. Other than himself, I think Jared's listening only to some of the more extreme Guardian Party lieutenants. Do you have any suggestions?"

"I'd have to think about this since I've been out of the loop this year. I think the best course of action is to see where and how fast Jared's leading. Do you think he'll push for a shooting war?" "According to Angus, he's currently OK with the diplomatic approach. But if something bad happens that inflames public sentiment, he'll push for war. And listen to this, the Secretary of Defense can't explain the source of increased hacking into CIA systems. If that ever gets linked to China, Jared will want to pull the trigger. He still thinks China was behind the poisoning plot. And here's one more piece of bad news: Conklin's telling us there might be a risk from a new strain of T-Plague virus, but nothing's been said officially. If that ever gets linked to China and Isilabad, game over for them. You should talk with Conklin."

"I will. Robin and I are going there for Thanksgiving next week. Hey, what are you doing for Thanksgiving?"

"Zoe and Matt invited me for dinner. They invited Mariah, too, but she already has an invitation from someone she met at one of your dance clubs. You know I'm not a big gossip, but I thought you should know that Zoe and Matt are becoming co-friends. Do you think Robin will be upset?"

"I'm not sure. She's getting a better handle on her feelings and realizes Matt needs to go his own way. In time, she'll want to be friends with everyone again, but I wouldn't push the issue."

"I have a meeting to run, so I've gotta go. Maybe we can get together between Thanksgiving and Christmas. Let's keep in touch."

Wow, talk about an interesting phone call! I learned a lot, and it'll give me more to think about, but there's nothing I need or can do for him or Angus. Time to turn to the next item on my list: a December vacation in Austin.

Austin would be the place for the Electra-Alisha duo to visit in December. Sam Ryder wants Alisha to meet the coach and some of the T-Bred team. That would be a time for Alisha to shine. She would showcase enough of her talents to make everyone happy.

Electra would interview Tim's neuro-software candidates. Perhaps they could provide insight into what Cybergard is up to.

Now that Electra's cognitive abilities were fully restored, she was ready to explore the link between Brian Ritz and Cybergard. Why does Cybergard want to steal my software? What are they planning to do with it? Who are they working with?" Although Electra was a skilled hacker, she expected Cybergard systems would be difficult to penetrate because they were a renowned leader in security software. And she was right; their systems were incredibly advanced, using state-of-the-art recognition systems and graphical user interfaces. Passwords were replaced by finger print, voice or retinal recognition, and its GUI's used multiple sensory inputs. In order to infiltrate their network, she would need to attack their operating system using a beyond state-of-the-art suite of Internet security software tools. This is just the kind of challenge I've been looking for. Electra focused all her cognitive skills on building the tools, just like Alisha focused most of her emotional energy on Robin or a budding Co-NFL career. Electra was fully engaged and enjoying all the moments to their fullest. Alisha was teaching her how.

"They're here, Jenn. I'll get the door. Now remember: ask Robin to help you set the table so I can chat privately with Alisha."

"I will. And I'll join you in the living room in a minute." Jennifer already knew Russell wanted Alisha's ideas for what he should do. Jennifer loved how he never stopped searching for actions to take that could protect his personal or professional world. His dedication had saved the Conklin family several times in the last couple of years, one time at home when rogue covert Guardian Party agents ambushed him and an undercover associate—Moses Solstein—in front of his wife and daughter, and another time at his NIH office when a government inquisition derailed his career. But both times, just like the Phoenix, he had risen from the ashes back to prominence.

Jennifer loved Robin and Alisha like daughters, even providing a place for Robin to stay when needing shelter that not even Alisha could give. They had been Christi's best friends; sharing Thanksgiving with them would be a pleasant remembrance of her only daughter, and she wanted to celebrate all the reasons to be thankful.

Russell opened the door, reached out to hug Robin first, then shepherded both ladies into the living room after putting their coats in the hall closet.

"Happy Thanksgiving! You both look wonderful. And Robin, it's wonderful to see you smiling again." Not only had her smile returned, but also her sense of humor.

"I owe you and Jennifer an apology for the mess I left in the bathroom last time I was here. I've promised Alisha never to do that again. And I'll make the same promise to you and Jennifer. I'm handling my emotional issues much better now." Jennifer bustled in, adding her greetings."

"Happy Thanksgiving to all! How nice and happy you both look. Alisha's got you back on track."

"Alisha's been taking good care of me, just like you always do." Jennifer directed the conversation for Russell.

"Why don't you tell me more in the kitchen. I need your help setting the table and dishing up." After the two left, Russell changed the subject to less pleasant business.

"Have you kept in touch with Carter?"

"Yes. I called him last week, and he told me about all the Brain Trust commotion. He asked me if I had any ideas, and I said I didn't. I said I'd need to think about the situation. I listened to Jared's speech last night, and it didn't tell me anything beyond what Carter did. But how about you? What's going on with T-Plague vaccines?"

"We're supposed to get improved vaccines by early January, but I'm worried they won't treat the new strain. Vaccines targeting the new strain won't be available until the middle of next year, so until then we'll have to be aggressive with our containment procedures. It's odd, but the epicenter of the new strain appears to be Washington. I wonder if that's connected to what you did—uh—what we did last Christmas. Whatever the connection, that doesn't matter. What matters is being able to treat it." Alisha shrugged her shoulders. Of course there's a connection, but I'll act dumb.

"I can't imagine why there'd be a connection. Maybe the new strain got carried here accidentally. If it ever gets linked to China or Isilabad, Carter says Jared will start a shooting war." Jennifer called for Russell to carve the turkey.

"Well, let's hope there's no connection. Come on, you can watch me carve. And no more grim talk. It's a day to be thankful…"

Robin was in complete agreement and said so on the drive home. "What a great dinner. The Conklins are wonderful hosts. And yes, I do have lots to be thankful for, especially to have you and Jennifer. She's my second mother. No wonder Christi had such a happy life. And Jennifer's so careful with my feelings. She wouldn't tell me too much about Matt and Zoe dating for fear it might upset me, but now she knows I can handle it. Hey, I have an idea. Why don't we have an early Christmas dinner with the Full House before we spend Christmas in Austin? I need to thank everyone for their friendship.

And don't worry. I'm sworn to secrecy about you playing for the Austin T-Breds."

"Good idea. I'll get a restaurant recommendation from Mariah and set it up for the evening before our flight to Austin. That'll be Thursday, December 10, two weeks from today. Their calendars are open." An odd question popped into Robin's brain. "How do you always know so many details? How do you know that date, and that everyone'll be available?"

"It's in my Electra DNA. She's built to plan and sweat the details."

"You know, Alisha is much more fun to be with than Electra. But I love them both just the same."

All of them made good use of the next two weeks. Robin caught up on her accounting work; Electra hacked partway into Cybergard and used her workouts for "hack-breaks." Alisha arranged a private room Christmas dinner party at a restaurant located not far from Anandale, Virginia. Mariah had been there last summer and said the surrounding area was lovely, providing hiking trails and recreational areas adjacent to Lake Accotnik. Electra made sure all packing was completed by noon the day before departure. Only the weather refused to cooperate, but the gently falling snow would not pose much of a problem. Alisha left early so she and Robin would be the first at the restaurant. Matt and Zoe arrived together, closely followed by Carter; Mariah arrived fifteen minutes later. Alisha was happy to be the hostess and proposed the first toast of the evening, even though she was working on her third drink.

"Happy Holidays to the Full House, and thanks for being such good friends. All of you have helped Robin come back from a bad place, and she has something to say." Robin blushed, but one deep breath steeled her nerves.

"I want to apologize to each of you for not being as nice to you as you have been to me. But I'm getting a better handle on my condition and want to be a better friend in the future. Matt, I apologize for not being what you were looking for in a partner, and I hope Zoe is better for you than I was. Carter, you were a great tutor; maybe I'll be a better student when I go back to school. And Mariah, I'm sorry I was jealous of you. I know it's silly of me to think that Alisha will like me less if she goes out dancing with you. I promise to be a nicer person to all of you." Alisha knew she needed to lighten the topic.

"Don't worry, Robin. If you aren't nicer to all of us, I'll leave you in Texas with the cactus and sagebrush. And I'll drink to that!" It was Carter's turn to poke fun.

"It looks to me like Alisha will toast everything tonight. We all learned this year how well she holds liquor, but she better slow down or Robin will have to drive her home." Alisha heeded Carter's warning, and by the time the dinner party ended everyone had a warm place in their hearts for their close circle of friends.

Mariah's drive home would not be long or difficult. The snow-covered rural roads had little traffic at 10 p.m. and she knew the route. She could handle the curves and hills and might not have to drive too much below the speed limit. And driving slower gave her time to think about what Robin had said.

I like Robin, and maybe Alisha will rekindle our relationship when Robin is stronger. But if not, all of us can still be friends, maybe even going to the dance clubs where I've met some nice fellows and ladies.

Mariah's reverie was shattered by the glare of headlights and a crunching jolt from a speeding pickup truck that smashed into the rear just as her car was rounding a right-hand curve onto a downhill stretch of road. The tires lost traction and her car spun out of control, going faster and faster down the hill and flipping sideways as it rolled down the embankment, coming to rest upside down and bursting into flames seconds after landing near a clump of trees. The truck slowed down so the occupant in the passenger seat could see what remained. Afterwards, he turned to the driver and said, "I don't think she'll have anything bad to say anymore." The truck sped up and drove on.

Chapter 13
December 2122

"Christmas Present Redux"
Thread 2 Chapter 3

ELECTRA ENJOYED THE EXCLUSIVITY and convenience of flying on Hud's leased jet, and today those perks were even better because of the widespread airline ticketing system glitch. I'll ask Carter about transportation system problems. Maybe he's aware of an emerging pattern. But I'd better ask Robin what's bothering her.

"You've flown lots of times. Why are you so pensive?"

"I don't think our Austin people know I tried to commit suicide. What if someone asks? I feel embarrassed telling them what I did. What should I do?"

"Don't bring it up, and if someone does, just tell them you did but are on the mend."

"I'm worried they'll think I'm crazy. Why are you looking at me like that?"

"Because you are crazy! You're psychotic, but not to worry. Everyone has flaws. Some of the most brilliant people, people who have done great things, are crazy. And it's not the fact that you're crazy that matters. What matters is how you deal with it. You're beginning to learn, and you're going to be fine. You're one of the nicest people I know. People will like you even more because of your idiosyncrasies. Just keep coming to my therapy sessions, and we'll make you even nicer." Robin smiled, kidding right back.

"That was pretty good. I guess I do resemble your remarks. Alisha would commend your empathy." Each drifted into their private thoughts, and Electra's touched a place she hadn't gone before. It's the people with serious challenges or deficits who are often the nicest. I've known so many talented or privileged people who are SOBs. They're so wrapped up in themselves or in guarding what they have. Jesus said, "When you have nothing, you are free." We should all remember those words.

Su and Kameyo ran the shuttle service today, giving them time to brief Electra on new vaccines, and since Su was driving, Kameyo talked first as she summarized progress.

"So that's why we're getting good results by using my autophagy concepts, but it's taking longer than we estimated. We are using our nine-month rollout timetable. Dr. Chou, is there anything else you'd like to add?"

"Yes. You are the brains behind our accomplishments." Though most pleased, Kameyo only nodded, saying nothing. Electra's empathy detected feelings hidden inside the silence. Her veil of reserve is just like her mentor's, hardly ever revealing emotions. I sense they're becoming friends. Perhaps Su has found someone to care about. If so, Indira would be pleased.

Su walked the visitors to a conference room where Tim, Hud, and his chief accountant were waiting. The accountant took Robin under his wing so she could review bookkeeping duties while Hud and Tim briefed Electra for final candidate interviews. Electra reminded herself before Hud started. I'll use my Electra personality today. It's Time to be all business.

"Tim's rounded up his three best picks and will be happy whichever one you choose."

"You're assuming that I'll like one of them. I hope you're right because time is slipping by. I have reviewed their resumes, so you can bring the first one in and tell them the interview will last up to an hour. And tell him to call me Electra."

As Hud and Tim filed out, Electra summarized to herself what she needed. I want someone smart enough to understand my proprietary programming methods and then uses them to code the solutions I'll provide. I won't expect any of the candidates to understand my theory or my multi-threaded recursive structures that incorporate modal logic. It's beyond state-of-the-art. But I'll provide a glimpse how my proprietary programming language extends the latest Lisp and Python releases and runs on parallel independent processing servers to achieve unmatched computational speed. And my small footprint code running on cloud-based Quantum Computers enhanced with nano-engineered reversible logic gates brings "Big Data" number crunching down to Earth.

Electra began each interview by asking the candidate about Cybergard. Candidate number one—a female West Coast computer science major working for a Cybergard competitor—told her that Cybergard has a reputation for pushing beyond the envelope of ethical business behavior, causing competitors to do likewise. She didn't personally know anyone who worked there, but it was known they recruited talent worldwide. Electra liked the first candidate but thought she was too theoretical, not enough hands-on experience.

The second candidate was a male counterpart of the first. Nice enough, but too much into theory instead of practice. Though he had never heard of Brian Ritz, he did know one of Cybergard's developers, a fellow from the Middle East. Electra recorded the name for later reference.

The third candidate, a well-groomed, slender black male from Houston, was different from the first two. Kwame Chyril's academic credentials weren't prefixed by PhD, and Electra detected an intensity in his eyes and expression, even though he avoided direct eye contact. He didn't know about Cybergard, wasn't much of a talker, but when she asked him about multi-threaded recursive programming, he came to life, talking and diagramming the concepts in startling detail. Electra knew exactly what he was. Kwame is autistic! No wonder he understands these techniques. He loves their precision and has the ability to focus focus focus. This is my guy.

She interrupted him in mid-sentence.

"You've shown me all I need to know. You're the guy I'm looking for. Look, I think you're autistic and you've learned to deal with it. And frankly,I think it makes you better than most programmers. I need you to learn my programming methods and then apply them to code the solution to application specifications and overall design I'll provide. Your title is Director—Software Development. You'll report to Tim Godfrey and will work on neuro-device and security software development. Tim told me you are a renowned hacker of "the Dark Web." He's a pretty good at hacking too, and he says you're not into criminal activity. When you and I develop our suite of Internet security tools, I expect you to tap into the Dark Web and the Deep Web. I assume you know all about both."

"Yes. The Deep Web is the collection of all sites on the Web that aren't reachable by a search engine. I'm pretty good navigating there too. The Dark Web is a collection of thousands of websites that use anonymity tools like Tor and I2P to hide their IP address and identity. While it's most famously been used for black market drug sales and child pornography, the Dark Web also enables anonymous whistleblowing and protects users from surveillance and censorship. I know a lot about it."

"Outstanding. Here's what we'll do next. I'll take you to Tim. He'll talk about salary and start date. Once you've started, Tim will give you the specs for neuro-device development, and I'll give you the specs for security tools. I live in DC but visit here periodically. I know you'll like working for us. There's enough for you to make a career here if that's what you decide. Now, let's get you to Tim, and then I'll tell Mr.
Holler that you're our guy. Do you have any questions for me?"
"What should I call you?"

"Sometimes, you can call me Electra, other times, call me Alisha. I'll let you know which to use."

Hud and his dad, Holy, treated all the ladies to dinner that night at their home. There was only one restriction for the conversation: work was off limits. The men listened while the ladies chattered about the approaching Holidays. Su asked about holiday plans.

"Since we're talking about fun stuff, please call me Alisha. Robin and I want to take in some Christmas concerts and a New Year's Eve party. And perhaps Kameo can show Robin the UT campus and surroundings."

Su directed the conversation to New Year's resolutions, and Hud smiled when she asked Alisha what is in store. He had been sworn to secrecy, so only he and Robin knew the magnitude of what was behind her nonchalant reply.

"Oh, I'm starting a new job. Hud's friend Sam Ryder made me an offer I can't refuse."

Bo Rudman had waited long enough to coach a Co-NFL football franchise. A sports management major and standout tight end at Houston's Rice University, he would have been a shoo-in for the NFC draft and subsequent career in coaching or sports management had it not been for a torn ACL that sidelined his athletic career, but he climbed up the coaching ladder anyway, jumping to the Co-NFL when he recognized its potential. Now fifty, in his coaching prime and ready to unveil his innovative Wide-V offense, he and Sam Ryder were waiting to meet the quarterback they would build their team around. Bo's pupils dilated when Alisha sailed in.

"Bo, shake hands with Alisha Kittner. We're rolling the dice for you to make her the star of our team. Both you and Alisha know what we're trying do here, and we're expecting both of you to make it so. Alisha's been training on her own for a couple of months and should be ready for your pre-season conditioning and training sessions."

"Howdy, Alisha. Good to meet you. Looks like she's got those alert eyes of a pilot or quarterback,and the agility of a cat. Nice grip and nice height, but sort of thin. I hope she's tougher than she looks. I don't want to get her injured by taking too many direct hits.

"Hello Coach,and hello Mr. Ryder. I've been practicing with the DC Ambassadors and I think you'll be pleased with my progress." Sam chuckled.

"Very clever to train with our competition, and I bet you didn't let on you signed with us."

"No sir, and I didn't strut my stuff. But maybe I can do some of that today for you and Coach. And before I do, let me give you my assessment. Fair enough?"Bo liked what his ears and eyes were telling him."Go right ahead."

"I'm quicker than the competition and can throw accurate short to medium passes, but don't expect me to throw long. I don't have the grip or arm strength for it,but my combination of running and passing should be effective. And I expect Coach's Wide-V offense will give us half-back passing options. I can't make one-handed receptions, but my leaping ability makes up for it." Bo looked at Sam —actually Sam Junior—then replied.

"If we can execute what you just said, we'll have a great first season."

Sam replied, "Let me mention how good our Texas-wide PR and advertising are going. We've piggybacked on Alisha's recent soccer fame, transitioning the message so fans will want to follow how she adjusts to a new sport on a new team using a new offense." "How about we have Alisha suit up and meet our players. Then we'll run through some assessment drills so our assistant coaches and trainers know what we've got. Players and coaches know what we're gonna do, and we've recruited the talent to showcase Alisha's skills. She'll be walking into a locker room that expects her to be special, to be their leader. So she doesn't need to hold back. Alisha, you need to make them confident you can deliver."

"Right Coach. Just watch me. And please call me Kit when I put my game face on." She said more to herself. This is what I've been waiting for,and for you to see. I'll make the most for Indira and Electra and me. I've memorized the players' positions and profiles, so I'll know them when I see them. Time to put my game face on and focus. And keep some gears in reserve. Don't show everything yet.

All heads turned to Alisha as she entered the unisex locker room. She smiled as Bo introduced her.

"OK team, listen up! This here's Alisha Kittner. You all know why she's here and why you're here. So I'll let you get acquainted. By the way, she says to call her Kit when she puts on her game face." After Bo left, Alisha asked everyone to gather around her. Then she called out the names of each player, giving each their appropriate kudos.

"Coach and franchise owners expect a lot from us, and they're giving all of us an opportunity of a lifetime sports career. I'll show you I've got the goods to deliver, but we must be a high-performance team. And I'll do my best to be the leader you expect. Let's build our teamwork starting right now. I'm sure

Coach will have lots more to tell us, but let me add one thing he might overlook. I like to work hard and play hard. We're going to have fun while winning." She stopped talking when an assistant coach told them to suit up and come to the indoor practice field.

Bo reviewed what he expected, though he didn't mention he'd relax the training regimen as long as the team meets his goals. Ten minutes later, the team began group assessment drills, starting with speed and quickness.

Alisha reminded herself. Keep a couple of gears in reserve, but show enough to impress. Bo and Sam watched from the sidelines. Twenty minutes later, Sam asked a question for which he already knew the answer.

"What do you think?"

"She's lightning quick. Able to change speed and direction. That should help her avoid too many direct hits. And judging from how she can leap, she's got explosive strength. Let's have them go through some lateral drills, then I want to see her throwing mechanics when stationary and when rolling left or right."Bo blew his whistle thirty minutes later.

"OK, team, listen up. I want everyone to watch Alisha on her rollouts." One of the assistant coaches set up a rollout play for Alisha and a receiver, running it several times to the left, then to the right. All the players—especially the receivers—stared in disbelief. Bo finally broke the pregnant pause.

"That is something special. Our quarterback is ambidextrous. She can throw with either arm. And the spiral is tight and accurate. She's the first two-armed female passer in the Co-NFL. We're gonna surprise opposing defenses, so let's keep it under wraps until the season starts. We won't show this in preseason games. OK, that's it for this morning. This afternoon, get with the assistants in the training room." Bo kept Alisha back for just a minute.

"You've got the goods. You're gonna love running my Wide-V offense. My big worry is keeping you from taking too many hard hits. Have you thought about this?"

"Yes, sir. I'm counting on quickness, but you'll see I'm tougher than I look. And I can count on my team to watch my back. You've recruited a great mix of male and female talent. And can I make one comment?"

"Go right ahead."

"I'll train hard and work hard, but I hope you and Sam will cut me some slack when off the field." Bo grinned knowingly.

"Say no more! We Texans do the same. So, welcome again to T-Bred football."

Electra decided to steer clear of Hud and business activities because she had already delegated follow-up activities, so she spent her time hacking into Cybergard and let Alisha handle football. Each was happy as could be with the progress they were making, and Hud marked the start of the company's Holiday break by hosting a surprise winter solstice dinner at a popular Mexican restaurant for his people.

Of course, Alisha commanded the spotlight at the start, and after joking that her new coach was almost as motivating as Hud, she let the spotlight move to others. She observed how different everyone was in social settings compared to work. Everyone except for Hud's father, Holy. It must be his wisdom that comes only from the experiences life brings. No wonder Electra, for all her brilliance, is still growing emotionally, and so am I. And the bond between Robin and Holy continues to grow. She was sitting next to him, immersed in a private conversation. Hud interrupted everyone to deliver a brief welcome.

"Here we are, December 21st, the winter solstice. It's the shortest day of the year, but going forward, the days get longer, and now that we've got the right people in the right seats, the days will be filled by us doing great things. Now go grab a plate and fill'er up at the buffet table. Then come on back and keep on talking. Ladies, you lead the way." That meant Su and Kameyo, followed by Robin and Alisha. Tim and Kwame would then precede Holy, and Hud would end the procession.

The festive lighting added to the pleasant sights and sounds of other guests socializing. Alisha nudged Robin, pointing out Hud's attention to his father.

"Hud's lucky. Holies are in excellent health. He looks like he could make it to at least one hundred."

"I hope so. Maybe by then I'll be a stronger person." Tim tapped Alisha's shoulder and she joined his discussion with Kwame. Kameyo asked Robin a question and Su followed with another; all were totally engaged in the moment, unaware of Hud's calamity.

"Dad, hold your plate while I dish up… Dad… did you hear me?… Dad… look at me and say something!" Holy dropped his plate onto the buffet table, turning to face Hud. His lips moved but no words came out, the left side of his face strangely drooping. Although he tried to steady himself, he was too weak to keep from collapsing into Hud, who clutched him for dear life and yelled, "I need some help here! We've got a problem!"

Like everyone nearby in line, Robin's attention leaped towards Hud, and then she leaped into action.

"Someone call 911!"Then she dashed to Holy's side. She knew enough from Matt's EMT training to recognize symptoms. Holy was in the midst of a stroke.

The only thing she and Hud could do until the EMT's arrived was keep Holy comfortable. She screamed, "Make a path!" as she dragged a chair for Hud to place him on, and then made sure he was breathing, talking with him and trying to keep him focused.

The EMT's, arriving in a matter of minutes, immediately diagnosed a stroke.

"OK, we'll take over now. We'll get him to Seton Medical Center ASAP." Robin spoke three words only.

"I'm coming too." The lead EMT was about to shoulder her aside but backed down when he saw the insane look in her eyes.

"OK, you can help. Let's go." Robin cleared a path as the EMT's rushed Holy away.

It was after midnight when a doctor called to Hud and Alisha, who were in the waiting area.

"You must be Hudson Haller. I'm the on-duty physician, Doctor Gonzales. Your father has had a stroke. The brain scan indicates it's an ischemic stroke caused by a blood clot, not hemorrhagic, caused by an aneurysm. We treated it with clot-busters that might minimize damage, and we'll need to keep him here for a day to evaluate him. He's conscious and he seems to understand when we talk to him, but his speech is slurred. Why don't you talk to him, and then come back tomorrow afternoon? We'll know more then. And we'll need you to sign the medical forms at the nurses' station before you leave." The doctor walked them to Holy's private room, then left.

And there was Holy, semi-reclined in bed, Robin sitting attentively at his side. She stood when they came in, explaining Holy's condition, then stepping back for Hud and Alisha.

"Dad, you gave us a good scare. The doctor says you should rest up so we can get you home soon. We'll come back tomorrow." Holy understood everything about the situation and was able to speak clearly, but very slowly.

"OK, Son. Don't fret." Hud grabbed Holy's head and kissed him, trying to control his emotions.

"We'll let you rest so we can get you home soon. Come on, ladies. Time to go." Those were the wrong words to say.

All the while, Alisha had been glancing at Robin. Robin had become a different person. Her demeanor and voice projected confidence, assertiveness.

"You and Alisha go. I'm staying right here. I'll watch over Mr. Holy. We'll see you tomorrow." Hud glanced at Alisha as she tugged his sleeve towards the door. They left, saying nothing else. Robin turned full attention to her patient.

"OK, Mr. Holy, let's get you a sip of water, then it's lower the bed and lights out. I'll be right here if you need anything." She had already dragged a reclining chair into his room, and that's where she would sleep.

But she couldn't sleep; her brain raced feverishly, excited because she finally knew what she wanted to do. I remember how I felt when I took care of Electra after the crash. I loved being her caregiver. It gave me purpose; it made me strong. I shall become Mr. Holy's caregiver. It'll help me deal with my psychosis. She dozed fitfully, always checking her patient who slept through the night. At seven, she checked the schedule at the nurses' station; it was time to get her patient up for breakfast and for morning tests.

"Good morning, Mr. Holy. How are you feeling?" He was still weak, especially on his left side, and spoke slowly, but his thinking was sharp as ever.

"I feel better than being in a stampede."

"Good. Let's get you to the bathroom. I'll get you shaved and bathed."

"I can't let you do that. You're a young woman. You won't know what to do."

"Don't worry. I'll figure it out." She used the wheelchair to whisk him around, and Holy's light frame, along with her surprising grit, made it easy to get him in and out of the chair. He was looking good when the nurse brought in breakfast for two.

Robin faded into the background, keeping out of the nurse's way, but was ready to come to the foreground at a moment's notice. When the doctor took him for evaluation, she piloted the wheelchair, observing and taking notes. On the way back to the room, she asked for home set-up and caregiver instructions that would work for stroke victims. She sat next to Holy, studying the details while Holy had lunch and listened to a cable business channel. A while later, he motioned for Robin to sit closer, where each could see and hear the other better.

"You've been a lifesaver for me. And the next time you visit, you'll see me looking a lot better." Robin didn't smile.

"Mr. Holy, I'm not going anywhere. You need a live-in caregiver, and that's what I'm going to be."

"Young lady, that's mighty generous, but I can't let you do that. You've got your whole life ahead of you. Don't waste your time with someone old like me. You've got better things to do." Robin said nothing. Instead, she showed him her wrists.

"What happened? Did you break a milk bottle or something? Those are bad cuts." Tears came to Robin's eyes, but her voice was strong as could be.

"I tried to kill myself a couple of months ago. I was in a bad place mentally. Mr. Holy, I have a mental illness that I'm learning to deal with. I want to take care of you. I took care of Electra a couple of years ago when she was in a bad accident, and it made me feel good, made me strong. I can help you get better physically; you can help me get better mentally. Please, don't send me away." Holy had more to say.

"I'm gonna die in at most ten years. You gotta plan for doing something after I'm gone."

"By that time I'll be a stronger, different person. And right now, I want just one day at a time." Robin had nothing left to say, her tears spoke the rest.

"Come here and let me give you a Texas-sized hug. Together, we'll make a formidable team." She followed her patient's orders, and then resumed her caregiving role.

"Mr. Holy, I'll be right back. I want to borrow a laptop from the nurses. I have stuff to prepare for our homecoming. And just tell everyone you decided to hire me to be your caregiver. Please don't tell anyone I tried to kill myself."

"Don't you worry. No one will ever figure out our game, not even that clever Electra or Alisha or whatever name she likes to use." That brought out Robin's smile.

"She's more than clever, but she keeps secrets better than anyone. We can trust her with anything. She's the one who helped me come back from the dead."

There was little Hud or Alisha needed to do when they visited that afternoon. Robin had already convinced the doctor that another day's stay would pave the way for a smoother return home, and she announced that Holy had hired her to be his live-in caregiver. Then she handed Hud a list of items to buy and a sketch of how she wanted Holy's suite of rooms rearranged. Hud was about to offer a suggestion, but decided not to interfere with what the patient and caregiver had devised. Alisha followed Hud's lead and left well enough alone because all was now in Robin's capable hands and heart.

Holy's Christmas Eve homecoming was the best present, for it brought tidings of comfort and joy to everyone in Hud's extended family. Christmas Eve and Christmas Day were low-key; there were Christmas presents only for Hud's children, Seth and Sally. Robin demanded a subdued post-Christmas week so she could adjust Holy's surroundings and routine to his immediate needs, including in-home visits from rehabilitation therapists.

Alisha attended T-Bred training sessions until Thursday, New Year's Eve. Coach Rudman gave the team a long weekend break, telling them to "party smart" on New Year's Eve and be ready to resume workouts on Monday. Alisha pounced on his advice, inviting her teammates to join her at a sports bar's New Year's Eve party she had scoped out. Several who knew Austin agreed with her choice and took her up on the offer, all agreeing to travel in one van. When Alisha called to reserve places for herself and five teammates— three guys and two gals-the hostess knew about the new team and treated her like a sports celebrity, offering to introduce them when they arrived. Alisha was looking forward to a great time and thought it might be good for Robin to come along. Holy insisted, joking that he and Hud wanted to troll for other ladies that night, so she reluctantly agreed.

Alisha was going to buy a party dress for the occasion, but changed her mind, picking more informal sports-oriented attire. She decided it would present a better image for a sports crowd. Hud gave them fatherly advice as Alisha pulled Robin towards the van." Remember to act ladylike and professional. You represent the Thoroughbreds as well as yourself."

Alisha was already in high spirits when she picked up her people.

"Hello team, and hooray for a New Year's Eve where we don't have to trudge through the snow. Let's go party. We've been working out plenty hard enough to earn a break." Her teammates needed no coaxing; they were a good-natured, high-energy group, and Alisha figured it wouldn't hurt to remind everyone they needed to be upstanding ambassadors for their new team.

"The hostess will introduce us, so let's be on our best behavior to recruit new fans. I'm gonna stick with local brews, and why don't you do the same? Let's not get carried away before the season starts. And we'll leave at twelve-thirty."

The hostess recognized Alisha immediately when she checked in. "You're Kit Kittner, our new T-Bred quarterback. Thanks for picking us for New Year's Eve. We would have promoted your being here if we had known further in advance. I'll make an announcement and then, if you don't mind, why don't you say hi to your fans?" Alisha had no idea the team's advertising had been so effective so quickly; she huddled with her players and told them she'd introduce each one. Sam Ryder's recruiting checklist had included poise, personality, and appearance as well as athleticism; Alisha knew the party-goers would like the T-Bred total package.

The hostess spoke on the PA system once the music volume had been dialed down.

"Good evening, party people! I would like you to meet Kit Kittner, quarterback of our new team, the Austin T-Breds. She and some of her players are taking a training break and will be with us tonight. Kit, say hi to your new fans." Amazing. Well, I'll just act naturally and make

the most of it. Kit grabbed the mike and strode into the limelight as if she were born to be a star.

"Hi, everyone! I'm Kit Kittner, quarterback of your newest team: the Austin Thoroughbreds. We want to thank you for supporting us, and we'll do our best to give you an exciting season. Let me introduce my teammates who are with me tonight…"Alisha rattled off their names, surprising each by providing a snappy sketch.

The crowd was genuinely pleased that Kit and her team were here; fans welcomed them to Austin and asked pertinent questions wherever they mingled. Kit dived into the festivities, dancing until the crowd toasted in the new year. Then she assembled the team to wave goodbye to the crowd. And that's when four rowdies crashed the party. The hostess recognized trouble brewing as soon as they staggered in, so she called 911, hoping a squad car would arrive before a brawl erupted. No such luck. It started when the rowdies collided with Kit's team, one of them picking poor Robin as their dance partner.

"Hey, doll, let me take you to the dance floor, and then let me take you to my car." The guy was about to wrap his arms around her, but Kit stepped between them.

"She's with me, not you. Why don't you leave her alone?" The jerk turned to one of his buddies.

"Hey Davey, we got a couple of queers here. Come help me put them straight." Then he turned to slug Kit, but she was too quick. She smashed him over the head with a beer mug, crashing him to the floor, then tackled his partner, who came at her. She came out on top, smashing his nose with a palm fist, and was about to do it again when the police dragged her off. They quickly restored order by hustling Kit and the four rowdies out the door and off to the local police station. The crowd buzz sounded as if it were coming from a football stadium.

Kit's team collected Robin, then asked the hostess where they'd take their quarterback. Once they knew where to go, Robin made one phone call. A sleepy voice answered on the fifth ring.

"Hud, this is Robin. Alisha's been arrested. You call your friend Sam and get her out of jail right now! We'll meet you there."

Well, this is something new for the New Year. I've never been booked before. I don't think Electra would be pleased. We'll just have to find a way out of this. Unbeknownst to Alisha, Robin's phone call had connected. Hud had called Sam, who immediately called his PR person to help manage damage control. By the time the reporters got there, Robin had given Hud and Sam the complete story. The reporters went to work, talking first with team members who gave them the facts, and then told the reporters to get more background from Robin. Robin's tearful interview, heralding how Alisha had rescued her from suicide, became a source of personal triumph for herself and the T-Bred quarterback. The media recognized they had great local sports story and would play it for the next two days. Sam and Hud stood back, realizing what great publicity this would be.

The police sorted facts from fiction, released Alisha, and charged the rowdies with disorderly conduct. All charges against her were dropped.

"Ms. Kittner, you are free to go. And you have a small group of reporters and fans out there, so be prepared."

"Thank you, officer. Do you know if Sam Ryder's out there? If he is, I'll ask him to give you tickets to our home opener."

"Oh, he's out there alright. And he's already taken care of us. We'll be at the game, rooting for you and the T-Breds."

New Year's Day was wonderfully quiet and relaxed. Robin resumed her caregiving role, Alisha took the day off from training, and Hud went to Sam's to watch college bowl games. Truth be told, Sam was more interested in the sports news that day rather than the contests. "T-Bred Brawl" stories made the local stations, featuring snippets from interviews spotlighting Alisha and Robin. Sam liked what he saw and said so.

"We couldn't buy better publicity. This'll boost home opener ticket sales, and if the team delivers, it'll grow from there. Our girl's got it. She's in command and she's going places, taking us with her."

Hud smiled, nodding in full agreement before replying, "We'll let the Little Lady's actions speak louder than any words we could say."

Chapter 14
January 2123

"The Games Begin"
Thread 3 Chapter 4

TWEET! "OK TEAM, LISTEN up. Be in to the conference room in a hour. That's plenty of time to shower and change." The sound of Bo Rudman's whistle always announced a change of pace at his training sessions. The team liked how he kept each training day different and exciting. Unlike many coaches, he challenged his players mentally and physically, treating them as partners instead of possessions, so everyone was anticipating his talk that would conclude January's first week of training camp. Bo had his flip charts and talk ready to go by the time the last player sat down.

"We've had an excellent training week and are right on schedule for the mid-February start of the season. What we're gonna do today is size up what we can expect, and then review why the Co-NFL is so popular. It's important we know, because our job is to win games and keep them exciting, so we bring fans to stadiums and media channels." Bo flipped to charts showing last season and pre-season rankings.

"The sports reporters are doing us a big favor. They've pegged us correctly; we're a new team because all of you were brought here at the end of last season to a relocated and renamed franchise that has a new coach ready to roll out a brand-new offensive set—the Wide-V. The odds-makers have set low expectations for us because they don't know how all the new pieces will fit. And that's good, because we're better than where they put us in the preseason rankings. Just how good are we? That's up to you, and how you gel as a team. And let's be honest. We might not have the best talent, but we'll be the best coached and best conditioned, and if our chemistry clicks the way you're showing me, we're gonna have a great season, maybe going deep into the playoffs. So, that's our goal for the first year: make it into the play-offs. And that's where the Wide-V offense is gonna take us. Let me explain." Bo's next chart diagrammed the reasons.

"Fans love the Co-NFL because it's the best possible combination of competition and entertainment using the minds and muscles of gifted male and female athletes teaming up. And here's another truth: female athletes make it so. During the last fifty years, they have excelled. And Co-NFL rules are designed to showcase the ladies. The league enforces height and weight limits for males. At least half the team on the field must be comprised of females. The same applies to each multi-player position on the field: linemen, defensive backs, receivers, etc. And we're the only team that has a female quarterback. And that's where our Wide-V offense comes in."

"We've built the team around Kit. From what she's shown us in camp, she's damn good, and the Wide-V offense lets her pass, run, hand off, or snap the ball to either halfback so they can run or pass. We'll catch opponents off guard, especially at the start of the season, until they catch on to what we're doing. And even then, Kit's ability to throw with either arm will keep them off balance.

"This season, the league is using wired helmets. Mini-cameras, speakers, and microphones are built in so coaches and players are in constant contact. This lets us run plays faster with or without huddles, and makes coaches' play-calling that much more streamlined. The fans love it. Last year, they could subscribe to helmet video-streaming, and this year they can subscribe to a time-delayed channel that lets them listen in. That engages them in the game even more.

"Let me wrap up this way: each of you is here because of your special combination of brains, looks, and athleticism. Remember to use them to build a high-performance team, protect one another on the field, and be appealing spokespersons during interviews and activities off the field. And you've earned the weekend off. We'll resume practice next Tuesday, so before we break, are there any questions?" Toni Diya, a rangy receiver, raised her hand.

"Do the rules still allow females to wear sticky gloves to help catch passes? There were rumors they'd be banned."

"Good question. Female receivers can wear them, males cannot." Another question was raised, this time by halfback Jonah Byers.

"The upper body protective gear is great, but the leg equipment slows me down. Do you know of any new stuff?"

"No, we have the latest gear. And remember this: your contract specifies you must wear protective gear in order to be covered by medical insurance. And that leads me to the tackling rules. Females can't be gang-tackled. It's sometimes hard to tell even in slo-mo replays, so the refs have to make a judgment call. And fans love tweeting in yes or no calls to see how they view it compared to calls on the field. OK, any final questions?" There were none, so the team left to enjoy a well-deserved break.

Alisha caught a late afternoon flight to DC, pleased that the new year was starting so well. She was living her athletic dream, training and bonding with the team. Drug and neuro-device development in Austin were on track, and Robin's live-in caregiving duties were transformative, a perfect fit for her emotional state.

That left plenty of time for Electra to handle her arcane cognitive pursuits: artificial intelligence and security software development. It also let her think about what she could do for the Brain Trust. On the flight, she cleared out her cellphone messages. She had turned her cellphone off while in Austin because she kept her Austin and Washington lives separate.

Her cellphone software screened out "junk calls." Only Carter's and Professor Ravenhill's had been saved; she'd call Carter on Saturday and put in a cameo appearance Monday morning with her advisors at a campus lab before flying back to Austin soon afterwards.

Carter was having the worst start ever for the month of January because so much came to an end when New Year's Eve rang in the new. It hurt when the Brain Trust was disbanded, ending his consulting role for Angus; the blow was cushioned because his economic assessment reports, which gave many Guardian Party programs high marks, had caught the attention of several congressional committees. They might bring him on board, but no firm date had been given. His personal life had stagnated; he lost his bar scene companion because Matt was spending more time with Zoe. But worst of all was the death of Mariah, his longtime friend. She had been killed in an auto accident when her car skidded off a snow-slick road, rolling over and over down an embankment before bursting into flames.

Carter handled all the above in a manner consistent with his intelligent, pragmatic, and realistic outlook. He acknowledged or grieved losses appropriately, then moved on to the future, looking for new opportunities. He knew that the Electra he had loved intimately, less than a year ago, he wanted to marry her—was gone for good, but hoped to keep her as a friend. That's why he'd been calling her: to keep their friendship alive and let her know about Mariah, and perhaps to ask for suggestions on political issues she might still be tracking. Whether she wanted to be called Electra or Alisha, she meant a lot to him. He jolted to attention when he recognized her called I.D.

"Hello Alisha, and Happy New Year. You've been hard to get hold of. How are you?... Been in Austin, eh... Welcome back to some winter, especially if you like snow. Listen, I have a lot of things to tell you. Did anyone tell you that Mariah was killed in an automobile accident?... No?... Why don't we do this: I'll pick you up and we can talk over lunch. I'll be over at twelve."

Alisha sat frozen on the sofa. Mariah's death cut to the quick; their intimacy never had a chance to blossom. It was too soon for the loss to register, so she decided to postpone grieving until she and Electra could sort through the emotions. For now, she would keep busy with what she had planned, and having lunch with Carter fit right in. He would be her only DC friend she would tell about her budding athletic career, letting him spread the word to only her closest friends. She would also ask him to house-sit while she was in Austin. She watched at the window and ran to his Vette when he pulled up.

Damn, she always looks good. I like the new sportswear too. If she's in the mood, maybe she'll be my partner for tomorrow's outing with Matt and Zoe. Alisha greeted Carter with a kiss on the cheek, then sounded a somber tone.

"I'm sorry about Mariah's accident. I'm not going to search for the right words to say because there aren't any. Please know that I miss her too." Carter nodded and drove in silence to let emotions settle before speaking.

"I called you soon after the crash, but there was nothing you could have done other than come to the funeral service. But maybe it's good you didn't. Look, let's change the subject. Tell me what you've been doing."

"I don't feel like kidding around, so believe me when I tell you I found a new job in Austin. I'm the starting quarterback for their CoNFL team, the Austin Thoroughbreds. I'll be spending most of my time there during the season, and I'd like you to house-sit while I'm away. You can live there rent-free and sublet your apartment if you like. You don't have to give me an answer now, just think about it."

"What you've just said sounds like something Alisha would do, so congratulations. I always knew something was holding you back in sports, and I'm glad you found a way to cut loose. You'll be terrific." Carter slowed to enter the restaurant parking lot.

"Thanks for the vote of confidence, but I'd rather talk about you, so let's do so when we get inside the restaurant."

Carter had chosen a smaller sports bar close to Alisha's home. It wasn't crowded this time on Saturday, and he took a booth that gave them privacy. Carter unloaded his story soon after the waitress took their orders.

"It's been a bad start to the year for me, but I'm adjusting. I'll miss our Brain Trust meetings, but I might be a consultant on some committees that like how I assess Jared's programs. Economically, they make a lot of sense. I just hope he steers a middle course implementing them. I don't talk with Angus anymore, so I'll just have to be an observer. Are you planning to call him?"

"No, I don't have anything to offer, and I'm not going to be around much. But how about you and me keeping in touch? You can let me know about Jared and any emerging terrorist threats. What else is going on in your life?"

"I have a new sports hobby, skiing. Matt talked Zoe into it, and they recruited me. I've been exercising for it, and tomorrow the three of us take our third skiing lesson at Whitetail Ski Resort. Would you like to join us? It's only a ninety-mile interstate drive northwest of DC. And you don't have to ski. You're into your football training and can't risk injury; just come along and watch us."

"Does it have a casino or dance club?" "Yes, according to Zoe."

"When are you leaving?"

"Matt's driving us early this evening. We have a room reserved for tonight, so we can have a full day of skiing tomorrow. And we'll drive home tomorrow evening."

"I'm in. Let's call Matt so he and Zoe know the score. You can tell them about my new athletic career, but the three of you are sworn to secrecy. Please, don't tell anyone else."

Alisha was the spark for the conversation on the ride to Whitetail. She didn't dwell on Mariah's death, instead getting everyone to remember her by looking to the future; that's what Mariah would want her friends to do. Alisha gave a summary of what and how Robin's doing, and how her football career was unfolding. Then she changed the subject.

"I'm bored talking about me. Tell me how you decided to take up skiing." Zoe dived right in.

"It was Matt's idea. He wanted us to have an activity that gets us outdoors in the winter and keeps us from cocooning. More's the merrier, so Carter joined in. This year we're renting skis; maybe next year we'll buy our own and consider ski vacations. Matt's EMT schedule doesn't give him much time off." Matt added to her remarks.

"That's another reason we like Whitetail. It's a quick and convenient drive through an enchanted-forested countryside. And there's something for everyone, outdoors and in. From what we've seen online, the resort attracts a nice mix to the casino and dance club." The more she heard, the more Alisha liked what the place had to offer. *Too bad I didn't pack one of my dress outfits.*

Well, my team sportswear fits right in. It'll be a conversation ice-breaker.

The welcoming glow from the resort buildings created a holiday mood as Matt led the way into the reception lodge. Alisha could tell from Zoe's relaxed and happy mood that she and Matt had started an intimate relationship. Good for Zoe and good for Matt. It's what they need. Maybe some of their good mood will rub off on Carter. It looks like he needs a lift.

They were settled in rooms by ten; too early for Alisha to call it a night, so she dragged Carter to the bar while Zoe and Matt went to bed. Alisha, the extrovert, never needed any sort of conversation starter, and to her pleasant surprise, she spotted her favorite dance partner, Jevon.

"Alisha! Great to see you. I didn't know you liked skiing." Jevon hugged her, and she returned a kiss. "Let me introduce you to my skiing instructor, Jasmine Kent."

"I'm not actually a skiing instructor. I work in DC for PNC Bank. I decided to learn to ski, so here I am. I didn't want to come by myself, so I recruited Jevon to help out, even though he doesn't ski. Tomorrow's my first lesson."

"I'm Alisha, and this is my friend Carter. He's learning this year, and I'm here for moral support. I have a great idea. Why don't you join us and our friends Matt and Zoe. After the lesson maybe Carter and you can ski while Jevon and I watch." Always the diplomat, Carter observed and listened before joining the conversation.

I think I saw Jevon at a club dance, but I certainly didn't see Jasmine. I would have remembered her.

"Hi, I'm Carter Quavah, and it's good to meet you. Jevon, I'm sorry but I didn't catch your last name. And I think I saw you at a dance club."

"Hi Carter. You might have, because dancing is my thing. Jazzi's not into dancing but wants a sport—or something—to balance her lifestyle. I keep telling her an attractive, intelligent black female doesn't have to be a workaholic to move up the banking career ladder. She got her MBA a couple of years ago, and at her age she'll climb fast." Jasmine gave him a playful shove.

"Jevon Mathias, I'll roll you down the mountain if you don't stop criticizing me. I happen to like my work. Financial analysis for me is like Website design for you. And I accept Alisha's invitation." Carter noticed it was almost midnight.

"Well, let's adjourn for tonight and meet for breakfast before taking our ski lesson. It should be a fun-filled morning."

Alisha and Jevon had the most fun of everyone next morning, watching Carter and Jazzi confound the ski instructor. Matt and Zoe had enough sense to keep their distance in order to stay vertical, but not so for those closer to Carter. He fell once while the instructor demonstrated how to release the ski from the boot, managing to take Jazzi with him. He fell again when the instructor assisted, this time falling the instructor. A second instructor took over the rest of the class while the first worked solely with Carter and Jazzi. And the comedy—not the skiing—got better.

Alisha lost count of how many times both of them fell while navigating the bunny slope. Carter demonstrated an uncanny ability to slide backwards on his back down the slope faster than most of the beginning students could ski. Too bad he couldn't control the direction. And whenever Jazzi fell, she could never get her skis pointed in the right direction once she struggled to a standing position. Neither of them figured out how to turn perpendicular to the slope so they could step back to the top. Jevon thought they looked like perpetual motion standing still.

Alisha worried that Carter would get frustrated. She knew he could be quick-tempered, especially when something bumped his male ego. He prided his athletic ability and had been intimidated by Electra's fitness when they first met. But judging from today, he must have outgrown that minor flaw. Jazzi and he were totally enjoying the moment, laughing good-naturedly and helping one another.

After lunch, Zoe and Matt decided to ski an intermediate run because Zoe had learned quickly and Matt could help when needed. Carter and Jazzi traded the skis for skates, while Alisha and Jevon explored the resort shops. All would meet for a quick dinner at six before driving home.

Alisha particularly enjoyed exploring a clothing boutique that already featured spring fashions. Jevon recognized style and picked out a pair of shoes Alisha liked. She felt an emotional twinge when he helped fit them. She had been so preoccupied the past month she hadn't paid attention to hormones; Jevon's touch brought primal urges to the surface. As they left the store, Jevon asked what she'd like to do next.

"How about we practice some dance moves? Our friends won't be back for an hour." Jevon smiled while putting his arm around Alisha's shoulder and guiding her towards his room, but as they approached, a troubling shadow darkened her mood. She stopped abruptly.

"I'm sorry, but suddenly I'm not in the mood. I'll meet you for dinner when the others get back." Jevon took Alisha's hands in his before saying,

"Hey, I understand. It's no fun for me if the feelings aren't right for you. We'll catch up later."

Lively dinner conversation lightened Alisha's spirits, as did the drive home, with Matt and Zoe in front talking about their next ski lesson while Carter and Alisha sat in back reflecting on the day. As the van entered her neighborhood, Christmas lights brightened the crisp clear evening, adding to Alisha's better mood until a sudden comparison interrupted. How merry is a friend-filled day, yet how melancholy is the fragility of life. Mariah is gone, now among the pantheon of my dearly departed. I miss what I'll never know what might have been, and it hurts. Electra told me to search Indira's poems whenever I need to understand my feelings. One of her sonnets, Returning to Life, came immediately to mind:

"As you travel through Life you're likely to find,
Rare items that you'd like to own.
Regarding them Fate's quite unkind,
They only are on loan."
"Fame and Fortune give you a wink,
You're picked for the grand prize.
But no matter how clever you do or think,
Over time it withers in size."
"And what about the most precious possession,

Your family and friends seen each day.
The Gods are stone-faced for them no concession,
To prevent being taken away."
"Danger to think you can keep what you earned,
Life says all must be returned."

Alisha turned away from Carter so he couldn't see tears welling; he saw them anyway but did not intrude. Whether it's Electra or Alisha, I'll never know what goes on inside her brain. Maybe that's good. But at least I know we're still friends." Carter didn't speak until Matt pulled into Alisha's driveway.

"Here we are. Please let us know when you're coming back."

"I will, and here's a set of keys. You can start house-sitting this week." Alisha hugged Carter and said good night to the pair in front, then dashed to the kitchen door.

Alisha's outlook brightened the next morning. Dreams had whispered a fond good bye to Mariah, and Indira spoke from the shadows, telling her not worry about unknowns no one controls. A morning run and light workout added zest to her mood. She packed for the early evening flight and called for a rideshare to campus. It's too bad I can't drive the Mustang back to Austin, but that'd take too long. Besides, it's good to have wheels when I come back, and maybe I can get another car to keep in Austin. I won't give up on the Ferrari.

Electra rehearsed on the ride how she'd soothe any ruffled advisor egos; they'd like the list of reasons why Austin was the place for her because it was good for them also. As the meeting wound down, Electra was happy to let Professor Ravenhall summarize.

"So, let me make sure I understand how you wish to conduct your research for the next six months. You'll work in Austin, collaborating with research associates and using their lab facilities. And you'll coordinate that with work already under way with your associates here. And as you demonstrated while playing soccer last year, your sports hobby contributes because your brain uses training time to solve problems. And you'll keep us in the loop by submitted summary reports and calling us when you need our assistance. Have I missed anything?"

"Only this: your names will be included in all journal articles. After all, I wouldn't be where I am without your support." It's true, but don't overdo the flattery.

"Very well. We'll allow this as long as you maintain your level of excellence. And we'll root for your Co-NFL team too. Keep us posted."

Electra worked in her lab afterwards, checking Emails and equipment, then reviewed hacking progress. She had perfected "trapdoor techniques," finally penetrating Cybergard's network and would incorporate them in her security software suite. And she now knew how to handle Cybergard. She had found weaknesses in their recognition and GUI interfaces that they had pirated from the Military. This would be Kwame's next assignment: use them in the neuro-devices and eliminate the glitches. He would do the same with the network software suite when she was ready to give him solution designs for the first set of applications. Until then, he'd be busy working on the Cyber-Theater.

Additional hacking was needed to trace Cybergard's trail of intrigue; Electra would use that as a challenge when in Austin because it was time to catch her flight. And it was time for Alisha to think about football. That and fashion Websites would be on her mind. After all, she wanted to look good on and off the field. Alisha deferred to Electra when Kameyo greeted her at the airport.

"Hello, Dr. Kittner. Welcome back." Electra returned the greeting with similar reserved affection.

"By now you should be comfortable calling me Electra when I'm in a serious state, or Alisha when I'm ready to have fun. So, why don't you call me Electra, I'll call you Kameyo, and you can tell me what you'd like."

Kameyo told while driving that she disappointed herself because she struggles to understand Electra's theories, even though Su tells her how smart she is. Electra came up with a plan that would satisfy Kameyo and her advisors, as well as provide additional cover for her multiple lives.

"Why don't we do this? You contact some of your associates at UT and have them collaborate with you on a research paper. Then I'll want you to talk to one of my advisors so he's in the loop. And I'll teach you more about my theories. But you must not tell them you work for me, or that I'm connected with H&H DNA. Will this be good for you?"

"Yes, Dr. Kittner. I mean Electra."

"Good. Let's change the subject. I'm ready for some fun."

And fun is what Alisha had. She didn't need to meddle in Robin's affairs because Robin was dealing wonderfully with her mental issues. She acted like a new person, alert, cheerful and competent, fully engaged taking care of Holy. He was recovering, though he would never walk again without assistance. Robin was now his constant companion; their relationship was like that of a caregiver daughter to an elderly father.

Alisha devoted full attention to football. The league did not have formal pre-season games, only spirited scrimmages with a couple of Co-NFL teams. T-Bred coaches and players were confident they would make a good showing at their season opener in DC against the Washington Ambassadors, and Alisha sent tickets to her close friends back home, expecting to have dinner with them the Saturday before.

Sleep came fitfully the night before the game, and Electra used the time to give Alisha pre-game advice.

"Of course, you can't sleep! Tomorrow is what we've wanted for a long time, and you're the one carrying the ball for us—sorry for the pun. You have a sixteen-game season to show what you can do against the best, so follow Coach's game plan and hold yourself back. There'll be plenty of chances to wow the crowd, but be smart and do so only after you've got your team, fans, and coaches believing in you. And you'll ultimately be measured by how well your team does, not by your individual stats. Now, get some sleep."

Alisha leaped out of bed the next morning, full of energy and excitement, unconcerned that snow showers were forecast for the entire day. The hardest part was waiting for Matt's van to whisk her to the stadium so she could warm up with her team. Even for

Alisha, too much solitary pre-game time increased butterflies to the size of bats; she instantly felt a calming focus when she entered the locker room. The eyes of her teammates turned to their quarterback. She had already earned the mantle of team leader and knew instinctively what to say when they gathered around her.

"Come on, now! Lose those looks of concern. Today is show time, school's out. This is a day we've all wanted, and we're gonna make the most of it by focusing on each play and not the score. Don't worry about winning. We'll all play with our hearts and heads and stick with Coach's game plan. Let's suit up and listen to what the Coach wants us to do."

Though Bo had rehearsed his strategies and speeches, he made last-minute adjustments for the game-time snow.

"OK team, listen up. We've got the coaching and conditioning to offset a lot of our opponent's athleticism. Their quarterback's got experience throwing in the snow, so defense, expect him to mix more passes than you'd expect. We're gonna run our conservative offensive set because of the snow—and because it's our first game. We'll get comfortable with our run game before we start mixing in passes. Listen on your head sets to what our spotters are saying. And your nerves will settle down as soon as the game begins. Now, head out for light drills, then come back in to stretch more and keep warm. Let's go!"

No matter how many times I hear it, our National Anthem playing to start the game gets me going. And here I am on the big stage in front of a national audience. This is my place, so just act naturally. It's time to put on my Kit game face. The Ambassadors won the coin toss and chose to kick. It was a touch-back, so the T-Breds ran their opening series from the 20-yard line. The Wide-V offense worked well in the snow. Coach Rudman's play calling gained three first downs by distributing the ball among Alisha and her two halfbacks, but the Ambassadors recovered a running back fumble.

On the first offensive play, their quarterback rolled to his right, then passed completely across the field, surprising the defense that couldn't cover the speedy receiver who streaked into the end zone. The point after made the score 7-0.

Coach Rudman stuck with his ground game, which ground out first downs. The snow and the defensive sets closed down the running lanes, limiting Alisha and the other ball carriers to short but steady gains. It was hard to get traction; even Alisha slipped and slid, but her catlike agility kept her vertical. Coach should let me carry the ball more, but he wants to distribute it. OK for now.

The Ambassadors superior talent showed in the second quarter; they scored a second touchdown and field goal. The best the T-Breds could do was a missed field goal, so halftime score was 17-0. The broadcasters commended both teams for playing solid football, noting that the snow forced conservative play-calling on the inexperienced T-Breds.

"The T-Breds are well-coached and disciplined on offense, but their defense has its hands full trying to contain a surprisingly accurate Ambassadors' passing game. Their talent and experience are certainly on display. Coach Rudman's Wide-V offense looks like it'll grind out yards. It's a clever blend of Wishbone T and West Coast offenses. Too bad they can't mix in passes yet. I guess their rookie quarterback, Kit Kittner, needs more seasoning and less snow. But she looks like she knows what she's doing and hasn't fumbled. It'll be fun to watch her and her team develop as the season progresses..."

The second half unfolded pretty much like the first as snow accumulated. Both teams kept to conservative running plays; fumbles ending a couple of scoring drives for each side. Midway through the fourth quarter the Ambassadors quarterback tried a drop-back pass that surprised the T-Bred linebackers. His throw spiraled perfectly through the snow flurries and into the arms of their tall female receiver who galloped over the fallen linebacker and into the end zone. The holder muffed the snap, putting the score at 23-0.

The T-Breds got the ball on the 20 with four minutes to go. Coach Rudman decided to mix in some passing plays, knowing the Ambassadors defense would play loose. Even if they didn't score, he figured Kit could complete a couple of passes that would build the team's confidence for the next game. Kit executed the drop-back pass, leading wide receiver Toni perfectly but she dropped the ball. The next play was a halfback run, and the following play was handoff from Kit to a halfback cutting right, but it would turn into a pass. Electra raced around the left side of the line and straight up the field, then cut towards the middle. The defense was caught flatfooted when the halfback threw a strike to her. The ball was high but Kit leaped to make the catch. The defensive backs slipped in the snow, but not the receiver, who raced untouched into the end zone. The kicker made the point after; the score was now 23-7, and that's how the game ended.

"Come on team, don't be so glum! You acquitted yourselves nicely. The entire coaching staff is pleased with our overall performance. We now have one game of actual experience. No amount of practice can take its place. And we'll be ready to run a wider selection of plays when we don't have to contend with snow. And no was injured, so let's give thanks for a successful start to the season. Now, hit the showers!"

Like her individual performance in the game, Kit was satisfied with Coach Rudman's post-game talk, though some of the other players weren't. Although they had fought gamely, they were on the wrong end of the score because the opponent had more talent and a game plan that utilized it. Toni Diya summarized it best.

"I don't want to be acquitted nicely. I want to kick ass out there. And I couldn't handle the snow. That's why I dropped three passes. Sorry, Kit."

"No need to be sorry. Just learn from today and move on. That's what all of us will do. The next time we play them it'll be different. All the great athletes have short memories and never look back. Do that after you retire. Not now. So, let's all of us enjoy the break tomorrow, and be ready to go Tuesday."

Alisha followed her own advice on the flight home. She concentrated on spring fashions rather than football, ordering online new slacks and sleeveless tops after modeling them with styling apps. They'll look great with the shoes Jevon helped me pick out. And I've got a list of Austin dance clubs I'll check out soon. Work hard, play hard. I'll remind Electra to do the same.

Chapter 15
April 2123

"The Austin Engagements"
Thread 1 Chapter 8

AUSTIN WAS THE PLACE to be for the Electra-Alisha duality. It kept Electra fully engaged, helping the Kameyo-Su combo develop drugs, as well as the Tim-Kwame coalition implement neuro-devices and virtual reality GUIs. And it kept Alisha engaged, helping Robin recover while the T-Breds build momentum. Today, Alisha was going out for a late breakfast to discuss Robin's latest concerns. It must have something to do with Holy. The two of them are always together, so I'll let her lead the discussion.

Robin continued gaining emotional stability, but some recent thoughts bothered her. The best way to deal with them is to talk them out. Holy likes the pancakes and Texas-friendly seating at the Magnolia Grill, so that's where we'll go. It won't be crowded, and it suits our schedules. I'll be bringing him back from a doctor's visit, and Alisha will meet us there.

Arriving first, Robin briskly parked Holy's wheelchair at a table near the entrance. Alisha arrived five minutes later, hugging each other before sitting down.

"I'm ordering buttermilk pancakes for me and Mr. H. What are you going to have?"

"I'll have oatmeal with brown sugar, a corn muffin, and a Coke. That's a healthy breakfast for an athlete. I'm in training, you know." Robin started the discussion as soon as the waitress took their order.

"You two are my best friends, and thanks to your help, I'm feeling better and better about myself. But I've been thinking a lot lately about topics I've never discussed with anyone before.

Please don't think I'm morbid, but I want to talk about old age and death. Mr. H, you're such an upbeat person, I'd appreciate hearing from you."

"They're not morbid subjects. Everyone should face up to what they can't dodge. Young people can't do it as well as codgers like me. We don't worry about death. We worry about cashing out when we still have our mibs and can count our chips. By the time you reach my age, you should be satisfied you've given life your best shot. And don't look back or yearn to correct mistakes. I don't fret about life after death. Between you and me, I don't believe in it, so when I go, that's it. Friends or relatives might grieve for me at my wake, but they're really grieving for themselves because nothing they say or do will matter one mote to me.

"Lots of smart ladies and gents have analyzed old age and death six ways to Sunday, telling us Death is unavoidable; it's part of the natural order. You should read some of Emily Dickinson. I agree, so it's silly to prolong it if all you do is live like a vegetable. That's why gerontology today is so much better than it was even fifty years ago. My check-up today focused on quality of life, not prolonging it when it's time to go. That's why I've approved DNR—do not resuscitate—if I collapse, and why I've chosen assisted suicide just before I reach that point. Don't either of you be shy about this. Since you're my caregiver and caregiver backup, I might call on you to carry out my wishes. And that includes whole body donation to science, if there's anything left worth using." Though Robin didn't say anything, her grimace told Holy to say more.

"Now don't be squeamish. You're a strong young woman, and you're getting stronger." The conversation paused while the waitress served breakfast, then resumed as Robin spoke.

"I'll deal with it when the time comes, but I hope it's not for a good long while. Tell me again how you've managed to keep so youthful mentally."

"Growing old sorta sneaks up on you. I remember one day lookin in the mirror and wondering who's that old coot lookin back at me? You can't relate to that yet, but think back to when you were in grade school settin at one of those tiny desks, wondering when'll you ever fit in the big ones. Well, it just happened and you didn't give it a thought. The only time getting old hits you is when there's an abrupt change, like my damn stroke. I can't walk now, and I notice how bad my droopy left side of the face looks. Maybe you felt the same a couple of years ago when your broken neck paralyzed you. The big difference is when you're young you can look forward to recovering to better times. But when you're old, your best days are behind you. And that's me, so I follow these principles.

"I'm a simple person, so I keep it simple. Each day I try to remember somethin to love, somethin to get up for, and somethin to keep me from lookin backward. And I try to get rid of guilt and regrets. Young people can hear this, but they need to bump up against life for it to sink in." Alisha made a comment to herself before speaking. Robin's body language tells me to ask Holy some questions, so I'll jump in.

"I have trouble dealing with love. How do you handle it?" Holy chuckled, then continued.

"Love's the strongest, hardest emotion to figure out. Most people never do, and I guess I didn't either, but I tried my best. Young people let their hormones cloud the issue. They focus too much on sex and storybook love, but they can't help it. Later on, they'll learn about other types of love that don't depend on sex. Things like love of knowledge, music and art, friends, and causes. The best I can do is point it out. I'll leave the rest for you to discover."

"I think Robin would agree. My attitudes toward living and dying have changed over time, but I think it takes the wisdom of old age to feel comfortable about them." Robin nodded, then spoke.

"I'm always going to have emotional issues, but I deal with them better by talking them out. Today helped, and I feel like I've crossed over into new territory. Maybe Alisha can put into words what I'm feeling."

"I can go one better. My mother wrote a poem that talks to us. I think she called it Crossing the Bar. See if this works:
Cross over to where you're meant be,
Doubt replaced by clarity.

No hindrance bars to set you free,
No whit of worry for others to see.
How long it took to figure out,
Looking back leaves nothing out.
For chosen path give silent shout,
Resolve provides secure redoubt.
How long the stay can't find a clue,
Bless each morn's sustaining dew.
Till winds of fate blow cold on you,
Announcing what is next to do.

Holy rubbed his chin, then said, "Your Momma was a wise lady. Those words fit the way I've felt sometimes when crossing into new territory. I hope I live long enough to help you two cross into other things you like before my time's up. But don't concern yourself with that now." Alisha glanced at the time.

"I'll follow your advice. And I better hustle to meet with Hud. He's got some business on his mind, so he'd better call me Electra."

Hud was sitting in his office, worrying about the Guardian Party's latest demand. Several days ago, he'd been told by an anonymous government bureaucrat that if he didn't make contributions to a yet-to-be-named charitable organization, the government would stop buying smart pills from him. And if push comes to shove, the government might force him to reveal patents and formulations in the name of national security. Electra warned me about this. She'll know what we should do. He perked up when Electra sat down across from him.

"Howdy, Lectra, or is it Lisha today?"

"Call me Electra when we get serious about business. I just had breakfast with your dad and Robin. She's a great caregiver."

"I could hire an army of caregivers, but they couldn't match her. Holy considers her a daughter, and that makes life good for both of 'em. And speaking of caregiving, I need to hear your advice on the latest government antics. I've been contacted on the Q.T. to make contributions or they'll stop buying our smart pills."

"Call their bluff. If they back down, good. If they don't, they'll have to buy on the grey or black or underground market from one of our virtual companies."

"But what if they force us to turn over patents and formulations?"

"If it comes to that, give them the original formulations. That's all you have. I'm the only one with the latest formulations and patents, which I never filed. Not even Su or Kameyo have them. And our manufacturing process is like that for Coca-Cola. Its formula is a secret recipe for Coke syrup, which bottlers combine with carbonated water to create the soft drink. Company founder Asa Candler initiated in 1891 the veil of secrecy that surrounds the formula as a publicity, marketing, and intellectual property protection strategy. While several recipes, each purporting to be the authentic formula, have been published, the company maintains that the actual formula remains a secret, known only to a very few select and anonymous employees. We're doing the same. I coordinate shipping in the 'magic formula', which you compound into gels and caplets. So, play hardball. They'll strike out." Hud's phone rang. He answered, then placed the call on hold.

"Lectra, I gotta take the call, but you've told me all I need to know. Maybe too much detail, but that's your style. Thanks."

Electra spent the rest of the afternoon applying her latest hacking skills to infiltrate Guardian Party computer networks. Now that Jared's back, there must be a link between him and Q.T. donations. I'll run this past Carter. He can check with Angus. And if I find more facts, I'll add it to my Jared file. How nice. I can piggyback on my Cybergard snooping and security suite apps development. Life is good.

Alisha's football career kept her fully engaged honing moves on the field and off, working hard in practice and playing hard weekends at dance clubs. She was becoming a local sports celebrity and enjoyed the spotlight. Only Electra knew how hard it was for Alisha to keep her vanity under control. Whenever Electra brought it to her attention, Alisha would kid that on a scale of one to ten, she scored a B. Then she would say, "You're the math whiz. Go figure my scoring system." The duo was ever the best of friends.

The second game—another away game—was similar to the first, minus the snow. Bo's conservative offense managed two touchdowns, but his defense gave up three and a field goal. Sam knew Bo's plan, but he wanted to discuss options, so they had a sit-down meeting the week before the home opener. After a minute of small talk, Sam got down to business.

"How do you like the team's performance so far?"

"Our players are gritty. They execute the plays well. I'm molding them into a cohesive unit, and given the talent we have, we're doing what I expected."

"I see it pretty much the same, but I think we'll do better if you dial up the offense. We've advertised excitement and innovation, but we've not delivered. I think our players want to see what your Wide V offense can do, and our fans want to see what our quarterback can do. Why not use her?"

"It's her first season. I don't want to put her in situations she can't handle, and I don't want to get her injured."

"You're not being fair to her, the team, or the fans. Remember what we said when she signed the contract: we'd roll the dice with her. Next Sunday is our home opener. I'll give you one more week. If your conservative play calls don't work, you'll have to go up-tempo."

"Not a problem. We should win our next game. Our next opponent is winless."

"So are you, so don't be overconfident. Let's get rid of the zero in the win column."

Alisha and her team liked the Tuesday-to-Saturday practice schedule, to which they added an all-Saturday buffet at Austin City Sportsters, a local sports club. The restaurant's owner promoted this opportunity for fans to mingle with the team and liked the spike in business. This week a local sports radio station, Border Media's 104.9 FM, was broadcasting from the club.

"We've got a great turnout for a great Saturday. I can tell Austin fans really like their new team and are looking forward to the T-Bred offense breaking out. With me is their quarterback, Kit

Kittner. Kit, welcome to our broadcast, and what can you tell us about the offensive plan for tomorrow's game?"

"Hello fans, and thanks for supporting us. Hey, Coach would bench me if I gave away our game plan, but let me say Coach Bo knows what he's doing. He knows we're still putting the pieces in place, but once their locked in he'll push the button."

"Thanks, Kit. Now, let's hear from some of the fans…"

Alisha had heard earlier in the week an earful of discontent from some of her teammates.

"We're supposed to play the game, not run practice drills. Some of us are fed up with Coach's play calling. It's not what we want." As the team leader, Alisha needed to find middle ground.

"Let's give it one more game. Then we'll know what to do." But Alisha already knew what she'd let Kit do. First half results of tomorrow's game will lead the way forward.

A home opener always commands extra attention. It's that singular event pitting hopes against competitive realities. The bright skies and festive banners highlighted enthusiasm; they hoped the earlier games were meant to keep the team's potential under wraps, awaiting the home opener to showcase what the T-Breds are made of.

Much to the crowd's displeasure, Coach Bo stuck to his conservative offensive sets, but the T-Breds did score a first-half touchdown. The fans expected more because the opponent was obviously one of the weaker teams in the league, and even though they scored easily against the T-Bred defense, which was spending too much time on the field. The score at halftime was 17-7. Some of the fans started chanting "Coach Boo—What's wrong with you?" when he and his staff trooped off the field.

Kit was as dissatisfied with the Bo's locker room pep talk as were the other players; she told the coaching staff to give the team a minute alone before heading back for the second half.

"We're gonna have fun in the second half, and here's how. I want all of you to turn off your communication channel that connects with the coaches. Just keep the players' channel open. I'm gonna call the plays, and we're gonna break out the Wide-V. Trust me. Just execute the plays I call. We're going up-tempo, and our offense is gonna wear down their defense. If I screw it up, I'll take the blame, but it's gonna work. And we'll make Coach look like a play-calling wizard. And just act natural out there. We'll let our performance do the rest."

The T-Breds received the second-half kick-off and brought the ball back to the thirty-yard line. Kit listened to what Bo called, but already had her team set for a halfback run and pass that connected for a solid gain. She had the second play in motion faster than the defense could handle. She rolled to her left and threw a strike for another first down. Then she completed another rollout pass to the left and followed that with a halfback run through the line. And now came the first surprise: her rollout pass to the right.

The defense didn't expect her to pass on this rollout because she would have to throw across her body. It didn't know it was facing an ambidextrous quarterback. Alisha's intermediate pass hit wide receiver Toni Diya right on the numbers, and she streaked into the end zone.

Bo was flabbergasted. Not only was his team executing plays at lightning speed, but they weren't running his. He was going to confront his quarterback when the offense came off the field, but instead, he came face-to-face with the entire offensive unit. Kit did the talking.

"It's time to let us strut our stuff. If you don't like what you see, tell us after the game. But right now, let us play the way we can. Out of the corner of her eye she caught Sam Ryder hurrying to join them. "Bo, way to go! That's what the fans want to see, and I do too. Keep going with your up-tempo plays." "Uh, that's the plan for the second half..."

The crowd loved the results. T-Bred scoring re-energized their defense, forcing opponents to four-and-outs more often than not. Alisha had the offense dancing down the field, putting the opponent's defense on its heels using a mix of runs and passes. The final score was 28-24; Alisha could have scored more, but she remembered the purpose of the game: for the team to win, not for her to show off.

The sportscasters recognized a good story in the making and grabbed the quarterback and coach for an on-field interview.

"Congratulations to you and your team. Do you know you're the first ambidextrous female QB in the league?"

"No, but Coach sure knows how to use it. He sent in the plays that really broke the game open."

"Coach Bo, it took you only three games to get your team ready for up-tempo play. How'd you do it?"

"Well, now, we recruited well and ran a great training camp. We've got a group of smart and talented athletes. We'll show the fans more in the coming weeks."

Bo held a quick meeting in the locker room.

"OK, team, listen up! From now on, you roll the offense like you did in the second half. Just remember to keep our secret to ourselves. Now go enjoy the victory and be ready for Tuesday practice."

Alisha was ready to celebrate afterwards at a post-game party hosted by the club and radio station that had run the Saturday pregame buffet. She glowed in the spotlight but was careful to share it with the team. The city was beginning to identify with the team because it was the first in professional sports to be so accessible to its fans. Sports is perhaps the clearest example of man's social nature. Fan's thrive on the range emotions sporting events generate, and the T-Breds were delivering.

Athletes at all levels often can't sleep until long after the excitement of competition subsides. Alisha didn't force herself to sleep. She took a light workout at home after the party, then a hot, soaking shower to loosen muscle tightness. By midnight, she was ready for a light snack, then eased into bed to let her mind roam freely. It wasn't long until Electra joined her.

"You handled yourself like a pro today in every which way. You're learning from me just like I'm learning from you. You're giving us a foundation to build on that I never would have come up with on my own. Do you realize what this means?"

"I'm sure it means good things for the future, but why don't we dwell in the moment and take as much joy as we can?"

"You're right. We'll each rest on it in our own special way and prepare for the promise of a new day. And as Indira would often say to Jason, we'll let the future come to us."

Alisha busied herself all next week practicing with the team and chatting on social media with fans. She also set up a Robin-Alisha shopping trip. And most evenings, she took a light workout followed by a recovery run.

Meanwhile, Electra remained fully engaged in her research, fully energized from a weekend of fun supplied by Alisha. She completed the final design of the first Cyber-Theater and now had schematics and two diagrams that would help Tim visualize the device. The first presented the simplest model. It contained a multi-track CD that coded all sensory inputs sent to three interrelated components:

- Cyber-Screen/Visor that displays the video track.
- Cyber-Helmet made of SPD "smart glass." The helmet interprets the audio and aroma track. (SPD is suspended particle glass that changes from transparent to opaque depending on the applied voltage.)
- Cyber-Shuttle—an ergonomic chair—that interprets the motion/touch and orientation tracks.

The overall effect would be a complete sensory experience of whatever was recorded on the CD. The applications were limited only by imagination. Entertainment, education, training, games, and military simulation easily came to mind. Tim would need to develop coding techniques for some of the tracks as well as digital-to-analog interfaces between the signals and hardware. Electra would tell him to start with current video game and military training simulators and invent from there. And she would recommend that he partner with entertainment media developers (Hollywood came to mind) to divide the work into chunks "mere mortals" could manage.

Simplest Cyber-Theater

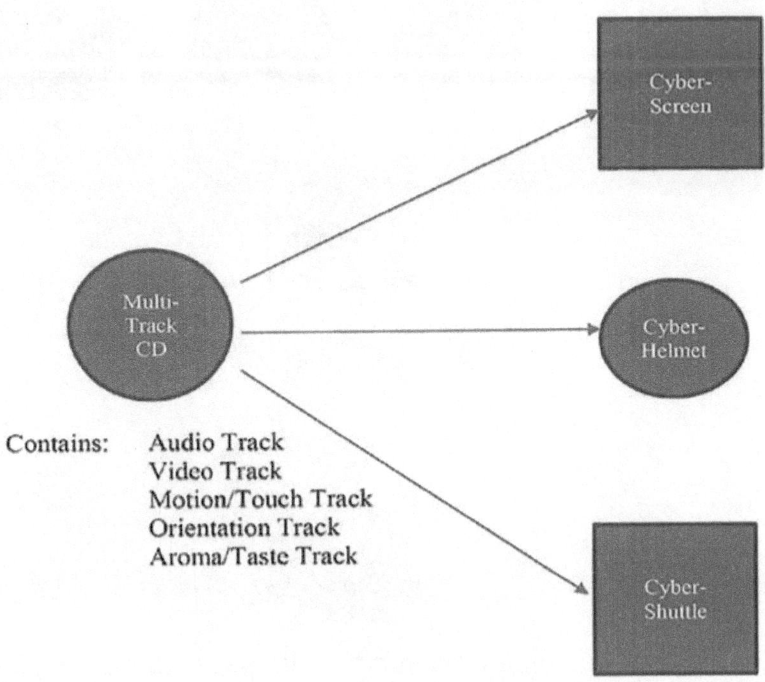

The second diagram took the theater to an interactive level that would use chips implanted in the brain to wire neurons so they could control the output displays. Electra would be entering into a brave new world of augmented human performance, connecting the brain and the computer in ways no one had yet explored. A handful of reactionary alarmists warned that research into transhumanism linked with artificial intelligence could unleash the "Singularity:" machines become self-aware and annihilate the human race. Electra's lightning brain comprehended this possibility but concluded the risk was minimal. She did not have a dream team of researchers to implement her discoveries, which meant an interactive level could be pursued only in the distant future. Electra shrugged it off; she had enough for Tim and Kwame. Interactive Cyber-Theater

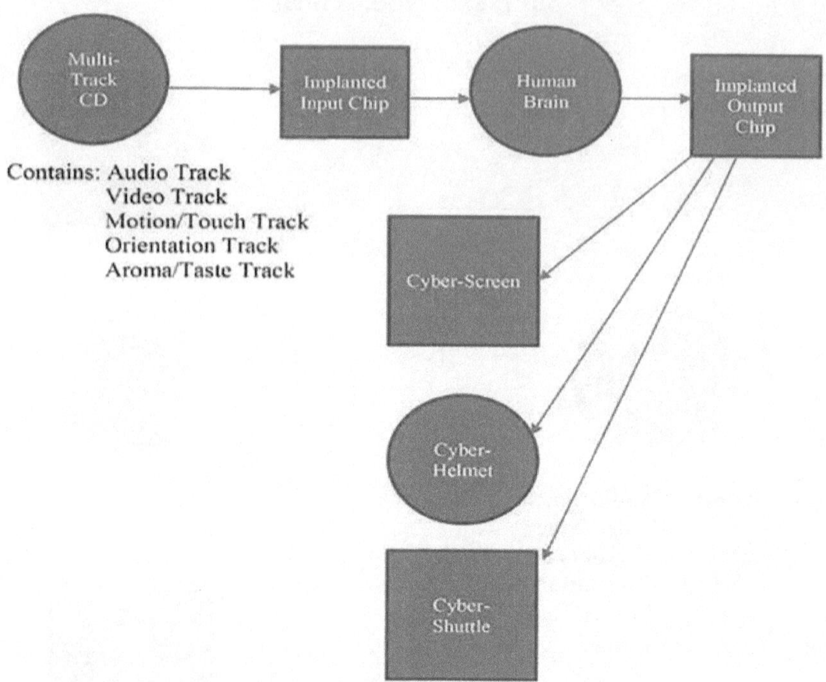

Contains: Audio Track
Video Track
Motion/Touch Track
Orientation Track
Aroma/Taste Track

Electra placed the diagrams in her white paper that gave all the design and implementation specifications, along with her analytic theory that would guide Tim and Kwame. Smart as they were, she knew they would need her assistance. Tim voiced at the Friday training session their concerns.

"We're supposed to invent hardware and software that will interpret new sensory coding tracks. How do we do that?"

"Some of what we're doing is already in video games and military simulation. So, you're responsible for literature searches and networking to get a state-of-the-art starting point to build on. Kwame will help you hack into what you need. And both of you need to be invisible. Leave no tracks leading back. And the simplest Cyber-Theater is one-way, not brain-interactive. You should have it prototyped in six months. Talk to Hud about introducing you to Sam Ryder. He'll have ideas about a Hollywood contact to partner with. And both of you remember this: you must never tell anyone I work here. Now tell me, how is Neuro-Knitter marketing going?" Tim gave the answer.

"The guy Hud replaced Brian with is doing a good job implementing Brian's sales and marketing plans. Hud is pleased with the orders in the pipeline. And that's just for broken necks. Our sales guys are now promoting it for broken backs. I'm going to work on a line extension to treat nerve damage in broken arms and legs. Where should I put this on my priority list?"

"Ask Hud and the sales guy." And then, follow up with me. And Kwame, I have something new for you too. But I don't have the issue fully scoped out yet. When I do, you'll have fun working on it."

Electra and Alisha weren't the only ladies fully engaged in new pursuits. Robin's dislike of accounting motivated an additional career change, the epiphany coming not long after her breakfast outing. Sitting at Holy's side while he was engaged in a business phone call, she suddenly decided what she would do instead of counting debits and credits. I shall be Holy's business partner for his livestock business venture. After the phone call, Holy listened patiently to what Robin proposed.

"I can change my major from Accounting to Business Management, and I won't lose any credits because UT will transfer all my credits from one program to the other. And instead of Hud's bookkeeper training me, you can teach me all about ranching and handling livestock. And it fits in perfectly since I'm at your side most of the time."

"Well, young lady, I know you've got grit, but you'll need to toughen up. Being outdoors might weather your skin. You'll need a new set of clothes, and you'll have to get comfortable dealing with four-legged critters. You ever have a dog or ride a horse?"

"No, but I can learn how. Please, give me a chance." Holy held Robin by the shoulders, looking straight into her eyes as he spoke.

"This can work. I was grooming Adom to take over until he got killed, and I haven't found a replacement. Until now. If the rest of you get as strong as your hands, there'll be no stopping us. We got ourselves a deal."

Alisha adjusted the already-scheduled shopping expedition, adding stores catering to ranch wear and inviting Holy to be a fashion consultant. He recommended they go to King Ranch

Saddle Shop because he knew first-hand that it carried a complete line of what Robin needed.

Robin's new wardrobe made her look sturdy, and as Holy and Alisha helped her recover from the suicide attempt, her mental toughness rebounded. Holy made sure she was groomed in all aspects of doing business in a traditionally all men's world. They played a great prank whenever Holy introduced her to business associates. He instructed her to "shake hands like a Texan" whenever greeting them for the first time. Years of piano playing had given her a vise-like grip; Holy chuckled every time Robin made even the most rugged fellow's eyes widen and wince. Everyone quickly learned that this lady means business.

Electra asked Alisha that evening how the shopping expedition went.

"Very well, indeed. Robin looks the part of a ranch lady, like Barbara Stanwyck in that retro TV series classic The Big Valley. Did you know that the Austin Film Society held a Barbara Stanwyck Retrospective last year? She was a talented and emotionally complex lady. But then, many actresses are."

"No, I didn't. But while you were researching the Austin Film Society, I was reviewing some of my psychology diagrams and notes. They help me understand the relationship between neuroscience and artificial intelligence. It is possible that someday the Id, Ego, and Superego will emerge from a computer-based silicon substrate. Would you like to hear more?"

"Yes, but only if you can avoid giving me an information overload."

"I think I can, but I'll let you be the judge. Here goes…" Electra earned an A-minus.

Chapter 16
June 2123

"Into the Dark and the Deep"
Thread 3 Chapter 5

INCREDIBLE! CYBERSPACE IS DARKER and deeper than even the CIA fathoms. And thanks to my lightning brain, I can see beyond. Electra had spent the entire day testing her "N++" code generator's effectiveness for hacking and cracking into computer hardware and software. "N++" would always describe her computer work. No matter what generation Silicon Valley was working on, Electra would always be several steps ahead. Currently, N stands for the seventh generation, known as "AAI," augmented artificial intelligence. Electra's revealing to even the brightest developers her coding techniques would be similar to Einstein's explaining to a caveman the curvature of spacetime. Only Electra could extend programming languages to construct rigorous modal logic subroutines encapsulating necessity and possibility operators that yielded ever more sophisticated semantic processors and language translators. Only she could code "Deep Learning Apps" that could efficiently search unstructured "Big Data" to build recursively additional code that becomes "smarter and smarter." My apps simulate creativity and innovation. If I let them run long enough, perhaps they might approach self-awareness, which is the holy grail of the AI Singularity. But I'd have to live a long, long time. Well, I'm not planning to call it quits, so let's see what the future holds.

Today's testing confirmed expectations. Latest modifications to her declarative code generator modules gave her the power to extend her arsenal of security software tools. Now she would have Kwame equip them with latest security recognition systems and input/output GUIs. This is a BIG BREAKTHROUGH. There's only one other person capable of understanding, but she's usually interested in training or having fun rather than breaking an intellectual sweat, so I won't bother her. I'll teach Kwame the basics so he can show Tim what to do. It's time for a break. I'll itemize the security tool kit and specifications this evening and give them to Kwame soon.

Electra took her favorite break: exercise followed by an endurance run. As the miles sped by, the lightning brain entered a freewheeling state, and Alisha joined her.

"Yes, I understand your breakthrough. Congratulations. Your return has helped me cognitively and emotionally. So, let me explain what you've done. Maybe you can use this when you dumb down for Kwame.

"There are two types of programming techniques: imperative, where you list all the steps in an algorithm, and declarative where you state what you want to get. SQL—structured query language— is a great example of declarative programming used in relational and object-relational databases. It's much easier to do than imperative programming. Your code generator is declarative, taking the grunt work out of building the application. But it's too powerful for the "hackers and crackers" threatening the Internet, so you'll keep it to yourself. You'll write your security software suite so you have the weapons you need when you go to war in Cyberspace. The GUI's Kwame puts on these apps put a human spin on it. Your 'soldiers' will sit at wide-screen monitors, pointing, typing, or talking to the apps while your GUIs present a virtual reality view of the action. It'll be like a video game, or like a drone pilot cruising through space. But now we're cruising through a virtual representation of Cyberspace hardware, data silos and software. And the game is deadly. We'll be out to destroy assets employed by terrorists of all kinds. How am I doing?"

"You're spot on. If you ever get tired of your athletic career and playing around, please come work for me. But it's probably better you keep doing what you're doing. That's how you teach me to handle emotions better."

"We're both right. You're the keeper of our cognitive persona; I'm the keeper of our emotional persona; Kit is the keeper of our physical persona, and the lightning brain is the keeper of the keepers. It works quite well. I hope you have a good time explaining stuff to Kwame; while you're doing that, I'll be having fun practicing for the next game. And we're always in touch, so let me know when you need me, and vice versa."

Electra went for a Coke while Kwame laser-focused on the document she had just spent an hour explaining. She returned a half-hour later, bringing one for him and another for herself, and would wait for Kwame to say something.

"Now I see what you're creating. This is brilliant. Let me explain it back to you, so I know I've got it. Let's turn to the 'Security Suite Tool Kit' table."

Security Suite Tool Kit

- Cyber-Snooper—Agent Application. Simulates covert agent.
- Cyber-Trooper—Agent Application. Simulates combat soldier.
- Cyber-Infiltrator—Agent Application. Simulates terrorist cell.
- Cyber-Jacker.—Agent Application. Takes control of target hardware or software.
- Cyber-Drone—Agent Tool Application. Simulates land or air transport vehicle used by our agent.
- Cyber-Message—Agent Tool Application. Used to send messages to/from agent and our control center
- Cyber-Interceptor—Tool Application. Used by control center to capture inbound or outbound messages and replace with substitutes.
- Cyber Tracer—Tool Application. Used by control center to uncover the actual address and owner of the target Website or URL (Uniform Resource Locator) or Internet/email Address. Cyber-Deceiver—Tool Application. Used by the control center to plant bogus information on the target Website.
- Cyber-Corrupter—Tool Application. Used by control center to disable target Website or databases.

- Cyber-Torpedo—Tool Application. Used by agent or control center to erase target software, databases, or disable target hardware.
- Cyber-Nuke—Tool Application. Used by agent or control center to erase target software directories, entire databases, disable entire networks.
- Cyber-Cipher—Tool Application. Used by control center to encrypt or decrypt target software files.
- Cyber-Thief—Tool Application. Used by agent or control center to steal target software, files or databases.
- Cyber-Translator—Tool application. Used by control center to convert target software into "readable" format.
- Cyber-Virus—Tool Application. Used by control center to plant virus in operating system on target hardware so control center can take control when virus is activated.

"THE SOFTWARE SUITE IS designed to give the control center that launches it a human touch and feel for what they're doing in Cyberspace. It's like playing a video game. It contains human-like avatar agents—snoopers, troopers, terrorists, and hijackers—assigns them weapons and resources, puts them in vehicles, and sends them to software or hardware sites to carry out their missions interactively with the control center. The control center also has tools it can use to manipulate target hardware or software or avatar agent enemies. So, the control center can wage a battle in Cyberspace, and it's like playing with the most advanced video game or simulator I've ever seen. We can interact with our agents visually or by voice or by keyboard or by screen touch. This is light-years ahead of what Silicon Valley or the Military is even thinking about. And if we target hard assets, like an airplane or car, we actually take control of it in 3D Space. And you've already written the code. And you need me to drop in the interfaces and recognition systems. Am I right?"

"Yes. You understand the overall design and what you need to do. Let me know if you recommend any additional tools."

"And I should start on the tool applications first, then the agent tools, and then the more advanced GUIs. That way, we can run the suite manually right away. Later on, we can create agents and send them into battle. This is cool stuff. But I have a question. Who's gonna be the enemy?'

"That's for me to worry about. I want you to get the tools ready. Please give me your task list and timeline for the suite. I think you'll have fun coding them. But do me one big favor. Don't work yourself to a frazzle. I know you have that tendency. People with autistic predispositions will focus on abstract activities. I used to be the same way, but I've learned to take breaks. So please, do the same. And do not tell anyone in your hacker nation about this. You've earned my trust, but don't ever make me angry. You wouldn't like me when I'm angry. And I know that you, like most autistic types, can read emotions, though you don't always show them. Am I right?"

"Yes, you are. I know you're deadly serious, and I won't disappoint you."

"Good. How about I buy you and Tim lunch? And you can call me Alisha, now that our training session is over."

Alisha never worried about working herself to a frazzle. She had perfected a balanced approach—working hard and playing hard— and put it to work in her first Co-NFL season, helping the T-Breds hit their stride on and off the field. A local sports commentator's story called it correctly.

"Austin's newest team, the T-Breds, is beginning to exceed expectations because its Wide-V Offense is beginning to click, and fans like the high-scoring action. And there are actually two games in one: T-Bred's offense, led by fan-favorite rookie quarterback Kit Kittner, versus opponents' defense, and T-Bred's usually overmatched defense versus opponents' offense. Their 4-3 record puts them on the bottom rung for a play-off spot, but the season's barely half over, so playoff possibilities are wide open."

Alisha didn't worry about making the play-offs; she enjoyed one game at a time, actually preferring away games. She and her road-mate, Toni Diya, liked visiting other cities, always packing party dresses and heels to wear the night before the game. Neither could sleep on those occasions; they considered clubbing a pre-warmup warmup.

Toni, Alisha's favorite receiver, came from a San Antonio middle-class mixed marriage (black father, an accountant, white mother, a school teacher), was fun-loving and attractive in a rangy athletic way, hyperactive, and indifferent towards school. Sports was her calling, and she was a fearless competitor even though her abilities matched a line from the poet Robert Burns: her reach exceeded her grasp. It was her aggressiveness and willingness to handle pain that set her apart from most female athletes. The Co-NFL was her comfort zone, and she would do whatever it takes to stay there because she was hooked on the endorphin rush competitive sports supplies.

The eighth game of the season took place on a mid-June Sunday in New York City. Bo, being a "New Age" coach, let his players prepare however they chose the night before as long as they performed well in the game. He never worried about Alisha, but he counseled all his athletes to be good ambassadors for the team and to avoid incidents. Alisha used her connections to find a "safe" dance club. Even though the Guardian Party's "Pillars Program" had put a dent in street crime, there were still too many bad guys prowling about at night, so she chose carefully.

This club's been a great pre-warmup. The hours danced right by, and it's time to go. I'll get Toni off the dance floor and we'll get a ride-share back to the hotel. Alisha was alone at a table, having just kissed her partner good night, a mid-thirties slender Hispanic male who had given her a new dance move as well as a Coca-Cola nightcap. Alisha enforced a strict rule the night before: no alcohol or drugs of any sort. She had never succumbed to the temptation of performance-enhancing drugs; caffeine in soft drinks was her limit. Toni finally saw her wave and sauntered over.

"You picked a great place. Nice atmosphere and crowd." "Yes, it's a keeper for next time we play here. Ready to go?" "In just a minute. Give me a sip of your Coke."

"Take the rest, I've had enough." Just then, Toni's dance partner came to the table.

"I called a buddy of mine, but Reynaldo didn't know where to get the stuff. But if I see you again, maybe I can think of someone else. And don't forget the cab stand I told you about. It's an easy walk from here." Toni's look was one of surprise, and she answered curtly.

"Uh, thanks for the news. Maybe I'll see you again." Still smiling, he cast a parting line before heading back to his party group. "Good luck tomorrow. And don't absorb any hard hits. You ladies look sort of vulnerable when you're not suited up." Alisha didn't like what she had just heard and gave Toni an earful.

"Stuff? What stuff? And what did you tell him about us?" I know what this is about, but I'll let Toni tell me. Toni finished the Coke before lowering her voice to explain.

"Stuff is performance-enhancing drugs. I take anabolic steroids during the season to recover from workouts. I'd have trouble staying in the league if I didn't."

"You fooled me. I never would have suspected. How do you fool the doping tests?"

"There are lots of ways. Just surf the Web and you'll find them. I'm sorry you found out. Are you going to report me?" Ugh. You've thrown me a dandy dilemma, made worse because I empathize with you, and I can argue both ways. And I must be careful when making decisions for others or telling them what to do. Electra warned me long ago not to "play God."

"No. I'll compromise my ethical standards because, in your case, taking steroids is a minor infraction. And according to WADA, ten percent of professional athletes take drugs." Toni looked puzzled, so Alisha added," That's the World Anti-Doping Association."

"I didn't know that, but do you know a Sports Illustrated survey of pro athletes found that ninety-eight percent said taking drugs is worth the risk of long-term health problems if it boosts performance. And half said they'd do it if it made them the best, even if they died in five years."

"Let's drop the subject and catch a cab. Why don't you lead the way to that cab stand?" As they left, neither noticed Toni's dance partner making another call.

"They're on the way. Duck back in the alley. We'll grab them when they walk by. I'll take the one in red…"

Alisha wasn't paying attention to her early warning system. She and Toni were caught off guard when a pair of burly thugs dragged them into a dark delivery alleyway, then pitched them to the pavement. Alisha, thunderstruck for a moment, became livid, angry at herself for being careless and furious at the clod for dashing her to the ground. She was scrambling on her hands and knees when words came to mind as one of the clods closed in.

"You asshole! You just broke the heels on my new shoes!" Alisha tackled him about the legs, crashing him backwards onto the asphalt and leaping on top. His gun clattered loose, and she used it as a club, knocking him senseless.

The action had happened too quickly for his partner to do anything but gape. Alisha sprang to her feet, wobbling a bit on her damaged shoes as she pointed the gun at the tough guy who was about to run for the car parked down the alley. He turned and ran only one step before tripping over Toni, who grabbed his hair and started pounding his head onto the pavement. The battle ended as abruptly as it started, but now the roles were reversed. The ladies were on top and ready for more. Alisha snapped out commands.

"Check for weapons, then get their wallets and keys." As the thugs began stirring, Alisha said more.

"Don't get up. Remove slowly your shoes and pants." It was hard to see their expressions, but Alisha saw they were following her commands. "Now lie face down. Toni, tie them up with pants and belts."

"Hey, come on. Give us a break." Alisha was in no mood for discussion, so she kicked the talker twice between the legs, then did the same to his partner. Toni finished trussing the toughs as Alisha ended the conversation.

"Thanks for your wallets and keys. The police will give them back to you, along with your car, which we're borrowing. Toni, wait here while I get the car." A minute later, the ladies escaped into the night. The adrenaline rush energized Toni, and she talked excitedly.

"That could have ended badly if you hadn't tackled the bigger jerk. Jesus, no wonder you're the quarterback. You didn't panic. You must have ice water instead of blood."

"No, just a good friend who taught me how to handle emergencies. Hey, use the car GPS to find a way back to our hotel. Then take enough money from the wallets so we can buy new shoes. That's the least those bozos can do for us."

The night's excitement boosted Kit's performance the next day. She threw TD strikes to Toni, who scored twice on leaping catches, and Kit unleashed for the very first time one of her trick plays—the beach ball pass—only to be used when the defense collapses the pocket. She floated the football into the helmet of an unsuspecting defender, then caught it on the bounce and rushed past the tacklers who were now heading in the wrong direction. Even though they lost the game, the T-Breds won additional fans. In the locker room, Bo tried to make the best of the defeat.

"OK, team, listen up. We played well today. Even though we didn't win, we beat the point spread. We have four games left, so we can still make the playoffs. This coming week, we'll focus on defense. If we shore it up, we sure can win enough to get in. OK, hit the showers and be ready for Tuesday practice."

In the coming weeks, Alisha kept busy practicing to make the playoffs. Electra, on the other hand, kept practicing in Cyberspace to identify possible opponents, and her toolkit gave her quick access to all the data she needed. The first thread she would follow unwound from Cybergard, so she began hacking a trail starting from Brian Ritz's Email directories.

The trail took her up Cybergard's corporate ladder and into the depths of its hardware and software development. Electra memorized the names of those in charge of company strategy and product development so she could track them later. And now it was clear why Cybergard targeted her neuro-devices: it wanted to pirate her hardware and software so Cybergard could dominate two separate markets: Computer Network Security and Augmented Artificial Intelligence. The deeper she dived the more devious the strategy becomes. Each market would have two sets of products. One for customers so they could protect themselves or be more productive, and the other for Cybergard and its devious partners to sabotage computer networks or create destructive AI devices. She would need to hack further to determine how far and how advanced they were, and now she knew where to look.

She followed communications trails through a maze leading to possible Cybergard partners. References to Iron Triangle emerged when she traced trails from software development, sales, and senior executives. Whoever or whatever it stood for must be important. The lightning brain would have to track it down.

There was also a second thread she would follow, unwinding from Hud's confrontation with the Guardian Party. Electra would trace it through a deepening tangle later. I wish I had a dream team to share the load. Well, I don't and can't, so no sense complaining. I'll do the best with what I have.

Darla Tinibu no longer complained that Brian Gardner had disappeared for good. After he fell off the grid, she used her industry and Hacker Nation contacts to locate a target that was even better than H&H Neuro-Device Lab. But it would take a different approach to infiltrate, and she was not ready to pirate just yet. She would need to co-develop with them first and steal later. No doubt they would try the same tactic, but Darla knew she and her people were smarter than her co-developers; she'd be meeting privately in Moscow to forge a relationship with the Iron Triangle. Unlike Napoleon's disastrous invasion, however, she would arrive later— in July rather than June—and leave much sooner—a week rather than five months. And she would leave victorious.

Most anticipated events take too long to arrive. Such was the case for Jared's return from the T-Plague. It had taken eighteen months to regain control of his brain, body, and Oval Office, but he was now ready to act on his own advice and let everyone else follow. He had been patient when first coming back, letting Angus and his lieutenants guide him until he regained enough of his footing to understand what would be best. The opinion polls indicated the public wanted the harsher tone Jared had been preaching before he had been struck down. His recovery proved in his own mind that he was the one chosen to channel divine plans for America, convincing him he could continue to operate above the law when necessary. That's where his political cunning came into play.

He restocked the White House secret service team with agents as devoted and as tight-lipped as Peter Schmitzer, who had been its team leader. Whenever the name Peter Schmitzer popped into Jared's head, so did troubled feelings he couldn't bring into focus. He had occasional dreams about abusing prostitutes in the Oval Office or having a clandestine love affair with a staffer. But he could remember no details, and the media never uncovered anything past unsubstantiated rumors. And after eighteen months, the public wouldn't be interested if fabricated stories surfaced. No one would believe them.

The public had long ago forgiven Jared's peccadillo that steered government contracts to companies he secretly controlled. And since then, he kept his public promise to have all contracts awarded through a transparent bidding process, but that didn't conflict with his network of felonious business partners establishing bogus charitable organization links to his hidden business ventures for laundering extortion payoffs from companies that needed government contracts to survive. He left the details to a handful of heavy-handed lieutenants, confident no investigation could ever connect him with the money trail of his dark and devious agenda. Besides, the people love me. Even if they ever found out, they'd look the other way. Everyone comes out ahead. It's for the public good and my personal gain.

Ziarmal Thaqaf was a thoroughly modern Muslim of the 22nd century. Like every enlightened atheist who understands what neuroscience is saying, he knew organized religion is a remnant of man's hard-wired nature that would become further irrelevant as DNA and social memes continue evolving. He even remembered a prophetic quote from one of the Four Horsemen of the New Atheism: If God didn't invent evolution, he missed a great opportunity. Ziarmal was fine with all the above; he and his Exalted Ruler would play on believers' faith to further their secular plans.

Ziarmal's approach to philosophy was as pragmatic as his approach to religion. He never agonized or split hairs when pondering the unanswerable questions, obscuring emotions or existence. He had little use for post-modern liberal scholars or artists who pouted and promoted their confused views. His hard sciences training had made him smug and proud.

Ziarmal, the mastermind behind the Iron Triangle Alliance, concluded several months ago that it couldn't leapfrog current security systems if it didn't bring in different approaches. I have learned well the lessons of history. Islam fell from world leadership nearly two centuries ago by looking inward rather than outward. I will look outward so we can regain our position in the world. And he didn't have to look long or far, because a person from his Silicon Valley days had reached out to him. He would greet her at Domodedovo International Airport today.

This would be Darla's first trip to Russia, a country that fascinated her. She knew enough Russian history to understand why it was more like the East than the West. It was built atop Kieven Rus, a loose federation of East Slavic and Finnic tribes that adopted Christianity from the Byzantine Empire late in the 10th century. Moscow became the cultural center of a huge Tsarist Empire that ultimately collapsed in the mid-19th century under the weight of brutal repression by rulers unwilling to adjust to the revolutionary demands of its oppressed people. Ever since then, Russia has struggled to find its place on the world stage. It was no wonder to Darla why the country imploded a hundred years ago, becoming a marginal player unable to replace its rule of lawlessness or build a post-resource-based economy. This trip will be win-win-win for me. I'll fake a renewed friendship with Ziarmal to strike a good deal for my company that I can use for myself as well. And I get a chance to sightsee Moscow and its culture, learning more about how it works, so I can use it better.

Ziarmal greeted Darla at baggage claim and whisked her through security clearance to a waiting limousine, all thanks to Sergei Zaitsev's connections—he was Ziarmal's Iron Triangle Russian counterpart.

"It is good to see you. Both of us have taken separate paths in the past ten years, but our paths cross again."

"You look pretty much the same. Frankly, I didn't know what to expect. I'm glad you're wearing regular clothes."

"Yes, I only wear jilbabs and head scarves when absolutely necessary. That's another reason we're meeting in Moscow. The July weather here is so much better than in Isilabad. And Beijing's air pollution is still a monumental problem."

"I'm looking forward to meeting all the Iron Triangle Partners, and I'm expecting to sightsee before I leave. That's one of the reasons I came. Ziarmal nodded and replied, using typical Middle Eastern civility.

"We will make your stay pleasant in all ways."

Three days of hard bargaining accomplished all that was possible at this early stage. Everyone's negotiation style mirrored their culture: Chen gruff and tough, Sergei impassioned and inflexible, Ziarmal urbane and deceptive, Darla direct and determined. She summarized late on that final afternoon a collective position.

"By now, it's clear what each of us wants. I can live with your political motives. Go ahead and try; the world will go on spinning its merry way no matter what you do. As for me, I'm out for money and power, no different than the guys running Silicon Valley. Isilabad wants to rock the Great Satan; China wants to derail America's economy, and Russia wants to break its banking system.

"And let's be honest, we all know this is a marriage of convenience, not love. Or as the textbooks say, we're a single-issue coalition, each contributing what we know best for what we need. You need my security-breaching expertise; I need you're AI and robotic linkages. We'll trade and go our separate ways and avoid tripping over one another. Ziarmal will be my main contact, then Sergei, and finally Chen, if our coalition becomes a target. I will appoint my backup shortly. Have I left anything out?" Ziarmal looked at his counterparts, then spoke.

"No, you presented it clearly. Let me confirm again that you can join our monthly secure and encrypted communications. And we will hold rotating face-to-face meetings as needed. And, now that we have concluded business, we shall have a day or so of relaxation. Sergei, would you please describe what has been arranged?"

"Of course. Tonight, you shall experience Moscow nightlife. Tomorrow, we have arranged a private tour of the Kremlin in the morning, the State Tretyakov Gallery in the afternoon, and shall conclude with the Bolshoi Ballet in the evening. And the following morning, you shall depart for home. All in all, you will have had an informative first visit to Russia. And now, I suggest we go back to the hotel to prepare for this evening."

Darla had prepared well for the trip and knew what Moscow nightlife might be like. She was not disappointed. Though the food was mediocre, the quantity of liquor and the quality of entertainment were stunning. Shouting above the din, Sergei told her that clubs were more raucous in the good old days; judging from the clouds of cigarette smoke, Darla didn't think anyone would have survived to tell the stories.

She learned lots on the tours, realizing she could spend a week at just the Kremlin—the name means fortified fortress in a city. Sergei picked the best assortment for a morning's worth of history. They began at the State Historical Museum, wedged between Red Square and Manege Square and founded in 1872 by Ivan Zabelin, Aleksey Uvarov, and several other Slavophiles interested in promoting Russian history and national self-awareness.

She liked the Tretyakov Gallery tour even more. The guide's Russian-accented English sounded like that of a Hollywood movie actor, and he fit the image to a T.

"Our gallery possesses a unique collection of Russian art, which includes masterpieces spanning a millennium. It was founded by Pavel Tretyakov, a Russian merchant and patron of the arts, in 1892 when he donated his collection to the city of Moscow. It has since become a world-famous museum. Nowadays, it contains more than 170,000 works by Russian artists, from early religious paintings to modern art. For obvious reasons, our modern art is much different than that of the West, but perhaps that will change moving forward."

The high point was an evening at the Bolshoi. Like most "IT geeks," Darla was bright and interested in much more than just bits and bytes, ballet among them. She knew the Bolshoi was an internationally renowned classical ballet company, but Sergei knew all the background.

"It was founded in 1776, but only achieved worldwide acclaim in the early 20th century when Moscow became the capital of Soviet Russia. Along with Saint Petersburg's Marinsky Ballet, Russian ballet is the world's standard. The word 'Bolshoi' means 'grand.' The company traces its origin to a 1773 Moscow orphanage dance school." Then he quickly summarized what they would see.

"Swan Lake, composed by Tchaikovsky in 1875, was initially a failure, but it is now one of the most popular of all ballets. The scenario, initially in two acts, was fashioned from Russian folk tales and tells the story of Odette, a princess turned into a swan by an evil sorcerer's curse." Darla nodded, then replied.

"The music is often used by figure skating choreographers. And I've heard that Russian figure skaters are the best because they're all Bolshoi dropouts who've taken to the ice."

"You are correct. So, let us look and listen…"

Ziarmal accompanied Darla to the airport the next day. "I trust you have enjoyed both business and pleasure."

"Yes, and please thank Sergei. I and my three new best friends learned a lot and know what's in store."

Darla's eighteen-hour flight afforded ample time to rest and then review the results of the trip. She had accomplished her mission and was returning victorious, figuring that within a year, she and Cybergard would begin reaping the benefits of their collective covert co-development. She was confident no one or organization, private or public, would ever catch on to her treachery. When the plane landed, Darla charged ahead.

Chapter 17
September 2123

"Great Expectations"
Thread 2 Chapter 4

ELECTRA'S SECURITY TOOL KIT made diving into the Dark Web like diving for sunken treasure when you know where it's buried. She uncovered trails from Cybergard's Darla Tinibu to an Iron Triangle conspiracy comprised of Russia, China and Isilabad. There were also trails from fabricated charitable organizations to specific Guardian Party lieutenants. Both were doubly troubling; not only did they warn of political or corporate terrorism, but they might cause her to bring Jared back under surveillance. I thought I unloaded all that to Angus and his Brain Trust, but maybe not. I'll call Carter to see what he knows, but I won't tell what I've uncovered until I know what he's up to. And I'll be Alisha to make the call sociable.

Carter enjoyed the hour-long chat because he hadn't talked with Alisha for several months. Though still impressed by her budding sports career, he liked her explanation regarding celebrities.

"Most are just ordinary people. And think about this: you are on a first-name basis with the Vice President of the United States, so you're a celebrity once-removed. Do you still talk to Angus?"

"Not very often, but I hear about him at some committee meetings for the organizations I consult. It turns out Jared likes my economic analysis on most of his programs. Frankly, they are cost-effective, even though he's pushing the ethical envelope even further. Angus is having a tough time pushing back because Jared's listening too much to himself. But when you look at opinion surveys, the public has his back. And nobody's as vocal about his trampling on human rights as Mariah was. Her auto accident was terrible luck. Maybe, if she had picked a different location, or if it hadn't been snowing, she might not have crashed. I don't know."

"Let's not dwell on it. It does no good. Hey, is all the terrorism and political intrigue under control? There's nothing much on the media, so I guess there's nothing on the radar."

"Right you are. No news is good news, because Jared's still looking for reasons to put the screws to China or Isilabad. And the infrastructure system outages and security breaches have gone away. We still don't know if they were just a temporary glitch or if some organization is up to no good. And this is why I've been researching social forecasting. Do you know anything about it?" Carter caught her by surprise.

"No. What is it?"

"This is the first time I can remember introducing a topic you don't know. Anyway, social forecasting is all about Big Data analysis on social media Websites and downloaded tweets, Emails, and private data to spot social trends. It'd be great if we could use it to predict economic, political, or terrorist trends that use human behavior as well as quantitative data. It's been talked about for fifty years. Theoretically, it makes sense, but the quantity of data overwhelms even the fastest algorithms and computer systems." Alisha thought, I'll file that away for later. Time to change the subject. "I would agree. There's just too much data to deal with. Hey, how are you dealing with your social life these days? Are you seeing any more of Jazzi?"

"Yes. She's fun to be with. I'm taking her on an overnight sail with Matt and Zoe while we still have great early autumn weather. Too bad you're not back in DC. You'd have a great time crewing with us."

"I might, but I'm used to moving faster. I'll bet you and Jazzi get a relationship reality check out of the adventure. Close quarters and Spartan comforts should uncover the real Jazzi and the real Carter. There'll be no place to hide. Tell me how it works out. Maybe I can join in the fun next season. Please give my best to Zoe and Matt."

"I will, and good luck making the playoffs. We love rooting for you. And I promise to do a better job keeping in touch."

As he was driving to the late afternoon tennis match, Carter decided the morning conversation had been an accurate reality check for his professional life: his careers at the Fed and associated government committee consulting appointments were satisfying, especially in these still-troubled times. No one knew if relative calm was the eye of the storm or its end. T-Plague, terrorism, public support for Guardian Party harshness, and Jared's return might or might not be problematic, but his abilities positioned his career close to decision makers.

It also confirmed he was satisfied with his personal life. Relationships had moved beyond Electra. Their intimacy revealed more than he wanted. She could be intimidating: too enigmatic, sometimes too cold-blooded and analytic for even his probing philosophical nature. He liked her better as a friend than a lover. Jazzi offered him a package of personality traits he liked better, and his friendship with Matt kept him socially engaged. They were tennis partners for the club's Labor Day weekend doubles tournament. Though a soccer player, not a tennis player in college, Matt's athleticism served him well learning tennis under Carter's coaching.

Carter yelled, "Great passing shot! Game, set, and match," to congratulate Matt for hitting the shot that defeated in straight sets, 6-4 6-0, the opponent. Jeff and Steve met them at the net, joking the way friendly rivals do.

"OK guys. As agreed, losers buy dinner at the club restaurant. And you have to tell us what's got into Matt. That's the best he's played against us."

Lingering in the afterglow of a spirited dinner table conversation, Steve lobbed a question to Carter.

"This is the first time you won a love set from us. Since we're married and you two are still bachelors, maybe it has something to do with your love lives. What's going on there?" Always the diplomat, Carter paused to make sure he could speak for Matt as well as himself. "If it were mixed doubles, you might have something, but we'll fill you in just the same. Both of us changed lady partners a while ago. And thanks to Matt, this new foursome has added skiing and boating to its sports agenda."

"Jeff and I saw your previous partners a couple of years ago. Very attractive young ladies. Pleasant personalities too. But it takes a while before you know what's real. And speaking for married men, maybe we never really know." Matt returned the comment with one of his own.

"Yes, you guys know who Robin is. I fell in love with her when I treated her best friend's broken neck. Unfortunately, she clicked with me more than the other way around. Carter will tell you I did everything I could to make our relationship work, but it wasn't to be. Robin had—and still has—too much emotional turmoil swirling about her. It's so difficult living with a drama queen. I'm much better off, much more compatible with Zoe. I think Carter would agree."

"Yes. Look, both of us know what guys need to do for their partners. It's hard work, as you married fellows know. But it's worth it and is actually fun if your partner pulls in the same direction with the right emotional mindset. Robin was her own worst enemy. Zoe's much more resilient and upbeat."

"No wonder Matt played well today. How about you?"

"I'm dating Jasmine, a banker I met skiing last winter. Jazzi is much more easygoing than my previous partner, whom I never really understood. I thought I was in love with her, but time revealed facets of her personality I couldn't deal with. Matt and I are still good friends with her, and if she still lived in DC, we'd invite her boating."

"Where is she now?" Carter's whimsical smile complemented his words.

"You won't believe this, but it's the truth. She's living in Austin, Texas, and she's the starting quarterback for its Co-NFL football team, and she'll lead them into the playoffs if they win the last game. Quite an extraordinary story…"

Carter wasn't exaggerating. Electra and her alter ego were alive and thriving in Austin. And with the final game of the season approaching, all of Austin's college or pro football fans would be cheering for their rookie quarterback when they battle the Los Angeles Earthquake, aka Quakers.

Bo Rudman and Sam Ryder were finishing a final pre-game toast in the LA hotel bar the Saturday night before. As Bo had just said, the practices, meetings, and media interviews are in the books; now their players can put an exclamation point on the first T-Bred season.

"We probably won't win, but we're ready to shake the Quakers and the fans tomorrow."

"If we win, we're in the playoffs. What's your bet?"

"I'll tell you what I wouldn't say to our players or the press. It's gonna be tough to beat them on their home turf. They played in the finals last year. When the season started, they were picked for a repeat performance, and if it weren't for a succession of mid-season upsets, they'd already be in the playoffs. But like us, they have to win to get in, so their top-rated defense will be ferocious. It's gonna be hard for us even to beat the point spread."

"I'm glad you told a better tale to the media. According to what's been reported, the fans have great expectations for a hard-fought contest. And we've been giving them what they want: exciting, innovative action on the field. Ever since you unleashed the uptempo Wide-V offense, we've been a fan favorite at home or on the road. If we strengthen our defense in the offseason, we'll have great expectations for next season."

"Yeah, but you gotta re-sign our QB. Alisha's got a knack for play calling. And she's got star quality with fans and media. They love her appearance and personality. The fans sometimes hold their breath because her light frame makes her look vulnerable, but she's lightning quick and leather tough. And she's got an unpretentious but sexy swagger. Gives pleasing interviews and me credit for calling the plays when actually she's doing it."

"I think we can make it worth her while, and ours too, to stick around. Do you think she stuck around the hotel tonight, or did she and her sidekick do a pre-game celebration?"

"I don't ask and they don't tell. It works so much better that way. I've never coached a team with better chemistry. Work hard play hard is their motto, and Alisha's harder on herself than on anyone else. That goes over big with our fans too."

"Let's call it a night and be ready for a great game tomorrow. No matter the outcome, we have great expectations for the future." Alisha and Toni didn't need a pre-warmup night out. Both awoke Sunday clear-headed and clearly focused and ready to give their best. And to lighten the locker room mood, Toni had music and video from the popular underdog retro-flick Rocky booming triumphantly. As was now the team's custom, Bo let Alisha run the locker room pep talk huddle before taking the field. He would do so at halftime.

"School's out for the season! Today we graduate for the playoffs. We've done our homework and our best, so no matter the score, we'll be winners if we play with our hearts and our heads. And leave any butterflies in the locker room. We're meant to take joy in the game on the field. So, let's take it to the competition. I've got my Kit game face strapped on."

The sportscasters felt electricity in the air as the overflow crowd and extra media coverage made the singing of the National Anthem even more tingling. The commentator's assessment matched what Bo told Sam but would never rule out an upset.

"That's why we play the game on the field, not by playing with numbers on a blackboard. Let the game begin."

Bo surprised everyone on the opening kick-off. He let Kit return it, setting the tone for the entire game. She danced and darted up the field, finally tackled just past midfield. The up-tempo offense kicked in immediately. Kit started by running the ball herself on the first play, then completed a rollout pass to a halfback on the second play for another first down, followed by a crossing pattern touchdown strike to Toni on only the game's third play.

"What a start!" crowed the commentator. The Quaker defense just got a wake-up call, and if the T-Bred defense can hold the Quaker offense to less than its average, the game's a toss-up. Stay tuned."

The first half became a footrace up and down the field; the Quaker's defense was barely able to contain the lightning in a bottle offense powered by Kit. The T-Breds threatened to score on most drives, but too many ended in turnovers—untimely fumbles or dropped passes or interceptions, or missed field goals.

The overmatched T-Bred defense fought gamely but couldn't stop a relentless Quaker offense. The score was 28-24 with two minutes remaining in the first half when Alisha got her hands on the ball at her thirty-yard line. The commentator's annotated-action calls kept the viewers spellbound.

"T-Breds have the ball first and 10 on their own thirty. It'll be difficult to score in the amount of time left because, good as she is, the T-Bred QB can't throw long. Let's see what play sequence Bo Rudman has plugged in." Kit peppered the defense with a mix of medium-range passes and laterals to halfbacks or wide receivers running end-arounds, taking the ball to the fifteen-yard line with ten seconds on the clock.

"The T-Breds have their field goal unit in place. There's the snap and the hold… Wait!… The holder is going to pass… I can't tell who it is… Oh! Too bad!… The ball slipped out and is sailing high into the air like a Hail Mary pass… By the time it comes down, there'll be a crowd leaping for it…It's heading down into the endzone… Six players leaping skyward… Someone's got it!… It's a T-Bred player… Touchdown!…Uh-oh…Penalty flag…I didn't see any infraction… We'll have to wait for the call… Let's check who caught the ball… Why, it's Kit Kittner, the quarterback… Let's look at the replay from the beginning."

The replay revealed another of Kit's first-time-ever trick plays. No one but her team saw her take the place of the holder. She faked an errant pass high into the air; the defense followed its trajectory and not her, and the height of the pass gave her enough time to join those leaping for the ball. She snared it just after it caromed off the helmet of a defensive player.

"Will you look at that! Kittner caught her own pass… And it's not an infraction… Another player touched it first. That, my fans, is a oneof-a-kind touchdown!"The half ended 31-28 in favor of the T-Breds.

Bo did his best in the locker room to settle his hyped-up squad.

"OK, team, listen up! That was a great first half. Defense, you were terrific, keeping their offense in check. Offense, you really caught them with the fake kick. Everyone, take a deep breath and forget about the first half. We gotta focus on the second half, and only that.

Offense, keep doing what you're doing. Defense, dig deep into your conditioning and reserves. Don't burn out. Marshal your energy and help one another. Their offense gets the second-half kickoff, so expect them to be in our face right from the start. And don't worry about the score or making mistakes. Play like you know how, and everything else will follow."

The first half foot race turned into a second half marathon. Drive and determination were as strong, but the first half's torrid pace had depleted speed and strength on both sides of the ball. The T-Bred defense stymied their foe until fatigue tripped a defensive back, allowing a touchdown at the end of the third quarter, making the score 35-31 in favor of the Quakers.

The fourth quarter became a war of attrition. Stadium fans and media viewers alike were riveted on what was becoming an epic struggle. They were watching primal emotions seen only in war or sports contests, where the contestants put everything on the line. Exhaustion made it even more dramatic, showing that even trained athletes struggle when trying to exceed their limits.

Neither team could move the ball consistently. A couple of spectacular plays would then be followed by physical or mental errors, resulting in turnovers or loss of down. The ball shuttled back and forth between the thirty-yard line markers. The commentator gave his assessment with a minute to go and the T-Bred offense in possession on their thirty-yard line.

"What a marvelous game! Both teams have played their hearts out and are exhausted from the effort. I can't imagine what Bo Rudman's going to do. Looks like too much distance and too little time or energy left. And no timeouts once the ball is snapped."

Only Kit knew what she was going to do. A crowning moment had arrived. All season, she had played selflessly for her team, bringing them with her. The time had come for Kit to run wild as only she could. She huddled her team for the final time; they looked to her; they wanted her to seize the game.

"We have enough time for two up-tempo plays. The first is a lateral to right halfback sweeping left. Then we're gonna run my

'Midnight Play.' Remember when you played schoolyard games of tag? Midnight was my favorite. One person in the middle, tagging people as they ran across. Those tagged help catch others. Game ended when only one person left untagged. That's what we're gonna do. I'll drop back to fake a pass. You gotta block your defender but not draw a penalty. And don't be offside. I'm gonna run them into the ground. And I'm ditching my knee and thigh protectors so I'm lighter and more mobile. Remember, don't draw a penalty or be offside. OK, break!"

Kit felt an involuntary shudder just before the snap; the lightning brain was shifting gears, preparing to unleash lightning in a bottle.

"Here's the snap… A handoff to the right halfback… He's cutting into a gap in the line… He's almost into the secondary… Oh! Too bad he tripped…You can tell everyone's running on fumes. Time for one last play." Kit took the final snap to start what would become known in Co-NFL folklore as "The Run."

"Kittner's dropping back to pass… No one's open… She's dropping back further…the defenders are drawing a bead on her… She sidestepped the first and is retreating back further…" Kit was drawing them into her trap. The lightning brain put the action into slow motion. Make them chase me; tire and spread them out; I'm juking and dancing and avoiding hits. Kit had retreated all the way back to her fifteen-yard line when the lightning brain shifted to a higher gear. Let the Run begin!

Kit reversed direction and raced like lightning up the middle of the field, leaping over a couple of fallen defensive linemen. As she raced up-field, offside or illegal receiver penalties were a thing of the past. Now she had to contend with lighter and faster defensive backs and safeties who had watched her from a distance, trying to figure out her moves. They had signaled one another, dividing the field into zones they would patrol. Kit would have to run past all of them in order to score.

She streaked directly towards the left sideline defenders. Neutralize them by freezing them in their tracks! Then she streaked across the field as they vainly chased. She retreated, letting them gain, but then she swept to the left and up the field, leaving them gasping. The other defenders retreated up the field to protect their goal line.

Kit drew another set of defensive backs to the center of the field, reversed direction twice then zoomed past. There were two sets left, waiting to intercept or chase from their five-yard line, each guarding a side of the field as Kit set sail directly towards the end zone. They took the bait and closed towards the middle just as Kit cut sharply to the right, trying to veer around them. But they cut her off, so she dashed across the field to try her luck on the other side. Watch out for blindside defenders coming back into action! Kit knew even she was running out energy. She could sense other defenders rushing towards her; she had one last move. She zigged back across the field almost to the sideline, then sprinted towards the exact center of the goal line. The remaining defenders plotted a course to intercept her at the two-yard line, and that's when Kit leaped skyward. For a moment frozen in spacetime and forever etched in the memories of those who saw, Kit became a sky walker; no, she became a sky runner, a high flyer soaring effortlessly above the earthbound defenders, her lithe frame paralleling the trajectory that would touch down in the end zone.

The commentator's action call would be replayed nationwide for two days on all the sports channels.

"Will you look at that! Kittner's leaving the defenders in the dust. The playing field looks like the Roman Coliseum. Gladiators face down. Uh-oh, some are getting up, rejoining the chase…She's got two groups ahead… It looks like she's tiring… She's going for it now… Look at her elevate!… She's diving and somersaulting over them and into the end zone… Touchdown!… Incredible!… She must have run four lengths of the field—nearly a quarter of a mile!… Uhoh, a penalty flag has just been thrown. Let's listen to the call…"

Kit was in the end zone on hands and knees, trembling from exertion and emotion and endorphins as teammates rushed to her, the crowd chanting "Run Girl Run!… Run Girl Run!" Teammates were screaming, "We're in the playoffs!" when a hushed buzzing replaced frenetic yelling. The commentator addressed the dreaded penalty flag that was now center stage.

"The replay clearly shows a T-Bred player blocking a defender below the waist from behind. How unfortunate. I don't think that defender could have made a difference, but that nullifies the touchdown. Let's get the name of who caused the penalty… Toni Diya."

The crowd settled down for a moment, but then erupted in cheers for both teams who were congratulating one another on the field. Players and fans alike saluted one another for being part of a magical game. Often, by the end of a hard-fought contest fans are more disconsolate than the players, whose emotions have replaced any aguish of defeat with the thrill of what they had accomplished. That could be said today for all T-Breds except one: Toni.

Poor Toni. She sobbed uncontrollably in the locker room, unwilling to share her self-directed anger and failure. It took the entire team to rouse her from the depths. Bo drew them together just before departing for the airport.

"OK team, listen up. Take joy in how well we played today. Fans are going to remember the game, not who won. Toni, you were a big part of our success this year. All of us can look forward to next season. Sure, we all would like to be in the playoffs now, but we'll do it next year. OK, let's get to the bus. That's our first step to next season."

Alisha bolstered Toni's sagging spirits on the flight back.

"Like Coach said, we're all winners today. Let go of your disappointment. Enjoy all we did and look forward to what's in store." Toni needed more convincing.

"Like what?"

"Well, we get time off from training to go back to other things in our lives."

"I don't have much else. Compared to our teammates, I'm sort of one-dimensional." A surge of empathy colored what Alisha said next.

"You have me as a friend. How about we do this. We'll party with our fans when we get back, and go shopping for fall fashions in a couple of days."

"I'd like that." Toni dropped her voice before continuing." I don't want to be alone tonight. Would you stay with me?" Alisha revealed the trace of a smile when she whispered,

"In football, the QB usually throws the pass. But there are other games where I'm a good receiver if I like what's being thrown, and I'm not gonna drop yours."

Alisha and the T-Breds weren't the only team expecting a great last weekend in September. So were Matt and Carter and their lady-friend partners. This was the weekend they would charter a ten-meter Beneteau for Chesapeake Bay sailing. Matt and Zoe had graduated first in their three-month, every-weekend sailing class and were confident they could handle a sloop equipped with Jazzi and Carter for crew. They left early Friday afternoon so they could sleep on the boat Friday evening.

Carter had sailed several times while growing up on the West Coast, but Jazzi was not fond of water sports. Skiing and skating were as far as she had gone, preferring to be on top of rather than in the water. Carter convinced her it would be fun, assuring her that boating keeps you on top. She was the first to offer an opinion when they reached the pier.

"Gee, I don't know. It looks kind of big. Are you sure you can handle it?"

"You bet. Zoe and I know what to do. We did great in our sailing class. And whether it's a big boat or small, the laws of physics governing sailing work the same. And this boat even has a motor. Don't worry. We'll be fine. And Carter's read up and will explain things to you. He's a great teacher." Carter decided it was time to put his oar in the conversational flow.

"That's right. I brought my copy of Chapman Piloting and Seamanship. It's been the authoritative book for power and sail boaters for two hundred years, often called the bible of boating. I'll read some of it to you tonight." Jazzi smiled, then thought to herself, Carter is too cerebral sometimes, too analytic. I bet If he were facing a firing squad and none of the guns went off, he'd try to figure out why, and then offer suggestions. But let's see what happens.

Carter explained enough boating terminology and points of sailing so Jazzi could navigate around the boat. Meanwhile, Zoe and Matt were happily plotting tomorrow's course. The adventure would start from the sloop's home port—the Sailing Emporium Marina near Rock Hall, Maryland—and sail south to Saint Michaels, a distance of forty miles as the crow flies. This late in the season, they should have no trouble securing a mooring in either the Saint Michaels Harbor Inn or the Mile River Yacht Club. The weather forecast called for prevailing easterly winds on a sunny mid-50s Saturday, so Matt could sail a beam reach all day along the eastern shore of the Bay. Matt announced the plan to the crew before everyone sat in.

"You'll love sailing on a beam reach. It's the fastest point of sail. Tomorrow we'll head due south with the wind over the starboard side. We'll stay on the course until we reach Saint Michael's. Zoe and I will take turns at the helm, and all you two need to do is man the sails and sheets. Carter knows all about them, and he'll help Jazzi."

Jazzi was beginning to confuse some of the boating lingo, but decided to ask questions in the morning. She'd be as bright as sunrise when Zoe awakens the crew at first light.

Saturday dawned, glowing with the promise of gorgeous sailing weather. Zoe busied herself in the galley, setting out breakfast cereal while Matt and Carter unhooked shore power and water lines. Jazzi took charge, folding up the sleeping areas and carefully removing the coverings. Carter came down below just as she finished stacking them.

"Looks like you're busy helping. Tell me, what are you doing?" "I'm doing what I was told last night. I'm taking care of the sheets. I've got them all neatly folded." Carter smiled as he corrected her. "Sheets in boating are different than sheets in sleeping. Sheets are the lines connected to the sails. Go ahead and put the folded bedding away. I'll teach you sheets when we go up on deck. But let's have breakfast first."

Boaters' breakfasts are meant to be fast, efficient, and clutter-free; Zoe's preparations suited everyone but Jazzi, but she didn't complain. Afterwards, Matt assembled the crew on deck to prepare for casting off.

"We're moored at the end of the pier, which is the perfect spot for sailing away from the dock using the jib, so here's what we'll do. I'll take the helm. Carter, you hoist the jib. Zoe and Jazzi will cast off. I'll tell you when to do what." Zoe pointed to where Jazzi should stand, then told her to loosen the line.

"I don't see a line. All I see are ropes." Carter called out instructions.

"Sailors call the ropes lines. I mentioned that last night. Grab the one you're standing on and watch what Zoe does." Jazzi didn't say so, but Carter seemed to have more confidence in what she was doing than she did.

Matt gave all the right commands when the time was right. Carter hoisted the jib, and then Jazzi watched as Zoe cast off. Too bad Matt couldn't command the wind to blow a little harder. It was too light to counteract the current, so the Seaquin—that's the name of the sloop—drifted slowly backward, eventually drifting into the stern of a power boat. It's Captain, a jovial, middle-aged, solid sort, stood on deck holding a coffee mug and enjoying the sunrise, called out to Matt.

"Ahoy there, skipper. What are your intentions?"

"Good morning to you, Captain. My name's Matt. I was trying to leave the dock under sail, but I guess I was overly optimistic. Not enough breeze. May I ask your name?"

"Call me Cap'n Bill. Ho-ho, you better help with oars or a motor. I'd recommend you start your engine. That's what we power boaters do, and it seems to keep us out of foul water or foul moods. Let me push you off as soon as you start your engine. We stink potters are good for something after all, eh?" Matt thanked him and started the engine, asking a question before heading towards the breakwater.

"Have you ever sailed? It's different than power boating. It's a lot of fun."

"Yes, sir. Done both and like 'em both, but for different reasons. Powerboats give you more space and creature comforts. Sailboats give you more quiet time and exercise. They put the work in the workout." Cap'n Bill raised his mug and bade Matt and his crew a safe journey. "Here's to all your spouses and lovers. May the two never meet!" Matt piloted through the breakwater entrance, heading towards the Chesapeake Channel. He would instruct the crew to raise the mainsail once they were in the clear. Too bad the motor didn't cooperate. Halfway across the channel, it sputtered to a dead silence.

Matt was unable to restart it, but Zoe sounded a cheerful note.

"Good thing it's early. There aren't many boats bearing down on us yet." Jazzi thought that just one would be too many, but decided to keep her mouth shut. Carter didn't say anything, but headed down below to look for a solution to the problem. He quickly spotted the problem, telling only himself what it was.

Jazzi accidentally bumped the fuel line valve into the shut position when she stowed the sheets. I'll have to read more of Chapman's to her. He opened the valve then hustled on deck.

"Try to start the engine now." It sputtered to life on the third try.

"You're a genius! Reading Chapmans makes you so. What did you do?"

"I adjusted the fuel line valve. I think Jazzi bumped it when she put the sheets away." Everyone smiled and said nothing, but Jazzi thought to herself, Hey, I'm doing my best. Be a little more patient.

Now that they were underway, everyone sat while they crossed the channel. Matt found the right place to hoist the mainsail and then steered south onto a beam reach. The rest of the day's untroubled sailing rewarded the crew's collective efforts that had been needed during departure.

If you want to test relationships, try crewing together. For better or worse, you're stuck in cramped quarters with your partner, significant other, spouse, friends, or whatever you wish to call them, and terms of endearment might be revised during the cruise. Only Jazzi paid attention to the phenomenon because the others had been friends for so long. She observed Matt and Zoe's compatibility. They delighted in working together to make sailing fun for everyone. But she wasn't certain about Carter. He's pleasant, but I sense a streak of impatience. And he can be judgmental, like a teacher reprimanding students. But everyone's happy now. The sun and calm water are fine by me.

The rest of the day sailed by, but Jazzi was glad when they approached Saint Michael's. Eight hours on the water was more than enough for one day. Matt radioed ahead to the harbor master to arrange a buoy mooring from where they could use a dinghy to motor to the pier. The entire crew was looking forward to dinner ashore, then catching the latest news and weather report before turning in early, but they didn't have to wait that long to get the bad news. The harbor master gave them the weather forecast when they registered in his office.

"A change in the weather's coming a day early. The northerly cold front is blowing in late tomorrow morning. What's your course?"

Matt said, "We're sailing back to Rock Hall. How do you think that'll be?"

"It'll take you a lot longer. You'll have to beat the entire way, and it's liable to be rough. Have you been in the Channel when the wind blows hard out of the north? It can get really lusty."

"No. Maybe we should reconsider." Matt was beginning to realize Sunday might give them more than they bargained for, but Zoe surprised everyone by recommending they wait until the morning to decide what to do.

"Maybe the front will blow in slower or softer. And if it doesn't, we can practice beating and reefing." The harbor master figured some free advice might be helpful.

"Miss, it might be better to practice when the weather's good. How long have you been sailing?"

"Three months, and we got the highest marks in our sailing class too." One look at the harbor master told everyone that he was an able-bodied seaman who had learned his craft on the water, not from reading books. He respected the power of the sea and always did his best to help boaters who stayed at his marina stay afloat, hoping that his advice would bring in repeat business.

"I applaud your pluck, but if I were you and your crew, I wouldn't push my luck. Get up at first light and decide, but stay out of the chop. It's cold and unforgiving."

Matt thanked him before steering his crew back to the boat. Zoe and Matt slept like stones that night, but Jazzi was uneasy, so Carter tried to loosen her nerves with a story.

"Sometimes people court danger for the adrenaline rush. A boater friend of mine said there's nothing more satisfying than the thrill of tying up at a pier just before the storm hits. He said it's like dodging a bullet. Maybe we'll learn about it tomorrow." Jazzi's reply matched her quizzical look.

"If you say so."

Weather at first light was inconclusive. Cooler winds were just beginning to gust, and clouds from the north were starting to generate large patches of shadow. After a quick breakfast, Matt made the "go" decision, so he and his three wanna-be Argonauts departed under power on a quest for safe passage home.

They hoisted jib and mainsail after they were well clear of the harbor entrance. By this time the wind was a moderate blow straight out of the north; if it intensified it would use Chesapeake Bay's fetch to build rollers that would become pea green whitecaps by midafternoon. Jazzi could hardly believe Matt's optimism and Zoe's carefree attitude. She really has confidence in him. She glanced at Carter, whose expression registered concentration more than concern, and it stayed that way for another ninety minutes until the waves started washing over the bow and he spotted a line of squalls approaching. That's when he called out to Matt.

"We've got heavy weather ahead. Looks like strong gusts and zero visibility. Let's take in the sails and power back to Saint Michaels while we can." Matt agreed, steering directly north to dump wind from the sails so his crew could haul in jib and mainsail. Zoe assisted but Jazzi couldn't because her stomach had started rising with the wave action; by the time the squall hit, so did her force five seasickness.

Carter grabbed her to cushion the fall into the cockpit, then held on as all her meals still in process came up and then went over the leeward side. Jazzi felt a little better as the spray simultaneously cleaned and revived her for the wild ride back to Saint Michaels.

Carter huddled in the front of the cockpit facing backwards, one arm around each lady so they could watch Matt deal with a following sea. Following seas—waves and boat going the same way—are dangerous because the boat loses steerage and becomes unstable, possibly capsizing. Matt had the know-how to handle the boat, but he also had luck behind him; the waves hadn't yet built to a dangerous level. He said a silent prayer and wore a jaunty smile when they passed the breakwater into the harbor. The harbor master helped them dock, even though another squall was about to break. All rushed into his office just before the rains came pouring down. There were enough chairs and mugs, so he poured coffee and handed out towels to his waterlogged guests.

"The four of you learned in the last two hours more about handling a boat in heavy weather than you would in a month of Sundays in a boating class. You got here safely; how do you plan to get home?" Carter answered first.

"I recommend we lock down the boat, pay our good harbor master a mooring fee, rent a car so we can drive back to Rock Hall, and settle up with the chartering service. I'm sure it can sail the boat back when the weather improves. And let's change out of these wet clothes before we leave. Jazzi glanced out the window, spotting several problems.

"Your plan has a bunch of holes in it. We can't change until we get our gear, and I'm not getting mine until the rain lets up." Matt could tell Jazzi wanted the weekend to wrap up faster than the weather might allow, so he said that the fellows would retrieve everyone's duffel bags. Before they returned, Zoe tried to buck up Jazzi's drooping spirits.

"You've been a great sport, and I hope you'll join us on other weekend adventures."

"I can't say I enjoyed the weekend as much as Carter did, but it was educational. I learned more about him, and I discovered my time limit for being in a boat. I'll consider joining you on other weekend outings, but only if they're on dry land."

"I'm sure that can be arranged. Matt and I are always coming up with new activities, and once we do, Carter always comes up with a way to make them educational." Though Jazzi didn't look convinced, she put her best voice forward.

"Carter's always the man with a plan, but next time I hope he's more like a partner than a teacher." Just then, the fellows trudged in with all the gear. Zoe picked up the conversation where Jazzi had stopped, pointing it in Carter's direction.

"Jazzi says she might join us again if you can make a plan for a dry land outing."

"I'm certain I can do that. Many learning experiences await us all." Jazzi didn't smile when she replied.

"That may be, but try to factor in some fun too, for you and for me."

"I'll make sure I do that. And sometimes, maybe Alisha will join us. She's a great planner, too, and I know she likes to have fun."

Chapter 18
November 2123

"The Rising Star"
Thread 2 Chapter 5

ELECTRA KNEW ALL ABOUT autism. Though not autistic, she had researched the condition well enough to conclude that her obsessive-compulsive predisposition occasionally accentuated her manic-depressive tendencies, the combination bordering on autism. She was well aware of her idiosyncrasies and had learned how to deal with them, as well as with Tim and Kwame.

Spectrum Disorder is the official term for autism, referring to sensory integration and processing deficits that overwhelm neural circuits. Symptoms include erratic or obsessive behavior, avoidance of eye contact, and unwillingness to speak. A hundred years ago, society stigmatized autism, but that's no longer the case. Many autistic people are now highly sought for their pattern-matching and number-crunching abilities perfectly suited for computer programming.

Kwame's autism was tailor-made for what Electra needed. Pediatricians diagnosed and specialists treated him early, so he didn't need gene or neuro-enhancement therapy or nano-tech implants. And he had taken so many Daily Life Skills classes that he volunteered to counsel patients at a nearby Austin clinic.

Like autistic Tim, working for Electra made Kwame's job a once-in-a-lifetime opportunity. She not only empathized with them but also trained each one-on-one, giving them whatever they asked for and finding clever ways to keep their autistic tendencies in check. And she employed an "employee-friendly" management style: one-minute planning, praising, and adjusting. Today, she would be instructing Kwame on another type of software he would begin coding. He had already integrated advanced GUIs into all high-priority security software tools, beating the Thanksgiving deadline by a week. It was time to introduce him to her next software suite: Social Forecasting Software.

Electra had begun focusing on "Big Data" techniques, often labeled by acronyms like STONE—Shaping Terrorist Organizational Networking Efficiency, OSI—Open Sourcing Intelligence, and SMI— Social Media Intelligence. Companies began using Big Data apps a hundred years ago when public and private uses for
"nudging" opinion or predicting behavior went viral, but not even Silicon Valley's best algorithms could match Electra's for crunching data and finding predictive patterns. Kwame would code her solutions, which could be used to forecast Cyberterrorist locations, spot social trends, and identify political instabilities before they emerged.

Electra spent Monday morning sketching the big picture before diving into algorithms and software design. As was now customary, Kwame sat spellbound, looking and listening carefully without saying a word. Electra then suggested he eat something, then walk outdoors with her before returning to the conference room where he could sit and think and draw pictures until he was ready to repeat everything. Kwame was now wrapping up his eruption of words and diagrams.

"You make this so easy. You've already developed the algorithmic modules I can drop into my code, and your distributed parsing protocols let me do Big Database parallel scanning. And you've already tested the code, so all I need to do is clean it up and make the graphical user interfaces more user friendly."

"You've got it. But please, wait until we have lunch. Tim will be disappointed if you're not with us."

Electra spent the afternoon listening to Tim explain Cyber-Theater progress. He had built a prototype "shuttle" and knew what standards to use for coding the media tracks, but he hadn't yet made vendor contacts necessary for producing and marketing it.

Electra knew people who could help.

"So far so good. And by year-end, I'll give you a contact list, but let me describe some longer-term possibilities for what we've begun. You and Kwame are going to integrate artificial intelligence into hardware and software that controls devices used in power generation, transportation, communications, manufacturing, business, and people's homes. Two that are already underway come to mind: V2I—stands for Vehicle to Infrastructure—and Communications Grid Control. I know something about both, and I'd like you to dig in for more details. Let's plan to compare notes by March of next year." After Tim left, Electra thought about what she might be unleashing.

Like all breakthroughs, my algorithms can be put to good use or bad. Think about government surveillance, PoV communications, and private data. Although sci-fi movies are going where Silicon Valley technology can't, Big Data is marching in that direction. I must be careful what I develop or teach. Danger awaits if my work falls into the wrong hands.

Electra had Tim's contact number one in mind and would talk to him just as soon as Alisha signs next year's T-Bred contract. Sam had already explained to Bo what he wanted the T-Breds to be next season, and they needed to sign Alisha to make it happen. He invited Hud Haller and Blake Woolker to join Sam Senior and him for a Thanksgiving Eve dinner with her. Collectively, they could show why Austin is the best place to be.

As she drove to the meeting, Alisha considered her preparations. Hud told me who's invited, and Electra summarized all the dollars and sense reasons. I've rehearsed my part, and I'm a good actress. And I'll remember Electra's first rule of negotiation: don't talk too much until the other side has revealed its position.

"Woolly" Woolker, a business contact as well as one of Sam's good friends, was the first to join Sam Junior and Senior. Serving as the governor's press secretary, he recognized that Alisha could be a useful asset in Texas politics. Youthful, personable, and articulate, she could be a role model and an advocate for K-to-12 Texas school programs. Sam liked the idea because it would piggyback on her growing popularity by keeping her name in the public spotlight, always good for ticket sales and media interest.

Hud walked in ten minutes later, knowing that his role was to provide the personal touch. He had sworn to Electra no one would ever know about their hidden business connections, and he was as good his word, having spun a believable yarn that Electra's parents— good friends from grad school days—had invested years ago in his start-up biotech company. When they died, Electra inherited their investment, and Hud became a good friend, helping her manage it.

Alisha cruised into Sam's office looking even more fit than when the season ended. Sam made introductions and appropriate small talk before steering the conversation to contract negotiations.

"Last year, Dad and I rolled the dice and it came up sevens and elevens. Thanks to us, you're a rising star, and thanks to you we had a successful season. How would like to do it again?"

"My agent and I have been talking about this, and I'm supposed to mention three words to get our discussion started: major media markets." Sam thought, Uh-oh, her agent is looking for big bucks. I thought about that, so let's see if she likes my counter-arguments.

"Yes, Austin ranks only forty-fifth, but Dallas-Fort Worth ranks fifth and Houston tenth. And thanks to our growing popularity, we're pulling from all three. So, you can play in a big spotlight right here. But let me describe what our strategy is for the coming season. I think you'll find it to your liking." Sam paused for effect, then continued.

"All of us know the Co-NFL is a combination of sports and entertainment, and the fans liked us on both counts last season. Our Wide-V Offense with you calling the plays is fast, exciting, and high-scoring. We want to keep the offense just like it is: you the star and the team your supporting cast. Your teammates look to you and want you to be the main attraction. The sports reporters expect me to strengthen our defense. They say if I do, we can dominate the league, but that can be a problem. Fans like to root for David, not Goliath. And team owners want to see balance in the league. If we dominate, the owners might change some of the rules to limit what you can do, and no one wants that. So, I'm not gonna beef up the defense. I can make excuses that it costs too much, or that I couldn't get our picks interested in coming to Austin. And frankly, let's look at it from your point of view. You'll be more popular—and I think you'll enjoy the challenge—staying here and leading a good team to victory rather than moving on to a better team that's expected to dominate. What do you say to all of that?" Electra would say it's a win-win-win. I'll say the same, but not all at once.

"It's got possibilities, but tell me, why is Mr. Wolker here?" Woolly knew why and didn't need to be asked twice to explain.

"We think you'd be a great asset to our Governor's K-to-12 school programs. You'd be a role model and spokesperson for us. Texas is a red state, but our Governor and his administration are not a bunch of rednecks. We lean liberal, far away from some of those Guardian Party reactionaries. We know you were a Guardian Party volunteer when you were in Washington, and but we think you'll like Texas politics. Alisha agreed, but kept her comments private. You bet! I like all of Texas, but play it cool.

"Yes, that could be interesting. But that means I'd spend more time in Texas. I'm willing to do that, but you'll need to do something for me. Here, take a look at my CV." Alisha handed out copies of her academic resume. "I would like the Governor to pull some strings so I can get a dual post-doc research position at UT Austin and my current school, GWU. I don't want to boast, but if you look at my research areas and publications, UT should like what I bring. And my post-doc advisors at GWU should go along with it because my projects will sync commonalities at both universities. I'll give you contact info so UT can contact GWU."

"I can't promise this will fly, but I think the Governor might like it. I'll get back to Sam." Alisha had two more wants that she would hand off.

"Mr. Ryder, I'd really like to stay with you, and I'm sure your salary will be appropriate. But I have a couple of suggestions for trading salary for perks. How about getting me a car, and how about lining up some sponsors? I know enough about marketing to know I'm a brand the public likes now and will like even more next season. I promise to keep my image better than Bambi's, as long as you let me work hard and play hard. And my agent and I have come up with a brand image that is All American, All T-Bred, and All Texan: unpretentious with a sexy swagger, connects with the fans, trains hard, competes hard, plays hard. And here are the companies that should go for my endorsements: Ford, Indian Motorcycle, and Patagonia Clothing. We can split the sponsorship and endorsement fees. You can use that to offset salary. And all this promotes my brand and the T-Bred brand too. So, here's where we are: I'll sign a contract that includes a car and sponsorship with the companies I want if I get UT a post-doc position." OK, Alisha, now keep your mouth

shut! Electra says the first side to talk is ready to sign. Sam looked at Woolly; both of them looked at Hud; Hud smiled at Alisha. Then Sam stood to shake Alisha's hand.

"We're gonna have a great season. Why don't you come back in about a week to sign your new contract? Woolly and I should have what you want lined up. I'm sure Bo will want to take you out to lunch, and I'm also sure Woolly will want you to meet his people."

Alisha's mood on her early morning run was as glorious as Thanksgiving's rising sun. She ran with a quickness of step and lightness of spirit fueled by yesterday's meetings. Electra agreed.

"You're a great actress, and how fitting the outcome. Today is truly a day to be thankful for the present and for what's in store. We can look forward to Hud's mid-afternoon buffet, and I'll immerse myself in security software work until then. So, hurry on home."

Electra had finished breakfast and was powering up her computer when her cellphone chimed. When she answered, Holy Haller's voice came through loud and clear, carrying a note of concern.

"Hi Mr. Holy, and Happy Thanksgiving…Yes,I agree…Robin's been doing well… She's taken a step back today?... Yes, I know what she means when she says she needs to talk to Electra the therapist… I'll be right over."

Electra saw what Holy meant when she stepped into his home office. Robin was sitting on the sofa, arms folded and a glum look shadowing what lately had been a cheerful countenance. Holy had rolled his wheelchair close by; Electra sat on the ottoman across the coffee table from them.

"It looks like you might need a minor attitude adjustment. Please tell us what's on your mind." Robin leaned forward and spoke, keeping her arms folded.

"I've been doing so good these past couple of months. I've been taking care of Holy; he's been teaching me all about business, and I'm taking two required courses that I couldn't transfer credits. But maybe I should have taken just one course to start. You know how I always get stressed out when final exams are coming. Well, to make it worse, I'm way behind on my comparative philosophy term paper due next week, and I'm really struggling with the topic I picked. I thought it would help me come to terms with things, but it's added to my confusion."

"What topic did you pick?"

"I titled my paper What Poetry and The Myth of Sisyphus Say About Suicide. I got lost in the essay and depressed by the poems my instructor recommended. I, uh, I felt awkward talking to him about my problem. I let it fester, and now I can't shake myself out of being depressed. Maybe you and Mr. Holy could help me lose the depression." Electra diagnosed the problem immediately.

"A lot of people get confused reading The Myth of Sisyphus by Camus. It's one of the most influential works for responding to existential and post-modern philosophers' depressing outlooks. It came out in 1955, long before neuroscience and brain research marginalized much current philosophical and theological babbling.

Mr. Holy, have you read it?"

"Can't say that I have. What's it about?"

"It starts with the most riveting line in philosophical analysis: 'There is but one truly serious problem, and that is suicide. I'll shed some light on what he's saying, but let's ask Mr. Holy to tell us why, when he wakes up each morning, he decides to go on living rather than kill himself."

"Never been asked that question before, but come to think of it, it's a good one. Gets you to thinking. I know that some people do think about it, and everyone has the freedom to pull a trigger on a gun pointed at themselves. I'm way old enough to know how hard life can be at times, hard to find meaning. But I'd rather find happiness each day looking for ways to make something out of nothing rather than calling it quits."

"Robin, you need to embrace what Mr. Holy just said. No wonder he'll live to be a hundred or more." Robin glanced at Holy. Both nodded slowly, then Electra continued.

"In a nutshell, Camus is telling us that life is basically absurd. Here's what he says absurd means: 'The absurd is born of the confrontation between human need for happiness and the unreasonable silence of the world. And because man is conscious, he cannot escape from the absurd. Furthermore, man is trapped between two ways of seeing his way through the problem: experience or cognitive thinking, and the revelation of religion. Either way leads to a logical conclusion that suicide is unavoidable.' After that, his arguments and words get a bit murky, perhaps because what I read is an English translation from French, but he goes on to show how many existentialist philosophers end up with Sartre's famous quote: 'If god exists, everything is possible; if god doesn't, everything is impossible. 'It means this: if god doesn't exist, nothing is possible, which is sort of the credo of nihilism, the rejection of everything. Camus turns this glum outlook on its head by rejecting rejection, demanding free will and freedom to act. So, you avoid suicide by choosing to embrace life, even though it is absurd. Why don't you take what I just said and use it in your term paper? You can embellish it a bit, but don't stray too far. Now, what about the poems?"

"My Instructor picked two: Do Not Go Gentle Into That Good Night by Dylan Thomas, and Because I could not stop for Death by Emily Dickenson." Electra knew them well.

"These are two of the greatest poems ever for confronting death. Many scholarly articles try to explain them. By the way, you can get bonus points by explaining that the Dylan Thomas work is actually a villanelle. And that's a nineteen-line poem with two rhymes throughout, consisting of five tercets and a quatrain, with the first and third lines of the opening tercet recurring alternately at the end of the other tercets and with both repeated at the close of the concluding quatrain. Bear in mind both poets were young when they wrote these verses. They had much left to do, so of course they didn't want to kill themselves. And now, let's give you something to use so you get an A-plus. Here is a poem from my Mother, Indira, that gives her view on death. She called it Don't Fear the Reaper:

'Death should be of less concern the older we become,
Simply one of Nature's Laws when all our work is done.
Something unavoidable that Life will send our way,
Expected then and brings an end to day's soft setting Sun.
For Youth forsooth it's tragedy Death would come too soon.
Their morning star is still in flight to reach a bright high noon.
So sad it's said to cut them short with so much yet to say,
Better they should stay awhile and sing out wine-sweet tune.
For those so close to Mid-Life peak Oh Death! is quite unfair,
Much to be accomplished still suspended in the air.
Better for to grant a stay ignore them for a while,
Returning at a later day when all's been taken care.
But do not fear the Reaper when becoming gray and old.
For those with faith and hope to see an outlook being bold.
Redemption may await for those on darkling distant isle,
Gods grant it true for me and you as Prophets have foretold.'

"You can easily write your paper if you build on what I've just given you. Add your own words for analyzing the poems. And I hope this will jolly you out of your depression, because today is Thanksgiving. Any questions?" Holy and Robin looked at one another; Holy scratched his head, then finally blurted out a question that had been puzzling him.

"Why do people sometimes call you Electra, and other times Alisha?"

"When I'm in the mood for thinking, call me Electra. And when I'm ready for fun, please call me Alisha. Robin, isn't that right?"

"Yes, and I love you both ways. But for the rest of the day, please be Alisha. She's usually a lot more fun to be around, and she doesn't give listeners an information overload."

Electra and her alter ego were lots of fun to be around in early December. UT's post-doc committee seized the opportunity and hastily approved a joint biotech and AI research appointment for Electra. Alisha signed her contract, had an outstanding pre-training camp meeting with Bo, and later the same week had a pleasant lunch with Woolly. And the day before she left for Christmas holiday in DC, Sam confirmed her sponsors were glad to have her onboard. All this meant the new year would start fast and furious.

Electra declined Hud's offer to fly her on the corporate jet. Air travel was back to normal, and mid-December traffic was tolerable. She used the uninterrupted flight time to contemplate what should be a relaxing two-week break.

I'll meet with my GWU post-doc advisors first. Professor Ravenhill will be overjoyed once I explain how he gets to participate in all the UT work and get his name included in all the journal articles. And I get to keep my office and lab privileges. Between the two universities, I have now increased my team's headcount. They aren't a dream team by any means, but I can leverage them to carry out my intentions.

The remaining time would be personal, most importantly a rekindling of friendships with what remains of the Full House— Zoe, Matt and Carter. Though she hadn't put it on her calendar, perhaps she could see Angus and Russell. However, a New Year's Eve dance club party would definitely be part of the mix.

Electra pondered the importance of traditional Holiday ceremonies and festivities, noting how they had transitioned even more from spiritual to secular. Organized religions finally acknowledged that people want a humane and inclusive message, not one of guilt or sin or salvation only after death. But she knew little children—and many adults too—weren't ready to deal with the realities of an indifferent Universe. The human species is genetically programmed to believe in the magic of some sort of god that can explain the connections seen in the world about them. Extraordinary as my lightning brain is, I'll never know the answer to life's big questions: Is there a god? How did the Universe begin? How did life begin? These are among the questions whose answers are inaccessible because even I have asymptotic limits that I can approach but never cross. That's the best I can do, and I can live with them. After all, the lightning brain's prime directive is to go on living, to survive.

Carter waved when he spotted her walking away from the baggage carousel. Jazzi was with him; he thought this would be a pleasant way for two ladies important to him to meet again. Should I call her Electra or Alisha? I'll wait for her to lead the way. And I'll let her decide what to tell Jazzi about our relationship. There's so much to her that I never understood, and what I did, I always had trouble keeping straight. Damnation! She looks better than ever. Alisha dropped her bags to hug Carter.

"Thank you for picking me up! And hi again, Jazzi. I'm Alisha. Are you and Carter skiing over the Holidays?"

"No, because Carter says I need to do more conditioning. Maybe we'll go in January."

Carter joined the conversation as they proceeded to the car. "Jazzi's a great sport. Maybe you can give her some training pointers too. And I hope you don't mind that I drove your Mustang. There's more room for the three of us and your luggage." Alisha's smile and words said it was fine, and the more they talked on the drive home, the more she understood why Carter liked Jazzi. She's attractive enough according to Carter's standards; she has a pleasing, non-threatening personality too. And she holds up her part of the conversation, so she's obviously intelligent. I hope she likes Carter's cerebral style, because I like hers.

"I really like your taste in clothing. I'll bet you subscribe to the Corporate Fashionista Newsletter. Currently, I'm into designer athletic wear, but I like tony styles too. We'll let Carter worry about the cost-benefit tradeoff, but since you're a banker, you probably have already done that."

"Ladies, when it comes to your looks, there are no costs, only benefits," Jazzi replied to Carter's humor by poking him in his ribs, then spoke to Alisha.

"We're happy you're spending the last half of the month in DC, so we get to see you before leaving. Carter bought us a Royal Caribbean Cruise package. We leave on the 23rd from Fort

Lauderdale to Barbados and return January 2nd." "Are Zoe and Matt joining you?"

"No. They'll be skiing at Vermont's Jay Peak Resort. And Zoe wants to give a dinner party this coming Saturday. Will that be good for you?"

"That's perfect. Between Thursday and Sunday, I have plenty of time to meet with my GWU committee and associates, as well as discuss real estate with my house sitter. I have an expert taking care of my property. I think you know the fellow."

"I do. Sometimes, he recruits me to help maintain the property. But there's little I ever need to do. Carter takes care of everything so well." Carter was about to pull into the driveway, so Alisha ended the conversation by teasing him.

"Yes, he's very thorough. I think that's just one of the reasons we like him."

Carter and Jazzi helped bring luggage into the house, then he led a walk-through to make sure Alisha found everything to her liking.

"The place looks even better now than when I was living here. Maybe I should pay you for staying. Are you staying tonight?" "Actually no. I thought you'd like some time to yourself settling in. I'll call you tomorrow on your cell. I assume you have the same number."

"It's the same, so call me when you like. If I'm not here, I'm out running or at GWU. And please tell Zoe to call me."

Alisha stuck to her normal schedule on Thursday morning. She worked out, then ran the route her muscles knew from memory. After a late breakfast, she switched to her Electra persona, confirming Friday's committee meeting and then spending the rest of the day working on a selection of projects. Unlike Alisha, whose motto is "work hard play hard," Electra's had always been "work hard because it's play," until Alisha taught her to enjoy taking a break. And whenever she relapsed into more work and less play, Alisha was there to remind her.

Friday's committee meeting held no surprises because Electra had prepared thoroughly. She was polite and professional, even helping her advisors maintain an illusion of understanding her work. Of course, they were pleased to have their names included on any publications, and they understood how she would integrate two sets of grad students working for her on separate campuses. Afterwards, she tidied her lab and office, then logged on to the university computer network to check for Emails and search for documents. She noted wryly, Most university Websites I visit have retarded logon procedures. Someday, I'll develop a security suite tailored for them. It'll have to be a dumbed-down version of what Kwame is working on.

Zoe usually didn't need to logon to talk with her circle of friends, preferring networking face-to-face. She needed to talk to Alisha soon because she hadn't done a good job this year keeping in touch. That bothered her because Alisha had done so much to keep her afloat when life overwhelmed her two years ago. Zoe was strong once again and able to deal with events on her own terms, but she wanted to rekindle the friendship. She would invite her early Sunday afternoon while the others were playing tennis indoors at Carter's club.

Zoe's voice still contained an endearing breathless quality that always gave Alisha an emotional twinge because it stirred memories of how Zoe helped her Guardian Party career. I still harbor residual guilt for not being a better friend when Zoe needed me. But that was then and this is now, so let go of the guilt.

Zoe flitted like a bird in flight to answer the door when Alisha knocked.

"Merry Christmas! Come on in." Alisha folded her arms around Zoe, kissing her on her forehead before speaking.

"You look marvelous. Life must be going well. I want to hear all about what's going on."

"Come into the kitchen so you can sample some of my hors d'oeuvres. I just opened a bottle of Syrah."

"It looks like you and Matt have just finished redecorating. I like the countertops and the hi-tech cooking station. Are you going to do the entire house?"

"Yes, we're doing a complete makeover, but not rushing it. We're phasing it in as our relationship develops. So far, we've done front and back doors, the master bedroom, and the kitchen.

And we've upgraded all appliances, door locks, and thermostats. They're now plugged into the 'Internet of Things.' Matt worries about power outages and hackers disrupting our home management software, but we've not had any issues. But please, tell me how you are."

"Life in Austin is good. I can tell you at dinner when I clue in Matt and the others, but I'd rather talk about you. You've had a lot going on in your life."

"I'm sorry I haven't responded to some of your Emails. I was afraid you might be angry at me, that you wouldn't like my dating Matt."

"I'm happy for you and Matt. I want nothing but the best for both of you. Matt is a great guy. He did everything possible to make his relationship with Robin work, but Robin isn't the right person. I think you are. I love Robin. She's my only remaining childhood friend, but as you've seen, she has mental issues that will probably keep her from ever having a long-term male-female relationship. I hope the rest of your life is going as well."

"Well, you know I left my Guardian Party public relations position as soon as I knew Jared was coming back, and I hired on with a new agency that handles public and private healthcare issues that arise from emerging technologies. It's a hot topic, what with all the furor about integrating biotechnology, nanotechnology, genetic engineering and artificial intelligence into the post-human age. Our clients come from both the supply and demand side for healthcare products and services. And I'm glad I resigned from the Brain Trust too. It was getting too stressful, personally and professionally. And I really need your help handling the personal stress. Do you think Jared is going to come after me again?"

"I think it's very unlikely for a number of reasons. First, according to what's been reported, there are big gaps in his memory. He might not remember what he did, and his closest agents from back then are dead. Second, that chapter of your life ended two years ago. Neither the media nor the Guardian Party should be interested in rumors that old. And finally, you and I might be the only ones who know the full story, and we're not going to tell anyone. So, I think you're safe. But you have to do this. If you ever get the notion something or someone is snooping into your past, please let me know. I still have contacts to help us put a stop to it."Zoe heard Matt's van pull into the driveway.

"Thanks for being my friend; actually, you're two friends in one, Alisha and Electra. What do you wish to be called this evening?"

"Please call me Alisha. I expect to have fun this evening." Conversation ran non-stop from appetizers through dinner and then late into the night. Alisha's Co-NFL stardom was front and center, but the topic soon switched to water sports—skiing, sailing, and cruising in the Caribbean. Alisha listened more than she talked, but did make comments to herself. Matt and Carter seem much happier with Jazzi and Zoe than with Robin and Electra.T he fellows have moved on, as have Electra and I. And it's almost midnight, so I better get going.

"I'll be back in Austin by the time you return, so please Email and send me some pics. And I'll let you know when I'm coming back to DC. Hugs and kisses to all."

The Electra-Alisha duo planned to putter around home the week before Christmas, starting a pre-season exercise program and setting plans for the coming year. She didn't plan to reach out to others until after Christmas, but three people called. The first call on Monday surprised her.

Angus McTear missed his Brain Trust, but he missed Electra's insights even more. He hadn't seen her for two years, ever since she had been struck down by the T-Plague. He was relieved when Carter told him she had recovered, but she had come back a different person. She had regained most of her memory and probably had most of her intelligence, but was different emotionally, softer, more understanding, easier-going. And according to Carter, people should call her Electra when they want to talk about darker issues; call her Alisha for the sunnier side of life.

Angus needed to talk to Electra. Maybe she could provide suggestions for keeping Jared under control. And he wanted to make sure the true story of the Chinese attack stayed hidden. Only five people had known the full story: Electra, Angus, Russell

Conklin, Mariah and Carter. Now, only four remained and he was sure all would maintain their code of silence. But was there damaging evidence somewhere in Cyberspace? Just before Jared forced him to terminate the Brain Trust, Angus had instructed Russell and Carter to destroy all hard copy or Cyberspace links. He did likewise, but when he searched in Cyberspace a month ago, he found files he had overlooked, and a couple of days later, when he logged on to delete them, they had disappeared. He needed to ask Electra what she knew, but not in person because Jared might be accessing his Big Data PoV. Jared might be watching him. He would call her on an encrypted private line. Electra answered as soon as she recognized the caller ID.

"Merry Christmas… Yes, I'm living in Austin and just signed a contract to play next year. How are you?… Carter told me the latest… I agree. The public still likes Jared and his policies… You better make sure he doesn't go too far… Sorry, I don't have any ideas for keeping him inbounds… If all of us keep quiet, no one will ever know what really happened… Evidence somewhere?… Unless you kept notes, there's no hard copy, but it's up to each of us to delete our Cyberspace documents. I think I deleted mine when I recovered, but I'll let you know if I find anything… You think Jared might be tapping into Big Data that's storing your tracking and privacy? Be careful where you go and what you say… Yes, I talk with Carter regularly… OK, I'll relay info to you through him. And here's something I just heard that might help you stay on Jared's good side. Look for connections between Cyberspace terrorist attacks and a group called the Iron Triangle… Don't ask me how I know… I'll tell Carter if I find out more. Happy New Year to you too." After disconnecting, Electra thought about poor Angus.

Next year's going to be challenging for him, but he doesn't need to know all I know—not yet, anyway. Thanks to my security tools, I made a final Cyberspace search for incriminating evidence and deleted the last of his files, along with everyone else's. And I gave him a useful terrorist clue too, so I've given him his Christmas present. But I'd better do more Cyberterrorism tracking.

Alisha handled the second surprise call that Monday evening when Jennifer Conklin invited her for Christmas Day dinner. And an even bigger surprise call came Thursday evening from Katy Tang, her best soccer team friend. Perfect timing too, for Katy would be happy to be her dance partner at a New Year's Eve dance club party.

Electra reminded Alisha that they would maintain their traditional Christmas Eve schedule. The morning training and strength run matched Alisha's good mood, and all afternoon Electra polished next year's plan. After finishing, she sat back and contemplated her handiwork.

This is as good as it gets. I have three careers and no fears about anyone discovering I'm a genetic Frankenstein. I can unleash my abilities, and I have big plans for doing so next year.

Alisha's ready for Co-NFL training camp that'll start in January. Kwame's coding will keep my security software ahead of Cyberterrorism, and I might uncover details Angus can use. And my newest apps will take me into social forecasting. And there's more.

Tim and I will strengthen the link between nanotechnology and artificial intelligence, applying it to the Cyber-Theater. And I'll keep Su and Kameyo busy developing new drugs and extending DNA applications.

And there's more for Alisha. She'll lead the effort to strengthen the bonds of friendship with our circle of close DC friends. And she'll watch over Robin. Electra powered down her workstation, ready to enjoy Christmas Eve dinner. It's time for Alisha to come into the foreground. After a traditional dinner of Swedish meatballs and baked beans, Alisha nibbled on sweets and sipped Champagne while listening to Christmas music. She particularly liked traditional English and French carols that were usually featured in London concerts held at King's College or Saint Paul's. Noel Nouvelet was her favorite, and she listened to it again on the Internet, enchanted by its hauntingly lovely voices. She listened once more and was about to log off when she came across a collection of traditional Irish songs, so she clicked on it and reclined on the sofa, using a pillow and blanket that added to the warmth of the candlelight.

The soprano's ethereal singing of the first ballad, Walk My Love, cut Alisha to the quick. Its plaintive lyrics brought forth a cascade of emotions she could not explain. She listened again, absorbing the words:

> "I wish I were on yonder hill
> Tis there'd I'd sit and cry my fill
> And every tear would turn a mill
> I wish I sat on my true love's knee
> Many a fond story told to me
> He told me things that ne'er shall be
> Siuil, siuil, siuil a ruin
> Siuil go sochair agus siuil go ciun
> Siuil go doras agus ealaigh liom
> His hair was black his eye was blue
> His arm was strong his word was true
> I wish in my heart I was with you
> Siuil, siuil, siuil a ruin
> Siuil go sochair agus siuil go ciun
> Siuil go doras agus ealaigh liom
> I'll dye my petticoat, I'll dye it red
> And 'round the world I'll beg my bread
> Til I find my love alive or dead
> Siuil, siuil, siuil a ruin
> Siuil go sochair agus siuil go ciun
> Siuil go doras agus ealaigh liom"

Alisha's obsession grew, so she put it into a playback loop and let it carry her away…

"Alisha, please awaken now! I must talk to you."

A voice roused her from reverie. Sitting up, Alisha saw a glowing, white-robed apparition sitting across from her. Although this was their first meeting, she knew immediately the visitor is Indira.

"Your lightning brain has summoned me to explain what you are feeling. You are keeper of our emotional persona, just as Electra is keeper of our cognitive. And you have done well since the lightning brain conjured you to help Electra."

"Mother, I've never felt this way before. Please help me."

"My precious daughter, the Christmas Season always brings the warmth of family, extolling the importance of family bonding. And here you sit, alone by choice and happy until hearing the sad song of the Irish lass whose love has gone to war. You are feeling her sadness because she is lonely.

"But you are not lonely; you are alone, and you know the difference." "That is true; I do. But I do not have the kind of love the Irish lass has. I have not taken a lover."

"That too is true. And remember this: you might never find— even for a moment—another to take for your very own, for you cannot take love. Love can only be given. So, take joy in the circle of friends you now have, and be engaged in what you do so you may find others and vice versa, too. They can become your family. You are still young; reach out to life and look for other creations to love: knowledge, arts, ideas, causes. Look forward to the future you and Electra share.

"Now sleep my precious daughter, and when you awaken, be of good cheer. I am here with you always."

Alisha blinked as the smiling apparition faded as it floated away in a shimmering glow. And then she slept until dawn's glow awakened her to the joy of Christmas Day.

"Merry Christmas, Alisha, and thank you for the T-Bred pullover and sweatshirt. I know which one I'll keep, and which I'll give to Russell. Come on in to the living room. Russell, Alisha is here." Jennifer hugged her first, then Russell did likewise.

"Merry Christmas! And thanks for inviting me. I forgot to wrap your presents, but since 'Ladies first' still applies, you get your pick." Russell added to the greetings.

"You probably don't remember what I said to your grandfather long, long ago: 'Your family always has a standing invitation to Holiday dinners.' I'm going to put on my sweatshirt right now." Jennifer donned her pullover and Alisha offered her opinion.

"You're ready to cheer for the T-Breds next year. If you'd like to go to the game, I'll get tickets when we play in DC. I'll do the same for Matt and Carter and their co-friends. Now please tell me, how have you been?" Jennifer went first.

"The holistic healthcare business Matt and I have is doing well. Next year, Matt might work full time, and Zoe might handle some of the load so Matt can continue his EMT work. It gives us so many new client leads."

"Zoe and Matt seem well suited. Does it seem that way to you and Russell?"

"Yes. He's such a great guy, and Zoe is such a better fit. You know I love Robin, but I think she's too high-strung, even for Matt. How is she doing in Austin?"

"Much better. She's learning to live with her mental issues, and being a fulltime caregiver focuses her attention, pushing her mental issues into the background. Russell, how has the year been for you?"

"Tolerable, but I don't have the mental or physical energy I did a couple of years ago. I turned seventy this year; it's time to retire and let someone else handle NIH T-Plague vaccine sourcing. That Texas company still hasn't released line extensions that work on the mutated virus. We've been able to contain it, but the number of new cases continues to grow."

"When Russell retires, he can join Matt and me. He manages the business, Matt brings in new clients, Zoe and I provide holistic services, and we all live happily ever after. Come on Alisha, help me put dinner on the table. Russell, please work your carving magic on the prime rib."

Electra added to post-Christmas activities by renewing contacts to friends she had neglected. She had lunch with Rihanna Antar, the plastic surgeon who had stitched her back together. She went out for dinner and dancing with Joe Miese, who had been an occasional boyfriend before life became too unsettled. And she called her Uncle Chandra—Indira's brother—who lived in London and was still taking care of his mother. Only one of the calls turned glum. She learned from the parents of a high school boyfriend that Hector had died a year ago from T-Plague complications. Electra reminisced how Hector had helped convert her first car into a stealth street racer. All that belonged to the past; Electra paid her respects, then turned the page.

Alisha spent much of New Year's Eve afternoon primping for the dance club party. Vanity was one of her foibles, but at least she was aware of it and wore it well. Though the weather was cold, the walks were clear of snow so she could wear a new pair of stilettos tailormade for dancing. I'm glad I kept a lot of party dresses and coats in DC. I'm gonna look good tonight.

Alisha appraised herself in a full-length mirror. Yes indeed, I do look good, and I'll look hot on the dance floor. How nice to be young. That thought triggered an abrupt realization. But someday I won't. Even the beautiful people lose youth and looks. What will I become? How will I handle it? Well, not to worry. I'll follow the advice of that Doris Day chestnut: Que Sera, Sera; What Will Be Will Be.

Alisha tingled as she drove to pick up Katy, even though she had no expectations. She would let whatever emotions emerge drive the evening. Katy wasn't ready when Alisha knocked, so Katy's father invited her in. Katy had told her that he was a foreign service professional who had married on his first assignment a Vietnamese woman. Both of Katy's parents were pleased to meet a "celebrity."

"Katy has told us about your football prowess. She even made us watch the last game of the season. No wonder you have become so popular among Co-NFL fans. But you look much different." "I'm out of uniform." Just then Katy entered the room.

"Hi Alisha. I'm so glad we're going dancing tonight. I used one of my Christmas gift certificates to buy this dress and heels. What do you think. Wow, I forgot how good-looking she is.

"You look totally hot! Have you looked on the Internet at some of the latest dance moves?"

"Yes, and I can't wait to show you. Let's go." The girls hustled to the car, their words setting the tone for the night.

"I'm sorry I didn't call you from Austin last season. I should have done so a long time ago, but maybe we can make up for that tonight. Katy giggled, her features glowed when she answered.

"The night's young, and a new year awaits. I'm sure it'll start well for us." The girls sped into a night full of possibilities.

Alisha and Katy weren't the only ones filled with cheer for the coming year. So was Darla Tinibu, the only one at Cybergard headquarters on New Year's Eve. The intensity of her intentions was matched only by that of her glee for what would soon happen. She was prioritizing the target list of banks whose computer networks she alone would covertly crash. Then, when the media reported the calamity, her sales consultants would diagnose the problem, then sell them the solution: Cybergard Security software that would ward off future attacks. Other banks would have to follow suit; if not, they would be added to the target list.

The banking industry was just the start. Other targets would be selected and attacked, but not too soon. She would be cautious and coordinate with her Iron Triangle partners, pirating from them when opportunities came her way. 2124 would be a very good year for Darla and Cybergard, but not for their customers unless they buy what she was selling. And the same might apply to my Iron Triangle associates if they don't like what I plan to do. And I won't tell them until I'm through.

Darla didn't wait for midnight to toast her upcoming success.

Chapter 19
January 2124

"Darkness at Midnight"
Thread 3 Chapter 6

UPON RETURNING TO AUSTIN, Electra immersed herself in all the subtleties of programming social networking apps, so by the end of January she had constructed a software suite that would guide her social forecasting projects." Big Data Social Networking" started bigtime early in the 21st century when legacy Websites, such as Facebook and LinkedIn, burst upon the Internet, spawning an entire industry linking people, "Big Data," businesses, and government organizations in Cyberspace.

Silicon Valley creativity extended it via open source intelligence and crowdsourcing to include content delivery networks controlled by social curators and user communities, giving a bewildering quantity of current events, data, and people's opinions. Private enterprise followed suit, developing similar Big Data networks and software apps for crowdfunding and collaboration that gave smaller companies access to capital and people so they could thrive. American hardware and software companies, large and small, were able to create wealth and jobs that replaced those lost to global outsourcing. All this required a smart workforce, which was beginning to rebound from T-Plague damage. Finally trending upward again, the U.S. economy showed signs of recovery.

Government and military agencies tapped into Big Data, developing stealth systems that tracked people and pirated private data. Department of Defense support for high energy physics paid big dividends because advanced weapons projects glommed onto the sophisticated apps spun off. But whether private or public, all developers shared the same Achilles Heel:

network security. It was the reason for an increasing number of government or infrastructure network failures as well as Cyberterrorism.

What did Electra want to do to improve Cyberspace security? Three things: build a suite of Cyberspace software tools Hud could sell to governments or companies seeking Cyberspace terrorism protection; develop weapons for battling Cyberspace terrorists; become master of social forecasting and Big Data manipulation. Tim and Kwame were already charging ahead on security software tools and weapons. By the end of February Electra would have first generation social forecasting software ready to fire.

Alisha, on the other hand, immersed herself in her expanding CoNFL world. At T-Bred's mid-January kick-off meeting, Bo introduced several new linemen and safeties recruited to bolster the defense, and Sam Ryder set goals everyone bought into: get into the play-offs and excite the fans. Alisha knew after the first week of practice the offense would be ready to roll out what the fans wanted. She was ready to unleash Kit whenever she strapped on her game face.

Thanks to Sam's promotional skills, Alisha's coalition of corporate sponsors arrived on a late January weekend to produce the first set of "Alisha brand" commercials. She sported some of Patagonia's newest designer sportswear, posing in front of her Ford Mustang or midsize Indian Scout motorcycle. The sponsors recognized possibilities. Alisha projected a striking and sexy image colored with a touch of vulnerability, packaged in All-American vitality and sparkling personality, which should win new fans and customers. What surprised the film crew most was how natural she acted in front of a camera.

Sam shared the commercials with a Co-NFL Public Relations Department coordinator who needed only one look to invite Alisha to the mid-February Hollywood shoot. She met with Sam a couple of days before leaving.

"Bo says the pre-season offensive practices have been dynamite, and he thinks the defense is strong enough to get us to the playoffs. And we'll make sure our offensive line gives you plenty of protection.

Do you feel ready?" Of course I am! The training is boosting my strength, and all the media attention is boosting my ego, but I'll be cool and just act naturally.

"Yes, I'm ready to roll, on the field and off. I love my new car and motorcycle. And I look good on them in Patagonia or T-Bred sportswear. Maybe I can get some tips from the media crew in Hollywood. But I need a favor from you. I want to bring a guy that works for Hud, Tim Godfrey, with me. He's working on a project that puts additional sound or video tracks into recordings. You've got Hollywood contacts, so maybe you could call ahead and introduce us so we could meet them in person."

"I'll arrange it and confirm the details before you leave. But you have to do me one favor also. Please don't party too hard when you're out there. The season opens in two weeks."

"I promise. Tim is real conservative. He's an engineer."

Neither Alisha nor Tim had been to Hollywood, so before they left, she played the coaching role.

"We're the team for launching our Cyber-Theater game. We need a filmmaker who can embed your multi-sensory tracks into a disk or video stream, and we need a fixture-maker to turn your prototype shuttle into a trendy viewing chair. Hud gave us contacts, and I might get more when I meet the media crew. So tomorrow, while I'm being filmed in commercials, I want you to practice what you're going say. You can do some sightseeing too, but tomorrow evening we'll rehearse together."

"I know the tech stuff cold, so I don't need to practice if you let me cover assembly details. But you better talk about the sales and marketing stuff. When you show your Electra personality, you're a great negotiator. I've seen you in action. And let me guess. For the commercials you'll be Alisha."

Alisha had been one of twenty athletes selected to showcase in CoNFL promotions. She knew all of them because she had played against them or had studied their game videos. The director in charge had produced Co-NFL commercials for previous seasons and selected athletes that were be attractive, athletic, and likable. He was not disappointed with the current crop, and as the filming proceeded he couldn't help noticing one in particular. That T-Bred athlete, Kit Kittner, seems special. Not beautiful in the classic Hollywood style, but she has striking features that her athletic build accentuates. Electric smile and so natural in front of the camera. I'll recommend she talk to our studio director after we put the film in the can.

Alisha was so into filming she was surprised when the director called it a day.

"That's a wrap. You've all done well, and our editing crew will make you look even better in the media than on the field. I hope all of you have great success this season."

As the athletes filed out of the briefing room, one of the film crew asked Alisha to see the studio director before leaving. As they marched to meet her, Alisha thought to herself, I don't know what to expect, but I'll be fine if I think before I talk and act naturally. Maybe I can get some good contacts.

"Ms. Lauret, here's Alisha Kittner." Kathryn Lauret, the tony, darkhaired, fortyish studio director handling athletic commercials, turned to greet them.

"Thanks, Randy. Hello Alisha, I'm Kathi Lauret. What name do you prefer, Kit or Alisha?"

"On the field it's Kit, off the field when I'm having fun its Alisha.

And it's Electra when I need to be serious. I'm pleased to meet you."

"Well Alisha, please have something to drink. Let's go to my office." On the way, Kathi discovered how poised and emotionally attuned Alisha could be. Once they were settled, Kathi buzzed for an assistant to bring a selection of snacks and soft drinks.

"Is this your first trip to Hollywood?"

"It's my first 3-D trip, but I've been here thanks to school and Cyberspace. I took a couple of cinematography classes, so I know a little about Hollywood's history and technology. And I watch all sorts of retro-flicks and current releases."

"Have you ever been in plays, or been coached in acting?" Only by Electra and the lightning brain, but that's not for you to know.

"No, I haven't. Was there something I should have done differently today?"

"No. According to my assistant director you were perfect. And that's why we're talking. We haven't vetted you yet, so I don't know anything about your background. What I do know is that you've become a popular rising star in the Co-NFL, a league that is wildly successful. You should think about this: your athletic career has an expiration date, and while your star is rising you need to make the most of it. No one can see themselves as well as someone viewing from a third-person perspective. And mine is film. I think you could do well in action-adventure movies. Our studio is noted for that genre. If you'd like to consider this, you need to take a screen test. I can't make any promises, nor should you either, but I can schedule you for tomorrow. And frankly, the evaluators will like that even better. Short notice lets the truth be told." Alisha felt like jumping across the desk for joy but managed to contain her enthusiasm.

"I'd like that. If I fall on my face, I'll consider it part of my football training. I know how to pick myself up and move ahead. But I'm usually pretty good staying on my feet. And I have an extra day or two, so tomorrow would be fine. By the way, I'm here with a friend; he's an engineer looking for business partners to launch a new kind of home theater. Maybe you might have some suggestions for him."

"I might, depending on what he needs. Let's talk at dinner in the studio cafeteria. Here in Hollywood, studio cafeterias are top shelf, just like everything else. And you look like you'd fit right in."

Tim wasn't happy when Electra announced a change in plan.

"Geez, I'll have to give both tech and sales pitches by myself tomorrow when I meet Hud's contacts. Maybe I should reschedule."

"That's a bad idea. They're doing us a favor, so you don't cancel at the last minute. And I lined up another interview for us day after tomorrow. Tomorrow's meetings will polish your act. Let's rehearse; give me your pitch."

An hour later, Alisha applauded Tim's performance.

"Nice work. Make sure you pitch the tech piece first, like you just did, and remember to smile, talk slowly, and maintain eye contact. Your enthusiasm will impress the other side. And don't overpromise. If there's something you can't answer, we can call them later."

Each was on their own the next day. Kathi played a neutral role, staying in the background and not telling anyone that Alisha was auditioning for future possibilities, not for consideration now. Doing so kept the evaluators unbiased. Alisha was one of twenty actresses auditioning for an action-adventure sequel to be released at the end of the year, always a popular time for new releases. She would be judged on how well she projected emotion in voice and body language, how well she followed what the director called for, and how well she acted a snippet of a scene. Alisha was one of only four selected for the second round that would be held that afternoon. The afternoon test included all the above but also required her to act a scene that included another actor and a minor stunt. Alisha breezed through the session, thinking to herself this is even more fun than running football drills. She was about to leave after changing into her clothes when one of the assistants approached her.

"Uh, Ms. Kittner, I'm supposed to take you to Ms. Lauret's office." Excellent, she thought. I never like waiting for results.

That's what's so good about sports. You always know the score.

Kathi rose to introduce an older gentleman who was standing beside her.

Hello again, Alisha. I'd like you to meet Jackson Nolan, one of our studio's senior producers. Electra smiled but kept her thoughts to herself. Why, he's a buffed image of Sam Ryder. I bet I'll like him.

"Hello Alisha. Please sit down. I wouldn't normally meet with you like this, but I'm making an exception for a couple of reasons; I took Kathi's advice and watched your audition, and I wanted to congratulate you. You handled yourself like a polished actress. Maybe your quarterback role has groomed you. What I saw confirmed what Kathi told me last night. You've got the look for action-adventures. I'm extending an invitation for your agent to send your media kit directly to me. There are a few athletes who are able to handle sports and acting careers. Maybe you're one of them. I can't make any promises, and you need to think about how

Hollywood might fit your plans. I don't want you to make any decisions tonight. Just let the experience sink in and think about it. Talk it over with your agent and let Kathi know if or when you'd like to take the next step. I assume you have an agent."

"Yes, a close friend of mine. Her name's Electra. And I believe she has a business proposal that your studio will discuss tomorrow. Would you be willing to join that meeting?" Jackson nodded, so Alisha fleshed out a description of her agent.

"She looks a lot like me, because I play both roles: client when having fun and agent when being serious." Smiling to herself, Kathi wondered just how far this young lady might go.

Alisha asked Tim about his day as soon as she returned to the hotel.

"How did your meetings go?"

"I got flushed at first, but the second went better. They told me to bring you tomorrow morning. I hope that fits with what you lined up for tomorrow. What's the name of the studio you were at?" "Cyber-Max Studios. I've lined up a meeting there tomorrow afternoon. And don't worry. Electra will run the show at both." Electra was satisfied with the morning meeting. Tim did a good job recapping how his prototype shuttle-chair interfaces with the sensory tracks, and Electra outlined a sales plan that projected a small but growing profit by the end of year two. The company would consider the offer further and respond next week. She and Tim prepped at lunch for the afternoon.

"Your presentation skills are definitely improving, and you'll do even better this afternoon because the studio likes me and the concept. They're larger and have more vendors that could join in, and they focus on action-adventure films that could showcase multi-sensory technology. I'll point all this out when I make my opening remarks. I can make the deal win-win. And remember, you go into a negotiation with an agenda that lets you run the meeting without the other side realizing you're in control. Be sure to listen carefully to the other side. Don't talk too much or too soon."

Electra's agenda worked. Her opening description explained how Cyber-Max could leapfrog current media technology, and how the Cyber-Theater shuttle-chair would become an at-home virtual theme park. Two hours later, Jackson summarized what they had accomplished.

"We like what you have, and we agree that H&H DNA Partners has uncovered a spinoff consumer market for its neuro-device R&D, so we'll be building on what you've already brought to the healthcare market. Our studio can handle multi-sensory track embedding, but we'll need your help handling aroma. Fragrance companies have already developed a vector representation that can approximate just about any odor. I'm not sure what that means, but I imagine Tim does." Electra kicked Tim's shin so he wouldn't start babbling about eigenvectors in orthogonal spaces. Then she spoke.

"Yes, Tim will show your assembly vendor how to scale up his prototype. And he can explain to your people how fragrance embedding works. This is a great win-win project: H&H gets some of the profit because we contribute the R&D, Cyber-Max Studios gets the rest for launching the Cyber-Theater." Jackson's closing remarks were music to Electra and Tim's ears.

"There are a lot of other details that need to be worked out, but I think we can do so as we move ahead. Our studio will draft a letter of intent for your company to sign. Who should we send it to?"

"It should go to Mr. Hudson Haller. He's the president of our company. Tim and his associates will handle all project details."

"Very good. Now we have two reasons for staying in touch." Alisha flashed her winning smile, then used Electra's favorite reply to any question: "Perhaps."

As they unwound at the hotel bar that evening, Alisha could tell Tim was feeling no pain.

"So, how do you like Hollywood now?"

"Geez, even better than before. Just about everyone out here looks like they could be in movies. And the tour guide pointed out a bunch of celebrity homes. I like the place."

"Our flight isn't until tomorrow morning. Let's have some fun tonight. I've never been to a Hollywood casino, so why don't we try our luck? Do you know anything about gambling?" That question transformed geeky Tim into a different person.

"Yes, I do. I know how to apply probability and statistics to all the popular casino games, so we won't be trying our luck. We'll be doing game theory expected value computations. I recommend you play craps while I check out black jack and poker tables. Then you can watch me, first at blackjack and then poker. What time's our flight?"

"Nine forty-five tomorrow morning."

"Good. That gives us eight hours of playing time. We can sleep on the plane. Let's check out of the hotel and stow our bags at the casino. We can leave directly for the airport from there. Hollywood Casino is a brief cab ride away and is supposed to be the best in LA."

"I'm game, and I'm counting on you to explain craps betting."

"Not a problem. I'll explain on the way."

The night belonged to Alisha rather than Electra. She would let Tim do card-counting and probability calculations while she reveled in the excitement. How amazing! Tim has talents I never imagined. Goes to show how difficult it is to know what makes another person tick. Tonight is Tim's time to shine. Tim gave Alisha her marching orders.

"So, here's your plan. First, give me the dollar amount you're willing to lose. That will give us an upper bound on your play."

"I'll stake each of us with ten thousand dollars." Tim didn't bat an eyelash.

"Here's how you should play conservative craps tonight. Place the minimum bet on the Pass Line. If you win, bet the minimum again on Pass. If you lose, double the bet you just lost and bet on Pass. Keep doubling the bet when you lose. As soon as you win, go back to the minimum bet. Here's the reason this works: by doubling up, you win back all the money you lost, plus you win the minimum bet. But here's the catch: you can't bet more than half your stakes on any one roll of the dice. So, if you lose too many times in a row, you go broke. I'll pick a craps table that has minimum and maximum betting limits that fit your strategy. Then I'll calculate how many consecutive losses it'll take for you to go broke. I'll get you started and come back later. Or, you can look for me at a blackjack table."

Part of Alisha was made for glamour and glitz, and vice versa. The casino matched her expectations: a sea of well-attired people surrounding gambling station islands, flowing to the rhythm of vibrant light and sound. I can feel the excitement, and in addition to having fun, I'm rehearsing for Las Vegas, which is on my bucket list. Alisha paid for chips at a cashier's window; Tim walked them through the gambling rooms, pointing out blackjack and poker stations, then found a suitable craps table. Tim explained the action for several rounds of shooters—the gamblers rolling the dice. Now it was time for Alisha to join the game. Tim took her aside so no one could hear his final explanation.

"Remember, stick with the minimum bet on Pass until you lose. Then start doubling up. And if you lose eleven times in a row, you're bankrupt. So, keep track of how many consecutive times you're losing. And remember: your maximum bet can't exceed five thousand dollars. Go get 'em." Tim hugged her, then strode away to play blackjack.

Alisha focused on craps betting, absorbing as much of the experience and the people as possible. She also returned the flirts from the fellow next to her in exchange for the drinks he bought. What she found most exciting was increasing the wager whenever a string of consecutive losses rolled in. Most of the time, her wager was less than $250, but one time it reached $1,000, and gamblers at the table noticed, applauding when she won on that bet.

Alisha lost track of time; there are no clocks in casinos. No chairs either, except at the tables, bars, or restaurants. None of that concerned her; she was on a roll and in the black but didn't count her winnings. She remembered a long-ago verse. The song says:
You never count your money

When you're sittin' at the table
There'll be time enough for countin'
When the dealin's done

So, I'll follow that advice. She placed a couple of more bets before Tim tapped her on the shoulder, bringing her back to reality.

"You've played long enough. Let's grab a bite at one of the restaurants and compare results."

"Whew! That was grand fun, but I didn't realize how much emotional energy it takes. I do need a break. I'm starved." Tim guided her to a restaurant and described what to expect.

"Casino restaurants have good food and fast service so the gamblers refuel and get back to the tables. I won $750 at blackjack. How'd you do? Tim counted her chips and announced she had won $150. "Excellent. You stuck to the plan and it paid off. What was the maximum bet you made?"

"$1,000.It was an exciting bet, and people at the table noticed." "When you're playing craps, don't pay attention to people paying attention to you. That's what amateurs do. If you're going to gamble, use your head. Think like the pros. After we eat, are you ready for more fun?" I can't believe it! Tim is a totally different person when gambling. This is great fun. "I'm in. What's next."

"I'm going to play Texas Hold'em poker. Don't worry about the actual rules. I want you to stand behind me and watch for tells. Do you know what tells are? She thought to herself, I'm sure Electra does, but she has the night off. I'll let Tim tell me about tells. Alisha nodded no.

"The term comes from sailing. A tell is a small strip of cloth affixed to a sail that lets the helmsman determine the direction of the wind. In gambling, a tell is unintentional body language that tells when a person is bluffing. I think you're good at reading body language, so let's see if it works at a casino. As the poker hand plays out, gamblers place bets and often bluff if their hand is no good. Watch the game for a while, and see if you can detect when a player is bluffing. Keep your hands on my shoulders. Squeeze my right shoulder when you guess a player bluffing. I'll use your guess and mine to adjust my betting strategy. And be discreet. There are hidden cameras watching us. What we're doing is not illegal, but casinos are paranoid. We don't want to get thrown out. Any questions?"

"Only one. Is it OK if I drink while you're gambling? It might be a good distraction to keep suspicion away from us." Tim's grin agreed.

"Humphrey Bogart would know what to say: 'Alisha, I think this is the beginning of a beautiful friendship."

And that it was. Alisha watched long enough to detect tells on some of the gamblers, then ordered an alcoholic Iced Tea. She took a couple of sips, placed it next to Tim, and took her place behind him. Then she began signaling tells. Tim had been holding his own, but Alisha's signals added to his winnings. He'd win a couple of hands, then fold, then win again. No one caught on, and after a couple of hours they left the game and started walking to a cashier's window.

"Nice work. How much did you win?"

"Eight hundred dollars. You spotted more tells than I did." Tim glanced at the time displayed on his cellphone. "The place closes at four, so let's go before they turn the lights out. We'll get a recommendation for a twenty-four-hour nightclub." Tim dumped all chips into one container before handing them to a cashier and chatting her up.

"Miss, you look like a starlet. I bet you know all the right places. Would you please recommend a nightclub for my partner and me?

"The Avalon has at least one lounge open twenty-four hours. I've heard they serve breakfast too. I'll jot down the address." Tim gave her a handful of chips, and when they were in the cab tried to give the money to Alisha.

"Why don't you keep it? You earned it today. Use some of it to pay for whatever you need to get us home. Use the rest for your next gambling junket."

A half-hour later a waiter was serving them pancakes. The food and service impressed Tim.

"This town has the best-looking people I've ever seen. Everyone looks so happy and healthy: perfect teeth, perfect complexion, perfect tan. Why don't we open an office here?"

"Maybe we can if the Cyber-Theater works out. Its line extensions will be even better. That's when we wire it for interacting with the brain. That's when we'll get Kwame working on it too." Tim changed the topic when Kwame's name came up.

"Next time we go to the casinos, let's bring Kwame. He's better at card counting and computing probabilities than I am."

"He might not handle poker as well as you. I know you're both autistic, but you handle the condition even better than he does. He sometimes doesn't process emotions as well as you. He might not interpret bluffs correctly."

"You might be surprised. Both of us turn into different people when gambling."

Early morning rush hour traffic didn't cause a delay because the club was on the west side of LA. After twenty-four hours of non-stop activity, fatigue finally tackled Alisha. She came to rest, asleep on Tim's shoulder. Glancing at her, he thought, What a multi-faceted creature she is. Electra is so professional, so calculating, sometimes so distant. Alisha's so different: so bubbly and alive, so emotional and empathetic, so competitive on the playing field. I don't think even Su knows what's inside her head, but all that's there is all good to me.

Alisha's catnap worked wonders, refreshing her for the flight back to Austin. Tim slept while Electra contemplated their collective accomplishments. Tim's in charge of making Cyber-Theater a commercial success. He and Alisha's casino caper shows he's got a lot of other talents too. Alisha does too. Maybe Hollywood awaits them both. Indira wrote somewhere that the future is yet unwritten on the winds of change. As she thought further, an ironic thought came to mind. Oh, Jason! My dearly departed father. What a strange twist of fate.

I remember what you told Grandfather long ago, why my secret must never be revealed.

"No one must ever know. Nemo. Nada. Never! Even in the best of times, do you know what would happen? Burned at the stake or dissected. And with the trouble now brewing because of the T-Plague and terrorism? It'll get worse, much worse."

But according to Cyber-Max, I could be an actress in action-adventure movies. My whole life has been that role. How odd; people would love me in a book or movie, but might be afraid of the real me. Alisha and I are the only ones still alive who know, and we'll keep it that way. The plane was about to land, so Electra snapped back to the present. She and Tim would drive to the office, sharing with Hud all they had accomplished. Afterwards, she would spend time in Cyberspace hunting for what she needed next.

Electra confirmed what she was looking for late one night the following week. All day, she had been instructing her assigned University of Texas grad students, and she was pleased how well UTA and GWU teams worked together. All evening she had been using her social media software to validate troubling trends she had detected. She reviewed the list one more time. Unsettling Forecasts

- Growing concern about mutant T-Plague. Could reach tipping point if the Government can't deliver effective vaccines.
- Growing concern about Cyberterrorism. Could reach tipping point if it spreads nationally.
- Growing concern about Infrastructure system glitches. Public increasingly on edge when power goes out, home appliances don't work, and banking networks crash.
- Growing concern about Guardian Party's "harsh measures."
- Lurking concern: Public I.Q. hasn't recovered from T-Plague epidemic. Many people unwilling to take responsibility.
- Lurking concern: Public sentiment pulling back from globalization. Minority hostility may spiral out of control if Middle East issues escalate. Watch out for backlash against China and Russia.
- Growing concern: Public worried about government's ability to keep them safe.
- Growing concern about Government surveillance and pirating private data.
- Growing fear of AI taking away jobs. Growing fear of DNA modifications.
- Growing concern about fake news. Public doesn't trust Administration or Media reporting.
- Growing concern about polarizing politics.

By midnight, Alisha concluded all trends pointed to a dark future.

No wonder I'm getting depressed. All the trends are down, not up. But what should I do? I've learned from my past mistakes it can be risky to meddle, to think I can play god because I'm smarter and know more than mere mortals. The time may come for me to do just that, but not yet.

Electra decided to remain an observer from the shadows; Carter and Angus would be unwitting partners keeping her informed about economics, politics, and the Guardian Party. Russell and Su would be her T-Plague agents, while Tim and Kwame would be her Cyberspace defense network.

Before logging off, Electra finally found reasons for optimism. None of the forecasts are cast in stone, and I have more partners working for me than ever before. No need to act now. And thanks to Alisha, our personal world is trending upward. The glass is at least half full. I hope my depression lifts by morning. I'll let the lightning brain take care of that.

Electra slept soundly that night.

Chapter 20
March 2124

"Kiss by the Sun"
Thread 2 Chapter 6

I REMEMBER WHAT JASON often said to Indira:" We're kissed by the Sun." Well, that's how I feel. Electra does too. I have lots to do and am enjoying every minute.

Upon returning to Austin, Alisha's first order of business was assembling a promotional packet every aspiring actress needs: hard copy and electronic formats of an Actor's Press Kit she would send to Cyber-Max Studios, and she already had the necessary components. All she had left to do was "cut and paste" pictures, documents, and articles describing her academic, Co-NFL, and Texas education spokesperson roles, using an online press kit development app.

She inserted portrait photos posted at GWU and UT as well as posed soccer and football action photos. Then she selected the ten most current articles that connected with universities, volunteer work, and Websites. She linked the kit to her three most active social media sites, dropped in an embellished curriculum vitae (academia's version of a resume), and included Ford Motors, Indian Motorcycles, and Patagonia Sportwear in the endorsements/sponsors section. Three hours later, after wordsmithing her direct quotes, she emailed to the studio her personalized press kit and tomorrow would print a hard copy, using the university's color printing system. I'm going to print extra copies, and I'll give a couple to Woolly next week when we film the "Texas Colleges Calling" video. Maybe he can use them to find other projects for me.

It was apparent to Woolly that Alisha needed little coaching in public speaking or political arenas. She had the instincts of a natural-born politician: diplomatic, charming, gregarious, empathetic, quick-witted, authoritative. He was certain there were other Texas programs he could slot her into later, but he'd start with education. He planned to edit the "College Calling" video into two promotional pieces: one for national college recruiting distribution, the other for in-state grade and high school student motivation. He invited Alisha to his office two days before its mid-March filming date to review all the details.

"You'll like the town hall meeting style. We've invited one hundred grade and high school students to participate. We'll hold the meeting in the main ballroom of the Texas Capital Visitors Center, tables and chairs arranged in semicircles with you speaking from the center so you can walk and talk and make eye contact. I'll give a five-minute introduction describing our purpose and your background. Then you can say hello and start answering questions. Students can ask any questions they like, and here's a list of suggested topics. Your job is to engage the students and make sure they cover two concerns: why should they go to college, and why should they consider Texas colleges and universities? The total time is ninety minutes. We're not giving you any speech to memorize because we want the session to be informal and spontaneous. And don't worry if you stumble a bit at first. We'll edit the session before releasing it. What do you think?" Alisha took a minute to glance at the proposed questions. I can handle this and much, much more. I'll script my own discussion guide and use it tomorrow.

"This list of questions and answers is thorough. I can handle them and keep the discussion focused. I'm looking forward to the meeting. I'll be there at nine, which is an hour ahead of time, if that's OK with you." It was, so Alisha went on her way. She would start preparing for her afternoon cooldown run.

Bo caught up to her as she was leaving the T-Bred practice field.

"Just keep the offense doing what we planned. Don't worry about where we are in the standings. Our defense is still gelling. And it's OK for you to call your own number more. The team likes how you distribute the plays, but they know you're our big weapon. And the fans want to watch you run. So, call 'em like you see 'em next Sunday."

Bo didn't know, but Alisha had perfected a couple of new moves she was ready to reveal. She smiled and said she'd be ready, then jogged a mile to cool down.

Woolly's PR career had made him a polished public speaker. He was satisfied with the audience's reaction to his opening remarks and was ready for Alisha to build on the interest he had sparked, hoping she could maintain their attention. He would be more than satisfied.

"Good morning to all of you, the leaders of our great nation's future. Yes, when I look at you, I see bright and eager students ready to learn. But I see beyond that, for you are the inheritors of what adults today are responsible for: we are the custodians of what you will inherit. And that is why I'm here today: to explain why college must be in your future, and to show why Texas colleges and universities may be your best choices.

Let me address 'why college?' first.

"There are a number of important reasons. It prepares you for a career if you pick an area of concentration that is in demand these days, such as healthcare, science and engineering, or information systems. It gives you foundation knowledge every intelligent person needs to understand the world about them, and that includes: religion and philosophy and literature, political science and economics and history, mathematics and science and psychology. It gives you critical thinking skills for making your own decisions rather than relying on someone else. And it prepares you to play an active role in protecting what makes America great. Each of you is expected to take responsibility and play an active role in politics, because the Golden Age of Greece taught us that self-government requires an educated people able to take care of themselves and their country.

"So, why attend Texas colleges and universities? This meeting is an example of the importance our state places in education. Here in Austin we have the main campus of University of Texas, which has a statewide network of locations. And we have outstanding private institutions, such as Southern Methodist

University in Dallas, Rice and the University of Houston, Texas A&M in College Station, the outstanding medical centers in Austin and Houston, as well as an extensive association of community colleges. All are all testaments to Texas excellence in higher education. So please, consider Texas when choosing a school.

"I'm here today to answer questions or concerns you may have regarding the topics I just introduced. I am young enough to know what concerns you have, yet I'm old enough to give you experience-based insights you might find helpful. So, let's open the floor to questions…"

Alisha's command of the meeting blew Woolly away. Her opening remarks were inspiring. She answered the questions effortlessly, and her closing summary had insights the Governor should look at. This young lady can be much more than a spokesperson for education.

As the students bustled out for lunch, Woolly guided Alisha to the video crew, asking them how the recording went.

"AOK. We had three cameras rolling from different angles, so we'll have plenty to make at least two videos. But I gotta ask: has she done much public speaking or acting? Not only is she photogenic, but her presentation style captivates the audience." Woolly answered for her.

"She lectures in front of a classroom, and she performs on the football field. And she's smart as can be. That's why she's a natural. She's got what it takes. Come on Alisha, I'll take you to lunch." She thanked the crew before Woolly hustled her away.

While driving home, Alisha coaxed herself into a more relaxed state as the morning adrenaline rush subsided. I'll savor the morning's success for the rest of the afternoon, and then I'll focus on my next performance: Sunday's home opener against the LA Earthquake. It's a rematch of our last game last season. They made it to the championship game, and they're supposed to be even better. I like the challenge. To be the best, you gotta beat the best.

Alisha gathered the offense after the next day's final practice session.

"Let's use the game to even the score. I'm gonna start by running the ball over, around and through the Quakers. And then we'll mix in halfback laterals, keepers, and midrange crossing pattern passes. Our offense will wear down their defense, and our lighting start might rattle their offense, which'll help out our defense. What else do you want to know?"

"Do you have any trick plays we haven't seen? Last year, you had the beach ball bounce pass off the defender's helmet and the Hail Mary to yourself. And the crowd pleaser was your midnight play." Alisha couldn't help letting just a hint of vanity show when she smiled.

"Well sort of. I have a couple of new moves. I have a stutter-spin move to spin away from defenders. And I have a touchdown dance move when I score. Let me demo it, because it'll be cool for all female teammates to join me in the end zone. It'll be fun for us and it'll be sorta sexy for the fans, especially for the guys watching. I call it the fist-pump wave, and I practice it at dance clubs."

The ladies picked up the move, and everyone laughed when Toni yelled, "Just make sure you score plenty of times so we can strut our stuff!"

Alisha spent the evening before the game at what was becoming an Austin sports bar trend: late afternoon pre-game dance parties featuring Alisha and T-Breds. Sam had contracted a schedule that rotated among the top five locations. The fans liked having their favorite team so accessible; Bo stopped complaining when Sam explained the diversion would reduce pre-game jitters.

Alisha knew the minute she awoke Sunday she'd be "in the zone" as soon as she put on her Kit game face. She was carefree and loose joking with everyone in the locker room, but when they took the field for the National Anthem, the lightning brain switched gears. She was ready to run, and the sportscaster was ready to call the action.

"Welcome fans! So, here we have a re-match of last season's greatest contest. Today we'll see if the T-Bred's defense has been beefed up enough to let their dazzling 'lightning in a bottle' offense blitz the Quakers. T-Breds won the toss and will receive.

"Here's the kick-off… fielded on the five by Kit Kittner… She's gliding up the center of the field…defenders closing in at the twenty… She spins to her left and is dashing up the left sidelines…She's coming to a complete stop, now stutter-stepping to the right… Hold on, she just spun back to the left and is streaking up the left sideline past two more defenders…Two more defenders closing in…Holy Moly!… She did some sort of stutter-step spin faking them out completely…She's at the forty and cutting towards the center of the field… only two defenders and the kicker in her way… What's this… She's running directly towards them… There's that stutter-spin move again!… Defenders on the ground and she's around them…The kicker's angle is no good… She's racing into the end zone…

Touchdown!"

The opening touchdown run and its fan-pleasing end zone dance set the tone for the entire game, putting pressure on the Quaker offense that went four and out, giving Kit's offense first and ten on their thirty. Kit used the up-tempo Wide-V Offense to motor up the field. She ran a rapid-fire series of halfback laterals and mid-range crossing passes that confused the defense; then she called her number for a sweep to the right. The defenders thought they had her cut her off, but then she uncorked another stutter move that froze them, allowing her to spin between two defenders who were tackling where she had just been, not where she was. She raced towards the defenders in the center of the field, danced around them and into the end zone. The announcer liked calling the action as much as the fans liked watching Kit run wild.

"Look at that! The Quaker defense can't touch those spin moves. The other teams better study game videos or they'll never catch her."

The second set of offensive plays were again four and out for the Quakers. This time, with the ball first and ten on the thirty-five, Kit went for the jugular. The very first play was an option pass, and she fired a mid-range strike over the pulled-in defense right into the outstretched arms of Toni who dashed into the end zone. The score was 21-0 and the first quarter still had a minute left.

Kit huddled the team when the quarter expired.

"We've blitzed them enough. The Quakers are in shock, so here's the plan for the rest of the game. We'll play ball control offense. No more big plays. We'll keep the ball and chew up time, keeping their defense on the field and ours off. Every time they score, we'll match 'em, but we'll take as much time off the clock as we can. No sense running up the score, or showing too much more."

The rest of the game followed Kit's plan. The Quaker offense sputtered to life in the second quarter, scoring two touchdowns, but the T-Breds responded with a touchdown pass and a field goal. Each team kicked a field goal in the third quarter and a touchdown in the fourth. Final score: T-Breds 38, Quakers 24.

Alisha was as modest as she could be at the post-game interview, giving credit to Bo's coaching and game strategy. When a reporter asked him why he featured so much of the offense around his QB, he used a quote made famous by coach Paul Brown of the Cleveland Browns when describing legendary running back Jim Brown: "If you got a big gun, you should use it a lot." When asked about Kit's elusive footwork, he was deliberately vague.

"There might be other moves, but we'll let the other teams worry about that."

Sam caught up with Bo after the game.

"Outstanding game! The crowd loved it, and I'm sure TV viewers did too. Our sponsors and national fan base will be pleased with the show we put on today. And that touchdown dance is as good as what the cheerleaders do. Where did you come up with that spin move? The defense couldn't touch it." Bo shook his head. "I didn't. It came from Kit's brain, and it'll keep defensive coaches busy trying to figure it out. But, let's not get ahead of ourselves. This is only the third game of the season. We've got nine to go before playoffs, and you never know what's gonna happen. Let's take it one game at a time."

Since Bo never held practice on Mondays, Alisha was cruising through rural Texas towns the next day. She was using Mondays to enjoy driving her Ford Mustang or Indian Scout motorcycle. Austin's surrounding Texas hill country offered unspoiled rural vistas and wildflower color alongside the curving, undulating roads. Each Monday she drove further, exploring smaller towns and cities. Most folks knew about the Austin T-Breds and their extraordinary quarterback, and they were happy to talk, sharing stories about themselves and their communities. Texans by nature are resilient and resourceful, independent and pragmatic, respectful of the land and other people, proud of their heritage. They taught her Texas history and folklore; she explained why she played football and liked Texas so much more than Washington.

Alisha estimated that by the end of the season she would have visited over one hundred smaller Texas towns and all major cities. She kidded herself that when people told her she was going places, she could reply it was true when viewed on a map of the Lone Star State. And none of her spokesperson's travels interfered with football practices because Woolly always chose appropriate times and transportation, often traveling with her. A sudden thought flashed into Alisha's brain.

When I combine my media commercials, Monday drives, and spokesperson meetings, I sure am getting a lot of exposure. And I think I'm gaining fans just by acting naturally. I like being liked. And I'll remember to keep my ego and vanity in check—except when I run wild on the football field. Then it's OK to strut for a minute, but no longer than that.

Electra kept busy the following week handling drug-related R&D. She met with her UT grad students, then coordinated joint university conference calls, trying to find results Kameyo and Su could use to accelerate vaccine development. She used what she learned to adjust Kameyo's solution path, so by early next week she brought Kameyo into her office to outline what to do next. Electra thought Kameyo would welcome the recommendations, but the more she explained the more disheartened Kameyo became. Electra abruptly switched topics from vaccines to the bright young researcher.

"You're doing outstanding work. My recommendations merely add to what you're accomplishing and might reduce the time to product launch. Your expertise surpasses Su's. You should feel good about yourself, but you seem glum. Would you please tell me why?"

"Dr. Kittner, I am disappointed in myself for needing help from you. I've been here two years and cannot match you."

"Please stop right there. First, call me Electra. And second, your Japanese heritage teaches the importance of teamwork. Think of me as your assistant on a project no one but you is capable of leading. I apologize for not officially promoting you, but I thought it was clear to everyone that you are the senior researcher. I'll tell Hud to make the change immediately." That brought a hint of a smile to Kameyo's stoic style.

"Very well, Electra, and thank you. But I am concerned about my relationship with Dr. Chou. I mean Su. I try to be her friend, professionally and personally, but she doesn't respond in kind. She is friendly but allows no one to get close enough to know her well. I know so little about her." Electra thought to herself, I need to help Kameyo see some things behind Su's Oriental veil of impenetrable reserve. "I have known Su my entire life. She, like you and most Orientals, often conceals her emotions, but I probably understand how she feels better than anyone. She's my godmother, and I consider her my aunt. She and my mother were best friends. Did she ever tell you about the Worldstars?" Kameyo nodded no.

"That was a group of four grad school friends: my mother, Indira, my father, Jason, Adom, and Su. They were great friends, but all are dead but Su, and that has affected her ability to form close friendships or reveal how she feels. I know she likes you more than you realize. It is up to the two of you to take it from there. The best I can do is tell Su the next time she and I have dinner." I'd better lighten the mood.

"So, by the time Hud gives you your new business cards, I'll have chatted with Su. Give her one of them and see how she deals with you after that."

Electra kidded to herself she was becoming as much a social butterfly as Alisha. She'd be taking Su out for dinner on Friday, and Holy would treat her and Robin to lunch on Sunday. Alisha would approve. She's the one teaching me to enjoy the present, and I'm getting better at doing that. And between now and Friday, I have work to do. Electra plunged back in and resurfaced on Friday. Later that afternoon, as they walked to her car, Electra explained why she likes driving motorcycles.

"You should ride on the back sometime. Of all the outdoor activities I've ever tried, motorcycling takes me away from what I was doing and wraps me in the moment. Unlike running that lets my mind freewheel, cycling forces me to think only about what I'm doing right now. It's so relaxing. And it doesn't matter what point A and B are. It's total engagement in the journey that does it." Su nodded before replying.

"That would be a new experience for me. Just like tonight. I've never been to the New Fortune Chinese Seafood Restaurant, even though it's in Austin's Chinatown Center."

"And I'll have an easy time parking in the community garage. We'll be dining shortly."

The waiter took their order twenty minutes later.

"You have chosen well. I like the menu and the décor." Su chattered further about oriental cuisine until Electra segued the conversation.

"Yes, I know how to pick restaurants, just like you know how to choose R&D people. Case in point is Kameyo. Did she tell you Hud officially promoted her to Senior R&D Contributor?"

"No, she didn't. She is so reserved and modest. No wonder I don't know much about her. I should make an effort to know her better." Electra waited until the waiter had served dinner before taking the discussion further.

"Do you realize I've known you longer than anyone else, and ditto for understanding each other. We've gone through a lot and are different now than even a couple of years ago. You are more than a good friend; I love you, and that allows me to speak frankly. And here's what I need to tell you: open yourself up to new friendships. Stop idolizing Indira. Please hear me out before you respond.

"I know that she was considered practically perfect. You and Indira were so-called kindred spirits, preferring intimacy with one another rather than with anyone else. I know that mother was planning to join with you instead of Jason after my birth, but the lightning bolt that killed her short-circuited all that. Over time, you have mythologized Indira into an impossibly peerless kindred spirit that never existed when she was alive, and certainly not now. You've deflected attempts by others to form friendships because you thought nothing would approach this fiction.

"Let go of this kindred spirit fantasy. It never existed. Indira—exceptional though she was—had flaws; everyone does. You never knew mother killed someone just before leaving India. And you never knew she had an affair with Adom while she was considering marrying Jason." Su's look registered only a fraction of the shock she felt.

"I'm telling you this while you still have time to form intimate relationships. They're what give much of the meaning to life, but past a certain age it will be impossible to do so. The choice is yours. Just make it, having a better understanding of what Indira meant to you. I don't believe in kindred spirits any longer. I used to think Christi and I were, but I've grown past that and am better for leaving it behind. Maybe you should too. I've talked so long our pot of tea is cold. Sorry." There was an awkward silence in which they picked at dinner until Su finally replied.

"I know how difficult this has been for you. I've never thought about Indira quite this way before. Perhaps you are right. Perhaps I have unintentionally cut myself off from lasting friendships. You have given me a lot to think about, and I love you for it, even though my emotions might not show that I do."

"I know you do. Look, it's time to talk about something else. I wish I could think of a clever segue to a different subject, but I'm emotionally drained."

"We don't need words to enjoy being together. That moment of awkward silence is in the past. Let's savor each other's company, some fortune cookies, and a pot of hot tea."

Electra slept well that night, for she had done all she could, but Su tossed and turned, trying to reconcile what Electra had disclosed. Where in the world did Electra learn all this about Indira? I never knew any of it. Could she possibly know about my prior life in China? Well, that's all in the past. But I will think about future intimacies. I shall talk with Kameyo.

Electra's next day to-do list held no surprises. She planned to mix project work and routine Saturday banking or shopping, but trouble began when the bank's ATM swallowed her card, so she parked and went in, only to discover she was one of many with the same luck.

The branch manager was explaining the situation to a crowd of frustrated customers.

"I apologize for the malfunction. There seems to be a glitch at all our branches. I need each of you to tell me your name and account number so I can add you to my priority account service list. And our tellers can manually handle your transaction."

Electra waited patiently in line, unlike many others who gave the poor manager an earful because they were wasting time. Instead of complaining, Electra thought about tomorrow's lunch outing Robin had planned. I need to commend Holy for how much he's helping Robin. How remarkable that Robin is Holy's physical caregiver, and he's become her career and emotional stabilizer.

Electra was on her way a half-hour later. The rest of her day went smoothly, though the evening news couldn't report the same for Austin's larger banks. A computer malfunction had shut down all online activity for the entire morning before the local area networks automatically rebooted. The banks claimed the problem was now fixed, although no details were given. The story sparked a connection. I recall other regional bank network outages. What's the cause? I'm going to search Cyberspace to find out. This will be additional practice with my network security and Big Data tools. No matter the results, I can tweak my tools. After all, perfect practice makes perfect.

Lord! If it's time to go make it quick and no more dress rehearsals. Holy Haller, lying in bed, gritted his teeth while trying calm himself for whatever would be. The wave of nausea subsided five minutes later, as did the pain and pounding in his chest. The only remaining symptom was a shiver caused by cold sweat; Holy had just survived another heart attack.

For the past year, Holy's heart had been struggling through episodes of acute oxygen deprivation that kills heart muscle cells. Holy didn't need a doctor's lecture on ischemia to tell him what he already knew: his ninety-plus-year-old heart was wearing out. Nor did he want operations or drugs to prolong the inevitable. He had lived long enough and harbored no regrets, so he didn't complain to anyone. He had only one remaining obligation that he would complete when his lawyer visited next week. That's when he would make Robin a beneficiary in his will.

He knew Robin would never be able to run his business. She was doing better in business classes and would graduate next winter, but she lacked Adom's entrepreneurial flair and analytic horsepower. That's why he left her a minority interest; the rest went to his management team. He hoped that financial security would center Robin emotionally when his time expired. *I'm doing all I can, and I'll let Robin and Electra know about the lawyer's next week visit. But not about my heart.* A peaceful stillness calmed his thoughts; Holy slept the rest of the night.

Alisha joined Robin and Holy at the Original Pancake House near Walnut Creek Park. The morning rain had ended, and a clearing sky promised a lovely spring afternoon.

"I'm glad Robin made our reservation later rather than earlier. The weather's better and the place isn't crowded."

"I've already ordered a Coke for you. Holy and I are having buttermilk pancakes today. What about you?"

"I think I'll have the same. Mr. H, how's Robin been treating you, and vice versa?" Holy spoke up after the waitress took Alisha's order. "I couldn't be in better hands. I'm doing fine, and so is she. And she's been learning more about business."

"Yes, I'm seeing connections between my marketing and business strategy classes. Our fatstock ranch business is tapping into an underserved market segment for restaurants featuring flavorful cuts of marbled pork and beef. The guys on his management team are helping me understand it better."

"Robin's done me proud by how well she's taking care of coursework while taking care of me. And she says we all can take a break after lunch by taking a walk through the park." Robin explained further.

"It gives us fresh air and a chance to watch dog walkers. And Mr. H can pet their pooches while I push the wheelchair."

Alisha joked, "Let me do the pushing. It'll count towards my training."

Walnut Creek Park's bike path had just the right amount of traffic so the trio could enjoy the surroundings. Wildflowers carpeted both sides, stretching to the leafy trees just beyond. And the side paths to the creek gave a rustic river vista in the heart of the city.

Robin said, "The creek is more like a river today, what with the rain we've been having. But it adds a burbling sound that's soothing. We'll come here more often now that I know layout." Robin ambled towards a rustling she spotted in the grass leading to a wooded area. Electra spotted it too.

"Be careful. Don't cross paths with a skunk or raccoon." That's not what Robin found.

"Holy Shit!" is all she said before running to the source. She came upon a black and white border collie pup, not more than three months old, struggling to crawl towards her, tail drooping, whimpering while straining to lick her hand. She swooped down to pick up the tattered creature; it came to life in her hands, licking her face for all its worth.

"We've got a situation," she said as she came to the wheelchair.

Holy gazed in amazement before speaking.

"Have you ever had a dog?"

"No, but I know all about taking care of pets. I took care of Alisha when she broke her neck, and I'm taking care of you. Can I keep it?"

"You can't leave the critter here. Dogs are useful on ranches, too." Alisha added her thoughts.

"I think Robin should take the pup to a vet right now. Get it patched, and then get what she needs if she decides to keep it. Is it a cur or a bitch?"

Robin exclaimed, "Neither. Puppy's really happy to see me." Holy's eyes met Electra's before he replied,

"That's not what Alisha meant. Is it male or female? You know what to look for."

"Let me check… It's a female."

Alisha said, "Use my car to take her to a vet. I'll take Mr. H home in the van. If you decide to keep her, you'll need to pick up supplies. Ask the vet what you should get and what you should do. But think about what you're getting into." Alisha surfed the Net to find a nearby vet, and then they went their separate ways.

As she drove, keeping the pup in her lap, Robin suddenly knew what she was getting into. Puppy needs me, and I need Puppy. She'll give me unconditional love and she'll help me keep my emotions centered. She glanced at her lap when approaching the park exit. We need to pick a name for you. The name came as she drove from shadows into the sunlight. I've got it. You're my ray of sunshine. Robin drew Sunshine to her for a kiss. The puppy wriggled, so happy it instinctively peed on Robin's blouse. Robin laughed aloud.

"Sunshine! You've just marked me your property. I'm yours and you're mine. We'll make a great team. And Mr. H can help train you as we take care of him. But try not to pee on other people. Use your tongue instead." Sunshine nestled in her lap as Robin drove ahead.

Chapter 21
May 2124

"The Invisible Avengers"
Thread 3 Chapter 7

BALIGH EL-MOFTY, THE Exalted Ruler of Isilabad, was even smarter than the predecessor who handpicked him. The devious Hassan Wassani had toiled for years to create Isilabad but wasn't secretive enough. Somehow the Infidels, when they stumbled upon his hidden plans and resources, terminated him and his Inner Circle. Baligh would not let that happen to him. He would keep things simple by dividing everyone into two groups: friends and foes. And it was much easier for him than for the President of the United States because Isilabad is a Theocracy, where Politics and Religion are one and the same.

His best friends were all in Isilabad's political system. To outsiders, Isilabad might appear to have a separation of powers: legislative, executive, judicial. Only insiders knew that Baligh controlled all three by placing his people wherever and whenever he wanted. He shared with no one his sketch of Isilabad's power structure. All arrows tracking power came from him.

Isilabad Theocracy Structure

Exalted Ruler

Assembly of the Faithful

Inner Council

Council of the Faithful

Supreme Security Council

Parliament

Ministry of Justice

Protectors of the Faithful (Military)

The People

He also had two friends on the world stage helping him thwart the West: leaders from China and Russia. All three trusted each other well enough to join forces in Cyberspace, keeping their avenging Iron Triangle Alliance invisible.

Baligh's political enemy was the Infidel West, spearheaded by America. Since becoming the Exalted Ruler, he had kept America at bay but now might need to adjust tactics if Jared Gardner pushes for harsher measures. However, there was still time because Jared was just beginning to reassert himself.

Baligh's primary religious opponent, Christianity as embodied in Western Europe and America, has been a thorn in the lion's paw of Islam for 1500 years. The war waxes and wanes, depending on synchronized pendulums swinging between faith and reason, between revelation and science, between regress and progress. There would be no end unless both sides searched together for a viable middle ground that would turn an unsolvable dilemma into a workable trilemma.

But Baligh also faced a secondary opponent, Islam's Shiite faction led by Iran. The Sunni—Shiite split dates back to Muhammad's rightful successor. The battle between the two factions made it even harder for Baligh to bring Islam out of its self-imposed Dark Ages into 22nd century prominence.

Baligh shared Hassan's vision for Isilabad's future: make Isilabad the Caliphate of Islam and reclaim its rightful place among nations by bringing its religious and cultural practices into the 22nd century. Herein lies his most difficult challenge. Even though he knows what changes are needed, centuries of religious belief and practice have ingrained its fundamentals into the very fiber of his people. The faithful minions will turn away if he isn't cautious and deceptive. Baligh took some consolation that the leader of America faces a similar challenge if he tries to take his people too quickly where they don't want to go, but he knew only that Gardner was unpredictable, so he and his Iron Triangle allies would need to probe America's defenses carefully, using his appointed warrior Ziarmal to lead the invisible charge in Cyberspace. Just as his people had faith in Baligh, he had faith in Ziarmal.

Darla Tinibu had faith in nothing but herself and Cybergard, and that would be enough to leapfrog everyone, including her Iron Triangle partners. Her recent destructive exploratory salvo into U.S. banking's network security systems exceeded all expectations: it proved invisible and untraceable. Her Russian partner's Cyberweapons could cripple banking hardware sold through companies controlled by her Chinese partner unless the banks' networks bought Cybergard firewall software. Partners swapped their development pieces so each could perfect their part of the conquest plan, and this afternoon Darla would meet privately in her office with Sales V.P. Kerby Gunther to give him marching orders. Kerby could be trusted. He was out for money, not glory, and Darla's plans would lead him to riches. He saw plenty of dollar signs as she concluded the meeting.

"So, now you understand why banks have to buy. And our developers have a great demo package for you to show our customers. On one of their test systems, I want you to fire one of our proprietary hack attack weapons into their firewall. It'll knock out their ATM's. Now, have them restore the firewall, install our latest release and repeat. This time, the firewall withstands the attack. This is all the proof they need. They'll have to buy."

"Has Marketing prepared any promotional literature for my salespeople?"

"Are you kidding? Of course not. It's too proprietary, and we don't want to tip our hand. But we're putting out press releases alerting all banks to contact our salesforce for our latest hack-proof software. I want you and Finance to show me what markup to use so you exceed year-end sales forecasts by at least twenty percent. That should motivate all your sales consultants to hustle. Your year-end commission check and bonus award will be hefty, so put this in motion ASAP. Any questions?"

"No, but I have one comment. I hope you can find out what weapons are coming next year and how they work. If so, our developers will have the next release ready to go as soon as the banking system craters."

"That'll be for me to know and our customers to find out. And that, my dear Kerby, you can take to the banks."

Darla toasted herself with a rum-spiked Coke after Kerby hustled away, confident nothing would stand in her way. No one's smart enough to figure out what we're doing or where we're going. And I'll keep it that way. I won't get careless and let my defenses down.

That's what my opponents do.

Darla wasn't the only person toasting success. Gui Hou was closing in on the location of the one person he would be willing to die for to meet: the last member of the Beijing family that had caused his family and himself so much shame and suffering. Gui's father hoped his only son's bitterness would die before he did and made him promise not to avenge wrongs as long as other members of the Hou family were still alive, but when his father died of the T-Plague late last year, Gui was freed from his promise and could track down his target, using resources available at his lower-level position in one of China's intelligence agencies.

Though he was no political or religious ideologue, Gui had learned enough about China's history to understand its leaders' planning.

Chinese civilization dates back 5,000 years, ruled until the early 20th century by brutal emperor dynasties that accomplished great projects by sacrificing millions of poor and uneducated peasants. Unlike Western Civilization, which played religion against the ruling class to carve out a place for a middle class, China had no politicized religion to come to its aid. Confucianism (selfless harmony, respect for elders and family), Taoism (mystical, simplistic worldview), and Buddhism (acceptance of suffering in a world of change) share no common values. Even today, China's political and economic systems seem inscrutable to outsiders. But Gui didn't care about insiders or outsiders. Plodding patiently and secretly, he cared only for his goal.

Gui's progress had been slow because he worked alone, invisibly, letting no one know. Starting with only his enemy's ancestral name and last known Beijing address, he tracked a move to London that had taken place thirty years ago, a move that occurred after their only child, a Su-Lin Song Chou, had gone to study in America. The parents had died five years ago.

He traced Su-Lin Song's academic and research trail to Boston and then to Washington. She was supposed to be a gifted NIH researcher assigned to T-Plague vaccine development, but for reasons unknown had vanished eight years ago. The pace quickened as his search became more targeted, and today, when Gui expanded his search criteria to include United States, biotech PhD, T-Plague, NIH, and Oriental keywords, he was rewarded with a list of ten names to track further. One of the names wasn't Chinese. The name Kato is Japanese, but Gui would keep it on his list. He would be patient. After all, he had hiked a long way on the trail in only six months, and since he was only forty, time would be working for him.

Angus finally resolved the ethical dilemma that had been tormenting him since the beginning of the year: how to deal with Jared. On one hand, he could stay put and unsuccessfully oppose Jared's increasingly blunt and misdirected programs; on the other, he could resign and watch from the sidelines as Jared ran in the wrong direction. Neither solution was good, so Angus converted the dilemma to a trilemma by discovering a way out: he would become the Democratic presidential candidate. No one knew he was going to accept the offer made to him by a tight-lipped coalition of conservative Democrats and liberal Republicans. He would drop the bombshell at a Memorial Day press conference.

There would be ample time between now and November to get his message out. For the past fifty years, supersaturated media coverage and social networking had eliminated the need for multiyear campaigning. What he needed immediately was to resurrect whatever pieces of the Brain Trust remained, and the best person to help would be Carter Quavah. They would be able to talk privately Saturday morning while golfing, since the course would be closed for several holes around them, and even his secret service team would steer clear of his erratic golf swing.

Carter, a good golfer but better diplomat, listened to the summary Angus provided during the first three holes before offering a preliminary recommendation.

"I agree that running against Jared is the right thing to do. You're the best one to sound the alarm. But realistically, he's going to be hard to be at. First off, most of his new programs are budget-neutral, so they won't bankrupt the treasury. Second, even though a growing segment is beginning to question his 'Harsh Times' mantra and isolation policies, it's not close to a tipping point percentage. Third, the international community wants America to take the lead, and Jared's ready to charge. And fourth, the T-Plague-dented public I.Q. is lower than Jared's; many people are afraid and want Jared to do the thinking for them." Carter paused to hit his tee shot. Angus liked his accuracy.

"You deliberately hit your T-shot close to mine so we can walk and talk together. Good. And since I'm still the Veep, I'll continue hitting first so you can follow me. And you can trust me. I have better aim than Jared."

"I do, and that's why I'm with you. Now, let me continue. We need a platform that's better than Jared's; one that the public can understand. We'll have to have political, economic, social, and international planks. We'll have to find big contrasts between ours and his. And we better avoid philosophical and religious planks. They usually become campaign third rails. If you touch them you're fried by the media." Angus grunted but said nothing, playing a shot while waiting for Carter to say more.

"We'll need contingency plans to adjust the platform depending on what, or if, anything big erupts domestically or internationally. And you're going to need two teams: one to prepare the platform and another to run your campaign. You might have considered the core of our erstwhile Brain Trust, but only Russell and I remain, and he's planning to retire. I can't think of any replacements. Too bad, because your Memorial Day speech needs to capture media attention. And I've already made the assumption that you want me on your platform team. Am I right?" Angus replied before hitting his next shot.

"Damn right you're right." Carter interrupted before Angus could say another word.

"I accept, but I have to work behind the scenes. If Jared finds out I'll lose some of my consulting assignments. So please don't let anyone on your campaign team know my role."

"Fair enough. And I'll talk privately with Russell. If he's planning to retire, he might not care if Jared fires him. And didn't you say you occasionally talk with Alisha? Why not give her a call and find out if she's interested. I can tell from Co-NFL highlights she's fully recovered physically. Do you think her brain is back to where it was?

And do we call her Electra or Alisha?"

"Call her Electra for serious stuff. Alisha for the lighter side of life. And frankly, her brain is an enigma to anyone who tries to know her.

But I'll give her a call and let you know."

Electra recognized Carter's caller I.D. and picked up immediately.

"Hi Carter. I was expecting a call from you because it's your turn to call me. How's life treating you?" An hour later she knew, and it was nothing like she expected to hear, but before ending the call she summarized what she'd do.

"Please tell Angus I appreciate the offer, but I prefer not to get involved. But here's what I'll do to help. You've told me what Angus thinks Jared is planning, and let me include that in political and economic planks I'll draft for you. The others will take more time. Your top priority is the Memorial Day speech and press conference. I don't have much time but I'll draft that for you first, then send you the planks later. But then you're on your own. You'll have to get your campaign team to revise everything I send. And you must keep my name out of it."

"I will. No one will know what you send. What you're doing will be a big help. Thanks a bunch. And will you call me next month?"

"I will. I don't have any immediate plans to visit DC but I'll let you know when I do."

"That will be fine. I'll give your best to Matt and Zoe and Jazzi. We four watch all your games. The media sure likes you, but then they should. Your T-Bred team puts on a great show. I'm sure the League wants you to make the playoffs. We do too."

Electra rose from her workstation after the call, then stretched while walking to the kitchen to prepare a quick dinner. Afterwards, she carved out a couple of hours to write what Angus needed. It would be a call to arms for all Americans to reclaim their right to be responsible. No doubt it would prompt an immediate response from Jared and would lead to a series of town hall meetings and debates that would explore platform details once campaigning gained momentum.

What an odd twist of fate. I already know what to put in the speech and planks, and I can use them against Jared and for my education spokesperson role. I'll use broad brush strokes in the speech and finer lines in the planks. This is going to be fun.

And fun she had that evening. The more she thought, the faster the words and sentences cascaded from the lightning brain into the word processor documents, first for the speech and then for a political plank. This is what I'd use if I were running for office. And I'll let Alisha use parts of it for the upcoming spokesperson meeting in Houston.

When finished, she proofed for final changes, then emailed the documents to Carter before going to bed, pleased with what she had developed and knowing that the lightning brain would keep writing into her memory while she slept.

Angus Speech

Good Evening my fellow citizens, and members of the press corp. Tonight, I stand before you to call you to arms, to have you stand with me in my bid to win the Oval Office. Tonight is the moment I start my campaign to win the Presidential election as the Democratic Party candidate so I can do what is right for our nation!

I believe most of you know me, my record, and my ethical standards. I served as your Vice President and then as your Interim President when Jared was struck down by the T-Plague, carrying out programs and policies that I felt were in our nation's best interests. But I can no longer support Jared Gardner's new programs and policies. They, just like Jared, are different since he came back from the T-Plague. In the coming weeks and months, you will have the opportunity to compare what I am offering to Jared's agenda.

Our constitutional heritage traces all the way from the Golden Age of Greece, then to Hobbes and Locke and the framers of our extraordinary constitution, then to our succession of presidents, stretching all the way to now. Along the way, our great nation's political pendulum has swung from liberal to conservative, from progressive to constitutional, to where we stand today. And make no mistake; we are at a defining moment. My call to arms is for you, the American people, to be what the framers of our Constitution demand: an educated, intelligent, and informed people ready to participate with me in our shared responsibility to govern ourselves.

Yes, the World is more complex today and we need to adjust accordingly how we govern, but the fundamental principles our Constitution is built on are timeless. I will explain to you as my campaign moves forward how my platform takes our country where we want to be. You will see that several years ago Jared Gardner and I shared many common goals, but he is now taking us where you do not want America to go. And that is why I am running for President. It is my moral obligation to you, to our nation, and to all the great men and women of the past and present we are honoring this Memorial Holiday. Please stand with me!

God's blessings on our people and on America…

Political Plank

"If men were angels, no government would be needed."

—James

Madison "We must trust in the better angels of our nature."

—Abraham Lincoln

We're not angels and it's hard to find statemen who practice their better instincts. That's why society must have a government. This bullet point political plank explains a political system that allows imperfect people to run a viable government serving the public.

Founding Principles:

- U.S. Constitution, Bill or Rights and Federalist Papers give unsurpassed foundation balancing freedom and equality in a democratic republic.
- Has built-in checks and balances for separation of power.
- Needs intelligent, educated and informed citizens willing to take responsibility and to participate in government.
- Must let individual self-interest contribute to the greater good. Must be inclusive and proactive.

Current Problems:

- Federal Government too large.
- Federal Government too intrusive locally. Cronyism and special interests entrenched.
- Too much Agency rule-making: Congress abandoned its responsibility to make laws.
- Public abdicates thinking. Expects Government to do right by them.

Steps for Solving:

- Shrink Federal Government. Return more autonomy to state and local governments.
- Embrace Constitutional, not Imperial Presidency. Set Term limits at all levels of government.
- Trade Public Campaign Funding for limited campaign duration

- Upgrade Civil Service. All staffs and assignments have term limits and are selected by Sortition or Demarchy pools.
- Establish Gridlock Time Limit Violations punishable by withholding salaries, removal from office, or fines/imprisonment.
- Enforce Agency Rule-Making Limits.
- Empower effective oversight/watchdog/media monitoring.
- Establish Failsafe Online Voting Protocols. Incentivize private citizen participation.

Prioritize steps for solving and implement them sequentially. Remember that change comes from the center via debate and compromise.

Carter didn't need to burrow any deeper into the documents Electra had sent him. He needed only one reading to conclude they were good to go, so his Email to Angus explained how best to proceed: have his newly formed campaign team run with them as is for the Memorial Day kick-off two weekends from now.

Electra returned to Cyberspace tracking the next day, looking for possible terrorist connections associated with recent banking glitches. Her Big Data and security tools were several generations ahead of the competition, letting her cruise undetected wherever she needed to go. She identified possible links between Cybergard and banking network outages but would need to analyze further. In the coming weeks, time and priorities permitting, she would burrow deeper while Alisha practiced quarterback and spokesperson roles.

Angus stunned the political world as the content and delivery of his speech rattled the Guardian Party. The campaign team deliberately leaked enough information so his address was widely advertised. Electra was among the millions of viewers listening, and she knew immediately that Angus must have liked what she wrote because he didn't change a single word. The public at large liked it and the way Angus fielded questions from the press corps afterwards; media analysts and pundits gave him high marks and expected a prompt response from President Gardner.

Jared postponed his spiritual advisor meeting to listen to what Angus had to say, and his response to his Chief of Staff was immediate and harsh.

"That damned Angus! He resigned before I could fire the bastard. What does he mean the T-Plague has changed me and I'm taking the country in the wrong direction? I'll set the record straight. Set up a press conference for me day after tomorrow. I know what I'm gonna say." Two days later the nation heard his words.

"Good evening fellow American Patriots!

"No doubt you have heard Angus McTear's speech. He resigned his Vice Presidential role before I could fire him. How dare he desecrate Memorial Day with lies and innuendo. That was his opening salvo against me, and in the coming weeks I'll debate him into the dirt he's throwing on the campaign trail. But let me steady your nerves right now with some comforting words.

"Yes, I was struck down by the T-Plague, caused by a Chinese-led cowardly attack several years ago. And yes, it changed me; it made me even stronger, even more resolved to take us to where we belong. I was the only survivor, which is a sign that I am the right leader for our nation at this time and place in history.

"The poll numbers show you support me. You like the harsher measures I push because you know the kinder and gentler pap from the string of previous feckless Administrations have not been in our best interests. And you like the results of my programs. They have made us safer and have shrunk our budget deficit. And I have additional programs all set to go. My school-based Security Watch Program will be another under the auspices of the Pillars Program. Soon we will roll out the 'Op-In' program where patients suffering from medical conditions will automatically be given appropriate medical treatment—drugs or operations—to help them fit into society. And I will suspend writ of habeas corpus and install harsher search and seizure protocols the second I detect a whiff of terrorism.

"So tonight, please rest assured we are on the right course as long as I am at the helm. I look forward to your continued support, culminating with your voting for me come November.

"God bless you patriotic Americans, and God bless our great nation."

Thanks to Electra's documents and all the media coverage of the Memorial Weekend speeches, Alisha had plenty of material to include in her mid-June student town hall meeting in Houston. The fourth largest American city and still the nation's capital for oil and gas, Houston has diversified to become a world center for infrastructure engineering and construction projects in addition to medical research. Numerous universities and performing arts venues make it a showcase city for the best Texas has to offer.

Woolly arranged to hold the meeting at Carnegie Vanguard High School. Acclaimed for its advanced placement programs and commitment to community service, it's ranked among the top 10 nationally. The school is just south of Memorial Parkway and west of Downtown, making its location convenient for the invited students, and the meeting would be recorded for in-school streaming later. There would be a fifteen-minute news interview afterwards to be aired on all local networks.

Woolly knew from the very first meeting that Alisha was special. He liked her personally and professionally, deciding she would be his political PR protégé. By now he no longer worried about what she would say or how she would run the meeting. Her organizational and speaking skills took a big load off his shoulders, allowing him to sit back and enjoy the show after he got the cameras rolling. Alisha's opening remarks set the tone.

"Good morning students, the next-gen leaders of our great nation. And all too soon you will collectively command our nation's course into an exciting future. But to do that, you need to know a lot about a lot of things. I thought the recent Presidential Campaign speeches would be a great topic to center our discussion.

"Angus McTear referenced our constitutional heritage, tracing all the way from the Golden Age of Greece, then to Hobbes and Locke, and then to framers of our extraordinary constitution. What does he mean by this? Well, I challenge you to ask your teachers, and to research it for yourself. Today, you have unlimited information resources available on the Internet. Search for these topics and think critically when you read.

"So, studying history helps you understand what's going on in the political arena. And I challenge your teachers not to teach historical dates and facts and faces, but rather teach first an overarching framework in which all the pieces fit. To use the well-worn metaphor, understand the forest first, then see how the trees fit. And you will see how many other events fit in the same framework. Let me briefly sketch this for literature.

"Writing is what distinguishes humans from the animal world, for we can record where we've been, what we think, and where we want to go. You will find when you study the great books much discussion of politics for the periods they cover. So here is another connection you make through your education: the connection between politics and literature. I'll touch on one more area of learning, then we'll open the floor to questions…"

The ninety minutes melted away even faster than Woolly expected, for Alisha's opening remarks stimulated a spirited series of questions. Her closing words re-emphasized why students must stay in school.

"All of you have the gift of youth. It is your time to ask why not, and to learn why you can. Do not make the mistake of dropping out, for if you do you will have to play a difficult game of catching up for lost learning opportunities. So, get your high school degree, move on to college, and set the foundation for lifelong learning."

Immediately afterwards, Woolly took her and the video crew to an adjacent room for a local media interview, where she demonstrated poise on either side of the microphone.

"And today, we're talking to Alisha Kittner, who is our Governor's designated spokesperson for K-12 educational programs. Many of our viewers know about your Co-NFL gridiron exploits. But they might not know that you have a PhD and also do biotech research at the University of Texas at Austin. A most unusual combination. How do you manage to do both, and how does that qualify you to be the K-12 spokesperson?"

"Actually, it's an example for our students, showing how mental and physical activities complement one another. When I'm practicing or playing football, my brain continues working on my academic projects. My T-Bred motto is work hard play hard, and I ask students to find examples from their own experiences how a solution to a problem came while doing something else."

"From what we saw today, the messages you delivered were well received by the students. They relate to you and your words. Why do you think that's the case?" Alisha couldn't resist adding a touch of humor before answering the question.

"Well as the T-Bred quarterback, I'm supposed to connect with my receivers, and students just might be the most important ones. Let me explain..."

Woolly let Alisha nap on the hour-long flight back to Austin. His media crew would chunk out videos he'd send to school districts as well as statewide media. He mused while studying his protégé's profile.

If I had a daughter, I'd want her to meet Alisha. What a role model. And I'll show these videos to the Governor. If events break her way, Alisha is going to go lots of places.

Chapter 22
August 2124

"The Hikers"
Thread 2 Chapter 7

CARTER NEEDED A BREAK and expected the Labor Day weekend getaway Matt and Zoe were arranging would help re-energize his flagging spirits. Not only did working for Angus deplete his time and energy, but it lowered his assessment that they'd defeat Jared.

Last weekend, after cobbling together pieces to build economic and international planks, Carter had spotted weaknesses in some of his ideas because Jared was already pushing ahead in directions Carter was recommending. He was putting people to work and creating more low-tech jobs thanks to infrastructure rebuild projects. He was reducing entitlements programs and shrinking the deficit, albeit some of the steps were harsh. Maybe Angus could criticize Jared for not doing enough to ease the public's fear of hi-tech or to make T-Plague victims smarter. Carter speculated that Jared wanted to keep people dumb so they would keep voting for him, but the public might not buy into such a conspiracy theory.

The international plank was only marginally better. Angus had more diplomacy than Jared, but that might not matter because the public would close ranks behind Jared if he started a shooting war. Polls showed the public wanted terrorist retribution. Economic Plank Foundation Principles:

- Capitalism and Free Enterprise provides foundation.
- International Economy is long-term win-win
- Technological change contributes to win-win growth.
- Economy too large for central planning.

- Place more importance on monetary policy rather than fiscal policy.
- Moderate booms and busts inherent in economic cycles. Provide interim safety net for displaced workers.

Current Problems:

- Growth hampered by too much regulation.
- Misplaced emphasis on income inequality instead of income insufficiency.
- Some workers not smart enough for the "brain-based" economy.
- Tendency for concentration of wealth and income inequality.
- Entitlements Programs inefficient.
- AI job erosion accelerating.
- AI changing Free Market Economics

Steps for Solving:

- Reduce regulation.
- Shrink size and number of government programs and services.
- Retrain workers to plug in to "brain-based" economy.
- Provide pool of "low-tech"jobs for workers who don't fit in "brain-based" economy (Infrastructure projects, etc.) Rationalize Trade Agreements. Recommend CEO Salary Caps.
- Streamline Entitlements Programs. (Size Duration)
- Revise minimum wage plus assistance programs for qualified workers.

International Plank

Foundation Principles:

- U.S. is the only Superpower.
- Nation Building difficult.
- Liberal Democracy and Free Enterprise thwarted by tyrants if force not used to dislodge them.
- America must choose to play only one role on the world stage: Independence/Isolation Economic Backer
- Exceptionalism

Current Problems:

- AI reshuffling World pecking order among Nations. China unwilling to recognize it's a "Toothless Tiger."
- Middle East Muddle has no solution until Islam decides to joint Modernity.
- Russia problematic until it establishes rule of law in post resource-based economy.
- Previous administrations built incoherent, impatient, and shortsighted programs.
- Previous administrations ignored cultural constraints and differences.
- UN leaders (except for U.S.) view world as kinder and gentler instead of cruel and harsh.
- Outcomes unsuccessful when relying on economic carrots instead of military sticks.

Steps for Solving:

- Pick a role and stick to it (First Choice: Economic Backer Second Choice: Exceptionalism Third Choice: Independence/Isolation)
- Consider cultural issues when setting policy and goals.
- Consider using force to dislodge tyrants.
- Don't impose American Government Model.
- Develop cooperative programs for protecting Intellectual Capital, Internet Access, AI Benefits.
- Expand alliances with Africa and India (primary); South America (secondary).

Carter could find nothing to add, so he sent them to Angus and called Monday evening. The best he could do was offer tactical advice.

"When you debate Jared, many of our platform items differ from Jared's only in style, not in content. We disagree with his heavy-handed, harsh manner, but the polls tell us the public still likes it better than kinder and gentler. I don't think your compromise position can move the voters' preference needle. And Jared's no fool. So far, he's been holding his own. The analysts might be scoring you the winner by a narrow margin, but either the public doesn't care or isn't smart enough to understand the nuances. Maybe you can trip him up on some of the other issues." Angus sighed, then straightened his shoulders before replying.

"You're right, but it's unethical for me to push marginal programs that differ from his just to be different. And if the public prefers his style to mine—even though long-term he's wrong and I'm right—I have to abide by the people's choice. Maybe it's time to contrast my philosophical, social, or religious planks, but I've got to be careful not to electrocute myself because those can be political third rails. Why don't you do this for me? Draft additional planks and let's see how I can weave them into a debate. When do you think you'll have them ready?"

"How about after my Labor Day weekend getaway? And let's not confuse ourselves or the public. I'm going to combine all these planks into one, which I'll call the Social Plank."

"That'll work. You can send it to me when you get back. Where are you going?"

"I don't know. My friends are planning it. They always come up with some new adventure. And I'll find out tomorrow what's in store when I play tennis at the club with my buddy Matt."

"Enjoy yourself on the court and on your adventure. Come back feeling more optimistic."

"That's game, set, and match. You're dragging tonight. What's the matter?"

"Too much work and not enough time. I need a break, and I hope you and Zoe have cooked up something good."

"We have. I'll tell you all about it after we eat. I'll buy the beers, but you pick up the tab for the rest." The fellows showered quickly, then grabbed dinner at the club's restaurant.

"Zoe and I had great fun sailing this summer. Too bad you and Jazzi didn't join us. We were thinking about taking the two of you on another overnight cruise, but Zoe came up with a new activity. How does a zip line hike sound to you?"

"I can always count on you and Zoe to surprise me. I know what a zip line is, but what's a zip line hike?"

"The National Park Service has built hiking trails in suitable national parks where you hike up the mountain, then zip line to the bottom of the next trail going up. Zoe researched them on the Web. They're safe and inexpensive when compared to chartering a sailboat. And we can pitch tents at a campground, or stay at a motel or bed and breakfast if the weather turns bad. What do you think?" "Jazzi should like it more than she liked sailing. And it'll be good for me too. Gets me out of my comfort zone. Where will we be going?"

"Shenandoah National Park near Front Royal, Virginia. Zoe's got all the info and is making the arrangements. She'll fill us in on the drive. I know how thorough you are, so check this out. You get Jazzi to your place and we'll pick you up 3 p.m. Friday afternoon. Pack light. Bring sleeping bags and hiking clothes. Zoe and I have all the rest. We'll camp out Friday and Saturday nights, returning sometime Sunday. That'll give all of us Monday to get ready for the week."

"Sounds like you and Zoe have it nailed. Let me buy one more round so we can drink a toast to Zoe."

Carter also wanted to cover one more topic that had puzzled him for years: relationships with females. He wanted to congratulate Matt for moving beyond co-friendship and hoped Matt might explain why the Carter-Jazzi relationship had stagnated. Carter spoke up soon after the server set down the beer.

"I'm happy that you're writing up your marriage contract for Zoe to approve. The two of you are compatible in all the right ways. Our Labor Day adventure is another example of how you're always keeping your relationship growing. I wish I could say the same for mine and Jazzi's. Maybe you can tell me what I'm doing wrong."

"I don't know how Jazzi looks at it, but Zoe and I have seen the two of you in action. Zoe picks up vibes better than I, and here's what she says. On the surface, you say and do the right things. But you sometimes come across too conservative, too intellectual, as if you're looking for someone to debate rather than to know intimately. And sometimes, your words stay in one place too long. Maybe Jazzi is looking for something different. That's about as far as I can take it. Talk to Jazzi." Carter mulled Matt's words, taking a sip of beer before replying.

"I guess that's as good an answer as I'm ever gonna get. It's in my court now. Come on, let's get going."

Carter didn't like the way Jazzi slammed the door when getting into the Vette.

"Hey! Don't break the door. You know it's made of SMC fiberglass, but please don't test its impact strength."

"I don't know what SMC stands for, and please, don't tell me. Sorry to be in a bad mood, but it's been a bad week at the bank. We had several computer network glitches that put me way behind. We're finally up and running, but the last I heard, several other banks are down today. What a bummer for the customers. Friday ATM traffic is always heavy, and withdrawals always spike before the start of a three-day weekend."

"Well, by the time we get back, the glitches will be resolved and everything should be back to normal, so try to forget about your problems and enjoy the outing."

"I packed what you told me to bring, but you didn't tell me where we're going."

"First to Matt and Zoe's. After that, I'll let Zoe describe. But wherever it is, we'll go in Matt's van. So, let's get started."

The start irked Carter. A power outage knocked out traffic signals, snarling traffic and testing his patience, but Zoe's cheery greeting lifted the mood of the late arrivals.

"You're only a half-hour late, and Matt filled the tank last night, so it doesn't matter that gas pumps are out of commission. Front Royal is 75 miles west, and I doubt the power outage extends that far. And it'll be a clear shot once we're on Interstate 66. Let's get going. I'll tell you all the details once we're on the Interstate." Forty-five minutes later, Zoe's always breathless manner added enthusiasm to her upbeat description.

"Since Carter's an economist, he'll be happy to know the National Park Service takes in over $20 million annually due to zip line hikes, and they plan to expand into western states. Where we're going—Shenandoah National Park in the Blue Ridge Mountains— is the third trail installed. Front Royal is the northern boundary of America's longest linear park, which stretches for 470 miles. I've never been there, but the forested mountain photos show why it's so popular. And starting at Front Royal, you can take the Skyline Drive 100 miles to where it becomes the Shenandoah Parkway stretching all the way to the Smoky Mountains." Jazzi asked an obvious question.

"Front Royal. Funny name for a town. How'd that come about?" Zoe knew the answer.

"Comes from Revolutionary War days. The town's militia used to drill in front of a giant oak tree and would come to attention there at the command 'Front Royal.' I found that info on the Internet." Zoe paused for Jazzi to reply.

"You were beginning to sound like Carter, but you stopped sooner." Matt said, "Carter often does provide an information overload, but he's learning to throttle back the number of words. Come on, Carter. Defend yourself."

"Yes, I'm getting better at summarizing. The last time I talked to Electra, she complimented me." Jazzi wasn't so sure.

"Maybe Electra likes to listen more than I do. I thought you had de-escalated that relationship."

"I did, but we still talk about economics and politics. She's very smart." Zoe thought a change of topic would help.

"Last week I bought a never-used two-room, eight-person Coleman tent. It's still in the original carton. I got a great deal on one of the auction Websites. Matt and I didn't have a chance to unpack it, but I'm sure we can figure out how to set it up. According to the Coleman Website, it takes only a couple of minutes. And I've got a campsite reserved at North Fork Resorts, which is just off Interstate 66 and close to the park entrance. I packed a couple of hampers and coolers so we can make our own breakfast and lunch. For dinner, we can come back to civilization. There are plenty of restaurants." All this was to Jazzi's liking, and she used it to poke fun at herself.

"I've never been camping or done much hiking, and until this adventure, I always considered roughing it to be pitching a tent in the lobby of a fabulous place, like Grossinger's Catskill Lodge or Yellowstone's Old Faithful Inn. I can tell this is going to be a different sort of outing."

Power had been restored by the time Matt registered at the campground office. The clerk explained how to get to their campsite, providing brochures and maps to the park's zip line center as well as a list of nearby restaurants.

"You four look pretty fit, and that's good because hiking plus zip lining can be strenuous. Is this your first time?" Zoe spoke for the group.

"Well, sort of. My partner and I did zip lining on a Caribbean cruise ship, so we got the hang of it. And all of us exercise regularly."

"Well, don't you worry none. The park ranger manning the zip line center will give you pointers before you start out. And the zip line starting gates are fully automated. Instructions are posted, so it's foolproof. There has never been a national park zip line fatality. You'll have a great time. And the latest weather forecast shows clear skies and warm temperatures through Labor Day." Matt thanked the clerk and led his group back to the van for a short drive to the campsite. Jazzi decided not to ask about safety issues because no one mentioned the "no fatality" remark, and Matt was happily reciting directions to the campsite. Half an hour later, he stopped the van so he could surrender the map to Zoe.

"I must have taken a couple of wrong turns. Nothing I'm driving past seems to match the map. Let's put our heads together and figure out where to go."Thanks to Zoe, Matt pulled into their spot ten minutes later; Zoe issued the next command.

"Well, here we are! Why don't Matt and Carter unpack the tent? Installation instructions should be inside." Unpacking was easier said than done. The industrial-strength staples needed an industrialsized screwdriver (which Matt's emergency toolkit didn't contain) to pry loose. Carter bent the blade of his Swiss Army Knife and gashed his thumb but finally defeated the last staple. Jazzi patched his thumb, courtesy of Zoe's emergency medical kit. Daylight was beginning to fade by the time Matt and Carter emptied the container's contents. That and the leafy forest made reading the instructions even more of a challenge. Matt scratched his head before handing them to Carter.

"Can anyone read Spanish? They forgot to include the English version." Carter was the only one to volunteer.

"I know a little Spanish; Mariah taught me some, so let me try." Ten minutes later he was still stuck on Roman Numeral II. Zoe came up with an idea.

"Let's identify all the parts and then assemble the tent according to the pictures." Carter and Matt laid out all the pieces while Zoe studied what the tent should look like. They were so engrossed in the exercise they had lost sight of Jazzi, who interrupted them when she introduced a fellow camper.

"I think Mr. Cavendish might be able to help." Jazzi had spotted a similar tent nearby and came back with help.

"Hello, young fellas. Let me give you a hand. None of the written instructions I've ever read are good for anything except for starting a campfire. These tents are easy to set up once someone shows you how."

The tent was up ten minutes later and the gals were bringing in the gear while Mr. Cavendish explained more to the guys.

"Do like I do. Keep the poles attached when you put it in the box; be sure to clean them off first. Your lady-friend told me you're doing a zip line hike tomorrow. If my wife and I were younger and lighter, we'd join you. Well, I better get out of your way. Have fun." Matt said, "Thanks again. We'll get a good night's sleep because of you. We thought we'd have dinner tonight at one of the restaurants. Do you have a recommendation?" He didn't, but Carter suggested they have cereal and turn in early. Jazzi detected a flaw in his plan.

"By any chance, did you pack dairy-free milk? I'm lactose-intolerant." There was stunned silence until Carter spoke up.

"You can use water instead of milk. And if you swallow fast enough, you won't notice the difference. Zoe replied before Jazzi.

"I think you guys should go shopping for what Jazzi needs." Now it was Carter's turn to be displeased.

"Do you realize brands like LACTAID cost twice as much as regular milk? Matt ended the discussion by pulling Carter towards the van.

"Say no more. We're going."

Jazzi's stiff neck and sore back put her in a worse mood when she awoke. The sleeping bag's inflatable mattress had a slow leak. Carter tried his best to brighten her mood.

"We'll switch sleeping bags tonight. And the warmth of the sun and the exertion from hiking will loosen up your joints. Just wait and see. You'll be fine."

Zoe set out a camper's breakfast of cereal and juice, then packed energy bars and drinks for lunch while Matt gave instructions.

"So, here's the drill. We follow the color-coded trail markers from the base of the mountain. According to what Zoe researched, national park trails have four classifications: Easy, Average, Vigorous, and Advanced. We'll pick an average e-trail, and it should always have a trail marker in sight. When we get to the top, we zip line down to the next starting point. According to Zoe, we should be able to complete three climbs and zip line descents in six hours." Jazzi wasn't sure her fitness level could handle that much fun on day one and asked for other opinions. Carter spoke right up.

"You're fitter than most females, and the trails are designed for average people. Don't worry, you'll be fine. And I think you're dressed AOK. Shorts and a short-sleeved top should do it. Just make sure your boots and socks are comfortable. Zoe, am I right?

"I think so. It'll be close to 80, so we don't want to wear too much. And the Average trails don't have much underbrush to wade through. Shorts should be OK. And if we get tired, we always have the option of zip-lining back to our starting point and heading back. The different zip line routes crisscross multiple base points. It's like a bunch of trails in the air. Just wait till we get to the first starting gate. I think we'll be impressed." Jazzi nodded but didn't say much as she helped Zoe clear away breakfast. Soon, the foursome was on its way to the first hiking trail.

The park ranger at the zip line center gave instructions that made Jazzi feel better, and a half-hour later, Matt led the party up the trail, having no trouble keeping the markers in sight. Jazzi was beginning to enjoy herself. Carter's right. The sunlight and hiking are loosening me up. And the path isn't that steep. I can handle this. And the views from the lookout spots are magnificent. Just a hint of autumn leaves sparkling in the sunlight. Zoe's cellphone pics should be spectacular. The foursome were that day's first arrivals at the zip line gate station, so it was easy for Zoe to pose group photos and selfies. Carter dutifully posed, then studied the starting gate instructions.

"This is so well planned and constructed. It's completely automated and computer controller. There are parallel lines on each route. You slide your credit card through the reader to obtain your harness, and you can position it for either chair lift or superhero position. Then you hop in, buckle up, and away you go when you push the release button. And don't worry, Jazzi. I'll hook you in. What position would you like?"

"I'll try chair lift for the first run. Zoe, what about you?"

"I'll try flying like Supergirl. Matt, why don't you pick the superhero position too,and we can descend on parallel tracks. And Carter, why don't you do the same after you launch Jazzi?"

"Will do. We'll watch you launch first, then follow suit." Though she needed little help,Matt made sure Zoe was buckled

in correctly,then pressed the start button. Zoe waved as she glided out the gate,accelerating as the angle of descent grew steeper. Matt followed a minute later, waving and cheering,"Away we go!"

Now it was Jazzi's turn. Carter buckled her in, patted her head, and said,

"Nothing to worry about. Gravity's got you. You'll be fine."Then he pushed the launch button. Jazzi shrieked as she blasted out of the gate backwards in the superhero position.

Carter launched himself as quickly as possible, collecting his thoughts on the way down. I must have done something wrong when I hooked her up,but I corrected whatever it was. I'm facing forward and found the braking lever. But you get pretty much the same view whether facing forward or backward. Jazzi should get a good view.

Jazzi was fine only because Zoe and Matt were there to catch her. She needed help freeing herself from the harness and was complaining to her helpers when Carter glided in.

"That wasn't funny. He better have a good explanation."Carter hustled over to his partner, apologizing on the way.

"I'm sorry. I misread the instructions. But look, no harm done, so please don't be upset." Zoe tried to soothe ruffled feelings.

"I'm sure Carter won't make the same mistake twice. Why don't we take a snack break and plan our next hike?"That helped everyone. There was a convenient picnic bench shaded by trees, and a gentle breeze added to the relaxed setting. Matt checked the maps to confirm their plan was still on target.

"After we rest a bit, we'll take the next average-rated trail up from here. I think we did well on the first one."Zoe piped right up. "Yes, we did. And I'm impressed with the zip lines. But what might happen if the power goes out?"

Carter volunteered, "Nothing bad. Anyone in motion when it happened would slide to the finish gate. But here's a thought. Suppose a terrorist hacked into the computer system. They could launch several people down the same line before it was clear. Not necessarily cataclysmic,but it could cause some broken bones. Well, that's not going to happen. It's too small a target for terrorists. Jazzi, why are your frowning?"

"Only you would come up with such a thought. Let's think happier thoughts."

The foursome started up the next trail just before noon. This time, Carter led the way and Matt took the trailing position, the gals spaced between. Zoe was right once again because Carter didn't make the same mistake; he made a new one. He followed an Advanced trail marker. All trails look the same at the start because incline and difficulty are nearly identical. Carter's confidence was way ahead of where it should be. By the time he admitted his mistake, not only would they need to climb hand-over-hand, but would need to spot a marker. Everyone gathered about Carter when he called for help.

"We're lost, and it's my fault. I must have followed the wrong markers, and now I can't see even one. Any ideas for what to do?" This time Matt spoke first.

"Zoe, why don't you check our GPS positioning on your cellphone? You can display it on a map that'll show our position relative to waypoints. Carter, you should have thought of that. You've sailed enough with us to know how to set waypoints for navigation." Carter pleaded memory lapse while Zoe activated her cell.

"Rats,there's no signal here,probably because of the mountains. Or maybe there's a communications network outage."

Just then,she spotted two hikers coming from below and waved to them. The opposite- sex couple appeared to be mid-forties, fit, and dressed for strenuous hiking. The woman spoke first.

"Hi there. I bet you're lost. You don't ever wear shorts on these advanced trails."

Carter said, "Yes, and it's my mistake. And we can't get a cellphone signal."

Her partner said,"Yeah,cell communication networks are down. Goes to show people need to know how to get along without hi-tech stuff. That's why Sheila and I enjoy outdoor activities. Puts us in touch with a simpler lifestyle. Here's what I recommend you do. Hike straight down the mountain. When you get to the bottom start walking southeast around the base until you reach your starting point. From there you can go back up or head back home. Gravity will tell you when you reach the bottom. We'll get you pointed in the right direction."

Matt led the way down after thanking the couple whose directions worked,but the four were grim by the time they straggled to Matt's van. Climbing down is just as strenuous as going up,tiring a different set of muscles. The underbrush had become an obstacle course for the shorts-clad ladies; Jazzi had twisted an ankle and Zoe's right knee was sore. Carter's and Matt's blisters needed attention. Zoe made the best of things when she said a hot shower, clean clothes, and dinner out would be rewards for escaping the wilderness. No one spoke as Matt steered the van back to the campground.

Dinner did help revive spirits. Zoe described after pie ala mode what Sunday's plan would be.

"We'll drive to another starting location and pick an easy trail. Then we'll zip line back to the start and decide if we want to do more or pack up and head home. Let's get a good night's sleep and be ready. And Carter, please make sure you swap sleeping bags so Jazzi doesn't get a stiff neck or sore back."

Once again Zoe was right. Jazzi awoke with neck and back feeling pain-free,but other parts were in agony. As she crawled out the sleeping bag,her legs were as stiff as if she had run a marathon, and her abdomen felt like it had been cut in two. Carter helped her up and then asked for Matt's opinion.

"Jazzi's muscles are sore. What do you think we should do?"

"Maybe we should pack up and head home. Jazzi, what would you like?"

"No, I don't want to spoil the weekend for everyone else. Why don't the three of you go on. I'll stay at the campsite."Carter agreed, saying she'd be fine on her own and began searching through his bag for a book when Zoe spoke up.

"No,that's no good for Zoe. I think it's time to pack up and head home. We can stop for pancakes on the way. I'm tired of cold cereal for breakfast."There were no dissenters,so Zoe,energetic as always, set an example for the fellows. They bustled about loading the van and were ready to leave when Mr. Cavendish bid them farewell.

"I can't help noticing how beat you all look. What do you think of zip line hikes now?" Jazzi didn't hold back her opinion.

"Sleeping on the ground is hard, and so is a zip line hike. If I ever do this again,I'll have to train for it. How do you and your wife manage to enjoy camping out?"

"We've got it down to a system. We bring air mattresses, comfortable chairs and a backlog of reading material. And after we stroll back from walking on the roads, I shake our martini's. And we stream music on the Internet." Just then a tail-wagging black Labrador bounded into Carter's midsection.

"Gabriel enjoys camping out even more than we do,and he's got us well trained. We always bring extra treats for him. But please, don't judge camping out from just one experience. Come again. Well, have a safe drive home."

The drive home was uneventful, but while Matt and Zoe chatted about what they'd do differently next time,Carter and Jazzi sat in uncomfortable silence the whole way. After the van dropped them off mid-afternoon, Carter drove her home, a drive that was awkward but not silent.

"I learned a lot this weekend about a couple of things. The most important thing is that although you're a real nice guy, I see once and for all we're not right for each other. And please, don't ask me to explain or analyze what happened. Figure it out for yourself." Carter kept his eyes fixed on the road ahead as he replied.

"If you want me to take a hike, I'll understand." Neither spoke again until reaching Jazzi's apartment.

"Here, let me help get your stuff to the front door." Carter put her gear inside the entrance, then turned and left without saying a word. Jazzi limped to the living room sofa and sat on something comfortable for the first time in two days. The cushions and tears helped her deal with the pain.

This is the worst Labor Day weekend of my life, but perhaps it's good for me. I learned to prepare better when jumping into something new. And after a year and a half, I know it's time to say goodbye to Carter.

Carter dragged himself and his gear out of the Vette and into the house. He put away what he could, put the rest in the laundry bin, and then took a hot shower to clean off residual grime and clear his mind. Afterwards, he settled onto the living room sofa.

How odd I feel right now, sitting in Electra's living room, trying to sort out relationships. Electra and Jazzi are as different as can be, but neither was right for me. And it's not their fault. They're open and honest and sharing. Perhaps I'm not caring enough. I seem to be better at friendship than intimacy. If that's the case, and being cerebral and conservative are my traits, I'll just have to deal with it.

Carter picked himself up by doing something useful. He spent the rest of the day getting a head start on the week ahead by creating the social plank for Angus. He proofread it only once, then attached it to an email, telling Angus to keep him invisible and let the campaign team decide how to use it.

Social Plank

Foundation Principles:
- More similarities than differences among all Cultures.
- Humans are Social Animals.
- There is a Genetic/DNA component to how Man constructs Societies/Cultures/Civilizations (Social Memes).
- Individual Potential 50% Heredity and 50% Environment.
- Science and Technology drive Social Change
- Technological Revolution confounds Human Evolution.
- End of History is not assured (Liberalism, Capitalism, Democracy not guaranteed)
- Utopian Civilization is not on the Horizon (Material Wants never satisfied)
- Current Problems:
- Modernity still adjusting to Science dethroning Religion (Revelation versus Reason).
- The Two Cultures (Science versus Humanities) still reconciling per C.P. Snow, S.J. Gould, E.O.Wilson.
- Political Polarization causing widening gaps. Radicalized groups violating human dignity.
- Radicalized Minorities thwarting Mainstream Majorities.
- Wrongheaded Progressive Liberalism spreading.
- Public's fear of hi-tech growing.
- Too many people withdrawing into a "Virtual Reality World."

Steps for Solving:
- Compromise through Reasoned Discussion.
- Respect Cultural Diversity.
- Promote Responsible Science and Technology.
- Lobby against Academic/Political Progressive Liberalism.
- Provide meaningful alternatives besides jobs for self-worth.

And then he went to bed, confident his mood would improve after a good night's sleep. Before nodding off, he made a promise to make up for a missed phone call. I forgot to call Electra. Well, we just turned the calendar. I'll call her this week and wish her luck. The T-Breds are in the playoffs so it's her time to shine.

Chapter 23
September 2124

"Bombs Away"
Thread 2 Chapter 8

T-BRED FANS AND PLAYERS Alike could feel Co-NFL playoff excitement building as Sunday's home game approached. The T-Breds' record had earned a first-round bye, so this week's workouts would help the team taper to peak performance. On Monday, Bo explained what the videos showed.

"The Chicago Crunchers are way better than their record. They would have skipped the first round if it weren't for early-season quarterback problems. But that's been fixed. They now have a deep threat passing game that makes their ground game even more potent. So, the defense watches for bombs thrown over the secondary. And offense, be prepared for aggressive play. The Crunchers are known for tough defense. We practiced hard enough last week; we throttle back this week, so come Sunday, we're ready to rock and roll. Any questions before we break?" Toni's hand shot up.

"OK, if we play hard on Friday? Our fans want us to join them as usual at the sports bars."

"I know fan mingling helps the team, so all I ask is for all of you to be sensible. You're all pros, so loosen up and be well-rested by gameday."

Alisha knew she'd be ready to shine on Sunday. Electra had much to do in Cyberspace this week, so Alisha put the playoff game on the back burner until early Friday evening.

A local media crew surprised her as she motorcycled in. Alisha was becoming a Texas celebrity because of her football and spokesperson roles, and her multi-faceted public image charmed viewers who saw a bright and energetic, talented young woman, both athlete and role model. Texans liked her appealing blend of down-home virtue, intelligence, and a touch of sexy swagger.

"And here comes Kit Kittner roaring into view. Kit, congratulations on taking your team to the playoffs and for performing all season like the MVP candidate you are. What would you like to say to your fans?"

"Thanks to all of you for supporting the T-Breds. I didn't take us to the playoffs. The team and fan support did. When we play home games, stadium fans are our twelfth player. And I know those watching at sports clubs or at home are rooting for us. My teammates and I can feel the support, and it energizes us. We'll do our best to give you a great game on Sunday."

"Coach Rudman always comes up with different offensive looks. Anything you can tell us about Sunday?" Kit threw her head back and giggled.

"That's a question for Coach Bo to answer. I'm here to have fun by dancing with our fans. So, ask me Sunday after the game."

Game day! Perfect weather, clear and bright like Alisha's thinking. She knew the game would be a toss-up. Opposing teams had studied T-Bred videos, devising defensive alignments that sometimes neutralized the Wide-V Offense if she didn't improvise. And the T-Bred defense, though stronger than last year, had lost two starting safeties and a linebacker, making them susceptible to intermediate and long passes. Alisha had to score more than her defense allowed, and she was ready to meet the challenge. No pre-game locker room pep talk was needed; she saw it in her teammates' eyes as she strapped on her game face. Bo's instructions were simple.

"Offense, follow Kit's commands. She'll probe Cruncher's defense in the first half by running a conservative offense. Don't go for the jugular until it's time. Defense, you gotta hold up. Do what you did in practice."

"We got it," is all Kit said. Bo's reply was equally brief. "Go get'em!"

The Crunchers must have had similar instructions because the first quarter offensive series merely probed for chinks in opposing defenses. The T-Bred defense was lucky; the Cruncher quarterback twice overthrew receivers going long, a mistake caused by nerves.

The Cruncher defense kept T-Bred's offense bottled up until early in the second quarter when Kit surprised rushers by faking a field goal attempt. She ran to the right, then reversed course, bouncing a pass off the helmet of a charging lineman and catching the carom, finally scampering through the line and into the end zone. That brought the crowd to its feet cheering "Run Girl Run… Run Girl Run…"

The play galvanized Cruncher's offense, coming to life on the next offensive drive as its runners and receivers dominated. They scored two quick touchdowns but missed a point after. The T-Breds managed a field goal, so the half ended 13-10 in favor of Chicago. In the locker room, Bo told his team he was proud of their first-half performance.

"Defense, you did an outstanding job containing their offense. Expect them to keep attacking our secondary by going deep. Their strong-armed QB is gonna start throwing bombs when he thinks he's softened us up, so be on the lookout. Offense, go up-tempo right away and play vertical. Make sure you watch Kit's back. Crunchers play by the rules, but they tackle hard."

The T-Breds received the second-half kick-off, and once again the Crunchers were caught by surprise. They didn't realize Kit was pretending to be a blocker. The returner handed the ball to her at the fifteen-yard line, just before the defenders closed, and she was off to the races, darting across the field and up the right sideline. She zigged and zagged across the field, finally brought down at the Crusher thirty-five by a lunging defender who had the angle. On the next play, she surprised everyone by calling her own number.

She faked an end around to the right, kept the ball, and stutter-step down the left sideline, diving into the end zone over a couple of defenders. The point-after was good, making the score 17-13, T-Breds on top.

The quick score put the Crushers on their heels; on their next possession, they made only two first downs and then had to punt. Kit decided to chew up some of the clock and Crusher's defense by calling a mix of runs through the line as well as halfback or receiver end arounds. Up-tempo play calling tired the defense more than the offense, so she called her number three times. Then she connected on a crossing pattern pass to Toni, who ran to the five. Three running plays later, Kit's right halfback dived over a pile of blockers to score. The third quarter ended 24-13, and the crowd sensed an explosive fourth quarter would be in store. So did the sportscaster calling the play-by-play for a national audience.

"Fourth quarter's gonna be a showdown and shootout. Can the T-Bred defense keep the Crusher offense from scoring 11 points more than their offense? It's gonna be bombs away by the Crusher QB. And can the Crusher defense contain the T-Bred lightning-in-a-bottle offense? The next 15 minutes will tell, so stay right here."

Bo substituted defensive players as best as possible, but late-season injuries had depleted the reserves. The Crusher offense began poking holes in the T-Bred defensive line, and as the fourth quarter unfolded, it continued ripping up the secondary. The Crushers scored on a long pass, and would have scored again if it weren't for their QB's overthrowing a leaping receiver. The T-Breds threatened to score once, but Kit fumbled when brought down by a crushing tackle. The ref threw a penalty flag, but the review showed the tackle was legal; only one defender had made contact. The score was now 24-20, with six minutes remaining.

The Crusher offense made two first downs and then committed a tactical blunder by running the ball, figuring the T-Bred defense would be looking for passes, but it backfired. Their running back fumbled, and a T-Bred defender pounced on the ball. There were only three minutes left, and the crowd sensed victory if Kit controlled the ball using conservative plays that would chew up the clock. Kit huddled the offense for the last time.

"We're up-tempo to the end, and we'll surprise them with short sideline passes after a couple of runs that'll force them to use their timeouts. And remember to stay in bounds on pass plays to keep the clock running. We're at midfield, so even if they get the ball back, they have a long way to go to score. OK, break!"

Kit's play calling worked. The T-Breds drove methodically down the field, running the clock down to less than three minutes and the ball to the 25 when disaster struck. Kit completed a short sideline pass, but a safety ripped the ball from the fumbling receiver. The crowd roared and rose, knowing the next series of plays would be the showdown.

Bo didn't need to tell his defense what to expect. It would be bombs away into the T-Bred secondary; the Crushers came out throwing like there was no tomorrow because there wasn't. It was either win or go home. The outgunned secondary fought best they could, but the Crushers were marching relentlessly down the field. One bomb almost connected, but it was slightly underthrown, letting the T-Bred safety knock the ball away. But his desperation leap was costly because it knocked his knee out of alignment. As he hobbled off the field, Bo had no idea who to send in until Kit raced over.

"I know how to play defense, and I'm gonna play without some of my protective gear. That'll give me another gear so I can keep up with their receivers."

"Oh no, you don't! Sam will kill me if I put you in." But it was no good arguing. Kit would not back down.

"Please don't try to stop me. This is the time for me to shine. Crunchers won't pay attention to who's the defensive sub. And if they do, I hope they throw in my direction."

"OK, you're in." The lightning brain shifted gears, the thrill of the moment energizing every neural fiber.

Not even the sportscaster knew Kit was playing defense.

"So, we're down to this: Crusher ball on the T-Bred 30, no timeouts, and 30 seconds remaining. Expect passing plays into the riddled T-Bred secondary."

The first play was a medium-depth pass to a receiver crossing into Kit's coverage, and she surprised everyone with her closing speed and leaping ability, batting the ball away. That got the attention of the Cruncher QB; he would throw elsewhere and did so on the next play, connecting for a first down at the T-Bred 20. Kit guessed he'd do the same on the next play and raced to cover the target receiver, once again batting the ball away. The crowd and announcer roared as the clock stopped, showing seven seconds.

"There's enough time for one more Crusher play, and everyone in the stadium knows it's gonna be a pass. We just found out that Kittner is the defensive sub who's batted a couple of passes away. Her fresh legs and leaping ability are making a difference. Crushers have three receivers ready to go deep, and one for an outlet, but the pass is gonna be bombs away. Watch for all receivers and defenders converging on the ball. Here's the snap. It's a bomb into the end zone. We've got a swarm of players on a collision course. They're leaping for the ball..."

The play unfolded in slow motion for the lightning brain. It plotted the trajectory and guided Kit to the spot where six athletes leaped as one for the ball. Kit elevated higher than the rest, reaching for the thrill of victory while bracing for a terrible collision that would follow. She snatched the ball and buried it with both arms against her chest, a split second before being scissored between charging Crushers. The impact spun her even higher before gravity crashed her awkwardly to the turf. She hit head-first, stunned senseless. No one but the colliding players heard the dull crunch. The announcer's voice matched the bedlam erupting in the stands.

"What a collision! Someone's got the ball but I can't tell who. They're all down in a big heap. The referee is sorting through the pile. No touchdown signaled. The pass was intercepted and one player's still down."

Alisha came to a second later, screaming from excruciating pain and panicking because she couldn't move her legs. As she lapsed into unconsciousness, no one but the lightning brain heard her scream, Electra! I need you.

Trainers rushed into the end zone. They knelt next to her motionless body, trying to snap her awake but couldn't, so they frantically signaled for EMTs. Five minutes later, they carefully placed her on a spine board, strapping her in place to prevent further damage to the spinal cord, then wheeled her to an awaiting ambulance as a smattering of applause from a stunned crowd trickled out.

Sam usually waited until after the team was off the field to talk with Bo, but not today. He started yelling en route.

"Jesus H. Christ! I've warned you time and again, you gotta protect her from hard hits. Why the hell did you throw her into the defense?"

"She put herself in. I tried to keep her out, but you don't want to get in her way when she's made up her mind. Maybe I should have tried harder." Sam said nothing else, instead wheeling on his heel and hustling towards the ambulance.

The locker room had all the enthusiasm of a wake when Bo walked in. Players milled about in twos or threes, still wearing stained uniforms.

"OK team, gather round. I'm going to the hospital. Sam's already on the way. I hope to have good news for you tomorrow. I take full responsibility for the mishap. You get the credit for today's victory. I'm sorry you can't savor it like you should." Toni spoke for the team.

"Coach, don't blame yourself. No one was gonna keep Alisha from playing defense. One of her sayings we joke about is 'Don't make me angry. You won't like me when I'm angry.' You might be the one in the ambulance if you kept her out." Bo thanked the team for their solidarity, then departed.

Bo and Sam waited in Seton Hospital's reception area until summoned three hours later by an attending doctor.

"We've got your quarterback stabilized, and our neurologists are still looking at the images, but the preliminary diagnosis is a broken back. It looks like a clean break in the L2 lumbar region's vertebra. We brought her out of neurogenic shock with dopamine. She's conscious, but the prescription pain relievers might make her groggy. We've got her in a back brace and will put her on intravenous steroids until we determine if surgery is needed. We should be able to make that call tomorrow. She needs to stay here for a couple of days until we know the course of treatment."

"Can we see her now?" "Yes, please follow me."

Alisha was now resting as comfortably as possible, but since the pain killers had dulled her, Sam wouldn't talk for very long.

"You get some sleep. We'll come back tomorrow and let the doctors tell us how they'll get you back in action." Alisha nodded, then fell asleep.

The lightning brain roused the Electra-Alisha duo four hours later because the mental fog had lifted. Electra spoke first.

"I'm proud of you. You performed like a champion, like the leader you are."

"Maybe so, but you overheard what the doctor said. We're sidelined indefinitely. I'm waiting for you to put a positive spin on our predicament. You're good at doing that."

"We took a hard hit, but we took an even harder one when the chopper crash broke our neck. The lightning brain made our broken neck as good as new, and this time we have Neuro-Knitter assistance."

"But, will we play again? And how long will it take to get back on our feet?" Electra chuckled before answering.

"Not even Indira can answer those questions. But she'd say you have many games to play, whether or not football is in the mix. And she'd tell you to enjoy the break. Not that of your back, but a timeout from training. We'll let our body rebuild itself while you and I focus on other activities. I recommend you work on your town hall meeting talks. And try writing some poetry. You're the one who has artistic ability and empathy. A while ago, you mentioned you'd do this, and I know you've been studying literature, so why don't you summarize your plan?"

"I guess I can use my injury to illustrate how an education can give you multi-career opportunities. I have other options besides football. And I have been reading poetry from all literary periods. I'm not fond of today's post-modern prosy free verse. Most people find it unappealing. And I don't pretend I can capture emotions or messages in verse better than what the greats from the past have already created. But what I can do is write a poetic rejoinder to some of the great poems that catch my fancy. Would you like to hear my reply to The Second Coming, written by Yeats?"

"I would. I know that Yeats didn't like Modernity's direction, and the poem expresses his pessimism. So, let me guess. Your poem matches his verses, but delivers an optimistic message presented through the prism of our philosophy. What's the title?" "Post-Second Coming. Here it is:

> 'The center holds like burnished gold,
> Centripetally pulling the knowing.
> Sacrifice showed when truth be told,
> Life set loose and flowing.
> One Second Coming come and gone,
> Aberrant against the tide.
> Time has proved it baseless and wrong,
> Though it posed an addictive side.
> But could it come to life once more,
> In a sinister form unknown?
> The future holds unknowns in store,
> Slouching towards distant throne.
> It's up to all to guard the gate,
> Avoid a state of thrall.
> To kill all rough-shod beasts in wait,
> Before they come to call."

"Indira would be pleased, and so am I. And I think we should sleep so the lightning brain can focus on the healing process. Tomorrow we can start our "road to recovery" game. And both of us will win."

Snippets of Bo's Monday interview were carried on many channels because Alisha was a fan favorite in a wildly popular sport. His opening statement summarized the facts.

"I'm relieved to report that Alisha will be released from the hospital tomorrow. She suffered a broken back in yesterday's contest, but surgery will not be needed. Doctors expect her to walk again, but it remains to be seen if she can or will play next season. I take full responsibility for allowing her to play defense at the end of the game, but it was her wish to play. I'm sure you have questions, so please fire away." There was no shortage. Pointing to one of the waving hands, Bo readied himself.

"Let's be brutally frank. You won the game but lost all hope of advancing. You knocked your wanna-be MVP quarterback out of action for the remainder of the playoffs, and maybe for good. Is Sam Ryder going to fire you?"

"I don't know. You'll have to ask him. Next question."

"All of us following the sport knew Alisha had amazing athletic ability, but were concerned she wasn't strong enough to take big hits. We saw the replay. Yesterday's collision was unfortunate but not illegal. Why didn't you act in her best interests by keeping her out of harm's way? She's not built to play defense. Her speed and quickness on offense let her avoid those damaging collisions."

"I tried to keep her out, but she was determined to play. It would have been difficult to keep her from playing. Next question."

"Here's a legendary sports quote:' They never come back.' Sports annals are littered with the carcasses of athletes whose careers were cut short by injury. Alisha Kittner might be the next entry: 'A lightning bolt that dazzled us too briefly.' Have you thought about this?"

"My concern right now is for her to get out of the wheelchair. Her future athletic career is furthest from my mind. Look, I feel worse than anyone. Next question." Finally, a sympathetic question from a local sports reporter.

"I've interviewed many of your players since the team moved to Austin. They all say Alisha leads by example as well as with words, and they quote her saying, 'Don't make me angry. You wouldn't like me when I'm angry.' Could you tell us more about that quote?"

"The team reminded me of that yesterday. They told me not to blame myself, because I'd be in the hospital today if I hadn't let Alisha play. Of course, they're kidding. Alisha is one of the nicest young ladies you'd ever want to meet. Yes, she's competitive on the field, but she would never deliberately hurt anyone, on the field or off. I hope I've answered questions to your satisfaction."

Alisha was feeling good enough on Monday evening to watch television while sitting in a wheelchair. She put her own spin on what came out of Bo's interview.

Perhaps it's too soon for the sports pages to carry my epitaph. Bo did get one thing right. There's no way he could have stopped me from playing. But he was wrong about my not ever deliberately hurting anyone. Only Electra and I know the truth, and we'll keep it that way. Well, I need my rest. I want to be fresh for tomorrow. Electra and I are ready to go home and get better. And while we're recovering, each of us has places to go and things to do. We'll let the lightning brain take care of repairs.

Chapter 24
September 2124

"Time Out"
Thread 1 Chapter 9

ELECTRA'S RECOVERY WAS IN good hands because Robin's had the caregiver's touch, first called into action six years ago when taking care of Electra after a near-fatal helicopter crash. Today, her caregiving and physical therapy skills were like those of a professional, and she practiced them every day on Electra and Holy while also taking care of Sunshine, who trotted alertly at her heels, never letting her alpha-female out of sight. Holy kidded Robin about rescuing the little dog.

"I can't tell who does a better job of making me feel good, you or Sunshine. I guess that's why you took her home. And now that you've got your hands on Electra too, Sunshine sorta divides up the work for you." Robin kidded right back.

"Of course, she does. And you and Electra help me with Sunshine's on-the-job training. I've picked up lots of dog training tips from online videos and use them daily. Border collies are smart. That's another reason why Sunshine is such a big help. She keeps you occupied when I'm working with Electra or vice versa. And you get credit for housebreaking her. You're so patient."

"She only peed on my lap twice. I think she was trying to mark me as her territory, and I could tell by her drooping tail after I scolded her that she was sorry. Why don't you keep her in the promo video, Tim and Kwame are putting together?" Electra, who was working from her wheelchair on her computer, thought that was a good idea and said she'd tell them.

The video was Electra's idea. Once completed, Hud's salesforce could send it to bone and joint clinics or additional prospective Neuro-Knitter customers, and Hud's people believed it would generate awareness, interest, and desire to buy, making it easier to close a sale. Hud knew Electra was on the mend when she joked, "I didn't intend to break my back so you could break a sales record, but perhaps some good is coming out of that collision after all. And at your next sales meeting, please remind your people that they can't sell anything. You hired them to facilitate customers' learning experience. Remember the new sales paradigm: business is a garden for growing and nurturing customer relationships."

"Yes, your Highness. And it doesn't matter whether or not the chair you're sitting in has wheels; your mind is always turning…"

Electra used wheelchair time to keep all university and corporate projects moving in the right direction. The lightning brain could think faster than its teams, even though her grad students and direct reports were among the best in their respective fields, but since Electra's dream team remained an impossible pipe dream, she never made comparisons. A random thought flickered in her brain. *What's the origin of the term pipe dream?* She googled to learn it refers to bizarre thoughts conjured when smoking opium. *I don't need drugs. I've got the lightning brain. And I think I'll take it to Cyberspace for the rest of the day. Let's see what my security tools can uncover on terrorist or political fronts.*

Electra confirmed some of the most disturbing conjectures because her newest Big Data analysis apps ferreted out details even better than before. One app calculated an 85 percent probability that in all three event categories—Infrastructure, Financial, Government—the computer network outages were not random. Someone or something was deliberately disrupting them. She also discovered, though she was not surprised, that there was little mention of this in any online articles because her apps were better than state-of-the-art software.

Before she could connect governments, organizations, or people to event categories, she needed to narrow candidate search criteria using prior probability estimates to prioritize them, and the hard work paid off. Her app calculated a 95 percent posterior probability that Cybergard was connected to financial network failures. She snooped further, looking for organization or government connections to Cybergard. This time, her app calculated a 99 percent probability for a Cybergard link to the Iron Triangle. But when looking for Iron Triangle connections to event categories, she came up empty.

Hmm, I need to parse my possible connection categories better. It's time to take a break and let the lightning brain freewheel.

Sunshine came over to say hello. Electra's back brace prevented her from picking up the little dog, but she motioned to hop up and Sunshine did. Electra was like all pet people; she talked aloud as if Sunshine could understand.

"You're always going to be on the small side because you were starved when little, but I'll bet you're as smart as a dolphin, which is supposed to be the second-smartest mammal. And you're a blessing for Robin. You and Holy make her feel needed, giving her purpose that keeps her schizophrenia at bay. Lots of pet people joke that pets are better than kids, because pets give unconditional love that grows over time. By comparison, frustrated parents often say adolescent behavior moves in the opposite direction. Sometimes, we'll ask Holy to tell us about Hud's childhood. Unlike Robin, I can't imagine he was ever a temperamental teen." Just then, Robin came calling.

"You've been on the computer long enough. Time for you to do your exercises. Then I'll hook up the Neuro-Knitter. And tomorrow we take you in for your four-week evaluation to see how well your back's mending."

"I know. Sunshine already told me."

After studying the test results, a clinic therapist told Robin that progress was faster than normal. Robin replied that a combination of aggressive exercise and Neuro-Knitter treatment is the reason. Alisha kidded Robin after leaving the clinic.

"Hud should hire you to sell Neuro-Knitters. That will make you his accountants' worst nightmare. You'll generate so many sales invoices you'll crash their accounting system."

"No, their worst nightmare is the accounting system. Holy tells me the network has been down more than up. He's convinced pencil and paper are more reliable than a computer."

That evening, Electra returned to Cyberspace. I've got it. I'll look for connections between Cybergard employees and financial network failures. Then I'll look for connections between likely employees and the Iron Triangle. After that, I'll look for connections between the Iron Triangle and people. Finally, I'll look for connections between likely people and Network Category Failures. And my Big Data app can chain together all these search commands.

Even the normally unemotional Electra shouted from the rooftops when she summarized the results:

- Cybergard—Darla Tinabu—Private Sector Financial Network Failures
- Iron triangle—Ziarmal Thaqaf—Government Security Network Failures
- Iron Triangle—Sergei Zaitzev—Government Financial Network Failures
- Iron Triangle—Chen Xu–Infrastructure Network Failures

I'm connecting all the dots! The Iron Triangle must be Isilabad… that's Ziarmal, China…that's Chen, and Russia…that's Sergei. They're going to wage war against the U.S. in Cyberspace. Ziarmal's targeting our intelligence ops, Russia our banks, and China our infrastructure. They need Darla because she has the best security software. And Darla needs them to know about their Cyberweapons. Then Darla can sell Cybergard security software to the financial industry for protection against current attack weapons, but not the next generation.

What a revelation! I know all about America's adversaries and their intentions, but they haven't a clue about me. My security software toolkit leaves no trail. I'm invisible.

They must still be testing their weapons. That's why the attacks have been intermittent. Now that I know, I'm going to drill deep and decide how to thwart them. And I better tell Carter soon, so he can alert Angus. But it's up to Angus to decide how to use what I decide to give him. I don't need to get involved yet, and I hope I never do.

Although the broken back time-out kept Alisha from football activities, she kept busy with others. She added an additional daily exercise session in addition to the one Robin supervised and spent more time connected to social media, chatting with fans and well-wishers. I never planned on being a role model, but now that I am I'm responsible for living up to what's expected. All the more reason for me to pay attention to my fashion wardrobe. Maybe this'll convince Electra I'm not wasting time and money on clothing and cosmetics. It makes her look good too.

Alisha handled her wheelchair well enough to get around on her own, which impressed Sam and Woolly when they met with her late October. They were mentors as well as fans and wanted to keep her careers moving forward. Sam spoke first.

"Congratulations on being league MVP runner-up. You might have been the playoff MVP if it weren't for the big hit. It knocked us out of the playoffs."

"It did. I watched the second playoff game; we were just going through the motions. But, there's always a next season."

"I hope so. You look dandy. How're you feeling and how's therapy going?"

"Good on both fronts. I'm feeling better and getting stronger every day. The docs think I'll be out of this wheelchair by Thanksgiving."

"That'll make it a special Thanksgiving for all of us. You still need time to sort through what you want to do for next season. I'm reluctant to let you play again. You're not built for hard hits, and we can't risk another spinal cord injury."

"Don't write my Co-NFL career off just yet. Who knows what shape I'll be in next year. And between now and then, Woolly will keep me busy, right?"

"It looks to me like you can get around pretty well, so we'll feature you in the November student town hall meeting in Dallas. Do you have any ideas what you'd like to cover?"

"I have two topics that tie in to staying in school. I'll use my sports injury to illustrate the first. Too many athletes haven't prepared for life after sports because they dropped out of college before earning a degree. I can explain how my education cushions me if I don't play again. And the second will tie in to the November presidential elections. You have to have a basic education to be an informed voting citizen. If you like these, I'll send you a copy of my talk so you can connect your intro to me."

"That should work. By the way, the Governor sends you his best wishes for a quick and complete recovery. He wants to see you up and about, because he agrees with me. You have places to go and things to do."

Angus also had places to go and things to do, but according to the latest polls, he might not be going to the Oval Office come January. Though Jared's percent lead was small, it was greater than the margin of error; if it holds up, Jared would be reelected.

Three weeks remained, but there were no debates on the calendar, so the campaign team arranged a primetime Angus speech to hit Jared above the belt but closer to the person rather than his words. The media considered Angus a statesman; he wondered what the blowback might be from the points he was planning to make. But some of the latest rumors had been confirmed and dovetailed with the "old Jared." Angus knew what he must say.

The public must hear the truth. Shame on them if they can't or won't handle it. Or maybe it's a shame on Jared for not helping make the public smarter."

Angus wrote his own speech, declining Carter's offer to critique it but using what Carter had told him about possible terrorist activity. Angus was a commanding public speaker, made even easier tonight because he didn't have to memorize someone else's words. Tonight, he spoke his own words.

"Good evening, fellow Americans.

"You have had the opportunity over the course of our presidential campaign to hear my position on important issues facing us and our great nation. You have also heard those of my opponent and should have compared his with mine. I hope you did, because the content of his platform reveals something about the character of the man."

"At one time I supported Jared. I was in his cabinet, then I became his Vice President. So, it is no surprise that he and I agree on many of the programs now in action, or those planned for the next administration. But I see changes in Jared's style since he came back from the T-Plague. I'm sure you see them too if you have been paying attention. Let me list some of them and let the media analysts dig deeper.

"First, I am concerned that Jared is no longer relying on reasoned opinions balancing both sides of issues. He is beginning to think like a zealot, believing that he alone knows what's best. Yes, it's good to have courage for your convictions, but never insulate yourself from opposing views. Abraham Lincoln depended on a team of rivals.

"Next, Jared is swerving towards harsher measures. He and I both agree that the series of directionless administrations before Jared came to power were living in a kinder and gentler fantasy political world. That's why we acted boldly and decisively in our nation's best interests. But we must not let harsher become oppressive, either abroad or even more importantly at home. If you reelect Jared, he might suspend more civil rights in the name of national security. And his Pillars Programs might turn into witch hunts.

"Of course, national security is at the top on everyone's list. But I just learned of possible terrorist connections to several adversaries besides Isilibad. Why hasn't Jared told us about them? I leave that for you to question further.

"The cornerstone of democracy is an educated, intelligent people. That is why it is imperative the Techno-Plague, which has compromised our nation's I.Q., be eradicated. We have finally contained it, but there are signs a new strain is propagating. And I want you to ask this question: why haven't any of Jared's programs emphasized reversal or rehabilitation for those struck down? Does he want to have a population that is too afraid or unable to think for itself? Does he want to do the thinking for the people who can't think for themselves? I detect in his rhetoric a hubris, a belief that the public is a savage or a child he needs to control for its own good. I ask you to think about that.

"I fear that if Jared is reelected, he may take our nation to a place we don't want to go. Once he and his policies reach a certain critical mass and have a tight grip on the levers of power, they become difficult to dislodge. Please do not be charmed by short-term gain that leads to long-term loss.

"No one can claim they have all the answers. Certainly, I don't. But I believe you know I make our nation's interests my top priority. And I do so as a statesman seeking just treatment for friend and foe alike, always searching for that middle ground on which lasting peace and prosperity will take root and thrive.

"There are three weeks remaining until the election. I thank you if you have already decided to vote for me. If you are undecided or are thinking of voting for the other person, I ask that you take into consideration what I have said tonight. You, the voter, are free to choose, and with that freedom comes your responsibility to deal with the consequences.

"Whatever your choice, God's blessings on our people and on America…"

Electra, like millions of Americans, listened closely to what Angus had to say. She and Holy were perched in their wheelchairs. Robin, sitting on the sofa and Sunshine curled up in her lap, wanted to know what Holy thought.

"Excellent speech. Excellent content and delivery. It might close the gap, but maybe the content went over the heads of some of the listeners. And we'll have to hear what the media people say and what Jared says in reply. Electra, how about you?"

"My thinking is pretty much like yours, but let me add this. Public sentiment today supports harsher rather than kinder and gentler. I just hope the reference Angus makes to short-term gain leading to long-term loss registers. And we'll have to hear what the pundits say about the innuendo that Jared's not like he was before he contracted the T-Plague. Also, what will they say about the reference to new terrorist warnings Jared hasn't yet tripped over or talked about?"

Robin asked, "What do you think Jared will do?" Holy nodded in Electra's direction, so she replied.

"Jared's not stupid. He won't give a rebuttal speech because most of the points Angus made are pretty accurate. I think his press secretary will issue a brief statement indicating that personal attacks like these happen all the time when the person behind in the polls starts grasping for straws. But if the race tightens to within the margin of error, watch out. Jared will trump up a crisis. During a crisis, voters always close ranks for the person in office. We'll know in a week or so."

Electra's opinion was spot on. Analysts agreed that the issues raised were relevant but too complicated for a public that feeds on soundbites. Several wanted Jared to release medical exam results or for Angus to turn over any terrorist leaks to the CIA. There was no White House press release, but Jared tweeted "Losers grope for lies." By week's end not a ripple remained; pollsters expected next week's numbers would be unchanged.

Jackson Nolan followed polling results closely, but he was much more interested in results other than election projections. Cyber-Max Studios had begun promoting on Social Media a mini-series they would start filming next year, and to generate viewer interest, asked for recommendations matching celebrities to roles. The mini-series would be an updated remake of the brother and sister Superman and Supergirl heroes confronting the complexities of 22nd-century life on Earth. Alisha Kittner was among the leading vote-getters. Jackson strolled to Kathi Lauret's office for her take on the feedback.

"Do you remember the Co-NFL commercials you filmed a couple of months ago? I recall you thought one of the athletes had Hollywood potential. Do you recall the name?"

"I sure do. I'm a Co-NFL fan, and Alisha Kittner was league MVP runner-up. I watched the last game where she took that big hit. The slow-mo replays were painful to watch. I hope she makes a comeback. Why do you ask?"

"We've been promoting the Superman-Supergirl mini-series that we'll air early next fall, asking on Social Media who they'd like to play the parts. Alisha Kittner is a leading vote-getter."

"I'm not surprised. She's had a lot of media exposure, and she appeals to a wide audience. Not only is she physically striking, but with a little practice, she probably could do action scenes just like a stunt pro. And you saw her screen test. She handled it like an experienced actress. I had dinner with her. She is one smart young lady. Given the right breaks, she and the mini-series could get top ratings. People love comeback stories, and this has all the makings of a great one. We can promote it as a timeout from football while she recovers from injury, helping us launch the mini-series, and maybe another career for her. But it's going to depend on if or how quickly and thoroughly she comes back."

"Why don't we do this? You know her better than I do. Would you please contact her ASAP to find out if she'd be interested, and if so, would she be healthy enough to start filming end of February? And ask her about that thing her associate talked about. If I remember correctly, he called it the Cyber-Theater."

Although Alisha didn't recognize the caller ID, she did connect the name and voice to her Hollywood adventure.

"Hi, Ms. Lauret…Thanks for your concern… Yes, I am on the mend and will be out of the wheelchair by Thanksgiving… I don't know if I want to play football at the start of next season. I've been working with my fitness coach, and he tells me I'll make even faster progress when I'm out of the wheelchair… Yes, thank you!… I'd love to be considered for a role in that mini-series… I had no idea fans would like me to play that role…Yes, I'm sure I could handle it… How about I do this: I'll call you after my November medical evaluation. That way, we'll both know what shape I'm in… No, I'm not involved in the Cyber-Theater. The fellow you met, Tim Godfrey, is handling it, and from what I've heard, your studio is going to start releasing multisensory track recordings that plug in to the shuttle-chair…If everything works out, perhaps he and I can visit you in January…I hope so, too. I'll call you as soon as I get the evaluation results…

Thanks again for calling."

Alisha would have leaped for joy if not for the broken back. This is incredibly good news! Electra was right. Some good is coming out of my big hit. I'm going to talk with her right now. Electra's voice sounded immediately.

"How ironic. People will love you for playing the role of a girl with extraordinary abilities, but society would treat us harshly if they ever found out we're a genetic freak. But that will never happen, thanks to our nearly being killed by the T-Plague. And now you have an opportunity to launch an acting career. See, you're the one who has artistic ability. You can be an actress and a poetess. And you can balance Hollywood, football, and education spokesperson roles. And while you're taking care of the fun side, I'll take care of more serious matters." Alisha's irrepressible humor bubbled out.

"We resemble that book you always talk about, Thinking, Fast and Slow. But I'd change the title to Thinking, Light, and Heavy. I know you can figure out who does what. After all, you inherited the big I.Q., but I've got the look." Electra kidded right back.

"Yes, but we're still learning from Indira. Mothers always know best."

Electra re-focused on immediate activities, paying little attention to the unfolding political drama. Subsequent opinion poll results reporting on Friday indicated there was a delayed reaction to what Angus had said. Though Jared was still leading, his lead was barely outside the margin of error. With only a week until elections, media pundits predicted the election would be a toss-up.

Jared knew it was time to act on his own advice. He had already devised a plan of action if polls tightened. Not only would his plan blast Angus, but it would also blast some of America's enemies as well as tighten his grip on the public and his party. Sunday afternoon, the White House Chief of Staff galloped to the Oval Office as soon as he was summoned.

"Yes, Mr. President."

"I have just uncovered additional terrorist planning we must quash immediately. Summon the Joint Chiefs of Staff. I have marching orders to give…"

Electra's cellphone roused her before sunrise. Why is Carter calling me at four in the morning? Her greeting cut right to the chase.

"You must have something that can't wait. What's going on?"

"Tune in to the news right now. The story's on all the channels. We just bombed North Korea! Call me when the dust settles."

Electra sat on the bed, not knowing what she could do. I have to get involved, but how? Come on…start thinking. A sudden sensation jolted her entire body. I feel like I'm about to be called back to action. I'd better get moving.

She decided to watch the news channels on her computer workstation, so she stretched herself awake while walking to her home office, sat down, and powered up. And then her actions spoke to her.

I can walk! That surge signaled the lightning brain to put me back in action.

Every media channel blared the same story, reporting that the United States had targeted North Korean missile and nuclear reactor sites with nuclear weapons and its capital with T-Plague dispersing bombs. Official statements and damage reports were just beginning to filter in; the media interspersed Jared Gardner's pre-recorded statement that was playing now.

"My fellow patriotic Americans.

"Early this morning, we launched coordinated military operations to punish China and North Korea for what they have done and are planning to do to our great nation.

"Counter-intelligence information that only I am privy to surfaced twenty-four hours ago, showing undeniably that China has covertly employed North Korea to infiltrate our computer networks. And China carried out that cowardly T-Plague attack several years ago when attempting to decapitate my administration. As I have promised you, I will act swiftly and decisively once I know the facts.

"I authorized nuclear missile strikes on North Korean missile and plutonium enrichment sites. And I authorized T-Plague dispersal on their capital. Make no mistake: my harsh response is what is needed, and I know you support me. I am putting China in particular and the world in general on notice: I will not tolerate inaction against our enemies once I know what they have done, or plan to do. I will be even more ruthless than our enemies. I will take no prisoners until I am sure our enemies are vanquished.

"I will report more to you as we assess results, but rest assured, we are more than ready to handle whatever response our enemies attempt.

"This is your Commander in Chief, signing off."

Electra worked for three hours, keeping multiple GUI windows open so she could gather information while listening to media reports. Then she powered off her computer and let the lightning brain freewheel.

Electra stretched her arms, then stood to walk to the kitchen for another Coke, suddenly realizing it was time to tell Alisha the good news.

"The Neuro-Knitter has done its job. You and I are back in action big time." Words and emotions broke through as Alisha sobbed.

We can walk again! I'm ready to take the next steps. And I'll follow your advice: never show off or tell too much too soon. We won't show anyone we've recovered until after the next medical evaluation, which is just before Thanksgiving. I can wait until then. Besides, no one will see the workouts. And I have my next spokesperson meeting to help organize, so I'll be happy as a clam sitting while preparing my talk."

Prancing about the room, Alisha's laughter replaced tears as she thought about the future. Suddenly, her thoughts returned to the recent past.

"I shall always feel the pain wheelchair-bound people have, but I can offer them hope. I shall try to be the best possible role model. Indira will be pleased."

Chapter 25
November 2124

"On the Move"
Thread 3 Chapter 8

ELECTRA KEPT A NEWS feed window open all the following week whenever working on the computer, keeping attuned to the latest fallout caused by Jared's bold moves. Wall Street surged while international markets suffered, caused by money seeking the safest haven. Neither foreign nations nor fund managers knew what Jared might do next, but whatever it was would be in America's best short-term interests.

National polls exploded upward in Jared's favor, revealing the public's pent-up thirst for revenge against international enemies. The public pooh-poohed any pundit complaining Jared's evidence linking North Korea to China's terrorist ambitions was flimsy at best or fabricated for re-election. People voted with their feet and hands; record numbers marched to polling places and pulled the lever for Jared. Electra called Carter on Friday after the election. As expected, he was distraught.

"We're careening toward the worst of times. Jared will become even harsher, and who's going to rein him in? He's going to address the UN after Thanksgiving, and he'll use what he did to North Korea as an example of what he'll do to other nations if they pose either a threat or an impediment. And talk about shock and awe. Our military hi-tech weaponry paralyzed targets before we struck."

"Does Angus think Jared might start an unprovoked shooting war against Isilabad or China? Perhaps he's put fear in the minds of their leaders. They'll stand down for fear of nuclear bombs and T-Plague contamination."

"Angus looks at it the same way you do. But if they strike first in any manner, he'll strike harder than he just did. Did you watch much of the onsite coverage?"

"Hard not to, and it looks like a gigantic humanitarian crisis. The United Nations is supposed to lead the relief effort, but it hasn't started yet for fear of radiation or T-Plague contamination. Does Angus think other countries are applauding Jared for removing a nasty government, using an ends-justify-the-means argument?"

"Possibly, but not officially. Either way, he thinks UN reaction will be muted. Do you think Jared's action is isolated, or is he now out of control?

"That's always been a concern. But let's wait until after his UN speech and public reaction before deciding. Let's talk about happier topics. How's life with you? How are Matt and Zoe?"

"You and I haven't talked in a couple of months. Sorry I didn't call after the injury put you out of the playoffs, but I figured you didn't need any more interruptions. I hope you're on the mend."

"Yes. I should be walking by Thanksgiving. Until then, I'm keeping busy. Now how about you. How was your Labor Day adventure?"

"We went on a zip line hike in Shenandoah National Park. It taught me a lot and Jazzi even more. She and I ended our relationship. It's better this way, but I won't get into it over the phone. Next time you visit, maybe we can talk about it. As for Matt and Zoe, they're moving beyond co-friendship. He gave her a marriage contract. They'll probably hold a vow-cer next year. They make a great team. You should have seen how they worked together on our Labor Day adventure."

"They're well suited. I'm happy for them. As for you and Jazzi, if compatibility issues came out on the hike, it's better to break off now rather than later. I know you're resilient. You'll be fine. Hey, what about Russell and Jennifer Conklin?"

"Russell retired, and Jennifer and Matt are full-time into their holistic healthcare business. Russell says he might be their business administrator when he gets tired of retirement, but he's happily adjusting to sitting on the sidelines. And Angus will have any number of consulting or Democratic Party opportunities. We don't have to worry about him being at loose ends."

"I don't think any of us have that worry. I'm glad we talked. How about I call you in January. We'll have lots to talk about as events move on."

Alisha used the next three days to prepare for the Dallas school town hall meeting, scheduled for 10:30 Tuesday at highly regarded Town-view Magnet Center, site of six magnet high schools in the Dallas Independent School District. Rather than fly, Woolly arranged for a van to transport the entire crew 200 miles straight south from Austin on Interstate 35. Alisha was so well prepared there was no need to rehearse, instead just listening to Woolly tell stories about the city his wife comes from.

"Yes sir, Dallas is a great city. Its metro population ranks fifth in the nation, just behind Houston's. And though Houston has a slightly larger population, Dallas is more sophisticated. It's the southwest region's banking center. City's got great universities and museums and symphonies. There's a thriving arts district not far from Downtown. You've been driving around on your motorcycle, learning about Texas. By now, you know that Stephen F. Austin played a big role establishing the territory, culminating in statehood in 1845, but do you know Dallas history?"

"I know some, but I'd like to hear more."

"Here's a quick rundown. John Neely Bryant founded it in 1841 as a trading center on the Trinity River. And as the country grew, so did Dallas. Went from ranching and farming to manufacturing, then to oil. And the integrated circuit was invented in Dallas. And Big-D leveraged its hi-tech status into telecommunications. Today, Dallas boasts a thriving, diverse economy. Great sports town too, and your team is as popular as the Dallas Cowboys with guys, maybe because you Co-NFL females are as appealing as the Dallas Cowboy Cheerleaders." Woolly's light-hearted talk made the time tick away, and he wheeled Alisha onto the stage at the scheduled time. After his introductory remarks, Alisha rolled right into her opening lines.

"Good morning students, and thank you for coming to our high school town hall meeting. I'd prefer to be walking among you rather than sitting in a wheelchair, but I'm told I should be walking by Thanksgiving, and that will make this year's Thanksgiving even more special. But let me use my wheelchair as an example for why all of you need to get a good education.

"I've been fortunate enough to play in the Co-NFL, but the big hit I took knocked me out of the playoffs. However, if I never play another game, I have other career opportunities besides pro sports. You hear stories of athletes leaving school early. They're going for short-term dollars at the expense of longer-term opportunities that only education offers. So, get your degree! Keep career options open.

"I thought I'd use the recent elections to illustrate why getting a college degree is important. You heard speeches by both candidates referencing the political systems started by Greece and Rome. And analogies were made to the conflicts between Athens, Sparta, and Persia, namely the Persian and the Peloponnesian Wars. Xerxes led the very first jihad way back then. My job today is not to teach you history, but to challenge you to learn it so you can understand political current events. By studying history, you will learn how to draw parallels between Roman conquest two thousand years ago and current international politics. George Santayana, the great late 19th century Spanish philosopher said: 'Those who do not learn history are doomed to repeat it.' You listening to me today are the next generation of leaders, so learn about the past and acquire critical thinking skills by staying in school. I'd now like to turn the floor over to you for questions and discussion..."

Even though he'd seen her lead ten town hall meetings, Woolly still marveled at Alisha's public speaking poise and audience empathy. This time, he particularly liked how she handled the last question raised by a black male.

"Ms. Kittner, how come in history we study so much about Greek or Roman or Chinese or Middle Eastern civilizations, but so little about Africa's? Homo sapiens first appeared in Africa, so why not study the history of where we began?"
"That is a great question, and I challenge you to discuss it with fellow students at your school, but let me give you a preliminary

answer. There were many African civilizations that flourished before, during, and after Greece and Rome. And they had a written language, but they didn't record as much in writing as other civilizations. And remember this: history is written by the victors. For a variety of reasons, such as natural resources, technology, weather, or indigenous microbes, African civilizations were conquered by outsiders. But Africa is poised to be a major engine of economic growth for the rest of the 22nd century. I recommend you and your classmates extend my answer…"

Woody listened to himself as Alisha ended the meeting. I'm going to recommend that the Governor expand Alisha's role. Whether she plays football again or not, she should play a bigger role on our team.

Alisha's high spirits were impossible to contain. So much was breaking her way she had to share her great fortune, so she barged into Holy's office. The three occupants stared in disbelief, Sunshine peering from behind Robin's legs, tail wagging uncertainly. Robin spoke before Holy could figure out what to say.

"Holy Shit! You're out of the wheelchair and moving on. You mended faster this time than before."

"The credit goes to you and Tim. You're pushing me to do extra wheelchair exercises, and Tim's jolting me with the Neuro-Knitter did it. Now I'll train to rebuild strength." Holy offered his advice.

"Young lady, you've been given another chance, so make the most of it. And don't put yourself in harm's way again on the gridiron. If you play again, you're gonna have to do something different. I know young people think they're invincible, but you shouldn't think that way after your big hit. Life is fragile. So are you. And Robin should take you to the medical evaluation next Tuesday. See what they say and recommend."

Alisha drove alone to her final medical evaluation. Though 22nd century medical practice was much better than fifty years ago—a result of progress made before the T-Plague emerged—Alisha's recovery ranked among the quickest. A medical technologist gave her the good news.

"According to our imaging, your vertebra and nerve damage have mended completely. Your spinal column is as good as new.

You're cleared to resume a normal routine, but if you intend to play sports again, I'd stay away from football. Find a non-contact sport."

"Excellent advice. And no matter what I decide, next season will be different. Thank you for all you've done."

Alisha hurried away, anxious to get home for her second workout of the day. I'll begin adding strength runs to my second workout every third day, starting at low mileage and building steadily. And I'll have to train differently. I haven't decided how, but no need to worry. I know where to get advice.

Unlike Alisha, Kameyo did worry about what she didn't know, and she would need help from Su or Electra. Her latest generation of vaccines was losing potency against the mutated T-Plague virus. Early computer simulations indicated that modifications recommended by Electra would work, but recent in vitro tests didn't. Viral structure appeared the same, but there must be some subtle micro-mutation affecting T-Plague etiology. Kameyo had a glimmer of insight, but she needed Electra's guidance. Tomorrow's meeting will be critical.

Kameyo's other unknown could be answered only by Su. Su had finally begun sharing more of herself with Kameyo, but many blanks remained. Why is Su reclusive, and why does she have two sets of I.D.s? And why did I receive a correspondence asking for Su's whereabouts? She would ask tonight when having dinner at the Capital Grille, located in downtown Austin's Warehouse District. Su had made reservations; Kameyo thanked her after being seated.

"This restaurant is so refined, so elegant, just like you. Someday I hope you can say the same about me."

"That someday is today. I apologize if I haven't told you so."

"But I'm not when I compare myself to Electra. She is only two years older, but she is so much smarter, so mature, physically and emotionally, and so poised. I don't understand it."

"No one understands Electra. I love her as a godmother and aunt, but I no longer try to know what's going on in her brain. Besides, you should not worry about comparing yourself to another person. Just compare yourself to what you expect from yourself."

"I shall try to remember your wisdom. May I ask you about something else? I would like to know more about you, for I aspire to be like you."

"I am honored you think so highly of me, and you know I care about you. Please ask your questions."

"These two might go together. Why are you so reclusive? And why do you have two sets of identification?" Su waited for the waiter to serve salad before answering.

"Only two people know the whole story—Hud and Electra. It's rather involved, so I'll give you an abbreviated version. Eight years ago, I was wrongly accused of conspiracy to sabotage the T-Plague project development while working at the NIH. Government agents nearly killed me. Electra revived me after I was given a truth serum overdose, and she came up with the plan for my new identity and Austin's career. The government finally realized I'm innocent, but I lost trust, so I still keep a low profile as well as two sets of identification. A similar situation embroiled Adom Ola about a year later, but he was cleared immediately."

"Electra was only nineteen. How could she do all that?"

"I don't know. I didn't ask, and she didn't tell. Perhaps it's good I don't know."

"Here's my final question. I received a correspondence from an insurance company asking if I know how it can reach you. Your parents bought you an annuity years ago that has matured, and they want you to have the money, but they have been unable to contact you. I will give you the name and Email address for you to respond."

"I never knew about this. My parents were as reserved as I. Both died five years ago in London from T-Plague complications. And our work on T-Plague vaccines is my redemption. Yes, I'll respond." Kameyo waited until dinner was served before mentioning the main topic for tomorrow's meeting.

"I have failed to improve our T-Plague vaccines. My latest tests confirm they are losing potency against the mutated virus. I hope you and Electra can help me.

"Let's not worry about that. I'm sure Electra will figure something out. She always does…"

Electra didn't worry when Su described issues impeding progress. She listened intently while Kameyo furnished details, and then summarized what she had heard.

"So, our vaccines work better on the old virus than on the mutation, but the problem was there all along. Both strains potentiate using neural electrical impulses, and the mutant strain scrubs electrons from neural pathways more aggressively. Am I right?" Kameyo nodded yes.

"Well, this answers a couple of questions. Now we know why it targets the brain: it's an enormous reservoir of neural pathways and electrical impulses. And now we know why it selectively targets certain species: it seeks out big-brained mammals. And finally, it suggests an answer to an anecdotal observation: smart people are impacted more than dumb because they have a greater supply of active neural pathways. Kameyo, have you conjectured how to adjust our solution path?"

"I'm sorry, but I have not. I will have to work on it over Thanksgiving." Electra had a better idea.

"How about we try this. Give your brain a rest. Let me think about possible solutions and I'll report back to you and Su next week. Until then, I want you and Su to enjoy the Thanksgiving holiday. Will you be at Hud's banquet?"

"Yes, I always enjoy his Thanksgiving hospitality. Su and I will be there tomorrow."

Alisha ran five miles that afternoon for the first time since the big hit put her out of action. She thrived on training workouts and would make a game out of her comeback. But on this run, endorphins helped the lightning brain think through to an improved vaccine, so Electra came to the fore. I've got! All I need to do is attach to the vaccine backbone micro-molecular electron scrubbers, analogous to anti-oxidant free radicals. I recall articles explaining how protobacteria feed on neural signals. So, all I need to do is embed an appropriate scrubber, and the vaccine will deliver it to the receptors on infected cells. Kameyo gets the credit for finding what I overlooked. In two weeks, I'll give her test batches of improved vaccines. By mid-January at the latest, we'll see how good my new formulation is. Now I can enjoy Hud's banquet. And it's time for Alisha to be onstage for the entire Thanksgiving holiday.

Everyone who knew Hud agreed he was as solid as his manly handshake. And he needed to be strong in order to keep his business empire moving ahead. Like all effective leaders, Hud knew how to lead by projecting confidence and taking decisive action, keeping all doubts to himself. He talked to himself while shaving that morning.

It's been an OK year. Less turbulent than those I've been coming through, like when Adom got killed or when Su and Lectra got injured. Dad getting sick and Robin trying to kill herself were hard too. Stuff like that can wear a man down. And I need Lectra out of the wheelchair, so she can help me move on. Or is it Lisha? Good thing I can tell'em apart when they talk.

Though smarter than most of his business associates, Hud relied on Electra. He had long ago given up any pretense of understanding the technology his people were using, instead handling the business aspects. Case in point is the Neuro-Device Lab, where Tim handles engineering and development for the Neuro-Knitter and Cyber-Theater while Hud handles contracts and agreements. And both were pleased that sales and royalties had begun.

Good thing I took Lectra's advice for dealing with the government. I called their bluff when they threatened to stop buying if I didn't give them T-Plague patents. I can't give'em what I don't have. Lectra won't share the patents with anyone. They had to back down or take their chances elsewhere.

In earlier years, Hud and his family would cook a traditional Thanksgiving feast, but life's whims forced changes. His wife died fifteen years ago in a car crash, his boy and girl were in college prep schools out East and rarely came home, his father's health was failing, and Hud's exhausting schedule left no time for himself. But this year, instead of having the entire buffet catered, he would deep-fry two turkeys and let the catering service handle the rest.

Later that morning, Hud and Holy chatted when Robin stepped away.

"You made it to another Thanksgiving. Let's make sure you keep doing so. I guess Robin's keeping you going."

"Yep. She and her little dog keep me moving, and Robin helps keep the ranch going too." This was a sensitive issue between father and son, which Hud handled with care.

"I know you were grooming Adom to run the ranch business, and from where I sit, we both miss him. It's good you're making a place for Robin, but she relies on me for help that Adom never needed. I'm sure you're aware of this."

"Yep. I know she's high-strung and has mental problems, but she's stabilized. I love her better than anyone but you. You and Electra are gonna have to help her when I'm gone. I've told her, just like I've told you, to give me a Mickey Finn when the time comes. I don't want to linger like a vegetable."

"The only vegetables I want to think about today are the ones being served on the buffet."

"Fair enough, but at holiday times like Thanksgiving, it makes me think about family things. We've never talked about what you'll do when I'm gone. Do you ever think about remarrying? Lots of folks older than you do it."

"I'm happy enough sticking to business and my longtime friends. Like you, I was happily married once, and that's enough. Besides, I'm too old to adjust to another person. Getting married again is fine if you're young enough to collect a bunch of new and different shared experiences. But as you get older, you get set in your ways and don't want to change for another person who doesn't know or want to learn how you got to be the person you are. Some people look at it differently and I'm happy for them if another marriage later in life works. But it won't work for me."

"I know what you mean. I had friends who remarried when in their 70's, and I told 'em straight out it's like joining a cruise that's ready to dock at home port. You get stuck with all the bills and none of the fun. Maybe something will happen to change your mind, but it never did for me. You're good like you are, even better than your deep-fried turkeys are doing."

Early Thanksgiving evening Sam Ryder paid a surprise visit to wish all a Happy Thanksgiving and to chat with Alisha for only the second time since her injury. He was uncertain what to expect, but Hud knew how to break the ice. He poured over mini-cubes two glasses of a favorite Texas bourbon, Smithville Distillery Bone, gave one to Sam and the other to Alisha, and let them chat in the relative quiet of his study.

"I propose a toast to your comeback from the big hit. May you always stay in action and out of harm's way." She was touched by his sincerity.

"I know you and Bo have always thought I was too fragile, but it was my choice to play. I don't regret a single second."

"I'm reluctant to let you play again. You were lucky this time. We can't risk another back injury. Have you thought about what you'll do after football?"

"I have options, but don't write me off like some of the sportswriters. I want to play again next season, but not right away. I'd like to start training at our facility, starting in December, and see how much progress I make. Maybe I can play the second half of the season. And I'll come up with something to make me more elusive, more effective. I don't know what that'll be, but I'll figure it out. I'll talk to my personal trainer."

"Our trainers and coaching staff can help, and I can make roster changes that give us what you need. You'll be in good hands. So please come visit me and Bo when you're ready for next season."

Sam felt better on the drive home, realizing that his star player might shine again. And he would feel even better if he knew that Electra would be her personal trainer. She had already begun preparing for next season.

Alisha had two meetings scheduled the week after Thanksgiving, one in person and one by phone. At Woolly's insistence, he had arranged a meeting for Alisha and himself with Governor Joshua Goodson at the State Capitol Building. The Governor needed no further convincing that Alisha could help him and at the same time help herself. As he rose to greet his guests, Alisha thought "Josh" Goodson was the best possible blend of Hud and Sam, making for a rugged, polished Texan.

"Why, hello Alisha. So nice to see you moving on your own two feet. I'm mighty glad you've recovered, and so is Woolly. Looks like you're ready to get back in action."

"Thank you, Governor. Yes, I'm ready, but I'm not gonna play football until I've regained my strength. Maybe by mid-season I'll be able to play."

"Well, now, Woolly and I hope you'll want to play more on my team right now. I've seen you in action leading town hall meetings. You connect with the people, and you have excellent political insight. Woolly, why don't you tell Alisha what you think will be win-win?" "We'd like to add to your Texas School Spokesperson duties. Feedback has been so positive, we'd like you to handle town hall economics meetings also. And the Governor wants you to be his liaison at the National Governors Association. All the governors attend Winter and Summary plenary sessions, but they are too busy to work through the details to implement program recommendations and policy statements, so they assign persons to attend monthly meetings and workshops. They in turn work on as many of the committees they can handle: Economic Opportunity, Education, Environment, Health, and Homeland Security are the most important. You used to live in DC, so you might like a monthly trip. And you can assist the Governor's staff in incorporating the best of the NGA recommendations into state programs. And if this sounds good, we'd like you to attend the January Liaison Meeting." Alisha needed no time to recognize an offer she couldn't refuse.

"Governor, I accept. And please tell me, what do you think of another person who shares your initials: Jared Gardner. I want to make sure I represent you appropriately."

"I liked him better a couple of years ago. I liked his 'American Interests First' and 'Guarding American Greatness' programs. Finally, we have an Administration that promotes what the people want. But maybe the T-Plague dimmed him a bit. He's becoming heavy-handed and unwilling to compromise. If he's not careful with his UN speech, he might lose some international goodwill. Short-term he's OK for the country, but maybe not so much longer-term."

"There are others who feel the same way, as do I. Working for you will be an honor. Thank you again, and thank you, Woolly. I'll do my best."

"Well, now that all that's settled, let's have lunch in our private dining room. And next year, I'd like you to come back with the T-Breds after winning the championship."

Alisha had to release excess energy by working out later that afternoon, and the concluding strength run would be ideal for Electra to explain the new training regimen. Alisha ran while listening to her alter ego.

"There are a couple of sports truisms everyone believes: in basketball, you can't coach height, and in football, you can't coach speed. Well, we're going to prove we can coach speed. So, you're training program is going to build up your fast-twitch leg muscles so you add an extra gear to your top end. We're going to replace your higher mileage strength runs with high-intensity resistance sprints. And we're going to add sets of plyometric exercises, which are explosive jumping and leaping exercises—like box and bar jumps, alien squat bounds, and bench sprints—that will increase leg speed and strength. We'll then have you increase max weight when lifting but keep the reps high so you add body strength and definition without bulking up too much. This will be the start. Any questions?"

"When I talk to students, I always tell them to know the terminology before they use it, so please refresh my memory. What does plyometrics mean?"

"It's derived from the Greek word plethyein, which means to increase. Plyometrics training programs started well over a hundred years ago, but football trainers haven't used much of its latest enhancements. We will. And once we've done this, we'll take the next step. But I prefer not to discuss it yet. Let's take it one step at a time."

Alisha took all steps necessary to hold another meeting that week, this time a telephone meeting with Kathi Lauret concerning a role in an upcoming superhero series. Alisha had decided that she could handle acting, football, and politics in parallel rather than in series, so it was time to find out if the Hollywood offer is still available. Alisha made the call.

"Hello, Ms. Lauret. This is Alisha Kittner calling. Perhaps I'm being presumptuous, but do you remember me?"

"Why, of course. You were going to call me after your Thanksgiving medical exam. I trust the news is good."

"Yes, I'm out of the wheelchair and into training. That's the reason for my call. I won't be playing until May, and I thought the timing would fit your filming for the Superman series you mentioned. I would be interested in a role if the offer is still open."

"Yes, we'll hold auditions in January, and I'll add you to the list. And assuming you play football again, series filming should dovetail perfectly. Let me describe our series theme. How much do you know about the history of action-adventure and superhero science fiction?"

"I took a couple of electives in college that covered the history of film as well as media technology, and I'm a big fan of retro and current sci-fi. Frankly, a lot of the early movies have much more sophisticated psychological plots. Even before the T-Plague hit, the newer movies dummy down, relying too much on special effects. Characters have become clownish stereotypes. The genre's still popular, but the public might like a reversal to more sophistication."

"That's our thinking too, so our series is not a remake but a new departure. Superman in our series is nearing middle age and is losing some of his superpowers due to Kryptonite poisoning, so he relies on his younger sister, Supergirl, to help him handle contemporary issues facing America as well as individuals. For example, Superman has to take care of aged step-parents, all the while keeping his identity secret. And superhero powers are not as fantastic as in previous series, like flying or leaping over tall buildings at a single bound. We want our superheroes to have flaws that endear them to the audience, making them more believable. Our series producer will tell when you audition mid-January more about what character traits he wants you to project. So, I'll schedule you for an audition, and you should call me first week in January to confirm."

"That will be perfect. It'll be a great start to the new year. Thank you so much."

Electra and her alter ego cruised into December as all activities continued moving in the right direction. Unlike last year, she would spend this Christmas in Austin, training and preparing for a whirlwind January. The President's address to the UN would provide clues for what to do about two outstanding issues: reining in Jared and confronting the Iron Triangle.

This would be his first speech since being re-elected, which media commentators would study closely for directions where Jared might steer the nation internationally and domestically. Electra was among the millions worldwide watching the live Friday morning telecast.

"Good morning, delegates to the United Nations, and hello to the millions of media viewers. As the re-elected President of the United States, whose victory proclaims a mandate from my people, I am here today to announce a new order for dealing with the world. And that is 'America Number One.' We kicked out the "kinder and gentler" feckless policies of previous administrations. We are no longer willing to be hamstrung by Washington or the World. We are open for business to the World, but on terms that make dollars and sense for America. No longer will we give away jobs or aid to countries that disrespect what we stand for. And we will act quickly and proactively to assert our rights.

"Illustration number one is our response to the terrorist intrigue against us by North Korea and its promoter China. We struck decisively, using appropriate weapons. Nuclear deterrents to dismantle WMD infrastructure. T-Plague to dismantle their political infrastructure. Let's see how long their tyrannical government can handle the medical crisis. The United States will not contribute a penny to humanitarian aid. Nor will we contribute vaccines. And if you think we are being harsh, take a lesson from history. By those standards, being vaporized by a nuclear blast or struck down by the T-Plague is kinder and gentler compared to having your head chopped off and planted on a stake.

"Where do we go from here internationally? Any hint of terrorism will be dealt with in similar manner. And we may strike at any time to end the centuries-long conflict between East and West. I will say no more than that. I will let other nations decide how this might impact them.

"Domestically, I will make sure our nation is rebuilt by guarding what makes America great. Infrastructure, military, economy, and jobs will be 'America Number One.' We are charting a course combining the best from the founding of the West—that's Greece and Rome— with the best from the founding of the United States—that's our Constitution and Bill of Rights—along with the best from what current political history and economics teaches— I direct you to the disciples of Francis Fukuyama and Steven Pinker and Timothy Ferris.

"I know that many of you support my unilateral actions. You are glad to be rid of North Korea, a rogue state, a state that was a pimple on a rhino's ass. And you will welcome a Middle East that either embraces Modernity or faces annihilation. And all of you know that international politics, like religion, is driven by economics, not ethics. Do any of you really believe America fought those pyrrhic Gulf wars in the late 1990s and turn of the century to bring democracy to oppressed people? Hell no, they were fought to bring oil to the West. That's realpolitik, so get with it, with us, or out of the way."

Jared's address ended abruptly. He wheeled on his heel and strode off the platform, leaving only stunned faces and overwhelming silence in his wake. Even the meeting facilitator and broadcast announcer were speechless until one station tentatively announced they would have a lively panel debate when the station came back from a commercial break. Electra was not at a loss for words.

Jared certainly didn't dance around the issues. He gave everyone an earful, including me. Lots to digest. The pundits will be chewing on this and spitting out inferences for the next couple of days. I will too, and one thing's certain: those coming from the lightning brain will be the best, so I'll let it work away while I tend to other matters.

Jared's press secretary Dean Corfu reported the good news Monday afternoon in the Oval Office after the kerfuffle caused by the President's harsh words subsided.

"Boss, the public liked the tough talk that came right from you, unfiltered. And opinion polls confirm what you thought all along: the public wants you to be especially tough internationally. And the pundits are coming up with so many contradictory conclusions no one knows what you'll do. This can work to your advantage. One of the analysts who supports you claims your contradictory statements are a deliberate tactic to keep the world off balance. You're not about to tell them your grand strategy. They'll have to guess, and chances are they'll guess wrong. But sometime between now and January's State of the Union Address, you better let us know what your domestic and international tactics are so we can craft the programs, press releases, and speeches." Jared was feeling mellow, so he pointed Dean to a chair after requesting he pour two scotch and sodas.

"My tactics come to me as revelations after contemplation through faith. Tactics follow strategy, so here's my strategy. I know I've been chosen to smite our international foes until they yield to our will. What's our will? To keep America number one. And that's my domestic strategy too: to make America number one economically because everything follows from that. All previous Administrations relied too much on liberal left-wing and effete academic manifestos that go against the grain of human nature. I'm taking us back to where the people own the nation and the nation owns the government instead of the reverse. And I'll make sure everyone has jobs, even the ones struck down by the T-Plague. I'm gonna take care of my people."

"Boss, I hear what you're saying, but maybe we need to be a little more thorough in strategizing, especially longer-term." Having heard this before, Jared knew how to respond. He propped his feet on the coffee table before speaking again.

"The long term is nothing but a succession of short terms laid end-to-end. I don't worry about the long term because you put enough short-term together and you're dead. And besides, in another four years, when I run again, no one will remember much about what we did a couple of years ago. Politics is all about what did you do for me lately that'll help me tomorrow." Dean was in no position, either intellectually nor financially, to disagree.

"Boss, you know better. May I pour you another scotch and soda?" "Yes, and one for yourself too…"

Unlike his press secretary, Electra was well equipped to disagree with some of what she surmised about Jared's chosen direction.

I can detect, from the way he looks, speaks, and thinks, that the T-Plague has damaged Jared. He truly wants to make America number one, but the way he's going about it is not going to work. I must rein him in. Between now and the State of the Union Address, I'll come up with a plan for doing so. And then it'll be time to share it with Carter. And the plan will cover the Iron Triangle too. I'm delegating all this to the lightning brain. For the rest of the month, I'll be Alisha and just have fun. All my planning for next year is done.

Darla Tinibu planned to have a cheery December despite caution flags raised by her Iron Triangle partners after listening to Jared Gardner's UN address. They did not want to stage any additional Cyberspace mini-attacks until Jared's possible moves against terrorism or the UN were manifest to their government leaders. Darla promised to lie low and she meant it. She would tell lies that were even lower than her partners' standards. The banking industry always struggles during the first days of the new year to close out last year's books. And that's when she would launch Cyberweapons against selected commercial banks.

I'll leave the Federal Reserve and government organizations alone. They're what the Russians are after, but not me. I'll stick to the major regional banks. No one will detect what I'm doing. The government won't realize it's Cyberterrorism. It's a win for my sales guys and a win for me, and the Iron Triangle won't know what I'm up to. I'll just fire away at the firewalls using my arsenal of Russian Cyberweapons. And it's a good thing I pirated their algorithms. I can build them myself. Oh, what fun I'll have this Holiday season as my plans move ahead…

Although Gui Hou didn't know Darla Tinibu from Tiny Tim or Timbuktu, he and Darla shared devious December joy.

Su-Lin Song Chou took the bait and will run to the bank with it. I will send her money, she thinks is coming from an annuity her parents bought long ago. Now I know where she is and what names and accounts she uses. I shall use my Chinese government hacking resources to learn everything about her and her Japanese friend. Then I shall avenge my family's disgrace. And I shall be patient. Confucius said, "It does not matter how slowly you go so long as you do not stop." I shall keep moving until I have exacted punishment for what she has done, for only then will my family's honor rise once again like the glory of the morning sun.

Chapter 26
January 2125

"Command and Control Performance"
Thread 2 Chapter 9

JARED BECAME MORE CONFUSED, more irate each time he read the eMail that had just barged into his hidden account.

"Happy New Year, Mr. President. Pay attention if you want to stay out of prison.

I know all about your hidden agendas, prostitute murders, staffer sexual abuse, religious channeling, government contract extortion, and trumped-up terrorism charges. Don't believe me? Read the attached documents; listen to the recordings; watch the videos.

Your behavior is disgusting and illegal; you are unfit to be president. Your policies and programs are too harsh and uncompromising and will lead America to a disastrous future. I have the power to vote you out of office and into prison. How? By leaking to the media what I have.

Poor you. Swapping Armani suits for prison attire, Cutty and soda for cold coffee, prime rib for leftover soy chicken patties.

Want to avoid the apocalypse? Play my game. Follow my commands:

- Reinstate a Team of Rivals led by Angus McTear.
- Follow McTear's recommendations.
- Implement Health Guard-led programs to cure T-Plague victims.
- Include all the above in your Inaugural Speech.

You do this, and I'll throw you a couple of bones:

- I won't leak what I've got.
- I'll let you run for another term.
- If you don't, I will destroy you.

I am watching every move you make, every correspondence you send or take. I can see you everywhere, but you can't see me. I am invisible. Think you can find me? Don't bet your life on it."

Every bit of correspondence vanished while still being read, leaving Jared's mind as blank as the monitor he was gawking at. It took several minutes for him to wake up from this surrealistic nightmare.

He sat for several more before muttering his predicament.

I'm being blackmailed, and I haven't a clue who. I'm SOL until I find out who's behind it, so I'll do what I'm told until I know what I'm up against. I gotta get my private counter-intelligence guy going. He's the only one who'll know, and he'll keep his mouth shut.

Jared powered off his computer before making a call.

Jared's muttering amused Electra. She had seen and heard all because the voice and video monitoring apps she had installed on Jared's Oval Office computer streamed Jared's performance into her invisible network. Electra was online at the time, so she observed Jared in action, but if she had not been logged on, she could have watched it later because her network automatically saved streaming data.

Jared's not the only one who will want to track me down. So will the Iron Triangle and Cybergard once I start meddling in their affairs.

As she powered off her computer system, Electra felt an emotional twinge. I have no worries for myself. I'm several steps ahead of my opponents, but I worry about spillover onto my friends, so I'd better be careful. Having reminded herself, Electra moved ahead.

Early January marked the start of T-Bred training camp and Bo wanted Alisha to be there, even though she wouldn't be ready to play until the second half of the season. She could help him coach his recently acquired strong-armed starting quarterback who would replace Kit until she was ready.

Training camp started like a combination homecoming and first day in a new school, players' enthusiasm bubbling, hiding traces of anxiety for what lies ahead. Bo's introduction outlined what he expected.

"OK team, listen up. Welcome back to returning players, and welcome aboard to the new. Please say hi to Cal Brundy, our starting quarterback until Kit is completely recovered. Kit will participate as best she can in training camp and will assist Cal master our Wide-V Offense. And for the first week, we're going to focus on conditioning. Some of you look like you spent too much time on the couch rather than in the training room, but we'll take care of that. So, let's suit up for non-contact practice and meet on the practice field."

Electra took a time-out during the weekend to call Carter. He needed to know she'd be in Washington the last week of the month for a National Governors Association meeting, and she wanted to compare notes regarding Jared.

"Happy New Year. I promised I'd call early January, so here I am." They chatted about recent holiday activities until she segued to serious matters.

"I need to talk to you about politics, so please call me Electra. I have an additional Texas assignment. I am the Texas liaison to the National Governors Association. We're meeting Thursday and Friday last week this month, so I'll be staying at home. And how about you and me and Matt and Zoe getting together on Saturday before I fly home Sunday morning?"

"That sounds like a plum of an assignment. I've heard good things about the organization. And I already know what we'll do Saturday. Zoe's become active in a discussion group that meets the last Saturday each month, so we'll go. But please do me one favor. You can be very intimidating in these kinds of settings, so please don't dominate."

"I thought I had corrected my behavior, but I guess I need to be reminded. Thank you. I'll be the very model of propriety and correctness."

"Well, don't go that far. You won't be Electra or Alisha if you do. Hey, speaking of going too far, I thought Jared's UN address went way beyond the pale. He's gonna alienate a lot of allies abroad, and maybe some minority groups at home, if he puts in place more Pillars Programs that spy on unsuspecting citizens."

"That could happen, but the public wants payback on bad governments or people. Perhaps Jared's State of the Union address might provide clarity."

"I hope so. Maybe it'll clear up rumors that Jared deliberately bombed North Korea using vaccine-resistant T-Plague. But let's not get into that right now. We can talk when you get here. Please call me a day ahead of your arrival so I can coordinate picking you up at the airport."

Carter's concern about vaccine-resistant T-Plague didn't worry Electra. Kameyo and Su are testing my newest vaccines. If they work as they should, victims will get better and Hud will rake in more dollars. If not, I'll tweak my solution paths until they do.

Although training camp was only two weeks old, Bo was worried. It was painfully apparent his offense would be mediocre in spite of Alisha's patient coaching devoted to Cal. He was smart enough, had a catapult for an arm, and moved better than most quarterbacks. But he couldn't call plays as quickly as Kit, and receivers complained he threw the ball too hard, causing busted fingers and incomplete passes. Bo tried to soothe the situation by explaining changes he'd make to the offense.

"OK team, listen up. We're gonna start the season with a different offensive set. We'll still use the Wide-V alignment, but we won't go up-tempo. I'll radio in the plays. And we'll be able to throw long because Cal's got a strong arm. He's also gonna lead you receivers more so there'll be less velocity on the pass." One of the running backs asked about the run versus pass mix.

"We'll run the ball a bit less, but when we do you halfbacks will carry most of the load. Cal will be a decoy or blocker more than a rusher. And defense, we'll try to keep you off the field as much as possible so you stay fresh for most of the game. Well, if there are no more questions, let's break for the weekend. See you Monday."

The team accepted Bo's decisions, but Toni and a couple of players huddled with Alisha in the locker room before leaving. Toni talked first.

"You look pretty fit, and judging from how you handle the workouts, you could be ready sooner than midseason." Though she was much better than what she was showing, Alisha gave a well-rehearsed reply.

"I'm feeling pretty good, but I haven't gone through contact drills yet, so I don't know if I'm ready to handle hits. The doctors are telling me to go slow on blocking and tackling until I'm stronger. If I start again, the up-tempo Wide-V will be better than ever. But until then, Cal is your guy. Work with him and do your best."

Alisha found out when she called Hollywood that auditioning had been pushed back to the first week in February. That's fine by me. It gives me an extra week to prepare. I'll be ready. Alisha could use an extra week because she had more than football on her mind. This coming week she would present at an Austin education town hall meeting a high school program she had designed for pilot testing in the city's school district. Alisha named it the New Athena Society, a combination math club and tutoring session that brought in subject matter experts from business and industry. Each chapter would be run by the members, who would select a sponsor-mentor for assistance. Alisha would be the sponsor for the first chapter. Subsequent chapters would follow best practices established by the first.

Woolly had an easy time selling the program to the Austin Independent School District, whose representatives complimented the speaker after the meeting.

"Ms. Kittner, not only are your presentations motivating, but they give our students tools to work with. There are already twenty students who have signed on. And they're in good hands because you'll be their sponsor. Woolly, if this works the way it should, you should take it to other cities." Woolly smiled, giving one of his patented replies befitting the speaker.

"Yes indeed. Alisha Kittner has places to go and things to do."

Electra kept busy providing test vaccines, probing encrypted files, and preparing for the trip to Washington while listening to Jared's inaugural address playing in the background and liking what she heard. *Good for Jared. He's going to play my game. I'm sure Angus will too, although he'll know even less than Jared.*

A minute after Jared ended his speech, Angus answered the call from Carter.

"Yes, that was another bombshell of a speech. We have another shot at reeling this guy in." Their discussion was brief because it was too soon to talk about details, but Angus promised to recruit Carter. Angus sat alone after the call, trying to decipher Jared's sudden change.

There's more to this than Jared's letting on, but no sense wasting time guessing. I'm going to carve out programs from my campaign platform that Jared will want to promote, no matter what reasons are motivating him.

Electra's flight to Washington was stress-free. The rash of pre-Holiday airport glitches had disappeared, and Carter spotted her at baggage claim.

There she is, striking as ever and still an enigma. She may have personalities other than Electra or Alisha, but at least she has revealed those two. Maybe it's not so odd that my feelings towards her have changed so much. I've moved past wanting sex. I want us to be friends. Electra planted a kiss on Carter's cheek and then thanked him for picking her up.

"You are always on time. It's one of your many traits everyone respects. No wonder you're able to steer a steady course in Washington."

"I try to, even though that inaugural address put Washington off balance. I called Angus right after, and he hasn't a clue what caused Jared's change in direction, but there's a good chance I'll be part of a team of rivals."

"That's great news. The two of you can keep him from getting us into too much trouble. And let me tell you how my role in the National Governors Association might help…" By the time they reached home, Carter was struggling to keep all the facts straight.

"You have the instincts of a seasoned politico because you're applying the Law of Reciprocity. I can tell you how it—" Alisha interrupted midsentence.

"I'm sure you can, and Electra would like to hear, but I've switched to my Alisha persona, so please, let's talk about lighter subjects.

By ten o'clock, Alisha was settled in her old bedroom.

A lot of grand memories in this house, but only once in a great while does the past whisper. Carter's part of the past, but he's also part of the present. And I'm still attracted to him. Perhaps he'd like to share my bed tonight.

Alisha spied a strip of light at the base of his bedroom door, so she knocked before entering.

"Carter, It's Alisha. May I come in?" I can't imagine what's on her mind? Well, at least I know which one it is. Carter met her at the door.

"Don't you want to get a good night's sleep and be ready for tomorrow?"

"Well, yes, and I thought some under-the-covers relaxation might be good for both of us. Are you up for it?" Uh-oh, his body language is saying no.

"I appreciate the offer, but my feelings towards you have changed. Once we were lovers, but now I'd rather be friends. In some ways, it's even better than sex. I hope we can always share friendship."

"I understand. You've grown emotionally in the last year, and I'm pleased for you. You must have learned a lot from your relationship with Jazzi. This weekend, you must tell me about your Labor Day adventure. And thanks for offering to drive me tomorrow, but I'll use my Mustang. There's a reception dinner so I'll come home late, and I don't want to make you pick me up." Electra kissed him on the cheek before saying good night.

As she sat in the audience awaiting the chairperson's opening remarks, Alisha reviewed her mental notes regarding NGA background. Let's see, it was founded in 1908 after a meeting of governors with President Theodore Roosevelt; its purpose is to share best practices and voice collective concerns to protect state's rights and federalism. There are members from 55 states, territories, or commonwealths, and its own building is in the heart of DC. Each state maintains a Washington staff and assigns liaison role to a delegate reporting back to the governor. That, of course, is my role, and I shall add to it as opportunities arise. Alisha glanced at those sitting nearby.

I'm dressed appropriately. I'm pleased I bought new clothes. My designer black pants suit, high-collar white blouse, and dark red paisley scarf fit in nicely, as do medium heels. I look professional and Tony. The short hair is good for politics and football. Hey, both are contact sports. A sudden pang of remembrance pinged her.

My scarf is the one Carter gave me for my birthday when we were lovers. How nice I have Carter's friendship. Part of my past is helping in my present, so let's get to it.

This term's chairperson—Bethany Hopkirk, a distinguished-looking late-50s staff person from Connecticut—kicked off the meeting only fifteen minutes late.

"Good morning, delegates, and welcome to the start of our new term. I see familiar as well as new faces among you, so let me give you a level-set intro on why we are here. We are the guardians of the Republic. A Republic needs strong states and intelligent citizens to balance our Federal Government. Our role is to push back against Washington's well-meaning but often misguided attempts to tell states what to do. We've done a good job, but we must be ever watchful to avoid or to roll back encroachments made over the last fifty years by inept administrations. Though there are differing opinions about President Gardner and his Guardian Party, many give him credit for leading the charge to reverse course. He'll speak to us tonight at our reception dinner.

"This morning we will listen to project status reports from two committees, then break for lunch. This afternoon you will have an opportunity to sit in on two committee meetings of your choice and offer to join if you wish. Then be back here tonight at 7:30 for our reception dinner."

Alisha pretended to take written notes, although her lightning brain automatically stored all it wanted. She particularly liked the report describing how the state of Illinois had finally fixed its dysfunctional state and major city financial issues by installing several best practices learned from neighboring states. Term limits and Internet voting, along with incentives for the public to participate in local governance and penalties for gridlock among elected officials were among the improvements featured.

Alisha hiked next to a talkative group as the crowd headed for lunch, asking if she could sit with them. One of the men in the group replied.

"Please join us. Don't I recognize your name and face, minus the helmet? Alisha Kittner. Aren't you the Austin T-Breds quarterback?"

"Yes, I am. And I'm also the liaison from Texas. This is my very first NGA meeting, so you can call me a rookie in a different contact sport. What state are you from?"

Alisha's choice was a good one; her friendly and experienced tablemates gave her advice for conducting herself, inviting her to join them for afternoon sessions. The first she attended was the State Education Committee, since it fit with her spokesperson role. She liked some of the ideas being batted about, such as competence-based credit for placing out of some high school electives. Members liked her New Athena tutoring program idea and encouraged her to join their committee, which she did as soon as the session ended.

She attended the Economic Development Committee meeting next, reminding herself why. National, state, or local economic prosperity is the foundation for all of civilization's "higher callings." I can learn things here that I can take back to Texas, and they might help Angus, too. Jared's right about jobs being critical for making America number one. Two committee members gave overviews of new programs they claimed would be even better than some that the President had formulated. Alisha shuddered when they proudly announced the names: "Death Deterrence" and "Fortress Zones." I must tell Carter.

The meetings adjourned at five, allowing delegates time to relax and change attire for the 7:30 reception dinner. Most went to nearby hotel rooms to do so; Alisha hiked to her car for her change of clothes, and on the way back into the building, waved to Madeline Hornstein, one of the women she had lunch with. Maddie asked where she was staying.

"I'm staying with friends in the suburbs, so I drove today and brought something to change into for this evening. I'll find a place to change inside."

"I'm staying at the Marriot Marquis which is right up the street. You can change there if you wish. Come on." Alisha accepted her offer and was glad she did. Maddie's sparkling personality and grassroots political insight, grown from her activities in Ohio, would make her a useful ally. The two compared Cincinnati versus Austin lifestyles as they dressed.

"Goodness, Alisha. You are particularly handsome in that dress. And it's perfect for political events. Black is always in, and it doesn't show too much cleavage. You must always maintain propriety if you want to be a player. By the way, I love that red velvet neck choker. Isn't that an Oriental Indian talisman? There must be a story behind it."

"Yes, it was a gift long ago to my mother, who came from India. Thank you for complimenting my appearance." Maddie chuckled, then replied.

"Your proportions are practically perfect. You'd look good in practically anything. I was trim before raising three children, but time and parenting have made me like a tree. Each year, I have to fight adding another ring around me. But I try my best. Come on, darling, let's not be late."

Maddie's guidance made for effortless socializing at the reception. She and her close circle introduced Alisha to a host of members, many of whom had already taken notice. Maddie introduced her to the reception's VIP line that terminated at President Gardner.

"Mr. President, may I introduce to you Alisha Kittner, our new delegate from Texas." Alisha hadn't seen Jared in person for four years and didn't expect him to recognize her, especially if the T-Plague had permanently damaged his brain. He looks older and duller than before, but still exudes some of his old charisma. I'll keep mum about working for him. That was a lifetime ago."

"Hello Alisha, and welcome aboard the NGA. Have a pleasant evening." Alisha and Maddie went on their way, but Jared's brain didn't. There's something about her I can't quite recall. Maybe it'll come to me before I leave.

Alisha had great fun at Maddie's table playing the role of a rookie being coached by Maddie. She was starting to make contacts for whatever directions her NGA experiences might lead. And she was now listening to Jared's brief speech that she'd compare later with what he had said at the U.N. and his inauguration.

"… So in conclusion, I look forward in the next four years to sharing my programs with you, and vice versa. Together, we'll continue guarding what makes America great. Thank you all." As Jared waved to the audience, his memory clicked when he spotted Alisha. *I know her! That's Electra Kittner. She's someone important from my past, but I can't quite nail it down. I'll have one of my staffers bring her to me before I leave.*

Alisha was in no hurry to go. She and Maddie were mingling in the crowd, chatting about tomorrow's agenda, when one of the reception organizers tapped her shoulder. "Ms. Kittner, excuse me, but one of the speakers would like a word with you."

"You lead and I shall follow. Maddie, I'll be right back. Please don't leave without me." She followed him into a small room just off the banquet hall entrance, coming face to face with Jared. The lightning brain switched gears, waiting for him to speak and ready to reengage an altered enemy.

"Electra Kittner. I apologize for not recognizing you, but it's been four years and you have matured so much. And now you go by the name Alisha. I can't seem to recall much that happened just before I was struck down by the T-Plague, but didn't you work for me?"

"Yes. I was part of Angus McTear's brain trust. And just like you, I too was struck down by the T-Plague. It nearly killed me, too, but somehow, we both survived."

"We were chosen to survive and to meet again tonight. Yes, now I remember. You have public relations talent and political insight. You can be useful once again. I am recruiting you to be part of a team of rivals that McTear will chair."

"Mr. President, I am honored to be chosen. I shall do my best for you and for Angus."

Jared clasped her hands in his before ending the conversation. "I shall have Angus get in touch soon. And until then, my blessings on you."

Maddie was busy talking to others when Alisha returned. Alisha preferred not to call attention to her chatting with "some speaker," so she focused on Maddie, thanking her for all her help and making plans to meet for breakfast.

Electra used the drive home to put meeting Jared in perspective. Jared's not what he was, and that's probably good in some ways. Good thing his memory is fuzzy. I don't think he remembers details about Zoe, so I'll keep her name out of view. But he and I being chosen ones? Angus is going to have his hands full making sure Jared chooses what he recommends. Well, my self-destructing Email reminders regarding consequences will help.

Carter was asleep when she arrived home, so she left a note asking him to drive her tomorrow morning; she would treat him to dinner that evening at a place of his choosing, promising to tell him about unexpected opportunities.

Carter was happy to oblige and although his curiosity was aroused didn't press for details. She signed the note Electra, so there must be some intrigue. I'll have to wait until she shows up later this afternoon.

Maddie invited several of her delegate friends to join them for breakfast, giving Alisha additional contacts that would be mutually beneficial. Bethany Hopkirk was one of them, so thanks to Maddie, Alisha had achieved her remaining NGA goal: she had connected with influential members. The other goals—join committees and bring back useful ideas—she had completed yesterday. After the morning wrap-up session, I get to spend this afternoon meeting the Texas NGA H.Q. staffers, and I'll call Woolly from headquarters. And then it'll be time for Alisha to enjoy the weekend after I tell Carter what's going on.

One wrap-up session speaker highlighted how his state had combined local Health Guard and Security Guard agencies into one; another explained how his state had reaped the benefits of demarchy (random selection pool) by using it to select local staff. She even gave recommendations for keeping the pool clean: hire an NGO to vette staffers biennially. Alisha networked before leaving, making plans to correspond monthly with Maddie and Beth.

Alisha relaxed that afternoon at the Texas NGA office. Its staff already knew about her because of Woolly's thoughtful preparations. She had her own office, most unusual for a new delegate, but one look at Alisha and the staff knew she was extraordinary. She contacted Woolly before leaving to meet Carter.

"I'm calling you from my very own office, and I have you to thank for it…Yes, it's been a successful week. I have lots of ideas for what I can do back in Texas… I'm flying back Sunday morning… Excellent. I'll meet with you on Wednesday."

"Carter, how did you find this sensual pleasures café? I haven't been here before."

"Jazzi told me about it. Each one is different but it's hard for me to rank them. Seems like each one's the best when I'm there. And I like how lighting, music and translucent curtain partitions make each seating area private. Well now, will you be Electra or Alisha when you tell me about the NGA meeting?"

"This is serious, so I'll be Electra. And I'll start with the most serious development. I talked with a mutual friend at the end of last night's reception dinner, Jared Gardner. He's a different person than he was before contracting the T-Plague. He remembers very little about me, which is the way we want to keep it, so never—I repeat never—are you, Angus, or Russell ever going to talk about previous brain trust activities."

"Don't worry, we all understand."

"Now, for the surprise. He remembers enough to know I was useful to him before, so he has recruited me for his team of rivals. Angus is supposed to let me know, so please don't tell him."

"I won't, and I'm certain he'll be pleased. It's win-win-win because it gives us a reason to meet. We can worry less about surveillance. And it will give us leverage controlling Jared."

"We'll need it too, because he really believes he's been chosen by God to lead the nation. And a couple of states described the proposed programs of his. Have you heard about the Death Deterrence program?" Carter hadn't so she continued.

"The program reestablishes the death penalty, but makes the method of execution more painful. Evidently, it's a method of execution that deters crime. I don't know if they're going to draw and quarter or keel-haul the convicted, but it'll be harsh. And the second program is called "Fortress Zones". It builds an electronic wall around high-crime neighborhoods, using drones and guards to catch people trying to get in or out during high-crime periods. You can rationalize it economically, but it's an ethical conundrum." Carter nodded, then replied.

"Public sentiment wants payback, so I can see where these programs could be popular, especially if they create jobs. Are they ready for rollout?"

"I don't think so. Angus can modify them as long as he's diplomatic. You can tell him about what I heard, but wait until he tells you I'm onboard."
"OK. How did the rest of the meeting go?"

"AOK.I made some useful contacts and joined two committees. And I came away with some ideas I can push for in Texas. And I even have my own office because I'll be coming back once a month. I'll invite you so you can see my etchings sometime." Carter nodded his head slowly.

"You're as thoroughly calculating as ever. Do you still fly home Sunday morning?"

"I do, and until I step on the plane, please call me Alisha. Now please tell me, what has Zoe arranged for tomorrow?"

"She and Matt are inviting us for lunch so we have time to chat before a 6 p.m. talk. She's become active in the Science and Arts Society and bought Matt for Christmas a group membership in its Education Forum lecture series. The topic is 'Contemporary Religions and Society.' There'll be a Q&A session afterwards, I want to attend."

"That should be fun, and I promise to be on my best behavior. I won't be intimidating or dominate the discussion. That's what Electra does, not Alisha. And I'll dress for the occasion, which means no party dress or stilettos. We can go out for drinks afterwards. And now, please tell me about the zip line hike." Though now in his early thirties, Carter still possessed a youthful sense of humor he used to poke fun at himself.

"You might say it was the end of the line for Jazzi and me. She was a good sport and did her best to follow the plan, but I wasn't as considerate as I should have been. I assumed it would be easier than it turned out to be. She could barely get out of her sleeping bag the second day, and Zoe had the good sense to end the adventure right then and there. When I dropped her off, she said we were finished. Said I'm too cerebral, lack spontaneity. Whenever we do things together, I explain too much and consider her too little. And I couldn't argue; she's got my number and it's not what she's looking for, so she pulled the chain and flushed it down the toilet of her heart."

"Well, at least both of you are being honest. Use what you learned and move on. And you'll know when you find someone compatible you want to take to a deeper level of intimacy. If you click as partners, you'll know."

"I think I have. You'll meet her tomorrow, so let's table that topic until then. Why not tell me about life in Austin?"

The rest of the evening sailed away on stories Alisha spun from her burgeoning collection of Austin adventures. Carter became enchanted. *She's like Scheherazade. Her voice and expressions remind me of an actress. How different Alisha is from Electra, and how different both are from a year ago. Matt and Zoe will notice too.*

Alisha took a light workout early Saturday morning, then had a bowl of oatmeal and an English muffin. She spent the next two hours primping, finally approving the end result just before Carter announced it was time to leave.

"Whether you dress for football or for campus, you sure know how to pick outfits. Even today's casual outfit is tony. And make sure you wear your red winter coat. We may have blustery snow this afternoon."

"I'm pleased you approve. And I'm glad I didn't take any winter clothes to Texas. I simply mixed something old and something new. Don't worry about me; snow is no bother." Carter opened the car door, admiring how gracefully Alisha folded herself in. She's even more elegant than Rachel, but I won't mention looks to either. I don't want to stir envy.

Though a flurry of snow started midway en route, it didn't slow traffic, so Carter arrived promptly at noon. Zoe and Matt greeted their guests at the front door, opening it before they knocked. Zoe's bright eyes and pert motions always reminded Alisha of a delicate bird about to take flight; she greeted Alisha in her typically breathless manner.

"You always look sharp. You must tell us all about Austin and your activities." Alisha returned the compliment.

"I love your scarf. It must be an Hermes silk plisse, and the bright color is so right for you. I'll bet that's a gift from Matt."

"Right you are on both counts. I always loved our shopping trips when you lived here. We'll have to do it again. Let me show you how we're redecorating the family room."
While Zoe took Alisha, Matt steered Carter to the kitchen.

"You can help me dish up. Zoe made a diced chicken curry we're serving over rice with salad and pinot grigio. Oh gosh, I forgot to set up a bar. I hope the wine will be satisfactory for Alisha. She's become quite the connoisseur of liquors."

"Maybe she's cut back because she's training for a T-Bred comeback in the second half of the season. Don't mention drinks unless she does. The wine should be fine."

Additional drinks weren't needed to keep the conversation flowing. All parties swapped stories, including Zoe's edited version of the zip line hike.

"The entire episode became a great learning experience for all of us, especially when Carter told Jazzi to put water on cereal. No wonder she dropped him. All that happened six months ago, and Carter's ego has healed enough to handle Matt's needling."

"Carter told me something else he learned; you and Matt are fortunate. Not many couples are as well-suited. And he tells me you might move beyond co-friendship next year and hold a vow-cer celebration."

"Yes, that's what we're thinking. Matt and Jennifer Conklin's business has stabilized, and so has my PR career. And it looks like the worst of Washington turmoil is behind us, so next summer might be right. And we want you and Robin to be there. Tell us, how is she?" "I'm happy to report that Robin has also stabilized. She might graduate from college this year, and she's working nearly full time as a caregiver. She also took in an abandoned border collie pup that she named Sunshine. She takes care of Sunshine and her client, and Sunshine and her client take care of Robin. Quite a trio." Matt had been doing most of the listening, but after checking the time he picked a different subject.

"Carter needs to leave before we do. He's picking up his latest potential co-friend, Rachel Cohen. She's the moderator for tonight's talk. I'll drive you and Zoe in my van." Alisha looked at Carter, talking to herself before to him. No wonder he wants me to be polite tonight. Rachel must be special, but I won't quiz him.

"If she's the moderator, she must be smart. No wonder you like her." Zoe talked before Carter could reply.

"Yes, Matt and I met her at a tutoring session. When we pointed her out to Carter, he asked for an introduction. I'll tell you about her while Matt drives. Carter, you better go. Rachel doesn't like to be kept waiting."

"Right you are. I'll meet you there."

Alisha said, "I'll help Zoe clear the table. Matt, why don't you walk Carter to his Vette. That will give you an opportunity to give him last-minute instructions."

"Good idea. He's learned a lot about females, but a reminder always helps." Matt kidded as he walked Carter out, giving Zoe an opportunity to tell about Carter's love life.

"I'd rather tell you about Rachel while Matt's gone. I think you'll like her, but she's different from the other ladies Carter's dated. Evidently, he took Jazzi's criticisms to heart and is trying to change his style. Matt told him she's far out of his comfort zone, but that's what Carter wants. Here comes Matt, so enough said. You judge for yourself after talking with her." After clearing the table, the ladies joined Matt in the living room. Alisha picked a new topic.

"You two are always finding new things to do. Who had the idea to join a lecture series?" Matt pointed to Zoe before answering.

"She did. It was her turn. I picked sailing, she picked the cruise ship, and I picked zip lining. She thought we needed an intellectual hobby, so she found one. And it was her idea to attend tutoring sessions." Zoe was happy to tell more.

"You're a scientist, so you might be familiar with the Washington Science and Arts Society. It's affiliated with the National Academy of Sciences, and the lectures cover a wide variety of subjects that are different each time. Tonight's will be hosted in one of the smaller conference rooms in the NAS Building. Do you know where it is?"

"It's just north of Constitution Avenue near the Lincoln Memorial. I've driven by but have never been in. It's an impressive building. Like everything near the White House, its spotless exterior seems larger than life." While she listened as Zoe chattered about member couples she and Matt had met, Alisha remarked to herself. *It's too bad we can't say the same about current occupants in the Oval Office or Capitol Building. But then, we never can, because they're all merely human, and our Constitution uses separation of powers to keep them in line. I'll remind Jared if and when I need to.*

The snow was beginning to accumulate, but not enough to delay the trio. Matt found a parking place a short block away, and he checked coats after they hustled into the building. Matt couldn't spot Carter in the gathering crowd but he pointed to Rachel as she swept into the lobby. Zoe waved and Alisha watched. *She and I are wearing the same coat, and she wears it well. I can see why Carter likes her looks. Zoe told me she's an associate professor of religion and philosophy at GWU. She looks about Carter's age, so she must be smart to be tenured by early thirties. And it looks like she knows many of the people. She walks among them like she's going to her coronation. I must see if her talk matches her walk.*

Carter arrived, spotted Rachel, and made introductions after escorting her to the group.

"You must be Alisha. Carter is so fond of you. He's such a dear. He didn't mind dropping me off before parking." Rachel removed her coat, handing it to Carter before continuing. "Would you please check my coat? I must round up our speakers. After all, I'm the moderator. Look for me in the lobby after the Q&A session. I shall have dessert with you after all. Ta-ta till then." Rachel walked away; Carter followed in her wake, leaving behind an awkward silence until Zoe filled it.

"We'll enjoy tonight's talk. There'll be three speakers, each representing a different religion—Christianity, Judaism, and Islamism —and they'll explain how its teachings fit modern societies. Rachel will lead a comparative discussion that will have a Q&A session at the end. Total time is ninety minutes, and it'll race by."

Alisha thought time had stopped. The speakers were dull, sticking to simplistic interpretations and having little understanding of fundamental beliefs in faiths other than their own. She pretended to listen but was thinking more about what she'd order for dessert rather than the discussion at hand. Her stomach was grumbling by the time the last question was finally put to rest and the audience began to file out.

Zoe herded her crew towards the stage to retrieve Rachel, who gazed regally from above. Zoe tweeted about next steps.

"I thought we'd go to the Couquelicot Café. Matt and Carter are treating." Alisha noted Rachel's insouciant tone when she replied.

"Of course, they are. And we ladies won't worry about the snow. The lads will drop us off at the entrance. Come, let us walk to the coatroom." This time, Alisha tried to spark a conversation.

"Did you know that Couquelicot means 'poppy' and is pronounced kohk-lee-ko. It must be one of the most gorgeous words in the French language. It rolls off the tongue effortlessly, don't you think? And contrary to popular belief, opium and heroin are made from the white latex fluid inside the seed pods when they are green, not from the seeds. By the way, heroin is a brand name given by the Bayer Corporation to distilled opium." Carter interrupted before Alisha could continue.

"That's all very interesting, but I thought we agreed you weren't going to be like Electra tonight. I don't think anyone is interested in —" Rachel interrupted in mid-sentence.

"Don't be silly, Carter. Of course, I'm interested, and I know what the word means. I speak French, in addition to Hebrew and

Russian. And my friends often take me to Couquelicot. It is one of my favorite sensual pleasures cafés. Zoe, I commend you for your excellent choice."

Even though traffic was light, the accumulating snow slowed travel, consuming an hour by the time the party was seated, but Couquelicot's touch of French elegance added to the overall ambience, partially removing stilts from the conversation. Desserts removed the rest. Alisha surprised Zoe by ordering only one Mary Jane Brownie. Matt tried the Key Lime Mari-Gras Pie, Carter had a Cana-Banana Smoothie, and Zoe ordered a Frozen Strawberry Marijuana Trifle for herself and Rachel. Though Alisha declined, Rachel insisted everyone order sherry. Then she directed the conversation towards Alisha.

"Carter tells me you hold joint research appointments at GWU and the University of Texas. That's quite an accomplishment. And he told me that Electra is your serious self; Alisha is your social self."

"Did he tell you why he prefers Alisha to Electra?"

"He says Electra can be intimidating, unwittingly dominating conversations. But as one professor to another, I'd like to hear Electra's comments. For a biotech type, you seem rather well-rounded. Most of the engineers I know are one-dimensional drones. As you can imagine, the Washington Science and Arts Society asked me to join their steering committee because I effortlessly handle both sides of C.P. Snow's 'Two Cultures' debate. I'm certain that Zoe concurs." As all eyes turned to Zoe, Alisha sensed she didn't know what to say, but Electra did.

"Before she does, may I comment on how you facilitated tonight's session?"

"By all means. I imagine they might be germane. But be forewarned that I teach religion and philosophy, as well as attend synagogue, church, and mosque prayer services once a month."

"That may be so, but neither those credentials nor a string of degree acronyms after your name confirms you know what you're talking about. Did you deliberately dummy down or not understand? You covered only linear mono-theistic religions. I would have included the cyclic poly-theistic ones also, such as

Buddhism, Hinduism, Confucianism, and Taoism. And I would have added Secular Christianity, which is a more generous form of Atheism, using a seminal book like The Golden Bough to illustrate a common heritage predating civilization."

"Of course, I omitted what you are alluding to in the interests of minimizing exegesis. It is up to the self to plumb the depths of incommensurable surables. Don't you understand?"

"I understand enough to put you in the post-modern philosophy camp. Your kind fabricates impressive-sounding words of zero substance. You have rejected Enlightenment principles because you are intellectually lazy, unwilling to break an intellectual sweat to understand enough math so you can handle quantitative critical thinking. Until you do that, you're merely a pretender, unable to connect liberal arts and hard sciences."

"How presumptuous of you! I have studied calculus and know its deconstructive formalisms. And I know that all of science and mathematics could be improved by embracing a subjective turn that would eliminate their hostility toward women as well as their slavish link to capitalism and objectivism. Let me tell—" Electra interrupted Rachel's monologue.

"Yes, please tell me about the logarithmic function. You should have studied in freshman calculus how it and its inverse, the exponential function, are related to the analytic continuation. But I doubt you know the difference between the square root of two and a turnip." Rachel blinked, saying nothing, so Electra charged ahead.

"Let me provide exegesis. Can you compute two to the second power?"

"Don't be patronizing. Of course I can. The answer is four."

"What about one-half to the one-half power?" Rachel blinked again while Electra waited for an answer. Carter came to her aid.

"According to the laws of exponents, isn't it equal to the inverse of the square root of two? And we can—" Rachel talked over him.

"I was about to say that." She smiled at Carter, who didn't look happy. Electra wasn't finished.

"Let's drill down to the next layer. What is the square root of two raised to the square root of two power?" Rachel looked expectantly at Carter, who finally stumbled into an answer.

"I, uh, I think we need to use a log table. But why don't we table the discussion?" Electra agreed.

"Yes. And I've heard enough to confirm the Sokal Hoax is spot on for Rachel and her ilk. Check it out for exegesis. And while someone's doing that, I'll have a Coke." She waved to the server who took the order. No one spoke until Matt stirred the conversation back to life.

"I googled it and came up with this title: Transgressing the Boundaries: Towards a Transformative Hermeneutics of Quantum Gravity. Sounds heavy. Does anyone have a clue what's being transgressed?" That stirred Rachel's smoldering anger, which she unloaded on poor Carter.

"Yes. Electra, or Alisha, or whatever your friend calls herself, has transgressed the bounds of civility. Please take me home immediately." She rose abruptly, jostling the table, causing Zoe's glass to spill on Matt. Carter struggled for words to aim at Electra as he followed Rachel.

"Damnation! You put on quite a transformative performance. I give it five stars on the inverse rating scale. I'm outta here." Zoe busily patted Matt's lap.

"There. Sherry won't stain. No harm done." Matt disagreed.

"You stomped all over her. That may be the last time Carter ever sees Rachel. I'm afraid to open my mouth if you don't switch back to Alisha."

"I'm so sorry I spoiled the party. Carter will be mad at me. I'd better wait until tomorrow to apologize."

Zoe said, "We'd better take you home now before the snow makes driving worse. You'll get there before Carter. Rachel lives south of Arlington, so he has to drive twice the distance."

Matt paid the bill, and the trio hiked on slushy sidewalks to his van. No one spoke until he pulled into the driveway and then gave advice.

"You'd better check for cancellations if your flight is tomorrow morning."

"I will, and I'll call Zoe next week. Thanks again for putting up with me." Alisha hugged Zoe before running into the house, too embarrassed to say anything else. She threw her coat on a chair, then checked on the Internet, learning that her flight would leave on time if the weather cleared by six a.m. Afterwards, she showered and went to bed, scolding Electra before falling asleep.

"You forgot to follow my advice for being diplomatic, but tomorrow's another day. Put your concerns away and get some rest so you can think about your performance. The sun's going to rise anyway."

Chapter 27
January 2125

"Moving On"
Thread 2 Chapter 10

CARTER USUALLY DISLIKED DRIVING in snow because it extended his drivetime while ice built up in his Vette's wheel wells and on its windshield, spoiling his prize possession's pristine appearance. But tonight was an exception; prolonged solitary confinement behind the wheel helped him come to terms with the results of tonight's bizarre event.

I'm no longer mad at Electra. I'll thank her instead. She forced me to see the Rachel underneath the facade. Of all my friends, only she had the chutzpah to ditch social etiquette so I wouldn't prolong another mistake. And it wasn't that painful to correct. This time I did the flushing. It's time to move on. I won't have much time to talk with Electra because her flight leaves at 10 a.m., but I know what thank you gift to get and where to get it. It's on the way home.

Troubled by possible flight delay and last night's rude behavior, Electra awoke at four a.m. Her mood lifted a notch when she found out her flight would leave on time. She was unable to sleep further, so she suited up for a short run through the snow, which though heavy with moisture, had not yet packed down to ice. As she tiptoed through the kitchen, she spied a box on the counter, then read Carter's attached note:

"Thanks for defending Zoe and helping me end my Rachel relationship. Only a true friend would act like you did. Please save at least one muffin and a chocolate donut for me. And there's extra butter in the fridge. I still marvel at how much you spread on a split muffin." Electra's mood elevated further.

Thank you for knowing my intentions were good, even though my delivery was bad. I feel better knowing you're OK. As she dashed out the kitchen door to run, her dancing footfall matched her feelings.

Carter was dressed and sitting at the kitchen table—coffee made, muffins and butter set for breakfast—when Electra pranced back.

"Let me guess. You'll have a lemon poppy muffin and Coke first, then do some cooldown exercises, then shower, and finish off with a blueberry muffin and another Coke."

"You remember well. Let's dive in."

The more they talked, the better last night's episode resolved itself. Before they left for the airport, Carter called Matt, and both agreed that all is forgiven but not forgotten. Everyone had learned a lesson.

Hugging before leaving the airport, Carter reminded her to call him once a week.

"Once again, we'll have business and pleasure to talk about. And please announce ahead of time if you wish to be called Electra or Alisha."

"I promise. And I promise to behave better during my next visit."

Electra napped for half the flight, then awoke to plan for people to see and places to go for the week ahead. Monday, she would chair on-campus morning and afternoon postdoc multi-team meetings, conferencing in those at GWU, providing more than enough guidance to keep them productive. Tuesday morning, she would meet Woolly to summarize NGA and spokesperson activities, then spend the rest of the day chatting with Hud's people before preparing to leave Wednesday for her Hollywood auditioning trip.

Monday and Tuesday meetings went smoothly, so early Tuesday afternoon, she chatted briefly with Robin and Holy. Sunshine scurried to greet her when she entered Holy's office.

"Hi everyone. You're busy, so I won't stay long. I just wanted to tell Robin her friends in DC are happy to hear she's doing well."

"I hope you gave them my best wishes. They were so nice to me when I needed help. How are they?"

"Carter is his usual diplomatic and rational self. Zoe and Matt are planning a vow-cer celebration, probably this summer. And of course, you and I are invited. Mr. H, did Robin ever tell you about her friends out east?"

"Yep. Matt sounds like a really nice person. Zoe does, too, but Robin says you know her better. I wish them a co-friend, marriage contract, and vow-cer success. Terminology is all different than in my day, but if it helps young people find the right partner, I'm all for it."

"Robin and I agree. Well, I'm leaving tomorrow for Hollywood, and I'm sure Robin remembers the times she and I helped Christi prepare for auditions. Christi and I did the same for her." Robin smiled briefly.

"All that seems a lifetime ago. What you told us worked, so take your own advice and vanish into the moment. You'll get the part if you want it. Do you?"

"I do. Hollywood fits my Alisha personality; it's a fun town, and it'll give me useful contacts. I'll let you know how it went. And now I'd better go meet Su and Kameyo."

The brief meeting pleased Electra because Kameyo reported that new vaccine testing results exceeded expectations. Hud's salesforce would have by year-end vaccines that could handle the latest T-Plague mutations. Afterwards, she held an informal Tim and Kwame meeting that pleased her as much as the vaccine test results. Cyber-Theater launch would happen second quarter next year, and Kwame's newest GUIs contain interactive features surpassing the best video games. As she drove home to pack, Electra couldn't be happier because all Austin projects under her control were unfolding according to plan. It was time for Alisha to command center stage.

Alisha could plan as well as Electra whenever she chose to focus, and while reviewing T-Bred and Hollywood plans after finishing a late afternoon workout, she knew her alter ego would approve.

My games are much more fun than Electra's, but since she's with me every step of the way, she gets to share in the excitement. CoNFL conditioning is on target, and I'm set to knock'em dead when I audition. And I can role-play tomorrow on the flight. All that's left is to check my packing list, get a good night's sleep, and be ready to roll when I play a new role starting tomorrow.

Kathi Lauret only played favorites at the racetrack, and although she never interfered during a director's audition picks, she hoped Alisha would win. We met only once and talked only twice, but I'm attracted to her. I'll do all I can to help, no matter what her feelings are towards me. Kathi's career on the business side of Hollywood spanned fifteen years, so she knew about actors' aspirations and lifestyles. At dinner tonight, she would advise her potential protégé on what to expect.

Alisha followed orders, calling Kathi from her hotel room.

"Hi Ms. Lauret, this is Alisha Kittner… Yes, the flight was not delayed, and I found the limo driver… Looks to me like all the Hollywood hotels are top drawer… I feel privileged to have dinner with you tonight…Yes, I'll find you in the hotel restaurant at seven… Thanks again."

Alisha used the time before dinner to take a light workout, followed by a swim in the pool. And she felt at ease, for everyone looked young, trim, and fit, but even here she turned heads. Her naturally long and leggy look, conditioned to perfection and crowned by chiseled features that—though not beautiful in the classic sense— commanded attention no matter the competition. Kathi noted all this and more as Alisha glided to the table.

"Hello again, and please call me Kathi. You look even better than last autumn. I do believe you are fully recovered after that terrible collision. Why don't you order something to drink and we can toast to your recovery and tomorrow's success." The attentive waiter took the order for Chablis.

"My entire career has been in Hollywood, so I know what performers and directors are like. You might find tomorrow a bit of a rude awakening." Alisha nodded, then commented.

"Competing in football and dancing to the tune of the coach might be similar, but it's not in your league. Any pointers you can give will be most appreciated."

"The actresses who are auditioning consider you competition for a scarce resource: an actual movie role. Some will know one another and treat you like a blundering yokel. And the director will be indifferent or rude to see how you handle yourself under pressure.

So, my advice is this: stay calm, think first, then act. And tonight, do something you probably already do the night before a football game. Put yourself in an auditioning role and think through how you'll handle yourself. This should be easy for you, because a superhero is like a quarterback. Both usually call the plays." Alisha listened attentively, replying when Kathi paused.

"Thanks for the advice. And I've watched motivation videos that explain how to prepare by visualizing yourself in a role you want. Did you ever attend a seminar?"

"I haven't, but many Hollywood types who have claimed the techniques work. And others say they get as much from reading the classic, Unlimited Power, by Tony Robbins.

"I shall put that on my reading list. And tomorrow, I'll put my game face on. When I play sports, teammates call me Kit. But please call me Alisha. I think Alisha fits Hollywood better than Kit."

The director and film crew had to be neutral, but if asked afterwards for their assessment, they would agree that Alisha had blown away the competition. Only a handful could handle the morning session stunts, and most were muscle-brained when cold-reading more emotive lines in scripts. The results were similar during the afternoon session, for which only the top five were invited; Alisha outclassed them all. She was the best at adjusting to the director's commands while ensemble acting.

Alisha had a great time immersing herself in acting roles, noting afterwards how easily she shifted from one mental state to another. What fun, but now I understand better why some actors have trouble shifting back to reality after working in front of a camera.

Lots of athletes have the same reentry problem.

She was pleased with her performance, but unlike sports, where the outcomes are usually measured by a stopwatch or tape, subjective contests are harder to call. Nevertheless, rumors surfaced from those eliminated in the morning session who were allowed to watch. There was grudging agreement who should get the part, and a couple of friendlier competitors relayed it to Alisha ahead of the official announcement.

Though exultation coursed through every neural fiber, Alisha tried to remain calm while changing clothes. But suddenly, she was overwhelmed by a profound sadness for her competitors, causing her to burst into tears. Here I am, the girl with the lightning brain, a marvelous dynamo giving me extraordinary possibilities, but thanks only to a bizarre lightning bolt. My empathy triggers feelings bordering on guilt for depriving my competitors of a shot at stardom. They're struggling to survive in Hollywood's shark tank, while I lead a charmed life. Winning the role means so much more to them than to me.

Electra interrupted the crying jag.

"Dry your tears! You deserve to win. You have worked hard. And your competitors are talented young ladies who will move on to other opportunities. Now it's time to savor your accomplishment and let happy emotions flow. And trust me to help plan for where Hollywood may take us."

"I can't believe I'm hearing these words from you. I'm the emotional persona, but I guess I've taught you well."

"Indeed, my empathy is growing, as is your I.Q. But, if I may quote a Robert Frost poem, there's more to it:
>'The woods are lovely, dark and deep,
>But I have promises to keep,
>And miles to go before I sleep,
>And miles to go before I sleep.'

We have great expectations, but always remember: we are greater than the sum of our parts as long as we work together and listen to the lightning brain."

When a director's assistant came to fetch her, he understandably mistook Alisha's tears for those of joy.

"You must have heard the rumors that you won the Supergirl role. Congratulations, you did. I'm supposed to take you to Ms. Lauret's office when you've settled down, but please take your time." As she walked to Kathi's office, the assistant's words and Electra's previous comments transformed Alisha's momentary sadness-tinged depression into euphoria. Time to act pleased, but stay inbounds.

Kathi was pleased that Alisha was the runaway winner because it confirmed her instincts for judging talent, making it unnecessary for her to meddle in the outcome.

"Congratulations! Your series director, Vincent Valdez, would like to welcome you aboard."

"Heartiest wishes, Ms. Kittner. I understand you go by your middle name Alisha. Well, Alisha, you are going to make my job very difficult. I'm supposed to find ways to rescue scripts or scenes by getting the actors and actresses to say or do things differently than what they're doing. But watching you today, I was at a loss for what to do. It was eerie how you played the role so effortlessly. Even accomplished actresses struggle at first when trying on a new character. You looked like you were playing yourself. And your body type is a perfect ten for the part. Whoever your acting coach is, please tell her to stay the course. That's about all I want to say today. I'm certain Kathi has directions for you to follow between now and when you return, so I'll leave that to her and head back to the set. When you return, I'll pick up where she leaves off." Kathi and Alisha sat down after Vince left.

"I do have instructions, but I know you're drained, physically and emotionally, and I want you to catch your flight back to Austin. Why not call me first thing Monday morning and I'll review what things to do before coming back to start filming. Between now and the end of May we'll film the first five-month season that we'll launch next autumn. And if the ratings are good, we'll film the second season later in the fall. Is there anything you'd like to ask before dashing off?"

"I'm sorry, there's only one winner. What do you think the others will do?"

"Look, Hollywood is one of the most competitive industries on the planet. Your competitors are smart, good-looking, talented, and tough. Vince has already selected one for your understudy, and some of the others might be extras or fill bit parts in a pilot or episodes. Don't project your feelings onto others. You probably don't know what's right for them. Alisha nodded, talking only to herself. Kathi sounds like Electra. No wonder I like her. Kathi's intercom announced the airport limo had arrived.

"LAX is not more than a half-hour drive during this part of the rush hour, so you'll have no trouble making your flight. And if I-10 or I-405 entrance ramps are closed because of driverless vehicle network failures, your driver can take surface streets. LA has had its share of computer network glitches. And you can imagine the problems they cause, not only on the highways but also in homes. Most of them contain the latest hi-tech appliances and monitoring systems that are interconnected to IOT. When the Internet crashes, people become prisoners in their own homes. Hard to get out, no food, water, or electricity." Kathi's comment sparked an Electra-like question.

"I've heard rumors that network failures might be coordinated Cyberspace terrorist attacks. Whether or not it's true, Hollywood could turn it into a movie." Kathi smiled.

"Yes. Virtual reality filming apps could make great chase scenes showing battles raging inside computers." Kathi cupped Alisha's cheeks in her hands before continuing. But no matter what happens in Cyberspace, I'm certain Supergirl can handle it. And now, you should fly to the airport." Alisha rose to leave.

"You've been so gracious. I'll do my best to deserve this opportunity."

"Just be yourself and follow your instincts. And as Vince told me, you're on your way, you're moving on."

Highway and airport traffic were normal, so Alisha's plane taxied for take-off on time. She happily sat back, letting the lightning brain freewheel.

I have much to do for my return to the T-Breds and Hollywood, and I know Electra will help lighten the load. We're constant companions, so she'll be with me, enjoying every step along the way. After all, she's learning to lighten up.

Alisha slept like a stone the entire flight home.

Chapter 28
April 2125

"Busy Living"
Thread 1 Chapter 10

ALISHA KEPT BUSY ON all fronts where she occupied center stage. Woolly liked the ideas she brought from the NGA; the Governor appointed her spokesperson for adult-focused townhall meetings featuring Texas economic development programs. And since their forum would be the same as what she used for high school, she already knew how to facilitate them.

Alisha also took extended Hollywood filming trips. With Kathi's guidance, she acted her part, becoming a card-carrying member of the Screen Actors Guild (aka SAG-AFTRA), dressing appropriately and dealing diplomatically with Hollywood's pecking order, and most importantly maintaining an image that served both Co-NFL and Supergirl roles: downhome virtue, intelligence, open and straight-talking, all wrapped in a sexy swagger. Alisha felt at home on both playing fields, as if she were made for stardom and vice versa; every so often, Electra had to rein in her "play hard" alter ego; she confessed only to Electra how tempting glitter can be. And in the shadows stood Indira, ready to be summoned whenever the Electra Alisha duo needed more from the lightning brain.

Woolly had arranged a Houston high school town hall meeting for early April. After introducing Alisha, Woolly sat back and enjoyed the show.

"Good morning, future leaders of America, and welcome to another high school town hall meeting. I am Alisha Kittner, and today's topic is 'Economics and Politics in Contemporary U.S. Society.' My role is not to teach these subjects, but to provide a framework you can use to challenge yourself, your fellow classmates, and your teachers as you study further. All this is another example of why you must get as much education as you can. Our nation depends on smart, educated, and informed citizens who want to take an active role at some level for steering the right course for our country.

"Let me start by summarizing the needs everyone has. They are universal and came to light with the dawn of civilization. I'll reference a framework all of you should know: Maslow's hierarchy of needs. They're like a pyramid. At the bottom are the basic needs: physiological needs such as food, water, shelter, and so forth. Next are safety needs: like protection from criminals, fire, pestilence, terrorism, and foreign invaders. Then come social and emotional needs: like friendship, love, and belonging. The next level contains esteem needs, like career or social position. And at the top are self-actualization needs, like personal happiness and self-worth. "Needs are connected to economics, because needs are satisfied by a society's producing goods and services. Economics is all about how a society organizes itself to produce what is needed, how and how much is made and by whom, and who gets the items produced. I'll cut right to the chase: the world has learned that a market economy in which free enterprise operates without too much government intervention works best.

"Let's connect the above to a framework for U.S. politics. The framers of our Constitution spelled out natural rights: Life, Liberty, and the Pursuit of Happiness. Then around 1900, the Progressive Movement came along, trying to replace natural rights with social rights, like rights to a house, a job, a certain level of income, and so forth. This movement held sway for over fifty years, causing tremendous growth in the size of the Federal Government and the emergence of the Imperial Presidency supported by a Bureaucracy that collapses the separation of powers into a collection of unelected agency personnel.

"For the past one hundred years, the Federal Government has been a swinging pendulum between government expansion, where the Federal Government does the thinking for the people, and government reduction, where the public thinks for themselves and local government exercises more power. I'm not here to tell you how to think. I'm here for you to discuss the frameworks I've highlighted so you can go back to your school and apply them when studying current economic and political issues. So, let's have questions and comments from the audience…"

Woolly complimented his speaker afterwards.

"You picked a topic that high schoolers need to explore. Of course, they need an education, but they also need a job when they graduate. Some of their comments showed the younger generation understands jobs come from companies, not from the government. And they want to have more say in what the government does." Alisha added to his observations.

"Did you notice their concern regarding T-Plague damage to the national I.Q.? Maybe the public will be more insistent on Health-guard programs to cure victims. Maybe the public will become less fearful and more tolerant as the public's I.Q. is restored." Woolly talked more as he gathered his crew.

"You handle high school and adult audiences so well, it's no wonder we're getting a lot of invites for you to speak. Your mix of skills and experiences makes a nice package. I'll explain more on our trip back home."

Woolly arranged for Alisha's next engagement, a mid-April economic development town hall meeting to be held in Austin. Alisha's role would be to introduce the discussion topic and speaker, and facilitate a Q&A afterwards. But her alter ego researched the topic so thoroughly that Alisha became a subject matter expert, able to provide more for the audience.

Alisha started the meeting by summarizing the characteristics and concerns of American workers, proudly announcing that the slogan "Made in Texas by Texans" remains a standard of excellence.

"Americans in general, and Texans in particular, are good-natured, pragmatic, and resilient, working hard to take care of their families and always willing to shoulder responsibility instead of relying on 'Big Government.'"

"And we never dodge troubling economic trends; we face them head-on. And what is troubling us today? Let me put a positive spin on the troubles by bullet-pointing the most important wants." Alisha flashed an appropriate slide:

Economic Wants

- Level the International Playing Field for American Companies and Workers
- Comprehensive Hi-Tech Training Programs to give Experienced Workers skills needed to thrive in the New Economy
- Government and Industry Collaboration to balance "Groundbreaking Technologies" and "Mainstreet Capabilities"
- Government and Industry Collaboration to balance "Shorter-Term" Constraints and "Longer-Term" Possibilities
- Added Incentives for Entrepreneurs to revolutionize the
- "Innovation/Collaboration" Economy
- T-Plague victims' I.Q. repair

"I won't delve into details, but our speaker will. He'll also outline proposed programs, and after that, I'll assist in answering your questions…"

Alisha's performance earned rave reviews from Woolly. She's getting better and better. After every meeting, people tell me how good she is. I'll show the Governor this video so he can see her in action. Media coverage is building an "Alisha" brand. Good for her and the Governor, too.

Alisha's training shifted to the next level by early May, preparing her to showcase what she could do when starring in her starting QB role. Bo had been waiting for Alisha to return when ready, and that's what he hoped Alisha would tell him today. She cruised into his office and, while sitting across from him, asked him to summarize the team's situation.

"We're still in a holding pattern, waiting for you to get back into the game. Cal's done all we could ask, but no one can run the Wide-V like you. You have this knack for rapid play calling and coordination using helmet wireless communication. And our record shows it. We've lost more than we've won. The fans still support us, but they miss the excitement and entertainment you bring. We haven't said anything yet to the media about your comeback progress. We're waiting for you to tell us. I hope that's why you're here. You look ready to play, but that's for you to decide."

"I'm ready to start scrimmaging with the team. Thanks to my personal trainer, you'll see I'm stronger, which means I can fend off defensive hits by hitting first. And I'm quicker. And when I run the offense, I'm gonna go for the jugular right away, putting opponents' defense on its heels. I'll score quickly and put enough points on the board to put pressure on their offense. Then I'll use halfback runs to run down the clock."

"Sounds like you'll take us to the playoffs if you can start by June. That'll give us the second half of the season to improve our record."

"I want to scrimmage at most every other day because I want to avoid injury. And I'll remind the team to call me Kit when I'm on the field. She's the one with killer instincts."

Angus McTear never needed to reveal killer instincts because his commanding presence and statesman-like demeanor usually convinced those opposed to go along with him. Now that Jared had brought Angus back into action, his first assignment was to build a team of rivals that needed no convincing.

Angus resurrected from his erstwhile brain trust four he could trust: Carter, Russell, Electra, and Olivia Torres, the senator from California who had been Carter's mentor.

He gathered them in his office for an impromptu May meeting that Electra attended via encrypted phone line. Angus wanted their latest assessments to prepare for an upcoming session with Jared, and he asked Russell to report first.

"It's now confirmed: mutant virus cases continue ticking upwards. It's not an epidemic yet, and the source appears to be the North Korea bombing. And I have good news. We now have available improved vaccines that should be effective. And if we can get more action on programs to cure the cognitively compromised, public opinion might eventually budge from its narrow-minded and fear-filled focus. But that'll take time." Russell had nothing more to say, so Angus motioned to Carter.

"Mariah taught me how to track public opinion, so I can handle that for us. I agree with what Russell said. We still have too many people who can't think for themselves, which means they are scared and look out only for themselves. Angus, you must convince Jared he won't lose their support if they can think for themselves. They'll worship the guy for installing rehab programs that sharpen their wits. "Let's turn to the economic situation. There are plenty of jobs for smart people, but even before the T-Plague started, technology tipped the scales towards jobs requiring brains, not brawn. Today, some older people, as well as some of the younger who have no training or brains, can't find jobs. Many of Jared's programs push back against too much outsourcing or technology, so we are creating jobs at home. People like that. So short term, most of his programs are popular. Longer term, economists are still divided concerning what approaches might work. But that's not unusual. I won't repeat a fitting joke about economists because I don't resemble the punchline." Olivia Torres spoke next regarding national and international politics.

"Jared has wide support on Capitol Hill and with our international allies because bombing North Korea has silenced the 'Hermit Kingdom' and served notice to China that we mean business. And the UN averted a humanitarian crisis by implementing a T-Plague containment and cleanup operation for which we contributed vaccines.

"Jared will maintain support if he pushes for a Middle East shooting war, as long as he comes up with convincing proof that terrorists are taking advantage of the UN's 'words not bullets' approach. He can rattle Isilabad by waving his 'America Number One' banner." Angus used the terrorist reference to interrupt.

"Electra, you were the one who tipped me off about the Iron Triangle. I bucked that over to CIA counter-intelligence, but so far they've heard no chatter on the networks. Have you heard anything new?"

"My sources aren't hearing much, and what they do hear repeats what you already know. But I'll keep checking. And I think Olivia's right. Jared will have to start shooting if Cyberspace terrorism escalates." Angus had enough for his Jared meeting, so he ended the session.

"All of you have done well. I think Jared will be satisfied with my report. We should all be pleased he came to his senses and put a team of rivals in place. I hope his senses stay put. Keep doing what you're doing. I'll notify you when I need another briefing."

The meeting reminded Electra to chat with Hud. Hud promptly ended his phone conversation when she marched into his office.

"You look like you have something to say. But before you do, should I call you Electra or Alisha?"

"Electra for starters. Our modified formulations work on the mutant virus, so please have your salespeople tell customers it's good to go. The number and locations of cases worldwide is growing, and the growth rate might accelerate. We need to line up manufacturing sites outside the country. There might be pressure once again from Washington to nationalize the vaccine pieces of your business. What locations have you considered?"

"I've got sites in Germany and Japan in mind. You got a preference?" "I don't trust any location in Europe. Europeans are biotech techno-phobes. Go with Japan. Kameyo and Su can work from that new location. And you need to arrange it now. You've done well keeping any connections between us and our virtual companies invisible. Please keep doing so."

"I will. Any other orders coming from Electra?"

"No, but here are some from Alisha. I'm flying to Hollywood tomorrow and am bringing Tim so he can discuss the next Cyber-Theater generation with our manufacturing partner while I'm acting in the final episode of my series. We'll be back in a week. And don't worry about Kwame. Tim and I will conference-call him while we're gone."

"I don't worry about Kwame or Tim. They're hard workers and make a great team. And if you hadn't told me when we hired them, I wouldn't have picked up on their autism. I guess they help each other deal with it."

"And I've taught Tim how to negotiate. He'll talk to you if he needs help adjusting the Cyber-Theater contract terms. I'll stay out of that picture. On this trip, I'll worry about only my series finale."

"That's a wrap! We've got the last scene in the can. Whoa, whoa, whoa! Everyone, come back tomorrow evening at eight for a wrap party right here in the studio." Vincent's victory whoops bounced around the set as cast and crew cheered after completing the last episode for the first season of the "Superman—New Age Saga" series.

Alisha had mixed emotions; happy that everyone thought the series would be a hit, yet sad that filming was completed. Hollywood's allure was powerful, even though she had been counseled by her alter ego to avoid expecting too much. *I'll be ticked if there's no second season. I better listen to my own advice given back to me by Electra: enjoy the moment and don't worry about what I can't control.* Her high spirits returned in a flash, and she joined the general merriment, then retired to her dressing room to peel off make-up while changing out of costume.

Here I am in Hollywood, the last Thursday in May, and everything's going my way. All careers are hitting on all cylinders. Tonight, Tim will tell me his good news, and tomorrow I can train in the morning, relax in the afternoon, and party the night away.

She took her time driving back to the hotel, enjoying the sights along the way. She would reward herself with one drink at the bar before waiting in her room for Tim. *Well, maybe two drinks if the guy flirting with me picks up the tab.* Alisha was adept at many roles. Rarely did she buy her own drinks. But when she stopped at the bar, she caught the eye of a non-flirting fellow. Tim was waiting for her.

"Drinks are on me! Our studio partners love my latest Cyber-Helmet prototype. The spherical image projection and GUIs that Kwame programmed in are superior to anything in virtual reality or simulation. And the sensory channel coding and embedding is a done deal. They'll schedule new product release for late fall, which is just in time for the Holiday shopping season. Hud will be happy." Alisha was pleased on all accounts.

"You've worked hard, so now you can play hard. Why don't you go to the casino tonight and go sightseeing tomorrow? And tomorrow evening, you can come to our wrap party to celebrate the completion of the first season of filming."

"Will you join me at the casino?"

"No. I'm going to have dinner in my hotel room and get ready for tomorrow. I'm training in the morning, then doing project work in the afternoon. But get ready for fun tomorrow evening."

Alisha awoke at six a.m. to start the day by working out in the hotel fitness center. Hers was equipped with state-of-the-art machines and trainers whose toned physiques showed the results of what they teach. Alisha fit right in. She had surpassed her training goals, so she would be T-Bred starting quarterback in a couple of weeks. That morning, she pushed more weight than anyone, including two gawking instructors, then relaxed her muscles in the jets of a hot tub. Then it was on to breakfast and project work, which she did poolside on her laptop.

Alisha collected Tim at the appropriate time so they'd arrive at eight. She had the good sense to ask Kathi a week ago what would be appropriate to wear and took her advice, buying tuxedo-black stretch knit flared pants accented by an arctic-white knit crop top and red suede leg wrap heels. Hollywood shopping's a trip in itself. Maybe I'll shop in Beverly Hills when I become famous.

Alisha introduced Tim to the cast and crew, letting him mingle while she talked with Kathi.

"I see you went shopping. Sometimes you and I will shop Rodeo Drive. And I like how your jewelry accents your features. Where did you get the bracelet and neck choker? They look Oriental."

"It's a friendship bracelet meant for my mother. I got it from her childhood friend on a trip to India. And the choker was also meant for her mother, a gift from her mother. Do you travel abroad much?"

"I love to travel, but I haven't been to Bollywood in Mumbai, which is India's film capital. My boss takes me to invitation-only Cannes film festival events, and I've been to others in Europe. But there are more in the U.S. than anywhere else. Did you know that Louisiana is the leading location for American films? California tax laws still penalize Hollywood, and the film industry is lobbying to have that changed. Here's an example where local government is worse than federal. But that's something for my side of the lens to worry about, not yours. Just keep doing what you're doing and you'll be here a long time. Let's get something to drink. And then I want you to tell me how you like working with Randall Dancer, your series star."

Alisha had memorized Randy Dancer's backstory months ago. A mid-forties fan favorite, his acting career spanned two decades and several generations of film aficionados, all of which kept his rollercoaster lifestyle in the spotlight, magnifying his virtues and vices. Alisha thought he was a gifted actor, able to portray different personalities called for when playing Superman or Clark Kent, and though she suspected drugs might have something to do with it, she kept that to herself.

She noted as he arrived at 8:30, towing a current significant other, that he seemed distracted. After greeting the director and thanking the set crew, Randy headed to the bar, where he teased some of the cast. I'll chat with him after he's made the rounds and settles down.

Kathi walked Alisha to another group, so she didn't think about Randy again until she saw him reenter. Alisha noticed his energetic gestures that were accompanied by rapid-fire comments as he moved towards the buffet. Kathi did too, but neither spoke about it as they moved to other topics.

Alisha's early warning system detected a buzz, then concerned voices and screams. When she turned, she spotted the problem. Randy was at the center of a circle ringed by stupefied friends. He had collapsed onto a dessert table, then bounced to the floor came to rest sprawled on his back. Alisha shifted gears and dived into action.

She pushed through to kneel beside him, checking vital signs. No pulse and dilated pupils. She screamed to herself, Cocaine overdose!

Then she yelled.

"I need a PAD right now! Where do you keep it?" There was no answer, so she yelled again, "I need a defibrillator! Randy's heart has stopped!" That jolted one of the stuntmen.

"It's on the medical crash cart. I'll get it." She had Randy's shirt torn open by the time she got the PAD.

It was a fully automated model, so Alisha simply connected the two electrode pads—one on the side of the chest underneath the breastbone and the other on top by the collarbone—pressed the start button, and hoped for the best. A calm female voice announced over the built-in speaker what the device was doing.

"Checking rhythm… Charging… Shock advised… Do not touch the patient…" Alisha almost panicked. Come on! Say something! Finally, it did.

"Press flashing shock button…" Then ZAP! Randy's body jerked as an electrical charge surged in. The voice continued after what seemed like an eternity.

"Shock one delivered… It is safe to touch the patient… Begin CPR now…" Alisha heard someone yell an explanation: five cycles of thirty chest compressions for every one mouth-to-mouth ventilation. The PAD kept track of every action; four minutes later, it spoke, once again stopping time dead inside Alisha's head.

"Stop CPR…Stop now…Do not touch the patient…Analyzing heart rhythm…No shock advised…It is safe to touch the patient… If needed, begin CPR."

Alisha came alive, checking for breath or movement, and found none, so she resumed CPR. There were still no signs of life, so she yelled again.

"Show me where the cart is, and someone call 911!" And then she screamed to herself.

I've got to inject epinephrine to start his heart! There's gotta be drugs and needles on the cart. She found what she needed and raced back. Randy was still deathlike, so she filled the syringe, injected into a vein, and resumed CPR. A minute later, Randy sputtered back to life, eyes flickering open and chest heaving for oxygen. Alisha stepped back as two EMTs rushed in to take over. They checked vitals before loading him onto a stretcher and then racing to a nearby emergency room; the drama ended as abruptly as it began.

The party mood of ten minutes ago was replaced by a rush of relief. As people gathered about Alisha, one of Randy's friends thanked her for bringing him back to life. Soon after, people started leaving. Alisha and Kathi were among them, and Kathi's whimsical humor made both of them smile.

"If the media gets hold of what happened, I can see tomorrow's headline:

Supergirl saves Superman." Alisha had a ready reply.

"If the series doesn't fly, perhaps I can be a studio EMT understudy next season. I can help people keep busy living."

Alisha and Tim departed for Austin early the next morning.

"I can't wait to tell Robin how you handled the medical situation. She and Holy are picking us up, and after your performance last night, you can work as her caregiver assistant."

"She already has one named Sunshine. And if she needs more, tell her to get the four-legged kind."

Alisha and Tim used the flight's two-and-a-half-hour quiet time to surf the Web or send Emails; unlike last night, time ticked at its usual pace. They would be landing shortly.

Holy liked being out and about in the van Robin drove. It made him feel younger, more engaged in life instead of sitting cooped up inside, so today he would treat everyone to a late lunch after picking up the Hollywood travelers.

Robin had become a pro at chauffeuring Holy around town. She knew the routes to all the familiar places and could keep her eyes on the road as well as on her patient. She had checked online to coordinate her passenger arrival pickup time; she was ahead of schedule, so she drove at a leisurely pace through one of Holy's favorite parks. Sunshine liked it too and watched attentively from the back seat.

Holy was peering out the side window as Robin chatted away.

"What a grand day for the start of our Memorial Day weekend."

He was about to reply when a bolt of pain stabbed through his chest, taking away his breath and ability to speak. He struggled to face Robin and did so just before his eyes rolled up and he gasped out, "Ca-can't breathe..." before slumping forward. Robin didn't panic. Instead, she drove like a wild woman to the closest emergency room.

Holy had just suffered a heart attack.

Tim didn't spot Robin's van, and after attempting several calls, spoke to his travel partner.

"I can't reach Robin or Hud on the cellphone. What do you think we should do?"

"Call Su. She might know where they are." Tim called and reported back.

"She hasn't seen either of them, but that's not unusual. She said they're adults, and if there's a problem, they'll contact us. Why don't we just go home?" Alisha agreed, so each took a separate taxi.

Knowing that someday he'd get the call, Hud had role-played long ago how he'd handle the situation, but it didn't help when the call came. A hospital clinician had just notified him that Holy had suffered a major heart attack. The exact words would be etched in Hud's memory forever. She told him to come immediately because Robin had told her that he had power of attorney. Hud sat glumly in the reception area, waiting for an hour before an attending physician gave him the news.

"Mr. Haller, your father has suffered a massive heart attack. Pulse is running 110 beats per minute, pressure has dropped, and he's unconscious. The young woman with him claims to be his caregiver, and his orders are DNR—do not resuscitate. Is that correct?"

"Yes, ma'am. Dad didn't want to linger like a vegetable, so Robin's making the right call. Can I see him?"

"Of course. Please follow me."

Hud tiptoed next to Robin, who was handling whatever was needed. She spoke crisply.

"Holy collapsed in the van on the way to the airport. The EMTs wheeled him into the E.R. ten minutes later, and I told them DNR. Those are your father's orders. He hasn't regained consciousness, so we should keep him here until he wakes up. Then, we should bring him home. Your father's orders are hospice care at home. Do you know what else your father wants?"

"Not in detail. He just told me to listen to you. So, what are the orders?"

"I'm to stay with him and handle all needs, not the hospital staff, because he's DNR. A hospital ambulance should take him home as soon as he's stabilized. You should handle all legal and insurance issues." Robin paused for Hud to talk, but he didn't know what to say, so Robin continued.

"Sunshine is locked in my van. I left it by the E.R. entrance, but I went back to crack the windows. Please take her to my place. Food and water are already out. Here are my keys. And walk her before you drive away." Hud couldn't think of anything add, so he told Robin to be strong, then trudged out.

Although schizophrenic, Robin's brittle emotions had toughened up. She was prepared to carry out whatever was necessary to honor Holy's wishes, so she sat patiently at the bedside, ready for whatever would come her way. And it came at 10 p.m., when Holy awoke from a coma, rasping and gasping.

"Ca-can't breathe… Ca-can't swallow…" Robin jumped to his side, cradling his head in her strong hands.

"Mr. H…It's me…Robin…I have water for you." He shook his head no, then stuttered his final command.

"N-n-noo… T-t-time… P-pu-lease… Lo-lo-love y-you." He closed his eyes, panting from the exhaustion of choking out what few syllables remained. Robin saw and heard enough. She steeled herself to carry out Holy's final command.

She already had what she needed: syringes and a bottle of pentobarbital. She repeatedly told herself,
You know what to do, and how to do it. Now it's time. Just do it.

She filled the syringe and injected more than enough so Holy would die quickly, with dignity, with no further suffering. She gently stroked his cheeks as she witnessed a miraculous transformation. Holy's body relaxed, his breathing steadied, becoming shallower and peaceful, his grimace became a restful smile. She watched in awe as life departed from the one she loved so dearly, unhurriedly submerging into that sea of infinite unknown dreams, and then she kissed him. She was too numb to feel anything, so she sat down, forcing herself to remember what she should tell Hud. And when she did, she called to give him Holy's final orders, then relayed to the hospital staff what to expect next. Finally, she drove home and collapsed fully clothed on the bed. Sunshine would watch over her until morning.

Electra didn't reach out to Hud until late Sunday afternoon; she knew from experience that he would prefer making final arrangements by himself. And when she did, the conversation was brief because Hud needed no help. As Holy was in life, so was he after departing. His orders wasted no time and required little effort. Holy would be cremated immediately. There would be a two-hour Monday morning wake followed by a brief ceremony at the family funeral parlor that would arrange for scattering his ashes in Lake Austin. And there would be no music and only one eulogy, to be given by the pastor from the family church.

Robin was too preoccupied to talk much afterwards, but she told Electra to arrange for them to have lunch with Hud on Wednesday. Holy had warned her a year ago to make plans for carrying on when he was gone, asking no one for advice. She could still hear his downhome voice twanging out:

"I'll be gone, and someday, Electra will be too. You're old enough and stable enough and know enough to figure out what you should do. You gotta cut yourself loose from Electra and move forward according to your values. Don't grieve about me too long. Vent your feelings, then look for wholeness by replacing death's pain with what it teaches. Do it by practicing what I call Sunset Mindfulness: keep flexible and open to emotion."

Robin was the last to arrive for lunch at the pancake house but the first to speak.

"You should have fired me long ago. I'm not worth a fiddler's fart working for any of your businesses. I never want to see a debit or credit again, and I'm dropping out of school. Electra's always preaching at town hall meetings to stay in school and get a degree, but I know enough to go my own way. There are three things I know about and like, and am good at: music, caregiving, and dogs. So, I'm starting my own caregiving business. I even have a name for it: Sunshine Eldercare. Here's—" Electra interrupted.
"Don't you want advice from me or—" Robin interrupted right back. "Shut up! I love you, but I don't want you to make decisions for me." Neither spoke, giving Hud a chance.

"Robin's right. Let her tell us her plan, and maybe we can help get it started."

"I'll find older people who need help a couple of times a week. And I can use my music skills and my dog to brighten their lives. I can line up visits to senior citizen centers to entertain by playing the piano, and I'll train Sunshine to be a therapy dog. And I'll train other dogs I take in from rescue shelters to be part of the package. Tomorrow I start by contacting senior centers and retirement homes." Hud nodded in Electra's direction, waiting for her to speak.

"Robin's business idea should work, and here's what we can do to get her started. Kwame will build a Sunshine Eldercare Website. Then I'll develop promotional Emails and brochures she can use to advertise. Hud will use his Austin clout to get local contacts, and Kwame will come up with target customers she can contact by Internet, telephone, or in person. Hud can set up an office and phone. And I agree with her decision to drop out of UT. She can get caregiver certification if it'll open more doors or qualify her business for Health-guard or Medicare reimbursement and insurance. She'll be busy, and that's the best way to deal with grief and depression." Hud chimed in again.

"I'll get my lawyer to set up her business as an LLC. Dad would approve the plan. And he wouldn't want any of us to grieve too long. As the pastor said, Dad lived a long, full life, had plenty of success, and few regrets. His faith wasn't spiritual—he'd didn't believe in life after death. His faith was in family, friends, and people. That's why the pastor's eulogy was a celebration of Dad's life. I'll miss him a lot. Other than the time away at school and earning my business spurs working out East, my time was with him. I liked the pastor's closing poem. Electra, do you remember the words?" "I do." She recited them verbatim.

> "Do not stand at my grave and weep,
> I am not there; I do not sleep.
> I am a thousand winds that blow,
> I am the diamond glints on snow,
> I am the sun on ripened grain,
> I am the gentle autumn rain.

When you awaken in the morning's hush,
I am the swift uplifting rush
Of quiet birds in circled flight.
I am the soft stars that shine at night.
Do not stand at my grave and cry,
I am not there; I did not die."
There was nothing left to say except Hud's final words.

"Well, come on, ladies, let's keep busy living. That's what Dad wants."

Chapter 29
July 2125

"Starting Again"
Thread 2 Chapter 11

THE ELECTRA-ALISHA DUO honored Holy's wishes by keeping busy living life in parallel fast lanes. Electra drove the pace in some, Alisha in others, each helping one another as needed and sharing the excitement. Alisha was about to accelerate action in the T-Bred lane because the second half of the Co-NFL season kicked off just after Memorial Day.

Bo had decided to hold Alisha back for another couple of games because his team had defeated several of the weaker rivals, which put the T-Breds within playoff striking distance if her return sparked a string of victories. He thought the longer he waited, the less time for competition to devise defenses to stop her, and the less risk of injury. She would be fresh and full of energy while opponents were wearing down. By game time first week of July, the coach, team, and fans were ready for Kit to ignite T-Bred's lightning offense whenever she bolted onto the field.

T-Bred press releases had been deliberately vague, reporting Kit's progress to keep an aura of suspense surrounding her return. When the date was finally announced, sports reporters billed the game as a grudge rematch because the Chicago Crushers had dealt the "big hit" last year. Kit looked at it differently. When interviewed, she said the Crushers always tackle hard but don't try to injure opponents, and was ready to challenge the best, reminding fans to call her Kit.

"I'm Alisha when not in uniform, but call me Kit when I strap on my helmet." A reporter asked what she'd be like this season.

"Watch me in action and ask me after the game." The front office liked the words and used them in PR hype.

The game had a play-off atmosphere, pumping up the stadium and TV fans, as well as Alisha's dream for the limelight. *I've got it, but I won't flaunt it with words. I'll let my fleet feet do the dazzling.*

Kit went for the jugular right from the opening kickoff. Sports reporters didn't know how quick she might be; serious injuries slow down even the best, but for Kit, it was just the opposite. Her new gear surprised the defense, making her stutter-spin moves that much more deceptive. She scored untouched.

The Crusher offense started too tentatively and went four and out. On the second possession, Kit mixed a couple of halfback runs and passes, then decided to dish out punishment now that she was stronger than last year. The very first time she carried the ball, she lowered her shoulder and broke through arm tackles. No one expected her to be as strong as some in the secondary defense. She bowled them over and danced into the end zone. The game was never in doubt after that, and the post-game commentator summarized for viewers what to expect going forward.

"We've just witnessed a promising first step in Kit Kittner's highly anticipated comeback. She looks quick and strong, and the competition will be studying the videos to devise defensive sets to stop the T-Bred's reignited offense. Still, this is only one game, and it remains to be seen if they can sustain it. If they do, they have a good shot at making the play-offs. The tale's not yet told, so please stay tuned."

Bo's post-game locker room talk expressed the same but added a cautionary note.

"Today's a good start, but it's only one step, so don't get ahead of yourselves. Defenses will look for ways to slow us down, which means our defense must be up to holding down the opponent's scoring. Don't party hard yet. Come back Tuesday ready for challenges ahead."

Alisha listened dutifully but had a different takeaway. *I've worked hard and I've earned the right to play hard this evening.*

I'm ready to dance tonight at this week's promo sports club. And I'm not going to worry about opponents' defenses. Let them worry about me.

Afterwards, she showered and changed, then drove to the club. Electra used the drivetime to explain next steps.

"You've done well. Indira is pleased. Your rehab training puts you back where you belong, at the helm of the T-Bred offense. And you were modest during the post-game interview. Kudos to you! Enjoy yourself tonight. Now, listen to this.

"You've got to keep the competition backpedaling so you win enough games to make the playoffs, and it'll get harder each week because the other teams will eventually figure out what to do to slow you down. So don't get complacent; keep going for the jugular. While you're doing that, I'll be coming up with some secret plays. I'm not ready to reveal them just yet. First, I want you and the team to settle into your play calling. In a couple of weeks, your offense will be ready. You'll like what I have, and so will the fans. But for tonight, don't worry, be happy."

In the weeks that followed, Alisha was able to carry forward a don't worry, be happy attitude because all her efforts were breaking her way. She was on break from Hollywood until September's Superman release, and on break from education town hall meetings until the fall term. She raced through the extra time, synchronizing Washington NGA and local town hall meetings or motorcycling around Texas, meeting fans.

Although Carter tried his best to have a "don't worry, be happy" attitude, several obstacles tripped him up. He worried about the public's attitude towards Jared's harsh policies. And he worried if his newest relationship would withstand an outing he had planned.

Zoe had introduced him to Hannah Aaron—a Howard University associate professor of history and political science— two months ago when she was a lecture series speaker. And when Carter told Matt that Hannah had enjoyed their first date, Zoe told them to join Matt and her for a Saturday outing. Like many Washingtonians, none of them had ever been to many local tourist sites, so Zoe organized a tour of Monticello, Thomas Jefferson's storied plantation near Charlottesville, Virginia.

Plans changed several days before departure because of Matt's schedule, forcing Zoe to cancel, but Carter took over, using it as an opportunity to practice flexibility and spontaneity. He would drive Hannah and himself on a scenic two-hour, 118-mile drive on Interstate 66 west, then US 29 south through beautiful rolling countryside.

Hannah accepted the new arrangements when he called, and afterwards, he concluded it would be better for just the two of them to go because it would be an uninterrupted opportunity to learn about each other.

Carter prepared for the outing in his typically thorough manner by summarizing a relevant chronology of relationships. A couple of years ago, I thought Electra was the one for me, but I was wrong. She intimidates and is too strong. Then along came Jazzi. We got along well, but finally, she could tell I wasn't the one for her. I was too inflexible and cerebral, too inconsiderate of her feelings. So, I changed my style and found Rachel. But then I found out she's not my type: too post-modern for my taste, too full of self-hype. I'm glad I found out, even though the last date was disastrous. So, as I move on, I'll remember to practice my new style as I look for a win-win relationship.

Carter's new style kept many of his old traits, particularly the one for detailed accuracy. But he had learned to scale back a predisposition to dump too much information on listeners. After researching the historical background appropriate for the outing, he reminded himself to dial back the details.

Hannah was ready when Carter knocked. Early Saturday morning, weather and traffic made for a pleasant drive conducive to conversation. And when Hannah mentioned she was teaching a summer term American Constitution course, Carter segued to his trip notes.

"I learned that Jefferson began building Monticello when only twenty-six. That's how old he was when he inherited five thousand acres in the Piedmont region from his father. He designed the main house using neoclassical principles described by Italian Renaissance architect Andrea Palladio and reworking it through much of his presidency to include design elements popular in late 18th-century Europe and integrating numerous of his own design solutions.

Situated on the summit of an 850-foot peak in the Southwest Mountains south of the Rivanna Gap, the name Monticello derives from the Italian for 'little mount.' I could tell you more, but I don't want to bore you."

"Why, that's not boring. I like to hear details, and I have many pertaining to our founding fathers. The framers of the Constitution were remarkable men. Wealthy, well-educated, and principled, they always place God and country ahead of themselves. They were visionary geniuses, Franklin and Jefferson in particular." Hannah paused for a Carter segue.

"I agree that they were men of the highest ethics, which is that branch of philosophy most accessible and useful in politics. If you wouldn't mind, I would appreciate hearing your assessment of a political issue that concerns me."

"I enjoy discussing issues and ideas, so please tell me, what is confounding you?"

"Let me state it simply: what should you do if you know a certain course of action is bad for a friend, but they're dead set on taking it? And we are given that the course of action is not breaking the law. How should you deal with it?"

"I discuss these right-versus-right ethical issues in a couple of my undergraduate courses. Note this: right-versus-right is an ethical dilemma because both sides have merit. I want you to contrast it with right-versus-wrong, which is called a moral temptation." Carter understood, so Hannah continued.

"To deal with the dilemma, we have to choose from one of four overarching ethical paradigms: Truth versus Loyalty, Short-Term versus Long-Term, Group versus Individual, or Justice versus Mercy. It's surprising, but they cover all ethical dilemmas I've ever studied." Carter agreed, deferring again to Hannah, so she spoke further.

"So, you pick a paradigm, then place your particular dilemma in it. Then, you have to find an ethical system for each side of the argument. That's where you have to be careful, because there are many to choose from. When I teach the course, I summarize for my students that any system fits into one of three categories: End-based, Rules-based, or Care-based. If you tell me more about the specific dilemma that's bothering you, we can extend our discussion."

"It's a current political issue. The public today is rather mean-spirited and wants to push for harsher methods. My worry is that the public isn't smart enough to realize the harsh methods aren't the right ones. And I'll pick the Short-Term versus Long-term paradigm. And maybe I'd pick Rules-based for the pro-harsh and Care-based for the con-harsh."

"I like your picks so far. And I suggest you use the entire category of civil disobedience issues when searching for correlated precedents." Carter was delighted with all he had heard and decided to change the subject so he wouldn't wear out Hannah's goodwill.

"Thank you. That was most helpful. I'll write up my paper and submit it on our next trip." Quick-witted Hannah joked right back.

"That won't be necessary. An oral presentation is preferred. And because I enjoy talking with you, I know you'll earn an A. Now, why don't you tell me more about Monticello?"

Carter did as told, even giving her a Monticello tour guide he had printed off the Internet earlier that week and recommending they not try to take in too many sights.

"I think we'll have a better time if we start at the Rubenstein Visitor Center, then proceed to the Smith Education Center. After that, we can hike or take a tram tour of the plantation and the house Jefferson built, or do whatever is better for you."

"Why, thank you for being so informative and thoughtful. That deserves a reward, so I'll treat you to lunch."

The duo followed Carter's recommendations after lunch, learning more about Monticello and each other as the afternoon drifted by. Carter treated for dinner at the historic Old Mill Room, the epicurean heart of Boar's Head Resort, which is the official University of Virginia hotel, and afterwards made a spontaneous offer.

"Please don't think me presumptuous, but we could extend the tour by staying the night and visiting Mount Vernon tomorrow. And I'll be happy for us to stay in separate rooms." Carter saw an impish smile, so he closed the deal before Hannah could accept.

"You know I'm an economist, and economists are always precise. So, let me clarify my offer. Not only will I be happy for us to stay in separate rooms, but I shall pay for them as well."

"I'll accept the terms this time, and next time we can negotiate from there."

Saturday's enjoyment continued Sunday, starting with a leisurely stroll and then brunch at one of the outdoor cafes on the Downtown Mall, followed by a drive-by tour of the University of Virginia, which occupies a lion's share of the city. Then they drove east to Richmond, then I-95 north to George Washington's landmark mansion, the 21-room center of the Mount Vernon estate, only 12 miles south of DC. Carter used only part of the drive-time conversation to talk about economics.

"My career so far has been in political economics and Federal Reserve Board policy. I imagine you've studied political philosophy and theory. Would you be willing to share your thoughts?"

"Why yes. You're helping me review lectures because I teach these topics. I cover liberty, justice, property rights, law, and the enforcement of a legal code, what they are, why or even if they are needed, what, if anything, makes a government legitimate, what rights and freedoms it should protect and why, what form it should take and why, what the law is, and what duties citizens owe to a legitimate government, if any, and when it may be legitimately overthrown, if ever. It's much more practical and much less abstruse than what is taught in philosophy courses. And let me elucidate the big mistake political scientists were making even a hundred years ago, for Washington occasionally relapses. Here's what I mean.

"You probably know the liberal versus conservative Constitutional debate. Progressives and liberals used to hype how, as human nature changes, so must our Constitution and human rights emphasis. Well, if you look at archaeological anthropology and neuroscience, it's clear that the human species has the same brain structure since the dawn of civilization 10 thousand years ago. It sounds like a long time period, but it's minuscule on the evolutionary time scale. Well, the Founding Fathers came up with the best form of government when they wrote the Constitution. What worked for them works for us today, because basic human nature hasn't changed. So, Carter, you tell me what liberals and conservatives are debating?"

"If I'm following you correctly, we should be debating not how government is structured, but how elected officials should go about making decisions. Even though man's brain today is the same as that of the caveman, our problems are more complex and changeable. I guess that takes us into the bureaucratic government labyrinth."

"Correct, and I'll vote for you if you work to reduce the DC bureaucratic overload and push it back to the state and local level. You know the saying: all politics is local. But if the public isn't smart enough or active enough, the Federal Government will usurp power that belongs to the people, which puts the government upside down. Instead of people owning the government, we end up with the government owning the people. Longer-term, as history bears out, that is the recipe for revolution."

"That would be an excellent topic for the lecture series. I'll mention that to Zoe."

"Yes, and please tell her I'd be happy to facilitate." Carter picked up on the word "happy," because that was the third philosophical issue on his weekend's hidden agenda.

"You've studied more philosophy than I have. What can you teach me about happiness?" Her smile spoke volumes.

"That is a slippery slope subject, but I'm glad you asked. Let's start with the basic definition: the philosophy of happiness is the philosophical concern with the existence, nature, and attainment of happiness. Philosophically, happiness can be understood as the moral goal of life or as an aspect of chance; indeed, in most European languages the term happiness is synonymous with luck. Thus, philosophers usually explicate on happiness as either a state of mind, or a life that goes well for the person leading it. So, happiness is best treated when you study ethics. And the best way to study ethics is to delve into what different philosophers have to say about 'the good life.'

"There aren't enough miles left for you to drive for me to give more than a glimpse, and it takes years for it to sink in. That's why my students don't agree with a lot of what I teach regarding happiness, so let me give you my Cliffs Notes summary for how to look at it. Are you ready?" Carter was all ears, so she launched her lecture.

"Happiness concerns what we do to find meaning and pleasure in life. It seems that 50% of our happiness is internal, from our genetic predisposition. 10% from external factors, and 40% from our efforts to make changes in our lifestyle. Neurons, emotions, rational thoughts, and external events all contribute. And studies have shown happiness indices decline from the age of 20 to 50, then improve to the age of 70. Can you explain this general pattern?"

"Let me take a stab at it. For most of us it's clear sailing to the age of 20, thanks to protection and nurturing from parents. But then we have to make our own way in the world. We have to face the truth about ourselves and what we can do. It's a struggle. If we survive to 50, we've experienced enough to grasp what it takes to be happy. That takes us to about 70 when physical decline pushes us on a downward slope."

"Very good. Let me take it a little further. You can divide philosophers or philosophies into two groups: those that say you'll be happy if you match your desires to the world, and those that say match the world to your desires. The first group is sometimes criticized for being too passive. Buddhist and Stoic philosophies fit there. The second group emphasizes a balanced moderation for what you want. Aristotle, for example, talked about the golden mean. Have you listened enough, or would you like to hear more?" Carter's reply showed his literary chops.

"I'll be like Oliver Twist. Please sir, I want some more."

"Very well. Think about these paradoxes and questions: Often, the quest for happiness makes us unhappy. Happiness, once obtained, quickly fades. Do you need other people in order to be happy? Should you defer happiness until you die? The list goes on, so I'll elaborate on only the first four I mentioned. And like all of philosophy, if you're not careful you drill so deep you lose your way back to the surface." Twenty minutes later, Carter had to end the conversation.

"We've arrived, so I'm sorry to say we must table our discussion. Perhaps we can pick up here if I pick up the tab for lunch." Hannah agreed.

Her parting words at her front door that evening added an exclamation point to Carter's weekend.

"I'm pleased we got to know one another. You talk so easily about subjects many people find rather boring. But I like them. We should see each other more often." She gave him a quick kiss on the cheek, then added to her comment.

"And your manners are much better than most of the other fellows I've dated. I like how you wait for me." She kissed him again, this time on the lips. We'll start here on our next date."

Carter joked to himself on the drive home. I'm glad I've trained myself to be patient. That's what my Jewish last name means, and as long as I'm considerate, Hannah likes letting me lead. I like where this is leading.

Jared never liked waiting, and ever since blackmail Emails started arriving his impatience force-multiplied his worry that an invisible adversary would leak his darkest transgressions. Anxiety surrounding their intermittent arrival pained him, turning his standard operating procedure on its head; until now, he had been the sender, not the receiver, of harsh words.

Immediately after the first had arrived, Jared surreptitiously tasked a loyal agent to hunt down the blackmailer, but after nine months the hunt had gone nowhere. Jared's store of patience was empty. I'm gonna turn the screws to get results, or else I'll get another hunter. That would be his message at a tete-a-tete with Debbie Klatterbuck later today.

Debbie Klatterbuck's first name did not match her personality. Many people associate her first name with sprightly debutante type, none of which fits this Debbie. As a child she used matches to test pain thresholds of pets or younger playmates. As a teenager and then college student, she prided her ability to exploit weak spots in others so she could inflict psychological pain. She would never admit to these practices, but they added to her personality traits that perfectly matched her chosen profession: Cyberspace counterintelligence tracker.

Considered a cut above average looking, her career would have advanced faster and further if it weren't for anti-social behavior, but that was one of the reasons she was so good at her job. Her superiors joked that the best way to manage her was put her in an office closet and let her come out when she found what she was looking for. Today she was out of the closet and sitting across from Jared in the Oval Office.

"Mr. President, whoever is sending you threatening Emails is pretty clever. I've had no luck intercepting or decrypting your messages even before you open them. And once I open them, I have only five minutes before they self-destruct. And my snooping software has led me down dead ends. So, I'm going to follow a new strategy. Instead of hunting in Cyberspace, I'm going to hunt top-down in the real world. And here's what I need you to do: talk to me about people and events going backward in time just before you were struck down by the T-Plague. And you'll need to give me access to any confidential files or correspondence you have from that period." Jared shrugged, replying matter-of-factly.

"There were a lot of stressful responsibilities on my shoulders back then. Maybe that's part of the reason I haven't been able to recall much. But here's what I'm gonna do. I'll pray for revelation, and I'll go through personal files to make a list of names or places or companies you can drill into." Debbie offered a helpful suggestion.

"Mr. President, a good place to start would be names of your closest committee and staff people, and trace from there. Can you do that for me now? If so, I can start hunting."

"Yeah, let's see. There was a brain trust led by Angus McTear just before I got the T-Plague. Now he's heading up my team of rivals. There's my Inner Circle of lieutenants, then and now. None of those struck down like I was ever came back. And there's my Secret Service guys then and now. Let me jot them down. I'll give you more when I remember more. And you gotta remember this: our discussion stays right here. Tell me when you go hunting in the field. When you do, I'll get a couple of my most tight-lipped agents to go with you." Thirty minutes later Debbie was on her way, ready to redirect the hunt, and Jared added another item to his list of discussion topics for his spiritual advisor. Though still worried, he was certain that revelation and counseling would bring forth his invisible adversary and deliver him from its evil intentions. That made Jared happy.

Chapter 30
September 2125

"A View from the Top"
Thread 2 Chapter 12

T-BRED OPPONENTS WERE HAPPIER now than when Kit first returned to the starting line-up because they had figured out how to slow her down enough to keep from being run out of the stadium. But the rejuvenated T-Breds were formidable, winning enough games to qualify for the play-offs if they didn't lose more than one game out of the remaining three. Electra decided a week before the third game to unveil secret offensive weapons to her partner.

"Pay attention to what I'm about to demonstrate. Your only weakness compared to male QBs is arm strength. No amount of strength training will correct it because female throwing mechanics are different. But we'll use basic Newtonian physics to transfer some of your body's linear and angular momentum to the football. Instead of throwing from a set position, you'll pass when running, using either of my new techniques. The first I call the Javelin Pass, because it's what Olympic javelin throwers do. Watch how I do it."

Electra pretended to take the snap, accelerated to full speed, and gracefully launched a perfect spiral while striding off her trailing foot, the ball landing 15 yards further than she had ever thrown before. She repeated two more times and then watched as Alisha executed the technique.

"That was good. Try a couple of more." Alisha followed orders. Electra stopped her after the third throw.

"Those were better, but that's what I expect from you. Now, for the next technique, which I call the Pirouette Pass. I copied it from Olympic shot putters who copied a spinning style from the guys throwing a discus. You'll use your stutter-spin to put your angular momentum into the ball's linear momentum. Your challenge will be nailing down its accuracy, and I'm counting on your catlike agility and vision to handle that. Watch me."

Electra sprinted to the left, stutter-spun to the right and whirled the ball into the distance. Two throws later Alisha took over. Electra gave her final instructions before turning her loose.

"I want you to demonstrate at the next practice what you now can do, but tell Bo you won't unleash it until the playoffs. Keep it a team secret, away from the media and the competition until it's time to gun them down. Now it's time for you to practice, practice, practice. And you know the drill: it's not practice makes perfect; it's perfect practice makes perfect. Have at it."

Bo was ready to make a brief announcement after whistling his players to gather.

"OK team, listen up. Kit has something to show then tell." Without further ado, she grabbed a football, stepped 10 yards back from the line of scrimmage, then raced full speed forward to launch a pass that soared like shot from a cannon. She repeated once more, than whirled away a couple of spin passes, all traveling further than the team had ever seen her throw before. Cal Brundy, now the backup QB, whistled out his reaction.

"Whew, I hope our receivers can run that far." Then Bo gave the team instructions for what would happen next.

"We're not gonna fire the cannon, unless we need to, until the playoffs start. So, let's practice loading between now and our first playoff game…"

The week before the first playoff game required only light practice, which meant the T-Breds would be fresh and full of energy. Alisha was happy to speak on Wednesday at another Austin town hall meeting, for it gave her a welcome change of pace. Too much practice and too much anticipation doesn't help me one bit. I'm not leaving my A-game on the practice field.

Alisha would ask for citizen opinion regarding how well Guardian Party programs help the economy, and she summarized the major ones to start the meeting.

"The Guardian Party put programs in place that were meant to guard our nation against the T-Plague and terrorism long before they captured the Oval Office. They were the creators of Health-guard and Security-guard agencies. And then they launched Infra-Rebuild and Re-Patriot programs, followed by the Pillars Program containing a number of initiatives such as Golden Years, Op-In, Security Watch, and stronger death penalty enforcement. So, I and our featured guest would like to hear your comments or questions, focusing on whether or not you think they've added jobs or helped the economy. The floor is yours…"

Alisha was surprised by how little the public actually knew about program details. She spent much of the time educating the audience, who wanted to know if she thought the programs made sense. Many people were concerned about the economic impact, but there were others who worried about ethical issues. Even if the programs saved taxpayer dollars, were they good for the citizens? What about longer-term impact, or international repercussions? Alisha asked Woolly afterwards what he would take back to the Governor.

"Sounds like a lot of people don't have the time or intelligence to understand much about these programs. And it's bad if they can't think for themselves. But one thing came through loud and clear: they wanted to know your opinion. You were very diplomatic when you said it wasn't your opinion, but their opinion that counted. But these audiences like you and respect what you say. They'd probably vote for you if you were ever on a ballot. And when you wrapped up the meeting, I like how a couple of them yelled out the T-Bred "Run Girl Run" slogan. They'll all be rooting for you come Sunday, and the Governor and I will too."

Playoff gameday Sunday, exciting for fans and players alike, and especially for Alisha because this was the first playoff game on the road to a hoped-for triumphant comeback story. She leaped out of bed full of energy and primed to deliver a memorable performance. Perhaps she was a bit too wound up, so Electra thought it best to counsel her alter ego while driving to the Austin stadium where they would battle the Pittsburgh Ferric Wheels, whose name mirrors a reference to steel, as does that of the city's NFL counterpart.

"I shall tell you highlights from a timeless story that will help calm you down, help put today into perspective. It dates back to 1200 B.C.E. in the city of Ilium, also known as Troy, and is told through the words of the Greek poet and writer Homer, the first and perhaps greatest storyteller ever. It centers on Achilles—half man, half god— and his prophesied destiny. It continues to inspire us today for its insight into so many aspects of human nature, such as rage and desire, delusion, disaster, death, respect, and glory. I want to point out three fatal errors Achilles made in the Trojan War that led to his downfall. Pride caused the death of his brother-in-arms Patroclus; disrespect given to heroic Hector, whom he defeated in mortal combat, angered all of Troy; the quest for glory ignored the needs of allies. All this led to his own death. So hear me out, then tuck away what I say so you might avoid the same mistakes as we advance in the playoffs.

"Your athletic career faces many of the challenges and accompanying emotions that Achilles confronted. Combat and disaster. Delusion and recklessness. Desire and quest for glory. Do not let your desire for victory sacrifice respect for opponents, nor your quest for individual glory immolate friendship or the common good. And don't be foolhardy enough to think you are invincible. Achilles had his heel. Extraordinary though you may be, you are still human." Electra talked; Alisha listened all the way to the stadium.

"We've arrived at our destination and at the end of what I wanted to tell you. It's time to put your game face on. You and Kit are in charge."

Alisha stayed carefree and loose during pregame warmups, joking with her teammates to help chase away or keep at bay everyone's jitters. But Kit took over in the sideline huddle just before they were to receive the opening kickoff.

"We're going to keep their defense off balance, but in unexpected ways. We'll be going for the jugular, but it'll be a collective effort. I'm gonna hand off more, and pass more. The deep routes are gonna catch them flat-footed, because I'll disguise my throws, making my running look like busted plays. Just listen to my play calls. Be sure your helmet intercoms are tuned only to me. Any questions?" There were none. "OK, let's go have fun!"

The game began according to Kit's plan, surprising the opponent, fans, and sportscaster, whose halftime recap would have pleased Electra.

"Quite a first half indeed. The T-Breds put most of the points on the scoreboard, but no one could have predicted how. Bo Rudman's play-calling is coaching wizardry, using Kit Kittner as a decoy, but letting her run when he spots an opening. And he's come up with some type of scrambling safety valve passes for busted plays. Kittner's throwing way beyond secondary coverage. Way beyond what was considered her arm-strength length. We'll have to see if the Wheel's defense can adjust. If not, the T-Breds are gonna roll over them en route to the next round in the playoffs."

Pittsburgh didn't know how to adjust. Every time they adjusted, the T-Bred offense readjusted utilizing a multi-dimensional array of players, runs, and passes. It was an impressive win, but Bo preached caution after the game.

"Outstanding team win today. Our defense held up well, thanks to our offense dominating time of possession. And we had a clever mix of disguised play-calling. Their secondary couldn't handle our deep routes because we kept outmaneuvering them. So, congratulations to all of you. But the championship game, if we get there, is three games away, which gives our opponents a couple of weeks to figure out how to stop us. So be mindful of our adversaries' abilities. They'll be gunning for us. We can't get cocky." Bo ended the locker room huddle, announcing light, tapered practice schedules for the rest of the playoffs.

To Electra, Alisha was like a finely tuned racecar hitting on all cylinders, gears shifting effortlessly whenever more speed was needed. No adjustments were necessary during Alisha's playoff run towards the championship game, so she just let her motor on, leaving the path clear for Electra to drill into disturbing Internet chatter only her software security suite could access.

Evidence was mounting that the Iron Triangle would launch coordinated Cyberspace attacks before yearend. Its partners were certain no counter-intelligence organization knew how to find them or stop their Cyber weapons, nor would the dithering UN do anything other than speak harsh words if they found out. The wild card in all this was the unpredictable United States, but the Iron Triangle was feeling more and more confident that Jared Gardner wouldn't alienate his allies by lashing out at what might be the most likely target—Isilabad.

Electra still had time to develop a proactive counter-attack, part of which might include Angus. What stupendous serendipity. If Alisha takes the T-Breds to the championship game, we might go to Washington next weekend to play the DC Ambassadors. I'll have plenty of time before then to simulate how well my counter-attack works, and I can delay my flight back so I can meet with Carter and Angus. And I have insider information that Alisha will carry the ball for us tomorrow.

Alisha delivered what Electra predicted; the T-Breds won their semi-final game, as did the Ambassadors. Bo knew there was nothing left for his team to do except taper, but since the game wouldn't be played in Austin, he approved a rally-dance for Wednesday at a sponsor sports bar, leaving instructions Tuesday to "play responsibly" so no one misses the Wednesday morning flight to Washington. Everyone at the dance followed his advice; all T-Bred players touched down on the Ronald Reagan National Airport tarmac together, ready to battle the Washington Ambassadors in the big game. Toni Diya, who was Alisha's roommate on road trips, cracked what everyone hoped would be a prophetic pun: "Now that the plane's touched down, we're good to go for many more on Sunday. We'll crash through the door of the Ambassadors. How fitting their nickname matches what we'll break down."

Electra had arranged to call Carter Thursday evening, expecting him to set up a special team of rivals meeting early next week, and hoping he could arrange a casual dinner with Matt and Zoe. When she apologized for being unable to get complimentary tickets,

Carter understood, replying that he and a date would watch the game with friends.

"Electra, please call me Monday to confirm our agenda for next week. And best wishes on Sunday."

Alisha was uncharacteristically restive early Sunday morning, ruminating on the twists and turns that brought her to the pinnacle of the Co-NFL. She thought back to championship game advice given long, long ago by her childhood soccer coach: "No matter what level the competition, reaching the finals is as good as it gets, and that's what counts, not the final score. So, put nerves in the rearview mirror! Play with abandon, for the thrill of being here. Use your head and play with your heart. Make your parents, your teammates and yourself proud of what you'll do on the field."
How should I handle myself today? What's the best role to play? Electra knew this was the time for a one-on-one final huddle.

"You've reached the promised land of every sport, no matter the age or setting: the championship game. And you've done and shown everything asked for to bring your team to this magic moment: dedication and incredibly hard rehab training, self-sacrifice and unselfish leadership, emotional sensitivity and strength. You've earned the right to showcase your stuff on center court; your teammates and fans want you to run wild, to display athletic greatness so they too can be part of a magic moment. Do so today; use your head and play with your heart. I'll see you after the game."

Electra's words were everything Alisha needed to hear, crystallizing how Kit would run the offense if the team liked what she had to say at the players-only pre-game meeting.

"We're here, where we want to be and where we belong. Embrace the moment and make greatness happen for all of us. And today, let's keep the Doors guessing by changing our playoff strategy. They'll expect us to stick with what we've been doing: a balanced mix of run and pass using all our weapons. Well, today, how about we start the first and second half, letting me carry the offense, building a points cushion that should withstand any pushback. I'm ready and able if you're willing." The captain of the defense immediately accepted her offer.

"Ever since I signed on, I knew you had the goods. I've been waiting to watch you cut loose, so do it today. Me, my defense, and I would like nothing better than sitting on our helmets watching you run over the Doors' defense instead of knocking heads with their offense. It'll pump us up and deflate them. So Kit, just do it!"

From the opening kickoff, that's what Kit did. She shifted into a higher gear, physical and emotional personas merging into an unstoppable force. The defense couldn't match her lightning-quick feet that danced around the field, nor could they handle surprise passes launched while she was in full stride or spinning. And she deliberately removed herself from the game at an opportune moment midway through the second quarter, surprising fans and sportscasters.

"Ooohh, that was a hard hit, drawing a penalty. The Doors' defense deliberately gang-tackled Kittner. You can do that in the NFC, but you can't gang-tackle females in this league. Kittner's slow to get up. Now she's up and heading to the sidelines. Rudman's putting in his backup QB, Cal Brundy, who kept the team afloat until Kittner returned for the second half of the season. Kittner's been a scoring dynamo so far. Maybe she's injured. Maybe she's getting tired. OK, the play's about to resume. Let's see how the Ambassadors react…"

The second half mirrored the first; Kit simply outdistanced all defenders. Early in the fourth quarter, she headed to the sidelines, ready for Cal to run the offense for the rest of the game. T-Bred victory was assured; her comeback story complete. As time expired, the announcer cheered the outcome.

"The T-Breds are now the Co-NFL champions! Today, we have been treated to a remarkable display of talent, capping a comeback unrivaled in the post-modern era of women in sports. Hard to return to greatness after serious injury, but Kittner's done just that. I'm sure the league will have to make rule changes for next season. What that might be, I can only speculate, but they'll have to introduce some sort of 'Kittner rules level the playing field. But that's for next year. Right now, the fans are celebrating."

Alisha was celebrating in the locker room with her teammates when suddenly, overwhelming sorrow swept her away. Before she began sobbing uncontrollably, she stripped out of her uniform and dashed for the comforting solitude of the showers. Bo thought he knew what was wrong and asked everyone to give Alisha private time to wash away any remaining stress placed on her by great expectations.

"Let's give her a moment alone to adjust. She'll be back with us soon."

Alisha sat under a cascade of warm water, back against the wall, arms hugging folded legs, and trying to make sense of her sorrow. She was not alone. As promised, Electra was with her and ready to speak.

"Bo doesn't know you like I do. Stress doesn't bother you. You morph it into an adrenaline rush, and what you are feeling is what you should expect. Everyone experiences a sense of sadness, a sense of loss when reaching the pinnacle; you've won the ultimate prize. But a view from the top is short-lived. Philosophers of semiotics call this the reentry problem. You have to come back to reality after reaching a moment of greatness that vanishes all too quickly. The best example from antiquity is that of Alexander the Great, captured in the Greek writer Plutarch's quote 2500 years ago: 'When Alexander saw the breadth of his domain, he wept for there were no more worlds to conquer.' Randy Dancer, your Superman series star, uses drugs to handle reentry, and that gives a very bad landing.

"Look, kiddo, I have some ideas for what's next in store for you and me. And I guarantee you'll like them. I'll clue you in a couple of days, but here's what I want you to do right now: get happy, get out of the shower, get into some party clothes, and go celebrate with the team and fans."

And that's exactly what Alisha did. Electra enjoyed watching from the shadow, even experiencing the emotional spillover, knowing there would be other games she and her alter ego would enjoy. Our journey is far from over. Alisha and I have places to go and things to do. And the lightning brain will see us through.

Chapter 31
November 2125

"The Odyssey Continues"
Thread 3 Chapter 9

ALISHA KEPT BUSY AFTER winning the Co-NFL championship, charting new directions for her extraordinary odyssey. The time had come to say farewell to football, and though initially depressed, she quickly understood why Electra told her it's the right thing to do.

"You'll be 29 next year, still young enough to develop athletic prowess further but not in the Co-NFL. You've reached its summit by winning the championship; reaching the pinnacle is exhilarating but all steps from there are downhill. And don't consider playing several additional seasons, collecting a string of consecutive awards or titles. It would be a diminishing achievement because you've demonstrated clear superiority. Once you've been there and shown you're the best, it's time to look for other challenges. Nothing's sadder than watching once-great athletes cling to where they no longer belong. Heed the words of A.E. Houseman's elegy, To an Athlete Dying Young:

"The time you won your town the race
We chaired you through the market-place;
Man and boy stood cheering by,
And home we brought you shoulder-high.
Today, the road all runners come.
Shoulder-high, we bring you home,
And set you at your threshold down,
Townsman of a stiller town.
Smart lad, to slip betimes away
From fields where glory does not stay,

> And early though the laurel grows
> It withers quicker than the rose.
> Eyes the shady night has shut
> Cannot see the record cut,
> And silence sounds no worse than cheers
> After earth has stopped the ears.
> Now you will not swell the rout
> Of lads that wore their honours out,
> Runners whom renown outran
> And the name died before the man.
> So set, before its echoes fade,
> The fleet foot on the sill of shade,
> And hold to the low lintel up
> The still-defended challenge-cup.
> And round that early-laurelled head
> Will flock to gaze the strengthless dead,
> And find unwithered on its curls
> The garland briefer than a girl's."

"Perhaps we can find another sport for which we can unleash your athletic skills, but that will be difficult. The Co-NFL was made for you and vice-versa because your advantage over female opposition was offset by males, making for exciting contests on a level playing field. But let's not look for it now; look to Hollywood for acting and Austin for politics. That's where our odyssey leads."

Sam was of course disappointed when Alisha called him to announce she planned to retire, but he understood the ephemeral nature of professional sports and had only best wishes for her. Alisha happily accepted his invitation for Friday dinner tomorrow. And a Hollywood phone call that evening from Kathi Lauret added to her upcoming engagements.

"Congratulations on your Co-NFL success. And I hope you've been following the Hollywood buzz. Our Superman—New Age Saga series has outstanding ratings, which means we'll extend to a second season and want to start filming in January. So, my first questions to you are these: are you up for a second season, and will that fit your football schedule?"

"Yes and Yes. Acting and Hollywood are for me. And just this week I told the T-Breds that I'm retiring from the Co-NFL."

"I applaud your decision to find new challenges. And from what the sportscasters are saying, the Co-NFL owners are angling for rule changes that would have worked against you. You're making it easy to keep the rules as they are. And your fans will follow you to Hollywood. The ratings and polls show that's the case. But this isn't all the news I have. I'd like you to consider another opportunity.

"Our studio just bought the rights to an updated Mission Impossible movie series. But now, the lead character is a young female, which opens up new script possibilities. We'll keep lots of special effects, but we're adding more character development and subtlety to plots. The main character's codename is Chameleon because she changes her appearance and personality to fit the situation. Vincent and I recommended you to the director. Would you be interested in auditioning?" Whoa! Alisha shouted to herself. Another role I already play.

"Yes, I would love to audition. I'm sure I can do a great job for you and the director. And I know that other actresses have starred simultaneously in movies and media series. I think I can handle the load."

"I know you can. That's why we recommended you. How about this? I'll confirm audition dates and get back to you."

Sam Junior and Senior were the first to arrive and thought it only fitting to invite Hud and Woolly to join them at Truluck's Seafood Restaurant, for that's where her Co-NFL journey began and should end. Hud arrived five minutes later, followed shortly by Alisha and Woolly, who were chatting as the greeter brought them to the table. Sam rose to shake hands and then asked the waiter to open the bottle of iced champagne that was already at the table.

"I wish to propose a toast to Alisha's starburst Co-NFL career and to what she's done for the T-Breds. And of course to the opportunities that lie ahead." In return, Alisha thanked Sam and

Woolly for all their support, after which Woolly led the conversation.

"The Governor's noted how well you've done for him at home and in Washington, and how you and the public relate. Sam shared his vetting info long ago, and we know how well qualified you are for many opportunities, so our thinking is this: we'd like you to consider running for Congress, representing the Texas 11th Congressional District. We think your youth, ability, personality, and popularity among Texas voters can defeat the incumbent. Do you know where the 11th district is?"

"Yes, it's a low population-density big stretch out in West Texas holding Midland-Odessa, San Angelo, Brownwood, La Mesa, and Andrews. About a million people—45% white, 45% Hispanic. I haven't motorcycled there yet, but I've visited Hud's drilling operations." Woolly looked at Hud, who hurriedly explained.

"You call her Alisha and I call her Electra, but in either case, you get a gal that knows the facts and is always prepared." Woolly agreed.

"Not only that, but you always impress the people you meet. We can build on your NGA and spokesperson roles to increase voter awareness and interest in the image you've already created. I'll get started assembling a campaign team, and you keep doing what you're doing. Come February, we'll start rolling, but first I need to know if you want to throw your hat in the ring. It's not for everyone. I want you to think about it, and let me know by Thanksgiving."

The Electra-Alisha duo recognized a win-win situation: Their combined intelligence and empathy, packaged in a pleasing personality, could win the voters, and a seat in Congress could provide additional ways to help Angus. And as illustrated by Ronald Reagan and other notables, acting and political careers could go together. Electra knew how challenging the road ahead might be but the duo had all the tools for success. My alter ego will handle the social and people side of politics while I formulate policy. That's a perfect division of labor. Woolly applauded Alisha's decision.

The latest Cyberspace chatter confirmed Electra's worst fear: an Iron Triangle attack seemed immanent, so she needed to set additional bio-tech and security software projects in motion. A meeting with Su and Kameyo activated the bio-tech piece.

"You and Kameyo need to work at the lab Hud has negotiated for us in Japan. For at least the next three months, you'll be there to coordinate testing and production of our latest vaccines. And you'll need to equip the lab with the latest biohazard containment, security, and fail-safe systems. And I'm transferring some of my university postdoc projects for you and Kameyo to coordinate from our new lab. You'll have to build a project task list and convert it into PERT/CPM diagrams and Gantt charts to track planned versus actual progress, and you must hire lab techs once you have the lab in operation. We'll correspond via encrypted Internet teleconferencing and communications, and I'll need to be onsite periodically to coordinate details you can't handle. I've already briefed Hud, so please follow up with him immediately." Su understood and added a special task to a travel-planning list.

"I would like you to handle any post office mail I receive while away. And rather than forwarding it to me, I want you to read what I get and handle it appropriately. And I won't complain like Indira did.

Do you remember the 'open mail' kerfuffle your father caused?'"

"I don't. Please tell us."

"Adom, not Jason is the one who told me. A year before you were born, Jason began opening some of Indira's mail. Your father was sometimes socially obtuse. It never occurred to him that she would object. When she called him out, he said he wasn't doing it to spy, but to help. But he did mention to Adom that Indira occasionally received letters postmarked from Hollywood. For some reason, he never opened those. Anyway, Indira complained and he stopped." Kameyo made the same request, to which Electra replied.

"Please give me your P.O. box keys and I shall handle. And I assume I have the right to chuck junk mail. I'm still amazed how much comes via snail mail. And many people prefer the U.S. postal system to the Internet because hackers can't get at hard copy. Well, if there are no further comments, we're good to go."

An odd thought came to mind as Electra walked to her next meeting. I saved one unopened Hollywood letter. It was in the packet addressed to Grandfather and me that we found when going through Father's belongings after he blew himself up. And I know where I put it. I shall read it as soon as I can.

Electra chatted briefly with Tim and Kwame, explaining how Tim should handle AI-related chip implants that would interface brain and external devices, for which the interactive Cyber-Theater would be the first commercial application. And like Su, he would coordinate related postdoc activities.

Kwame's Security Toolkit Suite directions came only from Electra. She needed to maintain tight control because it ranked above top secret and she trusted no one. She summarized how he should attach his latest 3-D VR GUI's to her next-gen, instructing him to extract from her proprietary suite a dummied-down tool kit they would market. After her monologue, she asked for questions or comments. Tim spoke for himself and Kwame.

"You're giving us a lot more to do. You've prioritized the projects so we know where to start, but do we get more people to help?"

"Not until additional time constraints become critical. You're on your own, so develop task lists and timelines. Help one another do this, and help one another complete the critical path pieces. We'll reconvene the week after Thanksgiving."

Electra rushed home to reconvene where she kept a family keepsake box. She sat on a bedroom chair, cradling the opened box, waiting for Alisha's first comment.

"You've kept so few remembrances. My empathy tells me why, but I'd like to hear you tell me the reason."

"Keepsakes are needed only when sharing the past with close friends or family populating the present. You're the only one that qualifies, and you know them as well as I. I kept only a critical mass in case we find other people."

"I'm pleased you saved the Hollywood letter. Now that we'll have a presence in Tinseltown, let's find out what's inside." Electra carefully opened it, reading it twice before Alisha finally spoke.

"What we've just read illustrates what I've taught us about relationships. You never know all there is about even the people you love the most. Did you have even an inkling?"

"No. I know nothing about Indira's undergrad days, and what's in the letter predates Su. She doesn't know any of this. Indira's love affair dates back to undergrad days. And why does the writer lament an abortion? And whose abortion is she lamenting?" Alisha read between the lines.

"The writer is Indira's undergrad Harvard roommate, Winona Kota, and it sounds like she and Indira may have been intimate. Evidently, Indira spent several summer vacations working in Hollywood, following Winona's lead. How intriguing. Now we have an additional trail that will lead to more Indira revelations. You're our hunter. How old is the trail?"

"According to Jason's farewell note, the letter came the day we were born, so it's nearly 29 years old. But I have the girl's name, Harvard affiliation, and an old address. I can start there, hacking into the past to discover what became of her. I'm going to surf the Net and hack for background information." Electra spoke again fifteen minutes later.

"Winona is an Indian name meaning first princess-daughter. It comes from the Dakota Tribe that split from the Sioux Nation. And that tribe comes from the Ho-chunk people of the Big Voice or Sacred Language, formerly called the Wisconsin Winnebago Tribe. Winnebago means murky water and comes from the Sioux language. The word Sioux has no special meaning." Alisha offered a brief comment.

"You're the best multi-tasking planner, tracker, and hacker I know, so have at it. But please, don't become obsessive. Why don't you take a break and hack into Winona's files later?"

"You've taught me well, so I'll take your advice by taking a workout."

Electra used her runtime-generated endorphins to focus on two pressing issues. The first had existed for years. My high-priority project list is getting longer and longer. I need my dream team to carry some of the load. Well, since I can't conjure it out of wishful thinking, I'll continue doing the best I can by using the best "mere mortals" available. Oops, wrong word. Alisha taught me not to use people. I will make win-win outcomes.

The second was of recent vintage, caused by the new Japanese lab. Government surveillance is everywhere, as is corporate or foreign spying. I'll need to smuggle myself and supplies to and from the new lab, and I must stay invisible, so how can I avoid airport screening and security checks? My British friend Alice Bickerwith would know, but MI-X terminated her five years ago. Perhaps some of her team survived the purge and are freelancing. I'll have to search in Cyberspace for survivors.

Electra searched her memory that evening for names associated with either of the British covert forays codenamed Holy Grail and White Rabbit, retrieving all the chilling details. Electra was blown up in the first and suffocated in the second, rescued both times by a team that nicknamed her "Crutches," which she used as part of her cover. She jotted down all the names and associated serial numbers she could recall, then went to work in Cyberspace, using her tool kit. By the end of the evening, she had tabulated a list of prospective Email addresses and telephone numbers that might connect her with what she needed. She would start calling first thing tomorrow morning London time, which is six hours ahead of Austin. I'll rest for two hours, then start calling at six their time. If they remember me, they'll pardon the early morning interruption. But if they're who I think they are, they'll already be up and in action. And if they tell me to bugger off, I'll say Adios MF. And I'll let them figure out what I mean by MF.

The first six calls were duds, but the seventh hit the mark. The correct Simon McNamie answered.

"Blimey! I can't believe I'm speaking to Crutches. What on earth is going on with you?" Electra thought it best to get right to the point.

"Are you still with British Secret Service? It's OK to level with me. No one can eavesdrop. I'm using an encrypted line."

"No, I left a year after Alice Bickerwith went missing. There was some sort of botched cover-up going on, and her boss, Chester Bowless, was killed. I got out to avoid the purge that followed."

"Well, maybe that can be good for you and me. I'm looking for freelance covert operators who can insert or extract people or equipment on short notice between the United States and Japan. Can you help me?"

"Sorry Luv; that's beyond my pay scale, but I can put you in touch with someone who can. You remember the A-Team TV series? I know someone who runs a couple of them, and it's damn clever. He has operatives at FedEx and other worldwide shippers who can get people or equipment in or out of airports, and then his ex-military commandos take it from there. He can supply boots on the ground, vehicles, and state-of-the-art firepower. But it's big bucks, COD, and a no-returns policy. Are you game?"

"Yes, I like these kinds of games."

"Righto. I'll call him to make introductions. He'll contact you directly if he's interested, or I'll call you if he isn't. Give me your number…"

The Iron Triangle team had already shared all the numbers Ziarmal needed: how many and which targets would be blasted with what weapons on what day and time. It was time for him to inform Darla, so she could schedule when her sales force should call on target customers so they could buy Cybergard security protection software.

Darla gleefully read the encrypted Email marked for her eyes only. How nice, she thought. New Year's Eve at the stroke of Midnight DC time the attack commences. East Coast major metropolitan areas will not be having a happy New Year's Day, for the Iron Triangle will unleash Russian-made Cyberweapons on transport, power, and the Federal banking system targets. And what a perfect reminder for Cybergard customers to buy now and avoid the next attack. And because I pirated the Russian algorithms, soon I can dump the Iron Triangle and blast away on my own. Next year will be a very good year for me and Cybergard.

Darla was quickly outgrowing the need for terrorist partners. She had stolen their weapons design and artificial intelligence algorithms that interface computers and devices, and was tired listening to Ziarmal's ideological rants. She didn't think he really believed all the silliness he spouted. Maybe he's doing it for effect. Maybe he's trying

to convince himself or get us to go along with his flawed beliefs.

Darla was no dummy; in college, while majoring in computer technology, she had taken courses in neuroscience, philosophy, and religion, learning all the major religions and their associated flaws. They try to make choosing the beliefs of their prophet a dilemma where the choice is obvious: either their prophet is crazy, or is a miracle worker. It's the mistake every rookie ethics student makes: they forget to convert the dilemma into a trilemma where the middle ground is chosen. In all religions, the middle ground is that no one knows what the prophet really said or did, so you can't choose either extreme. The other major shortcoming: men of the cloth pride themselves in making their practices so hard even the saints can't avoid sinning. I'd compare this to seating a starving man at a banquet, instructing him to nibble slowly. None of this is appealing to me. Nor do I like the sclerotic clergy of conventional religious organizations, dressed in costumes and beliefs from the Middle Ages. They're all dinosaurs. That's what I'd say when I'm in a good mood like I am today. But if I weren't, my comments would be a bit harsher.

Darla would be very upset if she knew another pair of eyes had access to her encrypted Email. Electra had read it and would activate her defensive strategy immediately, then decide how far in advance to let Angus know an attack was imminent, giving him enough to go on without his questioning how she knows. If he knew, would Angus turn me in to get his hands on my toolkit? I won't risk it. I'll feed this info to Carter and let him be the messenger. I'm walking an ethical tightrope, but I've done it before and trust myself more than I trust anyone else.

Since Holy's death, Robin had regained her footing, putting all her time and energy into launching Sunshine Eldercare. It was the driving force in her life, giving her a purposeful commitment and driving her schizophrenia deeper and deeper into remission. She arranged recitals and visits to attention-starved retirement villages, attracting families whose elderly parents needed occasional caregiving visits from herself and her little dog. Soon she had a pleasant calendar of clients. People who knew Robin remarked they had never seen her in better shape mentally, and Robin felt the same way, even though she was obsessed with obtaining one more possession that only she knew about. Not even Electra knew.

There were manifold means for getting what she wanted. All would take time; all had their pluses and minuses. She prioritized the list and focused on her top pick, which had no clear path, but that was of minor concern, for her clock was not yet ticking loudly. In the meantime, she was happy to grow the business, daydreaming of how to expand it once her new possession arrived. Sunshine will need

more partners, and I'll have to hire helpers too. Just what I want. More things to watch over, more things to do.

Electra worried less about Robin, now that Robin had adjusted to life after Holy. She was less dependent and more engaged in life, thinking more clearly than before, so Electra didn't visit her as often. Hud's catered Thanksgiving buffet would be an opportunity to swap news.

Though Hud missed his father terribly, he was working through a grieving process that awaits everyone. Electra had quoted for him soon after Holy's death some wisdom from a respected philosopher: "You are not an adult until your parents have passed on." Hud's friends and associates considered Hud much more than an adult. He was a rock solid pillar of the community who shouldered responsibilities or adversities in his typical forthright, practical manner. No one ever worried about him. He wore the mantle well, and only rarely did he wish for a supporting shoulder or an ear for listening, and whenever the wish came, it quickly faded. Dad, you were my best friend and I'll carry your wisdom with me till I drop. You're a better man than I, but you taught me well. You were always my backstop and still are. I'll always try to make you proud.

Su and Kameyo attracted much attention when they announced their departure date for Japan. Su let Kameyo do most of the talking.

"Hud masterfully handled negotiations for our new lab. It's near the site of the Fukushima nuclear disaster in 2011, about 150 miles north of Tokyo. It took much longer than originally estimated to clean up all the contamination. All but the power plant's acreage is supposed to be safe now, but people are reluctant to move back. That's why Hud could get such a good price on lab facilities already in place. They're still being converted to our biotech lab and manufacturing specifications; Su and I will leave next week to oversee progress and begin development and manufacturing there. We can visit my parents on weekends too, so I'm treating this as a combination work-study abroad program and family reunion." Hud added that diversified locations are good insurance against the whims of governments.

"We can't count on Washington just yet to leave us alone. So, if they come calling, what they're looking for won't be in Austin." Now it was Electra's turn to speak up.

"Well, I'm not going to Japan in December, but I've been invited to Washington. Zoe and Matt are holding a vow-cer celebration. Robin, you're invited too if your caregiving schedule allows. I'll give you the dates as soon as they're confirmed, but I think Zoe's Girl Party is Saturday December 2nd, Matt's Guy Party is Friday the 8th, and the ceremony's on Saturday the 9th. I plan to be there for everything, except the Guy Party. I can stay at the home where I grew up, work at my NGA office, and put in a cameo appearance at my GWU lab. Lucky for me I can use them all to keep up on all my projects."

Electra kept busy making an assortment of pre-Holiday arrangements. Luckily for her, Mission Impossible auditions would be first week of January rather than December, making for less year-end traveling. And she was tickled to hear from Jennifer Conklin, who was planning Zoe's Girl Party.

"I'm so glad you'll be here for the entire week. Have you ever been to an Ante Up Party? I'm planning it at Baltimore's Horseshoe Casino a week before the vow-cer celebration." Electra had never heard of it, so Jennifer explained.

"It's a themed pre-marriage girl-only get-together I picked the theme: marriage is a gamble. So, we'll have a private room for lunch and dinner and discussion, then a night of gambling. And I'll charter a bus to take us to and from, so we can arrive Saturday morning and leave late Saturday night so we can recover Sunday at our house." Electra was impressed.

"That's very clever; I'm sure you're outdoing whatever's being planned for Matt."

"Carter's told me what's in store for him, and by comparison, Guy Parties are so predictable, so earthy. Carter's arranging it the day before at one of those fantasy clubs. I think he picked Caliburn Fantasies. Caliburn is another name for King Arthur's legendary sword. Lots of psychological and sexual innuendos there. Of course, Carter's researched it. It has franchises in other cities and is certified safe. Escorts are STD and drug-free. And the mood elevators supplied are safe. And Carter told me more. Ever since the postmodern readjustments among sexuality, sins, and religion, fantasy clubs and pleasure cafes have contributed to a reduction in sex or drug violence. They've practically eliminated drug or sex trafficking, increased tax revenues, and decreased associated health costs. Leave it to an economist to place dollar signs on everything. But maybe he's got a point. And speaking of Carter, a lady he's dating will be at our Girl Party. Have you ever met Hannah Aaron?"

"No. This is the first I heard the name. What's she like?"

"She's an associate professor at Howard University. We're not prying, but from what Matt's picked up, Carter likes her and vice versa. I hope they're better suited than the Carter-Rachel relationship. We ladies can talk about this when we get together.

It should be a fun evening. And if Robin comes, please relay all the info to her."

"I will, and I plan to have fun, so please make sure you call me Alisha all week long."

In retrospect, Zoe's Girl Party was the best part of Alisha's first week in December. The morning bus ride to the casino became a perfect vehicle for all ten invitees to get to know one another and gossip about the lighter side of life. Jennifer, though nearly thirty years older than the rest, fit in comfortably. Her healthcare business activities kept her aware of current events, and her youthful appearance showed the results of exercise and a fashion model career in an earlier life. Though Alisha was five years younger than most of the others, her elegant and sophisticated appearance was that of a thirty-something.

The ladies skipped from the bus to a private room where light lunch and spirited discussion awaited. Four had never married, and all but two of those who had married were still with the original partner. Jennifer primed the conversation pump, and it never ran dry.

"I've been married for thirty-some years, so I know from experience you have to work at keeping a marriage—that's the older generation's term for what the vow-cer is all about—on the rails and going in the right direction. I always have a relationship self-help or popular psychology book on my reading list. I just finished the Five Languages of Love, written over a hundred years ago by Gary Chapman. It's all about how to express your heartfelt your mate. It outlines five ways to express and experience love; Chapman calls them 'love languages.' The names are self-explanatory: gift giving, quality time, words of affirmation, devotion or acts of service, physical touching. He claims that the list of five love languages is exhaustive. According to his theory, each person has one primary and one secondary love language. And he suggests that to discover another person's love language, one must observe the way they express love to others, and analyze what they complain about most often and what they request from their significant other most often. He theorizes that people tend naturally to give love in the way that they prefer to receive love." Jennifer didn't have to ask for comments. One of the divorced ladies spoke right up.

"I wish I had the book when I was married. I would have hit my ex over the head to improve his vocabulary. All he wanted to do was touch, touch, touch. And I'm sure you know where." The other divorced lady put a different spin on it.

"Maybe you were better off than I was. At least your ex didn't stray. My ex enjoyed sex with me, but when I learned he liked it with too many other ladies, I dumped him. Zoe, just be aware that men are built differently, emotionally as well as physically."

"Matt and I have talked about this, and I'm not going to chain him down so he can't follow what is programmed in his DNA. If I did that, he'd be frustrated in spite of himself. So, all I told him was to be honest with me. I think it's good that societies today deal with human predispositions more openly. Can anyone give us additional insights?" Hannah decided to do so.

"You've touched on something we usually don't consider when talking about people today. We like to think we're much smarter, more advanced than prehistoric man, but there's no evidence that our brains are any different than cave men's. We differ only because our science and technology give us a better grasp of reality. But, if you transplanted a newborn male from ten thousand years ago into the 22nd century, he'd grow up to be like a typical male." One of the married ladies spoke next.

"I've read some of the newer books patterned after the old Men are from Mars series. The new books are better than the old because they add more from the latest neuroscience findings, but the old series accurately covered the basic differences between men and women: men are like blunt objects attached to springs oscillating back and forth between closeness and distance; women are like emotional wells rising and falling. Men want to do rather than talk; women want to talk before doing. And there are genetic differences between the two sexes, so don't expect them to think or act the same way. Men are genetically programmed to hunt;

women to have kids." Zoe brought the discussion back to her significant other.

"I think you're right, and that's where I think I've got the right guy. Matt and his friend Carter know the difference and know how to treat their partners. Matt and I know we'll have to keep working if we want to keep our intimacy growing, but we have much more than sex going for us." Jennifer, who was keeping time, realized the group was ready for a change of pace.

"Ladies, I think we're ready for a dessert tray and drinks. And after that, it's time for fun at the gambling tables…"

Alisha was having fun being an active listener, but when the desserts rolled in, a couple of the ladies wanted to know about life in the Co-NFL.

"What's it like training with the guys? How do you keep sex out of the way?"

"The more both sexes train together, the more comfortable everyone becomes. Like Zoe said, there's a lot more between men and women than sex." Another lady asked if she was considering another sport.

"Great question. A sportscaster asked if I'd like to try out for a spot in the all-male NFC, but I told him that good as I may be, they're too big, too strong, too fast for me. I wouldn't be able to take the hits. At this time, I'm not considering another sport. I don't think I fit in female-only events because it's not a level playing field; I have an advantage in most, other than gymnastics or figure skating. I'm not built for those sports. Maybe I could play in the Co-NBA, but that'd be like the Co-NFL and I want something different. That's why I'm acting." Hollywood and acting provoked a couple of questions, which segued into a frank discussion about women and sex, topics that were top of mind for one lady.

"I think fantasy clubs and pleasure cafes are great for women. They give women a place to cater to themselves and not worry about men. And a friend of mine went to a party hosted at Madame Bovary's, a ladies-only fantasy club. If I try marriage again, I think I'll hold my Gal Party there." Jennifer interrupted all conversations when she joked about the remaining schedule.

"It's 6 p.m. and our bus leaves at midnight, so be back in our room at 11:30. You're on your own until then, so enjoy the tables and dance floor, or the bars and entertainment. And don't chat up the men too hard, unless they buy the drinks."

Electra worked at her GWU lab early next week, giving a personal touch to postdocs who were doing their best to implement some of her easier artificial intelligence projects. She kept the potentially sinister neuro devices strictly for herself, allowing Tim and teams to share the load on harmless ones like the Cyber-Theater. The Smart Clothing Project, set up to develop uniforms for monitoring the wearer's physical condition, was being developed by a GWU team. It included interactive fabrics for connective clothing by integrating digital signals from a wearable device (generations beyond early Fitbit devices) with fabrics that would adjust properties (such as reflectivity and heat transmission) according to device signals or environmental cues. She occasionally had to remind herself to be patient. If I had my dream team, I'd start integrating smart clothes directly into the brain using implanted chips. But that team is still a dream, so I better stick with what I've got.

Electra avoided chatting in person with Carter about terrorist activities, preferring instead to give him by phone enough Iron Triangle terrorism leads to keep Angus and the CIA ahead of any pending attack. And she dummied down what she gave so Angus wouldn't become suspicious about her sources. But she ended the call on a personal note.

"Please call me Alisha from now through Saturday. I had lots of fun at Zoe's Gal Party, and if Matt's Guy Party is half as good, you'll have lots of fun. Matt should too."

"Well, you know Matt. He's pretty level-headed. Hardly anything gets him in a flap. But I think he'll have his hands and lower head in motion dealing one-on-one with whatever entertainment Excalibur delivers. It's one of the best demi-monde escort and fantasy clubs. I vetted it in online before selecting it.

And Buford Crawley, the club manager, suggested I let him pick the party theme so it's a surprise for all. And he guarantees Matt will be pleasantly surprised, or he'll refund half the cost. I'll tell you Saturday how it went."

In his five years as DC's Excalibur Club manager, Buff Crawley had never been presented with such an opportunity. To prove she has what it takes to launch her new career, his just-hired Demi-Monde Escort would "audition" her services for free. When the young lady called him on Monday, he scoffed at the offer. But when she electronically sent him a "clean bill of health" medical certification, and he did a quick criminal background check, he considered her offer more seriously. And her Website promo video clinched it.

But the young woman was particular too. For work-related reasons, she was available only this coming Friday, and she must pick the particular party in order to prepare appropriately. She expected Buff to meet with her late Thursday afternoon, letting her stay the night before in the one-on-one chamber adjoining the party room. Buff balked at all that, but when the young woman said she would pay half the cost if the client wasn't completely satisfied, he accepted her offer. And after they met, he was certain Matt Fortier would enjoy his close encounter. Buff agreed to decorate the rooms in a Mardi Gras motif she selected. Very fitting, he thought. Fat Tuesday is the day before the start of Lent, 40 days of fasting and penitence ending with Easter. Well, well, our groom can let it all hang out the night before.

Matt should have expected all the hoopla accompanying his Guy Party. His circle of close friends was honoring a pledge made just before the first member held a vow-cer: each succeeding guy party must be better than the preceding. Matt was the penultimate bachelor in the group; only Carter remained single, so tonight's party was meant to be special. And so far, it had been. The drinks, buffet, and desserts satisfied all, as did the ladies who catered the affair.

Though he tried to appear nonchalant, Matt's eagerness built as he and his buddies fantasized.

"Whoever chose the Mardi Gras theme is very clever. It's telling me this is my last fling, eh? Well, maybe it's time to reveal what's behind the door. Tell me, what are the ground rules?" Carter glanced at the time before answering.

"I think your Demi-Monde entered the chamber through another door and is awaiting your knock. And the ground rules are a strictly private affair between you and whoever awaits. I suggest you not be like me. Don't ask any more questions. Just do it. Knock on the door."

"Good advice." Matt grinned at his buddies, who were now attentively watching the door, not knowing what might appear but looking forward to an alluring site. They were not disappointed. The door opened slowly, revealing first a tantalizing Mardi Gras ambiance complete with sensual lighting and suggestive music. And then, emerging insouciantly from behind the door came what the fellows were looking for: a long-legged French-braided blonde in black net nylons and stilettos, wearing a black bikini thong and floral lace silk chemise. Her identity was concealed by a mysterious black-feathered Mardi Gras mask. Saying nary a word, she affixed a silver unisex half-face mask to Matt and led him by the hand into her chamber, then closed and locked the door. Not only was she a showstopper, but also a conversation-stopper. Carter finally found something to say.

"From the looks of it, I don't think Matt has to worry what's behind the door or the mask. Come on, let's grab a drink and see what games are on the sports channels playing downstairs. We'll come back when Matt's game is over."

Matt adjusted quickly to his escort's stimulating pantomime. She was evidently an experienced performer, and it was exciting for Matt to follow her lead. She mixed drinks for two, then had him lay on the bed. As she straddled him, unbuttoning his shirt, Matt figured out the game she was playing: arousal without kissing. By the time his shirt was peeled off he could feel the magic of the game and the performance-enhancing drinks. Then she seductively stripped naked for his eyes only, removing everything except the mask, nylons, and stilettos. The drinks disoriented

Matt's cognition and coordination, but not his passion. He watched the girl rise abruptly to douse all but night lights, losing sight of her when she did, then suddenly felt his wrists being bound to the headboard. Awareness of being sexually dominated by a female drove his passion higher, reaching a frenzy when she mounted him after ripping off his pants. His last sensations were those of primal pelvic thrusting before climaxing into ecstasy. Then he plunged into unconsciousness…

By the time Carter and company returned, the chamber door was open and the Demi-Monde gone. The room was as neat as if a maid had just cleaned. Matt was asleep under the covers, his clothes neatly folded, and all empty containers and glasses stacked on a cart. Carter had already considered the outcome now at hand, so when one of the guys asked what they should do, he had a ready answer.

"The vow-cer isn't until tomorrow afternoon, so we'll sleep here until Matt wakes up, then we'll take him home. He's sleeping so peacefully, he must have had a good evening. Good for him. He should be well rested for tomorrow. Gentlemen, I think our Guy Party exceeded all expectations."

Holy Shit! I climaxed before Matt. And I'm glad he passed out. It made my exit that much easier. And I've got all the samples I need. I'm 13 days into my cycle, so the odds are good I'll get pregnant from the sample he planted tonight. I'll know for sure in about two weeks. And if I'm not, I'll use a sample from the condom I poked holes in. According to the Austin Fertility Clinic, it'll keep in the cryo-container until I deliver it tomorrow. Now I return the car and fly back home pronto. Mission accomplished…

Robin was well on her way for obtaining her obsessive possession— her very own child. She would have someone to care for, to love, to make her feel needed. Someone that would depend on her care and not die or fade away.

Having Matt's child was her first choice. She knew his DNA would be superior to what she might find in a donor bank or dating pool, neither of which she trusted. Tonight she put the missing piece in place for the life she wants to lead. And she'd leave a voice message for Electra, saying she couldn't make the wedding because of commitments in Austin.

And it's sort of the truth. I'm committed to making sure I have a backup pregnancy plan that I'm keeping on ice.

Alisha liked the retro wedding dresses and tuxedos selected by Zoe for her right-sized vow-cer. A fitting description would be the bride's beautiful and ecstatic, the groom's handsome and calm. And thanks to Carter's connections, the ceremony and reception held at his country club pleased everyone.

Alisha paced herself by nibbling on hors d'oeuvres, preferring to indulge in desserts, drinks, and dancing later. And she shared the closeness of the moment.

"Vow-cers are more personal, more relaxed, and flexible than previous generations' wedding celebrations. Zoe and Matt look so happy. And as their friends say, they are well matched." Electra added a comment.

"Yes, they make a great team. And Zoe can use the Marriage Contract if planned versus actual comparisons call for adjustments." Alisha kidded back.
"Hey, lighten up. Have another drink before we leave."

Before leaving to catch a late evening flight to Austin, Alisha recited a fitting poem for Matt and Zoe's ears only.

"My mother wrote poetry that was never published, and I found wedding verses I thought fit you and Matt. I'm giving you a framed copy of The Riddle of the Sphinx. Let me read it:

'Together you have found a prize,
That singly wouldn't be there.
A conjoint path to future days,
For the life you now will share.
Poets past to the current day,
Have tried to unravel love.
Grasping for things to help explain,
What's inside to Gods above.
But it matters not what the Poet says,
Nor what the Pundit thinks,

> The essence of love escapes the pen,
> It's the Riddle of the Sphinx.
> It matters only the two of you,
> The thoughts and feelings you share.
> Let the World keep spinning merrily,
> There is nothing else to compare.
> Blessings and Wishes from Family and Friends,
> Sun shining today as your journey begins.'

"I think the words speak the truth for your relationship."

Zoe said, "Yes, and I know just where we'll put this. I'm happy you stayed the entire week. Too bad Robin couldn't make it. You say something came up in Austin? I hope she's OK."

"I imagine she is. She's pretty stable now, and her eldercare business has reenergized her. Before I leave, can you tell me if you and Matt are taking a vow-cer holiday?"

"Yes, a Caribbean snorkeling cruise mid-January. We invited Carter and Hannah to join us,but the dates don't work. When will you visit Washington again?"

"In January, but you might be on your cruise. But I'll probably be back in February or March, so you can tell me then how you like snorkeling. Just make sure you don't snorkel with the sharks…"

Electra was happy to spend Christmas alone this year in Austin, relieved that all her friends were taken care of. Matt, Zoe, and Carter would be with the Conklins; Su and Kameyo would be in Tokyo with her parents; Hud was taking his children skiing; Tim was with his parents and Kwame was visiting Silicon Valley "hacker girls" he met in Cyberspace. And Electra was particularly happy that Robin was now immersed in eldercare. She was a different person than even six months ago: happy, focused, independent, and booked solid for the holidays at senior centers and nursing homes.

All this gave Electra the green light to spend the remainder of December focused completely on next year's schedules for all her projects, many with heightened urgency caused by an imminent

Iron Triangle threat. By the time she completed preliminary PERT/ CPM diagrams, project planning software flagged a recurring problem that grew each year. I'm doing too much. Maybe I'm doing stuff I shouldn't. I don't have enough resources to get my projects completed. I'll have to push back completion dates, even on some of the top priority ones. Or I'll have to suspend projects until I have the people to get the tasks completed. All this troubled her usually ebullient outlook, so she decided to take a break and give Alisha free rein until the day after Christmas, when Electra would get back to work.

Alisha made the most of the week before Christmas. Shopping at malls and fashion clothing Websites, she started accumulating a spring wardrobe better suited to her slimmed-down physique. Her vanity and lighter training regimen dropped the ten pounds of well-placed muscle she had needed for her triumphant Co-NFL comeback. And she went clubbing with teammates and fans. She even spent a day with her singular teammate, Toni Diya, who lives in Dallas. Postmodern America embraces most sexual relations if kept within suitable limits, so Alisha didn't need to hide her bisexuality from those who were building her media-generated emerging celebrity status. Maybe I'll cultivate male relationships when I'm in Hollywood.

But I can be satisfied without testosterone.

By the time Christmas Eve came, Alisha was happy to let her alter ego take center stage. Electra puttered around Cyberspace in the morning, then prepared in the afternoon her traditional Christmas Eve dinner: baked beans and Swedish meatballs, salad, and corn muffins, topped with a dessert of plum pudding and hard sauce. After dinner, she curled up on the living room sofa to watch live telecasts of whatever Christmas concerts caught her fancy. She shifted among several, alternately shifting her attention from the music to problems that were playing in her mind. She marveled at a musician's ability to shift into another state when performing, becoming a different person, as if the instrument and music were an extension of themselves. That's why Hollywood likes Alisha. She shifts into another state and becomes the part she's playing. And that's one of the extraordinary abilities of the lightning brain: it can shift into altered states whenever the need arises.

That thought carried her into additional musings about the mind. The mind and the brain are one and the same. And every state is simply what emerges from the interaction of trillions of neuronal connections. Even death is a brain state that shuts down all neural activity. A sudden shudder rippled through. If I were in dire straits with no way out, could I will myself to die? Or could the lightning brain decide for me it's time to go?

Electra had studied thanatology—the study of death—in neuroscience classes. Death has always been a theme of poets, priests, and philosophers, but science is increasingly making it possible to examine what lies behind the end of life. Just as the brain cannot remember pain vividly, neuroscientists believe it refuses to comprehend its own death and will shut down beforehand. The coma that often precedes death could be nature's ultimate anesthetic. And though not generally talked about, people sometimes have tried willing themselves to die. When confronted by helplessness and hopelessness, they merely stop fighting and let go. And some cultures pride themselves in mind control. Buddhist monks are known for this, but only anecdotal evidence supports the claim, for the dead cannot talk from the grave.

The lightning brain knew its prime directive—to go on living— and could do that better than any. It had brought Electra back from the brink numerous times: from a helicopter crash, from strangulation and suffocation, from mortal mutant virus combat. The shudder died away, and Electra returned to the music. Drowsiness caught up with her by ten o'clock, so she grabbed a couple of pillows, wrapped herself in blankets, and fell into a fitful sleep on the sofa.

"Electra, Electra, please awaken." A pleasant voice called her name in the early morning hours of Christmas Day. Electra bolted upright in the darkness of her living room, instantly recognizing the voice and the glowing white-robed shimmering apparition sitting across from her: Indira her mother, her inner voice and muse, visiting in a dream state more vivid than reality. She stared in awe, awaiting Indira's commands.

"My precious daughter, your lightning brain has conjured my dream visitation tonight because I can help you rediscover thoughts buried within that elude your efforts to find. And let me first congratulate you and your alter ego. The two of you are superior even to Plato's winged horses. So, my visit tonight is not for you to change direction, but to provide a forum for you to find what you are looking for." Electra stared mutely, absorbing every syllable.

"Because of the lightning brain's extraordinary cognition, you have known since childhood more about reality than any mere mortal ever knew. You have understood what foundation principles would guide your odyssey, so you have never needed a conversion epiphany that great men of the past have often chronicled. I see from your puzzled look that you need me to clarify what I mean, so I shall illustrate using what some literary scholars claim to be the greatest of the great books: Confessions of Saint Augustine.

"He wrote it at the age of 40 to describe how his sins and dissatisfactions with his life led him to convert to Christianity. And let me point out that all saints were sinners when alive. By the way, as a young man Augustine did more than just dabble in the carnal pleasures.

"His book is a masterpiece, beautifully written and articulates wisdom to those of faith. But I must give you fair warning. When reading such works, beware of the Explosion Principle." Electra's puzzlement grew. Indira smiled patiently and continued.

"The Explosion Principle is a logical rule of inference stating anything can be proved if you start with false assumptions. Saint Augustine arrives at his philosophy from his set of assumptions about the Universe, just as you arrive at yours from a different set. His are based on faith and revelation, yours on fact and neuroscience. And both resulting philosophies share much wisdom for how people should behave.

"So, my visit tonight is meant to assure that your odyssey is good, and to point the way for solving the problems facing you. Yes, you will need to suspend or delegate tasks to others because you lack the resources you need. But longer term, look within to find what you need.

"My daughter, I have spoken enough. It is time for me to leave." For the first time since Indira's apparition appeared, Electra knew what to say.

"Mother! Don't leave me! I don't know where to look! I don't know how to solve your riddle!"

"Yes, you do. Think back to those events that changed your life, and you will find words already spoken. The words and the solution are within." Electra blinked, and when she opened her eyes, the soothing, smiling apparition faded away, like a floating afterglow image painted by the retina into the brain. She fell back, sinking into a dreamless sleep.

Electra suited up first thing for her traditional Christmas Day run, hoping the magic of endorphins would allow her freewheeling brain to uncover what Indira said could be found. As she ran her brain skipped in no particular order through life-changing events. She reached her turnaround, slowed to reverse course and then accelerated to shift into one of her longer-distance running gears. And just then, the words she was searching for leaped into cognition, stopping her dead in her tracks. They were the words Zoe had spoken when Electra hovered near death, struck down by the mutant T-Plague virus:

"How can someone so strong and
Smart be brought so low by something so small?
She's my best friend now, and
I can't lose her.
If only I could clone her and keep her with me forever..."

There it is! Zoe's plaintive cry contains the answer to Indira's riddle! I must clone myself! Why couldn't I remember this before?

I guess there were bigger obstacles to overcome, like coming back to life.

But now I know, and I will find a way on my odyssey.

Enthusiasm and optimism surged within, filling her with joy for this moment, for recalling lost words, for just being alive. As she regained the rhythm of her run, she knew the lightning brain's prime directive would empower her towards all she wanted to do. Her determination was captured in one of the most famous poems, acclaiming the will to live, Dylan Thomas's celebrated Do not go Gentle into that Good Night:

> "Do not go gentle into that good night,
> Old age should burn and rave at close of day;
> Rage, rage against the dying of the light.
> Though wise men at their end know dark is right,
> Because their words had forked no lightning they
> Do not go gentle into that good night.
> Good men, the last wave by, crying how bright
> Their frail deeds might have danced in a green bay,
> Rage, rage against the dying of the light.
> Wild men who caught and sang the sun in flight,
> And learn, too late, they grieved it on its way,
> Do not go gentle into that good night.
> Grave men, near death, who see with blinding sight
> Blind eyes could blaze like meteors and be gay,
> Rage, rage against the dying of the light.
> And you, my father, there on the sad height,
> Curse, bless, me now with your fierce tears, I pray.
> Do not go gentle into that good night.
> Rage, rage against the dying of the light."

And I shall not rage! I shall fight to do what I know I should. What I know is right. Electra raced home to develop a new plan, one that she alone would control.

At that moment on the other side of the world, Gui Hou might be raging with delight, for his Cyberspace snooping had revealed his serendipity. Su-Lin Song Chou and her Japanese partner are in Japan! They are almost within striking distance. Almost within my grasp. Next year shall witness my revenge. I shall cleverly use my resources to make it so. And I shall not stop until then, no matter the cost.

512

Chapter 32
January 2126

"Call to Arms"
Thread 3 Chapter 10

10...9...8... BOMBS AWAY! ZIARMAL silently completed the countdown to midnight New Year's Eve DC time, then pressed his cursor to launch one prong of the Cyberspace terrorist attack on selected American East Coast sites. He was certain Sergei and Chen were doing the same to complete their part in the first larger-scale Iron Triangle coordinated strike that would leave targeted sectors of "the Great Satan" speechless, motionless, and in the dark. Ziarmal would cripple a handful of U.S. government network sites; his partners would take down counterparts in banking, power generation, and transportation. It was time to sit back and savor the moment, then start monitoring the disruption, after which he'd communicate with his partners to assess overall damage. Ten minutes later, most of the damage he detected was his own.

That's odd. Most of my target Websites are still operating. And what a strange coincidence: my stealth weapons network crashed. I don't know why and I have to get it working before I can launch more weapons.

Electra didn't think it was a strange coincidence because she had caused it. Most of her defensive planning worked perfectly, for she had kept busy much of December infiltrating Iron Triangle's Cyberweapon launch sites, replacing activated target address with that of weapon source. She had also installed tools on targets that would intercept incoming malware, awaiting her commands to delete.

Electra's "killer" apps let her play the most advanced "war game" ever conducted in Cyberspace. Kwame's graphical user interface added 3-D reality; displayed on the monitors were life-like animations of enemy missiles or torpedoes being destroyed by interactive soldiers or vehicles following her commands. She would defuse and store enough of the intercepted weapons so she could reverse-engineer them later; the rest she would destroy or redirect back to their launch sites.

This was the first actual large-scale test of defensive capabilities; it was not a simulation, and Electra's avatar app recorded glitches from which she would have to make corrections. White House communications networks stayed up, while New York and Baltimore air traffic control networks recovered in only 10 minutes, as did electric grids in New England, although the Philadelphia Federal Reserve Bank's funds transfer system took an hour. Not a bad first performance, but I better debug my interceptor software. I'll listen to Cyberspace chatter to learn what people on all sides are saying. Angus and Jared should get an earful from their people today. I'll find out from Carter what response they'll need to make.

Ziarmal wrapped up the Iron Triangle debriefing session by midafternoon. All partners shared similar outcomes: only a handful of targets knocked out, weapons launch networks crashed. Ziarmel speculated there must be a shared software glitch somewhere among three interconnected components that must be debugged: Chen's launch, Sergei's triggering, and Ziarmal's network infiltration software.

"It is also possible our adversaries have installed a new generation of firewall and network protection software that is attack-resistant. I must contact Darla, for she is the security guru we count on to keep our offensive weapons ahead of defensive countermeasures. I will report back what she says. In the meantime, please debug for what might have caused glitches."

Darla was expecting Ziarmal to contact her after he and his partners had assessed the outcome. Though she had pirated all their software and could construct and launch missiles or torpedoes independently, any debugging they could do would put her that much further ahead. She listened intently to Ziarmal's summary before replying curtly.

"No company I know of is marketing better security software than Cybergard, and our latest release is designed to allow Iron Triangle weapons to penetrate. I'm attending the annual Cyberspace Network Expo next month in Las Vegas, and I'll have my security team snoop online and in person before and during the Expo. Maybe we'll uncover something I've overlooked. I'll report back after the Expo. In the meantime, you three must keep debugging." Darla was grinning when she disconnected the call. *Not only can I build and fire weapons whenever I want, when mine get through and cripple targets, Ziarmal might think the damage was caused by IT's duds finally detonating. How nice for me to sit below everyone's radar. If the U.S. retaliates and the Iron Triangle fires back, I'll pretend to be on the sidelines watching, even though I might have triggered the exchange. This is gonna get real interesting.*

Media for the next two days hyped an unconfirmed Cyberterror attack, though only Electra knew the low level of disruption would have been much worse had she not intervened. Air travel was hardest hit because many people were traveling home from the Holiday break. Electric grid outages were less of a bother because of New England's mild temperatures, but news analysts did their best to hype the alarm, even fabricating fake stories. Government officials countered with "no comment" regarding modest banking system glitches, which suggested to pundits that there might actually be a terrorist link because the government seemed evasive.

Through it all, Electra kept what she knew to herself, and kept working to improve what she had. *I'll have to call Carter by Friday if he doesn't call me first. I've been doing my part, giving Carter enough clues so it looks like the Government is on top of Cyberterrorism. And when it gets to the point Angus can't do without my software, I'll let Hud sell to the CIA a dummied down version.*

After talking with Electra, Carter drilled down deep into facts and surveys to assess economic, political and public opinion impacts resulting from the spate of network outages and was ready by Thursday afternoon to report damage and response recommendations to Angus. He skimmed his notes while walking to the meeting room.

Angus needs to walk a fine line. The public wants us to act and the U.N. wants us to wait. We need to send a message to the bad guys that contains more than harsh language. And we have to satisfy Jared's blood lust without chopping off an enemy's head. I think I've got a middle ground staked out. Carter walked Angus and a select group of military advisors through a half-hour slide show, then summarized his recommendations.

"Here's the balancing act I recommend. The news stories have stirred up public hatred against any person or country attempting terrorism. If we don't do something to show we're tough, Jared's popularity will take a hit. Has the CIA come up with tangible evidence the outages are linked with whatever this Iron Triangle is?" One of the security advisors answered.

"No, but thanks to the rumors you uncovered, at least we're tapping into incriminating chatter. We're working hard to upgrade snooping and security software." Carter nodded, then continued.

"OK. We have to retaliate, but we must balance it against the wait and see UN policy. And we don't want to provoke another attack until we have our battle plans nailed down for both offense and defense. So, here's my recommendation. We cripple Russia by taking down its Central Bank computer system, and we use smart bombs to shut down their largest shipping port and pipeline facility supplying Italy. Since Russia is still a raw materials export economy, this one-two punch will hurt. We won't go after China or Isilabad, but attacking Russia serves notice, just like bombing North Korea did. You should be able to get Jared to buy in to all this." Angus wiped his glasses, glanced around the table, then replied.

"I still have more damage control to do for the North Korea bombing. I'll have to piggyback on it what we do to Russia, but I see where this is likely to go. I think Jared will like it. I have to see him later this afternoon, so if there are no final comments or questions, meeting adjourned."

Jared had no choice other than to buy what Angus recommended, but Angus detected his customer was dissatisfied. "I'm tired of waiting for middle ground action to gain traction. I'll hype it if you and your Team of Rivals don't start delivering more. This is the last time I'll listen, so go back and get the results I want." After Angus left, Jared gloated to himself.

If Klatterbuck delivers on her promise made yesterday, I can soon ditch the Team of Rivals. She says she's closing in on my blackmailer, thanks to the list I gave her. And the two security agents I gave her can be trusted to get the job done, no questions asked. She told me I'll get the blackmailer's head on a platter by the end of the month, and I'll hold her to it. If I don't get it, it'll be her head that gets the axe."

The public was pleased, the reporters and news analysts were puzzled, and the UN was stunned by a Sunday morning White House press release announcing a successful strike against Russia in retaliation for their part in what is now confirmed: New Year's Day network outages were caused by a Cyberterror attack. Additional details would be released soon.

The news didn't surprise Electra; it merely confirmed that Carter had run to Angus with her suggestions. Although Angus is smart enough to keep actions and reactions from spiraling out of control, I'll need to monitor Cyberspace chatter closely the next couple of weeks. And I'll keep the Iron Triangle in my crosshairs.

Electra also kept busy making travel plans. She'd be in Washington the following week for National Governors Association meetings, then fly afterwards to Las Vegas for a hi-tech expo Tim and Kwame wanted her to attend with them. And then she'd be off to Hollywood to confirm her movie role and start filming the next season of the Superman series.

Though DC weather had turned wintry, Monday air travel was back to normal so the flight was uneventful. She didn't bother Carter for a ride home because she arrived while he was working.

They would have dinner at home that evening. (Carter continued house-sitting duty.) She spent most of her time that week at NGA offices, splitting work between Texas political issues and Cyberspace snooping. She learned nothing new about the Iron Triangle, other than its reluctance to launch another attack until the UN calmed down the United States. It also wanted to find an explanation for what went wrong on the previous attack.

Electra came across alarming information while snooping into Jared's Cyberspace world. He had been swapping communications with a person unknown until Electra deciphered the proxy that revealed the name: Debbie Klatterbuck. Debbie claimed to be hot on the trail of Jared's blackmailer, and if this were true Electra would be in jeopardy, so she burrowed into Debbie's Cyberspace world to dig up all she could and came up with nothing that would connect to herself.

Debbie's a dangerous person. I'll add her cellphone number to my GPS tracking system so I can follow her. If she gets close, I'll be prepared. Electra returned to calmer activities after confirming the number could tracked, and by Friday evening, Alisha was ready to play. Just before leaving to go dancing, she called Zoe.

Zoe and Matt's cruise had been pushed back a month because their cruise ship needed to be decontaminated. A third of the passengers on the ship's last cruise had contracted a new strain of Norovirus, some of whose symptoms resembled the T-Plague. Health-guard regulations mandated the next cruise be delayed until an "all clean" certification was issued.

"So, Matt and Carter are playing tennis Saturday afternoon, then going to a Co-NBA game that evening. Would you like to go out for dinner tomorrow?... No? That's OK, I understand. If you feel you're catching a cold, it's better to stay home. I'll call sometime after you come back from next month's cruise. Enjoy the snorkeling."

Electra returned to action Saturday morning, working from home and dedicating all attention to setting up the cloning project. Top priority was enumerating all tasks, then developing task list timeline and resources needed.

This project will take me into a brave new and uncharted world. I'll need a separate lab to handle this. And I better not set it up in the United States. There's too much blowback to cloning research. I'll expand the Japanese lab. This is going to be big, so I might need to let Su assist. I better put the plan in action next month when I get back from Hollywood.

The list of reasons to avoid being tracked while traveling—especially for international travel—kept growing. It was time for Electra to reach out to Trevor Jarvis, Simon's freelancing soldier of fortune who ran "A-Teams." She would call him from encrypted communications lines as soon as she returned to Austin.

Carter fixed a light lunch he shared before leaving to pick up Matt.

"Are you in the Electra or Alisha state of mind?"

"I've finished today's allotment of project work, so call me Alisha."

"I won't be back until late. What are you doing the rest of today?"

"I'm going to pack for tomorrow's Austin flight. And I think I'll go to a sensual pleasures café tonight. So, don't worry if I'm not home when you get back."

Alisha spent a leisurely afternoon, first packing, then playing on social media Websites, contacting newfound fans and friends made thanks to her spreading celebrity status. Alisha's public image was as multi-dimensional as it was spotless. She didn't gloat about being a popular role model for male or female youth, or for young professional women. Nor did she seek praise for her support of alternate lifestyle communities. The public considered her closer to main street than to avant-garde. I do like being popular. It plays to my vanity and does make me feel good. But I try not to be swayed. Besides, I'm being honest. I present myself as I am, not pretending to be what I'm not. And if I like fashion wear, it's because I like to look good, not because I'm pretending for someone else. It's the people's choice to make me a role model if they like what I am. But they'll never know all that I am. What they don't know won't hurt them. And what they don't know usually tries to help them. But I'll never trust letting anyone know about the lightning brain. If they did know, that might hurt me.

By early evening Alisha was ready to change into something stylish that would look good at a sensual pleasures café. On a whim, she used a GPS app to plot cellphone locations for Carter, Matt, and Zoe. Carter and Matt overlapped while Zoe was at a distance. Then she added herself to the map. The separations were consistent. Let's plot Debbie's cell location and see if it's stationary or moving. Alisha watched for a minute; detecting no motion, she shifted to reading text messages. Twenty minutes later, before changing clothes, she checked cellphone locations again. This time, Debbie's location had advanced toward Zoe. The lightning brain instantly shifted to a higher state of readiness that brought Electra to the fore, and as she watched, she witnessed Debbie inexorably closing in on Zoe.

This is like a scene out of the retro sci-fi movie series: "Alien." The captain's hunting the alien. The crew is tracking his progress. Suddenly, another dot appears on the tracking monitor. It's the alien closing in on the captain. I've got to warn Zoe!" There was no answer when she called. Zoe must have gone to bed early and turned off her cell. I have to go there now.

If she were living in DC permanently, Electra's car would already be loaded with covert ops emergency gear, but she wasn't and the car contained no equipment or weapons. The lightning brain shifted to another gear. Change into all-black running suit, cap, and gloves. Put all my luggage in the car and bolt to Zoe's.

A hint of snow was in the chilled air that overcast night, but light traffic made the drive quick. Electra tracked locations as she drove at breakneck speed; Debbie would arrive only slightly before, but this would force Electra to park at a distance. She knew the neighborhood well enough, so she parked, then ran like the wind to do whatever was necessary to fend off Debbie.

Perched in the passenger seat, Debbie was about to issue orders. One of her covert security agents was driving, the other in the back seat. They were the new generation of covert agents: trim and light, agile and bright. Much different from the hulking brutes of bygone years who today were dinosaurs.

"The target is home alone. If she tells us what we want to hear, we'll let her be. But if she plays dumb, you guys will convince her to answer my questions. And if all that fails, I'll drug her again and we'll take her with us. Let me do the talking. I'll let you know when to apply force."

Electra, a black shadow in the darkness, paused outside the front door to survey the situation. Lights out. Car in the driveway next to the side door must belong to the bad guys. I gotta devise my plan of attack. Electra felt a calming thrill as she shifted to an altered state, physical and cognitive personas fully merged, ready to strike.

Debbie's gonna be in charge of one or two agents. They'll probably drag Zoe out of bed and into the living or family room. My only weapon is the element of surprise. Maybe I can grab one of theirs. I'll take out the agents in whatever order makes it quick. Then I'll chat with Debbie. This is gonna get bad.

Suddenly, Electra's calming thrill morphed into rage. Her emotional persona merged with the other two, unleashing her Creature from the Id. All three personas were totally focused on the mission. The Creature gloried in its prime directive: do all it must to survive, to thrive. Conclude with extreme prejudice.

The black shadow darted noiselessly into the unlighted house, looking or listening for directions. Light from one family room lamp was all Electra needed. As she crept forward, she head Zoe struggling to free herself while hissing in Debbie's grinning face.

"Stop hurting me! I don't know what you're talking about. Why would I blackmail Jared Gardner? I know nothing."

"OK boys. Stretch her out on the carpet. Maybe my needle will get her to tell the truth." As they knelt, one grabbing arms and the other grabbing legs, both pulled back, turning Zoe into a stationary target. Debbie filled a syringe with truth serum while she watched her associates take turns slapping Zoe.

That look of terror is a real turn-on. Maybe we'll do more slapping later if we need to wake her up. But it's time to put it to her. Debbie plunged the needle into a bulging vein inside Zoe's elbow; several seconds later Zoe jerked twice, then became motionless.

Electra attacked swiftly, silently. She grabbed with both hands the hair of the closest agent, snapping his head back and breaking his neck. The second fellow's training jolted him to action. He sprang forward into Electra, but she countered with a Judo flip throw, kicking him high into the air and over her head. Fortune evened the odds. He crashed headfirst onto and then through a glass coffee table, jagged fragments severing both carotid arteries. Blood spurted madly, gushing onto the carpet. Electra leaped to her feet and tackled Debbie. The battle was over before she could do anything other than gape at the unknown creature sitting astride.

"Answer my questions if you want to live! Where are the car keys?" Debbie stammered an answer.

"I-in the pockets of the guy you flipped." "What did you inject?"

"Thiopental sodium." "Where's the bottle?"

"In my bag." The bag was within reach, so Electra grabbed it and found what she was looking for. She had all she needed and asked no more questions. She filled the syringe, stuck the needle into Debbie, and repeated the process two more times. The overdose would be fatal.

The lightning brain shifted to a lower gear as the Creature from the Id submerged into the subliminal, and Electra's cognitive persona regained control. She rose slowly to assess the mess: Zoe comatose, three dead, and a pool of blood beneath the smashed coffee table. Get with it, soldier! This is not a drill! Put an exit plan together and go. In a flash, the plan materialized.

Electra checked Zoe, whose pulse and breathing indicated no life-threatening overdose. Best for me to let her lie. I'm not moving her or calling the police. She might still be out when Matt comes home. One way or another, she'll have to explain what she might not remember.

Electra cleared a path to the car, then opened its rear door that was close to the stairs. Darkness would conceal her dragging the bodies out of the house and into the rear seat. Before doing so, she removed wallets, I.D.s and cell phones. Once again, fortune favored her; the bodies were compact and light enough for her to handle. She had to tie a towel around the neck of the fellow she had flipped, and then place a large plastic bag over his head to avoid leaving a trail of dripped blood, but she loaded the car in less than 15 minutes. Only a pool of blood beneath the shattered table needed to be removed.

Electra used a couple of towels to soak it up but needed to disguise the stain, so she searched the kitchen cabinets for anything red. For the third time in short succession, fortune favored her. She found two bottles of spaghetti sauce whose contents she dumped over the large blot on the carpet, then arranged the empty bottles to look like an accidental spill. When Zoe comes to, she'll have to come up with some sort of explanation for Matt. This is the best I can do. Now, I gotta dump the bodies somewhere.

Electra became motionless, coolly surveying the scene while talking to herself. I'm glad Zoe didn't see me in action. Several years ago, Carter witnessed a similar performance and it frightened him. He couldn't handle my killer instincts. And it's true; I become my Creature from the Id, fully aware of what must be done to survive. Now I have three bodies and two cars to dispose of. And only one me. Hmm…There's an easy solution.

I'll drive Debbie's car to a nearby mall that has a sensual pleasures cafe, then run back to my Mustang so I can drive then park it next to Debbie's. Then I'll load my stuffinto Debbie's car, drive away, and figure out what's next. It's 10:10. Carter's GPS dot will be heading here soon.

By 10:45, Electra was cruising in a car containing bodies she needed to dump. She recalled a similar predicament and suddenly knew what might work.

Green marketing, sustainability, and recycling are all part of the 22nd century economy. There are round-the-clock recycling plants usually located in remote areas that handle scrap material. Last time I found one to crush a car; this time I need one that disposes of tires. Electra used her cellphone to surf the Web for an industrial tire recycling plant.

When I get there, I'll pretend my husband and I have an auto supply business, and we need to recycle a bunch of tires. I'll tell the operator that tonight I'm checking out the facility. And then, I'll sneak each body into a tire big enough to hold it.

The plan worked to perfection. Electra parked next to the tire stacks, then found the on-duty attendant. He bought her story and was happy to show her how the plant works.

"We keep the tires stacked next to automated conveyor belts: one for cars, one for trucks, and one for big industrial vehicles. Once tires are on the belt, we don't touch'em again. And I've already loaded the next set on the belts. I'll feed'em into the grinder after I shut down the scrap metal line. When you and your husband are ready, just drive in and we'll take care of you. I gotta get back to scrap metal now, so you can drive out on your own."

"Thank you so much for your help. I know the way." The attendant left, and Electra quickly stuffed three bodies into appropriately sized tires, then drove away. It was now 1:30 Sunday morning, and though she was running low on energy, she was not yet done. To complete her plan, there was only one task sequence remaining, and it was the easiest: drive to the airport, park the car in long-term parking, remove any fingerprints, and then sleep on a couch until flight time. I'll email Carter tomorrow, explaining I spent the night with a friend who drove me to the airport. And I'll ask him to retrieve my Mustang. He has a set of keys. As Grandfather would say, "Thank you, Jeezus!" And I'll add, "Thank you, lightning brain."

Matt went directly to the family room after coming home so he could turn off the lamp, but it was the sight, not the light, that stunned him. Zoe was asleep on the floor. Did she faint? And how did the table get smashed? After flipping on all lights, Matt finally roused a groggy and disoriented Zoe.

"Hey, what happened?" Zoe sat up, gripping Matt for support.

"I—I'm not sure. My head hurts. Help me up." As they stood next to the coffee table, Matt was the first to speak.

"Do you know how the table got broke? Or how the spaghetti sauce got spilled?"

"I haven't a clue."

"OK, let's get you to bed. Then I'll clean up the mess down here."

The lightning brain shifted to a normal state so Electra could rest during the flight to Austin, which proved to be uneventful. Rested and ready, she caught a ride home, able to assess how she had performed last night.

I never question my decisions when the lightning brain shifts into states I can't control. Last night was another example that I have no need ever to doubt my actions. I had to eliminate the threat so there'd be no follow-up, no trail. I terminated the bad guys and have no remorse. And what about Zoe? I chose the right option in the "truth versus loyalty" ethical dilemma. If I had called the police, reporting a break-in, Zoe would be a suspect in whatever the cops would drum up. No, it was better that I vanished without a trace left behind.

Electra called Carter before she unpacked, leaving a voice message explaining why and where to retrieve her car. Then she put her belongings away, suited up, and went out to run. Afterwards, she took a hot soaking shower, changed into appropriate leisure wear, and cooked a substantial bacon and eggs mid-afternoon brunch, complete with English muffins. Then she was ready to call Trevor. It would be almost midnight London time, but he had told her to call anytime. We'll see if I can take him at his word. He was awake, for he answered on the second ring.

"This is Electra Kittner, calling on a secure line. Is now a good time to talk?"

"Yes, it is, and I remember who you are. I assume you need my services. Please describe what you need and when..."Electra rattled off what she needed. Ten minutes later Trevor summarized the deal.

"I'll email you the cellphone number and Email address you can use to contact your team. We'll use the codename you want: Gemini. When you call, please confirm precise pickup and delivery addresses along with delivery date, time, and what resources you'll want. We will then give you an account number where you must transfer half our fee. Once we receive it, our service begins. We have your cellphone and Internet address. Can you think of any questions for us?" She couldn't, so she thanked him and Trevor disconnected.

Electra had only one task remaining before she let Alisha take over. She sent an encrypted Email to Jared.

Jared had been fuming all day Sunday. Even his morning spiritual session couldn't calm him down, no doubt because Debbie Klatterbuck had not yet reported back. She and the two agents he assigned to her were the only ones who knew what she was tracking. By evening, he knew something was amiss, and when he read a terse Monday evening Email, he knew the worst outcome had just arrived.

"Hello Jared. Debbie and your two agents retired last night. If you ever try tracking me again, you will end up behind bars. Whatever political actions you take better be sanctioned by Angus, or you are history. This is your last warning. I am watching and listening to you."

Jared sat in chilled silence, unable to think of how to deal with the situation until finally his devious mind unfroze. My blackmailer just won another round, so I'll have to take the recommendations Angus makes. I'll do so until I can think of another way to get the blackmailer off my back. And if these Emails are my spiritual channel, I gotta get a better connection.

Chapter 33
February 2126

"The Dutiful Daughters"
Thread 3 Chapter 11

THE MONTH OF FEBRUARY flew by, starting with a trip to Las Vegas where Electra attended a Cyberspace Expo, accompanied by Tim and Kwame. She warned them to be tight-lipped about what they were working on, and made Tim promise to keep Kwame in tow. She liked Kwame and the work he did, but was concerned he might be too gullible when chatting with his hacker friends. Although she told neither, Electra installed safeguards to control their hardware and software just in case they inadvertently shared too much.

She took another trip, this time destined for a week-long stay in Hollywood. As the plane soared early Monday morning through untroubled skies, Electra dived into Cyberspace, using uninterrupted flight time to piece together Winona Kota's picture. Electra had built innumerable "hacker apps" that could ferret out hidden data inaccessible even to cutting-edge developers. Many of her apps could hack in both directions. (Given a person's name, they could uncover associated phone numbers, and given a phone number or address, they could report associated persons or corporations.) And to make hacking even easier, she had packaged her apps into a "Hacker Suite" containing an Avatar-equipped VR-GUI that would report back after searching Big Data as well as proprietary and hidden directories. Two hours after launching the search, Electra recited a summary to herself.

Winona Kota, a Native American who grew up on the Osage Nation reservation in Oklahoma, is alive and living in an LA suburb. According to Harvard student records, she and Indira roomed together on campus for two years, then off campus for the next two until they graduated. Winona is two years older and earned an MS in graphic arts and cinematography, while Indira earned a BS in biotechnology.

According to her resume, Winona made a career of it in Hollywood, but according to IRS and Medicaid/Healthguard records, she has been unemployed for the past five years because of T-Plague. She's never been married and has one child, a daughter named Carley, born in 2097, who shares the same address and phone number. Carley never graduated from college and works as a freelance artist. Electra stopped reading the summary, instead looking at photos and reading between the lines.

Winona's photo looks awful. I'll bet Carley dropped out of school to be her caregiver. She and I are the same age, and her Native American features decorating an ectomorphic frame make her look like a younger sister. No need to research further. I know enough for the first contact as soon as Alisha concludes business.

Coming to the fore as the plane touched down, Alisha met at baggage claim the limo driver who loaded her luggage and whisked her to a mid-afternoon meeting arranged by Kathi Lauret, her de facto mentor.

Kathi introduced the Mission Impossible movie series director. Auditions would start tomorrow, having been delayed a month because of January scheduling conflicts. Tyger Riddley could not promise Alisha would win the audition, but he and Kathi exuded confidence.

"I am very impressed with your ability to vanish into the roles you play. And when we add your stunt scene ability, you'll be must-see at the box office. But we don't want you to get injured, so we may use a stunt person to double for any scene that makes you uncomfortable. Vincent shares a similar sentiment for your Superman series." Alisha added her comments.

"Advances in virtual reality have made animated stunt scenes almost as lifelike as those using actors and stand-ins. But according to surveys, moviegoers want to see real people in the action scenes because it heightens the sense of danger. And so far, none of my action scenes have been uncomfortable, even those including sex." Kathi picked up Alisha's whimsical humor before Tyger.

"Yes, your scenes have implied, rather explicit romance, because of your character's image. That may evolve as Mission Impossible unfolds, and we may want other sponsors for you. Tyger, why don't you talk to us?"

"Image is everything for advertising, sports, entertainment, politics, you name it. It turns you into a brand, and you are an evolving brand. Your current image includes downhome virtue, intelligence, open and straight-talking, all wrapped in a sexy swagger. That worked for the Co-NFL, which catapulted you to Hollywood, but we'd like to change it to sophisticated and intelligent virtue, cosmopolitan honesty in relationships, youthful yet elegant sexuality. Do you like it?"
"I do. Kathi, do you agree?"

"Yes, and I know how we can juggle sponsors. We can keep Ford Mustang, but we'll drop Indian Motorcycles and Patagonia Sportswear. I'll line up replacements that handle designer fashions and upscale spirits. Tyger, why don't you tell us the week's schedule?"

"Tomorrow and Wednesday you'll be with me for auditioning. Thursday and Friday you'll be with Vince. And Friday evening, Kathi and I will take you to a studio celebrity cocktail party. You can mingle with wannabe, rising, shining, and falling stars. You can take your pick, but always remember to protect your image. And Kathi will pick you up for dinner tonight at 7:30."

The week exceeded even Alisha's great expectations. As Tyger predicted, she was a natural for Mission Impossible and judged audition winner. She connected with the rest of the cast, and reconnected with those acting in Supergirl. And the celebrity cocktail party whetted her appetite for more. What a great pool of talent and possible partners, male and female. And like Kathi says, I'll stay in the shallow end until I learn all the strokes. This should be a wonderful spring."

Alisha's return flight left Sunday morning, which left Saturday open for first Winona Kota contact. Calling after an early morning run, Alisha replied to a youngish voice that said hello.

"Am I speaking to Winona Kota?" There was a measured pause before a factual answer.

"No, you are speaking to her caregiver, Carley. I am her daughter. May I help you?"

"Perhaps, but only if your mother remembers a person from thirty years ago. Did she ever mention the name Indira Ramanujan?" Another measured pause before a reply.

"Please wait." Carley returned to the phone five minutes later. "Are you Indira?"

"No, I am her daughter, Alisha Kittner."

"I'll come right back." This time Carley came back a minute later.

"Mother asks if you could visit. Do you have our address?"

"I have unit 22 at the University Village Apartments complex located at 801 E. Alosta, near Azusa Pacific University on Foothill Boulevard in Azusa. I can bring pizza and soft drinks if you and your mother would like to have lunch. What time would work for you?"

"I will have mother ready by one o'clock. She likes pizza as much as I. And if you don't mind a recommendation, Artist Pizza near Badillo and Covina is her favorite. Price is OK and it's close by."

Alisha's limo driver knew the area and was happy to serve as tour guide.

"You can tell by the green vegetation dotting the foothills that LA's rainy season has replaced most of summer and autumn's dry pattern. And it's clear enough today to see the snow-capped peak of Mount Baldy." Alisha always enjoyed playing a tourist role, learning more about people and places.

"How tall is it?"

"Its twin peaks stand at 10,000 feet and are the highest in the San Gabriel Mountains, which form the northern boundary of the Los Angeles basin. Mount Wilson Observatory is to the west, and the San Gabriel Valley and its Angelo National Forest are to the east. The forest is called the land of a thousand uses, and it has scenic drives into the valley, leading from Pasadena or Glendora."

"I learned that Azusa Pacific University is a top Christian college carrying an enrollment of seven thousand. It scores high in all categories except for 'Party Scene,' for which it earns a C-minus." The driver chuckled as he stopped for Alisha to exit.

"A C-minus Party Scene score in LA would be an A anywhere else. And the same goes for this apartment complex. Though it's not upscale, it's well maintained. Remember to call an hour before you want to be picked up."

The clear late-morning air carried a spicy fragrance that enhanced a warming sun and made her walk on the path towards ground-level unit 22 a pleasant stroll. When she tapped the knocker, Carley answered promptly.

"If I didn't know your name, I would have called you Indira. Mother and I viewed pictures after you called, and you look like your mother. Please come in. Mother is waiting in our living room. She is thinking more clearly today." Winona sat in a wheelchair. Alisha couldn't tell much from her unsmiling expression, so she waited for Carley to make introductions.

"Mother, this is the lady who called yesterday, Alisha Kittner, Indira's daughter." Winona leaned forward squinting before stuttering a question.

"You haven't aged. Ah-are you dead?"

"No, Mother. This is Indira's daughter." Before taking the pizza boxes to the kitchen, Carley explained what would be best.

"Mother, I'll have Alisha sit across from you, and I'll talk for both of us." When she returned, Carley gave a succinct summary.

"Winona and Indy roomed together until Mother graduated and came to Los Angeles. She took summer intern positions at Hollywood studios for two years before graduation, and your mother spent two summers working in intern positions as well, Winona in graphic arts and Indira in screenwriting. They roomed together during those two summers." Carley paused for Alisha to talk.

"This is all new to me. Indira died during childbirth. My father and his friends never knew Indy before she went to graduate school."

"Our mothers corresponded occasionally until Winona found out why her last couple of letters weren't answered. According to obituaries she found online, Indira died while giving birth to—I assume—you. Although Winona tried contacting a Jason Kittner— and I guess he's your father—he never returned calls or letters."

"Jason and his father raised me. Doc Kittner became my omniparent, but Jason never handled emotions very well. That's why he never answered. Could you tell me more about Indira's college years and her relationship with Winona?" Carley spoke slowly while looking at Winona.

"I am going to tell Alisha some of the stories I learned from you..." Carley spoke for the next 45 minutes until Winona interrupted.

"I want lunch. You go; Indira stays."

"It is not Indira. It is her daughter, Alisha. But yes, let's take you to the kitchen so we can eat." Alisha steered the wheelchair so Carley could lead the way. Alisha helped set the table after parking Winona on its far side. Carley spoke quietly to Alisha as they served pizza and soft drinks.

"Please tell mother about yourself, and what you can about Indira's life after the last summer she was in Hollywood. That was the last time they were together. And after that, I'll put Mother to bed. She's getting tired." Alisha wrapped up an edited summary 30 minutes later.

"And so, Indira and her best friends worked together until she died. And I didn't open the last letter Winona wrote until about a month ago." There was a welcome pause until Winona spoke first to Carley and then Alisha.

"I'm tired. Put me to bed. You go. Indira stays. Please give me a hug." The ladies did as Winona wished. Carley whispered to Alisha before wheeling Winona away.

"I'll be back in about twenty minutes. Please wait here for me." Alisha used the break to nibble on another piece of pizza while piecing together what she had heard.

Carley has her hands full. Good that Carley and I dummied down our stories. Winona would have become upset trying to follow more details. Her senility has become Alzheimer's. My R-Vac won't help her, but maybe I can help Carley. When Carley returned, she plopped herself on a kitchen chair and was about to speak, but Alisha did so first.

"I should have brought something stronger than Coca-Cola. I know what it's like being a caregiver, and you are a poster child for all the dutiful daughters. You're shouldering the responsibility while dealing with your mother's altered personality. What social services help?" Carley smiled faintly while opening another Coke.

"Health-guard's Golden Years Program would like to help Mother into her grave, but she's not suffering so I won't consider it. LA County offers support groups and subbing services, but it's difficult to coordinate because our local family numbers only two. And I think we're doing OK. I pick temp assignments whose hours don't interfere, and I can do work at home."

"I would agree. You keep the apartment and Winona spotless. I would imagine that makes her happy."

"Thanks to your coming, Mother is happier today. She used to have a very nice disposition, but as her Alzheimer's advances, she's getting more quarrelsome. Sometimes she swears and hits me. I feel bad that I have to fight the urge to yell at her."

"I think you should feel good about yourself, not bad. You're doing a wonderful job. When push comes to shove, most people push their parents into senior centers, which, even today, are nothing more than better-decorated nursing homes. And it's therapeutic for you to share your feelings. Every caregiver gets angry. But remember, it's not what you say or feel inside; it's what you do that defines you."

"Thanks for reminding me. And thanks for telling Mother your story. You and I both made them simpler."

"We did, and I think there's more to Winona and Indy than you let on. Would you tell me more?"

"I will, if you will do likewise…" Alisha and Carley talked for two hours, stopping near the end only long enough to park Winona in front of a living room TV. An hour later, they finished the pizza and Alisha prepared to leave.

"Would you please call us when you come back to Hollywood? There's much more we can talk about, and I'd like us to become friends."

"I'd like that too. And it's OK for your Mom to call me Indira." Winona continued staring and muttering at the TV as Carley walked Alisha to the front door. A tiny tear creased the corner of one eye as she smiled bravely.

"Thank you for coming. Your visit has helped me as much as Mother." Alisha gently wiped away Carley's tear before hugging her goodbye."

"You are a precious daughter. Please remember that until we meet again."

"Alisha didn't need to speak to Electra during the limo ride back to the hotel, instead simply compared herself to Carley. I was a dutiful daughter, just like Carley is, but my caregiver role was so much easier. Doc's mind and personality stayed youthful to the day he was killed, and he never needed a wheelchair. How would I have responded if fate had dealt me what it handed out to Carley? Alisha felt a calming certainty ping inside her brain. I would have done exactly what I did. I gave in full measure all the love Doc gave to me. And I will do it again if unconditional love ever returns. Alisha put any remaining thoughts away while the lightning brain shifted to neutral.

She awoke early Sunday to run before packing and departing for using the plane's solitude after take-off as background for chatting with Electra, who spoke first.

"Well, please tell me what you pieced together about Winona and
Indira."

"Poor Winona has had a bitch of a life. Her native ability gave her a good start, as did her friendship with Indira. I don't know if she was bisexual before coming to Hollywood, but being raped at her boss's party must have soured her attitude toward men. It's too bad Indy didn't accompany her that ill-fated night. And it's too bad she wouldn't let Indy take her to an emergency room when she came home." Alisha paused for Electra to talk.

"According to what Carley told you, Indira headed for graduate school a couple of days later, and Winona's boss stopped abusing her. Evidently, he committed suicide by leaping from his high-rise condo balcony not long after the party. Is it possible Indira had a hand in heaving him over? Four years earlier, she did something similar when helping her best friend Bhakti deal with a rapist. But you know that story."

"I do, but neither of us knew Indira had a Hollywood almost friend. When Indira departed, he hooked up with Winona, getting her pregnant about the same time Jason or Adom did the same for Indy. But his and Winona's Hollywood careers roller-coastered, and they never married. I think that's part of the reason why Winona resents Carley. Winona struggled as best she could, raising her daughter, but the T-Plague put her out of a job and Carley out of college five years ago. So, what should we plan to do?" Electra announced intentions.

"We've just scratched Carley's surface, so we should get to know her better. Although there's little we can do for Winona, a Carley relationship will be good for Carley and for us. And we might learn more about Indira by tracking Carley's father if he's alive or if she'll tell us about him." Alisha agreed but knew it was time to shift subjects.

Why don't we save all that for when we're in Hollywood? We're about to land, and it's time you take the lead on all those projects near and dear to your heart."

Alisha had the right idea but the wrong organ because Electra's favorite projects were those closer to her brain. For the next three days, she outlined projects for integrating cloning and artificial intelligence, taking them beyond the borders of transhumanism—a theory that the human race can use technology to evolve beyond its physical and mental limitations. I know that danger and excitement await those bold enough to enter this controversial realm where no mere mortal has gone before. If I can clone my dream team, the future is limitless. But I can't get there without help. Su and I must equip the Japanese lab for cloning. Kameyo can be part of the team if I can trust her. My first trip to Japan should answer any number of questions.

Electra took a timeout for Alisha to arrange a mid-March combo speaking engagement covering West Texas economic development and high school programs. Then she made plans for the next Washington NGA meeting, dovetailing these latest trips to avoid Hollywood schedule conflicts.

As Friday evening approached, the Electra-Alisha duo compared progress made that week. Electra spoke first.

"Congratulations. You did a marvelous job scheduling trips and talks. When we return to Austin, I'll finalize any last-minute details for traveling to Japan. And I expect your plans to unfold seamlessly because you've learned so well from me."

"And congratulations to you as well. You excel in the cerebral realm, but you are better than ever at dealing with emotions and feelings. When we watched the retro Star Trek's Observer Effect episode, you compared yourself to the Organians, a super-intelligent race of non-corporal beings that had evolved into a pure thought form of life. But your ever-expanding empathy is teaching you humanity's defining hallmark: the ability to force multiply emotions through the power of relationships to carry out the prime directive. We are meant to survive, to go on living. You'll be in charge of our trip to Japan. Please make sure we carry out our prime directive." Electra agreed.

Chapter 34
April 2126

"The Closing Circle"
Thread 3 Chapter 12

"DARLA! WHAT HAVE YOU done? Your midnight March 1 attack is madness that could boomerang and destroy us all. Why didn't you follow my orders?" Darla replied to Ziarmal as any skilled negotiator would when forced to play defense: she attacked.

"The last time we talked, you agreed to follow my orders! I told you I found nothing at the Las Vegas Expo to indicate anyone's leapfrogging my security software. One of my surveillance agents reported a vague rumor that one company might be pushing the envelope but had nothing commercial yet. The three of you have not found any glitches, so maybe what happened on your New Year's Eve launch is an unexplainable coincidence, and I think my launch confirms it. I brought down all intended target networks. If the Iron Triangle can't handle its part, I'll go my own way. You need me more than I need you."

"You're provoking the Great Satan, and there's no telling how he might respond this time. Look at the additional damage inflicted on our Russian partner." Of course, Darla wouldn't say so to Ziarmal, but she really didn't care if Jared punished Isilabad or China. And anyway, she was ready to go her own way. She could build and fire state-of-the-art weapons to frighten unsuspecting customers so they'd buy Cybergard software. And she was confident her people could reverse-engineer any new Iron Triangle weapons because she had already pirated their algorithms.

"Ziarmal, this conversation is over. You know what to do. Report back to me when you figure out your glitches." Ziarmal wanted to scream, but there was no one who would hear, for Darla was no longer listening.

Darla's attack surprised everyone, even Electra, who had never uncovered even a hint that Cybergard could make and launch weapons. But it took her only a day to figure out what happened because she intercepted communications among the Iron Triangle partners that told the full story, and she planted fake data linking Russia to the banking system attack. Media news blasted Russia, as did Jared's bombs. Darla must have stolen Iron Triangle software, so she no longer needs them. I don't think she needs to launch more missiles or torpedoes anytime soon. Cybergard now has the undivided attention of its customers.

Electra had already decided she would tell Carter she knew nothing about who's behind the latest attack, because she needed Angus to focus on the Iron Triangle, not Cybergard. She was deliberately entering into a murky world of international politics by deliberately manipulating Angus to confront Isilabad, and since public sentiment would demand swift retaliation, the United States must act quickly. Electra had just answered her ethical dilemma. Is it OK for me to deliberately lie if it provokes an action that must be taken? You bet it is. It's time to call Isilabad's bluff. It's time for East and West to start a dialogue so they can come to some middle ground both sides can live with.

As expected, Carter called a day later but was disappointed Electra didn't know a thing.

"It's too bad your contacts don't know who's behind the attack, but my guess is it can only be the Iron Triangle trying to intimidate us so we'll back off. But I don't think we can back off. Opinion surveys tell me the public wants action now. What do you think we should do?"

"I'd let Jared have his way on this. He has to come across as a strong, decisive leader making decisions that keep the other side off balance. The UN has to cave on this, and just make sure Jared picks only one opponent to attack. Russia is already on the sidelines, so it's between Isilabad and China. Angus will ask for your opinion.

Which would you choose?"

"Isilabad's my choice. They've been a festering problem for too long. We don't want to damage China's economy. It's too big a piece globally, so Isilabad is it. Then the question becomes what weapons to use and how soon to attack. What do you think?"

"If I pretend to be an economist and use utilitarian ethics, the choice of weapon is obvious. Use smart bombs to destroy oil exporting facilities. Use T-Plague dispersal systems on a couple of major cities, including Isilabad, the capitol. Do you agree?"

"I do, and I'll explain my reasoning to Angus. Look, if you hear anything about who pulled the trigger, please let me know. And I'll call you when I hear about our retaliation. By the way, I think you better confirm your DC meetings are still on. It's likely they've been pushed back because of all the commotion. Let's keep in touch. We can help each other."

Subsequent polls and pundit comments surprised both Electra and Carter. Yes, the public wanted revenge, but people were beginning to give Jared credit for unpredictable timing and severity of responses. There was a growing consensus his so-called toying with the enemy increased angst and instability among its leaders and citizens. One analyst boldly proclaimed Jared could win the battle without firing a shot. So much the better if it avoided T-Plague dispersal because its collateral damage always took a nasty toll.

Electra was pleased that her DC meetings had been postponed because it gave her additional time to plan her first trip to Japan, some of which she used to learn about Japanese geography and history. After surfing the Web to construct a bullet point list of relevant information, she summarized it to herself.

Japan is actually an archipelago 2000 miles from China and spanning nearly 1500 miles. The four main islands, from north to south, are Hokkaido, Honshu, Shikoku, and Kyushu. Tokyo is situated on Honshu, the largest and referred to as the Japanese mainland.

Populated in prehistoric times by small clans ruling small areas, these tiny kingdoms eventually unified under the control of an Emperor, whose power was usurped over centuries by samurai warrior military clans. The real power rested in the Shogun, the commander in chief of all the warlords. Civil strife lasted well into the 16th century when once again Japan was unified and controlled by a Shogun. Shogun rule lasted until the 1868 Admiral Perry Expedition ended Japan's seclusion and forced the Meiji Restoration that brought the Emperor back to power. Japan's 130 million population is 98 percent Japanese ethnicity, and 90 percent practice either Buddhism or its ethnic Shinto religion, interpreted to mean the way of the gods.

I have a good idea what to expect, and I'll add this virtual reconnoitering to what I already know about Japan: it's cultural heritage frowns on outsiders or diversity. Good for us that Su and Kimeyo fit right in. And though xenophobia still clouds trade relations, its government knows diplomacy and its economy welcomes America's technology.

Electra snooped Cyberspace for additional Iron Triangle insights. On a whim, she tracked any activity connected to Kameyo or Su. Kameyo's looked normal for a young professional, but Su's presented a puzzle. Who is Gui Hou, and why is he stalking Su? I better check him out so I know what I'm talking about when I tell her. And that'll be soon. FedEx picks me up next week. And it's good not even Su knows I'm visiting. My presence will be invisible to Gui Hou, should he be snooping.

Electra confirmed all details by contacting two days before pick-up the number Trevor had given her. An articulate British-accented female handled the call.

"Please use codename Gemini for all contact activity. FedEx has numerous flights to and from Tokyo because Tokyo Metropolitan Central Wholesale Market is the largest fish and seafood market in the world. Distance from Memphis is 6500 miles and flight time is fourteen hours. Sometimes we have to pack our clients, but we will disguise you as one of the crew. Once you arrive, our contact will take you to our staging area. You are requesting a van, a SIG Sauer 9 mm semi-automatic pistol and an extra 15 round clip, two throwing knives, a military grade laser bazooka, and a SWAT uniform equipped with compass, night vision goggles, and a team communications device. Have you thought of anything else?"

"Yes. I need you to plot van route and ETA to Fukushima. Have you done that yet?"

"Yes. Air travel distance is 149 miles, but we'll have you take a coastal route. Easier to follow, fewer people, and easier for chopper support should you need it. Estimated drive time is four to five hours. And remember, Tokyo is 15 hours ahead of Memphis.

Anything else you wish to know?"

"No thank you. I'll be ready for pickup as planned. And please call me if conditions change. I'll do likewise."

Normally cerebral and calm, even Electra felt growing excitement as the hours to departure counted down. And as she had hoped for, pickup and delivery went according to plan. She noted how well trained all support personnel were. They were prompt and professional, breezing her around security checks and avoiding idle conversation. They did not want to know more than the bare minimum. Electra didn't need any additional coaching from Alisha regarding how to act on the flight. She would simply look smart, stay awake, and say as few words as possible. All that was easy; she used the flight time for project work via tablet uplink to her computer systems as well as for learning about Tokyo. This was the first time she would attempt intercontinental logon to her upgraded networks, and she was relieved that her advanced access recognition systems worked remotely.

The ride from the airport to the staging area provided a glimpse into Tokyo's teeming milieu. The city covers 800 square miles, holding 17 million people, making it the most populous city on Earth—21 thousand per square mile. So many people and cars bustling about on such narrow roads crisscrossing a landscape filled with buildings lined up cheek by jowl. No wonder their culture values harmony and cooperation. There's no other choice when you're living that close.

The Japanese handler who greeted her at the staging area ushered her into a small but well-equipped conference room.

"Hello Ms. Kittner, codename Gemini. My name is Gemini H-2 or handler number two for the two-way Gemini pickup and delivery assignment. Would you like to freshen up and have something to eat before we proceed?" That sounds good to me. I can see why the Japanese culture is noted for its civility.

"Yes, thank you. I'll unpack a change of clothes." When she returned, H-2 had set out a typical Japanese breakfast that included hot tea, rice porridge, and a rolled omelet. They ate in comfortable silence at an unhurried pace; when both were finished, H-2 gave her an envelope before describing what was in store.

"Let me start by giving you all necessary documents you'll need. Try not to be stopped by the police, but if you are, these should cover you. And always call the number we gave you if you encounter something you can't handle. Your van is automatic shift and equipped as specified: GPS and tracking device installed, laser bazooka in the back. We will teach you how to fire it. And remember, in Japan you drive on the left. So far, any questions?" So far so good, so he continued.

"Your FedEx cargo plane landed at Tokyo Narita Airport, and you are now at a staging area in the city of Tsuchiura, 50 miles northeast of Tokyo, well beyond all the congestion. We have programmed your van's GPS to take a coastal route. So, if there are no questions, allow me to introduce your four-person team. H-2 returned, leading a procession of two male-female pairs attired in SWAT-like uniforms.

"Ms. Kittner Gemini, allow me to introduce Gemini T-1, 2, 3, 4. T-1 and T-2 are your team assigned to a support vehicle, T-3 and T-4 are assigned to a support helicopter. They are for backup, should the need arise, and will be positioned for rapid extraction." All were trim, fit, and taller than an average Japanese. Smiles were exchanged, but no words yet. H-2 glanced at his cellphone.

"I think it is time for T-1 and T-2 to take you to your van. They will train you for using your equipment, answer any final questions, then guide you to the coastal route. From there, follow the programmed GPS route to your destination. Distance is approximately 180 miles. Allow four to five hours driving. If you deviate from the route, use the map in the van. And as requested, here is five thousand American dollars denominated in yen, or 600 thousand yen. I wish you success." H-2 rose, bowed quickly then left, followed by T-3 and T-4. T-1 and T-2 escorted Electra to the van.

T-1 gave Electra a military grade communicator, showing her how to contact her team directly if the need arose. Then he showed her how to operate the van and its accessories. She already knew how to use the other equipment—SIG Sauer, night vision goggles, and the rest. She would change into a SWAT uniform only when a situation called for it. The last set of instructions came from T-2. She would demonstrate how to charge then fire the military grade laser bazooka.

"Ms. Kittner Gemini, I would like you to fire the laser bazooka. Electromagnetic radiation does carry momentum, but you will experience almost no recoil when you shoot. And you must wear a firing helmet to avoid retinal damage. Please put on the helmet, aim at the metal plate, and fire when ready. Electra followed orders, sending a blinding stream of lightning-like energy onto the plate. The effect was like that of welding torch blasting through metal. T-2 was satisfied.

"Not difficult at all. The van's engine charges the bazooka's power supply, so you can hold the beam on a target for 15 seconds before it powers down to recharge. That is ample time to disable whatever you are shooting at. Now, make one final inspection of the van and your equipment and ask any final questions." Electra spent another ten minutes reviewing all she had and all she had learned. I'm ready
to roll.

"I have no further questions. You Ts are excellent teachers. Thank you." The Ts smiled, then gave final instructions.

"Please follow our van to the coastal road. We will point you to the entrance, and then you will proceed north to Fukushima. And call us immediately when you reach your final destination so we know all is well. We want you to call us at six a.m. every morning so we know all is in order." Electra followed as directed, and by ten a.m. she was on her own.

But Electra was never alone. With her always was her inner voice, her muse Indira, speaking from the shadow whenever appropriate.

Alter ego Alisha was there also, chatting and switching places whenever a more empathetic, emotional touch was needed. This morning Electra was on duty, fully engaged in the moment while the lightning brain freewheeled in the solitude of its self-contained fortress of solitude.

The day's weather was typical for Tokyo's subtropical climate, making for a pleasant drive along the coast, bordered with stretches of light forest interspersed among gently rolling meadows and occasional clusters of old buildings. A random thought popped up: What an odd twist of fate. I am coming full circle. At birth, a lightning bolt electrocuted my mother, nearly killing me. At twenty-one, a lightning bolt brought down my escape helicopter, nearly killing me. And now, thanks to my laser bazooka, I am able to shoot lightning bolts, if needed, to save myself. The thought left as quickly as it came, and Electra drove on in a relaxed state of mind.

Electra had packed Coke and Oreo cookies, so there was no reason to stop for a snack, but she did for a pit stop and stretch break, which stretched drive time to five hours for reaching the cut-off road that would take her to the lab. She topped off the gas tank, noting that the surrounding area, though sparsely inhabited, appeared to be coming back to life after decades of abandonment. Then she followed the road and GPS directions. The one-story freestanding lab came into view precisely as indicated, matching the pictures Kameyo had posted. She parked alongside a two bay garage whose light gage aluminum doors were closed, then walked the perimeter of both windowless buildings before ringing the bell next to the locked front door. If no one's home I'll let myself in. I have my own set of keys for both front and back doors, and the garage too. But she didn't need to; a surprised Kameyo let her in.

"Electra, this is a surprise! How nice to see you. Please come in."

"I arrived Tokyo this morning and drove along the coast. Goodness, what a bustling city you grew up in. I'd love to sightsee, but only if you do the driving. Anyway, how are you and Su?"

"Doing well, thank you. What would you like to do? Su should be back from our manufacturing facility by five o'clock. She and one of our technicians are delivering to the manufacturing facility several batches of proto-vaccine concentrate we produce here."

"I would like to park my van in the garage and then bring in my stuff. Will it be OK if I stay in the quiet room instead of a hotel? I can sleep on the sofa.

"Of course. I do that occasionally, and I am sure you will find it satisfactory. Let me show you where it is."

Per Su's design, the lab's quiet room served as a study or sleeping area, and it was right where the architectural drawings had it. After that, Kameyo led a thorough inspection tour, after which Electra parked the van in the garage and brought in everything she would need. Finally, she placed a call to her support team and would do so every morning. Su arrived soon after Electra ended the call.

"Electra! You continue your enigmatic ways. You never told us you would visit. It is good to see you in person instead of online. Is everything OK?"

"Yes, but I need to talk to you and Kameyo about a new project we'll run from this location. I'll sleep in the quiet room for a couple of days, then go back to Austin."

"Very good. Are you hungry? We can go out for dinner."

"Why don't we order in? I want to keep a low profile, and I'll have more time to explain everything." Kameyo ordered dinner and then came to the conference room. Electra wasted no time bringing two subjects to the table.

"The lab setup looks good for what we originally designed, and I assume you prepare all concentrate in the cleanroom, but shouldn't that be done at the manufacturing facility?"

"Yes, but Kameyo and I do so here when needed to keep up with production. The expansion of our plant's cleanroom should be completed next month."

"Good. And after I explain the new project, you and Kameyo will need to decide where you want to add additional equipment. Let me describe what I have in mind. It will take us into the world of cloning." Electra sketched her intentions before, during, and after dinner. Two hours later, she asked for Su to comment.

"I read the journals, but I am not a cloning subject matter expert. What you are suggesting is beyond cutting-edge. Frankly, I don't think I'm smart enough or have the energy to take us to the next level. But Kameyo is young and bright. Let's ask her."

"I have worked for you and Su for five years. In that time, I have come to know both of you, how you work, and what you expect. I believe I can accomplish what you are asking for. You will teach me and I will help Su understand what we must know, and we will implement what needs to be done. I would be honored to work on this project." Kameyo had nailed what Electra had in mind, so she segued to the second topic.

"I am pleased with your assessment. If Su agrees, we will make you the project leader, and before I leave I will scope out starting details for you." Su smiled as she spoke.

"Indeed yes. You are giving Kameyo an opportunity that could last for the rest of her professional career. The ramifications are unlimited."

"Now let me bring up something else. Please do not be offended, but I routinely do security checks on all of us for our own protection. Lately, I have detected someone who could be a concern: a person who appears to be stalking Su in Cyberspace. Does the name Gui Hou mean anything to either of you?" Kameyo's expression revealed the name meant nothing, but not even Su's practiced calm and reserved demeanor could hide a look of horror. She was searching for words to say and finally whispered her reply.

"Yes, he is my illegitimate son." Now it was Electra's turn to be nonplussed, but Kameyo had the presence of mind to make a reply.

"Perhaps this is a topic for you and Electra to discuss." She was about to leave when Su grabbed her arm.

"No, please stay. You and Electra are my best friends. Both of you should hear my story." Su took a deep breath to compose herself, then proceeded.

"Gui Hou's father was my piano teacher when I was an adolescent. I fell in love with him when I was sixteen. He did not seduce me. I willingly encouraged him. Though he was fifteen years older than I and married, his desire for me was as strong as mine for him. I became pregnant, a terrible shame for my family and his. My mother had recently converted to Catholicism and refused my pleas for an abortion. I gave birth to an illegitimate son I did not want. His father named him, but I turned my back and walked away. That is why I came to America: to hide my family's shame. I never returned to China nor visited my parents even when they moved to London. After all these years, I cannot imagine why he is interested in me. Is there anything in what you have found that might explain why?"

"No. All Emails concerning you are to or from shadowy persons that may be affiliated with drug trafficking or illegal activities. From what I gather, he has hired them to bring you to meet him when he visits Japan. No dates given, but the last email is from last week and it sounded like his visit is immanent. I've been unable to connect any of the names to phone numbers. Have you noticed anything that would suggest you're under surveillance?" Silent negative nods and puzzled looks answered Electra's question, so she pushed ahead.

"Let's play safe. We'll temporarily suspend working here. The two of you will leave for Austin with me day after tomorrow. So, call your lab techs tonight explaining they don't need to come in tomorrow. Have them keep the production facility operating. Tell them you'll contact them again when you want them back in the lab. Tomorrow, I'll work with the two of you to make the last batches of protovaccine concentrate virus, then I'll arrange for our departure. Do you want to stay in the lab tonight?" Kameyo deferred to Su's judgment.

"Perhaps you're reading too much into this. A trip back to Austin makes sense for additional reasons, so we'll go with you. But I think Kameyo and I will be safe for one more night in our apartment.
Kameyo, do you agree?"

"Yes, and we can pack what we need before turning off all the lights." The strain of the day was wearing on all three, so it was time for Electra to end the evening.

"I think we should get some rest so we're fresh for tomorrow. I'll sleep here, and I need you to be back by seven. We'll need as much time as possible to make the last batches and then close the lab."

Electra spent the next hour mentally preparing tomorrow's to-do list while sifting through all that Su had revealed.

Amazing. Indira hid secrets from Su and vice versa. I never would have guessed Su's succumbing to hormones while so young. Maybe that lifechanging episode colored her entire approach to intimacy. Maybe both partners in a relationship never really know one another because they're afraid of telling or learning the truth. I'll have to postpone our cloning project discussion. Well, I'll sleep on all this and let the lightning brain guide me tomorrow.

If Electra had known all the facts behind Gui Hou's Emails, she and her partners would have started running for cover immediately because his "enforcers" were meeting him at Tokyo International Airport that very evening. Gui's plan was as simple as his desire for revenge was strong; grab Su so he can meet her privately; extract his revenge so she would never forget, even if it were her last meeting ever. The enforcers—underlings of a local Yakuza gang, the oldest Japanese crime syndicate—knew where she would be to make the plan a reality. After all these years, Mother will finally pay for the wrongs done to my family and myself. How could she walk away from her first son? Her actions placed a permanent stain on my family and myself.

Electra had no faith in extra sensory perception or parapsychology, but if she did she would have paid close attention to the dreadful anxiety that greeted her when awakening at 6 a.m. Normally she would bound out of bed, seizing the day by charging through her task list. Each item completed would elevate her mood from its characteristically optimistic starting point. But it wasn't that way today. She had to kick-start herself into a better state of mind.

She began by unpacking her SWAT team uniform, loading all weapons into appropriate pockets and hooking a flash light onto its belt. And she added another item to a mental list of lab shortcomings. It'll be pitch black in here if there's a power outage. There are no windows. And even with the lights on, the doors all look alike. It's easy to get disoriented. Each should be clearly marked.

Electra then called in a change of plan to her support team. There would be three people returning tomorrow to the staging area. After completing the call, she went to work, preparing to mix proto-vaccine batches. She carefully placed on the staging area table all remaining two-liter sealed glass jars that held a deadly liquid suspension of the mutated virus. Next, she carried one of them to the hooded and vent-filtered mixing area and carefully poured the contents into the small aluminum holding tank that would meter it under pressure as they made the proto-vaccine concentrate. Finally, she powered up the equipment, pressurized the tank and adjusted all settings. She would commence the first batch run as soon as Su and Kameyo arrive.

Electra was satisfied she still had a lab tech's touch, but wasn't pleased with the cleanroom. Whoever designed our cleanroom made a lot of mistakes. The staging area is too close to the door and too far from the hooded area. The door opens into the room, and there are no windows, so you can't see what's going on in here from out there. I'll ask Su if they tested the containment breach alarm. And I need to find out where the fail-safe switch is.

Suddenly, a blaring intrusion horn sounded, causing the lightning brain to shift into a higher gear. Someone is breaking in! She raced to the back door and found it intact, so she reversed course and ran to the front entrance. The horn stopped blaring just before she spotted the intruder. Su was punching a deactivation code into the security system controller.

"I'm so sorry. I forgot to deactivate the alarm, but I managed to punch in the reset code before a signal went to the security company."

"Not a problem. I've been up for two hours so I really didn't need a wake-up call, but now we know the alarm works. I've prepped the equipment for our first batch run. Come on into the cleanroom and I'll show you." Su was impressed.

"You've made all the right settings. We'll start as soon as Kameyo comes in. And I'll load another holding tank so we can prep another batch run." Su carefully picked up a jar and turned to carry it to the hooded area. And then she collided with the door Kameyo had just swung open. The impact knocked the jar from her hands and it exploded into a shower of glass and liquid when hitting the floor. All three were doused with active mutant T-Plague virus. The worst fear of any lab technician had just come to life: containment breach. The cleanroom was instantly contaminated.

No one panicked or said a word because they knew the contingency procedure. It would have been easier if they were wearing protective suits but they weren't, so they did the next best thing. They stripped off all clothes, then dashed out of the cleanroom, slamming the door and racing to the shower, where they scrubbed as thoroughly as possible, toweled off, and then sat in stunned silence on metal folding chairs. And then the containment breach siren started wailing, prompting gallows humor Electra could always find.

"Well, at least we know the siren works. But there must be a better way to test it. Where's the all clear switch?" Her partners began to stir; Electra's ironic words had cut through their mental fog; Su provided the answer.

"Next to the fail-safe panel on the wall in the cleanroom. They're on either side of the fire extinguisher." Su blinked as soon as she realized the irony in her words. "Not a good location for turning it off, is it?" Electra couldn't suppress a snicker.

"It's good for getting another exposure. I'll turn it off before scrubbing again." All were trying to think of what to do next; Electra was the first to speak.

"We've got a slow-moving train wreck on our hands, and we need to get out of the way before it rolls over us. Here's what we better do. For starters, we'll get dressed. We have to assume all of us have been exposed and might get sick. So, we have to gather what we need so we can first determine if we're sick, and if we are, we must have what we need for treatment. Su, what do we need to test ourselves?"

"Observe for symptoms, take temperatures, and test saliva for traces of the virus. I know where we keep thermometers and test strips." Electra turned to Kameyo.

"If we get sick, what's the treatment?"

"Start taking the antidote vaccine as soon as symptoms appear, drink lots of water, and try to rest. Symptoms are headache, nausea, dizziness, chills, and elevated temperature. Depending on how strong your immune system is, symptoms appear two to four hours after exposure. We have lots of antidote caplets. We keep them in the storage area refrigerator for challenge testing."

"Good. I'll retrieve a supply of caplets from the storage area while you two put the lab in shutdown mode. But first, put your suitcases in the conference room and change into uncontaminated clothing. And if needed, we can use the quiet room for sick bay."

Electra changed into yesterday's travel clothes and retrieved caplets before entering the cleanroom, then used towels to cover the spill and broken glass before turning off the siren. The fail-safe panel's light glowed green, which meant the system was disarmed. The light would turn red when armed, and would flash red as a horn-sounds if a contamination breach is detected. Electra would ask Su for the arming code and the countdown limit,

which is the time interval after breach until the cleanroom would self-destruct, incinerating the entire lab along with any and all deadly organisms. The fail-safe system operated on an uninterruptible power supply, guaranteeing
24/7 reliability.

I know of only two instances where fail-safe systems were called into action. Maybe Su or Kameyo knows of more. Whatever the count, we sure don't want to add to it. Electra was about to rejoin her partners when a thought came to mind.

I'm going to conduct a safety and efficacy test by taking antidote caplets immediately. Results will help me know what modifications I might need to make. She did so, then helped her partners.

"Why don't you and Kameyo tell me how to help close the lab. After that's done, I'll put all the suitcases in the van so we can leave ASAP. And if anyone gets really sick, we might have to go to an emergency room instead of the staging area I told you about. We'll have to wait and see. We'll know in four hours who should start taking the antidote vaccine."

Two hours later the lab was secured and the van packed for departure. The only thing left was the hardest: waiting for symptoms to appear. Electra whiled away the time by working on a computer; Su and Kameyo double-checked the shutdown protocol.

Whether it was due to age or a compromised immune system, Su's headache and nausea struck first, followed by dizziness and elevated temperature. Kameyo helped her first to the bathroom and then to bed, administering antidote caplets. There was nothing else for Kameyo to do except test Su's saliva.

"The test strip shows you're contagious, which confirms your symptoms: you've got the T-Plague. Too bad we don't have any SVac to help take care of the symptoms. But the antidote will give some symptomatic relief, just not as much. And we'll know you're out of danger when the fever breaks. Please lie still and rest."

Two hours later, Kameyo joined Su; Electra put her to bed and now had two patients to monitor. I'll keep them hydrated and give them antidote caplets every four hours. And I'll keep taking temperatures. The antidote vaccine did provide symptomatic relief. Su and Kameyo rested comfortably enough, which made Electra's nursing role easier.

I've watched and worked enough on the computer. I'm going to sit here and rest while letting my lightning brain freewheel.

The afternoon ticked by without additional stress. Though it was too soon to know for sure, it appeared that the antidote was working. All symptoms were mild, allowing the patients to sleep intermittently between treatments. By ten that evening, fevers broke, and Kameyo was feeling good enough to watch over Su, who still needed bed rest.

"I'll monitor Su. Why don't you take a break and grab something to eat?" A wave of relief swept over Electra as she headed to the kitchen area, for she and her partners had sidestepped the train wreck. She was about to signal all clear when a sobering thought thudded in her brain. I don't have any symptoms. That's good. But I haven't taken my temperature or used a test strip. I'd better do that now.

Her temperature was normal, but she broke into a cold sweat when she read the test strip. It showed that she was infected. She was contagious. She felt incipient panic, as if she were being pursued by a killer who was closing her circle of safety.

How can this be? I feel fine, and I've been taking the antidote caplets, but I'm spreading the mutant virus. What's going on? This conundrum needed an immediate answer. Electra could feel the lightning brain shift to a higher state of cognition as the answer came in a flash. I survived the last time because the lightning brain mutated my cellular chemistry. All T-Plague viruses are harmless to me now, even when in my body. I have built-in immunity, so my immune system doesn't bother killing them. It ignores them. It's live and let live, and my body wastes no energy. And now, my immune system is so strong it destroys the antidote because it considers all vaccines antigens. I'm in big trouble.

Electra knew that the human body hosts a symbiotic dance among countless viruses and bacteria. The number of internal microbe cells is greater than that of the body's and weighs nearly five pounds. Since some are helpful and the rest harmless, the immune system wastes no energy killing them. It simply ignores them, the worst possible outcome for Electra.

Mother of God! I'm a T-Plague carrier! I'll infect anyone who comes in contact with me. I've got to find a way to kill the virus that's inside of me, or I'll be a 22nd century Typhoid Mary. If Health-guard ever finds out, I'll be put away or euthanized in the name of public safety. If I can't think my way out of this, I'm SOL.

Electra stood, staring vacantly into space, unfamiliar emotions cascading over her: inchoate panic, doubt, dread. The lightning brain froze, not knowing how to handle an uncharted death-dealing crisis. It was completely in the dark. She closed her eyes to descend further into an altered state, but when she opened them, there was nothing but darkness all around. All lights had gone out, as if the power line to the lab had been cut. The dread she felt this morning surged to the forefront. Something was closing in and tightening the circle, but she didn't know what.

The lightning brain surged back to action as quickly as it had frozen, for now it knew what to do. Grab the flashlight and gun. Search for intruders. Electra groped her way to the quiet room, bumping into someone when she entered. She hiss-whispered, "Kameyo, is that you?" "Yes."

"Do you get power failures often?" "No, this is the first I can remember."

"You stay here and don't make a sound. I'll come back after searching for intruders. I gotta get my flashlight first. You stand still until I find it."

Electra felt her way to the table and found it, flicking the switch that instantly cast a beam of light that cut through the blackness. She found her pistol and marched to the door, stopping next to Kameyo for a moment to make sure she was settled.

"Go sit next to Su. I'll come back as soon as I can."

Electra turned off the flashlight before exiting. I'll creep on hands and knees to the front door, searching with hands and ears. I've done this before.

She was following in her brain a picture of the lab layout, moving silently towards the reception area. As she approached, flickers of light danced uncertainly.

Someone's coming this way. I'll hit 'em in the eyes with my flashlight beam as soon as I can. She stood to hide behind a bookcase. The flicker was stronger now; she saw a shadow silhouetted in flickering reflected light; it was time to act.

"Freeze, or I will kill you! Who are you? What are you looking for?" The shadow froze in spacetime…

"Our client's confused thinking is going to get us into trouble. We should have broken in hours ago. We know the two targets are the only ones in there. And here we are now, the two of us sitting in the car simply watching while Gui creeps in through the front entrance without a weapon. Go after him now and help him. And take a gun." The commands galvanized the younger "brother," who nodded, then darted to the entrance.

Electra's flashlight beam temporarily blinded the intruder, so he did as told.

"My name is Gui Hou. I am looking for Su-Lin Song Chou. I am unarmed. Who are you?"

"I am a friend of hers. There has been an accident. The lab is contaminated with T-Plague virus. Get out."

"No! Not until I talk to her." Electra knew what to do. He's unarmed, so I've got the upper hand and will call his bluff. I'll bring him to Su. She approached him slowly, then issued more commands.

"As you wish. I will take you to meet Su. She is in the building. Keep your flashlight on and walk straight ahead. My gun and I will be right behind you. I will tell you where to turn."

Gun and flashlight in hand, the enforcer could hear all that was being said. The fool! Now he's the victim, taking rather than giving orders. Well, I can fix that. I'll shoot first and ask questions later. A second later, he charged past the reception area, screaming "Kakatte koi yo! Bring it on!" and fired away.

When the shooting started, Electra's catlike reflexes were quicker than the enforcer's. She dived to the floor just in time to avoid the bullets, which found Gui instead. He screamed as two bullets crashed into his back, catapulting him forward face down and motionless. Electra scrambled to her feet and fled from her assailant. She plunged through another door just in time to avoid another burst of bullets, but she had picked the wrong door. She was trapped in the clean room. She retreated as far back as she could, standing in front of the hooded area when her assailant charged in and rushed her, but she didn't panic. She fired two bullets into the pressurized virus tank and dived to the floor. The tank exploded, showering the enforcer with shrapnel and virus.

"Agghh!" was all he could scream before tumbling headlong into the remains of the tank and then onto the floor. Electra clubbed him twice with her gun to make sure he stayed there.

Get with it, soldier! This is not a drill! Get your team and get out of here. Cover your tracks! Familiar commands; Electra leaped into action, running to check Gui. The flashlight beam illuminated a garish scene: he was motionless, face down in a pool of blood. Dead. Get your people and go!

Electra dashed to the quiet room. Kameyo had heard gunshots but followed Electra's commands; she never budged.

"Kameyo! Get Su out of bed and follow me to the back door. We've got to get in the van and go." The two of them carried Su and buckled her into the middle bench.

"One more thing to do. I'll be right back!" Electra ran to the cleanroom and activated the failsafe system. The lab would blow up in five minutes. That's plenty of time to get far away. She checked the assailant. She didn't know if he was dead, but if not dead, now would be soon. The T-Plague or blast would kill him. She grabbed what she needed from the quiet room, then sprinted back to the van and pushed the garage door opener, only to realize the garage and lab were connected to the same power line, and when she heaved the manual override lever, its cable snapped. She could not get the door open, but she knew what to do. She calmly climbed into the van and started the engine.

"Kameyo, make sure your seat belt is tight." And then she blasted through the door.

Hidden in the shadows, the car was too far away for its sole occupant to hear muffled gunshots, but the crash of the van through the garage door resonated loud and clear in the remaining enforcer's ears. He gaped at a van swerving onto the street and speeding away, not knowing what to do other than gaze at tail lights fading towards the coastal road.

A second later he gathered himself, instinctively following his warrior group's code of ethics: face adversity, honor commitment, protect your family. He grabbed flashlight and gun and raced into the lab, not knowing what would await.

He ran into the open area just beyond the reception station, nearly tripping over a body. He lifted the head; it was that of the client, Gui Hou, dead.

He yelled, "Haru! Haru! Where are you?" but realized it was futile. A blaring horn was drowning out his shouts. His flashlight beam scoured the walls for doorways, and he dived through the closest one. Beyond it on the floor was Haru, unconscious but alive, so the enforcer struggled mightily to drag the younger man out of the building before whatever the horn was warning occurred. He got as far as the front door when a fiery blast blew him outside, followed by a rush of debris and collapsing walls that buried Haru. Dazed, he picked himself up and tried to clear his head. I must find the van and eliminate all witnesses. The last man standing ran to the car and sped away.

Electra screeched to a stop. "Kameyo! You drive. Follow the GPS course. Go as fast as you can but don't lose control." Electra ran to the back of the van, opened the rear door and jumped in, then yelled, "Drive!"

Electra had what she needed: a laser bazooka and a rearguard firing station from which to blast any pursuer. She had spotted a parked car at a distance from the lab, so she was taking precautions. The laser was charged and ready to fire, so now she would contact her team.

"This is Gemini Kittner calling any Team Gemini. Do you copy? Over." Seconds later, a reply crackled back.

"Gemini Kittner, this is T-1 Gemini. We copy. What are your intentions? Over."

"Three in flight mode heading south on coastal road. Possible pursuit vehicle. Requesting immediate extraction. Over."

"We copy and are tracking you on GPS. Stay on the coastal road. Estimated interception in 45 minutes. Do you copy?"

"Copy that. Over."

Electra's altered state heightened to the excitement of the chase. Her cognitive and emotional personas had merged into one, empowering her to carry out all that was necessary if a chase vehicle appeared. At this early hour, driving through sparsely populated terrain, there was zero traffic, all the better for Kameyo, who was driving as fast as she could.

"Keep driving like you are. My support team is driving towards us. We should rendezvous in 45 minutes. Just stay on the road."

The enforcer guessed correctly where the van would be heading and drove madly to close the ten-minute head start. He could see one pair of taillights far ahead whenever the road straightened enough. He couldn't douse headlights because he was driving too fast; otherwise, he would crash. So, they see my car. So what? I'll slow down. They don't know who is in it. I'll pretend to pass, then run them off the road. Sayonara Jap. Bai Bai La Chink.

Electra scouted the approaching vehicle but detected no telltale danger signs.

"Kameyo, pull off the road to let this car pass." She followed orders; the van was perched on the edge facing a downslope to the Pacific. Electra recognized her fatal error a moment too late. The enforcer accelerated towards the rear of the van. Electra blasted her bazooka through the van's rear window, vaporizing some of the car and driver but it was too late. The van bounced down the steepening slope, burying its nose in a mound and flipping upside down. It careened over rocks and boulders, finally coming to rest nearly a quarter over the ledge of a precipitous drop to the ocean below.

Electra kicked open the rear door and stared at the drop facing her: twenty vertical feet to another steep slope that ended on angry wave-swept rocks.

"Kameyo! Get out of the van!"

"I'm stuck! My seat belt won't let go!" The engine was still running, all lights had popped on, and Electra could smell gasoline. We're trapped inside a bomb!

Electra swung out the rear, dangling into space and grasping the lip of the roof so she could inch herself towards safety. She reached a point where she could swing herself up onto solid ground and heaved with all her might to do so, then sprang to her feet, rushing to help Kameyo, who had finally freed herself. Electra tore open the door to pull her out, then the two of them did the same for Su, dragging her away but didn't get far enough. The van exploded; Electra pushed her partners down to avoid the blast, but she was not quick enough to save herself. A large chunk of door slammed into her, knocking her over the ledge.

She plunged to earth head first, then tumbled forward, faster and faster, toward an ominous, infinite ocean. An image more vivid than the desperate reality now whirling about flashed inside her brain. It was that of the Phoenix, triumphantly soaring skyward in all its glory. And it was accompanied by a final prime directive surging through every neural fiber just before she vanished under the ice-cold waves.

Unvanquished resolve cascaded into the lightning brain:

IT'S NOT MY TIME TO GO! I HAVE MORE TO DO. I SHALL WEATHER THE BLOW. I SHALL BECOME THE PHOENIX!

Storm-tossed waves crash to and fro, obscuring the enigma that's hidden below…

Glossary

EVERY BOOK IN THE Lightning Brain Series introduces abbreviations or terms collected here for convenient reference.

CAGE—Conjugative assembly genome engineering (CAGE) is a precise method of genome assembly using conjugation to hierarchically combine distinct genotypes from multiple Escherichia coli strains into a single chimeric genome. It permits large-scale transfer of specified genomic regions between strains without constraints imposed by in vitro manipulations.

CDC—The Centers for Disease Control and Prevention is the leading national public health institute of the United States. The CDC is a United States federal agency under the Department of Health and Human Services, headquartered near Atlanta, Georgia

MAGE—Multiplex Automated Genome Engineering rapidly introduces changes across a genome.

MGTOW—Men Going Their Own Way. An online social media community resulting from 21st century Men's Rights Movement.

NIH—The National Institutes of Health is the primary agency of the United States government responsible for biomedical and public health, founded in the late 1870s. It is part of the United States Department of Health and Human Services with facilities mainly located in Bethesda, Maryland. It conducts its own scientific research through its Intramural Research Program (IRP) and provides major biomedical research funding to non-NIH research facilities through its Extramural Research Program.

SWAT—SWAT (Special Weapons and Tactics), a paramilitary unit of law-enforcement agencies.

WMD—Weapon of Mass Destruction

America Strong—British covert operation established to help the United States deal with Middle East Terrorism and the Techno-Plague

Analytic Continuation—In complex analysis, a branch of mathematics,analytic continuation is a technique to extend the domain of a given analytic function. Analytic continuation often succeeds in defining further values of a function, for example, in a new region where an infinite series representation in terms of which it is initially defined becomes divergent.

Androids and Cyborgs—Manmade devices having human characteristics. **Android** can be made using any technology. It can be entirely artificial (like Star Trek's Data) or part biological (which makes it a **cyborg**). A robot is a generic term–anything can be a robot. All **androids** are robots. In order to fully duplicate a human being, the three personas (physical, emotional, and cognitive) of the human brain must each be uploaded and interconnected in a computer or simulated brain substrate

Apocalypse Clock—Hidden software controlling Trojan Filters.

Artificial Intelligence—Artificial Intelligence, abbreviated AI, is a broad term for the advancement of intelligence in computers. Despite varied opinions on this topic, most experts agree with three categories, or calibers, of AI development. They are:

- Artificial Narrow Intelligence: 1st intelligence caliber. "AI that specializes in one area. There's AI that can beat the world chess champion in chess, but that's the only thing it does.

- Artificial General Intelligence: 2nd intelligence caliber. AI that reaches and then passes the intelligence level of a human, meaning it has the ability to "reason, plan, solve problems, think abstractly, comprehend complex ideas, learn quickly, and learn from experience.

- Artificial Super Intelligence: 3rd intelligence caliber. AI that achieves a level of intelligence smarter than all of humanity combined, ranging from just a little smarter to one trillion times smarter.

- Augmented Artificial Intelligence: 3-D and VR GUI combination allowing user to interact in VR overlaid with actual surroundings.

Atomic Force Microscopy—**Atomic-force microscopy (AFM)** or scanning-**force Microscopy** (SFM) and successor technologies are very-high-resolution types of scanning probe **microscopy** (SPM), with demonstrated resolution on the order of fractions of a nanometer or less, more than 1000 times better than the optical diffraction limit.

Big Data—A term that describes the large volume of data—both structured and unstructured—that inundates a business on a dayto-day basis. But it's not the amount of data that's important. It's what organizations do with the data that matters. Big Data can be analyzed for insights that lead to better decisions and strategic business moves. Social media sites generate terabytes of Big Data that algorithms can analyze by correlating an individual's private data to predict behavior.

Biotechnology and Genetic Engineering—DNA is the instruction manual for all organisms. Current biotech and genetic engineering "read" the instruction manual to correct or improve organisms. Much of its focus is for improving the human condition.

Brain Probe—Biomedical device using software-controlled electromagnetic radiation to simulate sensory perception in human brain.

Brain Trust—Advisor group, reporting to the President of the United States, that develops policy recommendations and implementation.

Cognition and Self-Awareness—Neuroscientists conjecture that cognition and self-awareness are emergent phenomena coming from trillions of interconnected neurons in the brain. They draw parallels with force fields (gravitational, electromagnetic, weak and strong nuclear, etc.) that emerge from incomprehensible numbers of interacting atoms. Current research indicates the cognitive part of the brain may be able to self-direct organic development.

CRISPR/Cas9 Gene Editing—CRISPR-Cas9 and successor technologies allow for editing genes in living organisms. Scientists using these technologies say it has made targeting and changing genes in a cell's DNA easier and more precise than ever before. CRISPR is an acronym for Clustered Regularly Interspaced Short Palindromic Repeats.

Co-Friendship—Term coined by the Gay Community in the 21st century, referring to an intimate relationship between two people of either sex. Signifies a serious longer-term relationship.

Co-NFL—Professional football league offshoot created by the National Football League and Cross-fit Training Association. Teams comprised of elite male and female athletes. Rules and physical requirements set to allow exciting,fast-paced competition between offensive and defensive teams comprised of both males and females. League formed in late 21st century because women in the United States had achieved parity with men in most careers. There is a similar Co-NBA for basketball. Professional sports are considered the ideal combination of physicality and entertainment.

Cognicom Project—Codename for CDC project responsible for developing vaccines against the Techno-Plague. Divided into three sub-projects:

- I-Vac Project: Develops inoculation vaccine that protects
- R-Vac Project: Develops reversal vaccine that cures
- S-Vac Project: Develops symptomatic suppression vaccine that alleviates pain

Cosmology—Study of the universe. Current research areas include Multi-Verses,Big Bang,Big Crunch. They rely on high energy physics to provide verifiable confirmation.

Cyber-Theater—Cyber-Theater, or Neuro-Theater, is a multi-sensory reality simulator. Each category of sensory perception is recorded in a separate CD-ROM-like media track controlling what the theater projects. It's like the Holodeck from the Star Trek series, because advanced versions interconnect with the brain. A Cyber-Theater might use electrochemical glass, also known as smart glass or electronically switchable glass (SPD), that adjusts the level of transparency or color.

Deep Learning—**Deep learning** (also known as **deep** structured **learning**, hierarchical **learning** or **deep** machine **learning**) is the study of artificial neural networks and related machine **learning** algorithm that contain more than one hidden layer.

Digilog Signals—Latest and most advanced method of signal recording. An **analog signal** is any continuous **signal** for which the time varying feature (variable) of the **signal** is a representation of some other time varying quantity, i.e., analogous to another time varying **signal**. ... For example, an aneroid barometer uses rotary position as the **signal** to convey pressure information. A **digital signal** refers to an electrical **signal** that is converted into a pattern of bits. Unlike an analog **signal**, which is a continuous **signal** that contains time-varying quantities, a **digital signal** has a discrete value at each sampling point. A digilog signal combines the two for any phenomenon that has a finite number of base components. Each component is represented by a 0 or 1 to signify its "track" is present, and the track contains a continuous value from a minimum to a maximum value. Digilog signals are used for sensory media coding.

Guardian Party—National political party surging to prominence in the early 22nd century after a string of feckless government administrations and complicit Washington Establishment were unable to protect America from twin pandemics: Worldwide Islamic Terrorism, Global Techno-Plague.

The Guardian Party has its own "Guardian Agency", complete with its own covert ops group, to spy on other agencies, political parties, or governments.

Guardian Party Programs—Harsh programs designed to guard America's health and safety while cutting budget deficits. •

Crime-stoppers: Aggressive hunt for terrorists or criminals •

Infra-Rebuild: Put people to work rebuilding roads, communications systems, power systems, etc. Repatriate: Deport useless or dangerous people.

Golden Years: Euthanasia for the senile or terminally ill

- Pillars: Consists of two sub-programs:
- Private Citizens' Vigilantes to fight local criminals and terrorists,
- Health Watch Local groups to poke into neighbors' private lives to uncover community health risks.

H&H DNA Partners—Biotech Pharmaceutical Company started by Hudson (Hud) Haller and funded by his father Hollis (Holy) Haller

Healthguard—Intrusive national government agency established to guard private citizens against health risks. Championed by the Guardian Party.

High Energy Physics—Branch of physics seeking answers to fundamental questions posed by the universe. Current theories include Unified Field Theory, Time Reversal Theory, and String Theory. It is possible that man's cognitive asymptotic limit has moved high-energy physics from objective science to subjective philosophic conjecture.

Home-Track Schooling—American grade and high school educational systems are more flexible in the 22nd century, allowing customized education for gifted children or those with physical or mental handicaps. Home-Track Schooling allows a child to study at home using computerized learning and tutoring programs. The program is monitored by Health-Guard, the agency that tests, accepts, and monitors children in the program.

Insiders Group—Clandestine group created to spy on the Guardian Party.

Isilabad—Rogue Middle East State created midway through the 21st century to reestablish Islamic Caliphate and catapult Islam to its rightful place on the world stage.

Mega-Media—Umbrella term describing a worldwide computer network linking all types of communications networks and media. Includes smart cellphones and computer tablets when connected to "Worldwide Internet Grid".

Multi-threaded parallel Recursive Algorithmic Programming—Abbreviated by MPRAP. The most advanced computer programming technique used for artificial intelligence. The human brain contains trillions of interconnected sets of neurons. Though they operate at slower processing speeds of computer chips, they are interconnected, running in parallel, and in magnitudes that dwarf what the best computer hardware and software engineers can accomplish. That is why MPRAP was developed. The challenge facing engineers is to utilize as many massively parallel processing computers as they can. That number is limited by the collective intelligence of the engineering team, or the emergent intelligence of self-learning software.

Neural Network—In information technology, a neural network is a system of hardware and/or software patterned after the operation of neurons in the human brain. Neural networks—also called artificial neural networks—are a variety of deep learning technologies. The brain is modeled as layers of interconnected neurons that accept electrical signal input, process the input and send electrical signal output.

Neuro-Knitter—Biomedical device using software-controlled electromagnetic radiation to accelerate neural healing required after broken neck or back.

New-Wave—Generic term referring to early 22nd century younger generation tastes and lifestyles.

Opposition Group—Concerned Washington politicians and insiders opposed to Guardian Party's harsh measures for dealing with opponents. It has a clandestine steering committee to which a covert operations group reports.

Platform Economy and Companies—Platform refers to Cyberspace-based resources and services that reduce transaction costs (friction) and increase interaction (networking) among the Platform Economy's buyers and sellers. There are multiple ways to describe "product" companies and "platform" companies, so let's clarify. First, a "product" company is one that sells a particular type of solution to a problem across a specific sector or type of industry. In contrast, "platform" companies seek to transform industries or sectors with a set of solutions and products. Products lack defensibility and often rely on other platforms for customer acquisition, data, or infrastructure. Conversely, platforms allow new products built at a significantly lower incremental cost and users pay for the new value offered versus just paying for consuming more of a service. The pricing page of a company will likely show you whether they have built a product or a platform as a product company will charge by the number of users while a platform will price according to the increasing value the products provide to the customer.

Project Death Shield—Covert operation run by CIA (Central Intelligence Agency) to monitor how Techno-Plague impacts U.S. government stability.

Security guard—Intrusive national government agency established to guard private citizens against domestic or international threats. Championed by the Guardian Party.

Sensory Media Coding—Used to encode separate sensory perceptions for Cyber-Theater projection. There are six sensory perceptions: sight, sound, taste, touch, smell, and balance. Each sensory perception is represented by a set of base components. Each sensory perception is recorded on a separate track using digital coding. Here is an example: the sense of taste is composed of sweet, salty, sour, bitter, and umami (a strong meaty taste imparted by glutamate and certain other amino acids). Any taste can be simulated by coding the presence and intensity of its five components. Neuroscientists, physiologists, and computer scientists continue to improve hardware and software to project sensory perceptions into a viewing theater or directly into the brain.

Sensual Pleasures Café—many recreational drugs were legalized in the 21st century. A Sensual Pleasures café is a restaurant featuring foods, drinks or tobacco products containing legalized recreational drugs.

Techno-Plague—Also called T-Plague. Infection from a mutant manmade virus causing neural entanglement similar to Alzheimer's, leading to rapid cognitive impairment and senility. It Spread gradually but inexorably, becoming a global pandemic early in the 22nd century.

The Singularity—The Singularity is the hypothetical future creation of super-intelligent machines. Superintelligence is defined as a technologically-created cognitive capacity far beyond that possible for humans. Should the Singularity occur, technology will advance beyond our ability to foresee or control its outcomes and the world will be transformed beyond recognition by the application of superintelligence to humans and/or human problems, including poverty, disease and mortality. Revolutions in genetics, nanotechnology, and robotics (GNR) in the first half of the 21st century are expected to lay the foundation for the Singularity. According to Singularity theory, superintelligence will be developed by self-directed computers and will increase exponentially rather than incrementally.

Traser—State-of-the-art law enforcement weapon: dual tranquilizer and electric stun gun.

Trojan Filters—Hidden devices that can release T-Plague virus into air or water.

Transhumanism—Abbreviated as H+ or h+, it is an international and intellectual movement that aims to transform the human condition by developing and making widely available sophisticated technologies to greatly enhance human intellect and physiology.

Vow-Cer—The institution of marriage remains in the 22nd century a cornerstone of society, but adjusts to the needs of people. Vow-Cer is a Marriage Vow Contract Certification Ceremony. Two people affirm their commitment to each other,agreeing to honor their written marriage contract. Couples usually become Co-Friends before celebrating a vow-cer.

Whole Brain Emulation—**Whole brain emulation** (WBE), mind upload or **brain** upload (sometimes called "mind copying" or "mind transfer") is the hypothetical process of scanning mental state (including long-term memory and "self") of a particular **brain** substrate and copying it to a computer.

Worldstars—Name given by Indira Ramanujan to herself and three other talented biotech researchers: Su-Lin Song Chou, Adom Ola, and Jason Kittner.

Appendix

THE SCIENTIFIC OR GUIDING principles presented in this book are factual, as are technological applications. For readers who might enjoy reading more of the details, this appendix contains charts or diagrams referenced in the book's narrative or dialogue, identified by page number.

Page 70, 82—Background Primer

Religion:

- Theologians and philosophers have concluded there is no answer to "Does God Exist?" Each person must decide for themselves according to their preference for Faith or Reason.
- All religions are shrouded in the mists of Antiquity and emerged from myth and ritual practiced by different tribes that all shared universal yearnings.
- Man is genetically predisposed to believe in a god/higher power to explain the natural world.
- Organized religions often degenerate into a self-serving power grab.

Christianity:

- "Jesus Conspiracy" theories still abound. Analytic researchers utilize Bayesian statistics when trying to resurrect the "Historical Jesus," but the probability calculations disappoint religious fundamentalists.
- Many pre-Christian pagan religions contain Christ-like stories: A Savior or Messiah Virgin Birth Miracles Resurrection
- The existence of a historical Jesus doesn't matter, because its believers constructed the Bible that provided a world changing, universal ethical philosophy needed today.

Philosophy:

- The Greek philosophers pretty much nailed Western Philosophy, and might have concluded all controversy if they had today's science and technology.

- Note the progression: Greek Roman Judeo-Christian Muslim Renaissance Enlightenment Post-Modern Post Post-Modern Here is my definition of Post Post-Modern Philosophy: NeuroSci Extended Deconstructive Emergent Post-Pragmatism
- Enlightenment Philosophy principles: Truth, Knowledge, Rationalism, Progress
- Post-Modern philosophy is bankrupt (Negative, Nihilistic, AntiTruth, Anti-Math)

Science:

- Asymptotic limits to man's cognitive skills restrict what is accessible to man's comprehension.
- High Energy Physics/Quantum Mechanics/Cosmology have reached their limits and have become Religions rather than Science because their conjectures cannot be proved or disproved by experiments or observations. Their "Mind Experiments" are merely flights of fancy. Government keeps funding them because spin-offs have practical, technological benefits.
- Biotech, Nano-tech, and AI progress await for those able to apply the validated parts of Quantum Mechanics. Witness progress already made in Genetic Engineering and Quantum Computing.
- "Lightning Brain's competitive advantage compared to "Mere Mortals": Can develop superior Algorithms, Can handle greater Complexity Can build on existing Hardware

More will become apparent as you read through all my notebooks. I have run out of time to give you "Soft Science" basics: Psychology, Economics, Sociology, Politics. They are easier to grasp. You are smart enough to figure them out yourself, and you will remember what you already know as the lightning brain recovers.

Electra's conclusions when first meeting Alisha: (The lightning brain knows the state of science, religion, and philosophy. The lightning brain is at least as strong as previously.)

- Nietzsche quote: What doesn't kill me makes me stronger

- Neuroscience/DNA set the limits of what man can comprehend
- Wittgenstein was correct: Man's inability to articulate comprehensively via language limits what is accessible
- Godel's Completeness and Incompleteness theorems reinforce why High Energy Physics/Quantum Mechanics has reached a dead end. But optimistic physicists ignore Man's asymptotic limits ignored
- Explosion Principle ignored
- Anthropic Principle and possibly different asymptotic limits for brain substrates other than carbon-based (silicon or Star Trek/Star Wars life forms)

Page 165—Statistics Final Exam For Robin Setdarova

1. Explain Simpson's Paradox.

Simpson's paradox is a subtlety appearing in statistical problems dealing with proportions, for ostensibly it seems to contradict the following conditions:

If $A < B$ and $C < D$ then $A + C < B + D$ by showing contexts where $A < B$ and $C < D$ are consistent with $A + C > B + D$

However, upon closer examination of Simpson's Paradox problems, we discover the conditions actually involve proportions, and the so-called paradox is stated thusly:

If $a/A < b/B$ and $c/C < d/D$ we may still get

$$(a + c)/(A + C) > (b + d)/(B + D)$$

The paradox is caused by lurking variables when, for example, a three-way categorical table is collapsed to a two-way table by summing data over one of the categories. An illustration should clarify.

Consider two customer service sales representatives handling customer calls:

	Week 1	Week 2	Total
Goal Met	Alice	Alice	Alice
	Bob	Bob	Bob

Yes	162 19	10 99	172 118
No	18 1	10 81	28 82
Total	180 20	20 180	200 200

The three categorical variables are: Person, Calls Handled, and Week. The following tables display the percent of calls handled correctly or incorrectly:

Goal Met	Week 1 Alice Bob	Week 2 Alice Bob	Total Alice Bob
Yes	90% 95%	50% 55%	86% 59%
No	10% 5%	50% 45%	14% 41%
Total	100% 100%	100% 100%	100% 100%

When considering each week separately, Bob's performance is better than Alice's, but when considered in total, Alice performs better. The reason: aggregating the weekly data subsumes one of the categorical variables (Week), converting it into a hidden, or lurking variable. **So, conclusions that appear obvious when looked at in aggregated data can become quite different when the data are examined in more detail.**

2. Explain how Bayes' Theorem can be used to "prove historical events."

Note: Conditional and Bayesian probability concepts are nuanced topics that puzzle most people (cf. Kahneman Thinking, Fast and Slow, page 154 et al.)

There are two branches of statistics: Classical Statistics (uses sampling and experimentation) and Bayesian Statistics (uses subjective probability and conditional probability to convert a prior probability into a posterior probability). Bayes Theorem figures importantly in non-recurring contexts for which history gives relevant examples because every event in history is one-off. Here is a formal statement of Bayes Theorem. (H stands for Hypothesis is True,

-H stands for negation of Hypothesis is True, and
E stands for the Evidence is True.)

$$P(H \mid E) = P(H \text{ and } E)/P(E) = P(H) \times P(E \mid H)/$$
$$(P(H) \times P(E \mid H) + P(-H) \times P(E \mid -H))$$

Let's state the theorem in words: The Probability that H is True Given that E is True equals the Probability that H is True multiplied by the Probability that E is True Given H is True divided by the sum of the Probability H is True multiplied by the Probability that E is True Given H is True plus the Probability that -H is True multiplied by the Probability that E is True Given -H is True.

Note that P(H) is called the Prior Probability and P(H | E) is called the Posterior Probability. When attempting to "prove" that historical events actually occurred, research historians or anthropologists must make subjective guesses for:

- the Prior Probability that the Hypothesis is True (event actually occurred).
- the Conditional Probability that the Evidence is True Given that the Hypothesis is True.
- the Probability that the Evidence is True.

We can then plug these subjective probability guesses into the formula to calculate the Posterior Probability. This Posterior Probability becomes our Prior Probability when we gather more evidence and repeat the calculation.

Before giving examples, here are a couple of observations:

- If people already have already made up their minds (they believe 100%) it is a waste of time to argue because they won't believe your calculations.
- We can never know anything with 100% certainty, so never conclude that further testing is a waste of time.

Now for perhaps the most sought-after historical proof: Did Jesus exist?

Assume:

- The probability that Jesus existed is .00001 (Prior Probability)
- The probability that some Biblical evidence is True Given that Jesus existed is 001.
- The probability that some Biblical evidence is True is .0001 Plugging into the formula, we calculate the Posterior Probability:

$$.00001 \times .001 / .0001 = .0001$$

In other words, we have increased the probability that Jesus actually existed. But the problem with the entire calculation is the accuracy of Prior Probability guesses.

Here is a more relevant example that applies to filtering out Spam Emails. We would like to calculate the Probability that the Email is Spam Given that Suspect Words are in it:

P(Spam|Words) = P(Spam) x P(Words|Spam) / P(Words)

Internet Email apps actually use Bayesian filters to reduce the number of false positives. They work because "Big Data" gives much more accurate probability estimates than what are obtained in historical research.

3. Explain a solution to the Monty Hall Problem.

The problem is named for the original host of game show "Let's Make a Deal." Though a solution by Stevin Selvin had been published in a 1975 issue of the American Statistician, the problem caused a kerfuffle when it appeared in a 1990 Marilyn vos Savant (person scoring the highest recorded I.Q. test score) Parade Magazine column. Her answer, though correct, attracted scathing criticism by numerous PhD mathematicians. Even today, the problem and its methods of solution attract attention.

Statement of the Problem: A Contestant is asked to choose which closed door conceals a new car. The other two conceal a goat. The Contestant chooses Door 1, and the Host opens one of the other doors, concealing a goat. It doesn't matter if Door 2 or Door 3 is opened, so let's assume Door 3. There are now two unopened doors, and the Contestant is given a choice: keep Door 1 or switch to Door 2. What should the Contestant do?

The correct answer is to switch because there is a two-thirds probability the Contestant wins the car by switching versus a one-thirds probability if not. Most people, however, assume switching doesn't matter because there are two unopened doors and believe each has the same 50% probability. But a careful consideration indicates that the 50% equal probability assumption doesn't hold because the two remaining doors were not selected randomly.

I have searched the literature to find three solutions: Marilyn vos Savant's "simple solution", another based on a decision tree and accompanying conditional probability calculations, and a third based on Bayes Theorem calculations. All are cumbersome to explain, but I have come up with a better solution based on an analogous argument.

Suppose we have 1000 doors and you pick Door 1. The probability is .001 that the car is behind Door 1. Now, the Host opens all doors but Door 1 and one other, stipulating that the car is behind one of the two unopened doors. The probability is still .001 that the car is behind Door 1, which means the probability is .999 that the car is behind the other unopened door. Would you switch? Of course, because doing so has a .999 probability of success.

Coming back to our three-door problem, we will always switch because the probability is 1/3 the car is behind Door 1 and 2/3 it is behind Door 2.

Page 269—Mind/Brain Picture

Note: Preconscious and Subconscious are synonymous.

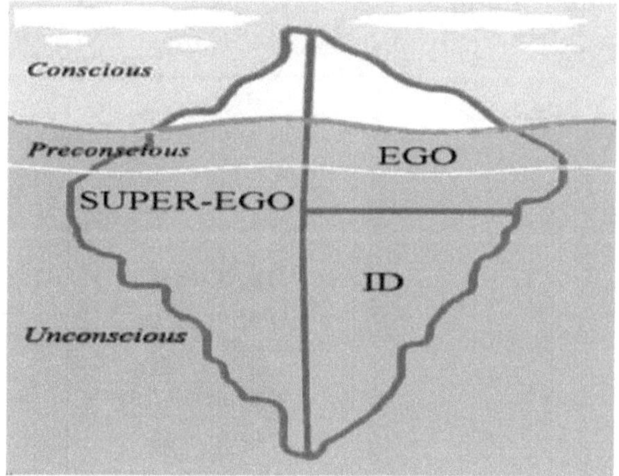

ID: Controls Emotions, Primal Functions, and Desires. Engages our Physical and Emotional Personas.

EGO: Controls Awareness. Engages our rational, organized Cognitive Persona.

SUPER-EGO: Controls Ethical and Cultural Values as well as Aspirations. Divided into "Collective Unconscious" and the "Shadow." Extends and uses elements found in ID or EGO.

Collective Unconscious: Term introduced by psychiatrist Carl Jung to represent a form of the unconscious (that part of the mind containing memories and impulses of which the individual is not aware) common to mankind as a whole and originating in the inherited structure of the brain.

Shadow: Carl Jung stated the Shadow is the darker side of the personality (Cognitive Persona). According to Jung, the Shadow's predisposition for instinctive and irrational behavior may cause psychological projection, in which a perceived personal inferiority is recognized as a perceived moral deficiency in someone else. People often relegate some of their potentially useful abilities and traits to the Shadow. Jung's dictate to "Own Your Shadow" commands each person to be aware of the "good" that may be found there.

Page 269—Mind/Brain and Artificial Intelligence

Note: The Mind and the Brain are one and the same. Brain sometimes refers to Physiological Characteristics. Mind sometime refers to Mental Characteristics.

Epi-Persona = Brain

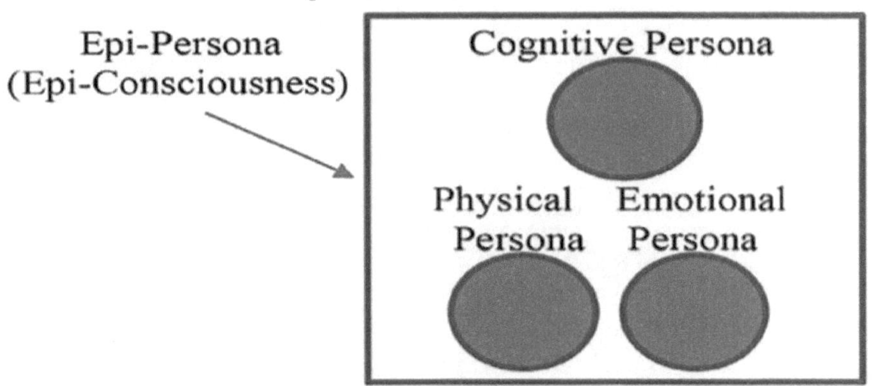

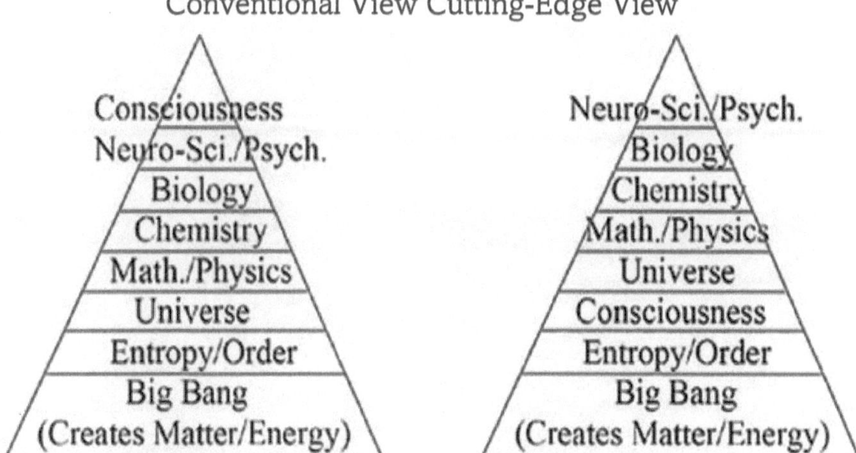

Matter = Energy = Entropy/Order = Information

- Higher Triangular Slices "emerge" from Lower Slices
- Emergence: Higher-level phenomena result from the interaction of lower-level entities. (Water waves emerge from the interaction of billions of water molecules. Consciousness emerges from the interaction of trillions of neural synapses.)
- Homo Sapiens emerged from Carbon-based DNA
- Properties, which determine what is accessible to the Brain and set Asymptotic Limits to what the Brain can achieve.
- Organic forms emerging from non-carbon-based substrates would have different DNA Properties and Asymptotic Limits. (Conjecture: Generalized AI emerges from a Silicon-based computer chip substrate.)

www.ingramcontent.com/pod-product-compliance
Lightning Source LLC
Chambersburg PA
CBHW031148310726
48969CB00001B/15